*The Editor*

DAN MCCALL is Professor of American Studies at Cornell University. He is the author of the novels *Jack the Bear*, which has appeared in fourteen languages, and *Triphammer*. His critical studies include *The Silence of Bartleby* and *Citizens of Somewhere Else*.

A NORTON CRITICAL EDITION

# MELVILLE'S
# SHORT NOVELS

## AUTHORITATIVE TEXTS
## CONTEXTS
## CRITICISM

*Selected and Edited by*

## DAN McCALL

CORNELL UNIVERSITY

W • W • NORTON & COMPANY • *New York* • *London*

Copyright © 2002 by W. W. Norton & Company, Inc.

The text of this book is composed in Fairfield Medium
with the display set in Bernhard Modern.
Composition by Publishing Synthesis.
Manufacturing by the Maple-Vail Book Manufacturing Group.
Book design by Antonina Krass.

Library of Congress Cataloging-in-Publication Data
Melville, Herman, 1819-1891.
[Novels. Selections]
Melville's short novels: authoritative texts, contexts, criticism / selected and
edited by
Dan McCall.
p. cm.—(Norton critical edition)
Includes bibliographical references.
Contents: Bartleby, the scrivener—Benito Cereno—Billy Budd.

**ISBN 0-393-97641-6 (pbk.)**

1. Melville, Herman, 1819-1891—Criticism and interpretation. 2. Sea stories,
American—History and criticism. 3. New York (N.Y.)—In literature. 4. New
York (N.Y.)—Fiction. 5. Slave trade—Fiction. 6. Sea stories, American. 7.
Copyists—Fiction. 8. Sailors—Fiction. I. McCall, Dan. II. Title.

PS2382 .M38 2001
813'.3—dc21

2001031490

W. W. Norton & Company, Inc. 500 Fifth Avenue, New York, N.Y. 10110
www.wwnorton.com
W. W. Norton & Company Ltd., Castle House, 75/76 Wells Street, London
W1T 3QT

3 4 5 6 7 8 9 0

# Contents

# Preface

Nearing his death in 1891 Herman Melville replied to a letter from an English admirer of his work that he was surprised anybody still knew his name. Forty years earlier he had published *Moby-Dick,* a commercial and critical failure at the time but today generally recognized as one of the greatest novels ever produced by an American.

This Norton Critical Edition presents three of Melville's short novels—or long stories, or novellas, or whatever we call them—all masterpieces. Some Melvilleans refer to them familiarly as "The Killer Bs": "Bartleby, The Scrivener," "Benito Cereno," and "Billy Budd." By 1853 Melville had published seven books (including *Moby-Dick*), but "Bartleby," published late in that year, was his first attempt at a short story. "Benito Cereno," the profoundest meditation on slavery in our literature, appeared two years later and was included in *The Piazza Tales* (1856). Soon thereafter Melville abandoned the writing of fiction altogether; he produced only poetry—some of it very fine poetry—during his long and tragic silence. He returned to storytelling only at the end of his life with the classic "Billy Budd."

All three short novels present textual problems, explored in the following pages, especially "Billy Budd," which was left in manuscript on Melville's writing desk when he died. Lively debates continue to focus on what Melville "really" meant, and some of the basic questions are included here. Readers will quickly see that the various interpretative essays often contradict each other; as editor I have not sought unanimity, but have tried to do justice to the wide and often bewildering variety of Melville commentary.

He read voraciously; in *Moby-Dick* he said, "I have swam through libraries." When he began to read Shakespeare, for example, something not altogether conscious or voluntary began happening to him. In *American Renaissance,* still the most valuable book on the period, F. O. Matthiessen concludes that

> Melville's imagination instinctively reshaped its impressions to suit his own needs. Shakespeare's
>
>> 'where a malignant and a turban'd Turk
>> Beat a Venetian and traduced the state,'
>
> is altered to 'No turbaned Turk, no hired Venetian or Malay, could have smote him with more seeming malice.' On such

levels the borrowed material has entered into the formation of
Melville's own thought. The most important effect of
Shakespeare's use of language was to give Melville a range of
vocabulary for expressing passion far beyond any that he had
previously possessed.

Matthiessen's great insight is his realization that "the borrowed material has entered into the formation of Melville's own thought." What
is going on is no isolated learned reference, no little allusion; the
process unfolding is a profound altering of the mind, for Melville is
acquiring a massive old language for a radical new way of seeing the
world. In Melville's hand at the end of his copy of *King Lear* there are
notes about Pip, Bulkington, Ishmael, and Ahab. Melville's reading
and Melville's writing are quite literally there, physically there on the
page together, so that meditation and creation become one.

To be sure, nothing Melville ever read altered his mind so radically
as Shakespeare did, unless it was the Bible. But almost anything he
read could mean something to him, and even a little story in the
newspaper could move him profoundly. His own linguistic resources
were marvelously extended and strengthened by his immersion in the
Elizabethans; that great experience had the consequence of working
in the other direction, too, so that anything he read found itself transformed into the massive instrument of his own language. It became
second nature to him and a kind of madness: when he sat down to
read, he found himself writing. "Bartleby, The Scrivener" clearly
comes from the Bible, Matthew 25, and when the narrator denies
Bartleby three times there are loud echoes of Peter's three denials of
Christ. We can hear Iago's last line in *Othello,* "From this time forth
I never will speak word" in the rebel Babo's final attitude in "Benito
Cereno": "His aspect seemed to say, since I cannot do deeds, I will not
speak words." In "Billy Budd" Captain Vere speaks of the ocean as
"the element where we move and have our being"; Acts 17: in the
Lord "we live and move and have our being." One's understanding of
Melville's genius is immensely enriched by considering his sources
and what he did with them.

We must be careful, though, not to use any of these as the key to
Melville's imagination but as an example of its deeply obsessive activity. He wrote to his literary friend and adviser Evert Duyckinck, "I
love all men who *dive!*" This most powerful of American minds was
swimming through libraries, and he happened to kick up all sorts of
things in the sand. They intrigued him; he picked them up and turned
them over in his "visible hands," way down there, deep down with
that "whole corps of thought-divers, that have been diving and coming up again with bloodshot eyes since the world began."

DAN MCCALL

# Acknowledgments

My gratitude to those who have faithfully given me encouragement and criticism, especially M. H. Abrams, Archie Ammons, Thomas R. Arp, Jonathan Bishop, Michael Colacurcio, Robert Dawidoff, Betty Friedlander, Lamar Herrin, Steve McCall, Reuben Munday, Joel Porte, Bert O. States, and especially to my dedicatee, without whom this book would not exist.

DMc

To Edgar Rosenberg

# The Texts of
# MELVILLE'S
# SHORT NOVELS

# Bartleby, The Scrivener

## A *Story of Wall-street*[1]

I am a rather elderly man. The nature of my avocations for the last thirty years has brought me into more than ordinary contact with what would seem an interesting and somewhat singular set of men of whom as yet nothing that I know of has ever been written:— I mean the law-copyists or scriveners. I have known very many of

1. When this story first appeared in *Putnam's Monthly Magazine* for November and December 1853, it was

Bartleby, The Scrivener
A Story of Wall-street

When Melville included the story in *The Piazza Tales*, he called it, simply, "Bartleby." Or did he? On January 19, 1856, he wrote to his publisher, Dix and Edwards, that the title of the book would be *Benito Cereno & Other Sketches*, and he proposed a "Table of Contents":

Benito Cereno
Bartleby
Bell-Tower
Encantadas
Lightning-Rod Man

On February 16 Melville wrote to his publisher to say that he had found a new title for the book, *The Piazza Tales*; after the opening piece of that name, "I think, with you, that 'Bartleby' had best come next." Did he really mean to shorten the title and cut out the subtitle? In both letters, as I read them, he is not deliberately abbreviating the title; he is simply referring to the place the story should occupy in the book. Some critics think "A Story of Wall-street" is too limiting, that it insists too much on the local setting of a work that has universal implications. Other readers argue the opposite: "Bartleby, The Scrivener" is a story about Wall Street, about economic pressures and class relationships; to remove the subtitle is to remove a cultural dimension from the story that was essential to its imaginative conception.

Melville clearly did mean to change one thing. When the story first appeared in *Putnam's*, the grub-man had a name, "Mr. Cutlets," and he asked Bartleby, "May Mrs. Cutlets and I have the pleasure of your company to dinner, sir, in Mrs. Cutlets' private room?" For *The Piazza Tales*, Melville cut both the name and the dinner invitation. Most modern editors respect these second thoughts. As do I. But should we? A wife, a "Mrs." Anybody, is surely an interesting person to mention in a story in which everybody seems to be a bachelor and the level of sexual energy is about as low as it can get. It does seem a little odd, though, to meet Dame Cutlets here. By the time we have reached this climactic point in the story, there is a woeful hush around everything, a sense of complete withdrawal and ultimate loss. One critic suggests that a note of "inappropriate slap-stick" is introduced by the name "Cutlets" and the reference to a woman's "private room." Then again, that might be just the reason to retain Cutlets and his Mrs. According to some critics, the name "Cutlets" is symbolically appropriate, altogether in keeping with the names of those other secondary characters "Turkey" and "Nippers" and "Ginger Nut." Other scholars think that is just what is wrong with it: our narrator tells us that the names of his three subordinates are "mutually conferred." Those nicknames belong to the office, and they express its special, feverish intimacy. To carry such names out into the anonymous world, especially to the cold impersonality of the Tombs, seems overclever and falsely insistent.

The punctuation of the story in the magazine is clearly preferable to the punctuation of the story in the book. The first paragraph has twelve commas in *Putnam's*, thirty in *The Piazza Tales*. On March 24, Melville wrote to his publisher: "There seems to have been a surprising profusion of commas in these proofs. I have struck them out pretty much; but hope that some one who understands punctuation better than I do, will give the final hand to it." Alas, Dix and Edwards ignored both Melville's own excisions and his request for help.

3

them, professionally and privately, and if I pleased, could relate divers histories, at which good-natured gentlemen might smile, and sentimental souls might weep. But I waive the biographies of all other scriveners for a few passages in the life of Bartleby, who was a scrivener the strangest I ever saw or heard of. While of other law-copyists I might write the complete life, of Bartleby nothing of that sort can be done. I believe that no materials exist for a full and sat-isfactory biography of this man. It is an irreparable loss to literature. Bartleby was one of those beings of whom nothing is ascertainable, except from the original sources, and in his case those are very small. What my own astonished eyes saw of Bartleby, *that* is all I know of him, except, indeed, one vague report which will appear in the sequel.

Ere introducing the scrivener, as he first appeared to me, it is fit I make some mention of myself, my *employées*, my business, my chambers, and general surroundings; because some such descrip-tion is indispensable to an adequate understanding of the chief character about to be presented.

Imprimis: I am a man who, from his youth upwards, has been filled with a profound conviction that the easiest way of life is the best. Hence, though I belong to a profession proverbially energetic and nervous, even to turbulence, at times, yet nothing of that sort have I ever suffered to invade my peace. I am one of those unambi-tious lawyers who never addresses a jury, or in any way draws down public applause; but in the cool tranquillity of a snug retreat, do a snug business among rich men's bonds and mortgages and title-deeds. All who know me, consider me an eminently *safe* man. The late John Jacob Astor,[2] a personage little given to poetic enthusiasm, had no hesitation in pronouncing my first grand point to be pru-dence; my next, method. I do not speak it in vanity, but simply record the fact, that I was not unemployed in my profession by the late John Jacob Astor; a name which, I admit, I love to repeat, for it hath a rounded and orbicular sound to it, and rings like unto bul-lion. I will freely add, that I was not insensible to the late John Jacob Astor's good opinion.

Some time prior to the period at which this little history begins, my avocations had been largely increased. The good old office, now extinct in the State of New York, of a Master in Chancery,[3] had been conferred upon me. It was not a very arduous office, but very pleas-antly remunerative. I seldom lose my temper; much more seldom

---

2. A dedicated philanthropist (1763–1848); when he died he was known as the richest man in America.
3. Courts of Chancery were abolished in New York State in the 1840s because they were viewed as an obstructive nuisance. The lawyer bemoans his loss of a "snug business among rich men's bonds and mortgages and title-deeds."

indulge in dangerous indignation at wrongs and outrages; but I must be permitted to be rash here and declare, that I consider the sudden and violent abrogation of the office of Master in Chancery, by the new Constitution, as a——premature act; inasmuch as I had counted upon a life-lease of the profits, whereas I only received those of a few short years. But this is by the way.

My chambers were up stairs at No.—Wall-street. At one end they looked upon the white wall of the interior of a spacious sky-light shaft, penetrating the building from top to bottom. This view might have been considered rather tame than otherwise, deficient in what landscape painters call "life." But if so, the view from the other end of my chambers offered, at least, a contrast, if nothing more. In that direction my windows commanded an unobstructed view of a lofty brick wall, black by age and everlasting shade; which wall required no spy-glass to bring out its lurking beauties, but for the benefit of all near-sighted spectators, was pushed up to within ten feet of my window panes. Owing to the great height of the surrounding buildings, and my chambers being on the second floor, the interval between this wall and mine not a little resembled a huge square cistern.

At the period just preceding the advent of Bartleby, I had two persons as copyists in my employment, and a promising lad as an office-boy. First, Turkey; second, Nippers; third, Ginger Nut.[4] These may seem names, the like of which are not usually found in the Directory. In truth they were nicknames, mutually conferred upon each other by my three clerks, and were deemed expressive of their respective persons or characters. Turkey was a short, pursy[5] Englishman of about my own age, that is, somewhere not far from sixty. In the morning, one might say, his face was of a fine florid hue, but after twelve o'clock, meridian—his dinner hour—it blazed like a grate full of Christmas coals; and continued blazing—but, as it were, with a gradual wane—till 6 o'clock, P.M. or thereabouts, after which I saw no more of the proprietor of the face, which gaining its meridian with the sun, seemed to set with it, to rise, culminate, and decline the following day, with the like regularity and undiminished glory. There are many singular coincidences I have known in the course of my life, not the least among which was the fact that exactly when Turkey displayed his fullest beams from his red and radiant countenance, just then, too, at the critical moment, began the daily period when I considered his business capacities as seriously disturbed for the remainder of the twenty-four hours. Not that he was absolutely idle, or averse to business then; far from it. The

---

4. The nicknames of the three employees all refer to food. "Nippers": crab or lobster claws.
5. Short of breath, overweight.

difficulty was, he was apt to be altogether too energetic. There was a strange, inflamed, flurried, flighty recklessness of activity about him. He would be incautious in dipping his pen into his inkstand. All his blots upon my documents, were dropped there after twelve o'clock, meridian. Indeed, not only would he be reckless and sadly given to making blots in the afternoon, but some days he went further, and was rather noisy. At such times, too, his face flamed with augmented blazonry, as if cannel coal had been heaped on anthracite. He made an unpleasant racket with his chair; spilled his sand-box; in mending his pens, impatiently split them all to pieces, and threw them on the floor in a sudden passion; stood up and leaned over his table, boxing his papers about in a most indecorous manner, very sad to behold in an elderly man like him. Nevertheless, as he was in many ways a most valuable person to me, and all the time before twelve o'clock, meridian, was the quickest, steadiest creature too, accomplishing a great deal of work in a style not easy to be matched—for these reasons, I was willing to overlook his eccentricities, though indeed, occasionally, I remonstrated with him. I did this very gently, however, because, though the civilest, nay, the blandest and most reverential of men in the morning, yet in the afternoon he was disposed, upon provocation, to be slightly rash with his tongue, in fact, insolent. Now, valuing his morning services as I did, and resolved not to lose them; yet, at the same time made uncomfortable by his inflamed ways after twelve o'clock; and being a man of peace, unwilling by my admonitions to call forth unseemingly retorts from him; I took upon me, one Saturday noon (he was always worse on Saturdays), to hint to him, very kindly, that perhaps now that he was growing old, it might be well to abridge his labors; in short, he need not come to my chambers after twelve o'clock, but, dinner over, had best go home to his lodgings and rest himself till tea-time. But no; he insisted upon his afternoon devotions. His countenance became intolerably fervid, as he oratorically assured me—gesticulating with a long ruler at the other end of the room—that if his services in the morning were useful, how indispensable, then, in the afternoon?

"With submission, sir," said Turkey on this occasion, "I consider myself your right-hand man. In the morning I but marshal and deploy my columns; but in the afternoon I put myself at their head, and gallantly charge the foe, thus!"—and he made a violent thrust with the ruler.

"But the blots, Turkey," intimated I.

"True,—but, with submission, sir, behold these hairs! I am getting old. Surely, sir, a blot or two of a warm afternoon is not to be severely urged against gray hairs. Old age—even if it blot the page— is honorable. With submission, sir, we *both* are getting old."

This appeal to my fellow-feeling was hardly to be resisted. At all events, I saw that go he would not. So I made up my mind to let him stay, resolving, nevertheless, to see to it, that during the afternoon he had to do with my less important papers.

Nippers, the second on my list, was a whiskered, sallow, and, upon the whole, rather piratical-looking young man of about five and twenty. I always deemed him the victim of two evil powers—ambition and indigestion. The ambition was evinced by a certain impatience of the duties of a mere copyist, an unwarrantable usurpation of strictly professional affairs, such as the original drawing up of legal documents. The indigestion seemed betokened in an occasional nervous testiness and grinning irritability, causing the teeth to audibly grind together over mistakes committed in copying; unnecessary maledictions, hissed, rather than spoken, in the heat of business; and especially by a continual discontent with the height of the table where he worked. Though of a very ingenious mechanical turn, Nippers could never get this table to suit him. He put chips under it, blocks of various sorts, bits of pasteboard, and at last went so far as to attempt an exquisite adjustment by final pieces of folded blotting-paper. But no invention would answer. If, for the sake of easing his back, he brought the table lid at a sharp angle well up towards his chin, and wrote there like a man using the steep roof of a Dutch house for his desk:—then he declared that it stopped the circulation in his arms. If now he lowered the table to his waistbands, and stooped over it in writing, then there was a sore aching in his back. In short, the truth of the matter was, Nippers knew not what he wanted. Or, if he wanted anything, it was to be rid of a scrivener's table altogether. Among the manifestations of his diseased ambition was a fondness he had for receiving visits from certain ambiguous-looking fellows in seedy coats, whom he called his clients. Indeed I was aware that not only was he, at times, considerable of a ward-politician, but he occasionally did a little business at the Justices' courts, and was not unknown on the steps of the Tombs.[6] I have good reason to believe, however, that one individual who called upon him at my chambers, and who, with a grand air, he insisted was his client, was no other than a dun,[7] and the alleged title-deed, a bill. But with all his failings, and the annoyances he caused me, Nippers, like his compatriot Turkey, was a very useful man to me; wrote a neat, swift hand; and, when he chose, was not deficient in a gentlemanly sort of deportment. Added to this, he always dressed in a gentlemanly sort of way; and so, incidentally, reflected credit upon my chambers. Whereas with respect to Turkey, I had much ado to keep him from being a reproach to me. His clothes

6. A prison in New York built during the Egyptian Revival of the 1830s. Note its role in the end of the story.
7. Bill collector.

were apt to look oily and smell of eating-houses. He wore his pantaloons very loose and baggy in summer. His coats were execrable; his
hat not to be handled. But while the hat was a thing of indifference to
me, inasmuch as his natural civility and deference, as a dependent
Englishman, always led him to doff it the moment he entered the
room, yet his coat was another matter. Concerning his coats, I reasoned with him; but with no effect. The truth was, I suppose, that a
man with so small an income, could not afford to sport such a lustrous face and a lustrous coat at one and the same time. As Nippers
once observed, Turkey's money went chiefly for red ink.[8] One winter
day I presented Turkey with a highly respectable looking coat of my
own, a padded gray coat, of a most comfortable warmth, and which
buttoned straight up from the knee to the neck. I thought Turkey
would appreciate the favor, and abate his rashness and obstreperous-
ness of afternoons. But no. I verily believe that buttoning himself up
in so downy and blanket-like a coat had a pernicious effect upon him;
upon the same principle that too much oats are bad for horses. In
fact, precisely as a rash, restive horse is said to feel his oats, so Turkey
felt his coat. It made him insolent. He was a man whom prosperity
harmed.

Though concerning the self-indulgent habits of Turkey I had my
own private surmises, yet touching Nippers I was well persuaded
that whatever might be his faults in other respects, he was, at least,
a temperate young man. But indeed, nature herself seemed to have
been his vintner, and at his birth charged him so thoroughly with an
irritable, brandy-like disposition, that all subsequent potations were
needless. When I consider how, amid the stillness of my chambers,
Nippers would sometimes impatiently rise from his seat, and
stooping over his table, spread his arms wide apart, seize the whole
desk, and move it, and jerk it, with a grim, grinding motion on the
floor, as if the table were a perverse voluntary agent, intent on
thwarting and vexing him; I plainly perceive that for Nippers,
brandy and water were altogether superfluous.

It was fortunate for me that, owing to its peculiar cause—indigestion—the irritability and consequent nervousness of Nippers,
were mainly observable in the morning, while in the afternoon he
was comparatively mild. So that Turkey's paroxysms only coming on
about twelve o'clock, I never had to do with their eccentricities at
one time. Their fits relieved each other like guards. When Nippers'
was on, Turkey's was off; and *vice versa*. This was a good natural
arrangement under the circumstances.

Ginger Nut, the third on my list, was a lad some twelve years old.
His father was a carman, ambitious of seeing his son on the bench

---

8. Wine.

instead of a cart, before he died. So he sent him to my office as student at law, errand boy, and cleaner and sweeper, at the rate of one dollar a week. He had a little desk to himself, but he did not use it much. Upon inspection, the drawer exhibited a great array of the shells of various sorts of nuts. Indeed, to this quick-witted youth the whole noble science of the law was contained in a nut-shell. Not the least among the employments of Ginger Nut, as well as one which he discharged with the most alacrity, was his duty as cake and apple purveyor for Turkey and Nippers. Copying law papers being proverbially a dry, husky sort of business, my two scriveners were fain to moisten their mouths very often with Spitzenbergs[9] to be had at the numerous stalls nigh the Custom House and Post Office. Also, they sent Ginger Nut very frequently for that peculiar cake—small, flat, round, and very spicy—after which he had been named by them. Of a cold morning when business was but dull, Turkey would gobble up scores of these cakes, as if they were mere wafers—indeed they sell them at the rate of six or eight for a penny—the scrape of his pen blending with the crunching of the crisp particles in his mouth. Of all the fiery afternoon blunders and flurried rashnesses of Turkey, was his once moistening a ginger-cake between his lips, and clapping it on to a mortgage for a seal. I came within an ace of dismissing him then. But he mollified me by making an oriental bow, and saying—"With submission, sir, it was generous of me to find you in stationery on my own account."

Now my original business—that of a conveyancer[1] and title hunter, and drawer-up of recondite documents of all sorts—was considerably increased by receiving the master's office. There was now great work for scriveners. Not only must I push the clerks already with me, but I must have additional help. In answer to my advertisement, a motionless young man one morning, stood upon my office threshold, the door being open, for it was summer. I can see that figure now—pallidly neat, pitiably respectable, incurably forlorn! It was Bartleby.

After a few words touching his qualifications, I engaged him, glad to have among my corps of copyists a man of so singularly sedate an aspect, which I thought might operate beneficially upon the flighty temper of Turkey, and the fiery one of Nippers.

I should have stated before that ground glass folding-doors divided my premises into two parts, one of which was occupied by my scriveners, the other by myself. According to my humor I threw open these doors, or closed them. I resolved to assign Bartleby a corner by the folding-doors, but on my side of them, so as to have

9. New York apples.
1. One who draws up deeds.

this quiet man within easy call, in case any trifling thing was to be done. I placed his desk close up to a small sidewindow in that part of the room, a window which originally had afforded a lateral view of certain grimy back-yards and bricks, but which, owing to subsequent erections, commanded at present no view at all, though it gave some light. Within three feet of the panes was a wall, and the light came down from far above, between two lofty buildings, as from a very small opening in a dome. Still further to a satisfactory arrangement, I procured a high green folding screen, which might entirely isolate Bartleby from my sight, though not remove him from my voice. And thus, in a manner, privacy and society were conjoined.

At first Bartleby did an extraordinary quantity of writing. As if long famishing for something to copy, he seemed to gorge himself on my documents. There was no pause for digestion. He ran a day and night line, copying by sun-light and by candle-light. I should have been quite delighted with his application, had he been cheerfully industrious. But he wrote on silently, palely, mechanically.

It is, of course, an indispensable part of a scrivener's business to verify the accuracy of his copy, word by word. Where there are two or more scriveners in an office, they assist each other in this examination, one reading from the copy, the other holding the original. It is a very dull, wearisome, and lethargic affair. I can readily imagine that to some sanguine temperaments it would be altogether intolerable. For example, I cannot credit that the mettlesome poet Byron would have contentedly sat down with Bartleby to examine a law document of, say five hundred pages, closely written in a crimpy hand.

Now and then, in the haste of business, it had been my habit to assist in comparing some brief document myself, calling Turkey or Nippers for this purpose. One object I had in placing Bartleby so handy to me behind the screen, was to avail myself of his services on such trivial occasions. It was on the third day, I think, of his being with me, and before any necessity had arisen for having his own writing examined, that, being much hurried to complete a small affair I had in hand, I abruptly called to Bartleby. In my haste and natural expectancy of instant compliance, I sat with my head bent over the original on my desk, and my right hand sideways, and somewhat nervously extended with the copy, so that immediately upon emerging from his retreat, Bartleby might snatch it and proceed to business without the least delay.

In this very attitude did I sit when I called to him, rapidly stating what it was I wanted him to do—namely, to examine a small paper with me. Imagine my surprise, nay, my consternation, when without moving from his privacy, Bartleby in a singularly mild, firm voice, replied, "I would prefer not to."

I sat awhile in perfect silence, rallying my stunned faculties. Immediately it occurred to me that my ears had deceived me, or Bartleby had entirely misunderstood my meaning. I repeated my request in the clearest tone I could assume. But in quite as clear a one came the previous reply, "I would prefer not to."

"Prefer not to," echoed I, rising in high excitement, and crossing the room with a stride, "What do you mean? Are you moon-struck? I want you to help me compare this sheet here—take it," and I thrust it towards him.

"I would prefer not to," said he.

I looked at him steadfastly. His face was leanly composed; his gray eye dimly calm. Not a wrinkle of agitation rippled him. Had there been the least uneasiness, anger, impatience or impertinence in his manner; in other words, had there been any thing ordinarily human about him, doubtless I should have violently dismissed him from the premises. But as it was, I should have as soon thought of turning my pale plaster-of-paris bust of Cicero[2] out of doors. I stood gazing at him awhile, as he went on with his own writing, and then reseated myself at my desk. This is very strange, thought I. What had one best do? But my business hurried me. I concluded to forget the matter for the present, reserving it for my future leisure. So calling Nippers from the other room, the paper was speedily examined.

A few days after this, Bartleby concluded four lengthy documents, being quadruplicates of a week's testimony taken before me in my High Court of Chancery. It became necessary to examine them. It was an important suit, and great accuracy was imperative. Having all things arranged I called Turkey, Nippers and Ginger Nut from the next room, meaning to place the four copies in the hands of my four clerks, while I should read from the original. Accordingly Turkey, Nippers and Ginger Nut had taken their seats in a row, each with his document in hand, when I called to Bartleby to join this interesting group.

"Bartleby! quick, I am waiting."

I heard a slow scrape of his chair legs on the unscraped floor, and soon he appeared standing at the entrance of his hermitage.

"What is wanted?" said he mildly.

"The copies, the copies," said I hurriedly. "We are going to examine them. There"—and I held towards him the fourth quadruplicate.

"I would prefer not to," he said, and gently disappeared behind the screen.

For a few moments I was turned into a pillar of salt,[3] standing at the head of my seated column of clerks. Recovering myself, I

---

2. Roman orator (106–43 B.C.E.).
3. The fate of Lot's disobedient wife (Genesis 19.26).

advanced towards the screen, and demanded the reason for such extraordinary conduct.

"*Why* do you refuse?"

"I would prefer not to."

With any other man I should have flown outright into a dreadful passion, scorned all further words, and thrust him ignominiously from my presence. But there was something about Bartleby that not only strangely disarmed me, but in a wonderful manner touched and disconcerted me. I began to reason with him.

"These are your own copies we are about to examine. It is labor saving to you, because one examination will answer for your four papers. It is common usage. Every copyist is bound to help examine his copy. Is it not so? Will you not speak? Answer!"

"I prefer not to," he replied in a flute-like tone. It seemed to me that while I had been addressing him, he carefully revolved every statement that I made; fully comprehended the meaning; could not gainsay the irresistible conclusion; but, at the same time, some paramount consideration prevailed with him to reply as he did.

"You are decided, then, not to comply with my request—a request made according to common usage and common sense?"

He briefly gave me to understand that on that point my judgment was sound. Yes: his decision was irreversible.

It is not seldom the case that when a man is browbeaten in some unprecedented and violently unreasonable way, he begins to stagger in his own plainest faith. He begins, as it were, vaguely to surmise that, wonderful as it may be, all the justice and all the reason is on the other side. Accordingly, if any disinterested persons are present, he turns to them for some reinforcement for his own faltering mind.

"Turkey," said I, "what do you think of this? Am I not right?"

"With submission, sir," said Turkey, with his blandest tone, "I think that you are."

"Nippers," said I, "what do *you* think of it?"

"I think I should kick him out of the office."

(The reader of nice perceptions will here perceive that, it being morning, Turkey's answer is couched in polite and tranquil terms, but Nippers replies in ill-tempered ones. Or, to repeat a previous sentence, Nippers's ugly mood was on duty, and Turkey's off.)

"Ginger Nut," said I, willing to enlist the smallest suffrage in my behalf, "what do *you* think of it?"

"I think, sir, he's a little *luny*," replied Ginger Nut, with a grin.

"You hear what they say," said I, turning towards the screen, "come forth and do your duty."

But he vouchsafed no reply. I pondered a moment in sore perplexity. But once more business hurried me. I determined again to postpone the consideration of this dilemma to my future leisure.

With a little trouble we made out to examine the papers without Bartleby, though at every page or two, Turkey deferentially dropped his opinion that this proceeding was quite out of the common; while Nippers, twitching in his chair with a dyspeptic nervousness, ground out between his set teeth occasional hissing maledictions against the stubborn oaf behind the screen. And for his (Nippers's) part, this was the first and the last time he would do another man's business without pay.

Meanwhile Bartleby sat in his hermitage, oblivious to every thing but his own peculiar business there.

Some days passed, the scrivener being employed upon another lengthy work. His late remarkable conduct led me to regard his way narrowly. I observed that he never went to dinner; indeed that he never went any where. As yet I had never of my personal knowledge known him to be outside of my office. He was a perpetual sentry in the corner. At about eleven o'clock though, in the morning, I noticed that Ginger Nut would advance toward the opening in Bartleby's screen, as if silently beckoned thither by a gesture invisible to me where I sat. That boy would then leave the office jingling a few pence, and reappear with a handful of ginger-nuts which he delivered in the hermitage, receiving two of the cakes for his trouble.

He lives, then, on ginger-nuts, thought I; never eats a dinner, properly speaking; he must be a vegetarian then, but no; he never eats even vegetables, he eats nothing but ginger-nuts. My mind then ran on in reveries concerning the probable effects upon the human constitution of living entirely on ginger-nuts. Ginger-nuts are so called because they contain ginger as one of their peculiar constituents, and the final flavoring one. Now what was ginger? A hot, spicy thing. Was Bartleby hot and spicy? Not at all. Ginger, then, had no effect upon Bartleby. Probably he preferred it should have none.

Nothing so aggravates an earnest person as a passive resistance. If the individual so resisted be of a not inhumane temper, and the resisting one perfectly harmless in his passivity; then, in the better moods of the former, he will endeavor charitably to construe to his imagination what proves impossible to be solved by his judgment. Even so, for the most part, I regarded Bartleby and his ways. Poor fellow! thought I, he means no mischief; it is plain he intends no insolence; his aspect sufficiently evinces that his eccentricities are involuntary. He is useful to me. I can get along with him. If I turn him away, the chances are he will fall in with some less indulgent employer, and then he will be rudely treated, and perhaps driven forth miserably to starve. Yes. Here I can cheaply purchase a delicious self-approval. To befriend Bartleby; to humor him in his strange wilfulness, will cost me little or nothing, while I lay up in my soul what will eventually prove a sweet morsel for my conscience. But this mood was not invariable with me. The passiveness of Bartleby sometimes irritated me. I felt strangely goaded on to encounter him in new opposition, to elicit some angry spark from him answerable to my own. But indeed I might as well have essayed to strike fire with my knuckles against a bit of Windsor soap. But one afternoon the evil impulse in me mastered me, and the following little scene ensued:

"Bartleby," said I, "when those papers are all copied, I will compare them with you."

"I would prefer not to."

"How? Surely you do not mean to persist in that mulish vagary?" No answer.

I threw open the folding-doors near by, and turning upon Turkey and Nippers, exclaimed in an excited manner—

"He says, a second time, he won't examine his papers. What do you think of it, Turkey?"

It was afternoon, be it remembered. Turkey sat glowing like a brass boiler, his bald head steaming, his hands reeling among his blotted papers.

"Think of it?" roared Turkey; "I think I'll just step behind his screen, and black his eyes for him!"

So saying, Turkey rose to his feet and threw his arms into a pugilistic position. He was hurrying away to make good his promise, when I detained him, alarmed at the effect of incautiously rousing Turkey's combativeness after dinner.

"Sit down, Turkey," said I, "and hear what Nippers has to say. What to do you think of it, Nippers? Would I not be justified in immediately dimissing Bartleby?"

"Excuse me, that is for you to decide, sir. I think his conduct quite unusual, and indeed unjust, as regards Turkey and myself. But it may only be a passing whim."

"Ah," exclaimed I, "you have strangely changed your mind then— you speak very gently of him now."

"All beer," cried Turkey; "gentleness is effects of beer—Nippers and I dined together to-day. You see how gentle *I* am, sir. Shall I go and black his eyes?"

"You refer to Bartleby, I suppose. No, not to-day, Turkey," I replied; "pray, put up your fists."

I closed the doors, and again advanced towards Bartleby. I felt additional incentives tempting me to my fate. I burned to be rebelled against again. I remembered that Bartleby never left the office.

"Bartleby," said I, "Ginger Nut is away; just step round to the Post Office, won't you? (it was but a three minutes walk,) and see if there is any thing for me."

"I would prefer not to."

"You *will* not?"

"I *prefer* not."

I staggered to my desk, and sat there in a deep study. My blind inveteracy returned. Was there any other thing in which I could procure myself to be ignominiously repulsed by this lean, penniless wight?—my hired clerk? What added thing is there, perfectly reasonable, that he will be sure to refuse to do?

"Bartleby!"

No answer.

"Bartleby," in a louder tone.

No answer.

"Bartleby," I roared.

Like a very ghost, agreeably to the laws of magical invocation, at the third summons, he appeared at the entrance of his hermitage.

"Go to the next room, and tell Nippers to come to me."

"I prefer not to," he respectfully and slowly said, and mildly disappeared.

"Very good, Bartleby," said I, in a quiet sort of serenely severe self-possessed tone, intimating the unalterable purpose of some terrible retribution very close at hand. At the moment I half intended something of the kind. But upon the whole, as it was drawing towards my dinner-hour, I thought it best to put on my hat and walk home for the day, suffering much from perplexity and distress of mind.

Shall I acknowledge it? The conclusion of this whole business was, that it soon became a fixed fact of my chambers, that a pale young scrivener, by the name of Bartleby, had a desk there; that he copied for me at the usual rate of four cents a folio (one hundred words); but he was permanently exempt from examining the work done by him, that duty being transferred to Turkey and Nippers, one of compliment doubtless to their superior acuteness; moreover, said Bartleby was never on any account to be dispatched on the most trivial errand of any sort; and that even if entreated to take upon him such a matter, it was generally understood that he would prefer not to—in other words, that he would refuse point-blank.

As days passed on, I became considerably reconciled to Bartleby. His steadiness, his freedom from all dissipation, his incessant industry (except when he chose to throw himself into a standing revery behind his screen), his great stillness, his unalterableness of demeanor under all circumstances, made him a valuable acquisition. One prime thing was this,—*he was always there*;—first in the morning, continually through the day, and the last at night. I had a singular confidence in his honesty. I felt my most precious papers perfectly safe in his hands. Sometimes to be sure I could not, for the very soul of me, avoid falling into sudden spasmodic passions with him. For it was exceeding difficult to bear in mind all the time those strange peculiarities, privileges, and unheard of exemptions, forming the tacit stipulations on Bartleby's part under which he remained in my office. Now and then, in the eagerness of dispatching pressing business, I would inadvertently summon Bartleby, in a short, rapid tone, to put his finger, say, on the incipient tie of a bit of red tape with which I was about compressing some papers. Of course, from behind the screen the usual answer, "I prefer not to," was sure to come; and then, how could a human creature with the common infirmities of our nature, refrain from bitterly exclaiming upon such perverseness—such unreasonableness. However, every added repulse of this sort which I received only tended to lessen the probability of my repeating the inadvertence.

Here it must be said, that according to the custom of most legal gentlemen occupying chambers in densely-populated law buildings, there were several keys to my door. One was kept by a woman residing in the attic, which person weekly scrubbed and daily swept and dusted my apartments. Another was kept by Turkey for convenience sake. The third I sometimes carried in my own pocket. The fourth I knew not who had.

Now one Sunday morning I happened to go to Trinity Church;[4] to hear a celebrated preacher, and finding myself rather early on the ground, I thought I would walk round to my chambers for a while. Luckily I had my key with me; but upon applying it to the lock, I found it resisted by something inserted from the inside. Quite surprised, I called out; when to my consternation a key was turned from within; and thrusting his lean visage at me, and holding the door ajar, the apparition of Bartleby appeared, in his shirt sleeves, and otherwise in a strangely tattered dishabille, saying quietly that he was sorry, but he was deeply engaged just then, and—preferred not admitting me at present. In a brief word or two, he moreover added, that perhaps I had better walk round the block two or three times, and by that time he would probably have concluded his affairs.

Now, the utterly unsurmised appearance of Bartleby, tenanting my law-chambers of a Sunday morning, with his cadaverously gentlemanly *nonchalance*, yet withal firm and self-possessed, had such a strange effect upon me, that incontinently I slunk away from my own door, and did as desired. But not without sundry twinges of impotent rebellion against the mild effrontery of this unaccountable scrivener. Indeed, it was his wonderful mildness chiefly, which not only disarmed me, but unmanned me, as it were. For I consider that one, for the time, is a sort of unmanned when he tranquilly permits

4. Episcopal church in Wall Street.

his hired clerk to dictate to him, and order him away from his own premises. Furthermore, I was full of uneasiness as to what Bartleby could possibly be doing in my office in his shirt sleeves, and in an otherwise dismantled condition of a Sunday morning. Was any thing amiss going on? Nay, that was out of the question. It was not to be thought of for a moment that Bartleby was an immoral person. But what could he be doing there?—copying? Nay again, whatever might be his eccentricities, Bartleby was an eminently decorous person. He would be the last man to sit down to his desk in any state approaching to nudity. Besides, it was Sunday; and there was something about Bartleby that forbade the supposition that he would by any secular occupation violate the proprieties of the day.

Nevertheless, my mind was not pacified; and full of a restless curiosity, at last I returned to the door. Without hindrance I inserted my key, opened it, and entered. Bartleby was not to be seen. I looked round anxiously, peeped behind his screen; but it was very plain that he was gone. Upon more closely examining the place, I surmised that for an indefinite period Bartleby must have ate, dressed, and slept in my office, and that too without plate, mirror, or bed. The cushioned seat of a rickety old sofa in one corner bore the faint impress of a lean, reclining form. Rolled away under his desk, I found a blanket; under the empty grate, a blacking box and brush; on a chair, a tin basin, with soap and a ragged towel; in a newspaper a few crumbs of ginger-nuts and a morsel of cheese. Yes, thought I, it is evident enough that Bartleby has been making his home here, keeping bachelor's hall all by himself. Immediately then the thought came sweeping across me, What miserable friendlessness and loneliness are here revealed! His poverty is great; but his solitude, how horrible! Think of it. Of a Sunday, Wall-street is deserted as Petra; and every night of every day it is an emptiness. This building too, which of week-days hums with industry and life, at nightfall echoes with sheer vacancy, and all through Sunday is forlorn. And here Bartleby makes his home; sole spectator of a solitude which he has seen all populous—a sort of innocent and transformed Marius brooding among the ruins of Carthage![5]

For the first time in my life a feeling of overpowering stinging melancholy seized me. Before, I had never experienced aught but a not-unpleasing sadness. The bond of a common humanity now drew me irresistibly to gloom. A fraternal melancholy! For both I and Bartleby were sons of Adam. I remembered the bright silks and sparkling faces I had seen that day in gala trim, swan-like sailing

---

5. A painting by the American artist John Vanderlyn, which won a gold medal—presented by Napoleon himself—at the Paris Salon in 1808. Vanderlyn went deeply into debt; stopped working; and died in 1852, the year before Melville published "Bartleby." *Marius* was an academic neoclassic painting of great size.

down the Mississippi of Broadway; and I contrasted them with the pallid copyist, and thought to myself, Ah, happiness courts the light, so we deem the world is gay; but misery hides aloof, so we deem that misery there is none. These sad fancyings—chimeras, doubtless, of a sick and silly brain—led on to other and more special thoughts, concerning the eccentricities of Bartleby. Presentiments of strange discoveries hovered round me. The scrivener's pale form appeared to me laid out, among uncaring strangers, in its shivering winding sheet.

Suddenly I was attracted by Bartleby's closed desk, the key in open sight left in the lock.

I mean no mischief, seek the gratification of no heartless curiosity, thought I; besides, the desk is mine, and its contents too, so I will make bold to look within. Every thing was methodically arranged, the papers smoothly placed. The pigeon holes were deep, and removing the files of documents, I groped into their recesses. Presently I felt something there, and dragged it out. It was an old bandanna handkerchief, heavy and knotted. I opened it, and saw it was a savings' bank.

I now recalled all the quiet mysteries which I had noted in the man. I remembered that he never spoke but to answer; that though at intervals he had considerable time to himself, yet I had never seen him reading—no, not even a newspaper; that for long periods he would stand looking out, at his pale window behind the screen, upon the dead brick wall; I was quite sure he never visited any refectory or eating house; while his pale face clearly indicated that he never drank beer like Turkey, or tea and coffee even, like other men; that he never went any where in particular that I could learn; never went out for a walk, unless indeed that was the case at present; that he had declined telling who he was, or whence he came, or whether he had any relatives in the world; that though so thin and pale, he never complained of ill health. And more than all, I remembered a certain unconscious air of pallid—how shall I call it?—of pallid haughtiness, say, or rather an austere reserve about him, which had positively awed me into my tame compliance with his eccentricities, when I had feared to ask him to do the slightest incidental thing for me, even though I might know, from his long-continued motionlessness, that behind his screen he must be standing in one of those dead-wall reveries of his.

Revolving all these things, and coupling them with the recently discovered fact that he made my office his constant abiding place and home, and not forgetful of his morbid moodiness; revolving all these things, a prudential feeling began to steal over me. My first emotions had been those of pure melancholy and sincerest pity; but just in proportion as the forlornness of Bartleby grew and grew to my imagination, did that same melancholy merge into fear, that pity into repulsion. So true it is, and so terrible too, that up to a certain point the thought or sight of misery enlists our best affections; but, in certain special cases, beyond that point it does not. They err who would assert that invariably this is owing to the inherent selfishness of the human heart. It rather proceeds from a certain hopelessness of remedying excessive and organic ill. To a sensitive being, pity is not seldom pain. And when at last it is perceived that such pity cannot lead to effectual succor, common sense bids the soul be rid of it. What I saw that morning persuaded me that the scrivener was the victim of innate and incurable disorder. I might give alms to his body; but his body did not pain him; it was his soul that suffered, and his soul I could not reach.

I did not accomplish the purpose of going to Trinity Church that morning. Somehow, the things I had seen disqualified me for the time from church-going. I walked homeward, thinking what I would do with Bartleby. Finally, I resolved upon this; I would put certain calm questions to him the next morning, touching his history, &c., and if he declined to answer them openly and unreservedly (and I supposed he would prefer not), then to give him a twenty dollar bill over and above whatever I might owe him, and tell him his services were no longer required; but that if in any other way I could assist him, I would be happy to do so, especially if he desired to return to his native place, wherever that might be, I would willingly help to defray the expenses. Moreover, if after reaching home, he found himself at any time in want of aid, a letter from him would be sure of a reply.

The next morning came.

"Bartleby," said I, gently calling to him behind his screen. No reply.

"Bartleby," said I, in a still gentler tone, "come here; I am not going to ask you to do any thing you would prefer not to do I simply wish to speak to you."

Upon this he noiselessly slid into view.

"Will you tell me, Bartleby, where you were born?"

"I would prefer not to."

"Will you tell me *any thing* about yourself?"

"I would prefer not to."

"But what reasonable objection can you have to speak to me? I feel friendly towards you."

He did not look at me while I spoke, but kept his glance fixed upon my bust of Cicero, which as I then sat, was directly behind me, some six inches above my head.

"What is your answer, Bartleby?" said I, after waiting a considerable time for a reply, during which his countenance remained immovable, only there was the faintest conceivable tremor of the white attenuated mouth.

"At present I prefer to give no answer," he said, and retired into his hermitage.

It was rather weak in me I confess, but his manner on this occasion nettled me. Not only did there seem to lurk in it a certain disdain, but his perverseness seemed ungrateful, considering the undeniable good usage and indulgence he had received from me.

Again I sat ruminating what I should do. Mortified as I was at his behavior, and resolved as I had been to dismiss him when I entered my office, nevertheless I strangely felt something superstitious knocking at my heart, and forbidding me to carry out my purpose, and denouncing me for a villain if I dared to breathe one bitter word against this forlornest of mankind. At last, familiarly drawing my chair behind his screen, I sat down and said: "Bartleby, never mind then about revealing your history; but let me entreat you, as a friend, to comply as far as may be with the usages of this office. Say now you will help to examine papers tomorrow or next day: in short, say now that in a day or two you will begin to be a little reasonable:—say so, Bartleby."

"At present I would prefer not to be a little reasonable," was his mildly cadaverous reply.

Just then the folding-doors opened, and Nippers approached. He seemed suffering from an unusually bad night's rest, induced by severer indigestion than common. He overheard those final words of Bartleby.

"*Prefer not*, eh?" gritted Nippers—"I'd *prefer* him, if I were you, sir," addressing me—"I'd *prefer* him; I'd give him preferences, the stubborn mule! What is it, sir, pray, that he *prefers* not to do now?"

Bartleby moved not a limb.

"Mr. Nippers," said I, "I'd prefer that you would withdraw for the present."

Somehow, of late I had got into the way of involuntary using this word "prefer" upon all sorts of not exactly suitable occasions. And I trembled to think that my contact with the scrivener had already and seriously affected me in a mental way. And what further and deeper aberration might it not yet produce? This apprehension had not been without efficacy in determining me to summary means.

As Nippers, looking very sour and sulky, was departing, Turkey blandly and deferentially approached.

"With submission, sir," said he, "yesterday I was thinking about Bartleby here, and I think that if he would but prefer to take a quart of good ale every day, it would do much towards mending him, and enabling him to assist in examining his papers."

"So you have got the word too," said I, slightly excited. "With submission, what word, sir," asked Turkey, respectfully crowding himself into the contracted space behind the screen, and by so doing, making me jostle the scrivener. "What word, sir?"

"I would prefer to be left alone here," said Bartleby, as if offended at being mobbed in his privacy.

"*That's* the word, Turkey," said I—"*that's* it."

"Oh, *prefer?* oh yes—queer word. I never use it myself. But, sir, as I was saying, if he would but prefer—"

"Turkey," interrupted I, "you will please withdraw." "Oh certainly, sir, if you prefer that I should."

As he opened the folding-door to retire, Nippers at his desk caught a glimpse of me, and asked whether I would prefer to have a certain paper copied on blue paper or white. He did not in the least roguishly accent the word prefer. It was plain that it involuntarily rolled from his tongue. I thought to myself, surely I must get rid of a demented man, who already has in some degree turned the tongues, if not the heads of myself and clerks. But I thought it prudent not to break the dismission at once.

The next day I noticed that Bartleby did nothing but stand at his window in his dead-wall revery. Upon asking him why he did not write, he said that he had decided upon doing no more writing.

"Why, how now? what next?" exclaimed I, "do no more writing?"

"No more."

"And what is the reason?"

"Do you not see the reason for yourself," he indifferently replied.

I looked steadfastly at him, and perceived that his eyes looked dull and glazed. Instantly it occurred to me, that his unexampled diligence in copying by his dim window for the first few weeks of his stay with me might have temporarily impaired his vision.

I was touched. I said something in condolence with him. I hinted that of course he did wisely in abstaining from writing for a while; and urged him to embrace that opportunity of taking wholesome exercise in the open air. This, however, he did not do. A few days after this, my other clerks being absent, and being in a great hurry to dispatch certain letters by the mail, I thought that, having nothing else earthly to do, Bartleby would surely be less inflexible than usual, and carry these letters to the post-office. But he blankly declined. So, much to my inconvenience, I went myself.

Still added days went by. Whether Bartleby's eyes improved or not, I could not say. To all appearance, I thought they did. But when I asked him if they did, he vouchsafed no answer. At all events, he would do no copying. At last, in reply to my urgings, he informed me that he had permanently given up copying.

"What!" exclaimed I; "suppose your eyes should get entirely well—better than ever before—would you not copy then?"

"I have given up copying," he answered, and slid aside.

He remained as ever, a fixture in my chamber. Nay—if that were possible—he became still more of a fixture than before. What was to be done? He would do nothing in the office: why should he stay there? In plain fact, he had now become a millstone[6] to me, not only useless as a necklace, but afflictive to bear. Yet I was sorry for him. I speak less than truth when I say that, on his own account, he occasioned me uneasiness. If he would but have named a single relative or friend, I would instantly have written, and urged their taking the poor fellow away to some convenient retreat. But he seemed alone, absolutely alone in the universe. A bit of wreck in the mid Atlantic. At length, necessities connected with my business tyrannized over all other considerations. Decently as I could, I told Bartleby that in six days' time he must unconditionally leave the office. I warned him to take measures, in the interval, for procuring some other abode. I offered to assist him in this endeavor, if he himself would but take the first step towards a removal. "And when you finally quit me, Bartleby," added I, "I shall see that you go not away entirely unprovided. Six days from this hour, remember."

At the expiration of that period, I peeped behind the screen, and lo! Bartleby was there.

I buttoned up my coat, balanced myself; advanced slowly towards him, touched his shoulder, and said, "The time has come; you must quit this place; I am sorry for you; here is money; but you must go."

"I would prefer not," he replied, with his back still towards me.

"You *must*."

He remained silent.

Now I had an unbounded confidence in this man's common honesty. He had frequently restored to me six pences and shillings carelessly dropped upon the floor, for I am apt to be very reckless in such shirt-button affairs. The proceeding then which followed will not be deemed extraordinary.

"Bartleby," said I, "I owe you twelve dollars on account; here are thirty-two; the odd twenty are yours.—Will you take it?" and I handed the bills towards him.

But he made no motion.

"I will leave them here then," putting them under a weight on the table. Then taking my hat and cane and going to the door I tranquilly turned and added—"After you have removed your things from these offices, Bartleby, you will of course lock the door—since every

6. "It were better for him that a millstone were hanged about his neck, and that he were drowned in the depth of the sea (Matthew 18.6)."

one is now gone for the day but you—and if you please, slip your key underneath the mat, so that I may have it in the morning. I shall not see you again; so good-bye to you. If hereafter in your new place of abode I can be of any service to you, do not fail to advise me by letter. Good-bye, Bartleby, and fare you well."

But he answered not a word; like the last column of some ruined temple, he remained standing mute and solitary in the middle of the otherwise deserted room.

As I walked home in a pensive mood, my vanity got the better of my pity. I could not but highly plume myself on my masterly management in getting rid of Bartleby. Masterly I call it, and such it must appear to any dispassionate thinker. The beauty of my procedure seemed to consist in its perfect quietness. There was no vulgar bullying, no bravado of any sort, no choleric hectoring, and striding to and fro across the apartment, jerking out vehement commands for Bartleby to bundle himself off with his beggarly traps. Nothing of the kind. Without loudly bidding Bartleby depart—as an inferior genius might have done—I *assumed* the ground that depart he must; and upon the assumption built all I had to say. The more I thought over my procedure, the more I was charmed with it. Nevertheless, next morning, upon awakening, I had my doubts,—I had somehow slept off the fumes of vanity. One of the coolest and wisest hours a man has, is just after he awakes in the morning. My procedure seemed as sagacious as ever,—but only in theory. How it would prove in practice—there was the rub. It was truly a beautiful thought to have assumed Bartleby's departure; but, after all, that assumption was simply my own, and none of Bartleby's. The great point was, not whether I had assumed that he would quit me, but whether he would prefer so to do. He was more a man of preferences than assumptions.

After breakfast, I walked down town, arguing the probabilities *pro* and *con*. One moment I thought it would prove a miserable failure, and Bartleby would be found all alive at my office as usual; the next moment it seemed certain that I should see his chair empty. And so I kept veering about. At the corner of Broadway and Canal-street, I saw quite an excited group of people standing in earnest conversation.

"I'll take odds he doesn't," said a voice as I passed.

"Doesn't go?—done!" said I, "put up your money."

I was instinctively putting my hand in my pocket to produce my own, when I remembered that this was an election day. The words I had overheard bore no reference to Bartleby, but to the success or non-success of some candidate for the mayoralty. In my intent frame of mind, I had, as it were, imagined that all Broadway shared in my excitement, and were debating the same question with me. I passed on, very thankful that the uproar of the street screened my momentary absent-mindedness.

As I had intended, I was earlier than usual at my office door. I stood listening for a moment. All was still. He must be gone. I tried the knob. The door was locked. Yes, my procedure had worked to a charm; he indeed must be vanished. Yet a certain melancholy mixed with this: I was almost sorry for my brilliant success. I was fumbling under the door mat for the key, which Bartleby was to have left there for me, when accidentally my knee knocked against a panel, producing a summoning sound, and in response a voice came to me from within—"Not yet; I am occupied."

It was Bartleby.

I was thunderstruck. For an instant I stood like the man who, pipe in mouth, was killed one cloudless afternoon long ago in Virginia, by summer lightning; at his own warm open window he was killed, and remained leaning out there upon the dreamy afternoon, till some one touched him, when he fell.

"Not gone!" I murmured at last. But again obeying that wondrous ascendancy which the inscrutable scrivener had over me, and from which ascendancy, for all my chafing, I could not completely escape, I slowly went down stairs and out into the street, and while walking round the block, considered what I should next do in this unheard-of perplexity. Turn the man out by an actual thrusting I could not; to drive him away by calling him hard names would not do; calling in the police was an unpleasant idea; and yet, permit him to enjoy his cadaverous triumph over me,—this too I could not think of. What was to be done? or, if nothing could be done, was there any thing further that I could assume in the matter? Yes, as before I had prospectively assumed that Bartleby would depart, so now I might retrospectively assume that departed he was. In the legitimate carrying out of this assumption, I might enter my office in a great hurry, and pretending not to see Bartleby at all, walk straight against him as if he were air. Such a proceeding would in a singular degree have the appearance of a home-thrust. It was hardly possible that Bartleby could withstand such an application of the doctrine of assumptions. But upon second thoughts the success of the plan seemed rather dubious. I resolved to argue the matter over with him again.

"Bartleby," said I, entering the office, with a quietly severe expression, "I am seriously displeased. I am pained, Bartleby. I had thought better of you. I had imagined you of such a gentlemanly organization, that in any delicate dilemma a slight hint would suffice—in short, an assumption. But it appears I am deceived. Why," I added, unaffectedly starting, "you have not even touched that money yet," pointing to it, just where I had left it the evening previous.

He answered nothing.

"Will you, or will you not, quit me?" I now demanded in a sudden passion, advancing close to him.

"I would prefer *not* to quit you," he replied, gently emphasizing the *not*.

"What earthly right have you to stay here? Do you pay any rent? Do you pay my taxes? Or is this property yours?"

He answered nothing.

"Are you ready to go on and write now? Are your eyes recovered? Could you copy a small paper for me this morning? or help examine a few lines? or step round to the post-office? In a word, will you do any thing at all, to give a coloring to your refusal to depart the premises?"

He silently retired into his hermitage.

I was now in such a state of nervous resentment that I thought it but prudent to check myself at present from further demonstrations. Bartleby and I were alone. I remembered the tragedy of the unfortuate Adams and the still more unfortunate Colt[7] in the solitary office of the latter; and how poor Colt, being dreadfully incensed by Adams, and imprudently permitting himself to get wildly excited, was at unawares hurried into his fatal act—an act which certainly no man could possibly deplore more than the actor himself. Often it had occurred to me in my ponderings upon the subject, that had that altercation taken place in the public street, or at a private residence, it would not have terminated as it did. It was the circumstance of being alone in a solitary office, up stairs, of a building entirely unhallowed by humanizing domestic associations—an uncarpeted office, doubtless, of a dusty, haggard sort of appearance;—this it must have been, which greatly helped to enhance the irritable desperation of the hapless Colt.

But when this old Adam of resentment rose in me and tempted me concerning Bartleby, I grappled him and threw him. How? Why, simply by recalling the divine injunction: "A new commandment give I unto you, that ye love one another."[8] Yes, this it was that saved me. Aside from higher considerations, charity often operates as a vastly wise and prudent principle—a great safeguard to its possessor. Men have committed murder for jealousy's sake, and anger's sake, and hatred's sake, and selfishness' sake, and spiritual pride's sake; but no man that ever I heard of, ever committed a diabolical murder for sweet charity's sake. Mere self-interest, then, if no better motive can be enlisted, should, especially with high-tempered men, prompt all beings to charity and philanthropy. At any rate, upon the occasion in question, I strove to drown my exasperated feelings towards the scriv-

---

7. A celebrated 1841 murder case in New York City; the crime scene was close to the setting of "Bartleby." John C. Colt killed Samuel Adams with a hatchet. Convicted of the murder, Colt stabbed himself to death before he could be hanged. Melville was aboard ship in the South Seas when the gruesome details were headlined in the New York newspapers.
8. Jesus to his disciples (John 13.34).

ener by benevolently construing his conduct. Poor fellow, poor fellow! thought I, he don't mean any thing; and besides, he has seen hard times, and ought to be indulged.

I endeavored also immediately to occupy myself, and at the same time to comfort my despondency. I tried to fancy that in the course of the morning, at such time as might prove agreeable to him, Bartleby, of his own free accord, would emerge from his hermitage, and take up some decided line of march in the direction of the door. But no. Half-past twelve o'clock came; Turkey began to glow in the face, overturn his inkstand, and become generally obstreperous; Nippers abated down into quietude and courtesy; Ginger Nut munched his noon apple; and Bartleby remained standing at his window in one of his profoundest deadwall reveries. Will it be credited? Ought I to acknowledge it? That afternoon I left the office without saying one further word to him.

Some days now passed, during which, at leisure intervals I looked a little into "Edwards in the Will," and "Priestley on Necessity."[9] Under the circumstances, those books induced a salutary feeling. Gradually I slid into the persuasion that these troubles of mine touching the scrivener, had been all predestined from eternity, and Bartleby was billeted upon me for some mysterious purpose of an all-wise Providence, which it was not for a mere mortal like me to fathom. Yes, Bartleby, stay there behind your screen, thought I; I shall persecute you no more; you are harmless and noiseless as any of these old chairs; in short, I never feel so private as when I know you are here. At least I see it, I feel it; I penetrate to the predestinated purpose of my life. I am content. Others may have loftier parts to enact; but my mission in this world, Bartleby, is to furnish you with office-room for such period as you may see fit to remain.

I believe that this wise and blessed frame of mind would have continued with me, had it not been for the unsolicited and uncharitable remarks obtruded upon me by my professional friends who visited the rooms. But thus it often is, that the constant friction of illiberal minds wears out at last the best resolves of the more generous. Though to be sure, when I reflected upon it, it was not strange that people entering my office should be struck by the peculiar aspect of the unaccountable Bartleby, and so be tempted to throw out some sinister observations concerning him. Sometimes an attorney having business with me, and calling at my office, and finding no one but the scrivener there, would undertake to obtain some sort of precise information from him touching my whereabouts; but without heeding his

9. Joseph Priestley (1733–1804), English scientist and theologian, author of *Doctrine of Philosophical Necessity* (1777). Jonathan Edwards (1703–1758), New England theologian and philosopher, author of *Freedom of Will* (1754). Some critics cite Edwards's doctrine of "Negative Preference" as a source for Bartleby's "I prefer not to."

idle talk, Bartleby would remain standing immovable in the middle of the room. So after contemplating him in that position for a time, the attorney would depart, no wiser than he came.

Also, when a Reference was going on, and the room full of lawyers and witnesses and business was driving fast; some deeply occupied legal gentleman present, seeing Bartleby wholly unemployed, would request him to run round to his (the legal gentleman's) office and fetch some papers for him. Thereupon, Bartleby would tranquilly decline, and remain idle as before. Then the lawyer would give a great stare, and turn to me. And what could I say? At last I was made aware that all through the circle of my professional acquaintance, a whisper of wonder was running round, having reference to the strange creature I kept at my office. This worried me very much. And as the idea came upon me of his possibly turning out a long-lived man, and keep occupying my chambers, and denying my authority; and perplexing my visitors; and scandalizing my professional reputation; and casting a general gloom over the premises; keeping soul and body together to the last upon his savings (for doubtless he spent but half a dime a day), and in the end perhaps outlive me, and claim possession of my office by right of his perpetual occupancy: as all these dark anticipations crowded upon me more and more, and my friends continually intruded their relentless remarks upon the apparition in my room; a great change was wrought in me. I resolved to gather all my faculties together, and for ever rid me of this intolerable incubus.

Ere revolving any complicated project, however, adapted to this end, I first simply suggested to Bartleby the propriety of his permanent departure. In a calm and serious tone, I commended the idea to his careful and mature consideration. But having taken three days to meditate upon it, he apprised me that his original determination remained the same; in short, that he still preferred to abide with me.

What shall I do? I now said to myself, buttoning up my coat to the last button. What shall I do? what ought I to do? what does conscience say I *should* do with this man, or rather ghost. Rid myself of him, I must; go, he shall. But how? You will not thrust him, the poor, pale, passive mortal,—you will not thrust such a helpless creature out of your door? you will not dishonor yourself by such cruelty? No, I will not, I cannot do that. Rather would I let him live and die here, and then mason up his remains in the wall. What then will you do? For all your coaxing, he will not budge. Bribes he leaves under your own paperweight on your table; in short, it is quite plain that he prefers to cling to you.

Then something severe, something unusual must be done. What! surely you will not have him collared by a constable, and commit his innocent pallor to the common jail? And upon what ground could you procure such a thing to be done?—a vagrant, is he? What! he a vagrant, a wanderer, who refuses to budge? It is because he will *not* be a vagrant, then, that you seek to count him *as* a vagrant. That is too absurd. No visible means of support: there I have him. Wrong again: for indubitably he *does* support himself, and that is the only unanswerable proof that any man can show of his possessing the means so to do. No more then. Since he will not quit me, I must quit him. I will change my offices; I will move elsewhere; and give him fair notice, that if I find him on my new premises I will then proceed against him as a common trespasser.

Acting accordingly, next day I thus addressed him: "I find these chambers too far from the City Hall; the air is unwholesome. In a word, I propose to remove my offices next week, and shall no longer require your services. I tell you this now, in order that you may seek another place."

He made no reply, and nothing more was said.

On the appointed day I engaged carts and men, proceeded to my chambers, and having but little furniture, every thing was removed in a few hours. Throughout, the scrivener remained standing behind the screen, which I directed to be removed the last thing. It was withdrawn; and being folded up like a huge folio, left him the motionless occupant of a naked room. I stood in the entry watching him a moment, while something from within me upbraided me.

I re-entered, with my hand in my pocket—and—and my heart in my mouth.

"Good-bye, Bartleby; I am going—good-bye, and God some way bless you; and take that," slipping something in his hand. But it dropped upon the floor, and then,—strange to say—I tore myself from him whom I had so longed to be rid of.

Established in my new quarters, for a day or two I kept the door locked, and started at every footfall in the passages. When I returned to my rooms after any little absence, I would pause at the threshold for an instant, and attentively listen, ere applying my key. But these fears were needless. Bartleby never came nigh me.

I thought all was going well, when a perturbed looking stranger visited me, inquiring whether I was the person who had recently occupied rooms at No.—Wall-street.

Full of forebodings, I replied that I was.

"Then sir," said the stranger, who proved a lawyer, "you are responsible for the man you left there. He refuses to do any copying; he refuses to do any thing; he says he prefers not to; and he refuses to quit the premises."

"I am very sorry, sir," said I, with assumed tranquillity, but an inward tremor, "but, really, the man you allude to is nothing to me— he is no relation or apprentice of mine, that you should hold me responsible for him."

"In mercy's name, who is he?"

"I certainly cannot inform you. I know nothing about him. Formerly I employed him as a copyist; but he has done nothing for me now for some time past."

"I shall settle him then,—good morning, sir."

Several days passed, and I heard nothing more; and though I often felt a charitable prompting to call at the place and see poor Bartleby, yet a certain squeamishness of I know not what withheld me.

All is over with him, by this time, thought I at last, when through another week no further intelligence reached me.

But coming to my room the day after, I found several persons waiting at my door in a high state of nervous excitement.

"That's the man—here he comes," cried the foremost one, whom I recognized as the lawyer who had previously called upon me alone.

"You must take him away, sir, at once," cried a portly person among them, advancing upon me, and whom I knew to be the land-lord of No.—Wall-street. "These gentlemen, my tenants, cannot stand it any longer; Mr. B—" pointing to the lawyer, "has turned him out of his room, and he now persists in haunting the building gen-erally, sitting upon the banisters of the stairs by day, and sleeping in the entry by night. Every body is concerned; clients are leaving the offices; some fears are entertained of a mob; something you must do, and that without delay."

Aghast at this torrent, I fell back before it, and would fain have locked myself in my new quarters. In vain I persisted that Bartleby was nothing to me—no more than to any one else. In vain:—I was the last person known to have any thing to do with him, and they held me to the terrible account. Fearful then of being exposed in the papers (as one person present obscurely threatened) I considered the matter, and at length said, that if the lawyer would give me a confidential interview with the scrivener, in his (the lawyer's) own room, I would that after-noon strive my best to rid them of the nuisance they complained of.

Going up stairs to my old haunt, there was Bartleby silently sit-ting upon the banister at the landing.

"What are you doing here, Bartleby?" said I.

"Sitting upon the banister," he mildly replied.

I motioned him into the lawyer's room, who then left us.

"Bartleby," said I, "are you aware that you are the cause of great tribulation to me, by persisting in occupying the entry after being dismissed from the office?"

No answer.

"Now one of two things must take place. Either you must do something or something must be done to you. Now what sort of business would you like to engage in? Would you like to re-engage in copying for some one?"

"No; I would prefer not to make any change."

"Would you like a clerkship in a dry-goods store?"

"There is too much confinement about that. No, I would not like a clerkship; but I am not particular."

"Too much confinement," I cried, "why you keep yourself confined all the time!"

"I would prefer not to take a clerkship," he rejoined, as if to settle that little item at once.

"How would a bar-tender's business suit you? There is no trying of the eyesight in that."

"I would not like it at all; though, as I said before, I am not particular."

His unwonted wordiness inspirited me. I returned to the charge.

"Well then, would you like to travel through the country collecting bills for the merchants? That would improve your health."

"No, I would prefer to be doing something else."

"How then would going as a companion to Europe, to entertain some young gentleman with your conversation,—how would that suit you?"

"Not at all. It does not strike me that there is any thing definite about that. I like to be stationary. But I am not particular."

"Stationary you shall be then," I cried, now losing all patience, and for the first time in all my exasperating connection with him fairly flying into a passion. "If you do not go away from these premises before night, I shall feel bound—indeed I *am* bound—to—to—to quit the premises myself!" I rather absurdly concluded, knowing not with what possible threat to try to frighten his immobility into compliance. Despairing of all further efforts, I was precipitately leaving him, when a final thought occurred to me—one which had not been wholly unindulged before.

"Bartleby," said I, in the kindest tone I could assume under such exciting circumstances, "will you go home with me now—not to my office, but my dwelling—and remain there till we can conclude upon some convenient arrangement for you at our leisure? Come, let us start now, right away."

"No: at present I would prefer not to make any change at all."

I answered nothing; but effectually dodging every one by the suddenness and rapidity of my flight, rushed from the building, ran up Wall-street towards Broadway, and jumping into the first omnibus was soon removed from pursuit. As soon as tranquillity returned I distinctly perceived that I had now done all that I possibly could, both in respect to the demands of the landlord and his tenants, and with regard to my own desire and sense of duty, to benefit Bartleby, and shield him from rude persecution. I now strove to be entirely care-free and quiescent; and my conscience justified me in the attempt; though indeed it was not so successful as I could have wished. So fearful was I of being again hunted out by the incensed landlord and his exasperated tenants, that, surrendering my business to Nippers, for a few days I drove about the upper part of the town and through the suburbs, in my rockaway;[1] crossed over to Jersey City and Hoboken, and paid fugitive visits to Manhattanville and Astoria. In fact I almost lived in my rockaway for the time.

When again I entered my office, lo, a note from the landlord lay upon the desk. I opened it with trembling hands. It informed me that the writer had sent to the police, and had Bartleby removed to the Tombs as a vagrant. Moreover, since I knew more about him than any one else, he wished me to appear at that place, and make a suitable statement of the facts. These tidings had a conflicting effect upon me. At first I was indignant; but at last almost approved. The landlord's energetic, summary disposition, had led him to adopt a procedure which I do not think I would have decided upon myself; and yet as a last resort, under such peculiar circumstances, it seemed the only plan.

As I afterwards learned, the poor scrivener, when told that he must be conducted to the Tombs, offered not the slightest obstacle, but in his pale unmoving way, silently acquiesced.

Some of the compassionate and curious bystanders joined the party; and headed by one of the constables arm in arm with Bartleby, the silent procession filed its way through all the noise, and heat, and joy of the roaring thoroughfares at noon.

The same day I received the note I went to the Tombs, or to speak more properly, the Halls of Justice. Seeking the right officer, I stated the purpose of my call, and was informed that the individual I described was indeed within. I then assured the functionary that Bartleby was a perfectly honest man, and greatly to be compassionated, however unaccountably eccentric. I narrated all I knew, and closed by suggesting the idea of letting him remain in as indulgent confinement as possible till something less harsh might be done— though indeed I hardly knew what. At all events, if nothing else could be decided upon, the alms-house must receive him. I then begged to have an interview.

Being under no disgraceful charge, and quite serene and harmless in all his ways, they had permitted him freely to wander about the prison, and especially in the inclosed grass-platted yards thereof. And so I found him there, standing all alone in the quietest of the yards, his face towards a high wall, while all around, from the narrow slits of the jail windows, I thought I saw peering out upon him the eyes of murderers and thieves.

1. An open carriage.

"Bartleby!"

"I know you," he said, without looking round,—"and I want nothing to say to you."

"It was not I that brought you here, Bartleby," said I, keenly pained at his implied suspicion. "And to you, this should not be so vile a place. Nothing reproachful attaches to you by being here. And see, it is not so sad a place as one might think. Look, there is the sky, and here is the grass."

"I know where I am," he replied, but would say nothing more, and so I left him.

As I entered the corridor again, a broad meat-like man, in an apron, accosted me, and jerking his thumb over his shoulder said—"Is that your friend?"

"Yes."

"Does he want to starve? If he does, let him live on the prison fare, that's all."

"Who are you?" asked I, not knowing what to make of such an unofficially speaking person in such a place.

"I am the grub-man. Such gentlemen as have friends here, hire me to provide them with something good to eat."

"Is this so?" said I, turning to the turnkey.

He said it was.

"Well then," said I, slipping some silver into the grubman's hands (for so they called him). "I want you to give particular attention to my friend there; let him have the best dinner you can get. And you must be as polite to him as possible."

"Introduce me, will you?" said the grub-man, looking at me with an expression which seemed to say he was all impatience for an opportunity to give a specimen of his breeding.

Thinking it would prove of benefit to the scrivener, I acquiesced; and asking the grub-man his name, went up with him to Bartleby.

"Bartleby, this is a friend; you will find him very useful to you."

"Your sarvant, sir, your sarvant," said the grub-man, making a low salutation behind his apron. "Hope you find it pleasant here, sir;—spacious grounds—cool apartments, sir—hope you'll stay with us some time—try to make it agreeable. What will you have for dinner today?"

"I prefer not to dine to-day," said Bartleby, turning away. "It would disagree with me; I am unused to dinners." So saying he slowly moved to the other side of the inclosure, and took up a position fronting the dead-wall.

"How's this?" said the grub-man, addressing me with a stare of astonishment. "He's odd, aint he?"

"I think he is a little deranged," said I, sadly.

"Deranged? deranged is it? Well now, upon my word, I thought that

friend of yourn was a gentleman forger; they are always pale and gen-
teel-like, them forgers. I can't help pity 'em—can't help it, sir. Did you
know Monroe Edwards?"[2] he added touchingly, and paused. Then,
laying his hand pityingly on my shoulder, sighed, "he died of consumption at Sing-Sing. So you weren't acquainted with Monroe?"

"No, I was never socially acquainted with any forgers. But I
cannot stop longer. Look to my friend yonder. You will not lose by it.
I will see you again."

Some few days after this, I again obtained admission to the
Tombs, and went through the corridors in quest of Bartleby; but
without finding him.

"I saw him coming from his cell not long ago," said a turnkey,
"may be he's gone to loiter in the yards."

So I went in that direction.

"Are you looking for the silent man?" said another turnkey
passing me. "Yonder he lies—sleeping in the yard there. 'Tis not
twenty minutes since I saw him lie down."

The yard was entirely quiet. It was not accessible to the common
prisoners. The surrounding walls, of amazing thickness, kept off all
sound behind them. The Egyptian character of the masonry
weighed upon me with its gloom. But a soft imprisoned turf grew
under foot. The heart of the eternal pyramids, it seemed, wherein,
by some strange magic, through the clefts, grass-seed, dropped by
birds, had sprung.[3]

Strangely huddled at the base of the wall, his knees drawn up,
and lying on his side, his head touching the cold stones, I saw the
wasted Bartleby. But nothing stirred. I paused; then went close up
to him; stooped over, and saw that his dim eyes were open; otherwise he seemed profoundly sleeping. Something prompted me to
touch him. I felt his hand, when a tingling shiver ran up my arm and
down my spine to my feet.

The round face of the grub-man peered upon me now. "His dinner
is ready. Won't he dine to-day, either? Or does he live without dining?"

"Lives without dining," said I, and closed the eyes.

"Eh!—He's asleep, aint he?"

"With kings and counsellors," murmured I.

\*    \*    \*    \*    \*    \*    \*    \*

There would seem little need for proceeding further in this history.
Imagination will readily supply the meagre recital of poor Bartleby's

---

2. A notorious swindler, imprisoned in the Tombs. He was characterized by Horace Greeley
   as "the most distinguished financier since the days of Judas Iscariot."
3. Compare this description of the prison yard with Melville's letter to Nathaniel
   Hawthorne, June 1851, "I am like one of those seeds taken out of the Egyptian Pyramids,
   which, after being three thousand years a seed and nothing but a seed, being planted in
   English soil, it developed itself, grew to greenness, and then fell to mould. So I."

interment. But ere parting with the reader, let me say, that if this little narrative has sufficiently interested him, to awaken curiosity as to who Bartleby was, and what manner of life he led prior to the present narrator's making his acquaintance, I can only reply, that in such curiosity I fully share, but am wholly unable to gratify it. Yet here I hardly know whether I should divulge one little item of rumor, which came to my ear a few months after the scrivener's decease. Upon what basis it rested, I could never ascertain; and hence how true it is I cannot now tell. But inasmuch as this vague report has not been without a certain strange suggestive interest to me, however sad, it may prove the same with some others; and so I will briefly mention it. The report was this: that Bartleby had been a subordinate clerk in the Dead Letter Office at Washington, from which he had been suddenly removed by a change in the administration. When I think over this rumor, I cannot adequately express the emotions which seize me. Dead letters! does it not sound like dead men? Conceive a man by nature and misfortune prone to a pallid hopelessness, can any business seem more fitted to heighten it than that of continually handling these dead letters and assorting them for the flames? For by the cartload they are annually burned. Sometimes from out the folded paper the pale clerk takes a ring:—the finger it was meant for, perhaps, moulders in the grave; a bank-note sent in swiftest charity:—he whom it would relieve, nor eats nor hungers any more; pardon for those who died despairing; hope for those who died unhoping; good tidings for those who died stifled by unrelieved calamities. On errands of life, these letters speed to death.

Ah Bartleby! Ah humanity!

# Benito Cereno[1]

In the year 1799, Captain Amasa Delano, of Duxbury, in Massachusetts, commanding a large sealer and general trader, lay at anchor, with a valuable cargo, in the harbor of St. Maria—a small,

1. The text is from the story's first printing in *Putnam's Monthly* (October, November, and December 1855) and includes Melville's revisions for its inclusion in *The Piazza Tales* (1856). An important source for the story is Chapter 18 of Amasa Delano's *Narrative of Voyages and Travels, in the Northern and Southern Hemispheres* (Boston, 1817), reprinted here on pp. 199–228. There is a substantial body of criticism devoted to the many changes Melville made in Delano's chapter. Among them: changing the date from 1805 to 1799, changing the names of the ships from the *Perseverence* and the *Tryal* to the *Bachelor's Delight* and the *San Dominick*. Modern readers see an allusion to the island of Santo Domingo, where Toussaint L'Overture led a slave rebellion in the 1790s. *San Dominick* may also refer to Dominican monks, the "Black Friars" prominent in the Spanish Inquisition. Delano's eighteenth chapter is fourteen thousand words; *Benito Cereno* is thirty-four thousand words.

desert, uninhabited island toward the southern extremity of the long coast of Chili. There he had touched for water.

On the second day, not long after dawn, while lying in his berth, his mate came below, informing him that a strange sail was coming into the bay. Ships were then not so plenty in those waters as now. He rose, dressed, and went on deck.

The morning was one peculiar to that coast. Everything was mute and calm; everything gray. The sea, though undulated into long roods of swells, seemed fixed, and was sleeked at the surface like waved lead that has cooled and set in the smelter's mold. The sky seemed a gray surtout. Flights of troubled gray fowl, kith and kin with flights of troubled gray vapors among which they were mixed, skimmed low and fitfully over the waters, as swallows over meadows before storms. Shadows present, foreshadowing deeper shadows to come.

To Captain Delano's surprise, the stranger, viewed through the glass, showed no colors; though to do so upon entering a haven, however uninhabited in its shores, where but a single other ship might be lying, was the custom among peaceful seamen of all nations. Considering the lawlessness and loneliness of the spot, and the sort of stories, at that day, associated with those seas, Captain Delano's surprise might have deepened into some uneasiness had he not been a person of a singularly undistrustful good nature, not liable, except on extraordinary and repeated incentives, and hardly then, to indulge in personal alarms, any way involving the imputation of malign evil in man. Whether, in view of what humanity is capable, such a trait implies, along with a benevolent heart, more than ordinary quickness and accuracy of intellectual perception, may be left to the wise to determine.

But whatever misgivings might have obtruded on first seeing the stranger, would almost, in any seaman's mind, have been dissipated by observing that, the ship, in navigating into the harbor, was drawing too near the land; a sunken reef making out off her bow. This seemed to prove her a stranger, indeed, not only to the sealer, but the island; consequently, she could be no wonted freebooter on that ocean. With no small interest, Captain Delano continued to watch her—a proceeding not much facilitated by the vapors partly mantling the hull, through which the far matin[2] light from her cabin streamed equivocally enough; much like the sun—by this time hemisphered on the rim of the horizon, and apparently, in company with the strange ship, entering the harbor—which, wimpled by the same low, creeping clouds, showed not unlike a Lima intriguante's

2. Early morning.

one sinister eye peering across the Plaza from the Indian loop-hole of her dusk *saya-y-manta*.[3]

It might have been but a deception of the vapors, but, the longer the stranger was watched, the more singular appeared her maneuvers. Ere long it seemed hard to decide whether she meant to come in or no—what she wanted, or what she was about. The wind, which had breezed up a little during the night, was now extremely light and baffling, which the more increased the apparent uncertainty of her movements.

Surmising, at last, that it might be a ship in distress, Captain Delano ordered his whale-boat to be dropped, and, much to the wary opposition of his mate, prepared to board her, and, at the least, pilot her in. On the night previous, a fishing-party of the seamen had gone a long distance to some detached rocks out of sight from the sealer, and, an hour or two before day-break, had returned, having met with no small success. Presuming that the stranger might have been long off soundings, the good captain put several baskets of the fish, for presents, into his boat, and so pulled away. From her continuing too near the sunken reef, deeming her in danger, calling to his men, he made all haste to apprise those on board of their situation. But, some time ere the boat came up, the wind, light though it was, having shifted, had headed the vessel off, as well as partly broken the vapors from about her.

Upon gaining a less remote view, the ship, when made signally visible on the verge of the leaden-hued swells, with the shreds of fog here and there raggedly furring her, appeared like a white-washed monastery after a thunder-storm, seen perched upon some dun cliff among the Pyrenees. But it was no purely fanciful resemblance which now, for a moment, almost led Captain Delano to think that nothing less than a ship-load of monks was before him. Peering over the bulwarks were what really seemed, in the hazy distance, throngs of dark cowls; while, fitfully revealed through the open port-holes, other dark moving figures were dimly descried, as of Black Friars pacing the cloisters.

Upon a still nigher approach, this appearance was modified, and the true character of the vessel was plain—a Spanish merchantman of the first class; carrying negro slaves, amongst other valuable freight, from one colonial port to another. A very large, and, in its time, a very fine vessel, such as in those days were at intervals encountered along that main; sometimes superseded Acapulco treasure-ships, or retired frigates of the Spanish king's navy, which, like superannuated Italian palaces, still, under a decline of masters, preserved signs of former state.

---

3. A woman's robe constructed to reveal only her face.

As the whale-boat drew more and more nigh, the cause of the peculiar pipe-clayed aspect of the stranger was seen in the slovenly neglect pervading her. The spars, ropes, and great part of the bulwarks, looked woolly, from long unacquaintance with the scraper, tar, and the brush. Her keel seemed laid, her ribs put together, and she launched, from Ezekiel's Valley of Dry Bones.[4]

In the present business in which she was engaged, the ship's general model and rig appeared to have undergone no material change from their original war-like and Froissart pattern. However, no guns were seen.

The tops were large, and were railed about with what had once been octagonal net-work, all now in sad disrepair. These tops hung overhead like three ruinous aviaries, in one of which was seen perched, on a ratlin, a white noddy, a strange fowl, so called from its lethargic, somnambulistic character, being frequently caught by hand at sea. Battered and mouldy, the castellated forecastle seemed some ancient turret, long ago taken by assault, and then left to decay. Toward the stern, two high-raised quarter galleries—the balustrades here and there covered with dry, tindery sea-moss—opening out from the unoccupied state-cabin, whose dead lights, for all the mild weather, were hermetically closed and calked—these tenantless balconies hung over the sea as if it were the grand Venetian canal. But the principal relic of faded grandeur was the ample oval of the shield-like stern-piece, intricately carved with the arms of Castile and Leon, medallioned about by groups of mythological or symbolical devices; uppermost and central of which was a dark satyr in a mask, holding his foot on the prostrate neck of a writhing figure, likewise masked.

Whether the ship had a figure-head, or only a plain beak, was not quite certain, owing to canvas wrapped about that part, either to protect it while undergoing a re-furbishing, or else decently to hide its decay. Rudely painted or chalked, as in a sailor freak, along the forward side of a sort of pedestal below the canvas, was the sentence, "Seguid vuestro jefe," (follow your leader); while upon the tarnished head-boards, near by, appeared, in stately capitals, once gilt, the ship's name, "SAN DOMINICK," each letter streakingly corroded with tricklings of copper-spike rust; while, like mourning weeds, dark festoons of sea-grass slimily swept to and fro over the name, with every hearse-like roll of the hull.

As at last the boat was hooked from the bow along toward the gangway amidship, its keel, while yet some inches separated from the hull, harshly grated as on a sunken coral reef. It proved a huge bunch of conglobated barnacles adhering below the water to the

4. Ezekiel 37.1–14.

side like a wen; a token of baffling airs and long calms passed some-where in those seas.

Climbing the side, the visitor was at once surrounded by a clam-orous throng of whites and blacks, but the latter outnumbering the former more than could have been expected, negro transportation-ship as the stranger in port was. But, in one language, and as with one voice, all poured out a common tale of suffering; in which the negresses, of whom there were not a few, exceeded the others in their dolorous vehemence. The scurvy, together with a fever, had swept off a great part of their number, more especially the Spaniards. Off Cape Horn, they had narrowly escaped shipwreck; then, for days together, they had lain tranced without wind; their provisions were low; their water next to none; their lips that moment were baked.

While Captain Delano was thus made the mark of all eager tongues, his one eager glance took in all the faces, with every other object about him.

Always upon first boarding a large and populous ship at sea, espe-cially a foreign one, with a nondescript crew such as Lascars or Manilla men, the impression varies in a peculiar way from that pro-duced by first entering a strange house with strange inmates in a strange land. Both house and ship, the one by its walls and blinds, the other by its high bulwarks like ramparts, hoard from view their interiors till the last moment; but in the case of the ship there is this addition; that the living spectacle it contains, upon its sudden and complete disclosure, has, in contrast with the blank ocean which zones it, something of the effect of enchantment. The ship seems unreal; these strange costumes, gestures, and faces, but a shadowy tableau just emerged from the deep, which directly must receive back what it gave.

Perhaps it was some such influence as above is attempted to be described, which, in Captain Delano's mind, hightened whatever, upon a staid scrutiny, might have seemed unusual; especially the conspicuous figures of four elderly grizzled negroes, their heads like black, doddered willow tops, who, in venerable contrast to the tumult below them, were couched sphynx-like, one on the starboard cat-head, another on the larboard, and the remaining pair face to face on the opposite bulwarks above the main-chains. They each had bits of unstranded old junk in their hands, and, with a sort of stoical self-content, were picking the junk into oakum, a small heap of which lay by their sides. They accompanied the task with a con-tinuous, low, monotonous chant; droning and druling away like so many gray-headed bag-pipers playing a funeral march.

The quarter-deck rose into an ample elevated poop, upon the for-ward verge of which, lifted, like the oakum-pickers, some eight feet

above the general throng, sat along in a row, separated by regular
spaces, the cross-legged figures of six other blacks; each with a rusty
hatchet in his hand, which, with a bit of brick and a rag, he was
engaged like a scullion in scouring; while between each two was a
small stack of hatchets, their rusted edges turned forward awaiting
a like operation. Though occasionally the four oakum-pickers would
briefly address some person or persons in the crowd below, yet the
six hatchet-polishers neither spoke to others, nor breathed a
whisper among themselves, but sat intent upon their task, except at
intervals, when, with the peculiar love in negroes of uniting industry
with pastime, two and two they sideways clashed their hatchets
together, like cymbals, with a barbarous din. All six, unlike the generality, had the raw aspect of unsophisticated Africans.

But that first comprehensive glance which took in those ten figures, with scores less conspicuous, rested but an instant upon them,
as, impatient of the hubbub of voices, the visitor turned in quest of
whomsoever it might be that commanded the ship.

But as if not unwilling to let nature make known her own case
among his suffering charge, or else in despair of restraining it for
the time, the Spanish captain, a gentlemanly, reserved-looking, and
rather young man to a stranger's eye, dressed with singular richness,
but bearing plain traces of recent sleepless cares and disquietudes,
stood passively by, leaning against the main-mast, at one moment
casting a dreary, spiritless look upon his excited people, at the next
an unhappy glance toward his visitor. By his side stood a black of
small stature, in whose rude face, as occasionally, like a shepherd's
dog, he mutely turned it up into the Spaniard's, sorrow and affection were equally blended.

Struggling through the throng, the American advanced to the
Spaniard, assuring him of his sympathies, and offering to render
whatever assistance might be in his power. To which the Spaniard
returned, for the present, but grave and ceremonious acknowledg-
ments, his national formality dusked by the saturnine mood of ill
health.

But losing no time in mere compliments, Captain Delano
returning to the gangway, had his baskets of fish brought up; and as
the wind still continued light, so that some hours at least must
elapse ere the ship could be brought to the anchorage, he bade his
men return to the sealer, and fetch back as much water as the
whale-boat could carry, with whatever soft bread the steward might
have, all the remaining pumpkins on board, with a box of sugar, and
a dozen of his private bottles of cider.

Not many minutes after the boat's pushing off, to the vexation of
all, the wind entirely died away, and the tide turning, began drifting
back the ship helplessly seaward. But trusting this would not long

last, Captain Delano sought with good hopes to cheer up the strangers, feeling no small satisfaction that, with persons in their condition he could—thanks to his frequent voyages along the Spanish main—converse with some freedom in their native tongue.

While left alone with them, he was not long in observing some things tending to highten his first impressions; but surprise was lost in pity, both for the Spaniards and blacks, alike evidently reduced from scarcity of water and provisions; while long-continued suffering seemed to have brought out the less good-natured qualities of the negroes, besides, at the same time, impairing the Spaniard's authority over them. But, under the circumstances, precisely this condition of things was to have been anticipated. In armies, navies, cities, or families, in nature herself, nothing more relaxes good order than misery. Still, Captain Delano was not without the idea, that had Benito Cereno been a man of greater energy, misrule would hardly have come to the present pass. But the debility, constitutional or induced by the hardships, bodily and mental, of the Spanish captain, was too obvious to be overlooked. A prey to settled dejection, as if long mocked with hope he would not now indulge it, even when it had ceased to be a mock, the prospect of that day or evening at furthest, lying at anchor, with plenty of water for his people, and a brother captain to counsel and befriend, seemed in no perceptible degree to encourage him. His mind appeared unstrung, if not still more seriously affected. Shut up in these oaken walls, chained to one dull round of command, whose unconditionality cloyed him, like some hypochondriac abbot he moved slowly about, at times suddenly pausing, starting, or staring, biting his lip, biting his finger-nail, flushing, paling, twitching his beard, with other symptoms of an absent or moody mind. This distempered spirit was lodged, as before hinted, in as distempered a frame. He was rather tall, but seemed never to have been robust, and now with nervous suffering was almost worn to a skeleton. A tendency to some pulmonary complaint appeared to have been lately confirmed. His voice was like that of one with lungs half gone, hoarsely suppressed, a husky whisper. No wonder that, as in this state he tottered about, his private servant apprehensively followed him. Sometimes the negro gave his master his arm, or took his handkerchief out of his pocket for him; performing these and similar offices with that affectionate zeal which transmutes into something filial or fraternal acts in themselves but menial; and which has gained for the negro the repute of making the most pleasing body servant in the world; one, too, whom a master need be on no stiffly superior terms with, but may treat with familiar trust; less a servant than a devoted companion.

Marking the noisy indocility of the blacks in general, as well as what seemed the sullen inefficiency of the whites, it was not without humane satisfaction that Captain Delano witnessed the steady good conduct of Babo.[5]

But the good conduct of Babo, hardly more than the ill-behavior of others, seemed to withdraw the half-lunatic Don Benito from his cloudy languor. Not that such precisely was the impression made by the Spaniard on the mind of his visitor. The Spaniard's individual unrest was, for the present, but noted as a conspicuous feature in the ship's general affliction. Still, Captain Delano was not a little concerned at what he could not help taking for the time to be Don Benito's unfriendly indifference towards himself. The Spaniard's manner, too, conveyed a sort of sour and gloomy disdain, which he seemed at no pains to disguise. But this the American in charity ascribed to the harassing effects of sickness, since, in former instances, he had noted that there are peculiar natures on whom prolonged physical suffering seems to cancel every social instinct of kindness; as if forced to black bread themselves, they deemed it but equity that each person coming nigh them should, indirectly, by some slight or affront, be made to partake of their fare.

But ere long Captain Delano bethought him that, indulgent as he was at the first, in judging the Spaniard, he might not, after all, have exercised charity enough. At bottom it was Don Benito's reserve which displeased him; but the same reserve was shown towards all but his faithful personal attendant. Even the formal reports which, according to sea-usage, were, at stated times, made to him by some petty underling, either a white, mulatto or black, he hardly had patience enough to listen to, without betraying contemptuous aversion. His manner upon such occasions was, in its degree, not unlike that which might be supposed to have been his imperial countryman's, Charles V.,[6] just previous to the anchoritish retirement of that monarch from the throne.

This splenetic disrelish of his place was evinced in almost every function pertaining to it. Proud as he was moody, he condescended to no personal mandate. Whatever special orders were necessary, their delivery was delegated to his body-servant, who in turn trans-

---

5. One of Melville's most dramatic changes was to combine into a single figure Delano's Mure, the servile companion to Don Benito, and Babo, the "captain of the slaves."

6. Spanish King and Holy Roman Emperor (1500–1558), who spent his last two years confined in a monastery. A popular book in America of the early 1850s was William Stirling's *The Cloister Life of the Emperor Charles the Fifth*. Parts of it were quoted in literary journals beside reviews of Melville's early books. In *The Wake of the Gods: Melville's Mythology* H. Bruce Franklin argues that "many of the phrases Melville uses to describe Benito Cereno are almost identical to the phrases Stirling uses to describe Charles V; many details of Cereno's physical and social environment have precise correspondents in the environment of Charles; almost every trait of Cereno is a trait of Charles. Benito Cereno is, in more than one sense, the ghost of Charles V . . . re-enacting Charles's abdication of the Holy Roman Empire and surrender of worldly power, and he finally becomes, like Charles himself, the symbolic ghost of all power." A significant addition Melville made to Delano's narrative, the shaving scene, is based on Stirling's book.

ferred them to their ultimate destination, through runners, alert
Spanish boys or slave boys, like pages or pilot-fish within easy call
continually hovering round Don Benito. So that to have beheld this
undemonstrative invalid gliding about, apathetic and mute, no
landsman could have dreamed that in him was lodged a dictatorship
beyond which, while at sea, there was no earthly appeal.

Thus, the Spaniard, regarded in his reserve, seemed as the involuntary victim of mental disorder. But, in fact, his reserve might, in
some degree, have procceded from design. If so, then here was
evinced the unhealthy climax of that icy though conscientious
policy, more or less adopted by all commanders of large ships,
which, except in signal emergencies, obliterates alike the manifestation of sway with every trace of sociality; transforming the man
into a block, or rather into a loaded cannon, which, until there is
call for thunder, has nothing to say.

Viewing him in this light, it seemed but a natural token of the perverse habit induced by a long course of such hard self-restraint,
that, notwithstanding the present condition of his ship, the
Spaniard should still persist in a demeanor, which, however harmless, or, it may be, appropriate, in a well appointed vessel, such as
the San Dominick might have been at the outset of the voyage, was
anything but judicious now. But the Spaniard perhaps thought that
it was with captains as with gods: reserve, under all events, must
still be their cue. But more probably this appearance of slumbering
dominion might have been but an attempted disguise to conscious
imbecility—not deep policy, but shallow device. But be all this as it
might, whether Don Benito's manner was designed or not, the more
Captain Delano noted its pervading reserve, the less he felt uneasiness at any particular manifestation of that reserve towards himself.

Neither were his thoughts taken up by the captain alone. Wonted
to the quiet orderliness of the sealer's comfortable family of a crew,
the noisy confusion of the San Dominick's suffering host repeatedly
challenged his eye. Some prominent breaches not only of discipline
but of decency were observed. These Captain Delano could not but
ascribe, in the main, to the absence of those subordinate deck-offi-
cers to whom, along with higher duties, is entrusted what may be
styled the police department of a populous ship. True, the old oakum-
pickers appeared at times to act the part of monitorial constables to
their countrymen, the blacks; but though occasionally succeeding in
allaying trifling outbreaks now and then between man and man, they
could do little or nothing toward establishing general quiet. The San
Dominick was in the condition of a transatlantic emigrant ship,
among whose multitude of living freight are some individuals, doubtless, as little troublesome as crates and bales; but the friendly remonstrances of such with their ruder companions are of not so much avail

as the unfriendly arm of the mate. What the San Dominick wanted was, what the emigrant ship has, stern superior officers. But on these decks not so much as a fourth mate was to be seen.

The visitor's curiosity was roused to learn the particulars of those mishaps which had brought about such absenteeism, with its consequences; because, though deriving some inkling of the voyage from the wails which at the first moment had greeted him, yet of the details no clear understanding had been had. The best account would, doubtless, be given by the captain. Yet at first the visitor was loth to ask it, unwilling to provoke some distant rebuff. But plucking up courage, he at last accosted Don Benito, renewing the expression of his benevolent interest, adding, that did he (Captain Delano) but know the particulars of the ship's misfortunes, he would, perhaps, be better able in the end to relieve them. Would Don Benito favor him with the whole story?

Don Benito faltered; then, like some somnambulist suddenly interfered with, vacantly stared at his visitor, and ended by looking down on the deck. He maintained this posture so long, that Captain Delano, almost equally disconcerted, and involuntarily almost as rude, turned suddenly from him, walking forward to accost one of the Spanish seamen for the desired information. But he had hardly gone five paces, when with a sort of eagerness Don Benito invited him back, regretting his momentary absence of mind, and professing readiness to gratify him.

While most part of the story was being given, the two captains stood on the after part of the main-deck, a privileged spot, no one being near but the servant.

"It is now a hundred and ninety days," began the Spaniard, in his husky whisper, "that this ship, well officered and well manned, with several cabin passengers—some fifty Spaniards in all—sailed from Buenos Ayres bound to Lima, with a general cargo, hardware, Paraguay tea and the like—and," pointing forward, "that parcel of negroes, now not more than a hundred and fifty, as you see, but then numbering over three hundred souls. Off Cape Horn we had heavy gales. In one moment, by night, three of my best officers, with fifteen sailors, were lost, with the main-yard; the spar snapping under them in the slings, as they sought, with heavers, to beat down the icy sail. To lighten the hull, the heavier sacks of mata were thrown into the sea, with most of the water-pipes lashed on deck at the time. And this last necessity it was, combined with the prolonged detentions afterwards experienced, which eventually brought about our chief causes of suffering. When——"

Here there was a sudden fainting attack of his cough, brought on, no doubt, by his mental distress. His servant sustained him, and drawing a cordial from his pocket placed it to his lips. He a little revived. But unwilling to leave him unsupported while yet imperfectly restored, the black with one arm still encircled his master, at the same time keeping his eye fixed on his face, as if to watch for the first sign of complete restoration, or relapse, as the event might prove.

The Spaniard proceeded, but brokenly and obscurely, as one in a dream.

—"Oh, my God! rather than pass through what I have, with joy I would have hailed the most terrible gales; but——"

His cough returned and with increased violence; this subsiding, with reddened lips and closed eyes he fell heavily against his supporter.

"His mind wanders. He was thinking of the plague that followed the gales," plaintively sighed the servant; "my poor, poor master!" wringing one hand, and with the other wiping the mouth. "But be patient, Señor," again turning to Captain Delano, "these fits do not last long; master will soon be himself."

Don Benito reviving, went on; but as this portion of the story was very brokenly delivered, the substance only will here be set down.

It appeared that after the ship had been many days tossed in storms off the Cape, the scurvy broke out, carrying off numbers of the whites and blacks. When at last they had worked round into the Pacific, their spars and sails were so damaged, and so inadequately handled by the surviving mariners, most of whom were become invalids, that, unable to lay her northerly course by the wind, which was powerful, the unmanageable ship for successive days and nights was blown northwestward, where the breeze suddenly deserted her, in unknown waters, to sultry calms. The absence of the water-pipes now proved as fatal to life as before their presence had menaced it. Induced, or at least aggravated, by the less than scanty allowance of water, a malignant fever followed the scurvy; with the excessive heat of the lengthened calm, making such short work of it as to sweep away, as by billows, whole families of the Africans, and a yet larger number, proportionably, of the Spaniards, including, by a luckless fatality, every remaining officer on board. Consequently, in the smart west winds eventually following the calm, the already rent sails having to be simply dropped, not furled, at need, had been gradually reduced to the beggar's rags they were now. To procure substitutes for his lost sailors, as well as supplies of water and sails, the captain at the earliest opportunity had made for Baldivia, the southermost civilized port of Chili and South America; but upon nearing the coast the thick weather had prevented him from so much as sighting that harbor. Since which period, almost without a crew, and almost without canvas and almost without water, and at intervals giving its added dead to the sea, the San Dominick had been battle-dored about by contrary winds, inveigled by currents, or grown weedy in calms. Like a man lost in woods, more than once she had doubled upon her own track.

"But throughout these calamities," huskily continued Don Benito, painfully turning in the half embrace of his servant, "I have to thank those negroes you see, who, though to your inexperienced eyes appearing unruly, have, indeed, conducted themselves with less of restlessness than even their owner could have thought possible under such circumstances."

Here he again fell faintly back. Again his mind wandered: but he rallied, and less obscurely proceeded.

"Yes, their owner was quite right in assuring me that no fetters would be needed with his blacks; so that while, as is wont in this transportation, those negroes have always remained upon deck—not thrust below, as in the Guineamen—they have, also, from the beginning, been freely permitted to range within given bounds at their pleasure."

Once more the faintness returned—his mind roved—but, recovering, he resumed:

"But it is Babo here to whom, under God, I owe not only my own preservation, but likewise to him, chiefly, the merit is due, of pacifying his more ignorant brethren, when at intervals tempted to murmurings."

"Ah, master," sighed the black, bowing his face, "don't speak of me; Babo is nothing; what Babo has done was but duty."

"Faithful fellow!" cried Capt. Delano. "Don Benito, I envy you such a friend; slave I cannot call him."

As master and man stood before him, the black upholding the white, Captain Delano could not but bethink him of the beauty of that relationship which could present such a spectacle of fidelity on the one hand and confidence on the other. The scene was hightened by the contrast in dress, denoting their relative positions. The Spaniard wore a loose Chili jacket of dark velvet; white small clothes and stockings, with silver buckles at the knee and instep; a high-crowned sombrero, of fine grass; a slender sword, silver mounted, hung from a knot in his sash; the last being an almost invariable adjunct, more for ornament than utility, of a South American gentleman's dress to this hour. Excepting when his occasional nervous contortions brought about disarray, there was a certain precision in his attire, curiously at variance with the unsightly disorder around; especially in the belittered Ghetto, forward of the main-mast, wholly occupied by the blacks.

The servant wore nothing but wide trowsers, apparently, from their coarseness and patches, made out of some old topsail; they were clean, and confined at the waist by a bit of unstranded rope, which, with his composed, deprecatory air at times, made him look something like a begging friar of St. Francis.

However unsuitable for the time and place, at least in the blunt-thinking American's eyes, and however strangely surviving in the midst of all his afflictions, the toilette of Don Benito might not, in fashion at least, have gone beyond the style of the day among South Americans of his class. Though on the present voyage sailing from Buenos Ayres, he had avowed himself a native and resident of Chili, whose inhabitants had not so generally adopted the plain coat and once plebeian pantaloons; but, with a becoming modification, adhered to their provincial costume, picturesque as any in the world. Still, relatively to the pale history of the voyage, and his own pale face, there seemed something so incongruous in the Spaniard's apparel, as almost to suggest the image of an invalid courtier tottering about London streets in the time of the plague.

The portion of the narrative which, perhaps, most excited interest, as well as some surprise, considering the latitudes in question, was the long calms spoken of, and more particularly the ship's so long drifting about. Without communicating the opinion, of course, the American could not but impute at least part of the detentions both to clumsy seamanship and faulty navigation. Eying Don Benito's small, yellow hands, he easily inferred that the young captain had not got into command at the hawse-hole, but the cabin-window; and if so, why wonder at incompetence, in youth, sickness, and gentility united?

But drowning criticism in compassion, after a fresh repetition of his sympathies, Captain Delano having heard out his story, not only engaged, as in the first place, to see Don Benito and his people supplied in their immediate bodily needs, but, also, now further promised to assist him in procuring a large permanent supply of water, as well as some sails and rigging; and, though it would involve no small embarrassment to himself, yet he would spare three of his best seamen for temporary deck officers; so that without delay the ship might proceed to Conception, there fully to refit for Lima, her destined port.

Such generosity was not without its effect, even upon the invalid. His face lighted up; eager and hectic, he met the honest glance of his visitor. With gratitude he seemed overcome.

"This excitement is bad for master," whispered the servant, taking his arm, and with soothing words gently drawing him aside.

When Don Benito returned, the American was pained to observe that his hopefulness, like the sudden kindling in his cheek, was but febrile and transient.

Ere long, with a joyless mien, looking up towards the poop, the host invited his guest to accompany him there, for the benefit of what little breath of wind might be stirring.

As during the telling of the story, Captain Delano had once or twice started at the occasional cymballing of the hatchet-polishers,

wondering why such an interruption should be allowed, especially
in that part of the ship, and in the ears of an invalid; and moreover,
as the hatchets had anything but an attractive look, and the han-
dlers of them still less so, it was, therefore, to tell the truth, not
without some lurking reluctance, or even shrinking, it may be, that
Captain Delano, with apparent complaisance, acquiesced in his
host's invitation. The more so, since with an untimely caprice of
punctilio, rendered distressing by his cadaverous aspect, Don
Benito, with Castilian bows, solemnly insisted upon his guest's preceding him up the ladder leading to the elevation; where, one on
each side of the last step, sat for armorial supporters and sentries
two of the ominous file. Gingerly enough stepped good Captain
Delano between them, and in the instant of leaving them behind,
like one running the gauntlet, he felt an apprehensive twitch in the
calves of his legs.

But when, facing about, he saw the whole file, like so many
organ-grinders, still stupidly intent on their work, unmindful of
everything beside, he could not but smile at his late fidgety panic.

Presently, while standing with his host, looking forward upon the
decks below, he was struck by one of those instances of insubordination previously alluded to. Three black boys, with two Spanish
boys, were sitting together on the hatches, scraping a rude wooden
platter, in which some scanty mess had recently been cooked.
Suddenly, one of the black boys, enraged at a word dropped by one
of his white companions, seized a knife, and though called to forbear by one of the oakum-pickers, struck the lad over the head,
inflicting a gash from which blood flowed.

In amazement, Captain Delano inquired what this meant. To
which the pale Don Benito dully muttered, that it was merely the
sport of the lad.

"Pretty serious sport, truly," rejoined Captain Delano. "Had such
a thing happened on board the Bachelor's Delight, instant punishment would have followed."

At these words the Spaniard turned upon the American one of his
sudden, staring, half-lunatic looks; then relapsing into his torpor,
answered, "Doubtless, doubtless, Señor."

Is it, thought Captain Delano, that this hapless man is one of
those paper captains I've known, who by policy wink at what by
power they cannot put down? I know no sadder sight than a commander who has little of command but the name.

"I should think, Don Benito," he now said, glancing towards the
oakum-picker who had sought to interfere with the boys, "that you
would find it advantageous to keep all your blacks employed, especially the younger ones, no matter at what useless task, and no
matter what happens to the ship. Why, even with my little band, I

find such a course indispensable. I once kept a crew on my quarter-deck thrumming mats for my cabin, when for three days, I had given up my ship—mats, men, and all—for a speedy loss, owing to the violence of a gale, in which we could do nothing but helplessly drive before it."

"Doubtless, doubtless," muttered Don Benito.

"But," continued Captain Delano, again glancing upon the oakum-pickers and then at the hatchet-polishers, near by. "I see you keep some at least of your host employed."

"Yes," was again the vacant response.

"Those old men there, shaking their pows from their pulpits," continued Captain Delano, pointing to the oakum-pickers, "seem to act the part of old dominies to the rest, little heeded as their admonitions are at times. Is this voluntary on their part, Don Benito, or have you appointed them shepherds to your flock of black sheep?"

"What posts they fill, I appointed them," rejoined the Spaniard, in an acrid tone, as if resenting some supposed satiric reflection.

"And these others, these Ashantee conjurors here," continued Captain Delano, rather uneasily eying the brandished steel of the hatchet-polishers, where in spots it had been brought to a shine, "this seems a curious business they are at, Don Benito?"

"In the gales we met," answered the Spaniard, "what of our general cargo was not thrown overboard was much damaged by the brine. Since coming into calm weather, I have had several cases of knives and hatchets daily brought up for overhauling and cleaning."

"A prudent idea, Don Benito. You are part owner of ship and cargo, I presume; but not of the slaves, perhaps?"[7]

"I am owner of all you see," impatiently returned Don Benito, "except the main company of blacks, who belonged to my late friend, Alexandro Aranda."[8]

As he mentioned this name, his air was heart-broken; his knees shook: his servant supported him.

Thinking he divined the cause of such unusual emotion, to confirm his surmise, Captain Delano, after a pause, said, "And may I ask, Don Benito, whether—since awhile ago you spoke of some cabin passengers—the friend, whose loss so afflicts you at the outset of the voyage accompanied his blacks?"

7. Several critics have demonstrated that the contrast between Captain Delano and Benito Cereno draws on a convention of plantation novels: Delano is a stock Yankee Traveler who visits Benito Cereno, an exhausted slaveowning aristocrat of the Old South.
8. The name may come from Pedro Aranda, a bishop during the reign of Charles V, who was divested of his power and imprisoned. Benito Cereno speaks of his "late friend, Alexandro Aranda" who permitted the slaves to walk freely, unchained, on the decks. Stirling writes that "it became necessary to remove the previous coverings" for Philip IV to come "face to face with his great ancestor," Charles. Something very similar occurs when the motto *Seguid vuestro jefe* is uncovered and we see the gruesome fate of Aranda's remains.

"Yes."

"But died of the fever?"

"Died of the fever.—Oh, could I but——"

Again quivering, the Spaniard paused.

"Pardon me," said Captain Delano lowly, "but I think that, by a sympathetic experience, I conjecture, Don Benito, what it is that gives the keener edge to your grief. It was once my hard fortune to lose at sea a dear friend, my own brother, then supercargo. Assured of the welfare of his spirit, its departure I could have borne like a man; but that honest eye, that honest hand—both of which had so often met mine—and that warm heart; all, all—like scraps to the dogs—to throw all to the sharks! It was then I vowed never to have for fellow-voyager a man I loved, unless, unbeknown to him, I had provided every requisite, in case of a fatality, for embalming his mortal part for interment on shore. Were your friend's remains now on board this ship, Don Benito, not thus strangely would the mention of his name affect you."

"On board this ship?" echoed the Spaniard. Then, with horrified gestures, as directed against some specter, he unconsciously fell into the ready arms of his attendant, who, with a silent appeal toward Captain Delano, seemed beseeching him not again to broach a theme so unspeakably distressing to his master.

This poor fellow now, thought the pained American, is the victim of that sad superstition which associates goblins with the deserted body of man, as ghosts with an abandoned house. How unlike are we made! What to me, in like case, would have been a solemn satisfaction, the bare suggestion, even, terrifies the Spaniard into this trance. Poor Alexandro Aranda! what would you say could you here see your friend—who, on former voyages, when you for months were left behind, has, I dare say, often longed, and longed, for one peep at you—now transported with terror at the least thought of having you anyway nigh him.

At this moment, with a dreary graveyard toll, betokening a flaw, the ship's forecastle bell, smote by one of the grizzled oakum-pickers, proclaimed ten o'clock through the leaden calm; when Captain Delano's attention was caught by the moving figure of a gigantic black, emerging from the general crowd below, and slowly advancing towards the elevated poop. An iron collar was about his neck, from which depended a chain, thrice wound round his body; the terminating links padlocked together at a broad band of iron, his girdle.

"How like a mute Atufal moves," murmured the servant.

The black mounted the steps of the poop, and, like a brave prisoner, brought up to receive sentence, stood in unquailing muteness before Don Benito, now recovered from his attack.

At the first glimpse of his approach, Don Benito had started, a resentful shadow swept over his face; and, as with the sudden memory of bootless rage, his white lips glued together.

This is some mulish mutineer, thought Captain Delano, surveying, not without a mixture of admiration, the colossal form of the negro.

"See, he waits your question, master," said the servant.

Thus reminded, Don Benito, nervously averting his glance, as if shunning, by anticipation, some rebellious response, in a disconcerted voice, thus spoke:—

"Atufal, will you ask my pardon now?"

The black was silent.

"Again, master," murmured the servant, with bitter upbraiding eying his countryman, "Again, master; he will bend to master yet."

"Answer," said Don Benito, still averting his glance, "say but the one word *pardon*, and your chains shall be off."

Upon this, the black, slowly raising both arms, let them lifelessly fall, his links clanking, his head bowed; as much as to say, "no, I am content."

"Go," said Don Benito, with inkept and unknown emotion.

Deliberately as he had come, the black obeyed.

"Excuse me, Don Benito," said Captain Delano, "but this scene surprises me; what means it, pray?"

"It means that that negro alone, of all the band, has given me peculiar cause of offense. I have put him in chains; I——"

Here he paused; his hand to his head, as if there were a swimming there, or a sudden bewilderment of memory had come over him; but meeting his servant's kindly glance seemed reassured, and proceeded:—

"I could not scourge such a form. But I told him he must ask my pardon. As yet he has not. At my command, every two hours he stands before me."

"And how long has this been?"

"Some sixty days."

"And obedient in all else? And respectful?"

"Yes."

"Upon my conscience, then," exclaimed Captain Delano, impulsively, "he has a royal spirit in him, this fellow."

"He may have some right to it," bitterly returned Don Benito, "he says he was king in his own land."

"Yes," said the servant, entering a word, "those slits in Atufal's ears once held wedges of gold; but poor Babo here, in his own land, was only a poor slave; a black man's slave was Babo, who now is the white's."

Somewhat annoyed by these conversational familiarities, Captain Delano turned curiously upon the attendant, then glanced inquiringly at his master; but, as if long wonted to these little informalities, neither master nor man seemed to understand him.

"What, pray, was Atufal's offense, Don Benito?" asked Captain Delano; "if it was not something very serious, take a fool's advice, and, in view of his general docility, as well as in some natural respect for his spirit, remit him his penalty."

"No, no, master never will do that," here murmured the servant to himself, "proud Atufal must first ask master's pardon. The slave there carries the padlock, but master here carries the key."

His attention thus directed, Captain Delano now noticed for the first time that, suspended by a slender silken cord, from Don Benito's neck hung a key. At once, from the servant's muttered syllables divining the key's purpose, he smiled and said:—"So, Don Benito—padlock and key—significant symbols, truly."

Biting his lip, Don Benito faltered.

Though the remark of Captain Delano, a man of such native simplicity as to be incapable of satire or irony, had been dropped in playful allusion to the Spaniard's singularly evidenced lordship over the black; yet the hypochondriac seemed in some way to have taken it as a malicious reflection upon his confessed inability thus far to break down, at least, on a verbal summons, the entrenched will of the slave. Deploring this supposed misconception, yet despairing of correcting it, Captain Delano shifted the subject; but finding his companion more than ever withdrawn, as if still sourly digesting the lees of the presumed affront above-mentioned, by-and-by Captain Delano likewise became less talkative, oppressed, against his own will, by what seemed the secret vindictiveness of the morbidly sensitive Spaniard. But the good sailor himself, of a quite contrary disposition, refrained, on his part, alike from the appearance as from the feeling of resentment, and if silent, was only so from contagion.

Presently the Spaniard, assisted by his servant, somewhat discourteously crossed over from his guest; a procedure which, sensibly enough, might have been allowed to pass for idle caprice of ill-humor, had not master and man, lingering round the corner of the elevated skylight, began whispering together in low voices. This was unpleasing. And more: the moody air of the Spaniard, which at times had not been without a sort of valetudinarian stateliness, now seemed anything but dignified; while the menial familiarity of the servant lost its original charm of simple-hearted attachment.

In his embarrassment, the visitor turned his face to the other side of the ship. By so doing, his glance accidentally fell on a young Spanish sailor, a coil of rope in his hand, just stepped from the deck to the first round of the mizzen-rigging. Perhaps the man would not have been particularly noticed, were it not that, during his ascent to one of the yards, he, with a sort of covert intentness, kept his eye fixed on Captain Delano, from whom, presently, it passed, as if by a natural sequence, to the two whisperers.

His own attention thus redirected to that quarter, Captain Delano gave a slight start. From something in Don Benito's manner just then, it seemed as if the visitor had, at least partly, been the subject of the withdrawn consultation going on—a conjecture as little agreeable to the guest as it was little flattering to the host.

The singular alternations of courtesy and ill-breeding in the Spanish captain were unaccountable, except on one of two suppositions—innocent lunacy, or wicked imposture.

But the first idea, though it might naturally have occurred to an indifferent observer, and, in some respect, had not hitherto been wholly a stranger to Captain Delano's mind, yet, now that, in an incipient way, he began to regard the stranger's conduct something in the light of an intentional affront, of course the idea of lunacy was virtually vacated. But if not a lunatic, what then? Under the circumstances, would a gentleman, nay, any honest boor, act the part now acted by his host? The man was an impostor. Some low-born adventurer, masquerading as an oceanic grandee; yet so ignorant of the first requisites of mere gentlemanhood as to be betrayed into the present remarkable indecorum. That strange ceremoniousness, too, at other times evinced, seemed not uncharacteristic of one playing a part above his real level. Benito Cereno—Don Benito Cereno—a sounding name. One, too, at that period, not unknown, in the surname, to supercargoes and sea captains trading along the Spanish Main, as belonging to one of the most enterprising and extensive mercantile families in all those provinces; several members of it having titles; a sort of Castilian Rothschild, with a noble brother, or cousin, in every great trading town of South America. The alleged Don Benito was in early manhood, about twenty-nine or thirty. To assume a sort of roving cadetship in the maritime affairs of such a house, what more likely scheme for a young knave of talent and spirit? But the Spaniard was a pale invalid. Never mind. For even to the degree of simulating mortal disease, the craft of some tricksters had been known to attain. To think, that, under the aspect of infantile weakness, the most savage energies might be couched—those velvets of the Spaniard but the silky paw to his fangs.

From no train of thought did these fancies come; not from within, but from without; suddenly, too, and in one throng, like hoar frost; yet as soon to vanish as the mild sun of Captain Delano's good-nature regained its meridian.

Glancing over once more towards his host—whose side-face, revealed above the skylight, was now turned towards him—he was struck by the profile, whose clearness of cut was refined by the thinness incident to ill-health, as well as ennobled about the chin by the beard. Away with suspicion. He was a true off-shoot of a true hidalgo Cereno.

Relieved by these and other better thoughts, the visitor, lightly humming a tune, now began indifferently pacing the poop, so as not to betray to Don Benito that he had at all mistrusted incivility, much less duplicity; for such mistrust would yet be proved illusory, and by the event; though, for the present, the circumstance which had provoked that distrust remained unexplained. But when that little mystery should have been cleared up, Captain Delano thought he might extremely regret it, did he allow Don Benito to become aware that he had indulged in ungenerous surmises. In short, to the Spaniard's black-letter text, it was best, for awhile, to leave open margin.

Presently, his pale face twitching and overcast, the Spaniard, still supported by his attendant, moved over towards his guest, when, with even more than his usual embarrassment, and a strange sort of intriguing intonation in his husky whisper, the following conversation began:—

"Señor, may I ask how long you have lain at this isle?"

"Oh, but a day or two, Don Benito."

"And from what port are you last?"|

"Canton."

"And there, Señor, you exchanged your seal-skins for teas and silks, I think you said?"

"Yes. Silks, mostly."

"And the balance you took in specie, perhaps?"

Captain Delano, fidgeting a little, answered—

"Yes; some silver; not a very great deal, though."

"Ah—well. May I ask how many men have you, Señor?"

Captain Delano slightly started, but answered—

"About five-and-twenty, all told."

"And at present, Señor, all on board, I suppose?"

"All on board, Don Benito," replied the Captain, now with satisfaction.

"And will be to-night, Señor?"

At this last question, following so many pertinacious ones, for the soul of him Captain Delano could not but look very earnestly at the questioner, who, instead of meeting the glance, with every token of craven discomposure dropped his eyes to the deck; presenting an unworthy contrast to his servant, who, just then, was kneeling at his feet, adjusting a loose shoe-buckle; his disengaged face meantime, with humble curiosity, turned openly up into his master's downcast one.

The Spaniard, still with a guilty shuffle, repeated his question:—

"And—and will be to-night, Señor?"

"Yes, for aught I know," returned Captain Delano,—"but nay," rallying himself into fearless truth, "some of them talked of going off on another fishing party about midnight."

"Your ships generally go—go more or less armed, I believe, Señor?"

"Oh, a six-pounder or two, in case of emergency," was the intrepidly indifferent reply, "with a small stock of muskets, sealing-spears, and cutlasses, you know."

As he thus responded, Captain Delano again glanced at Don Benito, but the latter's eyes were averted; while abruptly and awkwardly shifting the subject, he made some peevish allusion to the calm, and then, without apology, once more, with his attendant, withdrew to the opposite bulwarks, where the whispering was resumed.

At this moment, and ere Captain Delano could cast a cool thought upon what had just passed, the young Spanish sailor before mentioned was seen descending from the rigging. In act of stooping over to spring inboard to the deck, his voluminous, unconfined frock, or shirt, of coarse woollen, much spotted with tar, opened out far down the chest, revealing a soiled under garment of what seemed the finest linen, edged, about the neck, with a narrow blue ribbon, sadly faded and worn. At this moment the young sailor's eye was again fixed on the whisperers, and Captain Delano thought he observed a lurking significance in it, as if silent signs of some Freemason sort had that instant been interchanged.

This once more impelled his own glance in the direction of Don Benito, and, as before, he could not but infer that himself formed the subject of the conference. He paused. The sound of the hatchet-polishing fell on his ears. He cast another swift side-look at the two. They had the air of conspirators. In connection with the late questionings and the incident of the young sailor, these things now begat such return of involuntary suspicion, that the singular guilelessness of the American could not endure it. Plucking up a gay and humorous expression, he crossed over to the two rapidly, saying:— "Ha, Don Benito, your black here seems high in your trust; a sort of privy-counselor, in fact."

Upon this, the servant looked up with a good-natured grin, but the master started as from a venomous bite. It was a moment or two before the Spaniard sufficiently recovered himself to reply; which he did, at last, with cold constraint:—"Yes, Señor, I have trust in Babo."

Here Babo, changing his previous grin of mere animal humor into an intelligent smile, not ungratefully eyed his master.

Finding that the Spaniard now stood silent and reserved, as if involuntarily, or purposely giving hint that his guest's proximity was inconvenient just then, Captain Delano, unwilling to appear uncivil even to incivility itself, made some trivial remark and moved off; again and again turning over in his mind the mysterious demeanor of Don Benito Cereno.

He had descended from the poop, and, wrapped in thought, was passing near a dark hatchway, leading down into the steerage, when, perceiving motion there, he looked to see what moved. The same instant there was a sparkle in the shadowy hatchway, and he saw one of the Spanish sailors prowling there hurriedly placing his hand in the bosom of his frock, as if hiding something. Before the man could have been certain who it was that was passing, he slunk below out of sight. But enough was seen of him to make it sure that he was the same young sailor before noticed in the rigging.

What was that which so sparkled? thought Captain Delano. It was no lamp—no match—no live coal. Could it have been a jewel? But how come sailors with jewels?—or with silk-trimmed under-shirts either? Has he been robbing the trunks of the dead cabin passengers? But if so, he would hardly wear one of the stolen articles on board ship here. Ah, ah—if now that was, indeed, a secret sign I saw passing between this suspicious fellow and his captain awhile since; if I could only be certain that in my uneasiness my senses did not deceive me, then——

Here, passing from one suspicious thing to another, his mind revolved the strange questions put to him concerning his ship.

By a curious coincidence, as each point was recalled, the black wizards of Ashantee would strike up with their hatchets, as in ominous comment on the white stranger's thoughts. Pressed by such enigmas and portents, it would have been almost against nature, had not, even into the least distrustful heart, some ugly misgivings obtruded.

Observing the ship now helplessly fallen into a current, with enchanted sails, drifting with increased rapidity seaward; and noting that, from a lately intercepted projection of the land, the sealer was hidden, the stout mariner began to quake at thoughts which he barely durst confess to himself. Above all, he began to feel a ghostly dread of Don Benito. And yet when he roused himself, dilated his chest, felt himself strong on his legs, and coolly considered it—what did all these phantoms amount to?

Had the Spaniard any sinister scheme, it must have reference not so much to him (Captain Delano) as to his ship (the Bachelor's Delight). Hence the present drifting away of the one ship from the other, instead of favoring any such possible scheme, was, for the time at least, opposed to it. Clearly any suspicion, combining such contradictions, must need be delusive. Beside, was it not absurd to think of a vessel in distress—a vessel by sickness almost dismanned of her crew—a vessel whose inmates were parched for water—was it not a thousand times absurd that such a craft should, at present, be of a piratical character; or her commander, either for himself or those under him, cherish any desire but for speedy relief and refreshment? But then, might not general distress, and thirst in particular, be affected? And might not that same undiminished Spanish crew, alleged to have perished off to a remnant, be at that very moment lurking in the hold? On heart-broken pretense of entreating a cup of cold water, fiends in human form had got into lonely dwellings, nor retired until a dark deed had been done. And among the Malay pirates, it was no unusual thing to lure ships after them into their treacherous harbors, or entice boarders from a declared enemy at sea, by the spectacle of thinly manned or vacant decks, beneath which prowled a hundred spears with yellow arms ready to upthrust them through the mats. Not that Captain Delano had entirely credited such things. He had heard of them—and now, as stories, they recurred. The present destination of the ship was the anchorage. There she would be near his own vessel. Upon gaining that vicinity, might not the San Dominick, like a slumbering volcano, suddenly let loose energies now hid?

He recalled the Spaniard's manner while telling his story. There was a gloomy hesitancy and subterfuge about it. It was just the manner of one making up his tale for evil purposes, as he goes. But if that story was not true, what was the truth? That the ship had unlawfully come into the Spaniard's possession? But in many of its details, especially in reference to the more calamitous parts, such as the fatalities among the seamen, the consequent prolonged beating about, the past sufferings from obstinate calms, and still continued suffering from thirst; in all these points, as well as others, Don Benito's story had corroborated not only the wailing ejaculations of the indiscriminate multitude, white and black, but likewise—what seemed impossible to be counterfeit—by the very expression and play of every human feature, which Captain Delano saw. If Don Benito's story was throughout an invention, then every soul on board, down to the youngest negress, was his carefully drilled recruit in the plot: an incredible inference. And yet, if there was ground for mistrusting his veracity, that inference was a legitimate one.

But those questions of the Spaniard. There, indeed, one might pause. Did they not seem put with much the same object with which the burglar or assassin, by day-time, reconnoitres the walls of a house? But, with ill purposes, to solicit such information openly of the chief person endangered, and so, in effect, setting him on his guard; how unlikely a procedure was that? Absurd, then, to suppose that those questions had been prompted by evil designs. Thus, the same conduct, which, in this instance, had raised the alarm, served to dispel it. In short, scarce any suspicion or uneasiness, however apparently reasonable at the time, which was not now, with equal apparent reason, dismissed.

At last he began to laugh at his former forebodings; and laugh at the strange ship for, in its aspect someway siding with them, as it were; and laugh, too, at the odd-looking blacks, particularly those old scissors-grinders, the Ashantees; and those bed-ridden old knitting-women, the oakum-pickers; and almost at the dark Spaniard himself, the central hobgoblin of all.

For the rest, whatever in a serious way seemed enigmatical, was now good-naturedly explained away by the thought that, for the most part, the poor invalid scarcely knew what he was about; either sulking in black vapors, or putting idle questions without sense or object. Evidently, for the present, the man was not fit to be entrusted with the ship. On some benevolent plea withdrawing the command from him, Captain Delano would yet have to send her to Conception, in charge of his second mate, a worthy person and good navigator—a plan not more convenient for the San Dominick than for Don Benito; for, relieved from all anxiety, keeping wholly to his cabin, the sick man, under the good nursing of his servant, would probably, by the end of the passage, be in a measure restored to health, and with that he should also be restored to authority.

Such were the American's thoughts. They were tranquilizing. There was a difference between the idea of Don Benito's darkly pre-ordaining Captain Delano's fate, and Captain Delano's lightly arranging Don Benito's. Nevertheless, it was not without something of relief that the good seaman presently perceived his whale-boat in the distance. Its absence had been prolonged by unexpected detention at the sealer's side, as well as its returning trip lengthened by the continual recession of the goal.

The advancing speck was observed by the blacks. Their shouts attracted the attention of Don Benito, who, with a return of courtesy, approaching Captain Delano, expressed satisfaction at the coming of some supplies, slight and temporary as they must necessarily prove.

Captain Delano responded; but while doing so, his attention was drawn to something passing on the deck below: among the crowd climbing the landward bulwarks, anxiously watching the coming boat, two blacks, to all appearances accidentally incommoded by one of the sailors, violently pushed him aside, which the sailor someway resenting, they dashed him to the deck, despite the earnest cries of the oakum-pickers.

"Don Benito," said Captain Delano quickly, "do you see what is going on there? Look!"

But, seized by his cough, the Spaniard staggered, with both hands to his face, on the point of falling. Captain Delano would have supported him, but the servant was more alert, who, with one hand sustaining his master, with the other applied the cordial. Don Benito restored, the black withdrew his support, slipping aside a little, but dutifully remaining within call of a whisper. Such discretion was here evinced as quite wiped away, in the visitor's eyes, any blemish of impropriety which might have attached to the attendant, from the indecorous conferences before mentioned; showing, too, that if the servant were to blame, it might be more the master's fault than his own, since when left to himself he could conduct thus well.

His glance called away from the spectacle of disorder to the more pleasing one before him, Captain Delano could not avoid again congratulating his host upon possessing such a servant, who, though perhaps a little too forward now and then, must upon the whole be invaluable to one in the invalid's situation.

"Tell me, Don Benito," he added, with a smile—"I should like to have your man here myself—what will you take for him? Would fifty doubloons be any object?"

"Master wouldn't part with Babo for a thousand doubloons," murmured the black, overhearing the offer, and taking it in earnest, and, with the strange vanity of a faithful slave appreciated by his master, scorning to hear so paltry a valuation put upon him by a stranger. But Don Benito, apparently hardly yet completely restored, and again interrupted by his cough, made but some broken reply.

Soon his physical distress became so great, affecting his mind, too, apparently, that, as if to screen the sad spectacle, the servant gently conducted his master below.

Left to himself, the American, to while away the time till his boat should arrive, would have pleasantly accosted some one of the few Spanish seamen he saw; but recalling something that Don Benito had said touching their ill conduct, he refrained, as a ship-master indisposed to countenance cowardice or unfaithfulness in seamen.

While, with these thoughts, standing with eye directed forward towards that handful of sailors, suddenly he thought that one or two of them returned the glance and with a sort of meaning. He rubbed his eyes, and looked again; but again seemed to see the same thing. Under a new form, but more obscure than any previous one, the old suspicions recurred, but, in the absence of Don Benito, with less of panic than before. Despite the bad account given of the sailors, Captain Delano resolved forthwith to accost one of them. Descending the poop, he made his way through the blacks, his movement drawing a queer cry from the oakum-pickers, prompted by whom, the negroes, twitching each other aside, divided before him; but, as if curious to see what was the object of this deliberate visit to their Ghetto, closing in behind, in tolerable order, followed the white stranger up. His progress thus proclaimed as by mounted kings-at-arms, and escorted as by a Caffre guard of honor, Captain Delano, assuming a good humored, off-handed air, continued to advance; now and then saying a blithe word to the negroes, and his eye curiously surveying the white faces, here and there sparsely mixed in with the blacks, like stray white pawns venturously involved in the ranks of the chess-men opposed.

While thinking which of them to select for his purpose, he chanced to observe a sailor seated on the deck engaged in tarring the strap of a large block, with a circle of blacks squatted round him inquisitively eying the process.

The mean employment of the man was in contrast with something superior in his figure. His hand, black with continually thrusting it into the tar-pot held for him by a negro, seemed not naturally allied to his face, a face which would have been a very fine one but for its haggardness. Whether this haggardness had aught to do with criminality, could not be determined; since, as intense heat and cold, though unlike, produce like sensations, so innocence and guilt, when, through casual association with mental pain, stamping any visible impress, use one seal—a hacked one.

Not again that this reflection occurred to Captain Delano at the time, charitable man as he was. Rather another idea. Because observing so singular a haggardness combined with a dark eye, averted as in trouble and shame, and then again recalling Don Benito's confessed ill opinion of his crew, insensibly he was operated upon by certain general notions, which, while disconnecting pain and abashment from virtue, invariably link them with vice.

If, indeed, there be any wickedness on board this ship, thought Captain Delano, be sure that man there has fouled his hand in it, even as now he fouls it in the pitch. I don't like to accost him. I will speak to this other, this old Jack here on the windlass.

He advanced to an old Barcelona tar, in ragged red breeches and dirty night-cap, cheeks trenched and bronzed, whiskers dense as thorn hedges. Seated between two sleepy-looking Africans, this mariner, like his younger shipmate, was employed upon some rigging—splicing a cable—the sleepy-looking blacks performing the inferior function of holding the outer parts of the ropes for him.

Upon Captain Delano's approach, the man at once hung his head below its previous level; the one necessary for business. It appeared as if he desired to be thought absorbed, with more than common fidelity, in his task. Being addressed, he glanced up, but with what seemed a furtive, diffident air, which sat strangely enough on his weather-beaten visage, much as if a grizzly bear, instead of growling and biting, should simper and cast sheep's eyes. He was asked sev-

eral questions concerning the voyage, questions purposely referring
to several particulars in Don Benito's narrative, not previously corroborated by those impulsive cries greeting the visitor on first
coming on board. The questions were briefly answered, confirming
all that remained to be confirmed of the story. The negroes about
the windlass joined in with the old sailor, but, as they became talkative, he by degrees became mute, and at length quite glum, seemed
morosely unwilling to answer more questions, and yet, all the while,
this ursine air was somehow mixed with his sheepish one.

Despairing of getting into unembarrassed talk with such a cen-
taur, Captain Delano, after glancing round for a more promising
countenance, but seeing none, spoke pleasantly to the blacks to
make way for him; and so, amid various grins and grimaces,
returned to the poop, feeling a little strange at first, he could hardly
tell why, but upon the whole with regained confidence in Benito
Cereno.

How plainly, thought he, did that old whiskerando yonder betray
a consciousness of ill-desert. No doubt, when he saw me coming, he
dreaded lest I, apprised by his Captain of the crew's general misbe-
havior, came with sharp words for him, and so down with his head.
And yet—and yet, now that I think of it, that very old fellow, if I err
not, was one of those who seemed so earnestly eying me here awhile
since. Ah, these currents spin one's head round almost as much as
they do the ship. Ha, there now's a pleasant sort of sunny sight;
quite sociable, too.

His attention had been drawn to a slumbering negress, partly disclosed through the lace-work of some rigging, lying, with youthful
limbs carelessly disposed, under the lee of the bulwarks, like a doe
in the shade of a woodland rock. Sprawling at her lapped breasts
was her wide-awake fawn, stark naked, its black little body half
lifted from the deck, crosswise with its dam's; its hands, like two
paws, clambering upon her; its mouth and nose ineffectually
rooting to get at the mark; and meantime giving a vexatious half-
grunt, blending with the composed snore of the negress.[9]

The uncommon vigor of the child at length roused the mother.
She started up, at distance facing Captain Delano. But as if not at

9. Delano sees the slaves in terms of the animal kingdom. "Dam": a black woman who represents all black women, "unsophisticated as leopardesses; loving as doves." Later we are
   told that "Captain Delano took to negroes not philanthropically, but genially, just as other
   men to Newfoundland dogs." Delano thinks in the racist stereotypes of his time. He perceives a "certain easy cheerfulness, harmonious in every glance and gesture; as though
   God had set the whole negro to some pleasant tune." Blind to the reality of this reign of
   terror, Delano praises in blacks "the docility arising from the unaspiring contentment of
   a limited mind, and that susceptibility of blind attachment sometimes inherent in indisputable inferiors." An essay, "About Niggers," which appeared in *Putnam's Monthly* in
   December 1855 (the same issue in which the third installment of *Benito Cereno* was published) contains the assertion that the "nigger is a man, not a baboon."

all concerned at the attitude in which she had been caught, delight-
edly she caught the child up, with maternal transports, covering it
with kisses.

There's naked nature, now; pure tenderness and love, thought
Captain Delano, well pleased.

This incident prompted him to remark the other negresses more
particularly than before. He was gratified with their manners; like
most uncivilized women, they seemed at once tender of heart and
tough of constitution; equally ready to die for their infants or fight
for them. Unsophisticated as leopardesses; loving as doves. Ah!
thought Captain Delano, these perhaps are some of the very women
whom Ledyard[1] saw in Africa, and gave such a noble account of.

These natural sights somehow insensibly deepened his confidence and ease. At last he looked to see how his boat was getting
on; but it was still pretty remote. He turned to see if Don Benito had
returned; but he had not.

To change the scene, as well as to please himself with a leisurely
observation of the coming boat, stepping over into the mizzen-
chains he clambered his way into the starboard quarter-gallery; one
of those abandoned Venetian-looking water-balconies previously
mentioned; retreats cut off from the deck. As his foot pressed the
half-damp, half-dry sea-mosses matting the place, and a chance
phantom cats-paw—an islet of breeze, unheralded, unfollowed—as
this ghostly cats-paw came fanning his cheek, as his glance fell
upon the row of small, round dead-lights, all closed like coppered
eyes of the coffined, and the state-cabin door, once connecting with
the gallery, even as the dead-lights had once looked out upon it, but
now calked fast like a sarcophagus lid, to a purple-black, tarred-over
panel, threshold, and post; and he bethought him of the time, when
that state-cabin and this state-balcony had heard the voices of the
Spanish king's officers, and the forms of the Lima viceroy's daugh-
ters had perhaps leaned where he stood—as these and other images
flitted through his mind, as the cats-paw through the calm, gradually he felt rising a dreamy inquietude, like that of one who alone on
the prairie feels unrest from the repose of the noon.

He leaned against the carved balustrade, again looking off toward
his boat; but found his eye falling upon the ribboned grass, trailing
along the ship's water-line, straight as a border of green box; and
parterres of sea-weed, broad ovals and crescents, floating nigh and
far, with what seemed long formal alleys between, crossing the ter-
races of swells, and sweeping round as if leading to the grottoes
below. And overhanging all was the balustrade by his arm, which,

1. John Ledyard, *Proceedings of the Association for Promoting the Discovery of the Interior Parts of Africa* (1790).

partly stained with pitch and partly embossed with moss, seemed the charred ruin of some summer-house in a grand garden long running to waste.

Trying to break one charm, he was but becharmed anew. Though upon the wide sea, he seemed in some far inland country; prisoner in some deserted château, left to stare at empty grounds, and peer out at vague roads, where never wagon or wayfarer passed.

But these enchantments were a little disenchanted as his eye fell on the corroded main-chains. Of an ancient style, massy and rusty in link, shackle and bolt, they seemed even more fit for the ship's present business than the one for which she had been built.

Presently he thought something moved nigh the chains. He rubbed his eyes, and looked hard. Groves of rigging were about the chains; and there, peering from behind a great stay, like an Indian from behind a hemlock, a Spanish sailor, a marlingspike in his hand, was seen, who made what seemed an imperfect gesture towards the balcony, but immediately, as if alarmed by some advancing step along the deck within, vanished into the recesses of the hempen forest, like a poacher.

What meant this? Something the man had sought to communicate, unbeknown to any one, even to his captain. Did the secret involve aught unfavorable to his captain? Were those previous misgivings of Captain Delano's about to be verified? Or, in his haunted mood at the moment, had some random, unintentional motion of the man, while busy with the stay, as if repairing it, been mistaken for a significant beckoning?

Not unbewildered, again he gazed off for his boat. But it was temporarily hidden by a rocky spur of the isle. As with some eagerness he bent forward, watching for the first shooting view of its beak, the balustrade gave way before him like charcoal. Had he not clutched an outreaching rope he would have fallen into the sea. The crash, though feeble, and the fall, though hollow, of the rotten fragments, must have been overheard. He glanced up. With sober curiosity peering down upon him was one of the old oakum-pickers, slipped from his perch to an outside boom; while below the old negro, and, invisible to him, reconnoitering from a port-hole like a fox from the mouth of its den, crouched the Spanish sailor again. From something suddenly suggested by the man's air, the mad idea now darted into Captain Delano's mind, that Don Benito's plea of indisposition, in withdrawing below, was but a pretense: that he was engaged there maturing his plot, of which the sailor, by some means gaining an inkling, had a mind to warn the stranger against; incited, it may be, by gratitude for a kind word on first boarding the ship. Was it from foreseeing some possible interference like this, that Don Benito had, beforehand, given such a bad character of his sailors, while praising the negroes; though, indeed, the former seemed as docile as the latter the contrary? The whites, too, by nature, were the shrewder race. A man with some evil design, would he not be likely to speak well of that stupidity which was blind to his depravity, and malign that intelligence from which it might not be hidden? Not unlikely, perhaps. But if the whites had dark secrets concerning Don Benito, could then Don Benito be any way in complicity with the blacks? But they were too stupid. Besides, who ever heard of a white so far a renegade as to apostatize from his very species almost, by leaguing in against it with negroes? These difficulties recalled former ones. Lost in their mazes, Captain Delano, who had now regained the deck, was uneasily advancing along it, when he observed a new face; an aged sailor seated crosslegged near the main hatchway. His skin was shrunk up with wrinkles like a pelican's empty pouch; his hair frosted; his countenance grave and composed. His hands were full of ropes, which he was working into a large knot. Some blacks were about him obligingly dipping the strands for him, here and there, as the exigencies of the operation demanded.

Captain Delano crossed over to him, and stood in silence surveying the knot; his mind, by a not uncongenial transition, passing from its own entanglements to those of the hemp. For intricacy such a knot he had never seen in an American ship, or indeed any other. The old man looked like an Egyptian priest, making gordian knots for the temple of Ammon. The knot seemed a combination of double-bowline-knot, treble-crown-knot, back-handed-well-knot, knot-in-and-out-knot, and jamming-knot.

At last, puzzled to comprehend the meaning of such a knot, Captain Delano addressed the knotter:—

"What are you knotting there, my man?"

"The knot," was the brief reply, without looking up.

"So it seems; but what is it for?"

"For some one else to undo," muttered back the old man, plying his fingers harder than ever, the knot being now nearly completed.

While Captain Delano stood watching him, suddenly the old man threw the knot towards him, saying in broken English,—the first heard in the ship,—something to this effect—"Undo it, cut it, quick." It was said lowly, but with such condensation of rapidity, that the long, slow words in Spanish, which had preceded and followed, almost operated as covers to the brief English between.

For a moment, knot in hand, and knot in head, Captain Delano stood mute; while, without further heeding him, the old man was now intent upon other ropes. Presently there was a slight stir behind Captain Delano. Turning, he saw the chained negro, Atufal, standing quietly there. The next moment the old sailor rose, muttering, and, followed by his subordinate negroes, removed to the forward part of the ship, where in the crowd he disappeared.

An elderly negro, in a clout like an infant's, and with a pepper and salt head, and a kind of attorney air, now approached Captain Delano. In tolerable Spanish, and with a good-natured, knowing wink, he informed him that the old knotter was simple-witted, but harmless; often playing his odd tricks. The negro concluded by begging the knot, for of course the stranger would not care to be troubled with it. Unconsciously, it was handed to him. With a sort of congé, the negro received it, and turning his back, ferreted into it like a detective Custom House officer after smuggled laces. Soon, with some African word, equivalent to pshaw, he tossed the knot overboard.

All this is very queer now, thought Captain Delano, with a qualmish sort of emotion; but as one feeling incipient sea-sickness, he strove, by ignoring the symptoms, to get rid of the malady. Once more he looked off for his boat. To his delight, it was now again in view, leaving the rocky spur astern.

The sensation here experienced, after at first relieving his uneasiness, with unforeseen efficacy, soon began to remove it. The less distant sight of that well-known boat—showing it, not as before, half blended with the haze, but with outline defined, so that its individuality, like a man's, was manifest; that boat, Rover by name, which, though now in strange seas, had often pressed the beach of Captain Delano's home, and, brought to its threshold for repairs, had familiarly lain there, as a Newfoundland dog; the sight of that household boat evoked a thousand trustful associations, which, contrasted with previous suspicions, filled him not only with lightsome confidence, but somehow with half humorous self-reproaches at his former lack of it.

"What, I, Amasa Delano—Jack of the Beach, as they called me when a lad—I, Amasa; the same that, duck-satchel in hand, used to paddle along the waterside to the school-house made from the old hulk;—I, little Jack of the Beach, that used to go berrying with cousin Nat and the rest; I to be murdered here at the ends of the earth, on board a haunted pirate-ship by a horrible Spaniard?—Too nonsensical to think of! Who would murder Amasa Delano? His conscience is clean. There is some one above. Fie, fie, Jack of the Beach! you are a child indeed; a child of the second childhood, old boy; you are beginning to dote and drule, I'm afraid."

Light of heart and foot, he stepped aft, and there was met by Don Benito's servant, who, with a pleasing expression, responsive to his own present feelings, informed him that his master had recovered from the effects of his coughing fit, and had just ordered him to go present his compliments to his good guest, Don Amasa, and say that he (Don Benito) would soon have the happiness to rejoin him.

There now, do you mark that? again thought Captain Delano, walking the poop. What a donkey I was. This kind gentleman who here sends me his kind compliments, he, but ten minutes ago, dark-lantern in hand, was dodging round some old grind-stone in the hold, sharpening a hatchet for me, I thought. Well, well; these long calms have a morbid effect on the mind, I've often heard, though I never believed it before. Ha! glancing towards the boat; there's Rover; good dog; a white bone in her mouth. A pretty big bone though, seems to me.—What? Yes, she has fallen afoul of the bub-bling tide-rip there. It sets her the other way, too, for the time. Patience.

It was now about noon, though, from the grayness of everything, it seemed to be getting towards dusk.

The calm was confirmed. In the far distance, away from the influ-ence of land, the leaden ocean seemed laid out and leaded up, its course finished, soul gone, defunct. But the current from landward, where the ship was, increased; silently sweeping her further and further towards the tranced waters beyond.

Still, from his knowledge of those latitudes, cherishing hopes of a breeze, and a fair and fresh one, at any moment, Captain Delano, despite present prospects, buoyantly counted upon bringing the San Dominick safely to anchor ere night. The distance swept over was nothing; since, with a good wind, ten minutes' sailing would retrace more than sixty minutes' drifting. Meantime, one moment turning to mark "Rover" fighting the tide-rip, and the next to see Don Benito approaching, he continued walking the poop.

Gradually he felt a vexation arising from the delay of his boat; this soon merged into uneasiness; and at last, his eye falling continually, as from a stage-box into the pit, upon the strange crowd before and below him, and by and by recognising there the face—now composed to indifference—of the Spanish sailor who had seemed to beckon from the main chains, something of his old trepidations returned.

Ah, thought he—gravely enough—this is like the ague: because it went off, it follows not that it won't come back.

Though ashamed of the relapse, he could not altogether subdue it; and so, exerting his good nature to the utmost, insensibly he came to a compromise.

Yes, this is a strange craft; a strange history, too, and strange folks on board. But—nothing more.

By way of keeping his mind out of mischief till the boat should arrive, he tried to occupy it with turning over and over, in a purely speculative sort of way, some lesser peculiarities of the captain and crew. Among others, four curious points recurred.

First, the affair of the Spanish lad assailed with a knife by the slave boy; an act winked at by Don Benito. Second, the tyranny in Don Benito's treatment of Atufal, the black; as if a child should lead a bull of the Nile by the ring in his nose. Third, the trampling of the sailor by the two negroes; a piece of insolence passed over without so much as a reprimand. Fourth, the cringing submission to their master of all the ship's underlings, mostly blacks; as if by the least inadvertence they feared to draw down his despotic displeasure.

Coupling these points, they seemed somewhat contradictory. But what then, thought Captain Delano, glancing towards his now nearing boat,—what then? Why, Don Benito is a very capricious commander. But he is not the first of the sort I have seen; though it's true he rather exceeds any other. But as a nation—continued he in his reveries—these Spaniards are all an odd set: the very word Spaniard has a curious, conspirator, Guy-Fawkish[2] twang to it. And yet, I dare say, Spaniards in the main are as good folks as any in Duxbury, Massachusetts. Ah good! At last "Rover" has come.

As, with its welcome freight, the boat touched the side, the oakum-pickers, with venerable gestures, sought to restrain the blacks, who, at the sight of three gurried water-casks in its bottom, and a pile of wilted pumpkins in its bow, hung over the bulwarks in disorderly raptures.

Don Benito with his servant now appeared; his coming, perhaps, hastened by hearing the noise. Of him Captain Delano sought permission to serve out the water, so that all might share alike, and none injure themselves by unfair excess. But sensible, and, on Don Benito's account, kind as this offer was, it was received with what seemed impatience; as if aware that he lacked energy as a commander, Don Benito, with the true jealousy of weakness, resented as an affront any interference. So, at least, Captain Delano inferred.

In another moment the casks were being hoisted in, when some of the eager negroes accidentally jostled Captain Delano, where he stood by the gangway; so that, unmindful of Don Benito, yielding to the impulse of the moment, with good-natured authority he bade the blacks stand back; to enforce his words making use of a half-mirthful, half-menacing gesture. Instantly the blacks paused, just where they were, each negro and negress suspended in his or her posture, exactly as the word had found them—for a few seconds continuing so—while, as between the responsive posts of a telegraph, an unknown syllable ran from man to man among the perched oakum-pickers. While the visitor's attention was fixed by

2. Guy Fawkes (1570–1606), the leading figure in the Gunpowder Plot of 1605, was executed for attempting to blow up the Parliament of England and plotting a national Catholic rebellion.

this scene, suddenly the hatchet-polishers half rose, and a rapid cry came from Don Benito.

Thinking that at the signal of the Spaniard he was about to be massacred, Captain Delano would have sprung for his boat, but paused, as the oakum-pickers, dropping down into the crowd with earnest exclamations, forced every white and every negro back, at the same moment, with gestures friendly and familiar, almost jocose, bidding him, in substance, not be a fool. Simultaneously the hatchet-polishers resumed their seats, quietly as so many tailors, and at once, as if nothing had happened, the work of hoisting in the casks was resumed, whites and blacks singing at the tackle.

Captain Delano glanced towards Don Benito. As he saw his meager form in the act of recovering itself from reclining in the servant's arms, into which the agitated invalid had fallen, he could not but marvel at the panic by which himself had been surprised on the darting supposition that such a commander, who upon a legitimate occasion, so trivial, too, as it now appeared, could lose all self-command, was, with energetic iniquity, going to bring about his murder.

The casks being on deck, Captain Delano was handed a number of jars and cups by one of the steward's aids, who, in the name of his captain, entreated him to do as he had proposed: dole out the water. He complied, with republican impartiality as to this republican element, which always seeks one level, serving the oldest white no better than the youngest black; excepting, indeed, poor Don Benito, whose condition, if not rank, demanded an extra allowance. To him, in the first place, Captain Delano presented a fair pitcher of the fluid; but, thirsting as he was for it, the Spaniard quaffed not a drop until after several grave bows and salutes. A reciprocation of courtesies which the sight-loving Africans hailed with clapping of hands.

Two of the less wilted pumpkins being reserved for the cabin table, the residue were minced up on the spot for the general regalement. But the soft bread, sugar, and bottled cider, Captain Delano would have given the whites alone, and in chief Don Benito; but the latter objected; which disinterestedness not a little pleased the American; and so mouthfuls all around were given alike to whites and blacks; excepting one bottle of cider, which Babo insisted upon setting aside for his master.

Here it may be observed that as, on the first visit of the boat, the American had not permitted his men to board the ship, neither did he now; being unwilling to add to the confusion of the decks.

Not uninfluenced by the peculiar good humor at present prevailing, and for the time oblivious of any but benevolent thoughts, Captain Delano, who from recent indications counted upon a breeze within an hour or two at furthest, dispatched the boat back to the sealer with orders for all the hands that could be spared immediately to set about rafting casks to the watering-place and filling them. Likewise he bade word be carried to his chief officer, that if against present expectation the ship was not brought to anchor by sunset, he need be under no concern, for as there was to be a full moon that night, he (Captain Delano) would remain on board ready to play the pilot, come the wind soon or late.

As the two Captains stood together, observing the departing boat—the servant as it happened having just spied a spot on his master's velvet sleeve, and silently engaged rubbing it out—the American expressed his regrets that the San Dominick had no boats; none, at least, but the unseaworthy old hulk of the long-boat, which, warped as a camel's skeleton in the desert, and almost as bleached, lay pot-wise inverted amidships, one side a little tipped, furnishing a subterraneous sort of den for family groups of the blacks, mostly women and small children; who, squatting on old mats below, or perched above in the dark dome, on the elevated seats, were descried, some distance within, like a social circle of bats, sheltering in some friendly cave; at intervals, ebon flights of naked boys and girls, three or four years old, darting in and out of the den's mouth.

"Had you three or four boats now, Don Benito," said Captain Delano, "I think that, by tugging at the oars, your negroes here might help along matters some.—Did you sail from port without boats, Don Benito?"

"They were stove in the gales, Señor."

"That was bad. Many men, too, you lost then. Boats and men.—Those must have been hard gales, Don Benito."

"Past all speech," cringed the Spaniard.

"Tell me, Don Benito," continued his companion with increased interest, "tell me, were these gales immediately off the pitch of Cape Horn?"

"Cape Horn?—who spoke of Cape Horn?"

"Yourself did, when giving me an account of your voyage," answered Captain Delano with almost equal astonishment at this eating of his own words, even as he ever seemed eating his own heart, on the part of the Spaniard. "You yourself, Don Benito, spoke of Cape Horn," he emphatically repeated.

The Spaniard turned, in a sort of stooping posture, pausing an instant, as one about to make a plunging exchange of elements, as from air to water.

At this moment a messenger-boy, a white, hurried by, in the regular performance of his function carrying the last expired half hour forward to the forecastle, from the cabin time-piece, to have it struck at the ship's large bell.

"Master," said the servant, discontinuing his work on the coat sleeve, and addressing the rapt Spaniard with a sort of timid apprehensiveness, as one charged with a duty, the discharge of which, it was foreseen, would prove irksome to the very person who had imposed it, and for whose benefit it was intended, "master told me never mind where he was, or how engaged, always to remind him, to a minute, when shaving-time comes. Miguel has gone to strike the half-hour afternoon. It is *now*, master. Will master go into the cuddy?"

"Ah—yes," answered the Spaniard, starting, somewhat as from dreams into realities; then turning upon Captain Delano, he said that ere long he would resume the conversation.

"Then if master means to talk more to Don Amasa," said the servant, "why not let Don Amasa sit by master in the cuddy, and master can talk, and Don Amasa can listen, while Babo here lathers and strops."

"Yes," said Captain Delano, not unpleased with this sociable plan, "yes, Don Benito, unless you had rather not, I will go with you."

"Be it so, Señor."

As the three passed aft, the American could not but think it another strange instance of his host's capriciousness, this being shaved with such uncommon punctuality in the middle of the day. But he deemed it more than likely that the servant's anxious fidelity had something to do with the matter; inasmuch as the timely interruption served to rally his master from the mood which had evidently been coming upon him.

The place called the cuddy was a light deck-cabin formed by the poop, a sort of attic to the large cabin below. Part of it had formerly been the quarters of the officers; but since their death all the partitionings had been thrown down, and the whole interior converted into one spacious and airy marine hall; for absence of fine furniture and picturesque disarray, of odd appurtenances, somewhat answering to the wide, cluttered hall of some eccentric bachelor-squire in the country, who hangs his shooting-jacket and tobacco-pouch on deer antlers, and keeps his fishing-rod, tongs, and walking-stick in the same corner.

The similitude was hightened, if not originally suggested, by glimpses of the surrounding sea; since, in one aspect, the country and the ocean seem cousins-german.

The floor of the cuddy was matted. Overhead, four or five old muskets were stuck into horizontal holes along the beams. On one side was a claw-footed old table lashed to the deck; a thumbed missal on it, and over it a small, meager crucifix attached to the bulkhead. Under the table lay a dented cutlass or two, with a hacked harpoon, among some melancholy old rigging, like a heap of poor friars' girdles. There were also two long, sharp-ribbed settees of malacca cane, black with age, and uncomfortable to look at as inquisitors' racks, with a large, misshapen arm-chair, which, furnished with a rude barber's crotch at the back, working with a screw, seemed some grotesque engine of torment. A flag locker was in one corner, open, exposing various colored bunting, some rolled up, others half unrolled, still others tumbled. Opposite was a cumbrous washstand, of black mahogany, all of one block, with a pedestal, like a font, and over it a railed shelf, containing combs, brushes, and other implements of the toilet. A torn hammock of stained grass swung near; the sheets tossed, and the pillow wrinkled up like a brow, as if whoever slept here slept but illy, with alternate visitations of sad thoughts and bad dreams.[3]

The further extremity of the cuddy, overhanging the ship's stern, was pierced with three openings, windows or port holes, according as men or cannon might peer, socially or unsocially, out of them. At present neither men nor cannon were seen, though huge ring-bolts and other rusty iron fixtures of the wood-work hinted of twenty-four-pounders.

Glancing towards the hammock as he entered, Captain Delano said, "You sleep here, Don Benito?"

"Yes, Señor, since we got into mild weather."

"This seems a sort of dormitory, sitting-room, sail-loft, chapel, armory, and private closet all together, Don Benito," added Captain Delano, looking round.

"Yes, Señor; events have not been favorable to much order in my arrangements."

Here the servant, napkin on arm, made a motion as if waiting his master's good pleasure. Don Benito signified his readiness, when, seating him in the malacca arm-chair, and for the guest's convenience drawing opposite it one of the settees, the servant commenced operations by throwing back his master's collar and loosening his cravat.

There is something in the negro which, in a peculiar way, fits him for avocations about one's person. Most negroes are natural valets and hair-dressers; taking to the comb and brush congenially as to the castinets, and flourishing them apparently with almost equal satisfaction. There is, too, a smooth tact about them in this employment, with a marvelous, noiseless, gliding briskness, not ungraceful in its way, singularly pleasing to behold, and still more so to be the manipulated subject of. And above all is the great gift of good humor. Not the mere grin or laugh is here meant. Those were unsuitable. But a certain easy cheerfulness, harmonious in every

---

3. This paragraph can be seen as a description of a torture chamber.

glance and gesture; as though God had set the whole negro to some pleasant tune.

When to all this is added the docility arising from the unaspiring contentment of a limited mind, and that susceptibility of blind attachment sometimes inhering in indisputable inferiors, one readily perceives why those hypochondriacs, Johnson and Byron—it may be something like the hypochondriac, Benito Cereno—took to their hearts, almost to the exclusion of the entire white race, their serving men, the negroes, Barber and Fletcher. But if there be that in the negro which exempts him from the inflicted sourness of the morbid or cynical mind, how, in his most prepossessing aspects, must he appear to a benevolent one? When at ease with respect to exterior things, Captain Delano's nature was not only benign, but familiarly and humorously so. At home, he had often taken rare satisfaction in sitting in his door, watching some free man of color at his work or play. If on a voyage he chanced to have a black sailor, invariably he was on chatty, and half-gamesome terms with him. In fact, like most men of a good, blithe heart, Captain Delano took to negroes, not philanthropically, but genially, just as other men to Newfoundland dogs.

Hitherto the circumstances in which he found the San Dominick had repressed the tendency. But in the cuddy, relieved from his former uneasiness, and, for various reasons, more sociably inclined than at any previous period of the day, and seeing the colored servant, napkin on arm, so debonair about his master, in a business so familiar as that of shaving, too, all his old weakness for negroes returned.

Among other things, he was amused with an odd instance of the African love of bright colors and fine shows, in the black's informally taking from the flag-locker a great piece of bunting of all hues, and lavishly tucking it under his master's chin for an apron.

The mode of shaving among the Spaniards is a little different from what it is with other nations. They have a basin, specifically called a barber's basin, which on one side is scooped out, so as accurately to receive the chin, against which it is closely held in lathering; which is done, not with a brush, but with soap dipped in the water of the basin and rubbed on the face.

In the present instance salt-water was used for lack of better; and the parts lathered were only the upper lip, and low down under the throat, all the rest being cultivated beard.

The preliminaries being somewhat novel to Captain Delano, he sat curiously eying them, so that no conversation took place, nor for the present did Don Benito appear disposed to renew any.

Setting down his basin, the negro searched among the razors, as for the sharpest, and having found it, gave it an additional edge by expertly strapping it on the firm, smooth, oily skin of his open palm; he then made a gesture as if to begin, but midway stood suspended for an instant, one hand elevating the razor, the other professionally dabbling among the bubbling suds on the Spaniard's lank neck. Not unaffected by the close sight of the gleaming steel, Don Benito nervously shuddered, his usual ghastliness was hightened by the lather, which lather, again, was intensified in its hue by the contrasting sootiness of the negro's body. Altogether the scene was somewhat peculiar, at least to Captain Delano, nor, as he saw the two thus postured, could he resist the vagary, that in the black he saw a headsman, and in the white, a man at the block. But this was one of those antic conceits, appearing and vanishing in a breath, from which, perhaps, the best regulated mind is not always free.

Meantime the agitation of the Spaniard had a little loosened the bunting from around him, so that one broad fold swept curtain-like over the chair-arm to the floor, revealing, amid a profusion of armorial bars and ground-colors—black, blue, and yellow—a closed castle in a blood-red field diagonal with a lion rampant in a white.

"The castle and the lion," exclaimed Captain Delano—"why, Don Benito, this is the flag of Spain you use here. It's well it's only I, and not the King, that sees this," he added with a smile, "but"—turning towards the black,—"it's all one, I suppose, so the colors be gay;" which playful remark did not fail somewhat to tickle the negro.

"Now, master," he said, readjusting the flag, and pressing the head gently further back into the crotch of the chair; "now master," and the steel glanced nigh the throat.

Again Don Benito faintly shuddered.

"You must not shake so, master.—See, Don Amasa, master always shakes when I shave him. And yet master knows I never yet have drawn blood, though it's true, if master will shake so, I may some of these times. Now master," he continued. "And now, Don Amasa, please go on with your talk about the gale, and all that, master can hear, and between times master can answer."

"Ah yes, these gales," said Captain Delano; "but the more I think of your voyage, Don Benito, the more I wonder, not at the gales, terrible as they must have been, but at the disastrous interval following them. For here, by your account, have you been these two months and more getting from Cape Horn to St. Maria, a distance which I myself, with a good wind, have sailed in a few days. True, you had calms, and long ones, but to be becalmed for two months, that is, at least, unusual. Why, Don Benito, had almost any other gentleman told me such a story, I should have been half disposed to a little incredulity."

Here an involuntary expression came over the Spaniard, similar to that just before on the deck, and whether it was the start he gave, or a sudden gawky roll of the hull in the calm, or a momentary unsteadiness of the servant's hand; however it was, just then the razor drew blood, spots of which stained the creamy lather under the throat; immediately the black barber drew back his steel, and remaining in his professional attitude, back to Captain Delano, and face to Don Benito, held up the trickling razor, saying, with a sort of half humorous sorrow, "See, master,—you shook so—here's Babo's first blood."

No sword drawn before James the First of England, no assassination in that timid King's presence, could have produced a more terrified aspect than was now presented by Don Benito.

Poor fellow, thought Captain Delano, so nervous he can't even bear the sight of barber's blood; and this unstrung, sick man, is it credible that I should have imagined he meant to spill all my blood, who can't endure the sight of one little drop of his own? Surely, Amasa Delano, you have been beside yourself this day. Tell it not when you get home, sappy Amasa. Well, well, he looks like a murderer, doesn't he? More like as if himself were to be done for. Well, well, this day's experience shall be a good lesson.

Meantime, while these things were running through the honest seaman's mind, the servant had taken the napkin from his arm, and to Don Benito had said—"But answer Don Amasa, please, master, while I wipe this ugly stuff off the razor, and strop it again."

As he said the words, his face was turned half round, so as to be alike visible to the Spaniard and the American, and seemed by its expression to hint, that he was desirous, by getting his master to go on with the conversation, considerably to withdraw his attention from the recent annoying accident. As if glad to snatch the offered relief, Don Benito resumed, rehearsing to Captain Delano, that not only were the calms of unusual duration, but the ship had fallen in with obstinate currents; and other things he added, some of which were but repetitions of former statements, to explain how it came to pass that the passage from Cape Horn to St. Maria had been so exceedingly long, now and then mingling with his words, incidental praises, less qualified than before, to the blacks, for their general good conduct.

These particulars were not given consecutively, the servant at convenient times using his razor, and so, between the intervals of shaving, the story and panegyric went on with more than usual huskiness.

To Captain Delano's imagination, now again not wholly at rest, there was something so hollow in the Spaniard's manner, with apparently some reciprocal hollowness in the servant's dusky comment of silence, that the idea flashed across him, that possibly master and man, for some unknown purpose, were acting out, both in word and deed, nay, to the very tremor of Don Benito's limbs, some juggling play before him. Neither did the suspicion of collusion lack apparent support, from the fact of those whispered conferences before mentioned. But then, what could be the object of enacting this play of the barber before him? At last, regarding the notion as a whimsy, insensibly suggested, perhaps, by the theatrical aspect of Don Benito in his harlequin ensign, Captain Delano speedily banished it.

The shaving over, the servant bestirred himself with a small bottle of scented waters, pouring a few drops on the head, and then diligently rubbing; the vehemence of the exercise causing the muscles of his face to twitch rather strangely.

His next operation was with comb, scissors and brush; going round and round, smoothing a curl here, clipping an unruly whisker-hair there, giving a graceful sweep to the temple-lock, with other impromptu touches evincing the hand of a master; while, like any resigned gentleman in barber's hands, Don Benito bore all, much less uneasily, at least, than he had done the razoring; indeed, he sat so pale and rigid now, that the negro seemed a Nubian sculptor finishing off a white statue-head.

All being over at last, the standard of Spain removed, tumbled up, and tossed back into the flag-locker, the negro's warm breath blowing away any stray hair which might have lodged down his master's neck; collar and cravat readjusted; a speck of lint whisked off the velvet lapel; all this being done; backing off a little space, and pausing with an expression of subdued self-complacency, the servant for a moment surveyed his master, as, in toilet at least, the creature of his own tasteful hands.

Captain Delano playfully complimented him upon his achievement; at the same time congratulating Don Benito.

But neither sweet waters, nor shampooing, nor fidelity, nor sociality, delighted the Spaniard. Seeing him relapsing into forbidding gloom, and still remaining seated, Captain Delano, thinking that his presence was undesired just then, withdrew, on pretense of seeing whether, as he had prophecied, any signs of a breeze were visible.

Walking forward to the mainmast, he stood awhile thinking over the scene, and not without some undefined misgivings, when he heard a noise near the cuddy, and turning, saw the negro, his hand to his cheek. Advancing, Captain Delano perceived that the cheek was bleeding. He was about to ask the cause, when the negro's wailing soliloquy enlightened him.

"Ah, when will master get better from his sickness; only the sour heart that sour sickness breeds made him serve Babo so; cutting Babo with the razor, because, only by accident, Babo had given master one little scratch; and for the first time in so many a day, too. Ah, ah, ah," holding his hand to his face.

Is it possible, thought Captain Delano; was it to wreak in private his Spanish spite against this poor friend of his, that Don Benito, by his sullen manner, impelled me to withdraw? Ah, this slavery breeds ugly passions in man—Poor fellow!

He was about to speak in sympathy to the negro, but with a timid reluctance he now reëntered the cuddy.

Presently master and man came forth; Don Benito leaning on his servant as if nothing had happened.

But a sort of love-quarrel, after all, thought Captain Delano.

He accosted Don Benito, and they slowly walked together. They had gone but a few paces, when the steward—a tall, rajah-looking mulatto, orientally set off with a pagoda turban formed by three or four Madras handkerchiefs wound about his head, tier on tier—approaching with a saalam, announced lunch in the cabin.

On their way thither, the two Captains were preceded by the mulatto, who, turning round as he advanced, with continual smiles and bows, ushered them on, a display of elegance which quite completed the insignificance of the small bare-headed Babo, who, as if not unconscious of inferiority, eyed askance the graceful steward. But in part, Captain Delano imputed his jealous watchfulness to that peculiar feeling which the full-blooded African entertains for the adulterated one. As for the steward, his manner, if not bespeaking much dignity of self-respect, yet evidenced his extreme desire to please; which is doubly meritorious, as at once Christian and Chesterfieldian.[4]

Captain Delano observed with interest that while the complexion of the mulatto was hybrid, his physiognomy was European; classically so.

"Don Benito," whispered he, "I am glad to see this usher-of-the-golden-rod of yours; the sight refutes an ugly remark once made to me by a Barbardoes planter; that when a mulatto has a regular European face, look out for him; he is a devil. But see, your steward here has features more regular than King George's of England; and yet there he nods, and bows, and smiles; a king, indeed—the king of kind hearts and polite fellows. What a pleasant voice he has, too?"

"He has, Señor."

"But, tell me, has he not, so far as you have known him, always proved a good, worthy fellow?" said Captain Delano, pausing, while with a final genuflexion the steward disappeared into the

---

4. Philip Stanhope (1694–1773), fourth earl of Chesterfield, wrote to his son about the need for a worldly code less stringent than Jesus' absolute morality.

cabin; "come, for the reason just mentioned, I am curious to know."

"Francesco is a good man," a sort of sluggishly responded Don Benito, like a phlegmatic appreciator, who would neither find fault nor flatter.

"Ah, I thought so. For it were strange indeed, and not very creditable to us white-skins, if a little of our blood mixed with the African's, should, far from improving the latter's quality, have the sad effect of pouring vitriolic acid into black broth; improving the hue, perhaps, but not the wholesomeness."

"Doubtless, doubtless, Señor, but"—glancing at Babo—"not to speak of negroes, your planter's remark I have heard applied to the Spanish and Indian intermixtures in our provinces. But I know nothing about the matter," he listlessly added.

And here they entered the cabin.

The lunch was a frugal one. Some of Captain Delano's fresh fish and pumpkins, biscuit and salt beef, the reserved bottle of cider, and the San Dominick's last bottle of Canary.

As they entered, Francesco, with two or three colored aids, was hovering over the table giving the last adjustments. Upon perceiving their master they withdrew, Francesco making a smiling congé, and the Spaniard, without condescending to notice it, fastidiously remarking to his companion that he relished not superfluous attendance.

Without companions, host and guest sat down, like a childless married couple, at opposite ends of the table, Don Benito waving Captain Delano to his place, and, weak as he was, insisting upon that gentleman being seated before himself.

The negro placed a rug under Don Benito's feet, and a cushion behind his back, and then stood behind, not his master's chair, but Captain Delano's. At first, this a little surprised the latter. But it was soon evident that, in taking his position, the black was still true to his master; since by facing him he could the more readily anticipate his slightest want.

"This is an uncommonly intelligent fellow of yours, Don Benito," whispered Captain Delano across the table.

"You say true, Señor."

During the repast, the guest again reverted to parts of Don Benito's story, begging further particulars here and there. He inquired how it was that the scurvy and fever should have committed such wholesale havoc upon the whites, while destroying less than half of the blacks. As if this question reproduced the whole scene of plaque before the Spaniard's eyes, miserably reminding him of his solitude in a cabin where before he had had so many friends and officers around him, his hand shook, his face became hueless, broken words escaped; but directly the sane memory of the past seemed replaced by insane terrors of the present. With starting eyes he stared before him at vacancy. For nothing was to be seen but the hand of his servant pushing the Canary over towards him.[5] At length a few sips served partially to restore him. He made random reference to the different constitution of races, enabling one to offer more resistance to certain maladies than another. The thought was new to his companion.

Presently Captain Delano, intending to say something to his host concerning the pecuniary part of the business he had undertaken for him, especially—since he was strictly accountable to his owners—with reference to the new suit of sails, and other things of that sort; and naturally preferring to conduct such affairs in private, was desirous that the servant should withdraw; imagining that Don Benito for a few minutes could dispense with his attendance. He, however, waited awhile; thinking that, as the conversation proceeded, Don Benito, without being prompted, would perceive the propriety of the step.

But it was otherwise. At last catching his host's eye, Captain Delano, with a slight backward gesture of his thumb, whispered, "Don Benito, pardon me, but there is an interference with the full expression of what I have to say to you."

Upon this the Spaniard changed countenance; which was imputed to his resenting the hint, as in some way a reflection upon his servant. After a moment's pause, he assured his guest that the black's remaining with them could be of no disservice; because since losing his officers he had made Babo (whose original office, it now appeared, had been captain of the slaves) not only his constant attendant and companion, but in all things his confidant.

After this, nothing more could be said; though, indeed, Captain Delano could hardly avoid some little tinge of irritation upon being left ungratified in so inconsiderable a wish, by one, too, for whom he intended such solid services. But it is only his querulousness, thought he; and so filling his glass he proceeded to business.

The price of the sails and other matters was fixed upon. But while this was being done, the American observed that, though his original offer of assistance had been hailed with hectic animation, yet now when it was reduced to a business transaction, indifference and apathy were betrayed. Don Benito, in fact, appeared to submit to hearing the details more out of regard to common propriety, than from any impression that weighty benefit to himself and his voyage was involved.

---

5. "But, behold, the hand of him that betrayeth me is with me on the table" (Luke 22). "Canary": a wine from the Canary Islands.

Soon, his manner became still more reserved. The effort was vain to seek to draw him into social talk. Gnawed by his splenetic mood, he sat twitching his beard, while to little purpose the hand of his servant, mute as that on the wall, slowly pushed over the Canary.

Lunch being over, they sat down on the cushioned transom; the servant placing a pillow behind his master. The long continuance of the calm had now affected the atmosphere. Don Benito sighed heavily, as if for breath.

"Why not adjourn to the cuddy," said Captain Delano; "there is more air there." But the host sat silent and motionless.

Meantime his servant knelt before him, with a large fan of feathers. And Francesco coming in on tiptoes, handed the negro a little cup of aromatic waters, with which at intervals he chafed his master's brow; smoothing the hair along the temples as a nurse does a child's. He spoke no word. He only rested his eye on his master's, as if, amid all Don Benito's distress, a little to refresh his spirit by the silent sight of fidelity.

Presently the ship's bell sounded two o'clock; and through the cabin-windows a slight rippling of the sea was discerned; and from the desired direction.

"There," exclaimed Captain Delano, "I told you so, Don Benito, look!"

He had risen to his feet, speaking in a very animated tone, with a view the more to rouse his companion. But though the crimson curtain of the stern-window near him that moment fluttered against his pale cheek, Don Benito seemed to have even less welcome for the breeze than the calm.

Poor fellow, thought Captain Delano, bitter experience has taught him that one ripple does not make a wind, any more than one swallow a summer. But he is mistaken for once. I will get his ship in for him, and prove it.

Briefly alluding to his weak condition, he urged his host to remain quietly where he was, since he (Captain Delano) would with pleasure take upon himself the responsibility of making the best use of the wind.

Upon gaining the deck, Captain Delano started at the unexpected figure of Atufal, monumentally fixed at the threshold, like one of those sculptured porters of black marble guarding the porches of Egyptian tombs.

But this time the start was, perhaps, purely physical. Atufal's presence, singularly attesting docility even in sullenness, was contrasted with that of the hatchet-polishers, who in patience evinced their industry; while both spectacles showed, that lax as Don Benito's general authority might be, still, whenever he chose to exert it, no man so savage or colossal but must, more or less, bow.

Snatching a trumpet which hung from the bulwarks, with a free step Captain Delano advanced to the forward edge of the poop, issuing his orders in his best Spanish. The few sailors and many negroes, all equally pleased, obediently set about heading the ship towards the harbor.

While giving some directions about setting a lower stu'n'-sail, suddenly Captain Delano heard a voice faithfully repeating his orders. Turning, he saw Babo, now for the time acting, under the pilot, his original part of captain of the slaves. This assistance proved valuable. Tattered sails and warped yards were soon brought into some trim. And no brace or halyard was pulled but to the blithe songs of the inspirited negroes.

Good fellows, thought Captain Delano, a little training would make fine sailors of them. Why see, the very women pull and sing too. These must be some of those Ashantee negresses that make such capital soldiers, I've heard. But who's at the helm. I must have a good hand there.

He went to see.

The San Dominick steered with a cumbrous tiller, with large horizontal pullies attached. At each pully-end stood a subordinate black, and between them, at the tiller-head, the responsible post, a Spanish seaman, whose countenance evinced his due share in the general hopefulness and confidence at the coming of the breeze.

He proved the same man who had behaved with so shame-faced an air on the windlass.

"Ah—it is you, my man," exclaimed Captain Delano—"well, no more sheep's-eyes now;—look straightforward and keep the ship so. Good hand, I trust? And want to get into the harbor, don't you?"

The man assented with an inward chuckle, grasping the tiller-head firmly. Upon this, unperceived by the American, the two blacks eyed the sailor intently.

Finding all right at the helm, the pilot went forward to the forecastle, to see how matters stood there.

The ship now had way enough to breast the current. With the approach of evening, the breeze would be sure to freshen.

Having done all that was needed for the present, Captain Delano, giving his last orders to the sailors, turned aft to report affairs to Don Benito in the cabin; perhaps additionally incited to rejoin him by the hope of snatching a moment's private chat while the servant was engaged upon deck.

From opposite sides, there were, beneath the poop, two approaches to the cabin; one further forward than the other, and consequently communicating with a longer passage. Marking the servant still above, Captain Delano, taking the nighest entrance— the one last named, and at whose porch Atufal still stood—hurried on his way, till, arrived at the cabin threshold, he paused an instant, a little to recover from his eagerness. Then, with the words of his intended business upon his lips, he entered. As he advanced toward the seated Spaniard, he heard another footstep, keeping time with his. From the opposite door, a salver in hand, the servant was likewise advancing.

"Confound the faithful fellow," thought Captain Delano; "what a vexatious coincidence."

Possibly, the vexation might have been something different, were it not for the brisk confidence inspired by the breeze. But even as it was, he felt a slight twinge, from a sudden indefinite association in his mind of Babo with Atufal.

"Don Benito," said he, "I give you joy; the breeze will hold, and will increase. By the way, your tall man and time-piece, Atufal, stands without. By your order, of course?"

Don Benito recoiled, as if at some bland satirical touch, delivered with such adroit garnish of apparent good-breeding as to present no handle for retort.

He is like one flayed alive, thought Captain Delano; where may one touch him without causing a shrink?

The servant moved before his master, adjusting a cushion; recalled to civility, the Spaniard stiffly replied: "You are right. The slave appears where you saw him, according to my command; which is, that if at the given hour I am below, he must take his stand and abide my coming."

"Ah now, pardon me, but that is treating the poor fellow like an ex-king indeed. Ah, Don Benito," smiling, "for all the license you permit in some things, I fear lest, at bottom, you are a bitter hard master."

Again Don Benito shrank; and this time, as the good sailor thought, from a genuine twinge of his conscience.

Again conversation became constrained. In vain Captain Delano called attention to the now perceptible motion of the keel gently cleaving the sea; with lack-lustre eye, Don Benito returned words few and reserved.

By-and-by, the wind having steadily risen, and still blowing right into the harbor, bore the San Dominick swiftly on. Rounding a point of land, the sealer at distance came into open view.

Meantime Captain Delano had again repaired to the deck, remaining there some time. Having at last altered the ship's course, so as to give the reef a wide berth, he returned for a few moments below.

I will cheer up my poor friend, this time, thought he.

"Better and better, Don Benito," he cried as he blithely reëntered; "there will soon be an end to your cares, at least for awhile. For when, after a long, sad voyage, you know, the anchor drops into the haven, all its vast weight seems lifted from the captain's heart. We are getting on famously, Don Benito. My ship is in sight. Look through this side-light here; there she is; all a-taunt-o! The Bachelor's Delight, my good friend. Ah, how this wind braces one up. Come, you must take a cup of coffee with me this evening. My old steward will give you as fine a cup as ever any sultan tasted. What say you, Don Benito, will you?"

At first, the Spaniard glanced feverishly up, casting a longing look towards the sealer, while with mute concern his servant gazed into his face. Suddenly the old ague of coldness returned, and dropping back to his cushions he was silent.

"You do not answer. Come, all day you have been my host; would you have hospitality all on one side?"

"I cannot go," was the response.

"What? it will not fatigue you. The ships will lie together as near as they can, without swinging foul. It will be little more than stepping from deck to deck; which is but as from room to room. Come, come, you must not refuse me."

"I cannot go," decisively and repulsively repeated Don Benito.

Renouncing all but the last appearance of courtesy, with a sort of cadaverous sullenness, and biting his thin nails to the quick, he glanced, almost glared, at his guest; as if impatient that a stranger's presence should interfere with the full indulgence of his morbid hour. Meantime the sound of the parted waters came more and more gurglingly and merrily in at the windows; as reproaching him for his dark spleen; as telling him that, sulk as he might, and go mad with it, nature cared not a jot; since, whose fault was it, pray?

But the foul mood was now at its depth, as the fair wind at its hight.

There was something in the man so far beyond any mere unsociality or sourness previously evinced, that even the forbearing good-nature of his guest could no longer endure it. Wholly at a loss to account for such demeanor, and deeming sickness with eccentricity, however extreme, no adequate excuse, well satisfied, too, that nothing in his own conduct could justify it, Captain Delano's pride began to be roused. Himself became reserved. But all seemed one to the Spaniard. Quitting him, therefore, Captain Delano once more went to the deck.

The ship was now within less than two miles of the sealer. The whale-boat was seen darting over the interval.

To be brief, the two vessels, thanks to the pilot's skill, ere long in neighborly style lay anchored together.

Before returning to his own vessel, Captain Delano had intended communicating to Don Benito the smaller details of the proposed services to be rendered. But, as it was, unwilling anew to subject himself to rebuffs, he resolved, now that he had seen the San Dominick safely moored, immediately to quit her, without further allusion to hospitality or business. Indefinitely postponing his ulterior plans, he would regulate his future actions according to future circumstances. His boat was ready to receive him; but his host still tarried below. Well, thought Captain Delano, if he has little breeding, the more need to show mine. He descended to the cabin to bid a ceremonious, and, it may be, tacitly rebukeful adieu. But to his great satisfaction, Don Benito, as if he began to feel the weight of that treatment with which his slighted guest had, not indecorously, retaliated upon him, now supported by his servant, rose to his feet, and grasping Captain Delano's hand, stood tremulous; too much agitated to speak. But the good augury hence drawn was suddenly dashed, by his resuming all his previous reserve, with augmented gloom, as, with half-averted eyes, he silently reseated himself on his cushions. With a corresponding return of his own chilled feelings, Captain Delano bowed and withdrew.

He was hardly midway in the narrow corridor, dim as a tunnel, leading from the cabin to the stairs, when a sound, as of the tolling for execution in some jail-yard, fell on his ears. It was the echo of the ship's flawed bell, striking the hour, drearily reverberated in this subterranean vault. Instantly, by a fatality not to be withstood, his mind, responsive to the portent, swarmed with superstitious suspicions. He paused. In images far swifter than these sentences, the minutest details of all his former distrusts swept through him.

Hitherto, credulous good-nature had been too ready to furnish excuses for reasonable fears. Why was the Spaniard, so superfluously punctilious at times, now heedless of common propriety in not accompanying to the side his departing guest? Did indisposition forbid? Indisposition had not forbidden more irksome exertion that day. His last equivocal demeanor recurred. He had risen to his feet, grasped his guest's hand, motioned toward his hat; then, in an instant, all was eclipsed in sinister muteness and gloom. Did this imply one brief, repentent relenting at the final moment, from some iniquitous plot, followed by remorseless return to it? His last glance seemed to express a calamitous, yet acquiescent farewell to Captain Delano forever. Why decline the invitation to visit the sealer that evening? Or was the Spaniard less hardened than the Jew, who refrained not from supping at the board of him whom the same night he meant to betray?[6] What imported all those day-long enigmas and contradictions, except they were intended to mystify, preliminary to some stealthy blow? Atufal, the pretended rebel, but

6. Judas Iscariot at the Last Supper (Matthew 26).

punctual shadow, that moment lurked by the threshold without. He seemed a sentry, and more. Who, by his own confession, had stationed him there? Was the negro now lying in wait?

The Spaniard behind—his creature before: to rush from darkness to light was the involuntary choice.

The next moment, with clenched jaw and hand, he passed Atufal, and stood unharmed in the light. As he saw his trim ship lying peacefully at anchor, and almost within ordinary call; as he saw his household boat, with familiar faces in it, patiently rising and falling on the short waves by the San Dominick's side; and then, glancing about the decks where he stood, saw the oakum-pickers still gravely plying their fingers; and heard the low, buzzing whistle and industrious hum of the hatchet-polishers, still bestirring themselves over their endless occupation; and more than all, as he saw the benign aspect of nature, taking her innocent repose in the evening; the screened sun in the quiet camp of the west shining out like the mild light from Abraham's tent; as charmed eye and ear took in all these, with the chained figure of the black, clenched jaw and hand relaxed. Once again he smiled at the phantoms which he had mocked him, and felt something like a tinge of remorse, that, by harboring them even for a moment, he should, by implication, have betrayed an atheist doubt of the ever-watchful Providence above.

There was a few minutes' delay, while, in obedience to his orders, the boat was being hooked along to the gangway. During this interval, a sort of saddened satisfaction stole over Captain Delano, at thinking of the kindly offices he had that day discharged for a stranger. Ah, thought he, after good actions one's conscience is never ungrateful, however much so the benefited party may be.

Presently, his foot, in the first act of descent into the boat, pressed the first round of the side-ladder, his face presented inward upon the deck. In the same moment, he heard his name courteously sounded; and, to his pleased surprise, saw Don Benito advancing— an unwonted energy in his air, as if, at the last moment, intent upon making amends for his recent discourtesy. With instinctive good feeling, Captain Delano, withdrawing his foot, turned and reciprocally advanced. As he did so, the Spaniard's nervous eagerness increased, but his vital energy failed; so that, the better to support him, the servant, placing his master's hand on his naked shoulder, and gently holding it there, formed himself into a sort of crutch.

When the two captains met, the Spaniard again fervently took the hand of the American, at the same time casting an earnest glance into his eyes, but, as before, too much overcome to speak.

I have done him wrong, self-reproachfully thought Captain Delano; his apparent coldness has deceived me; in no instance has he meant to offend.

Meantime, as if fearful that the continuance of the scene might too much unstring his master, the servant seemed anxious to terminate it. And so, still presenting himself as a crutch, and walking between the two captains, he advanced with them towards the gangway; while still, as if full of kindly contrition, Don Benito would not let go the hand of Captain Delano, but retained it in his, across the black's body.

Soon they were standing by the side, looking over into the boat, whose crew turned up their curious eyes. Waiting a moment for the Spaniard to relinquish his hold, the now embarrassed Captain Delano lifted his foot, to overstep the threshold of the open gangway; but still Don Benito would not let go his hand. And yet, with an agitated tone, he said, "I can go no further; here I must bid you adieu. Adieu, my dear, dear Don Amasa. Go—go!" suddenly tearing his hand loose, "go, and God guard you better than me, my best friend."

Not unaffected, Captain Delano would now have lingered; but catching the meekly admonitory eye of the servant, with a hasty farewell he descended into his boat, followed by the continual adieus of Don Benito, standing rooted in the gangway.

Seating himself in the stern, Captain Delano, making a last salute, ordered the boat shoved off. The crew had their oars on end. The bowsman pushed the boat a sufficient distance for the oars to be lengthwise dropped. The instant that was done, Don Benito sprang over the bulwarks, falling at the feet of Captain Delano; at the same time, calling towards his ship, but in tones so frenzied, that none in the boat could understand him. But, as if not equally obtuse, three sailors, from three different and distant parts of the ship, splashed into the sea, swimming after their captain, as if intent upon his rescue.

The dismayed officer of the boat eagerly asked what this meant. To which, Captain Delano, turning a disdainful smile upon the unaccountable Spaniard, answered that, for his part, he neither knew nor cared; but it seemed as if Don Benito had taken it into his head to produce the impression among his people that the boat wanted to kidnap him. "Or else—give way for your lives," he wildly added, starting at a clattering hubbub in the ship, above which rang the tocsin of the hatchet-polishers; and seizing Don Benito by the throat he added, "this plotting pirate means murder!" Here, in apparent verification of the words, the servant, a dagger in his hand, was seen on the rail overhead, poised, in the act of leaping, as if with desperate fidelity to befriend his master to the last; while, seemingly to aid the black, the three white sailors were trying to clamber into the hampered bow. Meantime, the whole host of negroes, as if inflamed at the sight of their jeopardized captain, impended in one sooty avalanche over the bulwarks.

All this, with what preceded, and what followed, occurred with such involutions of rapidity, that past, present, and future seemed one.

Seeing the negro coming, Captain Delano had flung the Spaniard aside, almost in the very act of clutching him, and, by the unconscious recoil, shifting his place, with arms thrown up, so promptly grappled the servant in his descent, that with dagger presented at Captain Delano's heart, the black seemed of purpose to have leaped there as to his mark. But the weapon was wrenched away, and the assailant dashed down into the bottom of the boat, which now, with disentangled oars, began to speed through the sea.

At this juncture, the left hand of Captain Delano, on one side, again clutched the half-reclined Don Benito, heedless that he was in a speechless faint, while his right foot, on the other side, ground the prostrate negro; and his right arm pressed for added speed on the after oar, his eye bent forward, encouraging his men to their utmost.

But here, the officer of the boat, who had at last succeeded in beating off the towing sailors, and was now, with face turned aft, assisting the bowsman at his oar, suddenly called to Captain Delano, to see what the black was about; while a Portuguese oarsman shouted to him to give heed to what the Spaniard was saying.

Glancing down at his feet, Captain Delano saw the freed hand of the servant aiming with a second dagger—a small one, before concealed in his wool—with this he was snakishly writhing up from the boat's bottom, at the heart of his master, his countenance lividly vindictive, expressing the centred purpose of his soul; while the Spaniard, half-choked, was vainly shrinking away, with husky words, incoherent to all but the Portuguese.

That moment, across the long-benighted mind of Captain Delano, a flash of revelation swept, illuminating in unanticipated clearness, his host's whole mysterious demeanor, with every enigmatic event of the day, as well as the entire past voyage of the San Dominick. He smote Babo's hand down, but his own heart smote him harder. With infinite pity he withdrew his hold from Don Benito. Not Captain Delano, but Don Benito, the black, in leaping into the boat, had intended to stab.[7]

Both the black's hands were held, as, glancing up towards the San Dominick, Captain Delano, now with scales dropped from his eyes, saw the negroes, not in misrule, not in tumult, not as if frantically concerned for Don Benito, but with mask torn away, flourishing hatchets and knives, in ferocious piratical revolt. Like delirious black dervishes, the six Ashantees danced on the poop. Prevented by

---

7. In Delano's chapter Benito Cereno tries to stab a black man; in Melville's version Babo tries to stab Don Benito.

their foes from springing into the water, the Spanish boys were hurrying up to the topmost spars, while such of the few Spanish sailors, not already in the sea, less alert, were descried, helplessly mixed in, on deck, with the blacks.

Meantime Captain Delano hailed his own vessel, ordering the ports up, and the guns run out. But by this time the cable of the San Dominick had been cut; and the fag-end, in lashing out, whipped away the canvas shroud about the beak, suddenly revealing, as the bleached hull swung round towards the open ocean, death for the figure-head, in a human skeleton; chalky comment on the chalked words below, "*Follow your leader.*"

At the sight, Don Benito, covering his face, wailed out: "'Tis he, Aranda! my murdered, unburied friend!"

Upon reaching the sealer, calling for ropes, Captain Delano bound the negro, who made no resistance, and had him hoisted to the deck. He would then have assisted the now almost helpless Don Benito up the side; but Don Benito, wan as he was, refused to move, or be moved, until the negro should have been first put below out of view. When, presently assured that it was done, he no more shrank from the ascent.

The boat was immediately dispatched back to pick up the three swimming sailors. Meantime, the guns were in readiness, though, owing to the San Dominick having glided somewhat astern of the sealer, only the aftermost one could be brought to bear. With this, they fired six times; thinking to cripple the fugitive ship by bringing down her spars. But only a few inconsiderable ropes were shot away. Soon the ship was beyond the guns' range, steering broad out of the bay; the blacks thickly clustering round the bowsprit, one moment with taunting cries towards the whites, the next with upthrown gestures hailing the now dusky moors of ocean—cawing crows escaped from the hand of the fowler.

The first impulse was to slip the cables and give chase. But, upon second thoughts, to pursue with whale-boat and yawl seemed more promising.

Upon inquiring of Don Benito what fire arms they had on board the San Dominick, Captain Delano was answered that they had none that could be used; because, in the earlier stages of the mutiny, a cabin-passenger, since dead, had secretly put out of order the locks of what few muskets there were. But with all his remaining strength, Don Benito entreated the American not to give chase, either with ship or boat; for the negroes had already proved themselves such desperadoes, that, in case of a present assault, nothing but a total massacre of the whites could be looked for. But, regarding this warning as coming from one whose spirit had been crushed by misery, the American did not give up his design.

The boats were got ready and armed. Captain Delano ordered his men into them. He was going himself when Don Benito grasped his arm.

"What! have you saved my life, señor, and are you now going to throw away your own?"

The officers also, for reasons connected with their interests and those of the voyage, and a duty owing to the owners, strongly objected against their commander's going. Weighing their remonstrances a moment, Captain Delano felt bound to remain; appointing his chief mate—an athletic and resolute man, who had been a privateer's man—to head the party. The more to encourage the sailors, they were told, that the Spanish captain considered his ship good as lost; that she and her cargo, including some gold and silver, were worth more than a thousand doubloons. Take her, and no small part should be theirs. The sailors replied with a shout.

The fugitives had now almost gained an offing. It was nearly night; but the moon was rising. After hard, prolonged pulling, the boats came up on the ship's quarters, at a suitable distance laying upon their oars to discharge their muskets. Having no bullets to return, the negroes sent their yells. But, upon the second volley, Indian-like, they hurtled their hatchets. One took off a sailor's fingers. Another struck the whale-boat's bow, cutting off the rope there, and remaining stuck in the gunwale like a woodman's axe. Snatching it, quivering from its lodgment, the mate hurled it back. The returned gauntlet now stuck in the ship's broken quarter-gallery, and so remained.

The negroes giving too hot a reception, the whites kept a more respectful distance. Hovering now just out of reach of the hurtling hatchets, they, with a view to the close encounter which must soon come, sought to decoy the blacks into entirely disarming themselves of their most murderous weapons in a hand-to-hand fight, by foolishly flinging them, as missiles, short of the mark, into the sea. But ere long perceiving the stratagem, the negroes desisted, though not before many of them had to replace their lost hatchets with handspikes; an exchange which, as counted upon, proved in the end favorable to the assailants.

Meantime, with a strong wind, the ship still clove the water; the boats alternately falling behind, and pulling up, to discharge fresh volleys.

The fire was mostly directed towards the stern, since there, chiefly, the negroes, at present, were clustering. But to kill or maim the negroes was not the object. To take them, with the ship, was the object. To do it, the ship must be boarded; which could not be done by boats while she was sailing so fast.

A thought now struck the mate. Observing the Spanish boys still aloft, high as they could get, he called to them to descend to the yards, and cut adrift the sails. It was done. About this time, owing to causes hereafter to be shown, two Spaniards, in the dress of sailors and conspicuously showing themselves, were killed; not by volleys, but by deliberate marksman's shots; while, as it afterwards appeared, by one of the general discharges, Atufal, the black, and the Spaniard at the helm likewise were killed. What now, with the loss of the sails, and loss of leaders, the ship became unmanageable to the negroes.

With creaking masts, she came heavily round to the wind; the prow slowly swinging, into view of the boats, its skeleton gleaming in the horizontal moonlight, and casting a gigantic ribbed shadow upon the water. One extended arm of the ghost seemed beckoning the whites to avenge it.

"Follow your leader!" cried the mate; and, one on each bow, the boats boarded. Sealing-spears and cutlasses crossed hatchets and hand-spikes. Huddled upon the long-boat amidships, the negresses raised a wailing chant, whose chorus was the clash of the steel.

For a time, the attack wavered; the negroes wedging themselves to beat it back; the half-repelled sailors, as yet unable to gain a footing, fighting as troopers in the saddle, one leg sideways flung over the bulwarks, and one without, plying their cutlasses like carters' whips. But in vain. They were almost overborne, when, rallying themselves into a squad as one man, with a huzza, they sprang inboard; where, entangled, they involuntarily separated again. For a few breaths' space, there was a vague, muffled, inner sound, as of submerged sword-fish rushing hither and thither through shoals of black-fish. Soon, in a reunited band, and joined by the Spanish seamen, the whites came to the surface, irresistibly driving the negroes toward the stern. But a barricade of casks and sacks, from side to side, had been thrown up by the mainmast. Here the negroes faced about, and though scorning peace or truce, yet fain would have had respite. But, without pause, overleaping the barrier, the unflagging sailors again closed. Exhausted, the blacks now fought in despair. Their red tongues lolled, wolf-like, from their black mouths. But the pale sailors' teeth were set; not a word was spoken; and, in five minutes more, the ship was won.

Nearly a score of the negroes were killed. Exclusive of those by the balls, many were mangled; their wounds—mostly inflicted by the long-edged sealing-spears—resembling those shaven ones of the English at Preston Pans, made by the poled scythes of the Highlanders. On the other side, none were killed, though several were wounded; some severely, including the mate. The surviving negroes were temporarily secured, and the ship, towed back into the harbor at midnight, once more lay anchored.

Omitting the incidents and arrangements ensuing, suffice it that, after two days spent in refitting, the ships sailed in company for

Conception, in Chili, and thence for Lima, in Peru; where, before the vice-regal courts, the whole affair, from the beginning, underwent investigation.

Though, midway on the passage, the ill-fated Spaniard, relaxed from constraint, showed some signs of regaining health with freewill; yet, agreeably to his own foreboding, shortly before arriving at Lima, he relapsed, finally becoming so reduced as to be carried ashore in arms. Hearing of his story and plight, one of the many religious institutions of the City of Kings opened an hospitable refuge to him, where both physician and priest were his nurses, and a member of the order volunteered to be his one special guardian and consoler, by night and by day.

The following extracts, translated from one of the official Spanish documents, will it is hoped, shed light on the preceding narrative, as well as, in the first place, reveal the true port of departure and true history of the San Dominick's voyage, down to the time of her touching at the island of St. Maria.

But, ere the extracts come, it may be well to preface them with a remark.

The document selected, from among many others, for partial translation, contains the deposition of Benito Cereno; the first taken in the case. Some disclosures therein were, at the time, held dubious for both learned and natural reasons. The tribunal inclined to the opinion that the deponent, not undisturbed in his mind by recent events, raved of some things which could never have happened. But subsequent depositions of the surviving sailors, bearing out the revelations of their captain in several of the strangest particulars, gave credence to the rest. So that the tribunal, in its final decision, rested its capital sentences upon statements which, had they lacked confirmation, it would have deemed it but duty to reject.

I, Don Jose de Abos and Padilla, His Majesty's Notary for the Royal Revenue, and Register of this Province, and Notary Public of the Holy Crusade of this Bishopric, etc.

Do certify and declare, as much as is requisite in law, that, in the criminal cause commenced the twenty-fourth of the month of September, in the year seventeen hundred and ninety-nine, against the negroes of the ship San Dominick, the following declaration before me was made.

*Declaration of the first witness*, DON BENITO CERENO

*The same day, and month, and year, His Honor, Doctor Juan Martinez de Rozas, Councilor of the Royal Audience of this Kingdom, and learned in the law of this Intendency, ordered the captain of the ship San Dominick, Don Benito Cereno, to appear; which he did in his litter, attended by the monk Infelez; of whom he received the oath, which he took by God, our Lord, and a sign of the Cross; under which he promised to tell the truth of whatever he should know and should be asked;—and being interrogated agreeably to the tenor of the act commencing the process, he said, that on the twentieth of May last, he set sail with his ship from the port of Valparaiso, bound to that of Callao; loaded with the produce of the country beside thirty cases of hardware and one hundred and sixty blacks, of both sexes, mostly belonging to Don Alexandro Aranda, gentleman, of the city of Mendoza; that the crew of the ship consisted of thirty-six men, beside the persons who went as passengers; that the negroes were in part as follows:*

*[Here, in the original, follows a list of some fifty names, descriptions, and ages, compiled from certain recovered documents of Aranda's, and also from recollections of the deponent, from which portions only are extracted.]*

*One, from about eighteen to nineteen years, named José, and this was the man that waited upon his master, Don Alexandro, and who speaks well the Spanish, having served him four or five years; • • • a mulatto, named Francisco, the cabin steward, of a good person and voice, having sung in the Valparaiso churches, native of the province of Buenos Ayres, aged about thirty-five years. • • • A smart negro, named Dago, who had been for many years a grave-digger among the Spaniards, aged forty-six years. • • • Four old negroes, born in Africa, from sixty to seventy, but sound, calkers by trade, whose names are as follows:—the first was named Muri, and he was killed (as was also his son named Diamelo); the second, Nacta; the third, Yola, likewise killed; the fourth, Ghofan; and six full-grown negroes, aged from thirty to forty-five, all raw, and born among the Ashantees— Matiluqui, Yan, Lecbe, Mapenda, Yambaio, Akim; four of whom were killed; • • • a powerful negro named Atufal, who, being supposed to have been a chief in Africa, his owners set great store by him. • • • And a small negro of Senegal, but some years among the Spaniards, aged about thirty, which negro's name was Babo; • • • that he does not remember the names of the others, but that still expecting the residue of Don Alexandro's papers will be found, will then take due account of them all, and remit to the court; • • • and thirty-nine women and children of all ages.*

*[The catalogue over, the deposition goes on:]*

*• • • That all the negroes slept upon deck, as is customary in this navigation, and none wore fetters, because the owner, his friend Aranda, told him that they were all tractable; • • • that on the seventh day after leaving port, at three o'clock in the morning, all the Spaniards being asleep except the two officers on the watch, who were*

*the boatswain, Juan Robles, and the carpenter, Juan Bautista Gayete, and the helmsman and his boy, the negroes revolted suddenly, wounded dangerously the boatswain and the carpenter, and successively killed eighteen men of those who were sleeping upon deck, some with hand-spikes and hatchets, and others by throwing them alive overboard, after tying them; that of the Spaniards upon deck, they left about seven, as he thinks, alive and tied, to manœuvre the ship, and three or four more who hid themselves, remained also alive. Although in the act of revolt the negroes made themselves masters of the hatchway, six or seven wounded went through it to the cockpit, without any hindrance on their part; that during the act of revolt, the mate and another person, whose name he does not recollect, attempted to come up through the hatchway, but being quickly wounded, were obliged to return to the cabin; that the deponent resolved at break of day to come up the companionway, where the negro Babo was, being the ringleader, and Atufal, who assisted him, and having spoken to them, exhorted them to cease committing such atrocities, asking them, at the same time, what they wanted and intended to do, offering, himself, to obey their commands; that, notwithstanding this, they threw, in his presence, three men, alive and tied, overboard; that they told the deponent to come up, and that they would not kill him; which having done, the negro Babo asked him whether there were in those seas any negro countries where they might be carried, and he answered them, No; that the negro Babo afterwards told him to carry them to Senegal, or to the neighboring islands of St. Nicholas; and he answered, that this was impossible, on account of the great distance, the necessity involved of rounding Cape Horn, the bad condition of the vessel, the want of provisions, sails, and water; but that the negro Babo replied to him he must carry them in any way; that they would do and conform themselves to everything the deponent should require as to eating and drinking; that after a long conference, being absolutely compelled to please them, for they threatened him to kill all the whites if they were not, at all events, carried to Senegal, he told them that what was most wanting for the voyage was water; that they would go near the coast to take it, and thence they would proceed on their course; that the negro Babo agreed to it; and the deponent steered towards the intermediate ports; hoping to meet some Spanish or foreign vessel that would save them; within ten or eleven days they saw the land, and continued their course by it in the vicinity of Nasca; that the deponent observed that the negroes were now restless and mutinous, because he did not effect the taking in of water, the negro Babo having required, with threats, that it should be done, without fail, the following day; he told him he saw plainly that the coast was steep, and the rivers designated in the maps were not to be found, with other reasons suitable to the circumstances; that the best way would be to go to the island of Santa Maria, where they might water easily, it being a solitary island, as the foreigners did; that the deponent did not go to Pisco, that was near, nor make any other port of the coast, because the negro Babo had intimated to him several times, that he would kill all the whites the very moment he should perceive any city, town, or settlement of any kind on the shores to which they should be carried: that having determined to go to the island of Santa Maria, as the deponent had planned, for the purpose of trying whether, on the passage or near the island itself, they could find any vessel that should favor them, or whether he could escape from it in a boat to the neighboring coast of Arruco; to adopt the necessary means he immediately changed his course, steering for the island; that the negroes Babo and Atufal held daily conferences, in which they discussed what was necessary for their design of returning to Senegal, whether they were to kill all the Spaniards, and particularly the deponent; that eight days after parting from the coast of Nasca, the deponent being on the watch a little after day-break, and soon after the negroes had their meeting, the negro Babo came to the place where the deponent was, and told him that he had determined to kill his master, Don Alexandro Aranda, both because he and his companions could not otherwise be sure of their liberty, and that, to keep the seamen in subjection, he wanted to prepare a warning of what road they should be made to take did they or any of them oppose him; and that, by means of the death of Don Alexandro, that warning would best be given; but, that what this last meant, the deponent did not at the time comprehend, nor could not, further than that the death of Don Alexandro was intended; and moreover, the negro Babo proposed to the deponent to call the mate Raneds, who was sleeping in the cabin, before the thing was done, for fear, as the deponent understood it, that the mate, who was a good navigator, should be killed with Don Alexandro and the rest; that the deponent, who was the friend, from youth, of Don Alexandro, prayed and conjured, but all was useless; for the negro Babo answered him that the thing could not be prevented, and that all the Spaniards risked their death if they should attempt to frustrate his will in this matter or any other; that, in this conflict, the deponent called the mate, Raneds, who was forced to go apart, and immediately the negro Babo commanded the Ashantee Martinqui and the Ashantee Lecbe to go and commit the murder; that those two went down with hatchets to the berth of Don Alexandro; that, yet half alive and mangled, they dragged him on deck; that they were going to throw him overboard in that state, but the negro Babo stopped them, bidding the murder be completed on the deck before him, which was done, when, by his orders, the body was carried below, forward; that nothing more was seen of it by the deponent for three days; • • • that Don Alonzo Sidonia, an old man, long resident at Valparaiso, and lately appointed to a civil office in Peru, whither he had taken passage, was at the time sleeping in the berth opposite Don Alexandro's; that, awakening at his cries, surprised by them, and at the sight of the negroes with their bloody hatchets in their hands, he threw himself into the sea through a window which was near him, and was drowned, without it being in the power of the deponent to assist or take him up; • • • that, a short time after killing Aranda, they brought upon deck his german-cousin, of middle-age, Don Francisco Masa, of Mendoza, and the young Don Joaquin, Marques de Aramboalaza, then lately from Spain, with his Spanish servant Ponce, and the three young clerks of Aranda, José Morairi, Lorenzo Bargas, and Hermenegildo Gandix, all of Cadiz; that Don Joaquin and Hermenegildo Gandix, the negro Babo for purposes hereafter to appear, preserved alive; but Don Francisco Masa, José Morairi, and Lorenzo Bargas, with Ponce the servant, beside the boatswain, Juan Robles, the boatswain's mates, Manuel Viscaya and Roderigo Hurta, and four of the sailors, the negro Babo ordered to be thrown alive into the sea, although they made no resistance, nor begged for anything else but mercy; that the boatswain, Juan Robles, who knew how to swim, kept the longest above water, making acts of contrition, and, in the last words he uttered, charged this deponent to cause mass to be said for his soul to our Lady of Succor; • • • that, during the three days which followed, the deponent, uncertain what fate had befallen the remains of Don Alexandro, frequently asked the negro Babo where they were, and if, still on board, whether they were to be preserved for interment ashore, entreating him so to order it; that the negro Babo answered nothing till the fourth day, when at sunrise, the deponent coming on deck, the negro Babo showed him a skeleton, which had been substituted for the ship's proper figure-head, the image of Christopher Colon, the discoverer of the New World; that the negro Babo asked him whose skeleton that was, and whether, from its whiteness, he should not think it a white's; that, upon his covering his face, the negro Babo, coming close, said words to this effect: "Keep faith with the blacks from here to Senegal, or you shall in spirit, as now in body, follow your leader," pointing to the prow; • • • that the same morning the negro Babo took up succession each Spaniard forward, and asked him whose skeleton that was, and whether, from its whiteness, he should not think it a white's; that each Spaniard covered his face; that then to each the negro Babo repeated the words in the first place said to the deponent; • • • that they (the Spaniards), being then assembled aft, the negro Babo harangued them, saying that he had now done all; that the deponent (as navigator for the negroes) might pursue his course, warning him and all of them that they should, soul and body, go the way of Don Alexandro if he saw them (the Spaniards) speak or plot anything against them (the negroes)—a*

threat which was repeated every day; that, before the events last mentioned, they had tied the cook to throw him overboard, for it is not
known what thing they heard him speak, but finally the negro Babo
spared his life, at the request of the deponent; that a few days after, the
deponent, endeavoring not to omit any means to preserve the lives of
the remaining whites, spoke to the negroes peace and tranquillity, and
agreed to draw up a paper, signed by the deponent and the sailors who
could write, as also by the negro Babo, for himself and all the blacks,
in which the deponent obliged himself to carry them to Senegal, and
they not to kill any more, and he formally to make over to them the
ship, with the cargo, with which they were for that time satisfied and
quieted. • • • But the next day, the more surely to guard against the
sailors' escape, the negro Babo commanded all the boats to be
destroyed but the long-boat, which was unseaworthy, and another, a
cutter in good condition, which, knowing it would yet be wanted for
towing the water casks, he had lowered down into the hold.

• • • • • •

[Various particulars of the prolonged and perplexed navigation
ensuing here follow, with incidents of a calamitous calm, from which
portion one passage is extracted, to wit:]
—That on the fifth day of the calm, all on board suffering much from
the heat, and want of water, and five having died in fits, and mad, the
negroes became irritable, and for a chance gesture, which they
deemed suspicious—though it was harmless—made by the mate,
Raneds, to the deponent, in the act of handing a quadrant, they killed
him; but that for this they afterwards were sorry, the mate being the
only remaining navigator on board, except the deponent.

• • • • •

—That omitting other events, which daily happened, and which can
only serve uselessly to recall past misfortunes and conflicts, after sev-
enty-three days' navigation, reckoned from the time they sailed from
Nasca, during which they navigated under a scanty allowance of
water, and were afflicted with the calms before mentioned, they at last
arrived at the island of Santa Maria, on the seventeenth of the month
of August, at about six o'clock in the afternoon, at which hour they
cast anchor very near the American ship, Bachelor's Delight, which
lay in the same bay, commanded by the generous Captain Amasa
Delano; but at six o'clock in the morning, they had already descried
the port, and the negroes became uneasy, as soon as at distance they
saw the ship, not having expected to see one there; that the negro
Babo pacified them, assuring them that no fear need be had; that
straightway he ordered the figure on the bow to be covered with
canvas, as for repairs, and had the decks a little set in order; that for
a time the negro Babo and the negro Atufal conferred; that the negro
Atufal was for sailing away, but the negro Babo would not, and, by

*himself, cast about what to do; that at last he came to the deponent, proposing to him to say and do all that the deponent declares to have said and done to the American captain;* • • • • • *that the negro Babo warned him that if he varied in the least, or uttered any word, or gave any look that should give the least intimation of the past events or present state, he would instantly kill him, with all his companions, showing a dagger, which he carried hid, saying something which, as he understood it, meant that the dagger would be alert as his eye; that the negro Babo then announced the plan to all his companions, which pleased them; that he then, the better to disguise the truth, devised many expedients, in some of them uniting deceit and defense; that of this sort was the device of the six Ashantees before named, who were his bravoes; that them he stationed on the break of the poop, as if to clean certain hatchets (in cases, which were part of the cargo), but in reality to use them, and distribute them at need, and at a given word he told them that, among other devices, was the device of presenting Atufal, his right-hand man, as chained, though in a moment the chains could be dropped; that in every particular he informed the deponent what part he was expected to enact in every device, and what story he was to tell on every occasion, always threatening him with instant death if he varied in the least: that, conscious that many of the negroes would be turbulent, the negro Babo appointed the four aged negroes, who were calkers, to keep what domestic order they could on the decks; that again and again he harangued the Spaniards and his companions, informing them of his intent, and of his devices, and of the invented story that this deponent was to tell, charging them lest any of them varied from that story; that these arrangements were made and matured during the interval of two or three hours, between their first sighting the ship and the arrival on board of Captain Amasa Delano; that this happened about half-past seven o'clock in the morning, Captain Amasa Delano coming in his boat, and all gladly receiving him; that the deponent, as well as he could force himself, acting then the part of principal owner, and a free captain of the ship, told Captain Amasa Delano, when called upon, that he came from Buenos Ayres, bound to Lima, with three hundred negroes; that off Cape Horn, and in a subsequent fever, many negroes had died; that also, by similar casualties, all the sea officers and the greatest part of the crew had died.*

• • • • •

*[And so the deposition goes on, circumstantially recounting the fictitious story dictated to the deponent by Babo, and through the deponent imposed upon Captain Delano; and also recounting the friendly offers of Captain Delano, with other things, but all of which is here omitted. After the fictitious story, etc., the deposition proceeds:]*

• • • • • •

—that the generous Captain Amasa Delano remained on board all the
day, till he left the ship anchored at six o'clock in the evening, deponent speaking to him always of his pretended misfortunes, under the
fore-mentioned principles, without having had it in his power to tell
a single word, or give him the least hint, that he might know the truth
and state of things; because the negro Babo, performing the office of
an officious servant with all the appearance of submission of the
humble slave, did not leave the deponent one moment; that this was
in order to observe the deponent's actions and words, for the negro
Babo understands well the Spanish; and besides, there were thereabout some others who were constantly on the watch, and likewise
understood the Spanish. * that upon one occasion, while deponent
was standing on the deck conversing with Amasa Delano, by a secret
sign the negro Babo drew him (the deponent) aside, the act appearing
as if originating with the deponent; that then, he being drawn aside,
the negro Babo proposed to him to gain from Amasa Delano full particulars about his ship, and crew, and arms; that the deponent asked
"For what?" that the negro Babo answered he might conceive; that,
grieved at the prospect of what might overtake the generous Captain
Amasa Delano, the deponent at first refused to ask the desired questions, and used every argument to induce the negro Babo to give up
this new design; that the negro Babo showed the point of his dagger;
that, after the information had been obtained, the negro Babo again
drew him aside, telling him that the very night he (the deponent)
would be captain of two ships, instead of one, for that, great part of
the American's ship's crew being to be absent fishing, the six
Ashantees, without any one else, would easily take it; that at this time
he said other things to the same purpose; that no entreaties availed;
that, before Amasa Delano's coming on board, no hint had been given
touching the capture of the American ship: that to prevent this project the deponent was powerless; • • • —that in some things his
memory is confused, he cannot distinctly recall every event; • • • —
that as soon as they had cast anchor at six of the clock in the evening,
as has before been stated, the American Captain took leave to return
to his vessel; that upon a sudden impulse, which the deponent believes
to have come from God and his angels, he, after the farewell had been
said, followed the generous Captain Amasa Delano as far as the gunwale, where he stayed, under pretense of taking leave, until Amasa
Delano should have been seated in his boat; that on shoving off, the
deponent sprang from the gunwale into the boat, and fell into it, he
knows not how, God guarding him; that—

• • • • •

[Here, in the original, follows the account of what further happened at the escape, and how the San Dominick was retaken, and of
the passage to the coast; including in the recital many expressions of

*"eternal gratitude" to the "generous Captain Amasa Delano." The deposition then proceeds with recapitulatory remarks, and a partial renumeration of the negroes, making record of their individual part in the past events, with a view to furnishing, according to command of the court, the data whereon to found the criminal sentences to be pronounced. From this portion is the following:]*
—That he believes that all the negroes, though not in the first place knowing to the design of revolt, when it was accomplished, approved it. • • • That the negro, José, eighteen years old, and in the personal service of Don Alexandro, was the one who communicated the information to the negro Babo, about the state of things in the cabin, before the revolt; that this is known, because, in the preceding midnight, he used to come from his berth, which was under his master's, in the cabin, to the deck where the ringleader and his associates were, and had secret conversations with the negro Babo, in which he was several times seen by the mate; that, one night, the mate drove him away twice; • • that this same negro José, was the one who, without being commanded to do so by the negro Babo, as Lecbe and Martinqui were, stabbed his master, Don Alexandro, after he had been dragged half-lifeless to the deck; • • that the mulatto steward, Francisco, was of the first band of revolters, that he was, in all things, the creature and tool of the negro Babo; that, to make his court, he, just before a repast in the cabin, proposed, to the negro Babo, poisoning a dish for the generous Captain Amasa Delano; this is known and believed, because the negroes have said it; but that the negro Babo, having another design, forbade Francisco; • • that the Ashantee Lecbe was one of the worst of them; for that, on the day the ship was retaken, he assisted in the defense of her, with a hatchet in each hand, one of which he wounded, in the breast, the chief mate of Amasa Delano, in the first act of boarding; this all knew; that, in sight of the deponent, Lecbe struck, with a hatchet, Don Francisco Masa when, by the negro Babo's orders, he was carrying him to throw him overboard, alive; beside participating in the murder, before mentioned, of Don Alexandro Aranda, and others of the cabin-passengers; that, owing to the fury with which the Ashantees fought in the engagement with the boats, but this Lecbe and Yau survived; that Yau was bad as Lecbe; that Yau was the man who, by Babo's command, willingly prepared the skeleton of Don Alexandro, in a way the negroes afterwards told the deponent, but which he, so long as reason is left him, can never divulge; that Yau and Lecbe were the two who, in a calm by night, riveted the skeleton to the bow; this also the negroes told him; that the negro Babo was he who traced the inscription below it; that the negro Babo was the plotter from first to last; he ordered every murder, and was the helm and keel of the revolt; that Atufal was his lieutenant in all; but Atufal, with his own hand, committed no murder; nor did the negro Babo; • • that Atufal was shot, being killed in the fight with the boats,

*ere boarding; • • that the negresses, of age, were knowing to the revolt, and testified themselves satisfied at the death of their master, Don Alexandro; that, had the negroes not restrained them, they would have tortured to death, instead of simply killing, the Spaniards slain by command of the negro Babo; that the negresses used their utmost influence to have the deponent made away with; that, in the various acts of murder, they sang songs and danced—not gaily, but solemnly; and before the engagement with the boats, as well as during the action, they sang melancholy songs to the negroes, and that this melancholy tone was more inflaming than a different one would have been, and was so intended; that all this is believed, because the negroes have said it.*

*—that of the thirty-six men of the crew exclusive of the passengers, (all of whom are now dead), which the deponent had knowledge of, six only remained alive, with four cabin-boys and ship-boys, not included with the crew; • • —that the negroes broke an arm of one of the cabin-boys and gave him strokes with hatchets.*

*[Then follow various random disclosures referring to various periods of time. The following are extracted:]*

*—That during the presence of Captain Amasa Delano on board, some attempts were made by the sailors, and one by Hermenegildo Gandix, to convey hints to him of the true state of affairs; but that these attempts were ineffectual, owing to fear of incurring death, and furthermore owing to the devices which offered contradictions to the true state of affairs; as well as owing to the generosity and piety of Amasa Delano incapable of sounding such wickedness; • • • that Luys Galgo, a sailor about sixty years of age, and formerly of the king's navy, was one of those who sought to convey tokens to Captain Amasa Delano; but his intent, though undiscovered, being suspected, he was, on a pretense, made to retire out of sight, and at last into the hold, and there was made away with. This the negroes have since said; • • • that one of the ship-boys feeling, from Captain Amasa Delano's presence, some hopes of release, and not having enough prudence, dropped some chance-word respecting his expectations, which being overheard and understood by a slave-boy with whom he was eating at the time, the latter struck him on the head with a knife, inflicting a bad wound, but of which the boy is now healing; that likewise, not long before the ship was brought to anchor, one of the seamen, steering at the time, endangered himself by letting the blacks remark some expression in his countenance, arising from a cause similar to the above; but this sailor, by his heedful after conduct, escape; • • • that these statements are made to show the court that from the beginning to the end of the revolt, it was impossible for the deponent and his men to act otherwise than the did; • • • —that the third clerk, Hermenegildo Gandix, who before had been forced to live among the seamen, wearing a seaman's habit, and in all respects appearing to be one for the time; he, Gandix, was*

*killed by a musket-ball fired through a mistake from the boats before
boarding; having in his fright run up the mizzen-rigging, calling to the
boats—"don't board," lest upon their boarding the negroes should kill
him; that this inducing the Americans to believe he some way favored
the cause of the negroes, they fired two balls at him, so that he fell
wounded from the rigging, and was drowned in the sea;  • • •  —that
the young Don Joaquin, Marques de Arambaolaza, like Hermenegildo
Gandix, the third clerk, was degraded to the office and appearance of
a common seaman; that upon one occasion when Don Joaquin shrank,
the negro Babo commanded the Ashantee Lecbe to take tar and heat
it, and pour it upon Don Joaquin's hands;  • • •  —that Don Joaquin
was killed owing to another mistake of the Americans, but one impossible to be avoided, as upon the approach of the boats, Don Joaquin,
with a hatchet tied edge out and upright to his hand, was made by the
negroes to appear on the bulwarks; whereupon, seen with arms in his
hands and in a questionable attitude, he was shot for a renegade
seaman;  • • •  —that on the person of Don Joaquin was found secreted
a jewel, which, by papers that were discovered, proved to have been
meant for the shrine of our Lady of Mercy in Lima; a votive offering,
beforehand prepared and guarded, to attest his gratitude, when he
should have landed in Peru, his last destination, for the safe conclusion
of his entire voyage from Spain;  • • •  —that the jewel, with the other
effects of the late Don Joaquin, is in the custody of the brethren of the
Hospital de Sacerdotes, awaiting the disposition of the honorable
court;  • • •  —that, owing to the condition of the deponent, as well as
the haste in which the boats departed for the attack, the Americans
were not forewarned that there were, among the apparent crew, a passenger and one of the clerks disguised by the negro Babo;  • • •  —that,
beside the negroes killed in the action, some were killed after the capture and re-anchoring at night, when shackled to the ring-bolts on
deck; that these deaths were committed by the sailors, ere they could
be prevented. That so soon as informed of it, Captain Amasa Delano
used all his authority, and, in particular with his own hand, struck
down Martinez Gola, who, having found a razor in the pocket of an
old jacket of his, which one of the shackled negroes had on, was aiming
it at the negro's throat; that the noble Captain Amasa Delano also
wrenched from the hand of Bartholomew Barlo, a dagger secreted at
the time of the massacre of the whites, with which he was in the act of
stabbing a shackled negro, who, the same day, with another negro, had
thrown him down and jumped upon him;  • • •  —that, for all the
events, befalling through so long a time, during which the ship was in
the hands of the negro Babo, he cannot here give account; but that,
what he has said is the most substantial of what occurs to him at present, and is the truth under the oath which he has taken; which declaration he affirmed and ratified, after hearing it read to him.*

*He said that he is twenty-nine years of age, and broken in body and mind; that when finally dismissed by the court, he shall not return home to Chili, but betake himself to the monastery on Mount Agonia without; and signed with his honor, and crossed himself, and, for the time, departed as he came, in his litter, with the monk Infelez, to the Hospital de Sacerdotes.* BENITO CERENO DOCTOR ROZAS.

---

If the Deposition have served as the key to fit into the lock of the complications which precede it, then, as a vault whose door has been flung back, the San Dominick's hull lies open to-day.

Hitherto the nature of this narrative, besides rendering the intricacies in the beginning unavoidable, has more or less required that many things, instead of being set down in the order of occurrence, should be retrospectively, or irregularly given; this last is the case with the following passages, which will conclude the account:

During the long, mild voyage to Lima, there was, as before hinted, a period during which the sufferer a little recovered his health, or, at least in some degree, his tranquillity. Ere the decided relapse which came, the two captains had many cordial conversations—their fraternal unreserve in singular contrast with former withdrawments.

Again and again, it was repeated, how hard it had been to enact the part forced on the Spaniard by Babo.

"Ah, my dear," Don Benito once said, "at those very times when you thought me so morose and ungrateful, nay, when, as you now admit, you half thought me plotting your murder, at those very times my heart was frozen; I could not look at you, thinking of what, both on board this ship and your own, hung, from other hands, over my kind benefactor. And as God lives, Don Amasa, I know not whether desire for my own safety alone could have nerved me to that leap into your boat, had it not been for the thought that, did you, unenlightened, return to your ship, you, my best friend, with all who might be with you, stolen upon, that night, in your hammocks, would never in this world have wakened again. Do but think how you walked this deck, how you sat in this cabin, every inch of ground mined into honeycombs under you. Had I dropped the least hint, made the least advance towards an understanding between us, death, explosive death—yours as mine—would have ended the scene."

"True, true," cried Captain Delano, starting, "you saved my life, Don Benito, more than I yours; saved it, too, against my knowledge and will."

"Nay, my friend," rejoined the Spaniard, courteous even to the point of religion, "God charmed your life, but you saved mine. To think of some things you did—those smilings and chattings, rash pointings and gesturings. For less than these, they slew my mate,

Raneds; but you had the Prince of Heaven's safe conduct through all ambuscades."

"Yes, all is owing to Providence, I know; but the temper of my mind that morning was more than commonly pleasant, while the sight of so much suffering, more apparent than real, added to my good nature, compassion, and charity, happily interweaving the three. Had it been otherwise, doubtless, as you hint, some of my interferences might have ended unhappily enough. Besides, those feelings I spoke of enabled me to get the better of momentary distrust, at times when acuteness might have cost me my life, without saving another's. Only at the end did my suspicions get the better of me, and you know how wide of the mark they then proved."

"Wide, indeed," said Don Benito, sadly; "you were with me all day; stood with me, sat with me, talked with me, looked at me, ate with me, drank with me; and yet, your last act was to clutch for a monster, not only an innocent man, but the most pitiable of all men. To such degree may malign machinations and deceptions impose. So far may even the best man err, in judging the conduct of one with the recesses of whose condition he is not acquainted. But you were forced to it; and you were in time undeceived. Would that, in both respects, it was so ever, and with all men."

"You generalize, Don Benito; and mournfully enough. But the past is passed; why moralize upon it? Forget it. See, you bright sun has forgotten it all, and the blue sea, and the blue sky; these have turned over new leaves."[8]

"Because they have no memory," he dejectedly replied; "because they are not human."

"But these mild trades that now fan your cheek, do they not come with a human-like healing to you? Warm friends, steadfast friends are the trades."

"With their steadfastness they but waft me to my tomb, señor," was the foreboding response.

"You are saved," cried Captain Delano, more and more astonished and pained; "you are saved; what has cast such a shadow upon you?"

"The negro."

There was silence, while the moody man sat, slowly and unconsciously gathering his mantle about him, as if it were a pall.

There was no more conversation that day.

But if the Spaniard's melancholy sometimes ended in muteness upon topics like the above, there were others upon which he never spoke at all; on which, indeed, all his old reserves were piled. Pass over the worse, and, only to elucidate, let an item or two of these be

---

8. Cf. Daniel Webster's praise of the nation after the Compromise of 1850: "A long and violent convulsion of the elements has just passed away, and the heavens, the skies, smile upon us."

cited. The dress so precise and costly, worn by him on the day whose events have been narrated, had not willingly been put on. And that silver-mounted sword, apparent symbol of despotic command, was not, indeed, a sword, but the ghost of one. The scabbard, artificially stiffened, was empty.[9]

As for the black—whose brain, not body, had schemed and led the revolt, with the plot—his slight frame, inadequate to that which it held, had at once yielded to the superior muscular strength of his captor, in the boat. Seeing all was over, he uttered no sound, and could not be forced to. His aspect seemed to say, since I cannot do deeds, I will not speak words.[1] Put in irons in the hold, with the rest, he was carried to Lima. During the passage Don Benito did not visit him. Nor then, nor at any time after, would he look at him. Before the tribunal he refused. When pressed by the judges he fainted. On the testimony of the sailors alone rested the legal identity of Babo.

Some months after, dragged to the gibbet at the tail of a mule, the black met his voiceless end. The body was burned to ashes; but for many days, the head, that hive of subtlety, fixed on a pole in the Plaza, met, unabashed, the gaze of the whites; and across the Plaza looked towards St. Bartholomew's church, in whose vaults slept then, as now, the recovered bones of Aranda; and across the Rimac bridge looked towards the monastery, on Mount Agonia without; where, three months after being dismissed by the court, Benito Cereno, borne on the bier, did, indeed, follow his leader.

---

9. The imagery here strongly suggests that Benito Cereno has been rendered impotent.
1. See *Othello,* act V; Iago says, "From this time forth I never will speak word." We see Babo only two ways, as Sambo and then as Satan. We never hear him speak in his own voice. For the entire narrative he is the grinning, fawning, faithful slave; in the deposition he is an evil mastermind. Today, many readers see him as a tragic revolutionary hero.

# Billy Budd, Sailor

## (*An Inside Narrative*)[1]

### Dedicated to JACK CHASE[2] Englishman

Wherever that great heart may now be
Here on Earth or harbored in Paradise
Captain of the Maintop
in the year 1843
in the U.S. Frigate
*United States*

*1*

In the time before steamships, or then more frequently than now, a stroller along the docks of any considerable seaport would occasionally have his attention arrested by a group of bronzed mariners, man-of-war's men or merchant sailors in holiday attire, ashore on liberty. In certain instances they would flank, or like a bodyguard quite surround, some superior figure of their own class, moving along with them like Aldebaran[3] among the lesser lights of his constellation. That signal object was the "Handsome Sailor" of the less prosaic time alike of the military and merchant navies. With no perceptible trace of the vain-glorious about him, rather with the offhand unaffectedness of natural regality, he seemed to accept the spontaneous homage of his shipmates.

A somewhat remarkable instance recurs to me. In Liverpool, now half a century ago, I saw under the shadow of the great dingy street-wall of Prince's Dock (an obstruction long since removed) a common sailor so intensely black that he must needs have been a native African of the unadulterate blood of Ham[4]—a symmetric figure much above the average height. The two ends of a gay silk handkerchief thrown loose about the neck danced upon the displayed ebony of his chest, in his ears were big hoops of gold, and a Highland bonnet with a tartan band set off his shapely head. It was a hot noon in July; and his face, lustrous with perspiration,

---

1. Melville began work on *Billy Budd* in 1886 and was still working on it at his death in 1891. It was not published in any form until 1924. The best modern text is by Harrison Hayford and Merton M. Sealts Jr. (University of Chicago Press, 1962). For many years it has been listed as "forthcoming" in the Northwestern-Newberry complete edition of Melville's works. Several of the footnotes here are based on the Hayford-Sealts text and on Robert Milder's notes in the Oxford edition of *Billy Budd, Sailor (An Inside Narrative)*, a title now generally accepted as Melville's final choice rather than his earlier "Billy Budd, Foretopman."
2. Melville's shipmate on the *United States* and a character in the semi-autobiographical *White-Jacket*.
3. The brightest star in the constellation Taurus; it is the eye.
4. God's curse on Ham and all his descendants (Genesis 9.25). As Milder explains, the biblical passage became "interpreted as referring to the black race and commonly cited by Europeans and Americans as justification for Negro slavery."

beamed with barbaric good humor. In jovial sallies right and left, his white teeth flashing into view, he rollicked along, the center of a company of his shipmates. These were made up of such an assortment of tribes and complexions as would have well fitted them to be marched up by Anacharsis Cloots before the bar of the first French Assembly as Representatives of the Human Race. At each spontaneous tribute rendered by the wayfarers to this black pagod of a fellow—the tribute of a pause and stare, and less frequently an exclamation—the motley retinue showed that they took that sort of pride in the evoker of it which the Assyrian priests doubtless showed for their grand sculptured Bull when the faithful prostrated themselves.

To return. If in some cases a bit of a nautical Murat in setting forth his person ashore, the Handsome Sailor of the period in question evinced nothing of the dandified Billy-be-Dam, an amusing character all but extinct now, but occasionally to be encountered, and in a form yet more amusing than the original, at the tiller of the boats on the tempestuous Erie Canal[5] or, more likely, vaporing in the groggeries along the towpath. Invariably a proficient in his perilous calling, he was also more or less of a mighty boxer or wrestler. It was strength and beauty. Tales of his prowess were recited. Ashore he was the champion; afloat the spokesman; on every suitable occasion always foremost. Close-reefing topsails in a gale, there he was, astride the weather yardarm-end, foot in the Flemish horse as stirrup, both hands tugging at the earing as at a bridle, in very much the attitude of young Alexander curbing the fiery Bucephalus. A superb figure, tossed up as by the horns of Taurus against the thunderous sky, cheerily hallooing to the strenuous file along the spar.

The moral nature was seldom out of keeping with the physical make. Indeed, except as toned by the former, the comeliness and power, always attractive in masculine conjunction, hardly could have drawn the sort of honest homage the Handsome Sailor in some examples received from his less gifted associates.

Such a cynosure, at least in aspect, and something such too in nature, though with important variations made apparent as the story proceeds, was welkin-eyed[6] Billy Budd—or Baby Budd, as more familiarly, under circumstances hereafter to be given, he at last came to be called—aged twenty-one, a foretopman of the British fleet toward the close of the last decade of the eighteenth century. It was not very long prior to the time of the narration that follows that he had entered the King's service, having been impressed on the Narrow Seas from a homeward-bound English merchantman

5. A joke—the Erie Canal is calm.
6. Sky blue eyes.

into a seventy-four outward bound, H.M.S. *Bellipotent;*[7] which
ship, as was not unusual in those hurried days, having been obliged
to put to sea short of her proper complement of men. Plump upon
Billy at first sight in the gangway the boarding officer, Lieutenant
Ratcliffe, pounced, even before the merchantman's crew was formally mustered on the quarter-deck for his deliberate inspection.
And him only he elected. For whether it was because the other men
when ranged before him showed to ill advantage after Billy, or
whether he had some scruples in view of the merchantman's being
rather shorthanded, however it might be, the officer contented himself with his first spontaneous choice. To the surprise of the ship's
company, though much to the lieutenant's satisfaction, Billy made
no demur. But, indeed, any demur would have been as idle as the
protest of a goldfinch popped into a cage.

Nothing this uncomplaining acquiescence, all but cheerful, one
might say, the shipmaster turned a surprised glance of silent
reproach at the sailor. The shipmaster was one of those worthy mortals found in very vocation, even the humbler ones—the sort of
person whom everybody agrees in calling "a respectable man."
And—nor so strange to report as it may appear to be—though a
ploughman of the troubled waters, lifelong contending with the
intractable elements, there was nothing this honest soul at heart
loved better than simple peace and quiet. For the rest, he was fifty
or thereabouts, a little inclined to corpulence, a prepossessing face,
unwhiskered, and of an agreeable color—a rather full face,
humanely intelligent in expression. On a fair day with a fair wind
and all going well, a certain musical chime in his voice seemed to
be the veritable unobstructed outcome of the innermost man. He
had much prudence, much conscientiousness, and there were occasions when these virtues were the cause of overmuch disquietude in
him. On a passage, so long as his craft was in any proximity to land,
no sleep for Captain Graveling. He took to heart those serious
responsibilities not so heavily borne by some shipmasters.

Now while Billy Budd was down in the forecastle getting his kit
together, the *Bellipotent's* lieutenant, burly and bluff, nowise disconcerted by Captain Graveling's omitting to proffer the customary
hospitalities on an occasion so unwelcome to him, an omission
simply caused by preoccupation of thought, unceremoniously
invited himself into the cabin, and also to a flask from the spirit
locker, a receptacle which his experienced eye instantly discovered.
In fact he was one of those sea dogs in whom all the hardship and
peril of naval life in the great prolonged wars of his time never

---

7. At first Melville named the ship the *Indomitable;* he seems finally to have preferred the
   *Bellipotent.*

impaired the natural instinct for sensuous enjoyment. His duty he always faithfully did; but duty is sometimes a dry obligation, and he was for irrigating its aridity, whensoever possible, with a fertilizing decoction of strong waters. For the cabin's proprietor there was nothing left but to play the part of the enforced host with whatever grace and alacrity were practicable. As necessary adjuncts to the flask, he silently placed tumbler and water jug before the irrepressible guest. But excusing himself from partaking just then, he dismally watched the unembarrassed officer deliberately diluting his grog a little, then tossing it off in three swallows, pushing the empty tumbler away, yet not so far as to be beyond easy reach, at the same time settling himself in his seat and smacking his lips with high satisfaction, looking straight at the host.

These proceedings over, the master broke the silence; and there lurked a rueful reproach in the tone of his voice: "Lieutenant, you are going to take my best man from me, the jewel of 'em."

"Yes, I know," rejoined the other, immediately drawing back the tumbler preliminary to a replenishing. "Yes, I know. Sorry."

"Beg pardon, but you don't understand, Lieutenant. See here, now. Before I shipped that young fellow, my forecastle was a rat-pit of quarrels. It was black times, I tell you, aboard the *Rights* here. I was worried to that degree my pipe had no comfort for me. But Billy came; and it was like a Catholic priest striking peace in an Irish shindy.[8] Not that he preached to them or said or did anything in particular; but a virtue went out of him, sugaring the sour ones. They took to him like hornets to treacle; all but the buffer of the gang, the big shaggy chap with the fire-red whiskers. He indeed, out of envy, perhaps, of the newcomer, and thinking such a "sweet and pleasant fellow," as he mockingly designated him to the others, could hardly have the spirit of a gamecock, must needs bestir himself in trying to get up an ugly row with him. Billy forebore with him and reasoned with him in a pleasant way—he is something like myself, Lieutenant, to whom aught like a quarrel is hateful—but nothing served. So, in the second dogwatch one day, the Red Whiskers in presence of the others, under pretense of showing Billy just whence a sirloin steak was cut—for the fellow had once been a butcher—insultingly gave him a dig under the ribs. Quick as lightning Billy let fly his arm. I dare say he never meant to do quite as much as he did, but anyhow he gave the burly fool a terrible drubbing. It took about half a minute, I should think. And, lord bless you, the lubber was astonished at the celerity. And will you believe it, Lieutenant, the Red Whiskers now really loves Billy—loves him, or is the biggest hyp-

8. A brawl.

ocrite that ever I heard of. But they all love him. Some of 'em do his washing, dam his old trousers for him; the carpenter is at odd times making a pretty little chest of drawers for him. Anybody will do anything for Billy Budd; and it's the happy family here. But now, Lieutenant, if that young fellow goes—I know how it will be aboard the *Rights*. Not again very soon shall I, coming up from dinner, lean over the capstan smoking a quiet pipe—no, not very soon again, I think. Ay, Lieutenant, you are going to take away the jewel of 'em; you are going to take away my peacemaker!" And with that the good soul had really some ado in checking a rising sob.

"Well," said the lieutenant, who had listened with amused interest to all this and now was waxing merry with his tipple; "well, blessed are the peacemakers, especially the fighting peacemakers. And such are the seventy-four beauties some of which you see poking their noses out of the portholes of yonder warship lying to for me," pointing through the cabin window at the *Bellipotent*. "But courage! Don't look so downhearted, man. Why, I pledge you in advance the royal approbation. Rest assured that His Majesty will be delighted to know that in a time when his hardtack is not sought for by sailors with such avidity as should be, a time also when some shipmasters privily resent the borrowing from them a tar or two for the service; His Majesty, I say, will be delighted to learn that *one* shipmaster at least cheerfully surrenders to the King the flower of his flock, a sailor who with equal loyalty makes no dissent.—But where's my beauty? Ah," looking through the cabin's open door, "here he comes; and, by Jove, lugging along his chest—Apollo with his portmanteau!—My man," stepping out to him, "you can't take that big box aboard a warship. The boxes there are mostly shot boxes. Put your duds in a bag, lad. Boot and saddle for the cavalryman, bag and hammock for the man-of-war's man."

The transfer from chest to bag was made. And, after seeing his man into the cutter and then following him down, the lieutenant pushed off from the *Rights-of-Man*.[9] That was the merchant ship's name, though by her master and crew abbreviated in sailor fashion into the *Rights*. The hardheaded Dundee owner was a staunch admirer of Thomas Paine, whose book in rejoinder to Burke's arraignment of the French Revolution had then been published for some time and had gone everywhere. In christening his vessel after the title of Paine's volume the man of Dundee was something like his contemporary shipowner, Stephen Girard of Philadelphia, whose sympathies, alike

---

9. Hayford and Sealts note that "Thomas Paine published *The Rights of Man* in 1791 as a rejoinder to Edmund Burke's *Reflections on the Revolution in France* (1790): the opposing positions of the two men concerning the doctrine of abstract natural rights lie behind the dialectic of *Billy Budd*."

with his native land and its liberal philosophers, he evinced by naming his ships after Voltaire, Diderot, and so forth.

But now, when the boat swept under the merchantman's stern, and officer and oarsmen were noting—some bitterly and others with a grin—the name emblazoned there; just then it was that the new recruit jumped up from the bow where the coxswain had directed him to sit, and waving hat to his silent shipmates sorrowfully looking over at him from the taffrail, bade the lads a genial good-bye. Then, making a salutation as to the ship herself, "And good-bye to you too, old *Rights-of-Man*."

"Down, sir!" roared the lieutenant, instantly assuming all the rigor of his rank, though with difficulty repressing a smile.

To be sure, Billy's action was a terrible breach of naval decorum. But in that decorum he had never been instructed; in consideration of which the lieutenant would hardly have been so energetic in reproof but for the concluding farewell to the ship. This he rather took as meant to convey a covert sally on the new recruit's part, a sly slur at impressment in general, and that of himself in especial. And yet, more likely, if satire it was in effect, it was hardly so by intention, for Billy, though happily endowed with the gaiety of high health, youth, and a free heart, was yet by no means of a satirical turn. The will to it and the sinister dexterity were alike wanting. To deal in double meanings and insinuations of any sort was quite foreign to his nature.

As to his enforced enlistment, that he seemed to take pretty much as he was wont to take any vicissitude of weather. Like the animals, though no philosopher, he was, without knowing it, practically a fatalist. And it may be that he rather liked this adventurous turn in his affairs, which promised an opening into novel scenes and martial excitements.

Aboard the *Bellipotent* our merchant sailor was forthwith rated as an able seaman and assigned to the starboard watch of the foretop. He was soon at home in the service, not at all disliked for his unpretentious good looks and a sort of genial happy-go-lucky air. No merrier man in his mess: in marked contrast to certain other individuals included like himself among the impressed portion of the ship's company; for these when not actively employed were sometimes, and more particularly in the last dogwatch when the drawing near of twilight induced revery, apt to fall into a saddish mood which in some partook of sullenness. But they were not so young as our foretopman, and no few of them must have known a hearth of some sort, others may have had wives and children left, too probably, in uncertain circumstances, and hardly any but must have had acknowledged kith and kin, while for Billy, as will shortly be seen, his entire family was practically invested in himself.

2

Though our new-made foretopman was well received in the top and on the gun decks, hardly here was he that cynosure he had previously been among those minor ship's companies of the merchant marine, with which companies only had he hitherto consorted.

He was young; and despite his all but fully developed frame, in aspect looked even younger than he really was, owing to a lingering adolescent expression in the as yet smooth face all but feminine in purity of natural complexion but where, thanks to his seagoing, the lily was quite suppressed and the rose had some ado visibly to flush through the tan.

To one essentially such a novice in the complexities of factitious life, the abrupt transition from his former and simpler sphere to the ampler and more knowing world of a great warship; this might well have abashed him had there been any conceit or vanity in his composition. Among her miscellaneous multitude, the *Bellipotent* mustered several individuals who however inferior in grade were of no common natural stamp, sailors more signally susceptive of that air which continuous martial discipline and repeated presence in battle can in some degree impart even to the average man. As the Handsome Sailor, Billy Budd's position aboard the seventy-four was something analogous to that of a rustic beauty transplanted from the provinces and brought into competition with the highborn dames of the court. But this change of circumstances he scarce noted. As little did he observe that something about him provoked an ambiguous smile in one or two harder faces among the bluejackets. Nor less unaware was he of the peculiar favorable effect his person and demeanor had upon the more intelligent gentlemen of the quarter-deck. Nor could this well have been otherwise. Cast in a mold peculiar to the finest physical examples of those Englishmen in whom the Saxon strain would seem not at all to partake of any Norman or other admixture, he showed in face that humane look of reposeful good nature which the Greek sculptor in some instances gave to his heroic strong man, Hercules. But this again was subtly modified by another and pervasive quality. The ear, small and shapely, the arch of the foot, the curve in mouth and nostril, even the indurated hand dyed to the orange-tawny of the toucan's bill, a hand telling alike of the halyards and tar bucket; but, above all, something in the mobile expression, and every chance attitude and movement, something suggestive of a mother eminently favored by Love and the Graces; all this strangely indicated a lineage in direct contradiction to his lot. The mysteriousness here became less mysterious through a matter of fact elicited when Billy at the capstan was being formally mustered into the service. Asked by the officer, a small, brisk little gentleman as it chanced, among other questions, his place of birth, he replied, "Please, sir, I don't know."

"Don't know where you were born? Who was your father?"

"God knows, sir."[1]

Struck by the straightforward simplicity of these replies, the officer next asked, "Do you know anything about your beginning?"

"No, sir. But I have heard that I was found in a pretty silk-lined basket hanging one morning from the knocker of a good man's door in Bristol."

"*Found*, say you? Well," throwing back his head and looking up and down the new recruit; "well, it turns out to have been a pretty good find. Hope they'll find some more like you, my man; the fleet sadly needs them."

Yes, Billy Budd was a foundling, a presumable by-blow,[2] and, evidently, no ignoble one. Noble descent was as evident in him as in a blood horse.

For the rest, with little or no sharpness of faculty or any trace of the wisdom of the serpent, nor yet quite a dove, he possessed that kind and degree of intelligence going along with the unconventional rectitude of a sound human creature, one to whom not yet has been proffered the questionable apple of knowledge. He was illiterate; he could not read, but he could sing, and like the illiterate nightingale was sometimes the composer of his own song.

Of self-consciousness he seemed to have little or none, or about as much as we may reasonably impute to a dog of Saint Bernard's breed.

Habitually living with the elements and knowing little more of the land than as a beach, or, rather, that portion of the terraqueous globe providentially set apart for dance-houses, doxies,[3] and tapsters, in short what sailors call a "fiddler's green," his simple nature remained unsophisticated by those moral obliquities which are not in every case incompatible with that manufacturable thing known as respectability. But are sailors, frequenters of fiddlers' greens, without vices? No; but less often than with landsmen do their vices, so called, partake of crookedness of heart, seeming less to proceed from viciousness than exuberance of vitality after long constraint: frank manifestations in accordance with natural law. By his original constitution aided by the co-operating influences of his lot, Billy in many respects was little more than a sort of upright barbarian, much such perhaps as Adam presumably might have been ere the urbane Serpent wriggled himself into his company.

---

1. Some critics see an allegorical meaning here, namely, that Billy is Adam or Christ.
2. An illegitimate child. In Chapter 4 of *White-Jacket*, Jack Chase "must have been a by-blow of some British admiral of the blue."
3. Prostitutes.

And here be it submitted that apparently going to corroborate the doctrine of man's Fall, a doctrine now popularly ignored, it is observable that where certain virtues pristine and unadulterate peculiarly characterize anybody in the external uniform of civilization, they will upon scrutiny seem not to be derived from custom or convention, but rather to be out of keeping with these, as if indeed exceptionally transmitted from a period prior to Cain's city[4] and citified man. The character marked by such qualities has to an unvitiated taste an untampered-with flavor like that of berries, while the man thoroughly civilized, even in a fair specimen of the breed, has to the same moral palate a questionable smack as of a compounded wine. To any stray inheritor of these primitive qualities found, like Caspar Hauser,[5] wandering dazed in any Christian capital of our time, the good-natured poet's famous invocation, near two thousand years ago, of the good rustic out of his latitude in the Rome of the Caesars, still appropriately holds:

> Honest and poor, faithful in word and thought,
> What hath thee, Fabian, to the city brought?

Though our Handsome Sailor had as much of masculine beauty as one can expect anywhere to see; nevertheless, like the beautiful woman in one of Hawthorne's minor tales,[6] there was just one thing amiss in him. No visible blemish indeed, as with the lady; no, but an occasional liability to a vocal defect. Though in the hour of elemental uproar or peril he was everything that a sailor should be, yet under sudden provocation of strong heart-feeling his voice, otherwise singularly musical, as if expressive of the harmony within, was apt to develop an organic hesitancy, in fact more or less of a stutter or even worse. In this particular Billy was a striking instance that the arch interferer, the envious marplot of Eden,[7] still has more or less to do with every human consignment to this planet of Earth. In every case, one way or another he is sure to slip in his little card, as much as to remind us—I too have a hand here.

The avowal of such an imperfection in the Handsome Sailor should be evidence not alone that he is not presented as a conventional hero, but also that the story in which he is the main figure is no romance.

---

4. Genesis 4.17.
5. Hayford and Sealts explain that Caspar Hauser was a "mysterious foundling (1812?–33), perhaps a victim of amnesia, who appeared 'wandering dazed' in Nuremberg in 1828; he claimed to have been kept in a hole."
6. Georgiana in "The Birthmark." Georgiana has on her cheek "a visible blemish" that looks like the print of a tiny hand; Billy has "a vocal defect," a stutter.
7. Satan.

3

At the time of Billy Budd's arbitrary enlistment into the *Bellipotent* that ship was on her way to join the Mediterranean fleet. No long time elapsed before the junction was effected. As one of that fleet the seventy-four participated in its movements, though at times on account of her superior sailing qualities, in the absence of frigates, dispatched on separate duty as a scout and at times on less temporary service. But with all this the story has little concernment, restricted as it is to the inner life of one particular ship and the career of an individual sailor.

It was the summer of 1797. In the April of that year had occurred the commotion at Spithead followed in May by a second and yet more serious outbreak in the fleet at the Nore. The latter is known, and without exaggeration in the epithet, as "the Great Mutiny." It was indeed a demonstration more menacing to England than the contemporary manifestoes and conquering and proselyting armies of the French Directory. To the British Empire the Nore Mutiny was what a strike in the fire brigade would be to London threatened by general arson. In a crisis when the kingdom might well have antic-ipated the famous signal that some years later published along the naval line of battle what it was that upon occasion England expected of Englishmen; *that* was the time when at the mastheads of the three-deckers and seventy-fours moored in her own road-stead—a fleet the right arm of a Power then all but the sole free conservative one of the Old World—the bluejackets, to be num-bered by thousands, ran up with huzzas the British colors with the union and cross wiped out; by that cancellation transmuting the flag of founded law and freedom defined, into the enemy's red meteor of unbridled and unbounded revolt. Reasonable discontent growing out of practical grievances in the fleet had been ignited into irra-tional combustion as by live cinders blown across the Channel from France in flames.

The event converted into irony for a time those spirited strains of Dibdin—as a song-writer no mean auxiliary to the English govern-ment at that European conjuncture—strains celebrating, among other things, the patriotic devotion of the British tar: "And as for my life, 'tis the King's!"

Such an episode in the Island's grand naval story her naval histo-rians naturally abridge, one of them (William James) candidly acknowledging that fain would he pass it over did not "impartiality forbid fastidiousness." And yet his mention is less a narration than a reference, having to do hardly at all with details. Nor are these readily to be found in the libraries. Like some other events in every age befalling states everywhere, including America, the Great

Mutiny was of such character that national pride along with views of policy would fain shade it off into the historical background. Such events cannot be ignored, but there is a considerate way of historically treating them. If a well-constituted individual refrains from blazoning aught amiss or calamitous in his family, a nation in the like circumstance may without reproach be equally discreet.

Though after parleyings between government and the ring-leaders, and concessions by the former as to some glaring abuses, the first uprising—that at Spithead—with difficulty was put down, or matters for the time pacified; yet at the Nore the unforeseen renewal of insurrection on a yet larger scale, and emphasized in the conferences that ensued by demands deemed by the authori-ties not only inadmissible but aggressively insolent, indicated—if the Red Flag did not sufficiently do so—what was the spirit ani-mating the men. Final suppression, however, there was; but only made possible perhaps by the unswerving loyalty of the marine corps and a voluntary resumption of loyalty among influential sec-tions of the crews.

To some extent the Nore Mutiny may be regarded as analogous to the distempering irruption of contagious fever in a frame constitu-tionally sound, and which anon throws it off.

At all events, of these thousands of mutineers were some of the tars who not so very long afterwards—whether wholly prompted thereto by patriotism, or pugnacious instinct, or by both—helped to win a coronet for Nelson at the Nile, and the naval crown of crowns for him at Trafalgar. To the mutineers, those battles and especially Trafalgar were a plenary absolution and a grand one. For all that goes to make up scenic naval display and heroic magnificence in arms, those battles, especially Trafalgar, stand unmatched in human annals.[8]

## 4

In this matter of writing, resolve as one may to keep to the main road, some bypaths have an enticement not readily to be withstood. I am going to err into such a bypath. If the reader will keep me com-pany I shall be glad. At the least, we can promise ourselves that pleasure which is wickedly said to be in sinning, for a literary sin the divergence will be.

Very likely it is no new remark that the inventions of our time have at last brought about a change in sea warfare in degree corresponding to the revolution in all warfare effected by the original introduction

8. Melville owned Robert Southey's *Life of Nelson*; Admiral Horatio Nelson (1758–1805) defeated the French near the mouth of the Nile in 1798; he died during his victory at Trafalgar in 1805. Critics frequently compare Nelson to Captain Vere.

from China into Europe of gunpowder. The first European firearm, a clumsy contrivance, was, as is well known, scouted by no few of the knights as a base implement, good enough peradventure for weavers too craven to stand up crossing steel with steel in frank fight. But as ashore knightly valor, though shorn of its blazonry, did not cease with the knights, neither on the seas—though nowadays in encounters there a certain kind of displayed gallantry be fallen out of date as hardly applicable under changed circumstances—did the nobler qualities of such naval magnates as Don John of Austria, Doria, Van Tromp, Jean Bart, the long line of British admirals, and the American Decaturs of 1812 become obsolete with their wooden walls.

Nevertheless, to anybody who can hold the Present at its worth without being inappreciative of the Past, it may be forgiven, if to such an one the solitary old hulk at Portsmouth, Nelson's *Victory*, seems to float there, not alone as the decaying monument of a fame incorruptible, but also as a poetic reproach, softened by its picturesqueness, to the *Monitors* and yet mightier hulls of the European ironclads. And this not altogether because such craft are unsightly, unavoidably lacking the symmetry and grand lines of the old battleships, but equally for other reasons.

There are some, perhaps, who while not altogether inaccessible to that poetic reproach just alluded to, may yet on behalf of the new order be disposed to parry it; and this to the extent of iconoclasm, if need be. For example, prompted by the sight of the star inserted in the *Victory's* quarter-deck designating the spot where the Great Sailor fell, these martial utilitarians may suggest considerations implying that Nelson's ornate publication of his person in battle was not only unnecessary, but not military, nay, savored of foolhardiness and vanity. They may add, too, that at Trafalgar it was in effect nothing less than a challenge to death; and death came; and that but for his bravado the victorious admiral might possibly have survived the battle, and so, instead of having his sagacious dying injunctions overruled by his immediate successor in command, he himself when the contest was decided might have brought his shattered fleet to anchor, a proceeding which might have averted the deplorable loss of life by shipwreck in the elemental tempest that followed the martial one.

Well, should we set aside the more than disputable point whether for various reasons it was possible to anchor the fleet, then plausibly enough the Benthamites[9] of war may urge the above. But the *might-have-been* is but boggy ground to build on. And, certainly, in foresight as to the larger issue of an encounter, and anxious preparations for it—buoying the deadly way and mapping it out, as at

9. Followers of the English philosopher Jeremy Bentham (1748–1832), founder of Utilitarianism.

Copenhagen—few commandments have been so painstakingly cir-
cumspect as this same reckless declarer of his person in fight.

Personal prudence, even when dictated by quite other than selfish
considerations, surely is no special virtue in a military man; while an
excessive love of glory, impassioning a less burning impulse, the
honest sense of duty, is the first. If the name *Wellington* is not so
much of a trumpet to the blood as the simpler name *Nelson*, the
reason for this may perhaps be inferred from the above. Alfred in his
funeral ode on the victor of Waterloo ventures not to call him the
greatest soldier of all time, though in the same ode he invokes Nelson
as "the greatest sailor since our world began."

At Trafalgar Nelson on the brink of opening the fight sat down
and wrote his last brief will and testament. If under the presentiment of the most magnificent of all victories to be crowned by his
own glorious death, a sort of priestly motive led him to dress his
person in the jewelled vouchers of his own shining deeds; if thus to
have adorned himself for the altar and the sacrifice were indeed
vainglory, then affectation and fustian is each more heroic line in
the great epics and dramas, since in such lines the poet but
embodies in verse those exaltations of sentiment that a nature like
Nelson, the opportunity being given, vitalizes into acts.

## 5

Yes, the outbreak at the Nore was put down. But not every grievance was redressed. If the contractors, for example, were no longer
permitted to ply some practices peculiar to their tribe everywhere,
such as providing shoddy cloth, rations not sound, or false in the
measure; not the less impressment, for one thing, went on. By
custom sanctioned for centuries, and judicially maintained by a
Lord Chancellor as late as Mansfield, that mode of manning the
fleet, a mode now fallen into a sort of abeyance but never formally
renounced, it was not practicable to give up in those years. Its abrogation would have crippled the indispensable fleet, one wholly
under canvas, no steam power, its innumerable sails and thousands
of cannon, everything in short, worked by muscle alone; a fleet the
more insatiate in demand for men, because then multiplying its
ships of all grades against contingencies present and to come of the
convulsed Continent.

Discontent foreran the Two Mutinies, and more or less it lurk-
ingly survived them. Hence it was not unreasonable to apprehend
some return of trouble sporadic or general. One instance of such
apprehensions: In the same year with this story, Nelson, then Rear
Admiral Sir Horatio, being with the fleet off the Spanish coast, was
directed by the admiral in command to shift his pennant from the

*Captain* to the *Theseus*; and for this reason: that the latter ship
having newly arrived on the station from home, where it had taken
part in the Great Mutiny, danger was apprehended from the temper
of the men; and it was thought that an officer like Nelson was the
one, not indeed to terrorize the crew into base subjection, but to
win them, by force of his mere presence and heroic personality,
back to an allegiance if not as enthusiastic as his own yet as true.

So it was that for a time, on more than one quarter-deck, anxiety
did exist. At sea, precautionary vigilance was strained against
relapse. At short notice an engagement might come on. When it did,
the lieutenants assigned to batteries felt it incumbent on them, in
some instances, to stand with drawn swords behind the men
working the guns.

6

But on board the seventy-four in which Billy now swung his hammock, very little in the manner of the men and nothing obvious in
the demeanor of the officers would have suggested to an ordinary
observer that the Great Mutiny was a recent event. In their general
bearing and conduct the commissioned officers of a warship naturally take their tone from the commander, that is if he have that
ascendancy of character that ought to be his.

Captain the Honorable Edward Fairfax Vere, to give his full title,
was a bachelor of forty or thereabouts, a sailor of distinction even in
a time prolific of renowned seamen. Though allied to the higher
nobility, his advancement had not been altogether owing to influences connected with that circumstance. He had seen much service, been in various engagements, always acquitting himself as an
officer mindful of the welfare of his men, but never tolerating an
infraction of discipline; thoroughly versed in the science of his profession, and intrepid to the verge of temerity, though never injudi-
ciously so. For his gallantry in the West Indian waters as flag lieutenant under Rodney in that admiral's crowning victory over De
Grasse, he was made a post captain.

Ashore, in the garb of a civilian, scarce anyone would have taken
him for a sailor, more especially that he never garnished unprofessional talk with nautical terms, and grave in his bearing, evinced
little appreciation of mere humor. It was not out of keeping with
these traits that on a passage when nothing demanded his paramount action, he was the most undemonstrative of men. Any
landsman observing this gentleman not conspicuous by his stature
and wearing no pronounced insignia, emerging from his cabin to
the open deck, and noting the silent deference of the officers
retiring to leeward, might have taken him for the King's guest, a

civilian aboard the King's ship, some highly honorable discreet envoy on his way to an important post. But in fact this unobtrusiveness of demeanor may have proceeded from a certain unaffected modesty of manhood sometimes accompanying a resolute nature, a modesty evinced at all times not calling for pronounced action, which shown in any rank of life suggests a virtue aristocratic in kind. As with some others engaged in various departments of the world's more heroic activities, Captain Vere though practical enough upon occasion would at times betray a certain dreaminess of mood. Standing alone on the weather side of the quarter-deck, one hand holding by the rigging, he would absently gaze off at the blank sea. At the presentation to him then of some minor matter interrupting the current of his thoughts, he would show more or less irascibility; but instantly he would control it.

In the navy he was popularly known by the appellation "Starry Vere." How such a designation happened to fall upon one who whatever his sterling qualities was without any brilliant ones, was in this wise: A favorite kinsman, Lord Denton, a freehearted fellow, had been the first to meet and congratulate him upon his return to England from his West Indian cruise; and but the day previous turning over a copy of Andrew Marvell's poems had lighted, not for the first time, however, upon the lines entitled "Appleton House," the name of one of the seats of their common ancestor, a hero in the German wars of the seventeenth century, in which poem occur the lines:

> This 'tis to have been from the first
> In a domestic heaven nursed.
> Under the discipline severe
> Of Fairfax and the starry Vere.

And so, upon embracing his cousin fresh from Rodney's great victory wherein he had played so gallant a part, brimming over with just family pride in the sailor of their house, he exuberantly exclaimed, "Give ye joy, Ed; give ye joy, my starry Vere!"[1] This got currency, and the novel prefix serving in familiar parlance readily to distinguish the *Bellipotent's* captain from another Vere his senior, a distant relative, an officer of like rank in the navy, it remained permanently attached to the surname.

## 7

In view of the part that the commander of the *Bellipotent* plays in scenes shortly to follow, it may be well to fill out that sketch of him outlined in the previous chapter.

---

1. In *Benito Cereno* Captain Delano says to Don Benito, "I give you joy."

Aside from his qualities as a sea officer Captain Vere was an exceptional character. Unlike no few of England's renowned sailors, long and arduous service with signal devotion to it had not resulted in absorbing and *salting* the entire man. He had a marked leaning toward everything intellectual. He loved books, never going to sea without a newly replenished library, compact but of the best. The isolated leisure, in some cases so wearisome, falling at intervals to commanders even during a war cruise, never was tedious to Captain Vere. With nothing of that literary taste which less heeds the thing conveyed than the vehicle, his bias was toward those books to which every serious mind of superior order occupying any active post of authority in the world naturally inclines: books treating of actual men and events no matter of what era—history, biography, and unconventional writers like Montaigne,[2] who, free from cant and convention, honestly and in the spirit of common sense philoso-phize upon realities. In this line of reading he found confirmation of his own more reserved thoughts—confirmation which he had vainly sought in social converse, so that as touching most funda-mental topics, there had got to be established in him some positive convictions which he forefelt would abide in him essentially unmodified so long as his intelligent part remained unimpaired. In view of the troubled period in which his lot was cast, this was well for him. His settled convictions were as a dike against those invading waters of novel opinion social, political, and otherwise, which carried away as in a torrent no few minds in those days, minds by nature not inferior to his own. While other members of that aristocracy to which by birth he belonged were incensed at the innovators mainly because their theories were inimical to the privi-leged classes, Captain Vere disinterestedly opposed them not alone because they seemed to him insusceptible of embodiment in lasting institutions, but at war with the peace of the world and the true wel-fare of mankind.

With minds less stored than his and less earnest, some officers of his rank, with whom at times he would necessarily consort, found him lacking in the companionable quality, a dry and bookish gen-tleman, as they deemed. Upon any chance withdrawal from their company one would be apt to say to another something like this: "Vere is a noble fellow, Starry Vere. 'Spite[3] the gazettes, Sir Horatio" (meaning him who became Lord Nelson) "is at bottom scarce a better seaman or fighter. But between you and me now, don't you think there is a queer streak of the pedantic running through him? Yes, like the King's yarn in a coil of navy rope?"

2. Michel de Montaigne (1533–1592), French essayist known for his elegant skepticism. Melville frequently turned to Montaigne's essays.
3. A contraction of "despite" or "in spite of."

Some apparent ground there was for this sort of confidential criticism; since not only did the captain's discourse never fall into the jocosely familiar, but in illustrating of any point touching the stirring personages and events of the time he would be as apt to cite some historic character or incident of antiquity as he would be to cite from the moderns. He seemed unmindful of the circumstance that to his bluff company such remote allusions, however pertinent they might really be, were altogether alien to men whose reading was mainly confined to the journals. But considerateness in such matters is not easy to natures constituted like Captain Vere's. Their honesty prescribes to them directness, sometimes far-reaching like that of a migratory fowl that in its flight never heeds when it crosses a frontier.

## 8

The lieutenants and other commissioned gentlemen forming Captain Vere's staff it is not necessary here to particularize, nor needs it to make any mention of any of the warrant officers. But among the petty officers was one who, having much to do with the story, may as well be forthwith introduced. His portrait I essay, but shall never hit it. This was John Claggart, the master-at-arms. But that sea title may to landsmen seem somewhat equivocal. Originally, doubtless, that petty officer's function was the instruction of the men in the use of arms, sword or cutlass. But very long ago, owing to the advance in gunnery making hand-to-hand encounters less frequent and giving to niter and sulphur the pre-eminence over steel, that function ceased; the master-at-arms of a great warship becoming a sort of chief of police charged among other matters with the duty of preserving order on the populous lower gun decks.

Claggart was a man about five-and-thirty, somewhat spare and tall, yet of no ill figure upon the whole. His hand was too small and shapely to have been accustomed to hard toil. The face was a notable one, the features all except the chin cleanly cut as those on a Greek medallion; yet the chin, beardless as Tecumseh's,[4] had something of strange protuberant broadness in its make that recalled the prints of the Reverend Dr. Titus Oates, the historic deponent with the clerical drawl in the time of Charles II and the fraud of the alleged Popish Plot. It served Claggart in his office that his eye could cast a tutoring glance. His brow was of the sort phrenologically associated with more than average intellect; silken jet curls partly clustering over it, making a foil to the pallor below, a pallor tinged with a faint shade of amber akin to the hue of time-tinted marbles of old. This complexion, singularly contrasting with

4. Shawnee chief who sided with the British in the War of 1812.

the red or deeply bronzed visages of the sailors, and in part the result of his official seclusion from the sunlight, though it was not exactly displeasing, nevertheless seemed to hint of something defective or abnormal in the constitution and blood. But his general aspect and manner were so suggestive of an education and career incongruous with his naval function that when not actively engaged in it he looked like a man of high quality, social and moral, who for reasons of his own was keeping incog. Nothing was known of his former life. It might be that he was an Englishman; and yet there lurked a bit of accent in his speech suggesting that possibly he was not such by birth, but through naturalization in early childhood. Among certain grizzled sea gossips of the gun decks and forecastle went a rumor perdue that the master-at-arms was a *chevalier*[5] who had volunteered into the King's navy by way of compounding for some mysterious swindle whereof he had been arraigned at the King's Bench. The fact that nobody could substantiate this report was, of course, nothing against its secret currency. Such a rumor once started on the gun decks in reference to almost anyone below the rank of a commissioned officer would, during the period assigned to this narrative, have seemed not altogether wanting in credibility to the tarry old wiseacres of a man-of-war crew. And indeed a man of Claggart's accomplishments, without prior nautical experience entering the navy at mature life, as he did, and necessarily allotted at the start to the lowest grade in it; a man too who never made allusion to his previous life ashore; these were circumstances which in the dearth of exact knowledge as to his true antecedents opened to the invidious a vague field for unfavorable surmise.

But the sailors' dogwatch gossip concerning him derived a vague plausibility from the fact that now for some period the British navy could so little afford to be squeamish in the matter of keeping up the muster rolls, that not only were press gangs notoriously abroad both afloat and ashore, but there was little or no secret about another matter, namely, that the London police were at liberty to capture any able-bodied suspect, any questionable fellow at large, and summarily ship him to the dockyard or fleet. Furthermore, even among voluntary enlistments there were instances where the motive thereto partook neither of patriotic impulse nor yet of a random desire to experience a bit of sea life and martial adventure. Insolvent debtors of minor grade, together with the promiscuous lame ducks of morality, found in the navy a convenient and secure refuge, secure because, once enlisted aboard a King's ship, they were as much in sanctuary as the transgressor of the Middle Ages harboring

5. Swindler.

himself under the shadow of the altar. Such sanctioned irregularities, which for obvious reasons the government would hardly think to parade at the time and which consequently, and as affecting the least influential class of mankind, have all but dropped into oblivion, lend color to something for the truth whereof I do not vouch, and hence have some scruple in stating; something I remember having seen in print though the book I cannot recall; but the same thing was personally communicated to me now more than forty years ago by an old pensioner in a cocked hat with whom I had a most interesting talk on the terrace at Greenwich, a Baltimore Negro, a Trafalgar man. It was to this effect: In the case of a warship short of hands whose speedy sailing was imperative, the deficient quota, in lack of any other way of making it good, would be eked out by drafts culled direct from the jails. For reasons previously suggested it would not perhaps be easy at the present day directly to prove or disprove the allegation. But allowed as a verity, how significant would it be of England's straits at the time confronted by those wars which like a flight of harpies rose shrieking from the din and dust of the fallen Bastille. That era appears measurably clear to us who look back at it, and but read of it. But to the grandfathers of us graybeards, the more thoughtful of them, the genius of it presented an aspect like that of Camoëns' Spirit of the Cape, an eclipsing menace mysterious and prodigious. Not America was exempt from apprehension. At the height of Napoleon's unexampled conquests, there were Americans who had fought at Bunker Hill who looked forward to the possibility that the Atlantic might prove no barrier against the ultimate schemes of this French portentous upstart from the revolutionary chaos who seemed in act of fulfilling judgment prefigured in the Apocalypse.[6]

But the less credence was to be given to the gun-deck talk touching Claggart, seeing that no man holding his office in a man-of-war can ever hope to be popular with the crew. Besides, in derogatory comments upon anyone against whom they have a grudge, or for any reason or no reason mislike, sailors are much like landsmen: they are apt to exaggerate or romance it.

About as much was really known to the Bellipotent's tars of the master-at-arms' career before entering the service as an astronomer knows about a comet's travels prior to its first observable appearance in the sky. The verdict of the sea quidnuncs[7] has been cited only by way of showing what sort of moral impression the man made upon rude uncultivated natures whose conceptions of human wickedness were necessarily of the narrowest, limited to ideas of

6. The Book of Revelation.
7. Busybodies.

vulgar rascality—a thief among the swinging hammocks during a night watch, or the man-brokers and land-sharks of the seaports.

It was no gossip, however, but fact that though, as before hinted, Claggart upon his entrance into the navy was, as a novice, assigned to the least honorable section of a man-of-war's crew, embracing the drudgery, he did not long remain there. The superior capacity he immediately evinced, his constitutional sobriety, an ingratiating deference to superiors, together with a peculiar ferreting genius manifested on a singular occasion; all this, capped by a certain austere patriotism, abruptly advanced him to the position of master-at-arms.

Of this maritime chief of police the ship's corporals, so called, were the immediate subordinates, and compliant ones; and this, as is to be noted in some business departments ashore, almost to a degree inconsistent with entire moral volition. His place put various converging wires of underground influence under the chief's control, capable when astutely worked through his understrappers of operating to the mysterious discomfort, if nothing worse, of any of the sea commonalty.

9

Life in the foretop well agreed with Billy Budd. There, when not actually engaged on the yards yet higher aloft, the topmen, who as such had been picked out for youth and activity, constituted an aerial club lounging at ease against the smaller stun'sails rolled up into cushions, spinning yarns like the lazy gods, and frequently amused with what was going on in the busy world of the decks below. No wonder then that a young fellow of Billy's disposition was well content in such society. Giving no cause of offence to anybody, he was always alert at a call. So in the merchant service it had been with him. But now such a punctiliousness in duty was shown that his topmates would sometimes good-naturedly laugh at him for it. This heightened alacrity had its cause, namely, the impression made upon him by the first formal gangway-punishment he had ever witnessed, which befell the day following his impressment. It had been incurred by a little fellow, young, a novice after-guardsman absent from his assigned post when the ship was being put about; a dereliction resulting in a rather serious hitch to that maneuver, one demanding instantaneous promptitude in letting go and making fast. When Billy saw the culprit's naked back under the scourge, gridironed with red welts and worse, when he marked the dire expression in the liberated man's face as with his woolen shirt flung over him by the executioner he rushed forward from the spot to bury himself in the crowd, Billy was horrified. He resolved that never through remissness would he make himself liable to such a visitation or do or omit aught that might merit even verbal reproof. What then was his surprise and concern when ultimately he found himself getting into petty trouble occasionally about such matters as the stowage of his bag or something amiss in his hammock, matters under the police oversight of the ship's corporals of the lower decks, and which brought down on him a vague threat from one of them.

So heedful in all things as he was, how could this be? He could not understand it, and it more than vexed him. When he spoke to his young topmates about it they were either lightly incredulous or found something comical in his unconcealed anxiety. "Is it your bag, Billy?" said one. "Well, sew yourself up in it, bully boy, and then you'll be sure to know if anybody meddles with it."

Now there was a veteran aboard who because his years began to disqualify him for more active work had been recently assigned duty as mainmastman in his watch, looking to the gear belayed at the rail roundabout that great spar near the deck. At off-times the foretopman had picked up some acquaintance with him, and now in his trouble it occurred to him that he might be the sort of person to go to for wise counsel. He was an old Dansker long anglicized in the service, of few words, many wrinkles, and some honorable scars. His wizened face, time-tinted and weather-stained to the complexion of an antique parchment, was here and there peppered blue by the chance explosion of a gun cartridge in action.

He was an *Agamemnon* man, some two years prior to the time of this story having served under Nelson when still captain in that ship immortal in naval memory, which dismantled and in part broken up to her bare ribs is seen a grand skeleton in Haden's etching. As one of a boarding party from the *Agamemnon* he had received a cut slantwise along one temple and cheek leaving a long pale scar like a streak of dawn's light falling athwart the dark visage. It was on account of that scar and the affair in which it was known that he had received it, as well as from his blue-peppered complexion, that the Dansker went among the *Bellipotent's* crew by the name of "Board-Her-in-the-Smoke."

Now the first time that his small weasel eyes happened to light on Billy Budd, a certain grim internal merriment set all his ancient wrinkles into antic play. Was it that his eccentric unsentimental old sapience, primitive in its kind, saw or thought it saw something which in contrast with the warship's environment looked oddly incongruous in the Handsome Sailor? But after slyly studying him at intervals, the old Merlin's equivocal merriment was modified; for now when the twain would meet, it would start in his face a quizzing sort of look, but it would be but momentary and sometimes replaced by an expression of speculative query as to what might eventually befall a nature like that, dropped into a world not without some mantraps and against whose subtleties simple courage lacking experience and address, and without any touch of defensive ugliness, is of little avail; and where such innocence as man is capable of does yet in a moral emergency not always sharpen the faculties or enlighten the will.

However it was, the Dansker in his ascetic way rather took to Billy. Nor was this only because of a certain philosophic interest in such a character. There was another cause. While the old man's eccentricities, sometimes bordering on the ursine, repelled the juniors, Billy, undeterred thereby, revering him as a salt hero, would make advances, never passing the old *Agamemnon* man without a salutation marked by that respect which is seldom lost on the aged, however crabbed at times or whatever their station in life.

There was a vein of dry humor, or what not, in the mastman; and, whether in freak of patriarchal irony touching Billy's youth and athletic frame, or for some other and more recondite reason, from the first in addressing him he always substituted *Baby* for Billy, the Dansker in fact being the originator of the name by which the foretopman eventually became known aboard ship.

Well then, in his mysterious little difficulty going in quest of the wrinkled one, Billy found him off duty in a dogwatch ruminating by himself, seated on a shot box of the upper gun deck, now and then surveying with a somewhat cynical regard certain of the more swaggering promenaders there. Billy recounted his trouble, again wondering how it all happened. The salt seer attentively listened, accompanying the foretopman's recital with queer twitchings of his wrinkles and problematical little sparkles of his small ferret eyes. Making an end of his story, the foretopman asked, "And now, Dansker, do tell me what you think of it."

The old man, shoving up the front of his tarpaulin and deliberately rubbing the long slant scar at the point where it entered the thin hair, laconically said, "Baby Budd, *Jemmy Legs*"[8] (meaning the master-at-arms) "is down on you."

"*Jemmy Legs!*" ejaculated Billy, his welkin eyes expanding. "What for? Why, he calls me 'the sweet and pleasant young fellow,' they tell me."

"Does he so?" grinned the grizzled one; then said, "Ay, Baby lad, a sweet voice has Jemmy Legs."

"No, not always. But to me he has. I seldom pass him but there comes a pleasant word."

"And that's because he's down upon you, Baby Budd."

Such reiteration, along with the manner of it, incomprehensible

---

8. Shipboard term for the master-at-arms who was known by his official rattan, or walking stick. A kind of chief of police.

to a novice, disturbed Billy almost as much as the mystery for which he had sought explanation. Something less unpleasingly oracular he tried to extract; but the old sea Chiron, thinking perhaps that for the nonce he had sufficiently instructed his young Achilles, pursed his lips, gathered all his wrinkles together, and would commit himself to nothing further.

Years, and those experiences which befall certain shrewder men subordinated lifelong to the will of superiors, all this had developed in the Dansker the pithy guarded cynicism that was his leading characteristic.

10

The next day an incident served to confirm Billy Budd in his incredulity as to the Dansker's strange summing up of the case submitted. The ship at noon, going large before the wind, was rolling on her course, and he below at dinner and engaged in some sportful talk with the members of his mess, chanced in a sudden lurch to spill the entire contents of his soup pan upon the new-scrubbed deck. Claggart, the master-at-arms, official rattan in hand, happened to be passing along the battery in a bay of which the mess was lodged, and the greasy liquid streamed just across his path. Stepping over it, he was proceeding on his way without comment, since the matter was nothing to take notice of under the circumstances, when he happened to observe who it was that had done the spilling. His countenance changed. Pausing, he was about to ejaculate something hasty at the sailor,[9] but checked himself, and pointing down to the streaming soup, playfully tapped him from behind with his rattan, saying in a low musical voice peculiar to him at times, "Handsomely done, my lad! And handsome is as handsome did it, too!" And with that passed on. Not noted by Billy as not coming within his view was the involuntary smile, or rather grimace, that accompanied Claggart's equivocal words. Aridly it drew down the thin corners of his shapely mouth. But everybody taking his remark as meant for humorous, and at which therefore as coming from a superior they were bound to laugh "with counterfeited glee," acted accordingly; and Billy, tickled, it may be, by the allusion to his being the Handsome Sailor, merrily joined in; then addressing his messmates exclaimed, "There now, who says that Jemmy Legs is down on me!"

"And who said he was, Beauty?" demanded one Donald with some surprise. Whereat the foretopman looked a little foolish, recalling that it was only one person. Board-Her-in-the-Smoke, who

---

9. In the "ejaculate" and spilled soup several critics see sexual symbolism.

had suggested what to him was the smoky idea that this master-at-arms was in any peculiar way hostile to him. Meantime that functionary, resuming his path, must have momentarily worn some expression less guarded than that of the bitter smile, usurping the face from the heart—some distorting expression perhaps, for a drummer-boy heedlessly frolicking along from the opposite direction and chancing to come into light collision with his person was strangely disconcerted by his aspect. Nor was the impression lessened when the official, impetuously giving him a sharp cut with the rattan, vehemently exclaimed, "Look where you go!"

## 11

What was the matter with the master-at-arms? And, be the matter what it might, how could it have direct relation to Billy Budd, with whom prior to the affair of the spilled soup he had never come into any special contact official or otherwise? What indeed could the trouble have to do with one so little inclined to give offense as the merchant-ship's "peacemaker," even him who in Claggart's own phrase was "the sweet and pleasant young fellow"? Yes, why should Jemmy Legs, to borrow the Dansker's expression, be "down" on the Handsome Sailor? But, at heart and not for nothing, as the late chance encounter may indicate to the discerning, down on him, secretly down on him, he assuredly was.

Now to invent something touching the more private career of Claggart, something involving Billy Budd, of which something the latter should be wholly ignorant, some romantic incident implying that Claggart's knowledge of the young bluejacket began at some period anterior to catching sight of him on board the seventy-four—all this, not so difficult to do, might avail in a way more or less interesting to account for whatever of enigma may appear to lurk in the case. But in fact there was nothing of the sort. And yet the cause necessarily to be assumed as the sole one assignable is in its very realism as much charged with that prime element of Radcliffian romance, the mysterious, as any that the ingenuity of the author of *The Mysteries of Udolpho*[1] could devise. For what can more partake of the mysterious than an antipathy spontaneous and profound such as is evoked in certain exceptional mortals by the mere aspect of some other mortal, however harmless he may be, if not called forth by this very harmlessness itself?

Now there can exist no irritating juxtaposition of dissimilar personalities comparable to that which is possible aboard a great warship fully manned and at sea. There, every day among all ranks,

---

1. By Ann Radcliffe (1764–1823), English novelist known for her Gothic fiction.

almost every man comes into more or less of contact with almost every other man. Wholly there to avoid even the sight of an aggravating object one must needs give it Jonah's toss[2] or jump overboard himself. Imagine how all this might eventually operate on some peculiar human creature the direct reverse of a saint!

But for the adequate comprehending of Claggart by a normal nature these hints are insufficient. To pass from a normal nature to him one must cross "the deadly space between." And this is best done by indirection.

Long ago an honest scholar, my senior, said to me in reference to one who like himself is now no more, a man so unimpeachably respectable that against him nothing was ever openly said though among the few something was whispered, "Yes, X——is a nut not to be cracked by the tap of a lady's fan. You are aware that I am the adherent of no organized religion, much less of any philosophy built into a system. Well, for all that, I think that to try and get into X——, enter his labyrinth and get out again, without a clue derived from some source other than what is known as 'knowledge of the world'— that were hardly possible, at least for me."

"Why," said I, "X——, however singular a study to some, is yet human, and knowledge of the world assuredly implies the knowledge of human nature, and in most of its varieties."

"Yes, but a superficial knowledge of it, serving ordinary purposes. But for anything deeper, I am not certain whether to know the world and to know human nature be not two distinct branches of knowledge, which while they may coexist in the same heart, yet either may exist with little or nothing of the other. Nay, in an average man of the world, his constant rubbing with it blunts that finer spiritual insight indispensable to the understanding of the essential in certain exceptional characters, whether evil ones or good. In a matter of some importance I have seen a girl wind an old lawyer about her little finger. Nor was it the dotage of senile love. Nothing of the sort. But he knew law better than he knew the girl's heart. Coke and Blackstone[3] hardly shed so much light into obscure spiritual places as the Hebrew prophets. And who were they? Mostly recluses."

At the time, my inexperience was such that I did not quite see the drift of all this. It may be that I see it now. And, indeed, if that lexicon which is based on Holy Writ were any longer popular, one might with less difficulty define and denominate certain phenomenal men. As it is, one must turn to some authority not liable to the charge of being tinctured with the biblical element.

---

2. Jonah 1.15.
3. Sir Edward Coke (1552–1634) and Sir William Blackstone (1723–1780) were noted British jurists.

In a list of definitions included in the authentic translation of Plato, a list attributed to him, occurs this: "Natural Depravity: a depravity according to nature," a definition which, though savoring of Calvinism, by no means involves Calvin's dogma as to total mankind. Evidently its intent makes it applicable but to individuals. Not many are the examples of this depravity which the gallows and jail supply. At any rate, for notable instances, since these have no vulgar alloy of the brute in them, but invariably are dominated by intellectuality, one must go elsewhere. Civilization, especially if of the austerer sort, is auspicious to it. It folds itself in the mantle of respectability. It has its certain negative virtues serving as silent auxiliaries. It never allows wine to get within its guard. It is not going too far to say that it is without vices or small sins. There is a phenomenal pride in it that excludes them. It is never mercenary or avaricious. In short, the depravity here meant partakes nothing of the sordid or sensual. It is serious, but free from acerbity. Though no flatterer of mankind it never speaks ill of it.

But the thing which in eminent instances signalizes so exceptional a nature is this: Though the man's even temper and discreet bearing would seem to intimate a mind peculiarly subject to the law of reason, not the less in heart he would seem to riot in complete exemption from that law, having apparently little to do with reason further than to employ it as an ambidexter implement for effecting the irrational. That is to say: Toward the accomplishment of an aim which in wantonness of atrocity would seem to partake of the insane, he will direct a cool judgment sagacious and sound. These men are madmen, and of the most dangerous sort, for their lunacy is not continuous, but occasional, evoked by some special object; it is protectively secretive, which is as much as to say it is self-contained, so that when, moreover, most active it is to the average mind not distinguishable from sanity, and for the reason above suggested: that whatever its aims may be—and the aim is never declared—the method and the outward proceeding are always perfectly rational.

Now something such an one was Claggart, in whom was the mania of an evil nature, not engendered by vicious training or corrupting books or licentious living, but born with him and innate, in short "a depravity according to nature."

Dark sayings are these, some will say.[4] But why? Is it because they somewhat savor of Holy Writ in its phrase "mystery of iniquity"?[5] If they do, such savor was far enough from being intended, for little will it commend these pages to many a reader of today.

The point of the present story turning on the hidden nature of the

---

4. "I will open my mouth in a parable: I will utter dark sayings of old" (Psalm 78.2).
5. "The mystery of iniquity doth already work" (2 Thessalonians 2.7).

master-at-arms has necessitated this chapter. With an added hint or
two in connection with the incident at the mess, the resumed narrative must be left to vindicate, as it may, its own credibility.

## 12

That Claggart's figure was not amiss, and his face, save the chin,
well molded, has already been said. Of these favorable points he
seemed not insensible, for he was not only neat but careful in his
dress. But the form of Billy Budd was heroic; and if his face was
without the intellectual look of the pallid Claggart's, not the less
was it lit, like his, from within, though from a different source. The
bonfire in his heart made luminous the rose-tan in his cheek.

In view of the marked contrast between the persons of the twain,
it is more than probable that when the master-at-arms in the scene
last given applied to the sailor the proverb "Handsome is as handsome does," he there let escape an ironic inkling, not caught by the
young sailors who heard it, as to what it was that had first moved
him against Billy, namely, his significant personal beauty.

Now envy and antipathy, passions irreconcilable in reason, nevertheless in fact may spring conjoined like Chang and Eng in one birth.
Is Envy then such a monster? Well, though many an arraigned mortal
has in hopes of mitigated penalty pleaded guilty to horrible actions,
did ever anybody seriously confess to envy? Something there is in it
universally felt to be more shameful than even felonious crime. And
not only does everybody disown it, but the better sort are inclined to
incredulity when it is in earnest imputed to an intelligent man. But
since its lodgment is in the heart not the brain, no degree of intellect
supplies a guarantee against it. But Claggart's was no vulgar form of
the passion. Nor, as directed toward Billy Budd, did it partake of that
streak of apprehensive jealousy that marred Saul's visage perturbedly
brooding on the comely young David.[6] Claggart's envy struck deeper.
If askance he eyed the good looks, cheery health, and frank enjoyment of young life in Billy Budd, it was because these went along with
a nature that, as Claggart magnetically felt, had in its simplicity never
willed malice or experienced the reactionary bite of that serpent. To
him, the spirit lodged within Billy, and looking out from his welkin
eyes as from windows, that ineffability it was which made the dimple
in his dyed cheek, suppled his joints, and dancing in his yellow curls
made him pre-eminently the Handsome Sailor. One person excepted,
the master-at-arms was perhaps the only man in the ship intellectually capable of adequately appreciating the moral phenomenon presented in Billy Budd. And the insight but intensified his passion,

6. 1 Samuel 16.18.

which assuming various secret forms within him, at times assumed
that of cynic disdain, disdain of innocence—to be nothing more than
innocent! Yet in an aesthetic way he saw the charm of it, the courageous free-and-easy temper of it, and fain would have shared it, but
he despaired of it.

With no power to annul the elemental evil in him, though readily
enough he could hide it; apprehending the good, but powerless to
be it; a nature like Claggart's, surcharged with energy as such
natures almost invariably are, what recourse is left to it but to recoil
upon itself and, like the scorpion for which the Creator alone is
responsible, act out to the end the part allotted it.

## 13

Passion, and passion in its profoundest, is not a thing demanding
a palatial stage whereon to play its part. Down among the
groundlings, among the beggars and rakers of the garbage, profound
passion is enacted. And the circumstances that provoke it, however
trivial or mean, are no measure of its power. In the present instance
the stage is a scrubbed gun deck, and one of the external provoca-
tions a man-of-war's man's spilled soup.

Now when the master-at-arms noticed whence came that greasy
fluid streaming before his feet, he must have taken it—to some
extent wilfully, perhaps—not for the mere accident it assuredly was,
but for the sly escape of a spontaneous feeling on Billy's part more
or less answering to the antipathy on his own. In effect a foolish
demonstration, he must have thought, and very harmless, like the
futile kick of a heifer, which yet were the heifer a shod stallion
would not be so harmless. Even so was it that into the gall of
Claggart's envy he infused the vitriol of his contempt. But the incident confirmed to him certain telltale reports purveyed to his ear by
"Squeak," one of his more cunning corporals, a grizzled little man,
so nicknamed by the sailors on account of his squeaky voice and
sharp visage ferreting about the dark corners of the lower decks
after interlopers, satirically suggesting to them the idea of a rat in a
cellar.

From his chief's employing him as an implicit tool in laying little
traps for the worriment of the foretopman—for it was from the
master-at-arms that the petty persecutions heretofore adverted to
had proceeded—the corporal, having naturally enough concluded
that his master could have no love for the sailor, made it his business,
faithful understrapper that he was, to foment the ill blood by per-
verting to his chief certain innocent frolics of the good-natured foretopman, besides inventing for his mouth sundry contumelious epithets he claimed to have overheard him let fall. The master-at-arms

never suspected the veracity of these reports, more especially as to the epithets, for he well knew how secretly unpopular may become a master-at-arms, at least a master-at-arms of those days, zealous in his function, and how the bluejackets shoot at him in private their raillery and wit; the nickname by which he goes among them (Jemmy Legs) implying under the form of merriment their cherished disrespect and dislike. But in view of the greediness of hate for pabulum it hardly needed a purveyor to feed Claggart's passion.

An uncommon prudence is habitual with the subtler depravity, for it has everything to hide. And in case of an injury but suspected, its secretiveness voluntarily cuts it off from enlightenment or disillusion; and, not unreluctantly, action is taken upon surmise as upon certainty. And the retaliation is apt to be in monstrous disproportion to the supposed offense; for when in anybody was revenge in its exactions aught else but an inordinate usurer? But how with Claggart's conscience? For though consciences are unlike as foreheads, every intelligence, not excluding the scriptural devils who *"believe and tremble,"*[7] has one. But Claggart's conscience being but the lawyer to his will, made ogres of trifles, probably arguing that the motive imputed to Billy in spilling the soup just when he did, together with the epithets alleged, these, if nothing more, made a strong case against him; nay, justified animosity into a sort of retributive righteousness. The Pharisee is the Guy Fawkes[8] prowling in the hid chambers underlying some natures like Claggart's. And they can really form no conception of an unreciprocated malice. Probably the master-at-arms' clandestine persecution of Billy was started to try the temper of the man; but it had not developed any quality in him that enmity could make official use of or even pervert into plausible self-justification; so that the occurrence at the mess, petty if it were, was a welcome one to that peculiar conscience assigned to be the private mentor of Claggart; and, for the rest, not improbably it put him upon new experiments.

*14*

Not many days after the last incident narrated, something befell Billy Budd that more graveled him than aught that had previously occurred.

It was a warm night for the latitude; and the foretopman, whose watch at the time was properly below, was dozing on the uppermost deck whither he had ascended from his hot hammock, one of hundreds suspended so closely wedged together over a lower gun deck that there was little or no swing to them. He lay as in the shadow of

7. "The devils also believe, and tremble" (James 2.19).
8. See n. 2, p. 66.

a hillside, stretched under the lee of the booms, a piled ridge of spare spars amidships between foremast and mainmast among which the ship's largest boat, the launch, was stowed. Alongside of three other slumberers from below, he lay near that end of the booms which approaches the foremast; his station aloft on duty as a foretopman being just over the deck-station of the forecastlemen, entitling him according to usage to make himself more or less at home in that neighborhood.

Presently he was stirred into semiconsciousness by somebody, who must have previously sounded the sleep of the others, touching his shoulder, and then, as the foretopman raised his head, breathing into his ear in a quick whisper, "Slip into the lee forechains, Billy; there is something in the wind. Don't speak. Quick, I will meet you there," and disappearing.

Now Billy, like sundry other essentially good-natured ones, had some of the weaknesses inseparable from essential good nature; and among these was a reluctance, almost an incapacity of plumply saying *no* to an abrupt proposition not obviously absurd on the face of it, nor obviously unfriendly, nor iniquitous. And being of warm blood, he had not the phlegm tacitly to negative any proposition by unresponsive inaction. Like his sense of fear, his apprehension as to aught outside of the honest and natural was seldom very quick. Besides, upon the present occasion, the drowse from his sleep still hung upon him.

However it was, he mechanically rose and, sleepily wondering what could be in the wind, betook himself to the designated place, a narrow platform, one of six, outside of the high bulwarks and screened by the great deadeyes and multiple columned lanyards of the shrouds and backstays; and, in a great warship of that time, of dimensions commensurate to the hull's magnitude; a tarry balcony in short, overhanging the sea, and so secluded that one mariner of the *Bellipotent*, a Nonconformist old tar of a serious turn, made it even in daytime his private oratory.[9]

In this retired nook the stranger soon joined Billy Budd. There was no moon as yet; a haze obscured the starlight. He could not distinctly see the stranger's face. Yet from something in the outline and carriage, Billy took him, and correctly, for one of the afterguard.

"Hist! Billy," said the man, in the same quick cautionary whisper as before. "You were impressed, weren't you? Well, so was I"; and he paused, as to mark the effect. But Billy, not knowing exactly what to make of this, said nothing. Then the other: "We are not the only impressed ones, Billy. There's a gang of us.—Couldn't you—help— at a pinch?"

---

9. Prayer room. "Nonconformist": Protestant dissenter.

"What do you mean?" demanded Billy, here thoroughly shaking off his drowse.

"Hist, hist!" the hurried whisper now growing husky. "See here," and the man held up two small objects faintly twinkling in the nightlight; "see, they are yours, Billy, if you'll only——"

But Billy broke in, and in his resentful eagerness to deliver himself his vocal infirmity somewhat intruded. "D—d—damme, I don't know what you are d—d—driving at, or what you mean, but you had better g—g—go where you belong!" For the moment the fellow, as confounded, did not stir; and Billy, springing to his feet, said, "If you d—don't start, I'll t—t—toss you back over the r—rail!" There was no mistaking this, and the mysterious emissary decamped, disappearing in the direction of the mainmast in the shadow of the booms.

"Hallo, what's the matter?" here came growling from a forecastleman awakened from his deck-doze by Billy's raised voice. And as the foretopman reappeared and was recognized by him: "Ah, Beauty, is it you? Well, something must have been the matter, for you st—st—stuttered."

"Oh," rejoined Billy, now mastering the impediment, "I found an afterguardsman in our part of the ship here, and I bid him be off where he belongs."

"And is that all you did about it, Foretopman?" gruffly demanded another, an irascible old fellow of brick-colored visage and hair who was known to his associate forecastlemen as "Red Pepper." "Such sneaks I should like to marry to the gunner's daughter!"—by that expression meaning that he would like to subject them to disciplinary castigation over a gun.

However, Billy's rendering of the matter satisfactorily accounted to these inquirers for the brief commotion, since of all the sections of a ship's company the forecastlemen, veterans for the most part and bigoted in their sea prejudices, are the most jealous in resenting territorial encroachments, especially on the part of any of the afterguard, of whom they have but a sorry opinion—chiefly landsmen, never going aloft except to reef or furl the mainsail, and in no wise competent to handle a marlinspike or turn in a deadeye, say.

## 15

This incident sorely puzzled Billy Budd. It was an entirely new experience, the first time in his life that he had ever been personally approached in underhand intriguing fashion. Prior to this encounter he had known nothing of the afterguardsman, the two men being stationed wide apart, one forward and aloft during his watch the other on deck and aft.

What could it mean? And could they really be guineas, those two glittering objects the interloper had held up to his (Billy's) eyes? Where could the fellow get guineas? Why, even spare buttons are not so plentiful at sea. The more he turned the matter over, the more he was nonplussed, and made uneasy and discomfited. In his disgustful recoil from an overture which, though he but ill comprehended, he instinctively knew must involve evil of some sort, Billy Budd was like a young horse fresh from the pasture suddenly inhaling a vile whiff from some chemical factory, and by repeated snortings trying to get it out of his nostrils and lungs. This frame of mind barred all desire of holding further parley with the fellow, even were it but for the purpose of gaining some enlightenment as to his design in approaching him. And yet he was not without natural curiosity to see how such a visitor in the dark would look in broad day.

He espied him the following afternoon in his first dogwatch below, one of the smokers on that forward part of the upper gun deck allotted to the pipe. He recognized him by his general cut and build more than by his round freckled face and glassy eyes of pale blue, veiled with lashes all but white. And yet Billy was a bit uncertain whether indeed it were he—yonder chap about his own age chatting and laughing in freehearted way, leaning against a gun; a genial young fellow enough to look at, and something of a rattlebrain, to all appearance. Rather chubby too for a sailor, even an afterguardsman. In short, the last man in the world, one would think, to be overburdened with thoughts, especially those perilous thoughts that must needs belong to a conspirator in any serious project, or even to the underling of such a conspirator.

Although Billy was not aware of it, the fellow, with a side-long watchful glance, had perceived Billy first, and then noting that Billy was looking at him, thereupon nodded a familiar sort of friendly recognition as to an old acquaintance, without interrupting the talk he was engaged in with the group of smokers. A day or two afterwards, chancing in the evening promenade on a gun deck to pass Billy, he offered a flying word of good-fellowship, as it were, which by its unexpectedness, and equivocalness under the circumstances, so embarrassed Billy that he knew not how to respond to it, and let it go unnoticed.

Billy was now left more at a loss than before. The ineffectual speculations into which he was led were so disturbingly alien to him that he did his best to smother them. It never entered his mind that here was a matter which, from its extreme questionableness, it was his duty as a loyal bluejacket to report in the proper quarter. And, probably, had such a step been suggested to him, he would have been deterred from taking it by the thought, one of novice magnanimity, that it would savor overmuch of the dirty work of a telltale. He kept the thing to himself. Yet upon one occasion he could not forbear a little disburdening himself to the old Dansker, tempted thereto perhaps by the influence of a balmy night when the ship lay becalmed; the twain, silent for the most part, sitting together on deck, their heads propped against the bulwarks. But it was only a partial and anonymous account that Billy gave, the unfounded scruples above referred to preventing full disclosure to anybody. Upon hearing Billy's version, the sage Dansker seemed to divine more than he was told; and after a little meditation, during which his wrinkles were pursed as into a point, quite effacing for the time that quizzing expression his face sometimes wore: "Didn't I say so, Baby Budd?"

"Say what?" demanded Billy.

"Why, *Jemmy Legs* is *down* on you."

"And what," rejoined Billy in amazement, "has *Jemmy Legs* to do with that cracked afterguardsman?"

"Ho, it was an afterguardsman, then. A cat's-paw, a cat's-paw!" And with that exclamation, whether it had reference to a light puff of air just then coming over the calm sea, or a subtler relation to the afterguardsman, there is no telling, the old Merlin gave a twisting wrench with his black teeth at his plug of tobacco, vouchsafing no reply to Billy's impetuous question, though now repeated, for it was his wont to relapse into grim silence when interrogated in skeptical sort as to any of his sententious oracles, not always very clear ones, rather partaking of that obscurity which invests most Delphic deliverances from any quarter.

Long experience had very likely brought this old man to that bitter prudence which never interferes in aught and never gives advice.

### 16

Yes, despite the Dansker's pithy insistence as to the master-at-arms being at the bottom of these strange experiences of Billy on board the *Bellipotent*, the young sailor was ready to ascribe them to almost anybody but the man who, to use Billy's own expression, "always had a pleasant word for him." This is to be wondered at. Yet not so much to be wondered at. In certain matters, some sailors even in mature life remain unsophisticated enough. But a young seafarer of the disposition of our athletic foretopman is much of a child-man. And yet a child's utter innocence is but its blank ignorance, and the innocence more or less wanes as intelligence waxes. But in Billy Budd intelligence, such as it was, had advanced while yet his simple-mindedness remained for the most part unaffected.

Experience is a teacher indeed; yet did Billy's years make his experience small. Besides, he had none of that intuitive knowledge of
the bad which in natures not good or incompletely so foreruns experience, and therefore may pertain, as in some instances it too clearly
does pertain, even to youth.

And what could Billy know of man except of man as a mere
sailor? And the old-fashioned sailor, the veritable man before the
mast, the sailor from boyhood up, he, though indeed of the same
species as a landsman, is in some respects singularly distinct from
him. The sailor is frankness, the landsman is finesse. Life is not a
game with the sailor, demanding the long head[1]—no intricate game
of chess where few moves are made in straightforwardness and ends
are attained by indirection, an oblique, tedious, barren game hardly
worth that poor candle burnt out in playing it.

Yes, as a class, sailors are in character a juvenile race. Even their
deviations are marked by juvenility, this more especially holding true
with the sailors of Billy's time. Then too, certain things which apply
to all sailors do more pointedly operate here and there upon the
junior one. Every sailor, too, is accustomed to obey orders without
debating them; his life afloat is externally ruled for him; he is not
brought into that promiscuous commerce with mankind where
unobstructed free agency on equal terms—equal superficially, at
least—soon teaches one that unless upon occasion he exercise a distrust keen in proportion to the fairness of the appearance, some foul
turn may be served him. A ruled undemonstrative distrustfulness is
so habitual, not with businessmen so much as with men who know
their kind in less shallow relations than business, namely, certain
men of the world, that they come at last to employ it all but unconsciously; and some of them would very likely feel real surprise at
being charged with it as one of their general characteristics.

## 17

But after the little matter at the mess Billy Budd no more found
himself in strange trouble at times about his hammock or his
clothes bag or what not. As to that smile that occasionally sunned
him, and the pleasant passing word, these were, if not more frequent, yet if anything more pronounced than before.

But for all that, there were certain other demonstrations now.
When Claggart's unobserved glance happened to light on belted Billy
rolling along the upper gun deck in the leisure of the second dogwatch, exchanging passing broadsides of fun with other young promenaders in the crowd, that glance would follow the cheerful sea

1. Foresight.

Hyperion[2] with a settled meditative and melancholy expression, his eyes strangely suffused with incipient feverish tears. Then would Claggart look like the man of sorrows.[3] Yes, and sometimes the melancholy expression would have in it a touch of soft yearning, as if Claggart could even have loved Billy but for fate and ban. But this was an evanescence, and quickly repented of, as it were, by an immitigable look, pinching and shriveling the visage into the momentary semblance of a wrinkled walnut. But sometimes catching sight in advance of the foretopman coming in his direction, he would, upon their nearing, step aside a little to let him pass, dwelling upon Billy for the moment with the glittering dental satire of a Guise. But upon any abrupt unforeseen encounter a red light would flash forth from his eye like a spark from an anvil in a dusk smithy. That quick, fierce light was a strange one, darted from orbs which in repose were of a color nearest approaching a deeper violet, the softest of shades.

Though some of these caprices of the pit could not but be observed by their object, yet were they beyond the construing of such a nature. And the thews of Billy were hardly compatible with that sort of sensitive spiritual organization which in some cases instinctively conveys to ignorant innocence an admonition of the proximity of the malign. He thought the master-at-arms acted in a manner rather queer at times. That was all. But the occasional frank air and pleasant word went for what they purported to be, the young sailor never having heard as yet of the "too fair-spoken man."

Had the foretopman been conscious of having done or said anything to provoke the ill will of the official, it would have been different with him, and his sight might have been purged if not sharpened. As it was, innocence was his blinder.

So was it with him in yet another matter. Two minor officers, the armorer and captain of the hold, with whom he had never exchanged a word, his position in the ship not bringing him into contact with them, these men now for the first began to cast upon Billy, when they chanced to encounter him, that peculiar glance which evidences that the man from whom it comes has been some way tampered with, and to the prejudice of him upon whom the glance lights. Never did it occur to Billy as a thing to be noted or a thing suspicious, though he well knew the fact, that the armorer and captain of the hold, with the ship's yeoman, apothecary, and others of that grade, were by naval usage messmates of the master-at-arms, men with ears convenient to his confidential tongue.

But the general popularity that came from our Handsome Sailor's manly forwardness upon occasion and irresistible good nature, indi-

2. God of manly beauty.
3. Isaiah 53.3; a phrase often applied to Christ.

cating no mental superiority tending to excite an invidious feeling, this good will on the part of most of his shipmates made him the less to concern himself about such mute aspects toward him as those whereto allusion has just been made, aspects he could not so fathom as to infer their whole import.

As to the afterguardsman, though Billy for reasons already given necessarily saw little of him, yet when the two did happen to meet, invariably came the fellow's offhand cheerful recognition, sometimes accompanied by a passing pleasant word or two. Whatever that equivocal young person's original design may really have been, or the design of which he might have been the deputy, certain it was from his manner upon these occasions that he had wholly dropped it.

It was as if his precocity of crookedness (and every vulgar villain is precocious) had for once deceived him, and the man he had sought to entrap as a simpleton had through his very simplicity ignominiously baffled him.

But shrewd ones may opine that it was hardly possible for Billy to refrain from going up to the afterguardsman and bluntly demanding to know his purpose in the initial interview so abruptly closed in the forechains. Shrewd ones may also think it but natural in Billy to set about sounding some of the other impressed men of the ship in order to discover what basis, if any, there was for the emissary's obscure suggestions as to plotting disaffection aboard. Yes, shrewd ones may so think. But something more, or rather something else than mere shrewdness is perhaps needful for the due understanding of such a character as Billy Budd's.

As to Claggart, the monomania in the man—if that indeed it were—as involuntarily disclosed by starts in the manifestations detailed, yet in general covered over by his self-contained and rational demeanor; this, like a subterranean fire, was eating its way deeper and deeper in him. Something decisive must come of it.

## 18

After the mysterious interview in the forechains, the one so abruptly ended there by Billy, nothing especially germane to the story occurred until the events now about to be narrated.

Elsewhere it has been said that in the lack of frigates (of course better sailers than line-of-battle ships) in the English squadron up the Straits at that period, the *Bellipotent* 74 was occasionally employed not only as an available substitute for a scout, but at times on detached service of more important kind. This was not alone because of her sailing qualities, not common in a ship of her rate, but quite as much, probably, that the character of her commander, it was thought, specially adapted him for any duty where under unforeseen difficulties a prompt initiative might have to be taken in some matter demanding knowledge and ability in addition to those qualities implied in good seamanship. It was on an expedition of the latter sort, a somewhat distant one, and when the *Bellipotent* was almost at her furthest remove from the fleet, that in the latter part of an afternoon watch she unexpectedly came in sight of a ship of the enemy. It proved to be a frigate. The latter, perceiving through the glass that the weight of men and metal would be heavily against her, invoking her light heels crowded sail to get away. After a chase urged almost against hope and lasting until about the middle of the first dogwatch, she signally succeeded in effecting her escape.

Not long after the pursuit had been given up, and ere the excitement incident thereto had altogether waned away, the master-at-arms, ascending from his cavernous sphere, made his appearance cap in hand by the mainmast respectfully waiting the notice of Captain Vere, then solitary walking the weather side of the quarterdeck, doubtless somewhat chafed at the failure of the pursuit. The spot where Claggart stood was the place allotted to men of lesser grades seeking some more particular interview either with the officer of the deck or the captain himself. But from the latter it was not often that a sailor or petty officer of those days would seek a hearing; only some exceptional cause would, according to established custom, have warranted that.

Presently, just as the commander, absorbed in his reflections, was on the point of turning aft in his promenade, he became sensible of Claggart's presence, and saw the doffed cap held in deferential expectancy. Here be it said that Captain Vere's personal knowledge of this petty officer had only begun at the time of the ship's last sailing from home, Claggart then for the first, in transfer from a ship detained for repairs, supplying on board the *Bellipotent* the place of a previous master-at-arms disabled and ashore.

No sooner did the commander observe who it was that now deferentially stood awaiting his notice than a peculiar expression came over him. It was not unlike that which uncontrollably will flit across the countenance of one at unawares encountering a person who, though known to him indeed, has hardly been long enough known for thorough knowledge, but something in whose aspect nevertheless now for the first provokes a vaguely repellent distaste. But coming to a stand and resuming much of his wonted official manner, save that a sort of impatience lurked in the intonation of the opening word, he said "Well? What is it, Master-at-arms?"

With the air of a subordinate grieved at the necessity of being a messenger of ill tidings, and while conscientiously determined to be frank yet equally resolved upon shunning overstatement, Claggart at this invitation, or rather summons to disburden, spoke up. What he said, conveyed in the language of no uneducated man, was to the effect following, if not altogether in these words, namely, that during the chase and preparations for the possible encounter he had seen enough to convince him that at least one sailor aboard was a dangerous character in a ship mustering some who not only had taken a guilty part in the late serious troubles, but others also who, like the man in question, had entered His Majesty's service under another form than enlistment.

At this point Captain Vere with some impatience interrupted him: "Be direct, man; say *impressed men.*"

Claggart made a gesture of subservience, and proceeded. Quite lately he (Claggart) had begun to suspect that on the gun decks some sort of movement prompted by the sailor in question was covertly going on, but he had not thought himself warranted in reporting the suspicion so long as it remained indistinct. But from what he had that afternoon observed in the man referred to, the suspicion of something clandestine going on had advanced to a point less removed from certainty. He deeply felt, he added, the serious responsibility assumed in making a report involving such possible consequences to the individual mainly concerned, besides tending to augment those natural anxieties which every naval commander must feel in view of extraordinary outbreaks so recent as those which, he sorrowfully said it, it needed not to name.

Now at the first broaching of the matter Captain Vere, taken by surprise, could not wholly dissemble his disquietude. But as Claggart went on, the former's aspect changed into restiveness under something in the testifier's manner in giving his testimony. However, he refrained from interrupting him. And Claggart, continuing, concluded with this: "God forbid, your honor, that the *Bellipotent's* should be the experience of the——"

"Never mind that!" here peremptorily broke in the superior, his face altering with anger, instinctively divining the ship that the other was about to name, one in which the Nore Mutiny had assumed a singularly tragical character that for a time jeopardized the life of its commander. Under the circumstances he was indignant at the purposed allusion. When the commissioned officers themselves were on all occasions very heedful how they referred to the recent events in the fleet, for a petty officer unnecessarily to allude to them in the presence of his captain, this struck him as a most immodest presumption. Besides, to his quick sense of self-respect it even looked under the circumstances something like an attempt to alarm him. Nor at first was he without some surprise that one who so far as he had hitherto come under his notice had shown considerable tact in his function should in this particular evince such lack of it.

But these thoughts and kindred dubious ones flitting across his mind were suddenly replaced by an intuitional surmise which, though as yet obscure in form, served practically to affect his reception of the ill tidings. Certain it is that, long versed in everything pertaining to the complicated gun-deck life, which like every other form of life has its secret mines and dubious side, the side popularly disclaimed, Captain Vere did not permit himself to be unduly disturbed by the general tenor of his subordinate's report.

Furthermore, if in view of recent events prompt action should be taken at the first palpable sign of recurring insubordination, for all that, not judicious would it be, he thought, to keep the idea of lingering disaffection alive by undue forwardness in crediting an informer, even if his own subordinate and charged among other things with police surveillance of the crew. This feeling would not perhaps have so prevailed with him were it not that upon a prior occasion the patriotic zeal officially evinced by Claggart had somewhat irritated him as appearing rather supersensible and strained. Furthermore, something even in the official's self-possessed and somewhat ostentatious manner in making his specifications strangely reminded him of a bandsman, a perjurous witness in a capital case before a court-martial ashore of which when a lieutenant he (Captain Vere) had been a member.

Now the peremptory check given to Claggart in the matter of the arrested allusion was quickly followed up by this: "You say that there is at least one dangerous man aboard. Name him."

"William Budd, a foretopman, your honor."

"William Budd!" repeated Captain Vere with unfeigned astonishment. "And mean you the man that Lieutenant Ratcliffe took from the merchantman not very long ago, the young fellow who seems to be so popular with the men—Billy, the Handsome Sailor, as they call him?"

"The same, your honor; but for all his youth and good looks, a deep one. Not for nothing does he insinuate himself into the good will of his shipmates, since at the least they will at a pinch say—all hands will—a good word for him, and at all hazards. Did Lieutenant Ratcliffe happen to tell your honor of that adroit fling of Budd's, jumping up in the cutter's bow under the merchantman's stern when he was being taken off? It is even masked by that sort of good-humored air that at heart he resents his impressment. You have but noted his fair cheek. A mantrap may be under the ruddy-tipped daisies."

Now the Handsome Sailor as a signal figure among the crew had naturally enough attracted the captain's attention from the first. Though in general not very demonstrative to his officers, he had congratulated Lieutenant Ratcliffe upon his good fortune in lighting on such a fine specimen of the *genus homo*, who in the nude might have posed for a statue of young Adam before the Fall. As to Billy's adieu to the ship *Rights-of-Man*, which the boarding lieutenant had indeed reported to him, but, in a deferential way, more as a good story than aught else, Captain Vere, though mistakenly understanding it as a satiric sally, had but thought so much the better of the impressed man for it; as a military sailor, admiring the spirit that could take an arbitrary enlistment so merrily and sensibly. The foretopman's conduct, too, so far as it had fallen under the captain's notice, had confirmed the first happy augury, while the new recruit's qualities as a "sailor-man" seemed to be such that he had thought of recommending him to the executive officer for promotion to a place that would more frequently bring him under his own observation, namely, the captaincy of the mizzentop, replacing there in the starboard watch a man not so young whom partly for that reason he deemed less fitted for the post. Be it parenthesized here that since the mizzentopmen have not to handle such breadths of heavy canvas as the lower sails on the mainmast and foremast, a young man if of the right stuff not only seems best adapted to duty there, but in fact is generally selected for the captaincy of that top, and the company under him are light hands and often but striplings. In sum, Captain Vere had from the beginning deemed Billy Budd to be what in the naval parlance of the time was called a "King's bargain": that is to say, for His Britannic Majesty's navy a capital investment at small outlay or none at all.

After a brief pause, during which the reminiscences above mentioned passed vividly through his mind and he weighed the import of Claggart's last suggestion conveyed in the phrase "mantrap under the daisies," and the more he weighted it the less reliance he felt in the informer's good faith, suddenly he turned upon him and in a low voice demanded: "Do you come to me, Master-at-arms, with so foggy a tale? As to Budd, cite me an act or spoken word[4] of his confirmatory of what you in general charge against him. Stay," drawing nearer to him; "heed what you speak. Just now, and in a case like this, there is a yardarm-end for the false witness."

"Ah, your honor!" sighed Claggart, mildly shaking his shapely head as in sad deprecation of such unmerited severity of tone. Then, bridling—erecting himself as in virtuous self-assertion—he circumstantially alleged certain words and acts which collectively, if credited, led to presumptions mortally inculpating Budd. And for some of these averments, he added, substantiating proof was not far.

---

4. This phrase reminds many critics of Othello's demand for "ocular proof" to substantiate Iago's charges against Desdemona. Hayford and Sealts note "numerous verbal echoes of *Othello* here and elsewhere in the novel."

With gray eyes impatient and distrustful essaying to fathom to the bottom Claggart's calm violet ones, Captain Vere again heard him out; then for the moment stood ruminating. The mood he evinced, Claggart—himself for the time liberated from the other's scrutiny—steadily regarded with a look difficult to render: a look curious of the operation of his tactics, a look such as might have been that of the spokesman of the envious children of Jacob deceptively imposing upon the troubled patriarch the blood-dyed coat of young Joseph.[5]

Though something exceptional in the moral quality of Captain Vere made him, in earnest encounter with a fellow man, a veritable touchstone of that man's essential nature, yet now as to Claggart and what was really going on in him his feeling partook less of intuitional conviction than of strong suspicion clogged by strange dubieties. The perplexity he evinced proceeded less from aught touching the man informed against—as Claggart doubtless opined—than from considerations how best to act in regard to the informer. At first, indeed, he was naturally for summoning that substantiation of his allegations which Claggart said was at hand. But such a proceeding would result in the matter at once of getting abroad, which in the present stage of it, he thought, might undesirably affect the ship's company. If Claggart was a false witness—that closed the affair. And therefore, before trying the accusation, he would first practically test the accuser; and he thought this could be done in a quiet, undemonstrative way.

The measure he determined upon involved a shifting of the scene, a transfer to a place less exposed to observation than the broad quarter-deck. For although the few gun-room officers there at the time had, in due observance of naval etiquette, withdrawn to leeward the moment Captain Vere had begun his promenade on the deck's weather side; and though during the colloquy with Claggart they of course ventured not to diminish the distance; and though throughout the interview Captain Vere's voice was far from high, and Claggart's silvery and low; and the wind in the cordage and the wash of the sea helped the more to put them beyond earshot; nevertheless, the interview's continuance already had attracted observation from some topmen aloft and other sailors in the waist or further forward.

Having determined upon his measures, Captain Vere forthwith took action. Abruptly turning to Claggart, he asked, "Master-at-arms, is it now Budd's watch aloft?"

"No, your honor."

Whereupon, "Mr. Wilkes!" summoning the nearest midshipman.

5. Genesis 37.

"Tell Albert to come to me." Albert was the captain's hammock-boy, a sort of sea valet in whose discretion and fidelity his master had much confidence. The lad appeared.

"You know Budd, the foretopman?"

"I do, sir."

"Go find him. It is his watch off. Manage to tell him out of earshot that he is wanted aft. Contrive it that he speaks to nobody. Keep him in talk yourself. And not till you get well aft here, not till then let him know that the place where he is wanted is my cabin. You understand. Go.—Master-at-arms, show yourself on the decks below, and when you think it time for Albert to be coming with his man, stand by quietly to follow the sailor in."

## 19

Now when the foretopman found himself in the cabin, closeted there, as it were, with the captain and Claggart, he was surprised enough. But it was a surprise unaccompanied by apprehension or distrust. To an immature nature essentially honest and humane, forewarning intimations of subtler danger from one's kind come tardily if at all. The only thing that took shape in the young sailor's mind was this: Yes, the captain, I have always thought, looks kindly upon me. Wonder if he's going to make me his coxswain. I should like that. And may be now he is going to ask the master-at-arms about me.

"Shut the door there, sentry," said the commander; "stand without, and let nobody come in.—Now, Master-at-arms, tell this man to his face what you told of him to me," and stood prepared to scrutinize the mutually confronting visages.

With the measured step and calm collected air of an asylum physician approaching in the public hall some patient beginning to show indications of a coming paroxysm, Claggart deliberately advanced within short range of Billy and, mesmerically looking him in the eye, briefly recapitulated the accusation.

Not at first did Billy take it in. When he did, the rose-tan of his cheek looked struck as by white leprosy. He stood like one impaled and gagged. Meanwhile the accuser's eyes, removing not as yet from the blue dilated ones, underwent a phenomenal change, their wonted rich violet color blurring into a muddy purple. Those lights of human intelligence, losing human expression, were gelidly protruding like the alien eyes of certain uncatalogued creatures of the deep. The first mesmeristic glance was one of serpent fascination; the last was as the paralyzing lurch of the torpedo fish.

"Speak, man!" said Captain Vere to the transfixed one, struck by his aspect even more than by Claggart's. "Speak! Defend yourself!"

Which appeal caused but a strange dumb gesturing and gurgling in Billy: amazement at such an accusation so suddenly sprung on inexperienced nonage; this, and, it may be, horror of the accuser's eyes, serving to bring out his luking defect and in this instance for the time intensifying it into a convulsed tongue-tie; while the intent head and entire form straining forward in an agony of ineffectual eagerness to obey the injunction to speak and defend himself, gave an expression to the face like that of a condemned vestal priestess in the moment of being buried alive, and in the first struggle against suffocation.

Though at the time Captain Vere was quite ignorant of Billy's liability to vocal impediment, he now immediately divined it, since vividly Billy's aspect recalled to him that of a bright young schoolmate of his whom he had once seen struck by much the same startling impotence in the act of eagerly rising in the class to be foremost in response to a testing question put to it by the master. Going close up to the young sailor, and laying a soothing hand on his shoulder, he said, "There is no hurry, my boy. Take your time, take your time." Contrary to the effect intended, these words so fatherly in tone, doubtless touching Billy's heart to the quick, prompted yet more violent efforts at utterance—efforts soon ending for the time in confirming the paralysis, and bringing to his face an expression which was as a crucifixion to behold. The next instant, quick as the flame from a discharged cannon at night, his right arm shot out, and Claggart dropped to the deck. Whether intentionally or but owing to the young athlete's superior height, the blow had taken effect full upon the forehead, so shapely and intellectual-looking a feature in the master-at-arms; so that the body fell over lengthwise, like a heavy plank tilted from erectness. A gasp or two, and he lay motionless.

"Fated boy," breathed Captain Vere in tone so low as to be almost a whisper, "what have you done! But here, help me."

The twain raised the felled one from the loins up into a sitting position. The spare form flexibly acquiesced, but inertly. It was like handling a dead snake. They lowered it back. Regaining erectness, Captain Vere with one hand covering his face stood to all appearance as impassive as the object at his feet. Was he absorbed in taking in all the bearings of the event and what was best not only now at once to be done, but also in the sequel? Slowly he uncovered his face; and the effect was as if the moon emerging from eclipse should reappear with quite another aspect than that which had gone into hiding. The father in him, manifested towards Billy thus far in the scene, was replaced by the military disciplinarian. In his official tone he bade the foretopman retire to a stateroom aft (pointing it out), and there remain till thence summoned. This

order Billy in silence mechanically obeyed. Then going to the cabin
door where it opened on the quarter-deck, Captain Vere said to the
sentry without, "Tell somebody to send Albert here," When the lad
appeared, his master so contrived it that he should not catch sight
of the prone one. "Albert," he said to him, "tell the surgeon I wish
to see him. You need not come back till called."

When the surgeon entered—a self-poised character of that grave
sense and experience that hardly anything could take him aback—
Captain Vere advanced to meet him, thus unconsciously inter-
cepting his view of Claggart, and, interrupting the other's wonted
ceremonious salutation, said, "Nay. Tell me how it is with yonder
man," directing his attention to the prostrate one.

The surgeon looked, and for all his self-command somewhat
started at the abrupt revelation. On Claggart's always pallid complexion, thick black blood was now oozing from nostril and ear. To
the gazer's professional eye it was unmistakably no living man that
he saw.

"Is it so, then?" said Captain Vere, intently watching him. "I
thought it. But verify it." Whereupon the customary tests confirmed
the surgeon's first glance, who now, looking up in unfeigned concern, cast a look of intense inquisitiveness upon his superior. But
Captain Vere, with one hand to his brow, was standing motionless.
Suddenly, catching the surgeon's arm convulsively, he exclaimed,
pointing down to the body, "It is the divine judgment on Ananias![6]
Look!"

Disturbed by the excited manner he had never before observed in
the *Bellipotent's* captain, and as yet wholly ignorant of the affair, the
prudent surgeon nevertheless held his peace, only again looking an
earnest interrogatory as to what it was that had resulted in such a
tragedy.

But Captain Vere was now again motionless, standing absorbed in
thought. Again starting, he vehemently exclaimed, "Struck dead by
an angel of God! Yet the angel must hang!"[7]

At these passionate interjections, mere incoherences to the lis-
tener as yet unapprised of the antecedents, the surgeon was profoundly discomposed. But now, as recollecting himself, Captain
Vere in less passionate tone briefly related the circumstances
leading up to the event. "But come; we must dispatch," he added.
"Help me to remove him" (meaning the body) "to yonder compartment," designating one opposite that where the foretopman
remained immured. Anew disturbed by a request that, as implying a

---

6. Acts 5.3–5.
7. A key line for those critics who "disagree" with Captain Vere. They note he pronounces
   sentence before he convenes a court. Others see it as a declaration of tragic inevitability.

desire for secrecy, seemed unaccountably strange to him, there was nothing for the subordinate to do but comply.

"Go now," said Captain Vere with something of his wonted manner. "Go now. I presently shall call a drumhead court. Tell the lieutenants what has happened, and tell Mr. Mordant" (meaning the captain of marines), "and charge them to keep the matter to themselves."

## 20

Full of disquietude and misgiving, the surgeon left the cabin. Was Captain Vere suddenly affected in his mind, or was it but a transient excitement, brought about by so strange and extraordinary a tragedy? As to the drumhead court, it struck the surgeon as impolitic, if nothing more. The thing to do, he thought, was to place Billy Budd in confinement, and in a way dictated by usage, and postpone further action in so extraordinary a case to such time as they should rejoin the squadron, and then refer it to the admiral. He recalled the unwonted agitation of Captain Vere and his excited exclamations, so at variance with his normal manner. Was he unhinged?

But assuming that he is, it is not so susceptible of proof. What then can the surgeon do? No more trying situation is conceivable than that of an officer subordinate under a captain whom he suspects to be not mad, indeed, but yet not quite unaffected in his intellects. To argue his order to him would be insolence. To resist him would be mutiny.

In obedience to Captain Vere, he communicated what had happened to the lieutenants and captain of marines, saying nothing as to the captain's state. They fully shared his own surprise and concern. Like him too, they seemed to think that such a matter should be referred to the admiral.

## 21

Who in the rainbow can draw the line where the violet tint ends and the orange tint begins? Distinctly we see the difference of the colors, but where exactly does the one first blendingly enter into the other? So with sanity and insanity. In pronounced cases there is no question about them. But in some supposed cases, in various degrees supposedly less pronounced, to draw the exact line of demarcation few will undertake, though for a fee becoming considerate some professional experts will. There is nothing namable but that some men will, or undertake to, do it for pay.

Whether Captain Vere, as the surgeon professionally and privately surmised, was really the sudden victim of any degree of aberration, every one must determine for himself by such light as this narrative may afford.

That the unhappy event which has been narrated could not have happened at a worse juncture was but too true. For it was close on the heel of the suppressed insurrections, an aftertime very critical to naval authority, demanding from every English sea commander two qualities not readily interfusable—prudence and rigor. Moreover, there was something crucial in the case.

In the jugglery of circumstances preceding and attending the event on board the *Bellipotent*, and in the light of that martial code whereby it was formally to be judged, innocence and guilt personified in Claggart and Budd in effect changed places. In a legal view the apparent victim of the tragedy was he who had sought to victimize a man blameless; and the indisputable deed of the latter, navally regarded, constituted the most heinous of military crimes. Yet more. The essential right and wrong involved in the matter, the clearer that might be, so much the worse for the responsibility of a loyal sea commander, inasmuch as he was not authorized to determine the matter on that primitive basis.

Small wonder then that the *Bellipotent's* captain, though in general a man of rapid decision, felt that circumspectness not less than promptitude was necessary. Until he could decide upon his course, and in each detail; and not only so, but until the concluding measure was upon the point of being enacted, he deemed it advisable, in view of all the circumstances, to guard as much as possible against publicity. Here he may or may not have erred. Certain it is, however, that subsequently in the confidential talk of more than one or two gun rooms and cabins he was not a little criticized by some officers, a fact imputed by his friends and vehemently by his cousin Jack Denton to professional jealousy of Starry Vere. Some imaginative ground for invidious comment there was. The maintenance of secrecy in the matter, the confining all knowledge of it for a time to the place where the homicide occurred, the quarterdeck cabin; in these particulars lurked some resemblance to the policy adopted in those tragedies of the palace which have occurred more than once in the capital founded by Peter the Barbarian.

The case indeed was such that fain would the *Bellipotent's* captain have deferred taking any action whatever respecting it further than to keep the foretopman a close prisoner till the ship rejoined the squadron and then submitting the matter to the judgment of his admiral.

But a true military officer is in one particular like a true monk. Not with more of self-abnegation will the latter keep his vows of monastic obedience than the former his vows of allegiance to martial duty.

Feeling that unless quick action was taken on it, the deed of the foretopman, so soon as it should be known on the gun decks, would tend to awaken any slumbering embers of the Nore among the crew, a sense of the urgency of the case overruled in Captain Vere every other consideration. But though a conscientious disciplinarian, he was no lover of authority for mere authority's sake. Very far was he from embracing opportunities for monopolizing to himself the perils of moral responsibility, none at least that could properly be referred to an official superior or shared with him by his official equals or even subordinates. So thinking, he was glad it would not be at variance with usage to turn the matter over to a summary court of his own officers, reserving to himself, as the one on whom the ultimate accountability would rest, the right of maintaining a supervision of it, or formally or informally interposing at need. Accordingly a drumhead court was summarily convened, he electing the individuals composing it: the first lieutenant, the captain of marines, and the sailing master.

In associating an officer of marines with the sea lieutenant and the sailing master in a case having to do with a sailor, the commander perhaps deviated from general custom. He was prompted thereto by the circumstance that he took that soldier to be a judicious person, thoughtful, and not altogether incapable of grappling with a difficult case unprecedented in his prior experience. Yet even as to him he was not without some latent misgiving, for withal he was an extremely good-natured man, an enjoyer of his dinner, a sound sleeper, and inclined to obesity—a man who though he would always maintain his manhood in battle might not prove altogether reliable in a moral dilemma involving aught of the tragic. As to the first lieutenant and the sailing master, Captain Vere could not but be aware that though honest natures, of approved gallantry upon occasion, their intelligence was mostly confined to the matter of active seamanship and the fighting demands of their profession.

The court was held in the same cabin where the unfortunate affair had taken place. This cabin, the commander's, embraced the entire area under the poop deck. Aft, and on either side, was a small stateroom, the one now temporarily a jail and the other a deadhouse, and a yet smaller compartment, leaving a space between expanding forward into a goodly oblong of length coinciding with the ship's beam. A skylight of moderate dimension was overhead, and at each end of the oblong space were two sashed porthole windows easily convertible back into embrasures for short carronades.

All being quickly in readiness, Billy Budd was arraigned, Captain Vere necessarily appearing as the sole witness in the case, and as such temporarily sinking his rank, though singularly maintaining it in a matter apparently trivial, namely, that he testified from the ship's weather side, with that object having caused the court to sit on the lee side. Concisely he narrated all that had led up to the catastrophe, omitting nothing in Claggart's accusation and deposing as to the manner in which the prisoner had received it. At this testimony the three officers glanced with no little surprise at Billy Budd, the last man they would have suspected either of the mutinous design alleged by Claggart or the undeniable deed he himself had done. The first lieutenant, taking judicial primary and turning toward the prisoner, said, "Captain Vere has spoken. Is it or is it not as Captain Vere says?"

In response came syllables not so much impeded in the utterance as might have been anticipated. They were these: "Captain Vere tells the truth. It is just as Captain Vere says, but it is not as the master-at-arms said. I have eaten the King's bread and I am true to the King."

"I believe you, my man," said the witness, his voice indicating a suppressed emotion not otherwise betrayed.

"God will bless you for that, your honor!" not without stammering said Billy, and all but broke down. But immediately he was recalled to self-control by another question, to which with the same emotional difficulty of utterance he said, "No, there was no malice between us. I never bore malice against the master-at-arms. I am sorry that he is dead. I did not mean to kill him. Could I have used my tongue I would not have struck him. But he foully lied to my face and in presence of my captain, and I had to say something, and I could only say it with a blow, God help me!"

In the impulsive aboveboard manner of the frank one the court saw confirmed all that was implied in words that just previously had perplexed them, coming as they did from the testifier to the tragedy and promptly following Billy's impassioned disclaimer of mutinous intent—Captain Vere's words, "I believe you, my man."

Next it was asked of him whether he knew of or suspected aught savoring of incipient trouble (meaning mutiny, though the explicit term was avoided) going on in any section of the ship's company.

The reply lingered. This was naturally imputed by the court to the same vocal embarrassment which had retarded or obstructed previous answers. But in main it was otherwise here, the question immediately recalling to Billy's mind the interview with the afterguardsman in the forechains. But an innate repugnance to playing a part at all approaching that of an informer against one's own shipmates—the same erring sense of uninstructed honor which had stood in the way of his reporting the matter at the time, though as a loyal man-of-war's man it was incumbent on him, and failure so to do, if charged against him and proven, would have subjected him to the heaviest of penalties; this, with the blind feeling now his that nothing really was being hatched, prevailed with him. When the answer came it was a negative.

"One question more," said the officer of marines, now first speaking and with a troubled earnestness. "You tell us that what the master-at-arms said against you was a lie. Now why should he have so lied, so maliciously lied, since you declare there was no malice between you?"

At that question, unintentionally touching on a spiritual sphere wholly obscure to Billy's thoughts, he was nonplussed, evincing a confusion indeed that some observers, such as can readily be imagined, would have construed into involuntary evidence of hidden guilt. Nevertheless, he strove some way to answer, but all at once relinquished the vain endeavor, at the same time turning an appealing glance towards Captain Vere as deeming him his best helper and friend. Captain Vere, who had been seated for a time, rose to his feet, addressing the interrogator. "The question you put to him comes naturally enough. But how can he rightly answer it?— or anybody else, unless indeed it be he who lies within there," designating the compartment where lay the corpse. "But the prone one there will not rise to our summons. In effect, though, as it seems to me, the point you make is hardly material. Quite aside from any conceivable motive actuating the master-at-arms, and irrespective of the provocation to the blow, a martial court must needs in the present case confine its attention to the blow's consequence, which consequence justly is to be deemed not otherwise than as the striker's deed."

This utterance, the full significance of which it was not at all likely that Billy took in, nevertheless caused him to turn a wistful interrogative look toward the speaker, a look in its dumb expressiveness not unlike that which a dog of generous breed might turn upon his master, seeking in his face some elucidation of a previous gesture ambiguous to the canine intelligence. Nor was the same utterance without marked effect upon the three officers, more especially the soldier. Couched in it seemed to them a meaning unanticipated, involving a prejudgment on the speaker's part. It served to augment a mental disturbance previously evident enough.

The soldier once more spoke, in a tone of suggestive dubiety addressing at once his associates and Captain Vere: "Nobody is present—none of the ship's company, I mean—who might shed lateral light, if any is to be had, upon what remains mysterious in this matter."

"That is thoughtfully put," said Captain Vere; "I see your drift. Ay, there is a mystery; but, to use a scriptural phrase, it is a 'mystery of iniquity,' a matter for psychologic theologians to discuss. But what has a military court to do with it? Not to add that for us any possible investigation of it is cut off by the lasting tongue-tie of—him—in yonder," again designating the mortuary stateroom. "The prisoner's deed—with that alone we have to do."

To this, and particularly the closing reiteration, the marine soldier, knowing not how aptly to reply, sadly abstained from saying aught. The first lieutenant, who at the outset had not unnaturally assumed primacy in the court, now overrulingly instructed by a glance from Captain Vere, a glance more effective than words, resumed that primacy. Turning to the prisoner, "Budd," he said, and scarce in equable tones, "Budd, if you have aught further to say for yourself, say it now."

Upon this the young sailor turned another quick glance toward Captain Vere; then, as taking a hint from that aspect, a hint confirming his own instinct that silence was now best, replied to the lieutenant, "I have said all, sir."

The marine—the same who had been the sentinel without the cabin door at the time that the foretopman, followed by the master-at-arms, entered it—he, standing by the sailor throughout these judicial proceedings, was now directed to take him back to the after compartment originally assigned to the prisoner and his custodian. As the twain disappeared from view, the three officers, as partially liberated from some inward constraint associated with Billy's mere presence, simultaneously stirred in their seats. They exchanged looks of troubled indecision, yet feeling that decide they must and without long delay. For Captain Vere, he for the time stood—unconsciously with his back toward them, apparently in one of his absent fits—gazing out from a sashed porthole to windward upon the monotonous blank of the twilight sea. But the court's silence continuing, broken only at moments by brief consultations, in low earnest tones, this served to arouse him and energize him. Turning, he to-and-fro paced the cabin athwart; in the returning ascent to windward climbing the slant deck in the ship's lee roll, without knowing it symbolizing thus in his action a mind resolute to surmount difficulties even if against primitive instincts strong as the wind and the sea. Presently he came to a stand before the three. After scanning their faces he stood less as mustering his thoughts for expression than as one inly deliberating how best to put them to well-meaning men not intellectually mature, men with whom it was necessary to demonstrate certain principles that were axioms to himself. Similar impatience as to talking is perhaps one reason that deters some minds from addressing any popular assemblies.

When speak he did, something, both in the substance of what he said and his manner of saying it, showed the influence of unshared studies modifying and tempering the practical training of an active career. This, along with his phraseology, now and then was suggestive of the grounds whereon rested that imputation of a certain pedantry socially alleged against him by certain naval men of wholly practical cast, captains who nevertheless would frankly concede that His Majesty's navy mustered no more efficient officer of their grade than Starry Vere.

What he said was to this effect: "Hitherto I have been but the witness, little more; and I should hardly think now to take another tone, that of your coadjutor for the time, did I not perceive in you— at the crisis too—a troubled hesitancy, proceeding, I doubt not, from the clash of military duty with moral scruple—scruple vitalized by compassion. For the compassion, how can I otherwise than share it? But, mindful of paramount obligations, I strive against scruples that may tend to enervate decision. Not, gentlemen, that I hide from myself that the case is an exceptional one. Speculatively regarded, it well might be referred to a jury of casuists. But for us here, acting not as casuists or moralists, it is a case practical, and under martial law practically to be dealt with.

"But your scruples: do they move as in a dusk? Challenge them. Make them advance and declare themselves. Come now; do they import something like this: If, mindless of palliating circumstances, we are bound to regard the death of the master-at-arms as the prisoner's deed, then does that deed constitute a capital crime whereof the penalty is a mortal one. But in natural justice is nothing but the prisoner's overt act to be considered? How can we adjudge to summary and shameful death a fellow creature innocent before God, and whom we feel to be so?—Does that state it aright? You sign sad assent. Well, I too feel that, the full force of that. It is Nature. But do these buttons that we wear attest that our allegiance is to Nature? No, to the King. Though the ocean, which is inviolate Nature primeval, though this be the element where we move and have our being as sailors, yet as the King's officers lies our duty in a sphere correspondingly natural?[8] So little is that true, that in receiving our commissions we in the most important regards ceased to be natural free agents. When war is declared are we the commissioned fighters previously consulted? We fight at command. If our judgments approve the war, that is but coincidence. So in other particulars. So now. For suppose condemnation to follow these present proceedings. Would it be so much we ourselves that would condemn as it would be martial law operating through us? For that law and the rigor of it, we are not responsible. Our vowed responsibility is in this: That however pitilessly that law may operate in any instances, we nevertheless adhere to it and administer it.

"But the exceptional in the matter moves the hearts within you.

8. In the Lord "we live, and move, and have our being" (Acts 17.28).

Even so too is mine moved. But let not warm hearts betray heads that should be cool. Ashore in a criminal case, will an upright judge allow himself off the bench to be waylaid by some tender kinswoman of the accused seeking to touch him with her tearful plea? Well, the heart here, sometimes the feminine in man, is as that piteous woman, and hard though it be, she must here be ruled out."

He paused, earnestly studying them for a moment; then resumed.

"But something in your aspect seems to urge that it is not solely the heart that moves in you, but also the conscience, the private conscience. But tell me whether or not, occupying the position we do, private conscience should not yield to that imperial one formulated in the code under which alone we officially proceed?"

Here the three men moved in their seats, less convinced than agitated by the course of an argument troubling but the more the spontaneous conflict within.

Perceiving which, the speaker paused for a moment; then abruptly changing his tone, went on.

"To steady us a bit, let us recur to the facts.—In wartime at sea a man-of-war's man strikes his superior in grade, and the blow kills. Apart from its effect the blow itself is, according to the Articles of War, a capital crime. Furthermore——"

"Ay, sir," emotionally broke in the officer of marines, "in one sense it was. But surely Budd purposed neither mutiny nor homicide."

"Surely not, my good man. And before a court less arbitrary and more merciful than a martial one, that plea would largely extenuate. At the Last Assizes[9] it shall acquit. But how here? We proceed under the law of the Mutiny Act. In feature no child can resemble his father more than that Act resembles in spirit the thing from which it derives—War. In His Majesty's service—in this ship, indeed— there are Englishmen forced to fight for the King against their will. Against their conscience, for aught we know. Though as their fellow creatures some of us may appreciate their position, yet as navy officers what reck we of it? Still less recks the enemy. Our impressed men he would fain cut down in the same swath with our volunteers. As regards the enemy's naval conscripts, some of whom may even share our own abhorrence of the regicidal French Directory, it is the same on our side. War looks but to the frontage, the appearance. And the Mutiny Act, War's child, takes after the father. Budd's intent or non-intent is nothing to the purpose.

"But while, put to it by those anxieties in you which I cannot but respect, I only repeat myself—while thus strangely we prolong proceedings that should be summary—the enemy may be sighted and

9. The Last Judgment.

an engagement result. We must do; and one of two things must we do—condemn or let go."

"Can we not convict and yet mitigate the penalty?" asked the sailing master, here speaking, and falteringly, for the first.

"Gentlemen, were that clearly lawful for us under the circumstances, consider the consequences of such clemency. The people" (meaning the ship's company) "have native sense; most of them are familiar with our naval usage and tradition; and how would they take it? Even could you explain to them—which our official position forbids—they, long molded by arbitrary discipline, have not that kind of intelligent responsiveness that might qualify them to comprehend and discriminate. No, to the people the foretopman's deed, however it be worded in the announcement, will be plain homicide committed in a flagrant act of mutiny. What penalty for that should follow, they know. But it does not follow. *Why?* they will ruminate. You know what sailors are. Will they not revert to the recent outbreak at the Nore? Ay. They know the well-founded alarm—the panic it struck throughout England. Your clement sentence they would account pusillanimous. They would think that we flinch, that we are afraid of them—afraid of practicing a lawful rigor singularly demanded at this juncture, lest it should provoke new troubles. What shame to us such a conjecture on their part, and how deadly to discipline. You see then, whither, prompted by duty and the law, I steadfastly drive. But I beseech you, my friends, do not take me amiss. I feel as you do for this unfortunate boy. But did he know our hearts, I take him to be of that generous nature that he would feel even for us on whom in this military necessity so heavy a compulsion is laid."

With that, crossing the deck he resumed his place by the sashed porthole, tacitly leaving the three to come to a decision. On the cabin's opposite side the troubled court sat silent. Loyal lieges, plain and practical, though at bottom they dissented from some points Captain Vere had put to them, they were without the faculty, hardly had the inclination, to gainsay one whom they felt to be an earnest man, one too not less their superior in mind than in naval rank. But it is not improbable that even such of his words as were not without influence over them, less came home to them than his closing appeal to their instinct as sea officers: in the forethought he threw out as to the practical consequences to discipline, considering the unconfirmed tone of the fleet at the time, should a man-of-war's man's violent killing at sea of a superior in grade be allowed to pass for aught else than a capital crime demanding prompt infliction of the penalty.

Not unlikely they were brought to something more or less akin to that harassed frame of mind which in the year 1842 actuated the commander of the U.S. brig-of-war *Somers* to resolve, under the so-called Articles of War, Articles modeled upon the English Mutiny Act, to resolve upon the execution at sea of a midshipman and two sailors as mutineers designing the seizure of the brig. Which resolution was carried out though in a time of peace and within not many days' sail of home. An act vindicated by a naval court of inquiry subsequently convened ashore. History, and here cited without comment. True, the circumstances on board the *Somers* were different from those on board the *Bellipotent*. But the urgency felt, well-warranted or otherwise, was much the same.

Says a writer whom few know,[1] "Forty years after a battle it is easy for a noncombatant to reason about how it ought to have been fought. It is another thing personally and under fire to have to direct the fighting while involved in the obscuring smoke of it. Much so with respect to other emergencies involving considerations both practical and moral, and when it is imperative promptly to act. The greater the fog the more it imperils the steamer, and speed is put on though at the hazard of running somebody down. Little ween the snug card players in the cabin of the responsibilities of the sleepless man on the bridge."

In brief, Billy Budd was formally convicted and sentenced to be hung at the yardarm in the early morning watch, it being now night. Otherwise, as is customary in such cases, the sentence would forthwith have been carried out. In wartime on the field or in the fleet, a mortal punishment decreed by a drumhead court—on the field sometimes decreed by but a nod from the general—follows without delay on the heel of conviction, without appeal.

## 22

It was Captain Vere himself who of his own motion communicated the finding of the court to the prisoner, for that purpose going to the compartment where he was in custody and bidding the marine there to withdraw for the time.

Beyond the communication of the sentence, what took place at this interview was never known. But in view of the character of the twain briefly closeted in that stateroom, each radically sharing in the rarer qualities of our nature—so rare indeed as to be all but incredible to average minds however much cultivated—some conjectures may be ventured.

It would have been in consonance with the spirit of Captain Vere should he on this occasion have concealed nothing from the condemned one—should he indeed have frankly disclosed to him the

---

1. Melville himself.

part he himself had played in bringing about the decision, at the same time revealing his actuating motives. On Billy's side it is not improbable that such a confession would have been received in much the same spirit that prompted it. Not without a sort of joy, indeed, he might have appreciated the brave opinion of him implied in his captain's making such a confidant of him. Nor, as to the sentence itself, could he have been insensible that it was imparted to him as to one not afraid to die. Even more may have been. Captain Vere in end may have developed the passion sometimes latent under an exterior stoical or indifferent. He was old enough to have been Billy's father. The austere devotee of military duty, letting himself melt back into what remains primeval in our formalized humanity, may in end have caught Billy to his heart, even as Abraham may have caught young Isaac on the brink of resolutely offering him up in obedience to the exacting behest.[2] But there is no telling the sacrament, seldom if in any case revealed to the gadding world, whenever under circumstances at all akin to those here attempted to be set forth two of great Nature's nobler order embrace. There is privacy at the time, inviolable to the survivor; and holy oblivion, the sequel to each diviner magnanimity, providentially covers all at last.

The first to encounter Captain Vere in act of leaving the compartment was the senior lieutenant. The face he beheld, for the moment one expressive of the agony of the strong, was to that officer, though a man of fifty, a startling revelation. That the condemned one suffered less than he who mainly had effected the condemnation was apparently indicated by the former's exclamation in the scene soon perforce to be touched upon.

## 23

Of a series of incidents within a brief term rapidly following each other, the adequate narration may take up a term less brief, especially if explanation or comment here and there seem requisite to the better understanding of such incidents. Between the entrance into the cabin of him who never left it alive, and him who when he did leave it left it as one condemned to die; between this and the closeted interview just given, less than an hour and a half had elapsed. It was an interval long enough, however, to awaken speculations among no few of the ship's company as to what it was that

---

2. Genesis 22.1–18. Hayford and Sealts note the role of the father as military disciplinarian in *Redburn*, Chapter 14: the young sailor "had heard that some sea-captains are fathers to their crew; and so they are; but such fathers as Solomon's precepts tend to make— severe and chastising fathers, fathers whose sense of duty overcomes the sense of love." Note that in all three of Melville's short novels the "fathers" cannot save their "sons" from death. The Lawyer cannot reclaim Bartleby; Captain Delano cannot save Benito Cereno; and Captain Vere cannot acquit Billy Budd.

could be detaining in the cabin the master-at-arms and the sailor; for a rumor that both of them had been seen to enter it and neither of them had been seen to emerge, this rumor had got abroad upon the gun decks and in the tops, the people of a great warship being in one respect like villagers, taking microscopic note of every outward movement or non-movement going on. When therefore, in weather not at all temptestuous, all hands were called in the second dog-watch, a summons under such circumstances not usual in those hours, the crew were not wholly unprepared for some announcement extraordinary, one having connection too with the continued absence of the two men from their wonted haunts.

There was a moderate sea at the time; and the moon, newly risen and near to being at its full, silvered the white spar deck wherever not blotted by the clear-cut shadows horizontally thrown of fixtures and moving men. On either side the quarterdeck the marine guard under arms was drawn up; and Captain Vere, standing in his place surrounded by all the wardroom officers, addressed his men. In so doing, his manner showed neither more nor less than that properly pertaining to his supreme position aboard his own ship. In clear terms and concise he told them what had taken place in the cabin: that the master-at-arms was dead, that he who had killed him had been already tried by a summary court and condemned to death, and that the execution would take place in the early morning watch. The word *mutiny* was not named in what he said. He refrained too from making the occasion an opportunity for any preachment as to the maintenance of discipline, thinking perhaps that under existing circumstances in the navy the consequence of violating discipline should be made to speak for itself.

Their captain's announcement was listened to by the throng of standing sailors in a dumbness like that of a seated congregation of believers in hell listening to the clergyman's announcement of his Calvinistic text.

At the close, however, a confused murmur went up. It began to wax. All but instantly, then, at a sign, it was pierced and suppressed by shrill whistles of the boatswain and his mates. The word was given to about ship.

To be prepared for burial Claggart's body was delivered to certain petty officers of his mess. And here, not to clog the sequel with lateral matters, it may be added that at a suitable hour, the master-at-arms was committed to the sea with every funeral honor properly belonging to his naval grade.

In this proceeding as in every public one growing out of the tragedy strict adherence to usage was observed. Nor in any point could it have been at all deviated from, either with respect to Claggart or Billy Budd, without begetting undesirable speculations in the ship's company, sailors, and more particularly men-of-war's men, being of all men the greatest sticklers for usage. For similar cause, all communication between Captain Vere and the condemned one ended with the closeted interview already given, the latter being now surrendered to the ordinary routine preliminary to the end. His transfer under guard from the captain's quarters was effected without unusual precautions—at least no visible ones. If possible, not to let the men so much as surmise that their officers anticipate aught amiss from them is the tacit rule in a military ship. And the more that some sort of trouble should really be apprehended, the more do the officers keep that apprehension to themselves, though not the less unostentatious vigilance may be augmented. In the present instance, the sentry placed over the prisoner had strict orders to let no one have communication with him but the chaplain. And certain unobtrusive measures were taken absolutely to insure this point.

## 24

In a seventy-four of the old order the deck known as the upper gun deck was the one covered over by the spar deck, which last, though not without its armament, was for the most part exposed to the weather. In general it was at all hours free from hammocks; those of the crew swinging on the lower gun deck and berth deck, the latter being not only a dormitory but also the place for the stowing of the sailors' bags, and on both sides lined with the large chests or movable pantries of the many messes of the men.

On the starboard side of the *Bellipotent's* upper gun deck, behold Billy Budd under sentry lying prone in irons in one of the bays formed by the regular spacing of the guns comprising the batteries on either side. All these pieces were of the heavier caliber of that period. Mounted on lumbering wooden carriages, they were hampered with cumbersome harness of breeching and strong side-tackles for running them out. Guns and carriages, together with the long rammers and shorter linstocks lodged in loops overhead—all these, as customary, were painted black; and the heavy hempen breechings, tarred to the same tint, wore the like livery of the undertakers. In contrast with the funereal hue of these surroundings, the prone sailor's exterior apparel, white jumper and white duck trousers, each more or less soiled, dimly glimmered in the obscure light of the bay like a patch of discolored snow in early April lingering at some upland cave's black mouth. In effect he is already in his shroud, or the garments that shall serve him in lieu of one. Over him but scarce illuminating him, two battle lanterns swing from two massive beams of the deck above. Fed with the oil supplied by the war contractors (whose gains, honest or otherwise, are in every land an anticipated portion of the harvest of death), with flickering splashes of dirty yellow light they pollute the pale moonshine all but ineffectually struggling in obstructed flecks through the open ports from which the tampioned cannon protrude. Other lanterns at intervals serve but to bring out somewhat the obscurer bays which, like small confessionals or side-chapels in a cathedral, branch from the long dim-vistaed broad aisle between the two batteries of that covered tier.

Such was the deck where now lay the Handsome Sailor. Through the rose-tan of his complexion no pallor could have shown. It would have taken days of sequestration from the winds and the sun to have brought about the effacement of that. But the skeleton in the cheekbone at the point of its angle was just beginning delicately to be defined under the warm-tinted skin. In fervid hearts self-contained, some brief experiences devour our human tissue as secret fire in a ship's hold consumes cotton in the bale.

But now lying between the two guns, as nipped in the vice of fate, Billy's agony, mainly proceeding from a generous young heart's virgin experience of the diabolical incarnate and effective in some men—the tension of that agony was over now. It survived not the something healing in the closeted interview with Captain Vere. Without movement, he lay as in a trance, that adolescent expression previously noted as his taking on something akin to the look of a slumbering child in the cradle when the warm hearth-glow of the still chamber at night plays on the dimples that at whiles mysteriously form in the cheek silently coming and going there. For now and then in the gyved[3] one's trance a serene happy light born of some wandering reminiscence or dream would diffuse itself over his face, and then wane away only anew to return.

The chaplain, coming to see him and finding him thus, and perceiving no sign that he was conscious of his presence, attentively regarded him for a space, then slipping aside, withdrew for the time, peradventure feeling that even he, the minister of Christ though receiving his stipend from Mars, had no consolation to proffer which could result in a peace transcending that which he beheld. But in the small hours he came again. And the prisoner, now awake to his surroundings, noticed his approach, and civilly, all but cheerfully, welcomed him. But it was to little purpose that in the interview following, the good man sought to bring Billy Budd to some godly understanding that he must die, and at dawn. True, Billy himself freely referred to his death as a thing close at hand; but it was something in the way that children will refer to death in general,

---

3. Shackled or chained.

who yet among their other sports will play a funeral with hearse and mourners.

Not that like children Billy was incapable of conceiving what death really is. No, but he was wholly without irrational fear of it, a fear more prevalent in highly civilized communities than those so-called barbarous ones which in all respects stand nearer to unadulterate Nature. And, as elsewhere said, a barbarian Billy radically was—as much so, for all the costume, as his countrymen the British captives, living trophies, made to march in the Roman triumph of Germanicus. Quite as much so as those later barbarians, young men probably, and picked specimens among the earlier British converts to Christianity, at least nominally such, taken to Rome (as today converts from lesser isles of the sea may be taken to London), of whom the Pope of that time, admiring the strangeness of their personal beauty so unlike the Italian stamp, their clear ruddy complexion and curled flaxen locks, exclaimed, "Angles" (meaning *English*, the modern derivative), "Angles, do you call them? And is it because they look so like angels?" Had it been later in time, one would think that the Pope had in mind Fra Angelico's seraphs, some of whom, plucking apples in gardens of the Hesperides, have the faint rosebud complexion of the more beautiful English girls.

If in vain the good chaplain sought to impress the young barbarian with ideas of death akin to those conveyed in the skull, dial, and crossbones on old tombstones, equally futile to all appearance were his efforts to bring home to him the thought of salvation and a Savior. Billy listened, but less out of awe or reverence, perhaps, than from a certain natural politeness, doubtless at bottom regarding all that in much the same way that most mariners of his class take any discourse abstract or out of the common tone of the workaday world. And this sailor way of taking clerical discourse is not wholly unlike the way in which the primer of Christianity, full of transcendent miracles, was received long ago on tropic isles by any superior *savage*, so called—a Tahitian, say, of Captain Cook's time or shortly after that time. Out of natural courtesy he received, but did not appropriate. It was like a gift placed in the palm of an outreached hand upon which the fingers do not close.

But the *Bellipotent*'s chaplain was a discreet man possessing the good sense of a good heart. So he insisted not in his vocation here. At the instance of Captain Vere, a lieutenant had apprised him of pretty much everything as to Billy; and since he felt that innocence was even a better thing than religion wherewith to go to Judgment, he reluctantly withdrew; but in his emotion not without first performing an act strange enough in an Englishman, and under the circumstances yet more so in any regular priest. Stooping over, he kissed on the fair cheek his fellow man, a felon in martial law, one whom though on the confines of death he felt he could never convert to a dogma; nor for all that did he fear for his future.

Marvel not that having been made acquainted with the young sailor's essential innocence the worthy man lifted not a finger to avert the doom of such a martyr to martial discipline. So to do would not only have been as idle as invoking the desert, but would also have been an audacious transgression of the bounds of his function, one as exactly prescribed to him by military law as that of the boatswain or any other naval officer. Bluntly put, a chaplain is the minister of the Prince of Peace serving in the host of the God of War—Mars. As such, he is as incongruous as a musket would be on the altar at Christmas. Why, then, is he there? Because he indirectly subserves the purpose attested by the cannon; because too he lends the sanction of the religion of the meek to that which practically is the abrogation of everything but brute Force.

## 25

The night so luminous on the spar deck, but otherwise on the cavernous ones below, levels so like the tiered galleries in a coal mine—the luminous night passed away. But like the prophet in the chariot disappearing in heaven and dropping his mantle to Elisha,[4] the withdrawing night transferred its pale robe to the breaking day. A meek, shy light appeared in the East, where stretched a diaphanous fleece of white furrowed vapor. That light slowly waxed. Suddenly *eight bells* was struck aft, responded to by one louder metallic stroke from forward. It was four o'clock in the morning. Instantly the silver whistles were heard summoning all hands to witness punishment. Up through the great hatchways rimmed with racks of heavy shot the watch below came pouring, overspreading with the watch already on deck the space between the mainmast and foremast including that occupied by the capacious launch and the black booms tiered on either side of it, boat and booms making a summit of observation for the powder-boys and younger tars. A different group comprising one watch of topmen leaned over the rail of the sea balcony, no small one in a seventy-four, looking down on the crowd below. Man or boy, none spake but in whisper, and few spake at all. Captain Vere—as before, the central figure among the assembled commissioned officers—stood nigh the break of the poop deck facing forward. Just below him on the quarter-deck the marines in full equipment were drawn up much as the scene of the promulgated sentence.

At sea in the old time, the execution by halter of a military sailor

4. 2 Kings 2.9–15.

was generally from the foreyard. In the present instance, for special reasons the mainyard was assigned.[5] Under an arm of that yard the prisoner was presently brought up, the chaplain attending him. It was noted at the time, and remarked upon afterwards, that in this final scene the good man evinced little or nothing of the perfunctory. Brief speech indeed he had with the condemned one, but the genuine Gospel was less on his tongue than in his aspect and manner towards him. The final preparations personal to the latter being speedily brought to an end by two boatswain's mates, the consummation impended. Billy stood facing aft. At the penultimate moment, his words, his only ones, words wholly unobstructed in the utterance, were these: "God bless Captain Vere!"[6] Syllables so unanticipated coming from one with the ignominious hemp about his neck—a conventional felon's benediction directed aft towards the quarters of honor; syllables too delivered in the clear melody of a singing bird on the point of launching from the twig—had a phenomenal effect, not unenhanced by the rare personal beauty of the young sailor, spiritualized now through late experiences so poignantly profound.

Without volition, as it were, as if indeed the ship's populace were but the vehicles of some vocal current electric, with one voice from alow and aloft came a resonant sympathetic echo: "God bless Captain Vere!" And yet at that instant Billy alone must have been in their hearts, even as in their eyes.

At the pronounced words and the spontaneous echo that voluminously rebounded them, Captain Vere, either through stoic self-control or a sort of momentary paralysis induced by emotional shock, stood erectly rigid as a musket in the ship-armorer's rack.

The hull, deliberately recovering from the periodic roll to leeward, was just regaining an even keel when the last signal, a preconcerted dumb one, was given. At the same moment it chanced that the vapory fleece hanging low in the East was shot through with a soft glory as of the fleece of the Lamb of God seen in mystical vision,[7] and simultaneously therewith, watched by the wedged mass of upturned faces, Billy ascended; and, ascending, took the full rose of the dawn.

---

5. Hayford and Sealts note the "symbolic significance of the cruciform structure of the mainmast and mainyard."
6. The most famous single sentence of the work, variously interpreted as Christian resignation or cruel irony. One critic questions, "Is this not piercing?—as innocent Billy utters these words, does not the reader gag?" Hayford and Sealts explore the story's origin in the case of Elisha Small (1842), who cried out, just as he was hanged, "God bless that flag!," "the traditional ritual of the condemned man forgiving the official who is duty bound to order his death." See Newton Arvin's essay on p. 401 herein. Melville indicates that it is "a conventional felon's benediction directed aft towards the quarters of honor." Billy, the stutterer, speaks "words wholly unobstructed in the utterance."
7. See Revelation 1.14.

In the pinioned figure arrived at the yard-end, to the wonder of all no motion was apparent, none save that created by the slow roll of the hull in moderate weather, so majestic in a great ship ponderously cannoned.

## 26[8]

When some days afterwards, in reference to the singularity just mentioned, the purser, a rather ruddy, rotund person more accurate as an accountant than profound as a philosopher, said at mess to the surgeon, "What testimony to the force lodged in will power," the latter, saturnine, spare, and tall, one in whom a discreet causticity went along with a manner less genial than polite, replied, "Your pardon, Mr. Purser. In a hanging scientifically conducted—and under special orders I myself directed how Budd's was to be effected—any movement following the completed suspension and originating in the body suspended, such movement indicates mechanical spasm in the muscular system.[9] Hence the absence of that is no more attributable to will power, as you call it, than to horsepower—begging your pardon."

"But this muscular spasm you speak of, is not that in a degree more or less invariable in these cases?"

"Assuredly so, Mr. Purser."

"How then, my good sir, do you account for its absence in this instance?"

"Mr. Purser, it is clear that your sense of the singularity in this matter equals not mine. You account for it by what you call will power—a term not yet included in the lexicon of science. For me, I do not, with my present knowledge, pretend to account for it at all. Even should we assume the hypothesis that at the first touch of the halyards the action of Budd's heart, intensified by extraordinary emotion at its climax, abruptly stopped—much like a watch when in carelessly winding it up you strain at the finish, thus snapping the chain—even under that hypothesis how account for the phenomenon that followed?"

"You admit, then, that the absence of spasmodic movement was phenomenal."

"It was phenomenal, Mr. Purser, in the sense that it was an appearance the cause of which is not immediately to be assigned."

"But tell me, my dear sir," pertinaciously continued the other,

---

8. In Melville's draft the chapter has a title: "A Digression."
9. If death occurs because the spinal cord is snapped, rather than by asphyxiation, various parts of the hanged man may twitch and jump in "a dance of death." Many critics believe Melville means Billy did not ejaculate.

"was the man's death effected by the halter, or was it a species of euthanasia?"[1]

"*Euthanasia*, Mr. Purser, is something like your *will power:* I doubt its authenticity as a scientific term—begging your pardon again. It is at once imaginative and metaphysical—in short, Greek.—But," abruptly changing his tone, "there is a case in the sick bay that I do not care to leave to my assistants. Beg your pardon, but excuse me." And rising from the mess he formally withdrew.

## 27

The silence at the moment of execution and for a moment or two continuing thereafter, a silence but emphasized by the regular wash of the sea against the hull or the flutter of a sail caused by the helmsman's eyes being tempted astray, this emphasized silence was gradually disturbed by a sound not easily to be verbally rendered. Whoever has heard the freshet-wave of a torrent suddenly swelled by pouring showers in tropical mountains, showers not shared by the plain; whoever has heard the first muffled murmur of its sloping advance through precipitous woods may form some conception of the sound now heard. The seeming remoteness of its source was because of its murmurous indistinctness,[2] since it came from close by, even from the men massed on the ship's open deck. Being inarticulate, it was dubious in significance further than it seemed to indicate some capricious revulsion of thought or feeling such as mobs ashore are liable to, in the present instance possibly implying a sullen revocation on the men's part of their involuntary echoing of Billy's benediction. But ere the murmur had time to wax into clamor it was met by a strategic command, the more telling that it came with abrupt unexpectedness: "Pipe down the starboard watch, Boatswain, and see that they go."

Shrill as the shriek of the sea hawk, the silver whistles of the boatswain and his mates pierced that ominous low sound, dissipating it; and yielding to the mechanism of discipline the throng was thinned by one-half. For the remainder, most of them were set to temporary employments connected with trimming the yards and so forth, business readily to be got up to serve occasion by any officer of the deck.

Now each proceeding that follows a mortal sentence pronounced at sea by a drumhead court is characterized by promptitude not per-

---

1. Perhaps two meanings of the word co-exist here: first, the traditional Greek sense of the word, "willful sacrifice of one's self for one's country," and, second, Schopenhauer's sense of it as "an easy death, not ushered in by disease, and free from all pain and struggle."
2. In Chapter 23 of *The Scarlet Letter*, after Arthur Dimmesdale's "final word": "The multitude, silent till then, broke out in a strange, deep voice of awe and wonder, which could not as yet find utterance, save in this murmur that rolled so heavily after the departed spirit."

ceptibly merging into hurry, though bordering that. The hammock, the one which had been Billy's bed when alive, having already been ballasted with shot and otherwise prepared to serve for his canvas coffin, the last offices of the sea undertakers, the sailmaker's mates, were now speedily completed. When everything was in readiness a second call for all hands, made necessary by the strategic movement before mentioned, was sounded, now to witness burial.

The details of this closing formality it needs not to give. But when the tilted plank let slide its freight into the sea, a second strange human murmur was heard, blended now with another inarticulate sound proceeding from certain larger seafowl who, their attention having been attracted by the peculiar commotion in the water resulting from the heavy sloped dive of the shotted hammock into the sea, flew screaming to the spot. So near the hull did they come, that the stridor or bony creak of their gaunt double-jointed pinions was audible. As the ship under light airs passed on, leaving the burial spot astern, they still kept circling it low down with the moving shadow of their outstretched wings and the croaked requiem of their cries.

Upon sailors as superstitious as those of the age preceding ours, men-of-war's men too who had just beheld the prodigy of repose in the form suspended in air, and now foundering in the deeps; to such mariners the action of the seafowl, though dictated by mere animal greed for prey, was big with no prosaic significance. An uncertain movement began among them, in which some encroachment was made. It was tolerated but for a moment. For suddenly the drum beat to quarters, which familiar sound happening at least twice every day, had upon the present occasion a signal peremptoriness in it. True martial discipline long continued superinduces in average man a sort of impulse whose operation at the official word of command much resembles in its promptitude the effect of an instinct.

The drumbeat dissolved the multitude, distributing most of them along the batteries of the two covered gun decks. There, as wonted, the guns' crews stood by their respective cannon erect and silent. In due course the first officer, sword under arm and standing in his place on the quarter-deck, formally received the successive reports of the sworded lieutenants commanding the sections of batteries below; the last of which reports being made, the summed report he delivered with the customary salute to the commander. All this occupied time, which in the present case was the object in beating to quarters at an hour prior to the customary one. That such variance from usage was authorized by an officer like Captain Vere, a martinet as some deemed him, was evidence of the necessity for unusual action implied in what he deemed to be temporarily the mood of his men. "With mankind," he would say, "forms, measured forms, are everything; and that is the import couched in the story of

Orpheus with his lyre spellbinding the wild denizens of the wood."
And this he once applied to the disruption of forms going on across
the Channel and the consequences thereof.

At this unwonted muster at quarters, all proceeded as at the regular hour. The band on the quarter-deck played a sacred air, after
which the chaplain went through the customary morning service.
That done, the drum beat the retreat; and toned by music and religious rites subserving the discipline and purpose of war, the men in
their wonted orderly manner dispersed to the places allotted them
when not at the guns.

And now it was full day. The fleece of low-hanging vapor had vanished, licked up by the sun that late had so glorified it. And the cir-
cumambient air in the clearness of its serenity was like smooth
white marble in the polished block not yet removed from the
marble-dealer's yard.

## 28

The symmetry of form attainable in pure fiction cannot so readily
be achieved in a narration essentially having less to do with fable
than with fact. Truth uncompromisingly told will always have its
ragged edges; hence the conclusion of such a narration is apt to be
less finished than an architectural finial.

How it fared with the Handsome Sailor during the year of the
Great Mutiny has been faithfully given. But though properly the
story ends with his life, something in way of sequel will not be
amiss. Three brief chapters will suffice.

In the general rechristening under the Directory of the craft originally forming the navy of the French monarchy, the St. Louis line-
of-battle ship was named the Athée (the Atheist). Such a name, like
some other substituted ones in the Revolutionary fleet, while proclaiming the infidel audacity of the ruling power, was yet, though
not so intended to be, the aptest name, if one consider it, ever given
to a warship; far more so indeed than the Devastation, the Erebus
(the Hell), and similar names bestowed upon fighting ships.

On the return passage to the English fleet from the detached
cruise during which occurred the events already recorded, the Bellipotent fell in with the Athée. An engagement ensued, during which
Captain Vere, in the act of putting his ship alongside the enemy with
a view of throwing his boarders across her bulwarks, was hit by a
musket ball from a porthole of the enemy's main cabin. More than
disabled, he dropped to the deck and was carried below to the same
cockpit where some of his men already lay. The senior lieutenant took
command. Under him the enemy was finally captured, and though
much crippled was by rare good fortune successfully taken into

Gibraltar, an English port not very distant from the scene of the fight. There, Captain Vere with the rest of the wounded was put ashore. He lingered for some days, but the end came. Unhappily he was cut off too early for the Nile and Trafalgar. The spirit that 'spite its philosophic austerity may yet have indulged in the most secret of all passions, ambition, never attained to the fulness of fame.

Not long before death, while lying under the influence of that magical drug[3] which, soothing the physical frame, mysteriously operates on the subtler element in man, he was heard to murmur words inexplicable to his attendant: "Billy Budd, Billy Budd." That these were not the accents of remorse would seem clear from what the attendant said to the *Bellipotent's* senior officer of marines, who, as the most reluctant to condemn of the members of the drumhead court, too well knew, though here he kept the knowledge to himself, who Billy Budd was.

## 29

Some few weeks after the execution, among other matters under the head of "News from the Mediterranean," there appeared in a naval chronicle of the time, an authorized weekly publication, an account of the affair. It was doubtless for the most part written in good faith, though the medium, partly rumor, through which the facts must have reached the writer served to deflect and in part falsify them. The account was as follows:

"On the tenth of the last month a deplorable occurrence took place on board H.M.S. *Bellipotent.* John Claggart, the ship's master-at-arms, discovering that some sort of plot was incipient among an inferior section of the ship's company, and that the ringleader was one William Budd; he, Claggart, in the act of arraigning the man before the captain, was vindictively stabbed to the heart by the suddenly drawn sheath knife of Budd.

"The deed and the implement employed sufficiently suggest that though mustered into the service under an English name the assassin was no Englishman, but one of those aliens adopting English cognomens whom the present extraordinary necessities of the service have caused to be admitted into it in considerable numbers.

"The enormity of the crime and the extreme depravity of the criminal appear the greater in view of the character of the victim, a middle-aged man respectable and discreet, belonging to that minor official grade, the petty officers, upon whom, as none know better than the commissioned gentlemen, the efficiency of His Majesty's navy so largely depends. His function was a responsible one, at once

---

3. Opium.

onerous and thankless; and his fidelity in it the greater because of his strong patriotic impulse. In this instance as in so many other instances in these days, the character of this unfortunate man signally refutes, if refutation were needed, that peevish saying attributed to the late Dr. Johnson, that patriotism is the last refuge of a scoundrel.

"The criminal paid the penalty of his crime. The promptitude of the punishment has proved salutary. Nothing amiss is now apprehended aboard H.M.S. *Bellipotent*."

The above, appearing in a publication now long ago super-annuated and forgotten, is all that hitherto has stood in human record to attest what manner of men respectively were John Claggart and Billy Budd.

## 30

Everything is for a term venerated in navies. Any tangible object associated with some striking incident of the service is converted into a monument. The spar from which the foretopman was suspended was for some few years kept trace of by the bluejackets. Their knowledges followed it from ship to dockyard and again from dockyard to ship, still pursuing it even when at last reduced to a mere dockyard boom. To them a chip of it was as a piece of the Cross. Ignorant though they were of the secret facts of the tragedy, and not thinking but that the penalty was somehow unavoidably inflicted from the naval point of view, for all that, they instinctively felt that Billy was a sort of man as incapable of mutiny as of wilful murder. They recalled the fresh young image of the Handsome Sailor, that face never deformed by a sneer or subtler vile freak of the heart within. This impression of him was doubtless deepened by the fact that he was gone, and in a measure mysteriously gone. On the gun decks of the *Bellipotent* the general estimate of his nature and its unconscious simplicity eventually found rude utterance from another foretopman, one of his own watch, gifted, as some sailors are, with an artless *poetic* temperament. The tarry hand made some lines which, after circulating among the shipboard crews for a while, finally got rudely printed at Portsmouth as a ballad. The title given to it was the sailor's.

### BILLY IN THE DARBIES[4]

Good of the chaplain to enter Lone Bay
And down on his marrowbones here and pray
For the likes just o' me, Billy Budd.—But, look:
Through the port comes the moonshine astray!

4. Irons or handcuffs.

It tips the guard's cutlass and silvers this nook;
But 'twill die in the dawning of Billy's last day.
A jewel-block they'll make of me tomorrow,
Pendant pearl from the yardarm-end
Like the eardrop I gave to Bristol Molly—
O, 'tis me, not the sentence they'll suspend.
Ay, ay, all is up; and I must up too,
Early in the morning, aloft from alow.
On an empty stomach now never it would do.
They'll give me a nibble—bit o' biscuit ere I go.
Sure, a messmate will reach me the last parting cup;
But, turning heads away from the hoist and the belay,
Heaven knows who will have the running of me up!
No pipe to those halyards.—But aren't it all sham?
A blur's in my eyes; it is dreaming that I am.
A hatchet to my hawser? All adrift to go?
The drum roll to grog, and Billy never know?
But Donald he has promised to stand by the plank;
So I'll shake a friendly hand ere I sink.
But—no! It is dead then I'll be, come to think.
I remember Taff the Welshman when he sank.
And his cheek it was like the budding pink.
But me they'll lash in hammock, drop me deep.
Fathoms down, fathoms down, how I'll dream fast asleep.
I feel it stealing now. Sentry, are you there?
Just ease these darbies at the wrist,
And roll me over fair!
I am sleepy, and the oozy weeds about me twist.

# CONTEXTS

# Bartleby, The Scrivener

## JOHANNES DIETRICH BERGMANN

### "Bartleby" and "The Lawyer's Story"[†]

Hershel Parker has shown that newspaper items describing the Dead Letter Office in Washington were common during the year before *Putnam's Monthly* serialized Herman Melville's "Bartleby, the Scrivener" in November and December, 1853.[1] One or more of these often melancholy speculations about the human estrangement implied by dead letters may have suggested to Melville a way of portraying his narrator's sentimental arrangement of his emotions at the end of his story.[2] I would like to show here that a single newspaper item, appearing in both the New York *Tribune* and the New York *Times* for February 18, 1853, may have suggested to Melville a narrative structure he could use for "Bartleby."

The *Times* and the more widely read *Tribune* each carried a long advertisement headlined *The Lawyer's Story; Or, The Wrongs of the Orphans. By a Member of the Bar.* The advertisement is the complete first chapter of a novel, and the reader is referred to *The Sunday Dispatch* for its continuation. The *Dispatch* carried *The Lawyer's Story*, a chapter every week, until May 29, 1853. Later in the year H. Long & Brother issued the novel as a book, boasting that "No tale has ever been written which has attained greater popularity." In all the editions the author was anonymous, always to preserve the

† Reprinted by permission from *American Literature* 47.4 (November 1975): 432–36. Copyright 1975, Duke University Press. All rights reserved.

1. Hershel Parker, "Dead Letters and Melville's Bartleby," *Resources for American Literary Study*, IV (Spring, 1974), 90–99.
2. The newspaper speculations usually concentrate on the misery of unrelieved separation from loved ones. An illustration from the Albany *Evening Journal* for February 10, 1853: "How many anxious hearts have waited for the kind messages which a misdirection has sent to the dead letter office. . . . How many a warm heart has chilled beneath unexplained neglect, till mutual estrangement took the place of mutual love!" When the *Illustrated News* for March 19, 1853, reprinted the *Evening Journal* item, it remarked upon the Dead Letter Office clerks: "What an insight into character must those individuals obtain who have the examination of the letters!" The *Illustrated News* also reminded its readers that Charles Dickens's *Pickwick Papers* contains a reverie on "dead letters" (Chapter 49). See also, for a late example, "A Day in the Dead Letter Office," Francis Copcutt, *Leaves from a Bachelor's Book of Life* (New York, 1860), pp. 133–199.

effect that a prominent New York lawyer had written the account. In fact, the author was James A. Maitland, an accomplished popular novelist of the period.[3]

Like "Bartleby, the Scrivener," *The Lawyer's Story* is a successful New York lawyer's first-person narration of his interest in and involvement with an unusual, "extra" scrivener. We never learn the name of either Maitland's lawyer or Melville's lawyer: the impression is that we would recognize it were it given. The first sentence of *The Lawyer's Story* makes the general similarity between Maitland's novel and Melville's short story quite clear: "In the summer of 1843, having an extraordinary quantity of deeds to copy, I engaged, temporarily, an extra copying clerk, who interested me considerably, in consequence of his modest, quiet, gentlemanly demeanor, and his intense application to his duties."[4] Melville's lawyer too has had an increase in business, and his new scrivener is "singularly sedate [in] aspect"[5] and copies with "incessant industry." Maitland's lawyer's scrivener, named Adolphus Fitzherbert, uses Bartleby's famous verb (although not in its negative form) later in the first chapter when he begins the answer to a question with "I would prefer." He also has a characteristic which strongly suggests Bartleby: "the young man's countenance was shaded with constitutional or habitual melancholy—I judged the latter." "Habitual" melancholy is more understandable than "constitutional" melancholy because it implies a knowable cause, a beginning and history. But about his past life Adolphus is "reserved," and the lawyer does not at first press him. Bartleby's melancholy is, of course, more than "habitual" (if indeed the terms are applicable at all), but he too "declined telling who he was, or whence he came, or whether he had any relatives in the world."

When, after a few weeks, Maitland's lawyer no longer needs his extra scrivener's services, he lets him go. Adolphus, unlike Bartleby, leaves, but through a series of complicated coincidences the lawyer meets him again, and this time the lawyer actively investigates the mystery. He shares with Melville's lawyer a charitable and confident nature and a belief in the temporariness and ultimate explicability of human misery. His intervention in Adolphus's affairs, quite unlike Melville's lawyer's efforts with Bartleby, promises to succeed.[6] By

---

3. According to Lyle Wright's *American Fiction* (San Marino, Calif., 1965), James A. Maitland's other novels include *The Cabin Boy's Story* (1854), *The Cousins* (1858), *The Old Doctor* (1853), *Sartaroe* (1858), *The Wanderer* (1856), and *The Watchman* (1855).

4. This and all subsequent quotations from the first chapter of *The Lawyer's Story* are from the text as printed in the New York *Tribune* (Feb. 18, 1853), p. 3. The text of the first chapter of the H. Long & Brother book differs sometimes significantly from the *Tribune* text.

5. "Bartleby," in *Piazza Tales*, ed. Egbert S. Oliver (New York, 1948), Quotations are to this edition.

6. The charitable intervention of well-to-do and amiable New York lawyers and bachelors in the affairs of misused young people was a moderately common feature of the popular urban fiction of the period. John Treat Irving's highly successful "The Quod Correspon-

the end of the first chapter (and the newspaper advertisement) the lawyer has hints of the truth, but Adolphus's melancholy has transformed itself into an indifference like Bartleby's. Adolphus has learned of the disappearance of his beloved sister, his only friend or relative, and he is, despite the lawyer's efforts, "so completely paralyzed . . . that he appeared heedless regarding the matter, and careless as to what became of him." Adolphus, like Bartleby in his "long-continued motionlessness," expresses a lack of interest in the life around him and in the future.[7] Even in only the first chapter of *The Lawyer's Story*, however, the reader understands that Adolphus's "paralysis" is a direct consequence of separation from family, first from parents and then from sister. The crisis is a standard one in the popular novel of the period (*Uncle Tom's Cabin* is only the most obvious example), and, like most of those popular novels, *The Lawyer's Story* implicitly promises at any narrative moment that a resolution will come in time and subsequent event. Adolphus's paralysis is the middle of a story, but its beginning and end will be known. Bartleby's motionlessness, however initially similar, is timeless. In his constant repetition of a verb ("prefer") which has meaning only for the exact present, and not the past or the future, Bartleby eludes analysis or resolution.

After the first chapter, the action of *The Lawyer's Story* proceeds through four hundred pages toward an ultimate demonstration of the temporary nature of Adolphus's separation and of the success of the lawyer's intervention. That action has little to do with "Bartleby." Briefly, Maitland's lawyer narrates his discovery that the orphans Adolphus and Georgiana Fitzherbert are, without knowing it, the grandchildren of the Mrs. Fitzherbert who married the Prince of Wales in an illegal Roman Catholic ceremony in 1785.[8] A team of British lawyers has learned of the vast royal lands due the orphans and has enacted a complicated scheme to put impostors in their place. The New York lawyer and narrator methodically uncovers the

---

dence," originally serialized in the *Knickerbocker* between 1841 and 1844 and published separately as *The Attorney* (1842) and *Harry Harson: Or, the Benevolent Bachelor* (1844), is structured on such interventions.

7. The second chapter of *The Lawyer's Story*, which appeared only in *The Sunday Dispatch* and the H. Long & Brother book, contains an excellent example of Adolphus's hopelessness and the lawyer's clichéd temporal optimism. Adolphus announces that "Hope for the future is dead within me," to which the lawyer responds: "I . . . urge you to view the matter differently. You are a young man: brilliant prospects may be before you; happiness may yet await you. Time will blunt the keenest pangs of the grief you now feel on account of your sister's loss; your sister even may yet be restored to you. If not, recollect that others have suffered in a like degree, and if they have temporarily given way to despondency, it has not lasted forever" (New York, 1853), pp. 27–29.

8. See, at least, Anita Leslie, *Mrs. Fitzherbert* (New York, 1960), Shane Leslie, *Mrs. Fitzherbert: A Life Chiefly from Unpublished Sources* (New York, 1939), and W. H. Wilkins, *Mrs. Fitzherbert and George IV* (New York, 1905). Mrs. Fitzherbert's attachment to the Prince of Wales was, of course, the inspiration for many "lost heir" plots during the early nineteenth century.

mysteries and successfully defends Adolphus and Georgiana in an English court. Adolphus is reunited with his sister and with his royal inheritance. As much as all this implies the book that Melville is *not* writing, there seems to me little reason to suppose that Melville saw anything more of *The Lawyer's Story* than the first chapter which appeared in the *Tribune* and the *Times*.

The lawyer and narrator of Melville's "Bartleby" begins his tale by explaining that he could relate "divers histories" of law-copyists "at which good-natured gentlemen might smile and sentimental souls might weep." But he waives these popular biographies for a few "passages" in the life of Bartleby, for whom "no materials exist for a full and satisfactory biography." The lawyer naively thinks that the incompleteness is "an irreparable loss to literature." It seems to me that Melville may have found in the first chapter of *The Lawyer's Story* as it appeared in a newspaper advertisement a popular plot which, rendered "incomplete" in Melville's lawyer's sense, is turned back to its new readers as an intense tale of man without knowledge of beginning or end. *The Lawyer's Story* may have been the "satisfactory biography" of which "Bartleby" is the more important "passage."

# H. BRUCE FRANKLIN

## Bartleby: The Ascetic's Advent†

There are essentially three ethics available to man—action in and of the world, action in the world for other-worldly reasons, and non-action, that is, withdrawal from the world. We might call the extreme of the first the ethic of Wall Street, the extreme of the second the ethic of Christ, and the extreme of the third the ethic of the Eastern monk. Wall Street's ethic seeks the world as an end; Christ's ethic prescribes certain behavior in this world to get to a better world; the Eastern monk's ethic seeks to escape all worlds. *Bartleby* is a world in which these three ethics directly confront one another.

To read *Bartleby* well, we must first realize that we can never know who or what Bartleby is, but that we are continually asked to guess who or what he might be. We must see that he may be anything from a mere bit of human flotsam to a conscious and forceful rejecter of the world to an incarnation of God. When we see the first possibility we realize the full pathos of the story; when we see

† Reprinted from *The Wake of the Gods: Melville's Mythology*, by H. Bruce Franklin, with the permission of the publishers, Stanford University Press. © 1963 by the Board of Trustees of the Leland Stanford Junior University.

the last possibility we realize that the story is a grotesque joke and a parabolic tragedy.

But of course the possibility that Bartleby may be the very least of men does not necessarily contradict the possibility that Bartleby may be an embodiment of God. For as Christ explains in Matthew 25, the least of men (particularly when he appears as a stranger) is the physical representative and representation of Christ. Upon this identification depend the Christian ethic, the next world to which Christ sends every man, and the central meanings of *Bartleby*:

> 34 Then shall the King say unto them on his right hand, Come, ye blessed of my Father, inherit the kingdom prepared for you from the foundation of the world:
>
> 35 For I was ahungered, and ye gave me meat: I was thirsty, and ye gave me drink: I was a stranger, and ye took me in:
>
> 36 Naked, and ye clothed me: I was sick, and ye visited me: I was in prison, and ye came unto me.
>
> 37 Then shall the righteous answer him, saying, Lord, when saw we thee ahungered, and fed thee? or thirsty, and gave thee drink?
>
> 38 When saw we thee a stranger, and took thee in? or naked, and clothed thee?
>
> 39 Or when saw we thee sick, or in prison, and came unto thee?
>
> 40 And the King shall answer and say unto them, Verily I say unto you, Inasmuch as ye have done it unto one of the least of these my brethren, ye have done it unto me.
>
> 41 Then shall he say also unto them on the left hand, Depart from me, ye cursed, into everlasting fire, prepared for the devil and his angels:
>
> 42 For I was ahungered, and ye gave me no meat: I was thirsty, and ye gave me no drink:
>
> 43 I was a stranger, and ye took me not in: naked, and ye clothed me not: sick, and in prison, and ye visited me not.
>
> 44 Then shall they also answer him, saying, Lord, when saw we thee ahungered, or athirst, or a stranger, or naked, or sick, or in prison, and did not minister unto thee?
>
> 45 Then shall he answer them, saying, Verily I say unto you, Inasmuch as ye did it not to one of the least of these, ye did it not to me.

Christ is here saying that the individual comes to God and attains his salvation when he shows complete charity to a stranger, and he rejects God and calls for his damnation whenever he refuses complete charity to *one* stranger, even "the least of these." As the story of Bartleby unfolds, it becomes increasingly apparent that it is in part a testing of this message of Christ. The narrator's soul depends from his actions toward Bartleby, a mysterious, poor, lonely, sick stranger who ends his life in prison. Can the narrator, the man of our world, act in terms of Christ's ethics? The answer is yes and no. The narrator fulfills the letter of Christ's injunction point by point: he offers money to the stranger so that he may eat and drink; he takes him in, finally offering him not only his office but also his home; when he sees that he is sick, he attempts to minister to him; he, alone of all mankind, visits and befriends the stranger in prison. But he hardly fulfills the spirit of Christ's message: his money is carefully doled out; he tries to evict the stranger, offers his home only after betraying him, and then immediately flees from him in the time of his greatest need; it is his demands on the stranger which have made him sick; he visits the stranger in prison only once while he is alive, thus leaving him alone for several days before and after his visit, thus leaving him to die entirely alone. At the heart of both the tragedy and the comedy lies the narrator's view of the drama, a view which sees all but all in the wrong terms: "To befriend Bartleby; to humor him in his strange wilfulness, will cost me little or nothing, while I lay up in my soul what will eventually prove a sweet morsel for my conscience."

According to Christ's words in Matthew 25, it would make no difference to the narrator's salvation whether Bartleby is the Saviour incarnate or merely the least of his brethren. And certainly reading *Bartleby* with Matthew 25 in mind defines the central issues, no matter who Bartleby is. But the story repeatedly suggests that Bartleby may not be merely the least of Christ's brethren but may in fact be the Saviour himself. Again I wish to emphasize that we are certainly not justified in simply taking Bartleby to be an incarnation or reincarnation of Christ (except in the terms of Matthew 25). But if we do not entertain the possibility that Bartleby is Christ, although we still see most of the tragedy, we miss a great deal of the comedy. Bartleby's story is the story of the advent, the betrayal, and torment of a mysterious and innocent being; this is a tragic story no matter who the being is. These events carefully and pointedly re-enact the story of Christ, and there is nothing funny about this. Nor is there anything inherently funny about the fact that for all we know Bartleby may be God incarnate. The central joke of the story is that although the narrator comes close to seeing this possibility without ever seeing what he sees, his language continually recognizes and defines the possibility that Bartleby may be Christ. The narrator's own words define his own tragedy as cosmic and comic.

The narrator tells us that he is an "eminently *safe* man," an "unambitious" lawyer who, "in the cool tranquillity of a snug retreat," does "a snug business among rich men's bonds and mortgages and title-deeds." He tells of receiving the "good old office" of

"Master in Chancery," which greatly enlarges his business. This is the time which he significantly labels "the period just preceding the advent of Bartleby." After mentioning this office only once, he digresses for several pages. When he next mentions it, he calls it simply—and significantly—"the master's office." This joke introduces the pointedly ambiguous description of the advent of Bartleby:

> Now my original business . . . was considerably increased by receiving the master's office. There was now great work for scriveners. Not only must I push the clerks already with me, but I must have additional help.
>
> In answer to my advertisement, a motionless young man one morning stood upon my office threshold, the door being open, for it was summer. I can see that figure now—pallidly neat, pitiably respectable, incurably forlorn! It was Bartleby.

So Bartleby is a being who answers the narrator's call for "additional help" at a time of "great work for scriveners." The narrator responds by placing "this quiet man within easy call, in case any trifling thing was to be done."

Bartleby at first does an "extraordinary" amount of work, but, "on the third day," begins to answer "I would prefer not to" to the narrator's petty orders. Who is this being? The narrator can only tell us that "Bartleby was one of those beings of whom nothing is ascertainable, except from the original sources, and, in his case, those are very small."

As Bartleby, by merely standing, sitting, and lying still, step by step withdraws from the world, the narrator follows him, leaving behind, bit by bit, his worldly values. Slowly the narrator's compassion for Bartleby and his sense of brotherhood with him emerge, and as they emerge we see more and more clearly that the drama involves the salvation of both Bartleby—the poor, lonely stranger—and the narrator—the "safe" man who in many ways represents our world. As this drama becomes clear, the narrator's language becomes more and more grotesquely ironic.

At the beginning of his withdrawal, Bartleby is only saved from being "violently dismissed" because the narrator cannot find "anything ordinarily human about him." In the next stage of his withdrawal, Bartleby stands at the entrance of his "hermitage" and "mildly" asks "What is wanted?" when the narrator "hurriedly" demands that he proofread the copies, Bartleby answers that he "would prefer not to," and the narrator tells us that "for a few moments I was turned into a pillar of salt."

The narrator, as boss of the office, plays god. What he does not realize, but what his language makes clear, is that he may be playing this role with God himself. The narrator tells us that he "again advanced towards Bartleby" because "I felt additional incentives tempting me to my fate." "Sometimes, to be sure, I could not, for the very soul of me," he ironically admits, "avoid falling into sudden spasmodic passions with him."

The narrator even discovers "something superstitious knocking at my heart, and forbidding me to carry out my purpose . . . If I dared to breathe one bitter word against this forlornest of mankind." At this point we need hardly remember Matthew 25 or that Melville referred to Christ as the Man of Sorrows to see why the narrator should look to his salvation instead of his safety. But when the narrator surmises that Bartleby has "nothing else earthly to do," he blandly asks him to carry some letters to the post office.

The narrator then realizes that Bartleby is "absolutely alone in the universe," but his response to this cosmic loneliness is to tell Bartleby that "in six days' time he must unconditionally leave the office." On the appointed day, the narrator tries to dismiss Bartleby with words that become grotesquely ludicrous if they are seen as an inversion of the true roles of these two beings: "If, hereafter, in your new place of abode, I can be of any service to you, do not fail to advise me by letter." Perhaps the narrator has already received in very clear letters all the advice he needs, a description of what service Bartleby might be to him in his new place of abode, and what his own place of abode will be if he rejects the advice and denies the man. (But perhaps, as the last few paragraphs of the story hint, Matthew 25 and its entire context is now the Dead Letter Office.)

Shortly after saying these words, the narrator discovers that this very day is "an election day." Still, "a sudden passion"—the very thing which the narrator's words had recognized as endangering his "very soul"—makes him demand that Bartleby leave him. The scrivener gently replies, "I would prefer *not* to quit you." The narrator reminds Bartleby ironically that he has no "earthly right" to stay; Bartleby "answered nothing" and "silently retired into his hermitage."

This infuriates the narrator; as he says, the "old Adam of resentment rose in me and tempted me concerning Bartleby." But on this election day the narrator saves himself for the time being "simply by recalling the divine injunction: 'A new commandment give I unto you, that ye love one another.'" "Yes," he says, "this it was that saved me." But the narrator fails to grasp what he has seen; he defines this love "as a vastly wise and prudent principle"; "mere self-interest" becomes his most clearly perceived motive to "charity."

After some days pass in which he has had a chance to consult "Edwards on the Will" and "Priestley on Necessity," the narrator has his most complete revelation of his own drama:

Gradually I slid into the persuasion that these troubles of mine, touching the scrivener, had been all predestined from eternity, and Bartleby was billeted upon me for some mysterious purpose of an all-wise Providence, which it was not for a mere mortal like me to fathom. Yes, Bartleby, stay there behind your screen, thought I; I shall persecute you no more; you are harmless and noiseless as any of these old chairs; in short, I never feel so private as when I know you are here. At last I see it, I feel it; I penetrate to the predestinated purpose of my life. I am content. Others may have loftier parts to enact; but my mission in this world, Bartleby, is to furnish you with office-room for such period as you may see fit to remain.

According to Christ's own words in Matthew 25, the narrator is absolutely right; he has finally seen his mission in the world.

But the narrator's resolution of his dilemma is short-lived. It withers quickly under the "uncharitable remarks obtruded upon" him by his "professional friends." He confesses that the whispers of his professional acquaintance "worried me very much." When he then thinks of the possibility of Bartleby's "denying my authority," outliving him, and claiming "possession of my office by right of his perpetual occupancy," the narrator resolves to "forever rid me of this intolerable incubus." Even then, after he informs Bartleby that he must leave, and after Bartleby takes "three days to meditate upon it," he learns that Bartleby "still preferred to abide with" him, that "he prefers to cling to" him. This sets the stage for the narrator's denial of Bartleby, for he decides that "since he will not quit me, I must quit him."

To hear the full significance of his three denials of Bartleby, we must hear the loud echoes of Peter's three denials of Christ. Matthew 26:

> 70 But he denied before them all, saying, I know not what thou sayest.
> 72 And again he denied with an oath, I do not know the man.
> 74 Then began he to curse and to swear, saying, I know not the man.

Even closer are Peter's words in Mark 14:71: "I know not this man of whom ye speak."

The first denial:

> "Then, sir," said the stranger, who proved a lawyer, "you are responsible for the man you left there." . . .
> "I am very sorry, sir," said I, with assumed tranquillity, but an inward tremor, "but, really, the man you allude to is nothing to me."

The second denial:

> "In mercy's name, who is he?"
> "I certainly cannot inform you. I know nothing about him."

The third denial:

> In vain I persisted that Bartleby was nothing to me—no more
> than to any one else.

After the narrator's three denials of Bartleby, he belatedly makes
his most charitable gesture toward him, offering, "in the kindest
tone I could assume under such exciting circumstances," to permit him to come to his home. But Bartleby answers, "No: at present I would prefer not to make any change at all." The narrator
leaves; the new landlord has the police remove Bartleby to the
Tombs. The narrator then learns of Bartleby's procession to his
Golgotha:

> As I afterwards learned, the poor scrivener, when told that he
> must be conducted to the Tombs, offered not the slightest
> obstacle, but, in his pale, unmoving way, silently acquiesced.
> Some of the compassionate and curious bystanders joined
> the party; and headed by one of the constables arm in arm with
> Bartleby, the silent procession filed its way through all the
> noise, and heat, and joy of the roaring thoroughfares at noon.

"Quite serene and harmless in all his ways," Bartleby is, like Christ,
"numbered with the transgressors" (Mark 15:28). The world places
him in prison where, amidst "murderers and thieves," he completes
his withdrawal from the world.

When the narrator more or less meets the last condition laid
down in Matthew 25—visiting the stranger in prison—all his charity is shown to be too little and too late. Before Bartleby leaves the
world he says to the narrator, "I know you," and adds, without looking at him, "and I want nothing to say to you." At this point we can
hear new ironies in the narrator's attempt to dismiss Bartleby: "If,
hereafter, in your new place of abode, I can be of any service to you,
do not fail to advise me by letter." Thus, when the narrator retells
the rumor of Bartleby's having worked in the Dead Letter Office, he
describes in part himself, in part Bartleby, and in part the scriptural
letters which spell the hope of salvation. "The master's office" has
become the Dead Letter Office.

> Dead letters! does it not sound like dead men? . . . pardon for
> those who died despairing; hope for those who died unhoping;
> good tidings for those who died stifled by unrelieved calamities.
> On errands of life, these letters speed to death.
> Ah, Bartleby! Ah, humanity!

But all this is only half the story. For if the narrator is weighed and found wanting, what then of Bartleby himself? At least the narrator at times can show compassion, sympathy, and charity. Indeed, he at times much more than transcends the worldly ethics with which he starts and to which he tends to backslide. (One must bear in mind while evaluating the narrator's behavior that he is continually defending himself from two possible accusations—that he is too hard-hearted and that he is too soft-hearted.) Although he begins by strictly following horological time, he conforms more and more closely to chronometrical time. And he is after all certainly the most charitable character in the story. What time does Bartleby follow, and, finally, how charitable is he? Or is it possible to account for the actions of a being who is almost by definition enigmatic?

Because "Bartleby was one of those beings of whom nothing is ascertainable, except from the original sources, and, in his case, those are very small," he is almost as difficult to judge as to identify. But whether he is finally a god incarnate as a man or only a man playing the role of a crucified god, his behavior fits a pattern which implies an ethic.

If, as the Plotinus Plinlimmon pamphlet asserts in *Pierre*, chronometrical time is an impossibility for man, if man is left with the choice in the world between following chronometrical time and being destroyed or following horological time and being contemptible, if, then, no action in the world can be at the same time safe and worthy of salvation, what is there left for man to do? One answer is that man can try to live out of the world, can withdraw from the world altogether. This is the answer which forms the counterpoint with worldly ethics in both *Bartleby* and *Benito Cereno*, each of which dramatizes a particular and different kind of monasticism.

Bartleby's monkish withdrawal from the world has been described by Saburo Yamaya and Walter Sutton as essentially Buddhistic in nature. Yamaya shows the connections between Buddhist Quietism and the stone imagery of both *Pierre* and *Bartleby*, citing as one of Melville's sources this passage from Bayle's *Dictionary*:

> The great lords and the most illustrious persons suffered themselves to be so infatuated with the [Buddhist] Quietism, that they believed insensibility to be the way to perfection and beatitude and that the nearer a man came to the nature of a block or *a stone*, the greater progress he made, the more he was like the first principle, into which he was to return.

Sutton quite accurately perceives (apparently without reference to Yamaya) that Bartleby, in achieving "the complete withdrawal of the hunger artist," has attained what "in Buddhist terms . . . is Nirvana, extinction, or nothingness," and he suggests that at this point in his life Melville was unconsciously approaching Buddhism. But Melville was probably quite aware that Bartleby's behavior conforms very closely to a kind of Oriental asceticism which Thomas Maurice had spent about fifty pages describing.

The Oriental ascetic who most closely resembles Bartleby is the Saniassi, a Hindu rather than a Buddhist. It seems probable that once again Maurice's *Indian Antiquities* served as a direct source for Melville's fiction. Maurice describes in detail the systematic withdrawal from the world practiced by the Saniassi, and many details have a surprising—and grotesquely humorous—correspondence to the systematic withdrawal from the world practiced by Bartleby. For instance, in the fifth stage the Saniassi "eats only one particular kind of food during the day and night, but as often as he pleases." Bartleby "lives, then, on ginger-nuts . . . never eats a dinner, properly speaking; he must be a vegetarian, then, but no; he never eats even vegetables, he eats nothing but ginger-nuts." "During the last three days," the Saniassi "neither eats nor drinks." During Bartleby's last few days, he prefers not to eat.

The fact that external details of Bartleby's withdrawal closely parallel some of the external details of the Saniassi's withdrawal is not nearly so significant as this fact: Bartleby's behavior seems to be the very essence of Maurice's description of the Saniassi's behavior. In fact, Maurice's general description and judgment of the Saniassi often seems to be a precise description and judgment of Bartleby.

Most striking are the very things which Maurice claims are peculiar to the Saniassi. He observes that one of the principal ways in which the Saniassi is distinguished from the Yogi is "by the calm, the silent, dignity with which he suffers the series of complicated evils through which he is ordained to toil." The Saniassi "can only be fed by the charity of others"; "he must himself make no exertion, nor feel any solicitude for existence upon this contaminated orb." The Saniassis' design "is to detach their thoughts from all concern about sublunary objects; to be indifferent to hunger and thirst; to be insensible to shame and reproach."

Perhaps most important to the judgment of Bartleby is the Saniassis' "incessant efforts . . . to stifle every ebullition of human passion, and live upon earth as if they were already, and in reality, disembodied." This may at once help account for Bartleby's appearing as a "ghost" or as "cadaverous" to the narrator and explain what ethical time he follows, for "it is the boast of the Saniassi to sacrifice every human feeling and passion at the shrine of devotion." Like Bartleby, the Saniassi "is no more to be soothed by the suggestions of *adulation* in its most pleasing form, than he is to be terrified by the loudest clamours of *reproach* . . . By long habits of indifference, he becomes inanimate as a piece of wood or stone; and, though he mechanically respires the vital air, he is to all the purposes of active life *defunct.*"

*Bartleby* is, then, in part the story of a man of the world who receives "the master's office"; who advertises for help; who is thereupon visited by a strange being who in an "extraordinary" way at first does all that is asked of him; who treats this strange being with contempt; who nevertheless receives from this being what seems to be his purpose in life; who betrays this being; and who watches and describes the systematic withdrawal of this being. It is also in part the story of this strange being, who replays much of the role of Christ while behaving like an Hindu ascetic, and who ends by extinguishing himself and making dead letters of the scripture which describes his prototype.

\* \* \*

# RALPH WALDO EMERSON

## The Transcendentalist†

A Lecture read at the Masonic Temple, Boston, January 1842

The first thing we have to say respecting what are called *new views* here in New England, at the present time, is, that they are not new, but the very oldest of thoughts cast into the mould of these new times. The light is always identical in its composition, but it falls on a great variety of objects, and by so falling is first revealed to us, not in its own form, for it is formless, but in theirs; in like manner, thought only appears in the objects it classifies. What is popularly called Transcendentalism among us, is Idealism; Idealism as it appears in 1842. As thinkers, mankind have ever divided into two sects, Materialists and Idealists; the first class founding on experience, the second on consciousness; the first class beginning to think from the data of the senses, the second class perceive that the senses are not final, and say, the senses give us representations of things, but what are the things themselves, they cannot tell. The

† Melville heard Emerson lecture in the winter of 1848–49. Sophia Hawthorne wrote to her sister, Elizabeth Peabody, that one day in the early fall of 1850 Melville "shut himself into the boudoir and read Mr. Emerson's essays" all one morning. Clearly, from internal evidence alone, before Melville composed "Bartleby, The Scrivener," he read "The Transcendentalist" with considerable care. See Christopher W. Sten, "Bartleby the Transcendentalist: Melville's Dead Letter to Emerson," *Modern Language Quarterly* 35 (March 1974): 30–44.

materialist insists on facts, on history, on the force of circumstances, and the animal wants of man; the idealist on the power of
Thought and of Will, on inspiration, on miracle, on individual culture. These two modes of thinking are both natural, but the idealist
contends that his way of thinking is in higher nature. He concedes
all that the other affirms, admits the impressions of sense, admits
their coherency, their use and beauty, and then asks the materialist
for his grounds of assurance that things are as his senses represent
them. But I, he says, affirm facts not affected by the illusions of
sense, facts which are of the same nature as the faculty which
reports them, and not liable to doubt; facts which in their first
appearance to us assume a native superiority to material facts,
degrading these into a language by which the first are to be spoken;
facts which it only needs a retirement from the senses to discern.
Every materialist will be an idealist; but an idealist can never go
backward to be a materialist.

The idealist, in speaking of events, sees them as spirits. He does
not deny the sensuous fact: by no means; but he will not see that
alone. He does not deny the presence of this table, this chair, and
the walls of this room, but he looks at these things as the reverse
side of the tapestry, as the *other end*, each being a sequel or completion of a spiritual fact which nearly concerns him. This manner
of looking at things, transfers every object in nature from an independent and anomalous position without there, into the consciousness. Even the materialist Condillac, perhaps the most logical
expounder of materialism, was constrained to say, "Though we
should soar into the heavens, though we should sink into the abyss,
we never go out of ourselves; it is always our own thought that we
perceive." What more could an idealist say?

The materialist, secure in the certainty of sensation, mocks at
fine-spun theories, at star-gazers and dreamers, and believes that
his life is solid, that he at least takes nothing for granted, but knows
where he stands, and what he does. Yet how easy it is to show him,
that he also is a phantom walking and working amid phantoms, and
that he need only ask a question or two beyond his daily questions,
to find his solid universe growing dim and impalpable before his
sense. The sturdy capitalist, no matter how deep and square on
blocks of Quincy granite he lays the foundations of his banking-
house or Exchange, must set it, at last, not on a cube corresponding to the angles of his structure, but on a mass of unknown
materials and solidity, red-hot or white-hot, perhaps at the core,
which rounds off to an almost perfect sphericity, and lies floating in
soft air, and goes spinning away, dragging bank and banker with it
at a rate of thousands of miles the hour, he knows not whither,—a
bit of bullet, now glimmering, now darkling through a small cubic

space on the edge of an unimaginable pit of emptiness. And this wild balloon, in which his whole venture is embarked, is a just symbol of his whole state and faculty. One thing, at least, he says is certain, and does not give me the headache, that figures do not lie; the multiplication table has been hitherto found unimpeachable truth; and, moreover, if I put a gold eagle in my safe, I find it again to-morrow;—but for these thoughts, I know not whence they are. They change and pass away. But ask him why he believes that an uniform experience will continue uniform, or on what grounds he founds his faith in his figures, and he will perceive that his mental fabric is built up on just as strange and quaking foundations as his proud edifice of stone.

In the order of thought, the materialist takes his departure from the external world, and esteems a man as one product of that. The idealist takes his departure from his consciousness, and reckons the world an appearance. The materialist respects sensible masses, Society, Government, social art, and luxury, every establishment, every mass, whether majority of numbers, or extent of space, or amount of objects, every social action. The idealist has another measure, which is metaphysical, namely, the *rank* which things themselves take in his consciousness; not at all, the size or appearance. Mind is the only reality, of which men and all other natures are better or worse reflectors. Nature, literature, history, are only subjective phenomena. Although in his action overpowered by the laws of action, and so, warmly coöperating with men, even preferring them to himself, yet when he speaks scientifically, or after the order of thought, he is constrained to degrade persons into representatives of truths. He does not respect labor, or the products of labor, namely, property, otherwise than as a manifold symbol, illustrating with wonderful fidelity of details the laws of being; he does not respect government, except as far as it reiterates the law of his mind; nor the church; nor charities; nor arts, for themselves; but hears, as at a vast distance, what they say, as if his consciousness would speak to him through a pantomimic scene. His thought,— that is the Universe. His experience inclines him to behold the procession of facts you call the world, as flowing perpetually outward from an invisible, unsounded centre in himself, centre alike of him and of them, and necessitating him to regard all things as having a subjective or relative existence, relative to that aforesaid Unknown Centre of him.

From this transfer of the world into the consciousness, this beholding of all things in the mind, follow easily his whole ethics. It is simpler to be self-dependent. The height, the deity of man is, to be self-sustained, to need no gift, no foreign force. Society is good when it does not violate me; but best when it is likest to solitude. Everything real is self-existent. Everything divine shares the self-existence of Deity. All that you call the world is the shadow of that substance which you are, the perpetual creation of the powers of thought, of those that are dependent and of those that are independent of your will. Do not cumber yourself with fruitless pains to mend and remedy remote effects; let the soul be erect, and all things will go well. You think me the child of my circumstances: I make my circumstance. Let any thought or motive of mine be different from that they are, the difference will transform my condition and economy. I—this thought which is called I,—is the mould into which the world is poured like melted wax. The mould is invisible, but the world betrays the shape of the mould. You call it the power of circumstance, but it is the power of me. Am I in harmony with myself? my position will seem to you just and commanding. Am I vicious and insane? my fortunes will seem to you obscure and descending. As I am, so shall I associate, and, so shall I act; Cæsar's history will paint out Cæsar. Jesus acted so, because he thought so. I do not wish to overlook or to gainsay any reality; I say, I make my circumstance: but if you ask me, Whence am I? I feel like other men my relation to that Fact which cannot be spoken, or defined, nor even thought, but which exists, and will exist.

The Transcendentalist adopts the whole connection of spiritual doctrine. He believes in miracle, in the perpetual openness of the human mind to new influx of light and power; he believes in inspiration, and in ecstasy. He wishes that the spiritual principle should be suffered to demonstrate itself to the end, in all possible applications to the state of man, without the admission of anything unspiritual; that is, anything positive, dogmatic, personal. Thus, the spiritual measure of inspiration is the depth of the thought, and never, who said it? And so he resists all attempts to palm other rules and measures on the spirit than its own.

In action, he easily incurs the charge of antinomianism by his avowal that he, who has the Lawgiver, may with safety not only neglect, but even contravene every written commandment. In the play of Othello, the expiring Desdemona absolves her husband of the murder, to her attendant Emilia. Afterwards, when Emilia charges him with the crime. Othello exclaims,

> "You heard her say herself it was not I."

Emilia replies,

> "The more angel she, and thou the blacker devil."

Of this fine incident, Jacobi, the Transcendental moralist, makes use, with other parallel instances, in his reply to Fichte. Jacobi, refusing all measure of right and wrong except the determinations of the private spirit, remarks that there is no crime but has sometimes been a virtue. "I," he says, "am that atheist, that godless person who, in opposition to an imaginary doctrine of calculation, would lie as the dying Desdemona lied: would lie and deceive, as Pylades when he personated Orestes; would assassinate like Timoleon; would perjure myself like Epaminondas, and John de Witt: I would resolve on suicide like Cato; I would commit sacrilege with David: yea, and pluck ears of corn on the Sabbath, for no other reason than that I was fainting for lack of food. For, I have assurance in myself, that, in pardoning these faults according to the letter, man exerts the sovereign right which the majesty of his being confers on him; he sets the seal of his divine nature to the grace he accords."[2]

In like manner, if there is anything grand and daring in human thought or virtue, any reliance on the vast, the unknown: any presentiment; any extravagance of faith, the spiritualist adopts it as most in nature. The oriental mind has always tended to this largeness. Buddhism is an expression of it. The Buddhist who thanks no man, who says, "do not flatter your benefactors," but who, in his conviction that every good deed can by no possibility escape its reward, will not deceive the benefactor by pretending that he has done more than he should, is a Transcendentalist.

You will see by this sketch that there is no such thing as a Transcendental *party*; that there is no pure Transcendentalist; that we know of none but prophets and heralds of such a philosophy; that all who by strong bias of nature have leaned to the spiritual side in doctrine, have stopped short of their goal. We have had many harbingers and forerunners; but of a purely spiritual life, history has afforded no example. I mean, we have yet no man who has leaned entirely on his character, and eaten angels' food; who, trusting to his sentiments, found life made of miracles; who, working for universal aims, found himself fed, he knew not how; clothed, sheltered, and weaponed, he knew not how, and yet it was done by his own hands. Only in the instinct of the lower animals, we find the suggestion of the methods of it, and something higher than our understanding. The squirrel hoards nuts, and the bee gathers honey, without knowing what they do, and they are thus provided for without selfishness or disgrace.

Shall we say, then, that Transcendentalism is the Saturnalia or excess of Faith; the presentiment of a faith proper to man in his integrity, excessive only when his imperfect obedience hinders the satisfaction of his wish. Nature is transcendental, exists primarily, necessarily, ever works and advances, yet takes no thought for the

2. Coleridge's Translation [*Emerson*].

morrow. Man owns the dignity of the life which throbs around him in chemistry, and tree, and animal, and in the involuntary functions of his own body; yet he is balked when he tries to fling himself into this enchanted circle, where all is done without degradation. Yet genius and virtue predict in man the same absence of private ends, and of condescension to circumstances, united with every trait and talent of beauty and power.

This way of thinking, falling on Roman times, made Stoic philosophers; falling on despotic times, made patriot Catos and Brutuses; falling on superstitious times, made prophets and apostles; on popish times, made protestants and ascetic monks, preachers of Faith against the preachers of Works; on prelatical times, made Puritans and Quakers; and falling on Unitarian and commercial times, makes the peculiar shades of Idealism which we know.

It is well known to most of my audience, that the Idealism of the present day acquired the name of Transcendental, from the use of that term by Immanuel Kant, of Konigsberg, who replied to the skeptical philosophy of Locke, which insisted that there was nothing in the intellect which was not previously in the experience of the senses, by showing that there was a very important class of ideas, or imperative forms, which did not come by experience, but through which experience was acquired: that these were intuitions of the mind itself; and he denominated them *Transcendental* forms. The extraordinary profoundness and precision of that man's thinking have given vogue to his nomenclature, in Europe and America, to that extent, that whatever belongs to the class of intuitive thought, is popularly called at the present day *Transcendental*.

Although, as we have said, there is no pure Transcendentalist, yet the tendency to respect the intuitions, and to give them, at least in our creed, all authority over our experience, has deeply colored the conversation and poetry of the present day; and the history of genius and of religion in these times, though impure, and as yet not incarnated in any powerful individual, will be the history of this tendency.

It is a sign of our times, conspicuous to the coarsest observer, that many intelligent and religious persons withdraw themselves from the common labors and competitions of the market and the caucus, and betake themselves to a certain solitary and critical way of living, from which no solid fruit has yet appeared to justify their separation. They hold themselves aloof; they feel the disproportion between their faculties and the work offered them, and they prefer to ramble in the country and perish of ennui, to the degradation of such charities and such ambitions as the city can propose to them. They are striking work, and crying out for somewhat worthy to do![3]

---

3. This paragraph seems a likely source for the figure of Bartleby.

What they do, is done only because they are overpowered by the humanities that speak on all sides; and they consent to such labor as is open to them, though to their lofty dream the writing of Iliads or Hamlets, or the building of cities or empires seems drudgery.

Now every one must do after his kind, be he asp or angel, and these must. The question, which a wise man and a student of modern history will ask, is, what that kind is? And truly, as in ecclesiastical history we take so much pains to know what the Gnostics, what the Essenes, what the Manichees, and what the Reformers believed, it would not misbecome us to inquire nearer home, what these companions and contemporaries of ours think and do, at least so far as these thoughts and actions appear to be not accidental and personal, but common to many, and the inevitable flower of the Tree of Time. Our American literature and spiritual history are, we confess, in the optative mood; but whoso knows these seething brains, these admirable radicals, these unsocial worshippers, these talkers who talk the sun and moon away, will believe that this heresy cannot pass away without leaving its mark.

They are lonely; the spirit of their writing and conversation is lonely; they repel influences; they shun general society; they incline to shut themselves in their chamber in the house, to live in the country rather than in the town, and to find their tasks and amusements in solitude. Society, to be sure, does not like this very well; it saith, Whoso goes to walk alone, accuses the whole world; he declareth all to be unfit to be his companions; it is very uncivil, nay, insulting; Society will retaliate.[4] Meantime, this retirement does not proceed from any whim on the part of these separators; but if any one will take pains to talk with them, he will find that this part is chosen both from temperament and from principle; with some unwillingness, too, and as a choice of the less of two evils; for these persons are not by nature melancholy, sour, and unsocial,—they are not stockish or brute,— but joyous: susceptible, affectionate; they have even more than others a great wish to be loved. Like the young Mozart, they are rather ready to cry ten times a day, "But are you sure you love me?" Nay, if they tell you their whole thought, they will own that love seems to them the last and highest gift of nature; that there are persons whom in their hearts they daily thank for existing,—persons whose faces are perhaps unknown to them, but whose fame and spirit have penetrated their solitude,—and for whose sake they wish to exist. To behold the beauty of another character, which inspires a new interest in our own; to behold the beauty lodged in a human being, with such vivacity of apprehension, that I am instantly forced home to inquire

4. Note the repeated "lonely" and the "man of the world's" reaction to the "very uncivil, nay, insulting" talk.

if I am not deformity itself: to behold in another the expression of a love so high that it assures itself,—assures itself also to me against every possible casualty except my unworthiness;[5]—these are degrees on the scale of human happiness, to which they have ascended; and it is a fidelity to this sentiment which has made common association distasteful to them. They wish a just and even fellowship, or none. They cannot gossip with you, and they do not wish, as they are sincere and religious, to gratify any mere curiosity which you may entertain. Like fairies, they do not wish to be spoken of. Love me, they say, but do not ask who is my cousin and my uncle. If you do not need to hear my thought, because you can read it in my face and behavior, then I will tell it you from sunrise to sunset. If you cannot divine it, you would not understand what I say. I will not molest myself for you. I do not wish to be profaned.[6]

And yet, it seems as if this loneliness, and not this love, would prevail in their circumstances, because of the extravagant demand they make on human nature. That, indeed, constitutes a new feature in their portrait, that they are the most exacting and extortionate critics. Their quarrel with every man they meet, is not with his kind, but with his degree. There is not enough of him,—that is the only fault. They prolong their privilege of childhood in this wise, of doing nothing,—but making immense demands on all the gladiators in the lists of action and fame. They make us feel the strange disappointment which overcasts every human youth. So many promising youths, and never a finished man! The profound nature will have a savage rudeness; the delicate one will be shallow, or the victim of sensibility; the richly accomplished will have some capital absurdity; and so every piece has a crack. 'T is strange, but this masterpiece is a result of such an extreme delicacy, that the most unobserved flaw in the boy will neutralize the most aspiring genius, and spoil the work. Talk with a seaman of the hazards to life in his profession, and he will ask you, "Where are the old sailors? do you not see that all are young men?" And we, on this sea of human thought, in like manner inquire, Where are the old idealists? where are they who represented to the last generation that extravagant hope, which a few happy aspirants suggest to ours? In looking at the class of counsel, and power, and wealth, and at the matronage of the land, amidst all the prudence and all the triviality, one asks, Where are they who represented genius, virtue, the invisible and heavenly world, to these? Are they dead,—taken in early ripeness to the gods,—as as ancient wisdom foretold their fate? Or did the high idea die out of them, and leave their unperfumed body as its tomb and tablet, announcing to all that the celestial inhabitant,

5. Cf. the Lawyer's self-doubts.
6. Bartleby "declined telling who he was, or whence he came, or whether he had any relatives in the world."

who once gave them beauty, had departed? Will it be better with the new generation? We easily predict a fair future to each new candidate who enters the lists, but we are frivolous and volatile, and by low aims and ill example do what we can to defeat this hope. Then these youths bring us a rough but effectual aid. By their unconcealed dissatisfaction, they expose our poverty, and the insignificance of man to man. A man is a poor limitary benefactor. He ought to be a shower of benefits—a great influence, which should never let his brother go, but should refresh old merits continually with new ones; so that, though absent, he should never be out of my mind, his name never far from my lips; but if the earth should open at my side, or my last hour were come, his name should be the prayer I should utter to the Universe.[7] But in our experience, man is cheap, and friendship wants its deep sense. We affect to dwell with our friends in their absence, but we do not; when deed, word, or letter comes not, they let us go. These exacting children advertise us of our wants. There is no compliment, no smooth speech with them; they pay you only this one compliment, of insatiable expectation; they aspire, they severely exact, and if they only stand fast in this watchtower, and persist in demanding unto the end, and without end, then are they terrible friends, whereof poet and priest cannot choose but stand in awe; and what if they eat clouds, and drink wind, they have not been without service to the race of man.

With this passion for what is great and extraordinary, it cannot be wondered at, that they are repelled by vulgarity and frivolity in people. They say to themselves, It is better to be alone than in bad company. And it is really a wish to be met,—the wish to find society for their hope and religion,—which prompts them to shun what is called society. They feel that they are never so fit for friendship, as when they have quitted mankind, and taken themselves to friend. A picture, a book, a favorite spot in the hills or the woods, which they can people with the fair and worthy creation of the fancy, can give them often forms so vivid, that these for the time shall seem real, and society the illusion.

But their solitary and fastidious manners not only withdraw them from the conversation, but from the labors of the world; they are not good citizens, not good members of society; unwillingly they bear their part of the public and private burdens; they do not willingly share in the public charities, in the public religious rites, in the enterprises of education, of missions foreign or domestic, in the abolition of the slave-trade, or in the temperance society. They do not even like to vote. The philanthropists inquire whether Transcendentalism does

---

7. "Bartleby, The Scrivener" concludes with the Lawyer's prayer to the Universe, "Ah Bartleby! Ah Humanity!"

not mean sloth: they had as lief hear that their friend is dead, as that he is a Transcendentalist; for then is he paralyzed, and can never do anything for humanity. What right, cries the good world, has the man of genius to retreat from work, and indulge himself? The popular literary creed seems to be, 'I am a sublime genius; I ought not therefore to labor.' But genius is the power to labor better and more availably. Deserve thy genius: exalt it. The good, the illuminated, sit apart from the rest, censuring their dulness and vices, as if they thought that, by sitting very grand in their chairs, the very brokers, attorneys, and congressmen would see the error of their ways, and flock to them. But the good and wise must learn to act, and carry salvation to the combatants and demagogues in the dusty arena below.

On the part of these children, it is replied, that life and their faculty seem to them gifts too rich to be squandered on such trifles as you propose to them. What you call your fundamental institutions, your great and holy causes, seem to them great abuses, and, when nearly seen, paltry matters. Each 'Cause,' as it is called,—say Abolition, Temperance, say Calvinism, or Unitarianism,—becomes speedily a little shop, where the article, let it have been at first never so subtle and ethereal, is now made up into portable and convenient cakes, and retailed in small quantities to suit purchasers. You make very free use of these words 'great' and 'holy,' but few things appear to them such. Few persons have any magnificence of nature to inspire enthusiasm, and the philanthropies and charities have a certain air of quackery. As to the general course of living, and the daily employments of men, they cannot see much virtue in these, since they are parts of this vicious circle; and, as no great ends are answered by the men, there is nothing noble in the arts by which they are maintained. Nay, they have made the experiment, and found that, from the liberal professions to the coarsest manual labor, and from the courtesies of the academy and the college to the conventions of the cotillon-room and the morning call, there is a spirit of cowardly compromise and seeming, which intimates a frightful skepticism, a life without love, and an activity without an aim.

Unless the action is necessary, unless it is adequate, I do not wish to perform it. I do not wish to do one thing but once. I do not love routine.[8] Once possessed of the principle, it is equally easy to make four or forty thousand applications of it. A great man will be content to have indicated in any the slightest manner his perception of the reigning Idea of his time, and will leave to those who like it the multiplication of examples. When he has hit the white, the rest may shatter the target. Every thing admonishes us how needlessly long

---

8. We can hear Bartleby the *scrivener* in Emerson's young man: "I do not wish to do one thing but once. I do not love routine."

life is. Every moment of a hero so raises and cheers us, that a twelve-month is an age. All that the brave Xanthus brings home from his wars, is the recollection that, as the storming of Samos, "in the heat of the battle, Pericles smiled on me, and passed on to another detachment. "It is the quality of the moment, not the number of days, of events, or of actors, that imports.

New, we confess, and by no means happy, is our condition: if you want the aid of our labor, we ourselves stand in greater want of the labor. We are miserable with inaction. We perish of rest and rust: but we do not like your work.

'Then,' says the world, 'show me your own.'

'We have none.'

'What will you do, then?' cries the world.

'We will wait.'

'How long?'

'Until the Universe rises up and calls us to work.'

'But whilst you wait, you grow old and useless.'

'Be it so: I can sit in a corner and *perish*, (as you call it,) but I will not move until I have the highest command.[9] If no call should come for years, for centuries, then I know that the want of the Universe is the attestation of faith by my abstinence. Your virtuous projects, so called, do not cheer me. I know that which shall come will cheer me. If I cannot work, at least I need not lie. All that is clearly due to-day is not to lie. In other places, other men have encountered sharp trials, and have behaved themselves well. The martyrs were sawn asunder, or hung alive on meat-hooks. Cannot we screw our courage to patience and truth, and without complaint, or even with good-humor, await our turn of action in the Infinite Counsels?'

But, to come a little closer to the secret of these persons, we must say, that to them it seems a very easy matter to answer the objections of the man of the world, but not so easy to dispose of the doubts and objections that occur to themselves. They are exercised in their own spirit with queries, which acquaint them with all adversity, and with the trials of the bravest heroes. When I asked them concerning their private experience, they answered somewhat in this wise: It is not to be denied that there must be some wide difference between my faith and other faith; and mine is a certain brief experience, which surprised me in the highway or in the market, in some place, at some time,—whether in the body or out of the body, God knoweth,—and made me aware that I had played the fool with fools all this time, but that law existed for me and for all; that to me belonged trust, a child's trust and obedience, and the worship of ideas, and I should never be

9. The Lawyer's interrogations of Bartleby probably begin here in Emerson's imagined colloquies with the young man, "miserable with inaction," and Emerson's conclusion that "society must behold with what charity it can" such forlorn idealists.

fool more. Well, in the space of an hour, probably, I was let down from this height; I was at my old tricks, the selfish member of a selfish society. My life is superficial, takes no root in the deep world; I ask, When shall I die, and be relieved of the responsibility of seeing an Universe which I do not use? I wish to exchange this flash-of-lightning faith for continuous daylight, this fever-glow for a benign climate.

These two states of thought diverge every moment, and stand in wild contrast. To him who looks at his life from these moments of illumination, it will seem that he skulks and plays a mean, shiftless, and subaltern part in the world. That is to be done which he has not skill to do, or to be said which others can say better, and he lies by, or occupies his hands with some plaything, until his hour comes again. Much of our reading, much of our labor, seems mere waiting: it was not that we were born for. Any other could do it as well, or better. So little skill enters into these works, so little do they mix with the divine life, that it really signifies little what we do, whether we turn a grindstone, or ride, or run, or make fortunes, or govern the state. The worst feature of this double consciousness is, that the two lives, of the understanding and of the soul, which we lead, really show very little relation to each other, never meet and measure each other: one prevails now, all buzz and din; and the other prevails then, all infinitude and paradise; and, with the progress of life, the two discover no greater disposition to reconcile themselves. Yet, what is my faith? What am I? What but a thought of serenity and independence, an abode in the deep blue sky? Presently the clouds shut down again; yet we retain the belief that this petty web we weave will at last be overshot and reticulated with veins of the blue, and that the moments will characterize the days. Patience, then, is for us, is it not? Patience, and still patience. When we pass, as presently we shall, into some new infinitude, out of this Iceland of negations, it will please us to reflect that, though we had few virtues or consolations, we bore with our indigence, nor once strove to repair it with hypocrisy or false heat of any kind.

But this class are not sufficiently characterized, if we omit to add that they are lovers and worshippers of Beauty. In the eternal trinity of Truth, Goodness, and Beauty, each in its perfection including the three, they prefer to make Beauty the sign and head. Something of the same taste is observable in all the moral movements of the time, in the religious and benevolent enterprises. They have a liberal, even an æsthetic spirit. A reference to Beauty in action sounds, to be sure, a little hollow and ridiculous in the ears of the old church. In politics, it has often sufficed, when they treated of justice, if they kept the bounds of selfish calculation. If they granted restitution, it was prudence which granted it. But the justice which is now claimed for the black, and the pauper, and the drunkard is for Beauty,—is for a necessity to the soul of the agent, not of the beneficiary. I say, this is the tendency, not yet the realization. Our virtue totters and trips, does not yet walk firmly. Its representatives are austere; they preach and denounce; their rectitude is not yet a grace. They are still liable to that slight taint of burlesque which, in our strange world, attaches to the zealot. A saint should be as dear as the apple of the eye. Yet we are tempted to smile, and we flee from the working to the speculative reformer, to escape that same slight ridicule. Alas for these days of derision and criticism! We call the Beautiful the highest, because it appears to us the golden mean, escaping the dowdiness of the good, and the heartlessness of the true.—They are lovers of nature also, and find an indemnity in the inviolable order of the world for the violated order and grace of man.

There is, no doubt, a great deal of well-founded objection to be spoken or felt against the sayings and doings of this class, some of whose traits we have selected; no doubt, they will lay themselves open to criticism and to lampoons, and as ridiculous stories will be to be told of them as of any. There will be cant and pretension; there will be subtilty and moonshine. These persons are of unequal strength, and do not all prosper. They complain that everything around them must be denied; and if feeble, it takes all their strength to deny, before they can begin to lead their own life. Grave seniors insist on their respect to this institution, and that usage; to an obsolete history; to some vocation, or college, or etiquette, or beneficiary, or charity, or morning or evening call, which they resist, as what does not concern them. But it costs such sleepless nights, alienations and misgivings,—they have so many moods about it;—these old guardians never change *their* minds; they have but one mood on the subject, namely, that Antony is very perverse,—that it is quite as much as Antony can do, to assert his rights, abstain from what he thinks foolish, and keep his temper. He cannot help the reaction of this injustice in his own mind. He is braced-up and stilted; all freedom and flowing genius, all sallies of wit and frolic nature are quite out of the question; it is well if he can keep from lying, injustice, and suicide. This is no time for gaiety and grace. His strength and spirits are wasted in rejection. But the strong spirits overpower those around them without effort. Their thought and emotion comes in like a flood, quite withdraws them from all notice of these carping critics; they surrender themselves with glad heart to the heavenly guide, and only by implication reject the clamorous nonsense of the hour. Grave seniors talk to the deaf,— church and old book mumble and ritualize to an unheeding, preöccupied and advancing mind, and thus they by happiness of greater momentum lose no time, but take the right road at first.

But all these of whom I speak are not proficients; they are novices; they only show the road in which man should travel, when the soul has greater health and prowess. Yet let them feel the dignity of their charge, and deserve a larger power. Their heart is the ark in which the fire is concealed, which shall burn in a broader and universal flame. Let them obey the Genius then most when his impulse is wildest; then most when he seems to lead to uninhabitable desarts of thought and life; for the path which the hero travels alone is the highway of health and benefit to mankind. What is the privilege and nobility of our nature, but its persistency, through its power to attach itself to what is permanent?

Society also has its duties in reference to this class, and must behold them with what charity it can. Possibly some benefit may yet accrue from them to the state. In our Mechanics' Fair, there must be not only bridges, ploughs, carpenters' planes, and baking troughs, but also some few finer instruments,—raingauges, thermometers, and telescopes; and in society, besides farmers, sailors, and weavers, there must be a few persons of purer fire kept specially as gauges and meters of character; persons of a fine, detecting instinct, who betray the smallest accumulations of wit and feeling in the bystander. Perhaps too there might be room for the exciters and monitors; collectors of the heavenly spark with power to convey the electricity to others. Or, as the storm-tossed vessel at sea[1] speaks the frigate or 'line packet' to learn its longitude, so it may not be without its advantage that we should now and then encounter rare and gifted men, to compare the points of our spiritual compass, and verify our bearings from superior chronometers.

Amidst the downward tendency and proneness of things, when every voice is raised for a new road or another statute, or a subscription of stock, for an improvement in dress, or in dentistry, for a new house or a larger business, for a political party, or the division of an estate,—will you not tolerate one or two solitary voices in the land, speaking for thoughts and principles not marketable or perishable? Soon these improvements and mechanical inventions will be superseded; these modes of living lost out of memory; these cities rotted, ruined by war, by new inventions, by new seats of trade, or the geologic changes:—all gone, like the shells which sprinkle the seabeach with a white colony to-day, forever renewed to be forever destroyed. But the thoughts which these few hermits strove to proclaim by silence, as well as by speech, not only by what they did, but by what they forbore to do, shall abide in beauty and strength, to reorganize themselves in nature, to invest themselves anew in other, perhaps higher endowed and happier mixed clay than ours, in fuller union with the surrounding system.

---

1. Bartleby is "a bit of wreck in the mid Atlantic."

# Benito Cereno

## AMASA DELANO

## A Narrative of Voyages and Travels, Chapter XVIII[†]

*Particulars of the Capture of the Spanish Ship Tryal, at the island of St. Maria; with the Documents relating to that affair.*

In introducing the account of the capture of the Spanish ship Tryal, I shall first give an extract from the journal of the ship Perseverance, taken on board that ship at the time, by the officer who had the care of the log book.

"Wednesday, February 20th, commenced with light airs from the north east, and thick foggy weather. At six A.M. observed a sail opening round the south head of St. Maria, coming into the bay. It proved to be a ship. The captain took the whale boat and crew, and went on board her. As the wind was very light, so that a vessel would not have much more than steerage way at the time; observed that the ship acted very awkwardly. At ten A.M. the boat returned. Mr. Luther informed that Captain Delano had remained on board her, and that she was a Spaniard from Buenos Ayres, four months and twenty six days out of port, with slaves on board; and that the ship was in great want of water, had buried many white men and slaves on her passage, and that captain Delano had sent for a large boat load of water, some fresh fish, sugar, bread, pumpkins, and bottled cider, all of which articles were immediately sent. At twelve o'clock (Meridian) calm. At two P.M. the large boat returned from the Spaniards, had left our water casks on board her. At four P.M. a breeze sprung up from the southern quarter, which brought the Spanish ship into the roads. She anchored about two cables length to the south east of our ship. Immediately after she anchored, our captain with his boat was shoving off from along side the Spanish ship; when to his great surprise the Spanish captain leaped into the

† Amasa Delano, *A Narrative of Voyages and Travels, in the Northern and Southern Hemispheres: Comprising Three Voyages Round the World, Together with a Voyage of Survey and Discovery in the Pacific Ocean and Oriental Islands* (Boston: E. G. House, 1817). Reprinted by permission from William D. Richardson's *Melville's "Benito Cereno"* (Durham: Carolina Academic Press, 1987) 95–122.

boat, and called out in Spanish, that the slaves on board had risen
and murdered many of the people; and that he did not then command her; on which manoeuvre, several of the Spaniards who
remained on board jumped overboard, and swam for our boat, and
were picked up by our people. The Spaniards, who remained on
board, hurried up the rigging, as high aloft as they could possibly
get, and called out repeatedly for help—that they should be murdered by the slaves. Our captain came immediately on board, and
brought the Spanish captain and the men who were picked up in
the water; but before the boat arrived, we observed that the slaves
had cut the Spanish ship adrift. On learning this, our captain
hailed, and ordered the ports to be got up, and the guns cleared; but
unfortunately, we could not bring but one of our guns to bear on the
ship. We fired five or six shot with it, but could not bring her too.
We soon observed her making sail, and standing directly out of the
bay. We dispatched two boats well manned, and well armed after
her, who, after much trouble, boarded the ship and retook her. But
unfortunately in the business, Mr. Rufus Low, our chief officer, who
commanded the party, was desperately wounded in the breast, by
being stabbed with a pike, by one of the slaves. We likewise had one
man badly wounded and two or three slightly. To continue the misfortune, the chief office of the Spanish ship, who was compelled by
the slaves to steer her out of the bay, received two very bad wounds,
one in the side, and one through the thigh, both from musket balls.
One Spaniard, a gentleman passenger on board, was likewise killed
by a musket ball. We have not rightly ascertained what number of
slaves were killed; but we believe seven, and a great number
wounded. Our people brought the ship in, and came to nearly where
she first anchored, at about two o'clock in the morning of the 21st.
At six A.M. the two captains went on board the Spanish ship; took
with them irons from our ship, and doubled ironed all the remaining men of the slaves who were living. Left Mr. Brown, our second
officer, in charge of the ship, the gunner with him as mate, and
eight other hands; together with the survivors of the Spanish crew.
The captain, and chief officer, were removed to our ship, the latter
for the benefit of having his wounds better attended to with us, than
he could have had them on board his own ship. At nine A.M. the
two captains returned, having put every thing aright, as they supposed, on board the Spanish ship.

"The Spanish captain then informed us that he was compelled by
the slaves to say, that he was from Buenos Ayres, bound to Lima:
that he was not from Buenos Ayres, but sailed on the 20th of
December last from Valparaiso for Lima, with upwards of seventy
slaves on board; that on the 26th of December, the slaves rose upon
the ship, and took possession of her, and put to death eighteen

white men, and threw overboard at different periods after, seven more; that the slaves had commanded him to go to Senegal; that he had kept to sea until his water was expended, and had made this port to get it; and also with a view to save his own and the remainder of his people's lives if possible, by run[n]ing away from his ship with his boat."

I shall here add some remarks of my own, to what is stated above from the ship's journal, with a view of giving the reader a correct understanding of the peculiar situation under which we were placed at the time this affair happened. We were in a worse situation to effect any important enterprize than I had been in during the voyage. We had been from home a year and a half, and had not made enough to amount to twenty dollars for each of my people, who were all on shares, and our future prospects were not very flattering. To make our situation worse, I had found after leaving New Holland, on mustering my people, that I had seventeen men, most of whom had been convicts at Botany bay. They had secreted themselves on board without my knowledge. This was a larger number than had been inveigled away from me at the same place, by people who had been convicts, and were then employed at places that we visited. The men whom we lost were all of them extraordinarily good men. This exchange materially altered the quality of the crew. Three of the Botany-bay-men were outlawed convicts; they had been shot at many times, and several times wounded. After making this bad exchange, my crew were refractory; the convicts were ever unfaithful, and took all the advantage that opportunity gave them. But sometimes exercising very strict discipline, and giving them good wholesome floggings; and at other times treating them with the best I had, or could get, according as their deeds deserved, I managed them without much difficulty during the passage across the South Pacific Ocean; and all the time I had been on the coast of Chili. I had lately been at the islands of St. Ambrose and St. Felix, and left there fifteen of my best men, with the view of procuring seals; and left that place in company with my consort the Pilgrim. We appointed Massa Fuero as our place of rendezvous, and if we did not meet there, again to rendezvous at St. Maria. I proceeded to the first place appointed; the Pilgrim had not arrived. I then determined to take a look at Juan Fernandez, and see if we could find any seals, as some persons had informed me they were to be found on some part of the island. I accordingly visited that place, as has been stated; from thence I proceeded to St. Maria; and arrived the 13th of February at that place, where we commonly find visitors. We found the ship Mars of Nantucket, commanded by Captain Jonathan Barney. The day we arrived, three of my Botany bay men run from the boat when on shore. The next day, (the 14th) I was informed by Captain Barney, that some of my convict men had planned to run away with one of my boats, and go over to the main. This information he obtained through the medium of his people. I examined into the affair, and was satisfied as to the truth of it; set five more of the above description of men on shore, making eight in all I had gotten clear of in two days. Captain Barney sailed about the 17th, and left me quite alone. I continued in that unpleasant situation till the 20th, never at any time after my arrival at this place, daring to let my whale boat be in the water fifteen minutes unless I was in her myself, from a fear that some of my people would run away with her. I always hoisted her in on deck the moment I came along side, by which means I had the advantage of them; for should they run away with any other boat belonging to the ship, I could overtake them with the whale boat, which they very well knew. They were also well satisfied of the reasons why that boat was always kept on board, except when in my immediate use. During this time, I had no fear from them, except of their running away. Under these disadvantages the Spanish ship Tryal made her appearance on the morning of the 20th, as has been stated; and I had in the course of the day the satisfaction of seeing the great utility of good discipline. In every part of the business of the Tryal, not one disaffected word was spoken by the men, but all flew to obey the commands they received; and to their credit it should be recorded, that no men ever behaved better than they, under such circumstances. When it is considered that we had but two boats, one a whale boat, and the other built by ourselves, while on the coast of New Holland, which was very little larger than the whale boat; both of them were clinker built, one of cedar, and the other not much stouter; with only twenty men to board and carry a ship, containing so many slaves, made desperate by their situation; for they were certain, if taken, to suffer death; and when arriving along side of the ship, they might have staved the bottom of the boats, by heaving into them a ballast stone or log of wood of twenty pounds: when all these things are taken into view, the reader may conceive of the hazardous nature of the enterprise, and the skill and the intrepidity which were requisite to carry it into execution.

On the afternoon of the 19th, before night, I sent the boatswain with the large boat and seine to try if he could catch some fish; he returned at night with but few, observing that the morning would be better, if he went early. I then wished him to go as early as he thought proper, and he accordingly went at four o'clock. At sunrise, or about that time, the officer who commanded the deck, came down to me while I was in my cot, with information that a sail was just opening round the south point, or head of the island. I immediately rose, went on deck, and observed that she was too near the land, on account of a reef that lay off the head; and at the same time remarked to my people, that she must be a stranger, and I did not well understand what she was about. Some of them observed that they did not know who she was, or what she was doing; but that they were accustomed to see vessels shew their colours, when coming into a port. I ordered the whale boat to be hoisted out and manned, which was accordingly done. Presuming the vessel was from sea, and had been many days out, without perhaps fresh provisions, we put the fish which had been caught the night before into the boat, to be presented if necessary. Every thing being soon ready, as I thought the strange ship was in danger, we made all the haste in our power to get on board, that we might prevent her getting on the reefs; but before we came near her, the wind headed her off, and she was doing well. I went along side, and saw the decks were filled with slaves. As soon as I got on deck, the captain, mate, people and slaves, crowded around me to relate their stories, and to make known their grievances; which could not but impress me with feelings of pity for their sufferings. They told me they had no water, as is related in their different accounts and depositions. After promising to relieve all the wants they had mentioned, I ordered the fish to be put on board, and sent the whale boat to our ship, with orders that the large boat, as soon as she returned from fishing, should take a set of gang casks to the watering place, fill them, and bring it for their relief as soon as possible. I also ordered the small boat to take what fish the large one had caught, and what soft bread they had baked, some pumpkins, some sugar, and bottled cider, and return to me without delay. The boat left me on board the Spanish ship, went to our own, and executed the orders; and returned to me again about eleven o'clock. At noon the large boat came with the water, which I was obliged to serve out to them myself, to keep them [from] drinking so much as to do themselves injury. I gave them at first one gill each, an hour after, half a pint, and the third hour, a pint. Afterward, I permitted them to drink as they pleased. They all looked up to me as a benefactor; and as I was deceived in them, I did them every possible kindness. Had it been otherwise there is no doubt I should have fallen a victim to their power. It was to my great advantage, that, on this occasion, the temperament of my mind was unusually pleasant. The apparent sufferings of those about me had softened my feelings into sympathy; or, doubtless my interference with some of their transactions would have cost me my life. The Spanish captain had evidently lost much of his authority over the slaves, whom he appeared to fear, and whom he was unwilling in any case to oppose. An instance of this occurred in the conduct of the four cabin boys, spoken of by the captain. They were eating with the slave boys on the main deck, when, (as I was afterwards informed) the Spanish boys, feeling some hopes of release, and not having prudence sufficient to keep silent, some words dropped respecting their expectations, which were understood by the slave boys. One of them gave a stroke with a knife on the head of one of the Spanish boys, which penetrated to the bone, in a cut four inches in length. I saw this and inquired what it meant. The captain replied, that it was merely the sport of the boys, who had fallen out. I told him it appeared to me to be rather serious sport, as the wound had caused the boy to lose about a quart of blood. Several similar instances of unruly conduct, which, agreeably to my manner of thinking, demanded immediate resistance and punishment, were thus easily winked at, and passed over. I felt willing however to make some allowance even for conduct so gross, when I considered them to have been broken down with fatigue and long suffering.

The act of the negro, who kept constantly at the elbows of Don Bonito and myself, I should, at any other time, have immediately resented; and although it excited my wonder, that his commander should allow this extraordinary liberty, I did not remonstrate against it, until it became troublesome to myself. I wished to have some private conversation with the captain alone, and the negro as usual following us into the cabin, I requested the captain to send him on deck, as the business about which we were to talk could not be conveniently communicated in presence of a third person. I spoke in Spanish, and the negro understood me. The captain assured me, that his remaining with us would be of no disservice; that he had made him his confidant and companion since he had lost so many of his officers and men. He had introduced him to me before, as captain of the slaves, and told me he kept them in good order. I was alone with them, or rather on board by myself, for three or four hours, during the absence of my boat, at which time the ship drifted out with the current three leagues from my own, when the breeze sprung up from the south east. It was nearly four o'clock in the afternoon. We ran the ship as near to the Perseverance as we could without either ship's swinging afoul the other. After the Spanish ship was anchored, I invited the captain to go on board my ship and take tea or coffee with me. His answer was short and seemingly reserved; and his air very different from that with which he had received my assistance. As I was at a loss to account for this change in his demeanour, and knew he had seen nothing in my conduct to justify it, and as I felt certain that he treated me with intentional neglect; in return I became less sociable, and said little to him. After I had ordered my boat to be hauled up and manned, and as I was going to the side of the vessel, in order to get into her, Don Bonito came to me, gave my hand a hearty squeeze, and, as I thought, seemed to feel the weight of the cool treatment with which I had retaliated. I had committed a mistake in attributing his apparent coldness to neglect; and as soon as the discovery was made, I was happy to rectify it, by a prompt renewal of friendly intercourse. He continued to hold my hand fast till I stepped off the gunwale down the side, when he let it go, and stood making me compliments. When I had seated myself in the boat, and ordered her to be shoved off, the people having their oars up on end, she fell off at a sufficient distance to leave room for the oars to drop. After they were down, the Spanish captain, to my great astonishment, leaped from the gunwale of the ship into the middle of our boat. As soon as he had recovered a little, he called out in so alarming a manner, that I could not understand him; and the Spanish sailors were then seen jumping overboard and making for our boat. These proceedings excited the wonder of us all. The officer whom I had with me anxiously inquired into their meaning. I smiled and told him, that I neither knew, nor cared; but it seemed the captain was trying to impress his people with a belief that we intended to run away with him. At this moment one of my Portuguese sailors in the boat, spoke to me, and gave me to understand what Don Bonito said. I desired the captain to come aft and sit down by my side, and in a calm deliberate manner relate the whole affair[.] In the mean time the boat was employed in picking up the men who had jumped from the ship. They had picked up three, (leaving one in the water till after the boat had put the Spanish captain and myself on board my ship,) when my officer observed the cable was cut, and the ship was swinging. I hailed the Perseverance, ordering the ports got up, and the guns run out as soon as possible. We pulled as fast as we could on board; and then despatched the boat for the man who was left in the water, whom we succeeded to save alive.

We soon had our guns ready; but the Spanish ship had dropped so far astern of the Perseverance, that we could bring but one gun to bear on her, which was the after one. This was fired six times, without any other effect than cutting away the fore top-mast stay, and some other small ropes which were no hindrance to her going away. She was soon out of reach of our shot, steering out of the bay. We then had some other calculations to make. Our ship was moored with two bower anchors, which were all the cables or anchors of that description we had. To slip and leave them would be to break our policy of insurance by a deviation, against which I would here caution the masters of all vessels. It should always be borne in mind, that to do any thing which will destroy the guaranty of their policies, how great soever may be the inducement, and how generous soever the motive, is not justifiable; for should any accident subsequently occur, whereby a loss might accrue to the underwriters, they will be found ready enough, and sometimes too ready, to avail themselves of the opportunity to be released from responsibility; and the damage must necessarily be sustained by the owners. This is perfectly right. The law has wisely restrained the powers of the insured, that the insurer should not be subject to imposition, or abuse. All bad consequences may be avoided by one who has a knowledge of his duty, and is disposed faithfully to obey its dictates.

At length, without much loss of time, I came to a determination to pursue, and take the ship with my two boats. On inquiring of the captain what fire arms they had on board the Tryal, he answered, they had none which they could use; that he had put the few they had out of order, so that they could make no defence with them; and furthermore, that they did not understand their use, if they were in order. He observed at the same time, that if I attempted to take her with boats we should all be killed; for the negros were such bravos and so desperate, that there would be no such thing as conquering them. I saw the man in the situation that I have seen others, frightened at his own shadow. This was probably owing to his having been effectually conquered and his spirits broken.

After the boats were armed, I ordered the men to get into them, and they obeyed with cheerfulness. I was going myself, but Don Bonito took hold of my hand and forbade me, saying, you have saved my life, and now you are going to throw away your own. Some of my confidential officers asked me if it would be prudent for me to go, and leave the Perseverance in such an unguarded state; and also, if any thing should happen to me, what would be the consequence to the voyage. Every man on board, they observed, would willingly go, if it were my pleasure. I gave their remonstrances a moment's consideration, and felt their weight. I then ordered into the boats my chief officer, Mr. Low, who commanded the party; and under him, Mr. Brown, my second officer, my brother William, Mr. George Russell, son to major Benjamin Russell of Boston, and Mr. Nathaniel Luther, midshipmen; William Clark, boatswain; Charles Spence, gunner; and thirteen seamen. By way of encouragement, I told them that Don Bonito considered the ship and what was in her as lost; that the value was more than one hundred thousand dollars; that if we would take her, it should be all our own; and that if we should afterwards be disposed to give him up one half, it would be considered as a present. I likewise reminded them of the suffering condition of the poor Spaniards remaining on board, whom I then saw with my spy-glass as high aloft as they could get on the top-gallant-masts, and knowing that death must be their fate if they came down. I told them, never to see my face again, if they did not take her; and these were all of them pretty powerful stimulants. I wished God to prosper them in the discharge of their arduous duty, and they shoved off. They pulled after and came up with the Tryal, took

their station upon each quarter, and commenced a brisk fire of musketry, directing it as much at the man at the helm as they could, as
that was likewise a place of resort for the negroes. At length they
drove the chief mate from it, who had been compelled to steer the
ship. He ran up the mizen rigging as high as the cross jack yard, and
called out in Spanish, "Don't board." This induced our people to
believe that he favoured the cause of the negroes; they fired at him,
and two balls took effect; one of them went through his side, but did
not go deep enough to be mortal; and the other went through one
of his thighs. This brought him down on deck again. They found the
ship made such head way, that the boats could hardly keep up with
her, as the breeze was growing stronger. They then called to the
Spaniards, who were still as high aloft as they could get, to come
down on the yards, and cut away the robings and earings of the topsails, and let them fall from the yards, so that they might not hold
any wind. They accordingly did so. About the same time, the
Spaniard who was steering the ship, was killed; (he is sometimes
called *passenger* and sometimes *clerk*, in the different depositions,)
so that both these circumstances combined, rendered her unmanageable by such people as were left on board. She came round to
the wind, and both boats boarded, one on each bow, when she was
carried by hard fighting. The negroes defended themselves with desperate courage; and after our people had boarded them, they found
they had barricadoed the deck by making a breast work of the water
casks which we had left on board, and sacks of matta, abreast the
mainmast, from one side of the ship to the other, to the height of six
feet; behind which they defended themselves with all the means in
their power to the last; and our people had to force their way over
this breast work before they could compel them to surrender. The
other parts of the transaction have some of them been, and the
remainder will be hereafter stated.

On going on board the next morning with hand-cuffs, leg-irons,
and shackled bolts, to secure the hands and feet of the negroes, the
sight which presented itself to our view was truly horrid. They had
got all the men who were living made fast, hands and feet, to the
ring bolts in the deck; some of them had parts of their bowels hanging out, and some with half their backs and thighs shaved off. This
was done with our boarding lances, which were always kept exceedingly sharp, and as bright as a gentleman's sword. Whilst putting
them in irons, I had to exercise as much authority over the Spanish
captain and his crew, as I had to use over my own men on any other
occasion, to prevent them from cutting to pieces and killing these
poor unfortunate beings. I observed one of the Spanish sailors had
found a razor in the pocket of an old jacket of his, which one of the
slaves had on; he opened it, and made a cut upon the negro's head.

He seemed to aim at his throat, and it bled shockingly. Seeing several more about to engage in the same kind of barbarity, I commanded them not to hurt another of them, on pain of being brought to the gang-way and flogged. The captain also, I noticed, had a dirk, which he had secreted at the time the negroes were massacreing the Spaniards. I did not observe, however, that he intended to use it, until one of my people gave me a twitch by the elbow, to draw my attention to what was passing, when I saw him in the act of stabbing one of the slaves. I immediately caught hold of him, took away his dirk, and threatened him with the consequences of my displeasure, if he attempted to hurt one of them. Thus I was obliged to be continually vigilant, to prevent them from using violence towards these wretched creatures.

After we had put every thing in order on board the Spanish ship, and swept for and obtained her anchors, which the negroes had cut her from, we sailed on the 23d, both ships in company, for Conception, where we anchored on the 26th. After the common forms were passed, we delivered the ship, and all that was on board her, to the captain, whom we had befriended. We delivered him also a bag of doubloons, containing, I presume, nearly a thousand; several bags of dollars, containing a like number; and several baskets of watches, some gold, and some silver: all of which had been brought on board the Perseverance for safe keeping. We detained no part of this treasure to reward us for the services we had rendered:—all that we received was faithfully returned.

After our arrival at Conception, I was mortified and very much hurt at the treatment which I received from Don Bonito Sereno; but had this been the only time that I ever was treated with ingratitude, injustice, or want of compassion, I would not complain. I will only name one act of his towards me at this place. He went to the prison and took the depositions of five of my Botany bay convicts, who had left us at St. Maria, and were now in prison here. This was done by him with a view to injure my character, so that he might not be obliged to make us any compensation for what we had done for him. I never made any demand of, nor claimed in any way whatever, more than that they should give me justice; and did not ask to be my own judge, but to refer it to government. Amongst those who swore against me were the three outlawed convicts, who have been before mentioned. I had been the means, undoubtedly, of saving every one of their lives, and had supplied them with clothes. They swore every thing against me they could to effect my ruin. Amongst other atrocities, they swore I was a pirate, and made several statements that would operate equally to my disadvantage had they been believed; all of which were brought before the viceroy of Lima against me. When we met at that place, the viceroy was too great and too good a man to be misled by these false representations. He told Don Bonito, that my conduct towards him proved the injustice of these depositions, taking his own official declaration at Conception for the proof of it; that he had been informed by Don Jose Calminaries, who was commandant of the marine, and was at that time, and after the affair of the Tryal, on the coast of Chili; that Calminaries had informed him how both Don Bonito and myself had conducted, and he was satisfied that no man had behaved better, under all circumstances, than the American captain had done to Don Bonito, and that he never had seen or heard of any man treating another with so much dishonesty and ingratitude as he had treated the American. The viceroy had previously issued an order, on his own authority, to Don Bonito, to deliver to me eight thousand dollars as part payment for services rendered him. This order was not given till his Excellency had consulted all the tribunals holding jurisdiction over similar cases, except the twelve royal judges. These judges exercise a supreme authority over all the courts in Peru, and reserve to themselves the right of giving a final decision in all questions of law. Whenever either party is dissatisfied with the decision of the inferior courts in this kingdom, they have a right of appeal to the twelve judges. Don Bonito had attempted an appeal from the viceroy's order to the royal judges. The viceroy sent for me, and acquainted me of Don Bonito's attempt; at the same time recommending to me to accede to it, as the royal judges well understood the nature of the business, and would do much better for me than his order would. He observed at the same time, that they were men of too great characters to be biassed or swayed from doing justice by any party; they holding their appointments immediately from his majesty. He said, if I requested it, Don Bonito should be holden to his order. I then represented, that I had been in Lima nearly two months, waiting for different tribunals, to satisfy his Excellency what was safe for him, and best to be done for me, short of a course of law, which I was neither able nor willing to enter into; that I had then nearly thirty men on different islands, and on board my tender, which was then somewhere amongst the islands on the coast of Chili; that they had no method that I knew of to help themselves, or receive succor, except from me; and that if I was to defer the time any longer it amounted to a certainty, that they must suffer. I therefore must pray that his Excellency's order might be put in force.

Don Bonito, who was owner of the ship and part of the cargo, had been quibbling and using all his endeavors to delay the time of payment, provided the appeal was not allowed, when his Excellency told him to get out of his sight, that he would pay the money himself, and put him (Don Bonito) into a dungeon, where he should not see sun, moon, or stars; and was about giving the order, when a very respectable company of merchants waited on him and pleaded for Don Bonito; praying that his Excellency would favour him on account of his family, who were very rich and respectable. The viceroy remarked that Don Bonito's character had been such as to disgrace any family, that had any pretensions to respectability; but that he should grant their prayer, provided there was no more reason for complaint. The last transaction brought me the money in two hours; by which time I was extremely distressed, enought, I believe, to have punished me for a great many of my bad deeds.

When I take a retrospective view of my life, I cannot find in my soul, that I ever have done any thing to deserve such misery and ingratitude as I have suffered at different periods, and in general, from the very persons to whom I have rendered the greatest services.

The following Documents were officially translated, and are inserted without alteration, from the original papers. This I thought to be the most correct course, as it would give the reader a better view of the subject than any other method that could be adopted. My deposition and that of Mr. Luther, were communicated through a bad linguist, who could not speak the English language so well as I could the Spanish, Mr. Luther not having any knowledge of the Spanish language. The Spanish captain's deposition, together with Mr. Luther's and my own, were translated into English again, as now inserted; having thus undergone two translations. These circumstances, will, we hope, be a sufficient apology for any thing which may appear to the reader not to be perfectly consistent, one declaration with another; and for any impropriety of expression.

---

## OFFICIAL DOCUMENTS.

STAMP.

A FAITHFUL TRANSLATION OF THE DEPOSITIONS OF DON BENITO CERENO, OF DON AMASA DELANO, AND OF DON NATHANIEL LUTHER, TOGETHER WITH THE DOCUMENTS OF THE COMMENCEMENT OF THE PROCESS, UNDER THE KING'S SEAL.

I DON JOSE DE ABOS, and Padilla, his Majesty's Notary for the Royal Revenue, and Register of this Province, and Notary Public of the Holy Crusade of this Bishoprick, &c.

Do certify and declare, as much as requisite in law, that, in the criminal cause, which by an order of the Royal Justice, Doctor DON JUAN MARTINEZ DE ROZAS, deputy assessor general of this province, conducted against the Senegal Negroes,

that the ship Tryal was carrying from the port of Valparaiso, to
that of Callao of Lima, in the month of December last. There is
at the beginning of the prosecution, a decree in continuation of
the declaration of her captain, Don Benito Cereno, and on the
back of the twenty-sixth leaf, that of the captain of the American ship, the Perseverance, Amasa Delano; and that of the
supercargo of this ship, Nathaniel Luther, midshipman, of the
United States, on the thirtieth leaf; as also the Sentence of the
aforesaid cause, on the back of the 72d leaf; and the confirmation of the Royal Audience, of this District, on the 78th and
79th leaves; and an official order of the Tribunal with which the
cause and every thing else therein continued, is remitted back;
which proceedings with a representation made by the said
American captain, Amasa Delano, to this Intendency, against
the Spanish captain of the ship Tryal, Don Benito Cereno, and
answers thereto—are in the following manner—

### Decree of the Commencement of the Process.

In the port of Talcahuane, the twenty-fourth of the month of
February, one thousand eight hundred and five, Doctor Don
Juan Martinez de Rozas, Counsellor of the Royal Audience of
this Kingdom, Deputy Assessor, and learned in the law, of this
Intendency, having the deputation thereof on account of the
absence of his Lordship, the Governor Intendent—Said, that
whereas the ship Tryal, has just cast anchor in the road of this
port, and her captain, Don Benito Cereno, has made the declaration of the twentieth of December, he sailed from the port
of Valparaiso, bound to that of Callao; having his ship loaded
with produce and merchandize of the country, with sixty-three
negroes of all sexes and ages, and besides nine sucking infants;
that the twenty-sixth, in the night, revolted, killed eighteen of
his men, and made themselves master of the ship—that afterwards they killed seven men more, and obliged him to carry
them to the coast of Africa, at Senegal, of which they were
natives; that Tuesday the nineteenth, he put into the island of
Santa Maria, for the purpose of taking in water, and he found
in its harbour the American ship, the Perseverance, commanded by captain Amasa Delano, who being informed of the
revolt of the negroes on board the ship Tryal, killed five or six
of them in the engagement, and finally overcame them; that
the ship being recovered, he supplied him with hands, and
brought him to the port.—Wherefore, for examining the truth
of these facts, and inflict on the guilty of such heinous crimes,
the penalties provided by law. He therefore orders that this
decree commencing the process, should be extended, that
agreeably to its tenor, the witnesses, that should be able to give

an account of them, be examined—thus ordered by his honour, which I attest.—Doctor ROZAS

Before me, JOSE DE ABOS, and Padilla, his Majesty's Notary of Royal Revenue and Registers.

### Declaration of first Witness, DON BENITO CERENO.

The same day and month and year, his Honour ordered the captain of the ship Tryal, Don Benito Cereno, to appear, of whom he received before me, the oath, which he took by God, our Lord, and a Sign of the Cross, under which he promised to tell the truth of whatever he should know and should be asked—and being interrogated agreeably to the tenor of the act, commencing the process, he said, that the twentieth of December last, he set sail with his ship from the port of Valparaiso, bound to that of Callao; loaded with the produce of the country, and seventy-two negroes of both sexes, and of all ages, belonging to Don Alexandro Aranda, inhabitant of the city of Mendosa; that the crew of the ship consisted of thirty-six men, besides the persons who went [as] passengers; that the negroes were of the following ages,—twenty from twelve to sixteen years, one from about eighteen to nineteen years, named Jose, and this was the man that waited upon his master Don Alexandro, who speaks well the Spanish, having had him four or five years; a mulatto, named Francisco, native of the province of Buenos Ayres, aged about thirty-five years; a smart negro, named Joaquin, who had been for many years among the Spaniards, aged twenty six years, and a caulker by trade; twelve full grown negroes, aged from twenty-five to fifty years, all raw and born on the coast of Senegal—whose names are as follow,—the first was named Babo, and he was killed,—the second who is his son, is named Muri,—the third, Matiluqui,—the fourth, Yola,—the fifth, Yau,—the sixth Atufal, who was killed,—the seventh, Diamelo, also killed,—the eighth, Lecbe, likewise killed,—the ninth, Natu, in the same manner killed, and that he does not recollect the names of the others; but that he will take due account of them all, and remit to the court; and twenty-eight women of all ages;—that all the negroes slept upon deck, as is customary in this navigation; and none wore fetters, because the owner, Aranda told him that they were all tractable; that the twenty-seventh of December, at three o'clock in the morning, all the Spaniards being asleep except the two officers on the watch, who were the boatswain Juan Robles, and the carpenter Juan Balltista Gayete, and the helmsman and his boy; the negroes revolted suddenly, wounded dangerously the boatswain and the carpenter, and successively killed eighteen men of those who were sleeping upon deck,—some with sticks and daggers, and others by throwing them alive overboard, after tying them; that of the Spaniards who were upon deck, they left about seven, as he thinks, alive and tied, to manoeuvre the ship; and three or four more who hid themselves, remained also alive, although in the act of revolt, they made themselves masters of the hatchway, six or seven wounded, went through it to the cock-pit without any hindrance on their part; that in the act of revolt, the mate and another person, whose name he does not recollect, attempted to come up through the hatchway, but having been wounded at the onset, they were obliged to return to the cabin; that the deponent resolved at break of day to come up the companion-way, where the negro Babo was, being the ring leader, and another who assisted him, and having spoken to them, exhorted them to cease committing such atrocities—asking them at the same time what they wanted and intended to do—offering himself to obey their commands; that notwithstanding this, they threw, in his presence, three men, alive and tied, overboard; that they told the deponent to come up, and that they would not kill him—which having done, they asked him whether there were in these seas any negro countries, where they might be carried, and he answered them, no; that they afterwards told him to carry them to *Senegal*, or to the neighbouring islands of St. Nicolas—and he answered them, that this was impossible, on account of the great distance, the bad condition of the vessel, the want of provisions, sails and water; that they replied to him, he must carry them in any way; that they would do and conform themselves to every thing the deponent should require as to eating and drinking, that after a long conference, being absolutely compelled to please them, for they threatened him to kill them all, if they were not at all events carried to Senegal. He told them that what was most wanting for the voyage was water; that they would go near the coast to take it, and thence they would proceed on their course—that the negroes agreed to it; and the deponent steered towards the intermediate ports, hoping to meet some Spanish or foreign vessel that would save them; that within ten or eleven days they saw the land, and continued their course by it in the vicinity of Nasca; that the deponent observed that the negroes were now restless, and mutinous, because he did not effect the taking in of water, they having required with threats that it should be done, without fail the following day; he told them they saw plainly that the coast was steep, and the rivers designated in the maps were not to be found, with other reasons suitable to the circumstances; that the best way would be to go to the island of Santa Maria, where they might water and victual easily, it being a desert island, as the foreigners did; that the deponent did not go to Pisco, that was near, nor make any other port of the coast, because the negroes had intimated to him several times, that they would kill them all the very moment they should perceive any city, town, or settlement, on the shores to which they should be carried; that having determined to go to the island of Santa Maria, as the deponent had planned, for the purpose of trying whether in the passage or in the island itself, they could find any vessel that should favour them, or whether he could escape from it in a boat to the neighbouring coast of Arruco. To adopt the necessary means he immediately changed his course, steering for the island; that the negroes held daily conferences, in which they discussed what was necessary for their design of returning to Senegal, whether they were to kill all the Spaniards, and particularly the deponent; that eight days after parting from the coast of Nasca, the deponent being on the watch a little after day-break, and soon after the negroes had their meeting, the negro Mure came to the place where the deponent was, and told him, that his comrades had determined to kill his master, Don Alexandro Aranda, because they said they could not otherwise obtain their liberty, and that he should call the mate, who was sleeping, before they executed it, for fear, as he understood, that he should not be killed with the rest; that the deponent prayed and told him all that was necessary in such a circumstance to dissuade him from his design, but all was useless, for the negro Mure answered him, that the thing could not be prevented, and that they should all run the risk of being killed if they should attempt to dissuade or obstruct them in the act; that in this conflict the deponent called the mate, and immediately the negro Mure ordered the negro Matinqui, and another named Lecbe, who died in the island of Santa Maria, to go and commit this murder; that the two negroes went down to the birth of Don Alexandro, and stabbed him in his bed; that yet half alive and agonizing, they dragged him on deck and threw him overboard; that the clerk, Don Lorenzo Bargas, was sleeping in the opposite birth, and awaking at the cries of Aranda, surprised by them, and at the sight of the negroes, who had bloody daggers in their hands, he threw himself into the sea through a window which was near him, and was miserably drowned, without being in the power of the deponent to assist, or take him up, though he immediately put out his boat; that a short time after killing Aranda, they got upon deck his german-cousin, Don Francisco Masa, and his other clerk, called Don Hermenegildo, a native of Spain, and a relation of the said Aranda, besides the boatswain, Juan Robles, the boatswain's mate, Manuel Viseaya, and two or three others of the sailors, all of whom were wounded, and having stabbed them again, they threw them alive into the sea, although they made no resistance, nor begged for any thing else but mercy; that the boatswain, Juan Robles, who knew how to swim, kept himself the longest above water, making acts of contrition, and in the last words he uttered, charged this deponent to cause mass to be said for his soul, to our Lady of Succour; that having finished this slaughter, the negro Mure told him that they had now done all, and that he might pursue his destination, warning him that they would kill all the Spaniards, if they saw them speak, or plot any thing against them—a threat which they repeated almost every day; that before this occurrence last mentioned, they had tied the cook to throw him overboard for I know not what thing they heard him speak, and finally they spared his life at the request of the deponent; that a few days after, the deponent endeavoured not to omit any means to preserve their lives— spoke to them peace and tranquillity, and agreed to draw up a paper, signed by the deponent, and the sailors who could write, as also by the negroes, Babo and Atufal, who could do it in their language, though they were new, in which he obliged himself to carry them to Senegal, and they not to kill any more, and to return to them the ship with the cargo, with which they were for that satisfied and quieted; that omitting other events which daily happened, and which can only serve to recal their past misfortunes and conflicts, after forty-two days navigation, reck-oned from the time they sailed from Nasca, during which they navigated under a scanty allowance of water, they at last arrived at the island of Santa Maria, on Tuesday the nineteenth instant, at about five o'clock in the afternoon, at which hour they cast anchor very near the American ship Perseverance, which lay in the same port, commanded by the *generous captain Amasa Delano*, but at seven o'clock in the morning they had already descried the port, and the negroes became uneasy as soon as they saw the ship, and the deponent, to appease and quiet them, proposed to them to say and do all that he will declare to have said to the American captain, with which they were tranquilized warning him that if he varied in the least, or uttered any word that should give the least intimation of the past occurrences, they would instantly kill him and all his companions; that about eight o'clock in the morning, captain Amasa Delano came in his boat, on board the Tryal, and all gladly received him; that the deponent, acting then the part of an owner and a free captain of the ship, told them that he came from Buenos Ayres, bound to Lima, with that parcel of negroes; that at the cape many had died, that also, all the sea officers and the greatest part of the crew had died, there remained to him no other sailors than these few who were in sight, and that for want of them the sails had been torn to pieces; that the heavy storms off the cape had obliged them to throw overboard the greatest part of the cargo, and the water pipes; that consequently he had no more water; that he had thought of putting into the port of Conception, but that the north wind had prevented him, as also the want of water, for he had only enough for that day, concluded by asking of him supplies;—that the *generous captain Amasa Delano* immediately offered them sails, pipes, and whatever he wanted, to pursue his voyage to Lima, without entering any other port, leaving it to his pleasure to refund him for these supplies at Callao, or pay him for them if he thought best; that he immediately ordered his boat for the purpose of bringing him water, sugar, and bread, as they did; that Amasa Delano remained on board the Tryal all the day, till he left the ship anchored at five o'clock in the afternoon, deponent speaking to him always of his pretended misfortunes, under the fore-mentioned principles, without having had it in his power to tell a single word, nor giving him the least hint, that he might know the truth, and state of things; because the negro Mure, who is a man of capacity and talents, performing the office of an officious servant, with all the appearance of submission of the humble slave, did not leave the deponent one moment, in order to observe his actions and words; for he understands well the Spanish, and besides there were thereabout some others who were constantly on the watch and understood it also; that a moment in which Amasa Delano left the deponent, Mure asked him, how do we come on? and the deponent answered them, well; he gives us all the supplies we want, but he asked him afterwards how many men he had, and the deponent told him that he had thirty men; but that twenty of them were on the island, and there were in the vessel only those whom he saw there in the two boats; and then the negro told him, well, you will be the captain of this ship to night and his also, for three negroes are sufficient to take it; that as soon as they had cast anchor, at five of the clock, as has been stated, the American captain took leave, to return to his vessel, and the deponent accompanied him as far as the gunwale, where he staid under pretence of taking leave, until he should have got into his boat; but on shoving off, the deponent jumped from the gunwale into the boat and fell into it, without knowing how, and without sustaining, fortunately, any harm; but he immediately hallooed to the Spaniards in the ship, "Overboard, those that can swim, the rest to the rigging." That he instantly told the captain, by means of the Portuguese interpreter, that they were revolted negroes, who had killed all his people; that the said captain soon understood the affair, and recovered from his surprise, which the leap of the deponent occassioned, and told him, "Be not afraid, be not afraid, set down and be easy," and ordered his sailors to row towards his ship, and before coming up to her, he hailed, to get a cannon ready and run it out of the port hole, which they did very quick, and fired with it a few shots at the negroes; that in the mean while the boat was sent to pick up two men who had thrown themselves overboard, which they effected; that the negroes cut the cables, and endeavoured to sail away; that Amasa Delano, seeing them sailing away, and the cannon could not subdue them, ordered his people to get muskets, pikes, and sabres ready, and all his men offered themselves willingly to board them with the boats; that captain Amasa Delano wanted to go in person, and was going to embark the first, but the deponent prevented him, and after many entreaties he finally remained, saying, though that circumstance would procure him much honour, he would stay to please him, and keep him company in his affliction, and would send a brother of his, on whom he said he placed as much reliance as on himself; his brother, the mates, and eighteen men, whom he had in his vessel, embarked in the two boats, and made their way towards the Tryal, which was already under sail; that they rowed considerably in pursuing the ship, and kept up a musketry fire; but that they could not overtake them, until they hallooed to the sailors on the rigging, to unbend or take away the sails, which they accordingly did, letting them fall on the deck; that they were then able to lay themselves alongside, keeping up constantly a musketry fire, whilst some got up the sides on deck, with pikes and sabres, and the others remained in the stern of the boat, keeping up also a fire, until they got up finally by the same side, and engaged the negroes, who defended themselves to the last with their weapons, rushing upon the points of the pikes with an extraordinary fury; that the Americans killed five or six negroes, and these were Babo, Atufal, Dick, Natu, Qiamolo, and does not recollect any other; that they wounded several others, and at last conquered and made them prisoners; that at ten o'clock at night, the first mate with three men, came to inform the captain that the ship had been taken, and came also for the purpose of being cured of a dangerous wound, made by a point of a dagger, which he had received in his breast; that two other Americans had been slightly wounded; the captain left nine men to take care of the ship as far as this port; he accompanied her with his own until both ships, the Tryal and Perseverance, cast anchor between nine and eleven o'clock in the forenoon of this day; that the deponent has not seen the twenty negroes, from twelve to sixteen years of age, have any share in the execution of the murders; nor does he believe they have had, on account of their age, although all were knowing to the insurrection; that the negro Jose, eighteen years old, and in the service of Don Alexandro, was the one who communicated the information to the negro Mure and his comrades, of the state of things before the revolt;

and this is known, because in the preceding nights he used to come to sleep from below, where they were, and had secret conversations with Mure, in which he was seen several times by the mate; and one night he drove him away twice; that this same negro Jose, was the one who advised the other negroes to kill his master, Don Alexandro; and that this is known, because the negroes have said it; that on the first revolt, the negro Jose was upon deck with the other revolted negroes, but it is not known whether he materially participated in the murders; that the mulatto Francisco was of the band of revolters, and one of their number; that the negro Joaquin was also one of the worst of them, for that on the day the ship was taken, he assisted in the defence of her with a hatchet in one hand and a dagger in the other, as the sailors told him; that in sight of the deponent, he stabbed Don Francisco Masa, when he was carrying him to throw him overboard alive, he being the one who held him fast; that the twelve or thirteen negroes, from twenty-five to fifty years of age, were with the former, the principal revolters, and committed the murders and atrocities before related; that five or six of them were killed, as has been said, in the attack on the ship, and the following remained alive and are prisoners,—to wit—Mure, who acted as captain and commander of them, and on all the insurrections and posterior events, Matinqui, Alathano, Yau, Luis, Mapenda, Yola, Yambaio, being eight in number, and with Jose, Joaquin, and Francisco, who are also alive, making the member of eleven of the remaining insurgents; that the negresses of age, were knowing to the revolt, and influenced the death of their master; who also used their influence to kill the deponent; that in the act of murder, and before that of the engagement of the ship, they began to sing, and were singing a very melancholy song during the action, to excite the courage of the negroes; that the statement he has just given of the negroes who are alive, has been made by the officers of the ship; that of the thirty-six men of the crew and passengers, which the deponent had knowledge of, twelve only including the mate remained alive, besides four cabin boys, who were not included in that number; that they broke an arm of one of those cabin boys, named Francisco Raneds, and gave him three or four stabs, which are already healed; that in the engagement of the ship, the second clerk, Don Jose Morairi, was killed by a musket ball fired at him through accident, for having incautiously presented himself on the gunwale; that at the time of the attack of the ship, Don Joaquin Arambaolaza was on one of the yards flying from the negroes, and at the approach of the boats, he hallooed by order of the negroes, not to board, on which account the Americans thought he was also one of the revolters, and fired two balls at him, one passed through one of his thighs,

and the other in the chest of his body, of which he is now confined, though the American captain, who has him on board, says
he will recover; that in order to be able to proceed from the
coast of Nasca, to the island of Santa Maria, he saw himself
obliged to lighten the ship, by throwing more than one third of
the cargo overboard, for he could not have made that voyage
otherwise; that what he has said is the most substantial of what
occurs to him on this unfortunate event, and the truth, under
the oath that he has taken;—which declaration he affirmed and
ratified, after hearing it read to him. He said that he was twenty-
nine years of age;—and signed with his honour—which I certify.

BENITO CERENO.

DOCTOR ROZAS
*Before me.*—PADILLA.

### RATIFICATION.

In the port of Talcahuano, the first day of the month of March,
in the year one thousand eight hundred and five,—the same
Honourable Judge of this cause caused to appear in his presence
the captain of the ship Tryal, Don Benito Cereno, of whom he
received an oath, before me, which he took conformably to law,
under which he promised to tell the truth of what he should
know, and of what he should be asked, and having read to him
the foregoing declaration, and being asked if it is the same he has
given and whether he has to add or to take off any thing,—he
said, that it is the same he has given, that he affirms and ratifies
it; and has only to add, that the new negroes were thirteen, and
the females comprehended twenty-seven, without including the
infants, and that one of them died from hunger or thi[r]st, and
two young negroes of those from twelve to sixteen, together with
an infant. And he signed it with his honour—which I certify.

BENITO CERENO.

DOCTOR ROZAS.
*Before me.*—PADILLA.

### *Declaration of DOM AMASA DELANO.*

The same day, month and year, his Honour, ordered the captain of the American ship Perseverance to appear, whose oath
his Honour received, which he took by placing his right hand
on the Evangelists, under which he promised to tell the truth
of what he should know and be asked—and being interrogated
according to the decree, beginning this process, through the
medium of the interpreter Carlos Elli, who likewise swore to

exercise well and lawfully his office, that the nineteenth or twentieth of the month, as he believes, agreeably to the calculation he keeps from the eastward, being at the island of Santa Maria, at anchor, he descried at seven o'clock in the morning, a ship coming round the point; that he asked his crew what ship that was; they replied that they did not know her; that taking his spy-glass he perceived she bore no colours; that he took his barge, and his net for fishing, and went on board of her, that when he got on deck he embraced the Spanish captain, who told him that he had been four months and twenty six days from Buenoes Ayres; that many of his people had died of the scurvy, and that he was in great want of supplies—particularly pipes for water, duck for sails, and refreshment for his crew; that the deponent offered to give and supply him with every thing he asked and wanted; that the Spanish captain did nothing else, because the ringleader of the negroes was constantly at their elbows, observing what was said. That immediately he sent his barge to his own ship to bring, (as they accordingly did) water, peas, bread, sugar, and fish. That he also sent for his long boat to bring a load of water, and having brought it, he returned to his own ship; that in parting he asked the Spanish captain to come on board his ship to take coffee, tea, and other refreshments; but he answered him with coldness and indifference; that he could not go then, but that he would in two or three days. That at the same time he visited him, the ship Tryal cast anchor in the port, about four o'clock in the afternoon,— that he told his people belonging to his boat to embark in order to return to his ship, that the deponent also left the deck to get into his barge,—that on getting into the barge, the Spanish captain took him by the hand and immediately gave a jump on board his boat,—that he then told him that the negroes of the Tryal had taken her, and had murdered twenty-five men, which the deponent was informed of through the medium of an interpreter, who was with him, and a Portuguese; that two or three other Spaniards threw themselves into the water, who were picked up by his boats; that he immediately went to his ship, and before reaching her, called to the mate to prepare and load the guns; that having got on board, he fired at them with his cannon, and this same deponent pointed six shots at the time the negroes of the Tryal were cutting away the cables and setting sail; that the Spanish captain told him that the ship was already going away, and that she could not be taken; that the deponent replied that he would take her; then the Spanish captain told him that if he took her, one half of her value would be his, and the other half would remain to the real owners; that thereupon he ordered the people belonging to his crew, to embark in the two boats, armed with knives, pistols, sabres, and pikes, to pursue her, and board her; that the two boats were firing at her near an hour with musketry, and at the end boarded and captured her; and that before sending his boats, he told his crew, in order to encourage them, that the Spanish captain offered to give them the half of the value of the Tryal if they took her. That having taken the ship, they came to anchor at about two o'clock in the morning very near the deponent's, leaving in her about twenty of his men; that his first mate received a very dangerous wound in his breast made with a pike, of which he lies very ill; that three other sailors were also wounded with clubs, though not dangerously; that five or six of the negroes were killed in boarding; that at six o'clock in the morning, he went with the Spanish captain on board the Tryal, to carry manacles and fetters from his ship, ordering them to be put on the negroes who remained alive, he dressed the wounded, and [accompanied] the Tryal to the anchoring ground; and in it he delivered her up manned from his crew; for until that moment he remained in possession of her; that what he has said is what he knows, and the truth, under the oath he has taken, which he affirmed and ratified after the said declaration had been read to him,—saying he was forty-two years of age,—the interpreter did not sign it because he said he did not know how—the captain signed it with his honour—which I certify.

AMASA DELANO.

Doctor ROZAS.
    *Before me.*—Padilla.

---

### RATIFICATION.

The said day, month and year, his Honour ordered the captain of the American ship, Don Amasa Delano to appear, of whom his Honour received an oath, which he took by placing his hand on the Evangelists, under which he promised to tell the truth of what he should know, and be asked, and having read to him the foregoing declaration, through the medium of the interpreter, Ambrosio Fernandez, who likewise took an oath to exercise well and faithfully his office,—he said that he affirms and ratifies the same; that he has nothing to add or diminish, and he signed it, with his Honour, and likewise the Interpreter.

AMASA DELANO.

AMBROSIO FERNANDEZ.

Doctor ROZAS.
    *Before me.*—Padilla.

---

### Declaration of DON NATHANIEL LUTHER, Midshipman.

The same day, month and year, his Honour ordered Don
Nathaniel Luther, first midshipman of the American ship Perseverance, and acting as clerk to the captain, to appear, of
whom he received an oath, and which he took by placing his
right hand on the Evangelists, under which he promised to tell
the truth of what he should know and be asked, and being
interrogated agreeably to the decree commencing this process,
through the medium of the Interpreter Carlos Elli, he said that
the deponent himself was one that boarded, and helped to take
the ship Tryal in the boats; that he knows that his captain,
Amasa Delano, has deposed on every thing that happened in
this affair; that in order to avoid delay he requests that his declaration should be read to him, and he will tell whether it is
[con]formable to the happening of the events; that if anything
should be omitted he will observe it, and add to it, doing the
same if he erred in any part thereof; and his Honour having
acquiesced in this proposal, the Declaration made this day by
captain Amasa Delano, was read to him through the medium of
the Interpreter, and said, that the deponent went with his captain, Amasa Delano, to the ship Tryal, as soon as she appeared
at the point of the island, which was about seven o'clock in the
morning, and remained with him on board of her, until she cast
anchor; that the deponent was one of those who boarded the
ship Tryal in the boats, and by this he knows that the narration
which the captain has made in the deposition which has been
read to him, is certain and exact in all its parts; and he has only
three things to add: the first, that whilst his captain remained
on board the Tryal, a negro stood constantly at his elbow, and
by the side of the deponent, the second, that the deponent was
in the boat, when the Spanish captain jumped into it, and when
the Portuguese declared that the negroes had revolted; the
third, that the number of killed was six, five negroes and a
Spanish sailor; that what he has said is the truth, under the
oath which he has taken; which he affirmed and ratified, after
his Declaration had been read to him; he said he was twenty
one years of age, and signed it with his Honour, but the Interpreter did not sign it, because he said he did not know how—
which I certify,

NATHANIEL LUTHER.

DOCTOR ROZAS.
   *Before me.*—PADILLA.

## RATIFICATION.

The aforesaid day, month and year, his Honour, ordered Don Nathaniel Luther, first midshipman of the American ship Perseverance, and acting as clerk to the captain, to whom he administ[e]red an oath, which he took by placing his hand on the Evangelists, under the sanctity of which he promised to tell the truth of what he should know and be asked; and the foregoing Declaration having been read to him, which he thoroughly understood, through the medium of the Interpreter, Ambrosio Fernandez, to whom an oath was likewise administred, to exercise well and faithfully his office, he says that he affirms and ratifies the same, that he has nothing to add or diminish, and he signed it with his Honour, and the Interpreter, which I certify.

NATHANIEL LUTHER.

AMBROSIO FERNANDEZ.

Doctor ROZAS.
  *Before me.*—Padilla.

## SENTENCE.

In this city of Conception, the second day of the month of March, of one thousand eight hundred and five, his Honour Doctor Don Juan Martinez de Rozas, Deputy Assessor and learned in the law, of this intendency, having the execution thereof on account of the absence of his Honour, the principal having seen the proceedings, which he has conducted officially against the negroes of the ship Tryal, in consequence of the insurrection and atrocities which they have committed on board of her.—He declared, that the insurrection and revolt of said negroes, being sufficiently substantiated, with premediated intent, the twenty seventh of December last, at three o'clock in the morning; that taking by surprise the sleeping crew, they killed eighteen men, some with sticks, and daggers, and others by throwing them alive overboard; that a few days afterward with the same deliberate intent, they stabbed their master Don Alexandro Aranda, and threw Don Franciso Masa, his german cousin, Hermenegildo, his relation, and the other wounded persons who were confined in the berths, overboard alive; that in the island of Santa Maria, they defended themselves with arms, against the Americans, who attempted to subdue them, causing the death of Don Jose Moraira the second clerk, as they had done that of the first, Don Lorenzo Bargas; the whole being considered, and the consequent guilts resulting from those [heinous] and atrocious actions as an example to others, he ought and did condemn the negroes, Mure, Martinqui, Alazase, Yola, Joaquin, Luis, Yau, Mapenda, and Yambaio, to the common penalty of death, which shall be executed, by taking them out and dragging them from the prison, at the tail of a beast of burden, as far as the gibbet, where they shall be hung until they are dead, and to the forfeiture of all their property, if they should have any, to be applied to the Royal Treasury; that the heads of the five first be cut off after they are dead, and be fixed on a pole, in the square of the port of Talcahuano, and the corpses of all be burnt to ashes. The negresses and young negroes of the same gang shall be present at the execution, if they should be in that city at the time thereof; that he ought and did condemn likewise, the negro Jose, servant to said Don Alexandro, and Yambaio, Francisco, Rodriguez, to ten years confinement in the place of Valdivia, to work chained, on allowance and without pay, in the work of the King, and also to attend the execution of the other criminals; and judging definitively by this sentence thus pronounced and ordered by his Honour, and that the same should be executed notwithstanding the appeal, for which he declared there was no cause, but that an account of it should be previously sent to the Royal Audience of this district, for the execution thereof with the costs.

DOCTOR ROZAS.

*Before me.*—JOSE DE ABOS PADILLA.

*His Majesty's Notary of the Royal Revenue and Registers.*

---

### CONFIRMATION OF THE SENTENCE.

SANTIAGO, *March the twenty first, of one thousand eight hundred and five.*

Having duly considered the whole, we suppose the sentence pronounced by the Deputy Assessor of the City of Conception, to whom we remit the same for its execution and fulfilment, with the official resolution, taking first an authenticated copy of the proceedings, to give an account thereof to his Majesty: and in regard to the request of the acting Notary, to the process upon the pay of his charges, he will exercise his right when and where he shall judge best.—

*There are four flourishes.*

Their Honours, the President, Regent, and Auditors of his Royal Audience passed the foregoing decree, and those on the Margin set their flourishes, the day of this date, the twenty first of March, one thousand eight hundred and five;—which I certify,

ROMAN.

## NOTIFICATION.

The twenty third of said month, I acquainted his Honour, the King's Attorney of the foregoing decree,—which I certify,

ROMAN.

## OFFICIAL RESOLUTION.

The Tribunal has resolved to manifest by this official resolve and pleasure for the exactitude, zeal and promptness which you have discovered in the cause against the revolted negroes of the ship Tryal, which process it remits to you, with the approbation of the sentence for the execution thereof, forewarning you that before its completion, you may agree with the most Illustrious Bishop, on the subject of furnishing the spiritual aids to those miserable beings, affording the same to them with all possible dispatch.—At the same time this Royal Audience has thought fit in case you should have an opportunity of speaking with the Bostonian captain, Amasa Delano, to charge you to inform him, that they will give an account to his Majesty, of the generous and benevolent conduct which he displayed in the punctual assistance that he afforded the Spanish captain of the aforesaid ship, for the suitable manifestation, publication and noticety of such a memorable event.

God preserve you many years.

SANTIAGO, *March the twenty second, of one thousand eight hundred and five.*

JOSÉ De SANTIAGO CONCHA.

Doctor Don JUAN MARTINEZ De ROZAS,

*Deputy assessor, and learned in the law, of the Intendency of Conception.*

I the unde[r]signed, sworn Interpreter of languages, do certify that the foregoing translation from the Spanish original, is true.

FRANCIS SALES.

*Boston, April 15th, 1808.*

N.B. It is proper here to state, that the difference of two days, in the dates of the process at Talquahauno, that of the Spaniards being the 24th of February and ours the 26th, was because they dated theirs the day we anchored in the lower harbour, which was one day before we got up abreast of the port at which time we dated ours; and our coming by the way of the Cape of Good Hope, made our reckoning of time one day different from theirs.

It is also necessary to remark, that the statement in page 332, respecting Mr. Luther being supercargo, and United States midshipman, is a mistake of the linguist. He was with me, the same as Mr. George Russell, and my brother William, midshipmen of the ship Perseverance.

---

On my return to America in 1807, I was gratified in receiving a polite letter from the Marquis DE CASE YRUSO, through the medium of JUAN STOUGHTON Esq. expressing the satisfaction of his majesty, the king of Spain, on account of our conduct in capturing the Spanish ship Tryal at the island St. Maria, accompanied with a gold medal, having his majesty's likeness on one side, and on the other the inscription, REWARD OF MERIT. The correspondence relating to that subject, I shall insert for the satisfaction of the reader. I had been assured by the president of Chili, when I was in that country, and likewise by the viceroy of Lima, that all my conduct, and the treatment I had received, should be faithfully represented to his majesty Charles IV, who most probably would do something more for me. I had reason to expect, through the medium of so many powerful friends as I had procured at different times and places, and on different occasions, that I should most likely have received something essentially to my advantage. This probably would have been the case had it not been for the unhappy catastrophe which soon after took place in Spain, by the dethronement of Charles IV, and the distracted state of the Spanish government, which followed that event.

*Philadelphia, 8th September, 1806.*

Sir,

HIS Catholic Majesty the king of Spain, my master, having been informed by the audience of Chili of your noble and generous conduct in rescuing, off the island St. Maria, the Spanish merchant ship Tryal, captain Don Benito Cereno, with the cargo of slaves, who had mutinized, and cruelly massacred the greater part of the Spaniards on board; and by humanely supplying them afterwards with water and provisions, which they were in need of, has desired me to express to you, sir, the high sense he entertains of the spirited, humane, and successful effort of yo[u]rself and the brave crew of the Perseverance, under your command, in saving the lives of his subjects thus exposed, and in token whereof, his majesty has directed me to present to you the golden medal, with his likeness, which will be handed to you by his consul in Boston. At the same time permit me, sir, to assure you I feel particular satisfaction in being the organ of the grateful sentiments of my sovereign, on an occurrence which reflects so much honour on your character.

I have the honour to be, sir,

Your obedient servant,

(Signed)                    MARQUIS DE CASE YRUSO.
*Captain* AMASA DELANO, *of the American*
*Ship Perseverance, Boston.*

---

*Boston, August,* 1807

Sir,

WITH sentiments of gratitude I acknowledge the receipt of your Excellency's much esteemed favour of September 8th, conveying to me the pleasing information of his Catholic Majesty having been informed of the conduct of myself and the crew of the Perseverance under my command. It is peculiarly gratifying to me, to receive such honours from your Excellency's sovereign, as entertaining a sense of my spirit and honour, and successful efforts of myself and crew in saving the lives of his subjects; and still more so by receiving the token of his royal favour in the present of the golden medal bearing his likeness. The services rendered off the island St. Maria were from pure motives of humanity. They shall ever be rendered his Catholic Majesty's subjects when wanted, and it is in my power to grant. Permit me, sir, to thank your Excellency for the satisfaction that you feel in being the organ of the grateful sentiments of your sovereign on this occasion, and believe me, it shall ever be my duty publicly to acknowledge the receipt of such high considerations from such a source.

I have the honour to be

Your Excellency's most obedient,

And devoted humble servant,

(Signed)                    AMASA DELANO.
*His Excellency the Marquis* DE CASE YRUSO.

---

*Consular Office,* 30th *July,* 1807.

Sir,

Under date of September last, was forwarded me the enclosed letter from his Excellency the Marquis DE CASE

YRUSO, his Catholic Majesty's minister plenipotentiary to the United States of America, which explains to you the purport of the commission with which I was then charged, and until now have anxiously waited for the pleasing opportunity of carrying into effect his Excellency's orders, to present to you at the same time the gold medal therein mentioned.

It will be a pleasing circumstance to that gentleman, to be informed of your safe arrival, and my punctuality in the discharge of that duty so justly owed to the best of sovereigns, under whose benignity and patronage I have the honour to subscribe myself, with great consideration, and much respect, sir,

Your obedient humble servant,

(Signed)                    JUAN STOUGHTON,

Consul of his Catholic majesty,

Residing at Boston.

AMASA DELANO, *ESQ.*

---

BOSTON, AUGUST 8TH, 1807.

SIR,

I Feel particular satisfaction in acknowledging the receipt of your esteemed favour, bearing date the 30th ult. covering a letter from the Marquis DE CASE YRUSO, his Catholic Majesty's minister plenipotentiary to the United States of America, together with the gold medal bearing his Catholic Majesty's likeness.

Permit me, sir, to return my most sincere thanks for the honours I have received through your medium, as well as for the generous, friendly treatment you have shown on the occasion. I shall ever consider it one of the first honours publicly to acknowledge them as long as I live.

These services rendered his Catholic Majesty's subjects off the island St. Maria, with the men under my command, were from pure motives of humanity. The like services we will ever render, if wanted, should it be in our power.

With due respect, permit me, sir, to subscribe myself,

Your most obedient, and

Very humble servant,

(Signed)                    AMASA DELANO.

*To Don* JUAN STOUGHTON *ESQ.* HIS CATHOLIC MAJESTY'S CONSUL, RESIDING IN BOSTON.

# HERMAN MELVILLE

## [On Cannibals]†

But it will be urged that these shocking unprincipled wretches are cannibals. Very true; and a rather bad trait in their character it must be allowed. But they are such only when they seek to gratify the passion of revenge upon their enemies; and I ask whether the mere eating of human flesh so very far exceeds in barbarity that custom which only a few years since was practised in enlightened England—a convicted traitor, perhaps a man found guilty of honesty, patriotism, and such-like heinous crimes, had his head lopped off with a huge axe, his bowels dragged out and thrown into a fire; while his body, carved into four quarters, was with his head exposed upon pikes, and permitted to rot and fester among the public haunts of men!

The fiend-like skill we display in the invention of all manner of death-dealing engines, the vindictiveness with which we carry on our wars, and the misery and desolation that follow in their train, are enough of themselves to distinguish the white civilized man as the most ferocious animal on the face of the earth.

† *Typee,* Chapter XVII (1846).

# Billy Budd

## NATHANIEL HAWTHORNE

## [Hawthorne and Melville in Liverpool]†

*November 20 [1856] [Southport]*

A week ago last Monday, Herman Melville came to see me at the Consulate, looking much as he used to do (a little paler, and perhaps a little sadder), in a rough outside coat, and with his characteristic gravity and reserve of manner. He had crossed from New York to Glasgow in a screw steamer, about a fortnight before, and had since been seeing Edinburgh, and other interesting places. I felt rather awkward at first, because this is the first time I have met him since my ineffectual attempt to get him a consular appointment from General Pierce. However, I failed only from real lack of power to serve him; so there was no reason to be ashamed, and we soon found ourselves on pretty much our former terms of sociability and confidence. Melville has not been well of late; he has been affected with neuralgic complaints in his head and his limbs, and no doubt has suffered from too constant literary occupation, pursued without much success latterly; and his writings, for a long while past, have indicated a morbid state of mind. So he left his place at Pittsfield, and has established his wife and family, I believe, with his father-in-law in Boston, and is thus far on his way to Constantinople. I do not wonder that he found it necessary to take an airing through the world, after so many years of toilsome pen-labor following after so wild and adventurous a youth as his was. I invited him to come and stay with us at Southport as long as he might remain in this vicinity; and, accordingly, he did come, on the next day, taking with him, by way of luggage, the least little bit of a bundle, which, he told me, contained a nightshirt and a toothbrush. He is a person of very gentlemanly instincts in every respect, save that he is a little heterodox in the matter of clean linen.

He stayed with us from Tuesday till Thursday; and, on the intervening day, we took a pretty long walk together, and sat down in a

† From Hawthorne's journals for 1856.

hollow among the sandhills (sheltering ourselves from the high, cool wind) and smoked a cigar. Melville, as he always does, began to reason of Providence and futurity, and of everything that lies beyond human ken, and informed me that he had 'pretty much made up his mind to be annihilated'; but still he does not seem to rest in that anticipation, and, I think, will never rest until he gets hold of a definite belief. It is strange how he persists—and has persisted ever since I knew him, and probably long before—in wandering to and fro over these deserts, as dismal and monotonous as the sandhills amid which we were sitting. He can neither believe, nor be comfortable in his unbelief; and he is too honest and courageous not to try to do one or the other. If he were a religious man, he would be one of the most truly religious and reverential; he has a very high and noble nature and is better worth immortality than most of us.

# ROBERT M. COVER

## *From* Justice Accused[†]

Melville's Captain Vere in *Billy Budd* is one of the few examples of an attempt to portray the conflict patterns of Creon or Creon's minions in a context more nearly resembling the choice situations of judges in modern legal systems. Billy Budd, radical innocence personified, is overwhelmed by a charge of fomenting mutiny, falsely levied against him by the first mate Claggart. Claggart seems to personify dark and evil forces. Struck dumb by the slanderous charges, Billy strikes out and kills the mate with a single blow. Captain Vere must instruct a drumhead court on the law of the Mutiny Act as it is to be applied to Billy Budd—in some most fundamental sense "innocent," though perpetrator of the act of killing the first mate. In what must be, for the legal scholar, the high point of the novella, Vere articulates the "scruples" of the three officers (and his own) and rejects them.

> How can we adjudge to summary and shameful death a fellow creature innocent before God, and whom we feel to be so?— Does that state it aright? You sign sad assent. Well, I too feel that, the full force of that. It is Nature. But do these buttons that we wear attest that our allegiance is to Nature? No, to the King.

† From Robert M. Cover, *Justice Accused*, pp. 2–6. Copyright © 1975 by Yale University Press. Reprinted by permission of Yale University Press.

And, but a few paragraphs farther on, Vere asks the three whether "occupying the position we do, private conscience should not yield to that imperial one formulated in the code under which alone we officially proceed."

In Vere's words we have a positivist's condensation of a legal system's formal character. Five aspects of that formalism may be discerned and specified: First, there is explicit recognition of the role character of the judges—a consciousness of the formal element. It is a uniform, not nature, that defines obligation. Second, law is distinguished from both the transcendent and the personal sources of obligation. The law is neither nature nor conscience. Third, the law is embodied in a readily identifiable source which governs transactions and occurrences of the sort under consideration: here an imperial code of which the Mutiny Act is a part. Fourth, the will behind the law is vague, uncertain, but *clearly not* that of the judges. It is here "imperial will" which, in (either eighteenth- or) nineteenth-century terms as applied to England, is not very easy to describe except through a constitutional law treatise. But, in any event, it is not the will of Vere and his three officers. Fifth, a corollary of the fourth point, the judge is not responsible for the content of the law but for its straightforward application.

> For that law and the rigor of it, we are not responsible. Our vowed responsibility is in this: That however pitilessly that law may operate in any instances, we nevertheless adhere to it and administer it.

These five elements are part of Vere's arguments. But *Billy Budd* is a literary work and much that is most interesting about Vere is not in what he says but in what he is, in overtones of character. For example, we have intimations from the outset of a personality committed to fearful symmetries. His nickname, derived from Marvell's lines

> Under the discipline severe
> Of Fairfax and the starry Vere

suggests an impersonal and unrelaxed severity. And his intellectual bent, too, reinforces this suggestion of rigidity. He eschewed innovations "disinterestedly" and because they seemed "insusceptible of embodiment in lasting institutions." And he lacked "companionable quality." A man emerges who is disposed to approach life institutionally, to avoid the personal realm even where it perhaps ought to hold sway, to be inflexibly honest, righteous, and duty bound.

It is this man who, seeing and appreciating Budd's violent act, exclaimed, "Struck dead by an angel of God! Yet the angel must hang." And, characteristically, it is Vere who assumes the responsi-

bility of conveying the dread verdict to the accused. Melville's speculations on that "interview" are revealing. He stresses the likelihood
that Vere revealed his own full part in the "trial." He goes on to
speculate that Vere might well have assumed a paternal stance in
the manner of Abraham embracing Isaac "on the brink of resolutely
offering him up in obedience to the exacting behest." Such a religious conviction of duty characterizes our man. Neither conventional morality, pity, nor personal agony could bend him from a stern
duty. But in Vere's case the master is not God but the King. And the
King is but a symbol for a social order.

Righteous men, indeed, suffer the agonies of their righteousness.
Captain Vere betrayed just such agony in leaving his meeting with
Billy Budd. But there is no indication that Vere suffered the agony
of doubt about his course. When Billy died uttering "God Bless
Captain Vere," there is no intimation that the Captain sensed any
irony (whether intended or not) in the parting benediction. If Captain Vere is Abraham, he is the biblical version, not Kierkegaard's
shadow poised achingly at the chasm.

Melville has been astonishingly successful in making his readers
ask dreadful questions of Vere and his behavior. What deep urge
leads a man to condemn unworldly beauty and innocence? To
embrace, personally, the opportunity to do an impersonal, distasteful task? How reconcile the flash of recognition of "the angel must
die" and the seizing of the opportunity to act Abraham, with
declared protestations, unquestionably sincere, that only plain and
clear duty overcomes his sense of the victim's cosmic innocence?
We have so many doubts about a man who hears and obeys the
voice of the Master so quickly, and our doubts are compounded
when it is a harsh social system that becomes the Lord.

I venture to suggest that Melville had a model for Captain Vere
that may bring us very close to our main story. Melville's father-in-
law was Chief Justice Lemuel Shaw of the Massachusetts Supreme
Judicial Court. A firm, unbending man of stern integrity, Shaw dominated the Massachusetts judicial system very much as Captain Vere
ran his ship. The Chief Justice was a noted, strong opponent to slavery and expressed his opposition privately, in print, and in appropriate judicial opinions. Yet, in the great causes célèbres involving
fugitive slaves, Shaw came down hard for an unflinching application of the harsh and summary law. The effort cost Shaw untold personal agony. He was villified by abolitionists. I cannot claim that
Vere is Lemuel Shaw (though he might be), for there is no direct
evidence. I can only say that it would be remarkable that in portraying a man caught in the horrible conflict between duty and conscience, between role and morality, between nature and positive law,
Melville would be untouched by the figure of his father-in-law in

the *Sims Case*, the Latimer affair, or the Burns controversy. We
know Melville's predilection to the ship as microcosm for the social
order. He used the device quite plainly with respect to slavery in
*Benito Cereno*.

The fugitive slave was very Budd-like, though he was as black as
Billy was blonde. The Mutiny Act admitted of none of the usual
defenses, extenuations, or mitigations. If the physical act was that
of the defendant, he was guilty. The Fugitive Slave Act similarly
excluded most customary sorts of defenses. The alleged fugitive
could not even plead that he was not legally a slave so long as he
was the person *alleged* to be a fugitive. The drumhead court was a
special and summary proceeding; so was the fugitive rendition
process. In both proceedings the fatal judgment was carried out
immediately. There was no appeal.

More important, Billy's fatal flaw was his innocent dumbness. He
struck because he could not speak. So, under the Fugitive Slave
Acts, the alleged fugitive had no right to speak. And, as a rule, slaves
had no capacity to testify against their masters or whites, generally.
Billy Budd partakes of the slave, generalized. He was seized,
impressed, from the ship *Rights of Man* and taken aboard the *Bellipotent*. Aboard the *Bellipotent* the Mutiny Act and Captain Vere
held sway. The Mutiny Act was justified because of its necessity for
the order demanded on a ship in time of war. So the laws of slavery,
often equally harsh and unbending, were justified as necessary for
the social order in antebellum America. Moreover, the institution
itself was said to have its origin in war.

But most persuasive is Vere and his dilemma—the subject matter
of this book. For, if there was a single sort of case in which judges
during Melville's lifetime struggled with the moral-formal dilemma,
it was slave cases. In these cases, time and again, the judiciary
paraded its helplessness before the law; lamented harsh results; intimated that in a more perfect world, or at the end of days, a better
law would emerge, but almost uniformly, marched to the music,
steeled themselves, and hung Billy Budd.

Of course, *Billy Budd*, like any great work of literature, exists on
many levels. I would not deny the theology in the work, nor the
clash of elemental good and elemental evil in Budd and Claggart.
But the novella is also about a judgment, within a social system, and
about the man who, dimly perceiving the great and abstract forces
at work, bears responsibility for that judgment. It is about starry-
eyed Vere and Lemuel Shaw.

# CRITICISM

# Bartleby, The Scrivener

## LEO MARX

## Melville's Parable of the Walls[†]

> Dead,
> 25. Of a wall. . . . : Unbroken, unrelieved by breaks or interrup-
> tions; absolutely uniform and continuous.
> —*New English Dictionary*

In the spring of 1851, while still at work on *Moby Dick*, Herman Melville wrote his celebrated "dollars damn me" letter to Hawthorne:

> In a week or so, I go to New York, to bury myself in a third-story room, and work and slave on my "Whale" while it is driving through the press. *That* is the only way I can finish it now—I am so pulled hither and thither by circumstances. The calm, the coolness, the silent grass-growing mood in which a man *ought* always to compose,—that, I fear, can seldom be mine. Dollars damn me. . . . My dear Sir, a presentiment is on me,—I shall at last be worn out and perish. . . . What I feel most moved to write, that is banned,—it will not pay. Yet, altogether, write the *other* way I cannot.

He went on and wrote the "Whale" as he felt moved to write it; the public was apathetic and most critics were cool. Nevertheless Melville stubbornly refused to return to the *other* way, to his more successful earlier modes, the South Sea romance and the travel narrative. In 1852 he published *Pierre*, a novel even more certain not to be popular. And this time the critics were vehemently hostile. Then, the following year, Melville turned to shorter fiction. "Bartleby the Scrivener," the first of his stories, dealt with a problem unmistakably like the one Melville had described to Hawthorne.

There are excellent reasons for reading "Bartleby" as a parable having to do with Meville's own fate as a writer. To begin with, the story *is* about a kind of writer, a "copyist" in a Wall Street lawyer's

---

† First published in the *Sewanee Review* 61.4 (Autumn 1953). Copyright © 1953, 1981 by the University of the South. Reprinted with the permission of the editor.

office. Furthermore, the copyist is a man who obstinately refuses to go on doing the sort of writing demanded of him. Under the circumstances there can be little doubt about the connection between Bartleby's dilemma and Melville's own. Although some critics have noted the autobiographical relevance of this facet of the story, a close examination of the parable reveals a more detailed parallel with Melville's situation than has been suggested.[1] In fact the theme itself can be described in a way which at once establishes a more precise relation. "Bartleby" is not only about a writer who refuses to conform to the demands of society, but it is, more relevantly, about a writer who foresakes conventional modes because of an irresistible preoccupation with the most baffling philosophical questions. This shift of Bartleby's attention is the symbolic equivalent of Melville's own shift of interest between *Typee* and *Moby Dick*. And it is significant that Melville's story, read in this light, does not by any means proclaim the desirability of the change. It was written in a time of deep hopelessness, and as I shall attempt to show, it reflects Melville's doubts about the value of his recent work.

Indeed, if I am correct about what this parable means, it has immense importance, for it provides the most explicit and mercilessly self-critical statement of his own dilemma that Melville has left us. Perhaps it is because "Bartleby" reveals so much of his situation that Melville took such extraordinary pains to mask its meaning. This may explain why he chose to rely upon symbols which derive from his earlier work, and to handle them with so light a touch that only the reader who comes to the story after an immersion in the other novels can be expected to see how much is being said here. Whatever Melville's motive may have been, I believe it may legitimately be accounted a grave defect of the parable that we must go back to *Typee* and *Moby Dick* and *Pierre* for the clues to its meaning. It is as if Melville had decided that the only adequate test of a reader's qualifications for sharing so damaging a self-revelation was a thorough reading of his own work.

## I

"Bartleby the Scrivener" is a parable about a particular kind of writer's relations to a particular kind of society. The subtitle, "A Story of Wall Street," provides the first clue about the nature of the society.

---

1. The most interesting interpretations of the story are those of Richard Chase and Newton Arvin. Chase stresses the social implications of the parable in his *Herman Melville, A Critical Study* (New York, 1949), pp. 143–149. Arvin describes "Bartleby" as a "wonderfully intuitive study in what would now be called schizophrenia . . ." in his *Herman Melville* (New York, 1950), pp. 240–242. Neither Chase nor Arvin makes a detailed analysis of the symbolism of the walls. E. S. Oliver has written of the tale as embodying Thoreau's political ideas in "A Second Look at 'Bartleby'," *College English* (May, 1945), 431–439.

It is a commercial society, dominated by a concern with property and finance. Most of the action takes place in Wall Street. But the designation has a further meaning: as Melville describes the street it literally becomes a walled street. The walls are the controlling symbols of the story, and in fact it may be said that this is a parable of walls, the walls which hem in the meditative artist and for that matter every reflective man. Melville also explicitly tells us that certain prosaic facts are "indispensable" to an understanding of the story. These facts fall into two categories: first, details concerning the personality and profession of the narrator, the center of consciousness in this tale, and more important, the actual floor-plan of his chambers.

The narrator is a Wall Street lawyer. One can easily surmise that at this unhappy turning point in his life Melville was fascinated by the problem of seeing what his sort of writer looked like to a representative American. For his narrator he therefore chose, as he did in "Benito Cereno," which belongs to the same period, a man of middling status with a propensity for getting along with people, but a man of distinctly limited perception. Speaking in lucid, matter-of-fact language, this observer of Bartleby's strange behavior describes himself as comfortable, methodical and prudent. He has prospered; he unabashedly tells of the praise with which John Jacob Astor has spoken of him. Naturally, he is a conservative, or as he says, an "eminently *safe*" man, proud of his snug traffic in rich men's bonds, mortgages and deeds. As he tells the story we are made to feel his mildness, his good humor, his satisfaction with himself and his way of life. He is the sort who prefers the remunerative though avowedly obsolete sinecure of the Mastership of Chancery, which has just been bestowed upon him when the action starts, to the exciting notoriety of the courtroom. He wants only to be left alone; nothing disturbs his complacency until Bartleby appears. As a spokesman for the society he is well chosen; he stands at its center and performs a critical role, unravelling and retying the invisible cords of property and equity which intertwine in Wall Street and bind the social system.

The lawyer describes his chambers with great care, and only when the plan of the office is clearly in mind can we find the key to the parable. Although the chambers are on the second floor, the surrounding buildings rise above them, and as a result only very limited vistas are presented to those inside the office. At each end the windows look out upon a wall. One of the walls, which is part of a skylight shaft, is *white*. It provides the best light available, but even from the windows which open upon the white wall the sky is invisible. No direct rays of the sun penetrate the legal sanctum. The wall at the other end gives us what seems at first to be a sharply contrasting view of the outside world. It is a lofty brick structure within ten feet of the lawyer's window. It stands in an everlasting shade and

is *black* with age; the space it encloses reminds the lawyer of a huge
black cistern. But we are not encouraged to take this extreme black
and white, earthward and skyward contrast at face value (readers of
*Moby Dick* will recall how illusory colors can be), for the lawyer tells
us that the two "view," in spite of their colors, have something very
important in common: they are equally "deficient in what landscape
painters call 'life'." The difference in color is less important than the
fact that what we see through each window is only a wall.

This is all we are told about the arrangement of the chambers
until Bartleby is hired. When the lawyer is appointed Master in
Chancery he requires the services of another copyist. He places an
advertisement, Bartleby appears, and the lawyer hastily checks his
qualifications and hires him. Clearly the lawyer cares little about
Bartleby's previous experience; the kind of writer wanted in Wall
Street need merely be one of the great interchangeable white-collar
labor force. It is true that Bartleby seems to him peculiarly pitiable
and forlorn, but on the other hand the lawyer is favorably impressed
by his neat, respectable appearance. So sedate does he seem that
the boss decides to place Bartleby's desk close to his own. This is his
first mistake; he thinks it will be useful to have so quiet and apparently tractable a man within easy call. He does not understand
Bartleby then or at any point until their difficult relationship ends.

When Bartleby arrives we discover that there is also a kind of wall
inside the office. It consists of the ground-glass folding-doors which
separate the lawyer's desk, and now Bartleby's, from the desks of the
other employees, the copyists and the office boy. Unlike the walls outside the windows, however, this is a social barrier men can cross, and
the lawyer makes a point of telling us that he opens and shuts these
doors according to *his* humor. Even when they are shut, it should be
noted, the ground glass provides at least an illusion of penetrability
quite different from the opaqueness of the walls outside.

So far we have been told of only two possible views of the external world which are to be had from the office, one black and the
other white. It is fitting that the coming of a writer like Bartleby is
what makes us aware of another view, one neither black nor white,
but a quite distinct third view which is now added to the topogra-
phy of the Wall Street microcosm.

> I placed his desk close up to a small side-window in that part
> of the room [a corner near the folding-doors]—a window which
> originally had afforded a lateral view of certain grimy back
> yards and bricks, but which, owing to subsequent erections,
> commanded at present no view at all, though it gave some light.
> Within three feet of the panes was a wall, and the light came
> down from far above, between two lofty buildings, as from a
> very small opening in a dome. Still further to a satisfactory

arrangement, I procured a high green folding screen, which might entirely isolate Bartleby from my sight, though not remove him from my voice. And thus, in a manner, privacy and society were conjoined.

Notice that of all the people in the office Bartleby is to be in the best possible position to make a close scrutiny of a wall. His is only three feet away. And although the narrator mentions that the new writer's window offers "no view at all," we recall that he has, paradoxically, used the word "view" a moment before to describe the walled vista to be had through the other windows. Actually every window in the office looks out upon some sort of wall; the important difference between Bartleby and the others is that he is closest to a wall. Another notable difference is implied by the lawyer's failure to specify the color of Bartleby's wall. Apparently it is almost colorless, or blank. This also enhances the new man's ability to scrutinize and know the wall which limits his vision; he does not have to contend with the illusion of blackness or whiteness. Only Bartleby faces the stark problem of perception presented by the walls. For him external reality thus takes on some of the character it had for Ishmael, who knew that color did not reside in objects, and therefore saw beyond the deceptive whiteness of the whale to "a colorless, all-color of atheism." As we shall see, only the nature of the wall with which the enigmatic Bartleby is confronted can account for his strange behavior later.

What follows (and it is necessary to remember that all the impressions we receive are the lawyer's) takes place in three consecutive movements: Bartleby's gradually stiffening resistance to the Wall Street routine, then a series of attempts by the lawyer to enforce the scrivener's conformity, and finally, society's punishment of the recalcitrant writer.

During the first movement Bartleby holds the initiative. After he is hired he seems content to remain in the quasi-isolation provided by the "protective" *green* screen and to work silently and industriously. This screen, too, is a kind of wall, and its color, as will become apparent, means a great deal. Although Bartleby seems pleased with it and places great reliance upon it, the screen is an extremely ineffectual wall. It is the flimsiest of all the walls in and out of the office; it has most in common with the ground glass door—both are "folding," that is, susceptible to human manipulation.

Bartleby likes his job, and in fact at first seems the exemplar of the writer wanted by Wall Street. Like Melville himself in the years between *Typee* and *Pierre*, he is an ardent and indefatigable worker; Bartleby impresses the lawyer with probably having "been long famished for something to copy." He copies by sun-light and candle-light, and his employer, although he does detect a curiously silent and mechanical quality in Bartleby's behavior, is well satisfied.

The first sign of trouble is Bartleby's refusal to "check copy." It is customary for the scriveners to help each other in this dull task, but when Bartleby is first asked to do it, to everyone's astonishment, he simply says that he prefers not to. From the lawyer's point of view "to verify the accuracy of his copy" is an indispensable part of the writer's job. But evidently Bartleby is the sort of writer who is little concerned with the detailed accuracy of his work, or in any case he does not share the lawyer's standards of accuracy. This passage is troublesome because the words "verify accuracy" seem to suggest a latter-day conception of "realism." For Melville to imply that what the public wanted of him in 1853 was a kind of "realism" is not plausible on historical grounds. But if we recall the nature of the "originals" which the lawyer wants impeccably copied the incident makes sense. These documents are mortgages and title-deeds, and they incorporate the official version of social (property) relations as they exist at the time. It occurs to the lawyer that "the mettlesome poet, Byron" would not have acceded to such a demand either. And like the revolutionary poet, Bartleby apparently cares nothing for "common usage" or "common sense"—a lawyer's way of saying that this writer does not want his work to embody a faithful copy of human relations as they are conceived in the Street.

After this we hear over and over again the reiterated refrain of Bartleby's nay-saying. To every request that he do something other than copy he replies with his deceptively mild, "I would prefer not to." He adamantly refuses to verify the accuracy of copy, or to run errands, or to do anything but write. But it is not until much later that the good-natured lawyer begins to grasp the seriousness of his employee's passive resistance. A number of things hinder his perception. For one thing he admits that he is put off by the writer's impassive mask (he expresses himself only in his work); this and the fact that there seems nothing "ordinarily human" about him saves Bartleby from being fired on the spot. Then, too, his business preoccupations constantly "hurry" the lawyer away from considering what to do about Bartleby. He has more important things to think about; and since the scrivener unobtrusively goes on working in his green hermitage, the lawyer continues to regard him as a "valuable acquisition."

On this typically pragmatic basis the narrator has become reconciled to Bartleby until, one Sunday, when most people are in church, he decides to stop at his office. Beforehand he tells us that there are several keys to this Wall Street world, four in fact, and that he himself has one, one of the other copyists has another, and the scrub woman has the third. (Apparently the representative of each social stratum has its own key.) But there is a fourth key he cannot account for. When he arrives at the office, expecting it to be deserted, he finds to his amazement that Bartleby is there. (If this suggests, however, that Bartleby holds the missing key, it is merely an intimation, for we are never actually provided with explicit evidence that he does, a detail which serves to underline Melville's misgivings about Bartleby's conduct throughout the story.) After waiting until Bartleby has a chance to leave, the lawyer enters and soon discovers that the scrivener has become a permanent resident of his Wall Street chambers, that he sleeps and eats as well as works there.

At this strange discovery the narrator feels mixed emotions. On the one hand the effrontery, the vaguely felt sense that his rights are being subverted, angers him. He thinks his actual identity, manifestly inseparable from his property rights, is threatened. "For I consider that one . . . is somehow unmanned when he tranquilly permits his hired clerk to dictate to him, and order him away from his own premises." But at the same time the lawyer feels pity at the thought of this man inhabiting the silent desert that is Wall Street on Sunday. Such abject friendliness and loneliness draws him, by the bond of common humanity, to sympathize with the horrible solitude of the writer. So horrible is this solitude that it provokes in his mind a premonitory image of the scrivener's "pale form . . . laid out, among uncaring strangers, in its shivering winding sheet." He is reminded of the many "quiet mysteries" of the man, and of the "long periods he would stand looking out, at his pale window behind the screen, upon the *dead brick wall*." The lawyer now is aware that death is somehow an important constituent of that no-color wall which comprises Bartleby's view of reality. After this we hear several times of the forlorn writer immobilized in a "*dead*-wall revery." He is obsessed by the wall of death which stands between him and a more ample reality than he finds in Wall Street.

The puzzled lawyer now concludes that Bartleby is the victim of an "innate" or "incurable" disorder; he decides to question him, and if that reveals nothing useful, to dismiss him. But his efforts to make Bartleby talk about himself fail. Communication between the writer and the rest of Wall Street society has almost completely broken down. The next day the lawyer notices that Bartleby now remains permanently fixed in a "dead-wall revery." He questions the writer, who calmly announces that he has given up all writing. "And what is the reason?" asks the lawyer. "Do you not see the reason for yourself?" Bartleby enigmatically replies. The lawyer looks, and the only clue he finds is the dull and glazed look of Bartleby's eyes. It occurs to him that the writer's "unexampled diligence" in copying may have had this effect upon his eyes, particularly since he has been working near the dim window. (The light surely is very bad, since the wall is only three feet away.) If the lawyer is correct in assuming that the scrivener's vision has been "temporarily impaired"

(Bartleby never admits it himself) then it is the proximity of the colorless dead-wall which has incapacitated him. As a writer he has become paralyzed by trying to work in the shadow of the philosophic problems represented by the wall. From now on Bartleby does nothing but stand and gaze at the impenetrable wall.

Here Melville might seem to be abandoning the equivalence he has established between Bartleby's history and his own. Until he chooses to have Bartleby stop writing and stare at the wall the parallel between his career as a writer and Bartleby's is transparently close. The period immediately following the scrivener's arrival at the office, when he works with such exemplary diligence and apparent satisfaction, clearly corresponds to the years after Melville's return to America, when he so industriously devoted himself to his first novels. And Bartleby's intransigence ("I prefer not to") corresponds to Melville's refusal ("Yet . . . write the *other* way I cannot.") to write another *Omoo*, or, in his own words, another "beggarly 'Redburn'." Bartleby's switch from copying what he is told to copy to staring at the wall is therefore, presumably, the emblematic counterpart to that stage in Melville's career when he shifted from writing best-selling romances to a preoccupation with the philosophic themes which dominate *Mardi*, *Moby Dick* and *Pierre*. But the question is, can we accept Bartleby's merely passive staring at the blank wall as in any sense a parallel to the state of mind in which Melville wrote the later novels?

The answer, if we recall who is telling the story, is Yes. This is the lawyer's story, and in his eyes, as in the eyes of Melville's critics and the public, this stage of his career *is* artistically barren; his turn to metaphysical themes *is* in fact the equivalent of ceasing to write. In the judgment of his contemporaries Melville's later novels are no more meaningful than Bartleby's absurd habit of staring at the dead-wall. Writing from the point of view of the Wall Street lawyer, Melville accepts the popular estimate of his work and of his life.[2] The scrivener's trance-like stare is the surrealistic device with which Melville leads us into the nightmare world where he sees himself as his countrymen do. It is a world evoked by terror, and particularly the fear that he may have allowed himself to get disastrously out of touch with actuality. Here the writer's refusal to produce what the public wants is a ludicrous mystery. He loses all capacity to convey ideas. He becomes a prisoner of his own consciousness. "Bartleby the Scrivener" is an imaginative projection of that premonition of exhaustion and death which Melville had described to Hawthorne.

---

2. It is not unreasonable to speculate that Melville's capacity for entertaining this negative view of his work is in fact a symptom of his own doubts about it. Was there some truth to the view that he was merely talking to himself? He may have asked himself this question at the time, and it must be admitted that this fear, at least in the case of *Pierre* and *Mardi*, is not without basis in fact.

To return to the story. With his decision to stop copying the first, or "Bartleby," movement ends. For him writing is the only conceivable kind of action, and during the rest of his life he is therefore incapable of action or, for that matter, of making any choice except that of utter passivity. When he ceases to write he begins to die. He remains a fixture in the lawyer's chamber, and it is the lawyer who now must take the initiative. Although the lawyer is touched by the miserable spectacle of the inert writer, he is a practical man, and he soon takes steps to rid himself of the useless fellow.

He threatens Bartleby, but the writer cannot be frightened. He tries to bribe him, but money holds no appeal for Bartleby. Finally he conceives what he thinks to be a "masterly" plan; he will simply convey to the idle writer that he "assumes" Bartleby, now that he has ceased to be productive, will vacate the premises. But when he returns to the office after having communicated this assumption, which he characteristically thinks is universally acceptable, he finds Bartleby still at his window. This "doctrine of assumptions," as he calls it, fails because he and the writer patently share no assumptions whatsoever about either human behavior or the nature of reality. However, if Bartleby refuses to accept the premises upon which the Wall Street world operates, he also refuses to leave. We later see that the only escape available to Bartleby is by way of prison or death.

Bartleby stays on, and then an extraordinary thing happens. After yet another abortive attempt to communicate with the inarticulate scrivener the narrator finds himself in such a state of nervous indignation that he is suddenly afraid he may murder Bartleby. The fear recalls to his mind the Christian doctrine of charity, though he still tends, as Melville's Confidence Man does later, to interpret the doctrine according to self-interest: it pays to be charitable. However, this partial return to a Christian view leads him on toward metaphysical speculation, and it is here that he finds the help he needs. After reading Jonathan Edwards on the will and Joseph Priestley on necessity, both Christian determinists (though one is a Calvinist and the other on the road to Unitarianism), he becomes completely reconciled to his relationship with Bartleby. He infers from these theologians that it is his fate to furnish Bartleby with the means of subsistence. This excursion in Protestant theology teaches him a kind of resignation; he decides to accept the inexplicable situation without further effort to understand or alleviate the poor scrivener's suffering.

At this point we have reached a stasis and the second, or "lawyer's" movement ends. He accepts his relation to Bartleby as "some purpose of an allwise Providence." As a Christian he can tolerate the obstinate writer although he cannot help him. And it is an ironic commentary upon this fatalistic explanation of what has happened that the lawyer's own activities from now on are to be explicitly directed not, insofar as the evidence of the story can be taken as complete, by any supernatural force, but rather by the Wall Street society itself. Now it seems that it is the nature of the social order which determines Bartleby's fate. (The subtitle should be recalled; it is after all Wall Street's story too.) For the lawyer admits that were it not for his professional friends and clients he would have condoned Bartleby's presence indefinitely. But the sepulchral figure of the scrivener hovering in the background of business conferences causes understandable uneasiness among the men of the Street. Businessmen are perplexed and disturbed by writers, particularly writers who don't write. When they ask Bartleby to fetch a paper and he silently declines, they are offended. Recognizing that his reputation must suffer, the lawyer again decides that the situation is intolerable. He now sees that the mere presence of a writer who does not accept Wall Street assumptions has a dangerously inhibiting effect upon business. Bartleby seems to cast a gloom over the office, and more disturbing, his attitude implies a denial of all authority. Now, more clearly than before, the lawyer is aware that Bartleby jeopardizes the sacred right of private property itself, for the insubordinate writer in the end may "outlive" him and so "claim possession . . . [of his office] by right of perpetual occupancy" (a wonderful touch!). If this happens, of course, Bartleby's unorthodox assumptions rather than the lawyer's will eventually dominate the world of Wall Street. The lawyer's friends, by "relentless remarks," bring great pressure to bear upon him, and henceforth the lawyer is in effect an instrument of the great power of social custom, which forces him to take action against the non-conforming writer.

When persuasion fails another time, the only new strategem which the lawyer can conceive is to change offices. This he does, and in the process removes the portable green screen which has provided what little defense Bartleby has had against his environment. The inanimate writer is left "the motionless occupant of a naked room." However, it soon becomes clear to the lawyer that it is not so easy to abdicate his responsibility. Soon he receives a visit from a stranger who reports that the scrivener still inhabits the old building. The lawyer refuses to do anything further. But a few days later several excited persons, including his former landlord, confront him with the news that Bartleby not only continues to haunt the building, but that the whole structure of Wall Street society is in danger of being undermined. By this time Bartleby's rebellion has taken on an explicitly revolutionary character: "Everyone is concerned," the landlord tells the lawyer, "clients are leaving the offices; some fears are entertained of a mob. . . ."

Fear of exposure in the public press now moves the lawyer to seek a final interview with the squatter. This time he offers Bartleby a series of new jobs. To each offer the scrivener says no, although in every case he asserts that he is "not particular" about what he does; that is, all the jobs are equally distasteful to him. Desperate because of his inability to frighten Bartleby's "immobility into compliance," the lawyer is driven to make a truly charitable offer: he asks the abject copyist to come home with him. (The problem of dealing with the writer gradually brings out the best in this complacent American.) But Bartleby does not want charity; he prefers to stay where he is.

Then the narrator actually escapes. He leaves the city, and when he returns there is word that the police have removed Bartleby to the Tombs as a vagrant. (He learns that even physical compulsion was unable to shake the writer's impressive composure, and that he had silently obeyed the orders of the police). There is an official request for the lawyer to appear and make a statement of the facts. He feels a mixture of indignation and approval at the news. At the prison he finds Bartleby standing alone in the "inclosed grass-platted yards" silently facing a high wall. Renewing his efforts to get through to the writer, all the lawyer can elicit is a cryptic "I know where I am." A moment later Bartleby turns away and again takes up a position "fronting the dead-wall." The wall, with its deathlike character, completely engages Bartleby. Whether "free" or imprisoned he has no concern for anything but the omnipresent and impenetrable wall. Taking the last resort of the "normal" man, the lawyer concludes that Bartleby is out of his mind.

A few days pass and the lawyer returns to the Tombs only to find that they have become, for Bartleby, literally a tomb. He discovers the wasted figure of the writer huddled up at the base of a wall, dead, but with his dim eyes open.

In a brief epilogue the lawyer gives us a final clue to Bartleby's story. He hears a vague report which he asserts has a "certain suggestive interest"; it is that Bartleby had been a subordinate clerk in the Dead Letter Office at Washington. There is some reason to believe, in other words, that Bartleby's destiny, his appointed vocation in this society, had been that of a writer who handled communications for which there were no recipients—PERSON UNKNOWN AT THIS ADDRESS. The story ends with the lawyer's heartfelt exclamation of pity for Bartleby and humankind.

## II

What did Melville think of Bartleby? The lawyer's notion that Bartleby was insane is of course not to be taken at face value. For when the scrivener says that he knows where he is we can only believe that he does, and the central irony is that there was scarcely a difference, so far as the writer's freedom was concerned, between the prison and Wall Street. In Wall Street Bartleby did not read or write

or talk or go anywhere or eat any dinners (he refuses to eat them in
prison too) or, for that matter, do anything which normally would distinguish the free man from the prisoner in solitary confinement. And,
of course, the office in which he had worked was enclosed by walls.
How was this to be distinguished from the place where he died?

> The yard was entirely quiet. It was not accessible to the com-
> mon prisoners. The surrounding walls, of amazing thickness,
> kept off all sounds behind them. The Egyptian character of the
> masonry weighed upon me with its gloom. But a soft impris-
> oned turf grew under foot. The heart of the eternal pyramids,
> it seemed, wherein, by some strange magic, through the clefts,
> grass-seed, dropped by the birds, had sprung.

At first glance the most striking difference between the Wall
Street office and the prison is that here in prison there are four
walls, while only three had been visible from the lawyer's windows.
On reflection, however, we recall that the side of the office containing the door, which offered a kind of freedom to the others, was
in effect a fourth wall for Bartleby. He had refused to walk through
it. The plain inference is that he acknowledged no distinction
between the lawyer's chambers and the world outside; his problem
was not to be solved by leaving the office, or by leaving Wall Street;
indeed, from Bartleby's point of view, Wall Street *was* America. The
difference between Wall Street and the Tombs was an illusion of the
lawyer's, not Bartleby's. In the prison yard, for example, the lawyer
is disturbed because he thinks he sees, through the slits of the jail
windows, the "eyes of murderers and thieves" peering at the dying
Bartleby. (He has all along been persuaded of the writer's incorruptible honesty.) But the writer knows where he is, and he offers
no objection to being among thieves. Such minor distinctions do
not interest him. For him the important thing is that he still fronts
the same dead-wall which has always impinged upon his consciousness, and upon the mind of man since the beginning of time.
(Notice the archaic Egyptian character of the prison wall.) Bartleby
has come as close to the wall as any man can hope to do. He finds
that it is absolutely impassable, and that it is not, as the Ahabs of
the world would like to think, merely a pasteboard mask through
which man can strike. The masonry is of "amazing thickness."

Then why has Bartleby allowed the wall to paralyze him? The others in the office are not disturbed by the walls; in spite of the poor
light they are able to do their work. Is it possible that Bartleby's suffering is, to some extent, self-inflicted? that it is symptomatic of the
perhaps morbid fear of annihilation manifested in his preoccupation
with the dead-wall? Melville gives us reason to suspect as much. For
Bartleby has come to regard the walls as permanent, immovable parts

of the structure of things, comparable to man's inability to surmount the limitations of his sense perceptions, or comparable to death itself. He has forgotten to take account of the fact that these particular walls which surround the office are, after all, man-made. They are products of society, but he has imputed eternality to them. In his disturbed mind metaphysical problems which seem to be timeless concomitants of the condition of man and problems created by the social order are inextricably joined, joined in the symbol of the wall.

And yet, even if we grant that Bartleby's tortured imagination has had a part in creating his dead-wall, Melville has not ignored society's share of responsibility for the writer's fate. There is a sense in which Bartleby's state of mind may be understood as a response to the hostile world of Wall Street. Melville has given us a fact of the utmost importance: the window through which Bartleby had stared at the wall had "originally . . . afforded a lateral view of certain grimy backyards and bricks, but . . . owing to subsequent erections, commanded at present no view at all, though it gave some light." Melville's insinuation is that the wall, whatever its symbolic significance for Bartleby, actually served as an impediment to (or substitute for?) the writer's vision of the world around him. This is perhaps the most awesome moment in Melville's cold self-examination. The whole fable consists of a surgical probing of Bartleby's motives, and here he questions the value, for a novelist, of those metaphysical themes which dominate his later work. What made Bartleby turn to the wall? There is the unmistakable hint that such themes (fixing his attention on "subsequent erections") had had the effect of shielding from view the sordid social scene ("grimy backyards and bricks") with which Melville, for example, had been more directly concerned in earlier novels such as *Redburn* or *White Jacket*. At this point we are apparently being asked to consider whether Bartleby's obsession was perhaps a palliative, a defense against social experience which had become more than he could stand. To this extent the nature of the Wall Street society has contributed to Bartleby's fate. What is important here, however, is that Melville does not exonerate the writer by placing all the onus upon society. Bartleby has made a fatal mistake.

Melville's analysis of Bartleby's predicament may be appallingly detached, but it is by no means unsympathetic. When he develops the contrast between a man like Bartleby and the typical American writers of his age there is no doubt where his sympathies lie. The other copyists in the office accept their status as wage earners. The relations between them are tinged by competitiveness—even their names, "Nippers" and "Turkey," suggest "nip and tuck." Nevertheless they are not completely satisfactory employees; they are "useful" to the lawyer only half of the time. During half of each day each writer is industrious and respectful and compliant; during the other half he tends to be recalcitrant and even mildly rebellious. But fortunately for their employer these half-men are never aggressive at the same time, and so he easily dominates them, he compels them to do the sort of writing he wants, and has them "verify the accuracy" of their work according to his standards. When Bartleby's resistance begins they characteristically waver between him and the lawyer. Half the time, in their "submissive" moods ("submission" is their favorite word as "prefer" is Bartleby's), they stand with the employer and are incensed against Bartleby, particularly when his resistance inconveniences *them*; the rest of the time they mildly approve of his behavior, since it expresses their own ineffectual impulses toward independence. Such are the writers the society selects and, though not too lavishly, rewards.

One of Melville's finest touches is the way he has these compliant and representative scriveners, though they never actually enlist in Bartleby's cause, begin to echo his "prefer" without being aware of its source. So does the lawyer. "Prefer" is the nucleus of Bartleby's refrain, "I prefer not to," and it embodies the very essence of his power. It simply means "choice," but it is backed up, as it clearly is not in the case of the other copyists, by will. And it is in the strength of his will that the crucial difference between Bartleby and other writers lies. When Nippers and Turkey use the word "prefer" it is only because they are unconsciously imitating the manner, the surface vocabulary of the truly independent writer; they say "prefer," but in the course of the parable they never make any real choices. In their mouths "prefer" actually is indistinguishable from "submission"; only in Bartleby's does it stand for a genuine act of will. In fact writers like Nippers and Turkey are incapable of action, a trait carefully reserved for Bartleby, the lawyer, and the social system itself (acting through various agencies, the lawyers' clients, the landlord, and the police). Bartleby represents the only real, if ultimately ineffective, threat to society; his experience gives some support to Henry Thoreau's view that one lone intransigent man can shake the foundations of our institutions.

But he can only shake them, and in the end the practical consequence of Bartleby's rebellion is that society has eliminated an enemy. The lawyer's premonition was true; he finally sees Bartleby in death. Again the story insinuates the most severe self-criticism. For the nearly lifeless Bartleby, attracted neither by the skyward tending white wall, nor the cistern-like black wall, had fixed his eyes on the "dead" wall. This wall of death which surrounds us, and which Melville's heroes so desperately needed to pierce, has much in common with the deadly White Whale. Even Ahab, who first spoke of the whale as a "pasteboard mask" through which man might strike, sensed this, and he significantly shifted images in the middle of his celebrated quarter-deck reply to Starbuck:

All visible objects, man, are but as pasteboard masks. . . . If man will strike, strike through the mask! How can the prisoner reach outside except by thrusting through the wall? To me, the white whale is that wall, shoved near to me.

Like the whale, the wall will destroy the man who tries too obstinately to penetrate it. Bartleby had become so obsessed by the problem of the dead-wall that his removal to prison hardly changed his condition, or, for that matter, the state of his being; even in the walled street he had allowed his life to become suffused by death.

The detachment with which Melville views Bartleby's situation is perhaps the most striking thing about the fable. He gives us a powerful and unequivocal case against Wall Street society for its treatment of the writer, yet he avoids the temptation of finding in social evil a sentimental sanction for everything his hero thinks and does. True, the society has been indifferent to Bartleby's needs and aspirations; it has demanded of him a kind of writing he prefers not to do; and, most serious of all, it has impaired his vision by forcing him to work in the shadow of its walls. Certainly society shares the responsibility for Bartleby's fate. But Melville will not go all the way with those who find in the guilt of society an excuse for the writer's every hallucination. To understand what led to Bartleby's behavior is not to condone it. Melville refuses to ignore the painful fact that even if society shares the blame for Bartleby's delusion, it was nevertheless a delusion. What ultimately killed this writer was not the walls themselves, but the fact that he confused the walls built by men with the wall of human mortality.

## III

Is this, then, as F. O. Matthiessen has written, "a tragedy of utter negation"? If it is not it is because there is a clear if muted note of affirmation here which must not be ignored. In the end, in prison, we are made to feel that the action has somehow taken us closer to the mysterious source of positive values in Melville's universe. "And see," says the lawyer to Bartleby in the prison yard, "it is not so sad a place as one might think. Look, there is the sky, and here is the grass." To the lawyer the presence of the grass in the Tombs is as wonderful as its presence in the heart of eternal pyramids where "by some strange magic through the clefts, grass-seed, dropped by birds, had sprung." The saving power attributed to the green grass is the clue to Melville's affirmation.[3]

3. Recall that two years before, in the letter to Hawthorne which I quoted at the beginning of this essay, Melville had contrasted the unhappy circumstances under which he wrote *Moby Dick* to "the silent grass-growing mood in which a man *ought* always to compose." Later in the same letter he described his own development in the identical image which comes to the mind of the lawyer in "Bartleby":

The green of the grass signifies everything that the walls, whether black or white or blank, do not. Most men who inhabit Wall Street merely accept the walls for what they are—man-made structures which compartmentalize experience. To Bartleby, however, they are abstract emblems of all the impediments to man's realization of his place in the universe. Only the lawyer sees that the outstanding characteristic of the walls, whether regarded as material objects or as symbols, is that they are "deficient in . . . 'life'." Green, on the other hand, *is* life. The color green is the key to a cluster of images of fecundity which recurs in Melville's work beginning with *Typee*. It is the color which dominates that tropical primitive isle. It is the color of growth and of all pastoral experience. Indeed the imminent disappearance of our agrarian society is an important motive for Ishmael's signing on the Pequod. "Are the green fields gone?" he asks as *Moby Dick* begins. And later he says, in describing the ecstacy of squeezing sperm: "I declare to you that for the time I lived as in a musky meadow." So he gives a green tint to his redeeming vision of "attainable felicity," a felicity which he says resides in the country, the wife, the heart, the bed—wherever, that is, men may know the magical life-giving force in the world. And *Pierre*, published the year before "Bartleby," also begins with a vision of a green paradise. There Melville makes his meaning explicit. He compares a certain green paint made of verdigris with the "democratic element [which] operates as subtile acid among us, forever producing new things by corroding the old. . . ."

> Now in general nothing can be more significant of decay than the idea of corrosion; yet on the other hand, nothing can more vividly suggest luxuriance of life than the idea of green as a color; for green is the peculiar signet of all-fertile Nature herself.

By some curious quirk of the human situation, Bartleby's uncompromising resistance, which takes him to prison, also takes him a step closer to the green of animal faith. Melville deftly introduces this note of hope by having the lawyer compare the grass in the prison yard to the mystery of the grass within the pyramids. In time greenness, the lawyer suggests, may penetrate the most massive of walls. Indeed green seems virtually inherent in time itself, a somehow eternal property of man's universe. And in a Wall Street society it is (paradoxically) most accessible to the scrivener when he finds

---

I am like one of those seeds taken out of the Egyptian Pyramids, which, after being three thousand years a seed and nothing but a seed, being planted in English soil, it developed itself, grew to greenness, and then fell to the mould.

The fact that this same constellation of images reappears in "Bartleby" in conjunction with the same theme (the contrast between two kinds of writing) seems to me conclusive evidence of the relation between the parable and the "dollars damn me" letter.

himself in prison and at the verge of death. Why? If Bartleby's sui-
cidal obsession has taken him closer to grass and sky, are we to
understand that it has had consequences both heartening and
meaningful? Is Melville implying, in spite of all the reasons he has
given us for being skeptical of Bartleby's motives, that an understanding of his fate may show us the way to a genuine affirmation?
Before attempting to answer these questions, it is appropriate to
note here how remarkable a fusion of manner and content Melville
has achieved. While the questions are never explicitly asked, they
are most carefully insinuated. The unique quality of this tale, in
fact, resides in its ability to say almost nothing on its placid and
inscrutable surface, and yet so powerfully to suggest that a great
deal is being said. This quality of style is a perfect embodiment of
the theme itself: concealed beneath the apparently meaningless if
not mad behavior of Bartleby is a message of utmost significance to
all men.

While the presence of the grass at Bartleby's death scene is the
clue to Melville's affirmation, the affirmation can only exist outside
of the scrivener's mind. Green now means nothing to him. In the
Wall Street world he had known, the green fields *were* gone; he was
able to see neither grass nor sky from the walled-in windows. The
only green that remained was the artificial green painted upon his
flimsy screen, the screen behind which he did his diligent early
work. But the screen proved a chemical means of protection. Again
Melville seems to be pointing the most accusing questions at himself. Had not his early novels contained a strong ingredient of prim-
itivism? Had he not in effect relied upon the values implicit in the
*Typee* experience (values which reappeared in the image of the inaccessible "insular Tahiti" in *Moby Dick*) as his shelter from the new
America? Was this pastoral commitment of any real worth as a
defense against a Wall Street society? The story of Bartleby and his
green screen, like the letter to Hawthorne (dollars damn me!),
denies that it was. In this fable, artificial or man-made green, used
as a shield in a Wall Street office, merely abets self-delusion. As for
the other green, the natural green of the grass in the prison yard, it
is clear that Bartleby never apprehended its meaning. For one thing,
a color could hardly have meant anything to him at that stage. His
skepticism had taken him beyond any trust in the evidence of his
senses; there is no reason to believe that green was for him any less
illusory a color than the black or white of the walls. We know, moreover, that when he died Bartleby was still searching: he died with his
eyes open.

It is not the writer but the lawyer, the complacent representative
American, who is aware of the grass and to whom, therefore, the
meaning is finally granted. If there is any hope indicated, it is hope

for his, not Bartleby's, salvation. Recall that everything we understand of the scrivener's fate has come to us by way of the lawyer's
consciousness. From the first the situation of the writer has been
working upon the narrator's latent sensibility, gradually drawing
upon his capacity for sympathy, his recognition of the bond between
his desperate employee and the rest of mankind. And Bartleby's
death elicits a cry of compassion from this man who had once
grasped so little of the writer's problem. "Ah, Bartleby! Ah, humanity!" are his (and Melville's) last words. They contain the final revelation. Such deeply felt and spontaneous sympathy is the nearest
equivalent to the green of the grass within reach of man. It is an
expression of human brotherhood as persistent, as magical as the
leaves of grass. Charity is the force which may enable men to meet
the challenge of death, whose many manifestations, real and imagined, annihilated the valiant Bartleby.

The final words of the fable are of a piece with Melville's undevi-
ating aloofness from his hero: they at once acknowledge Bartleby's
courage and repudiate his delusion. If such a man as the lawyer is
ultimately capable of this discernment, then how wrong Bartleby
was in permitting the wall to become the exclusive object of his concern. The lawyer can be saved. But the scrivener, like Ahab, or one
of Hawthorne's genuises, has made the fatal error of turning his
back on mankind. He has failed to see that there were in fact no
impenetrable walls between the lawyer and himself. The only walls
which had separated them were the folding (manipulatable) glass
doors, and the green screen. Bartleby is wrong, but wrong or not, he
is a hero; much as Ahab's mad quest was the necessary occasion for
Ishmael's salvation, this writer's annihilation is the necessary occasion for Everyman's perception.

Among the countless imaginative statements of the artist's problems in modern literature, "Bartleby" is exceptional in its sympathy
and hope for the average man, and in the severity of its treatment
of the artist. This is particularly remarkable when we consider the
seriousness of the rebuffs Melville had so recently been given by his
contemporaries. But nothing, he is saying, may be allowed to relieve
the writer of his obligations to mankind. If he forgets humanity, as
Bartleby did, his art will die, and so will he. The lawyer, realizing
this, at the last moment couples Bartleby's name with that of
humanity itself. The fate of the artist is inseparable from that of all
men. The eerie story of Bartleby is a compassionate rebuke to the
self-absorption of the artist, and so a plea that he devote himself to
keeping strong his bonds with the rest of mankind. * * *
"Bartleby the Scrivener" is a counter-statement to the large and
ever-growing canon of "ordealist" interpretations of the situation of
the modern writer.

## ELIZABETH HARDWICK

### *From* Bartleby in Manhattan[†]

\* \* \* Bartleby seemed to me to be \* \* \* most of all an example of the superior uses of dialogue in fiction, here a strange, bone-thin dialogue that nevertheless serves to reveal a profoundly moving tragedy.

(Melville's brothers were lawyers, with offices at 10 Wall Street; a close friend was employed in a law office and seems to have been worn down by "incessant writing." About the story itself, some critics have thought of "Bartleby" as a masterly presentation of schizophrenic deterioration; others have seen the story as coming out of the rejection of Melville by the reading public and his own inability to be a popular "copyist." Some have found in the story the life of Wall Street, "walling in" the creative American spirit. All of these ideas are convincing and important. "Bartleby" may be one or all of these. My own reading is largely concerned with the nature of Bartleby's short sentences.)

Out of some sixteen thousand words, Bartleby, the cadaverous and yet blazing center of all our attention, speaks only thirty-seven short lines, more than a third of which are a repetition of a single line, the celebrated, the "famous," I think one might call it, retort: *I would prefer not to.* No, "retort" will not do, representing as it does too great a degree of active mutuality for Bartleby—*reply* perhaps.

Bartleby's reduction of language is of an expressiveness literally limitless. Few characters in fiction, if indeed any exist, have been able to say all they wish in so striking, so nearly speechless a manner. The work is, of course, a sort of fable of inanition, and returning to it, as I did, mindful of the old stone historical downtown and the new, insatiable necropolis of steel and glass, lying on the vegetation of the participial *declining* this and that, I found it possible to wish that "Bartleby, the Scrivener" was just itself, a masterpiece without the challenge of its setting, Wall Street. Still, the setting does not flee the mind, even if it does not quite bind itself either, the way unloaded furniture seems immediately bound to its doors and floors.

Melville has written his story in a cheerful, confident, rather optimistic, Dickensian manner. Or at least that is the manner in which it begins. In the law office, for instance, the copyists and errand-boy are introduced with their Dickensian *tics* and their tic-names: Nippers, Turkey, and Ginger Nut. An atmosphere of comedy, of small, amusing, busy particulars, surrounds Bartleby and his large, unofficial (not suited to an office) articulations, which are nevertheless clerkly and even, perhaps, clerical.

---

† From *"Bartleby in Manhattan" and Other Essays* by Elizabeth Hardwick. Copyright © 1983 by Elizabeth Hardwick. Reprinted by permission of Random House, Inc.

The narrator, a mild man of the law with a mild Wall Street business, is a "rather elderly man," as he says of himself at the time of putting down his remembrances of Bartleby. On the edge of retirement, the lawyer begins to think about that "singular set of men," the law-copyists or scriveners he has known in his thirty years of practice. He notes that he has seen nothing of these men in print and, were it not for the dominating memory of Bartleby, he might have told lighthearted professional anecdotes, something perhaps like the anecdotes of servants come and gone, such as we find in the letters of Jane Carlyle, girls from the country who are not always unlike the Turkeys, Nippers, and Ginger Nuts.

The lawyer understands that no biography of Bartleby is possible because "no materials exist," and indeed the work is not a character sketch and not a section of a "life," even though it ends in death. Yet the device of memory is not quite the way it works out, because each of Bartleby's thirty-seven lines, with their riveting variations, so slight as to be almost painful to the mind taking note of them, must be produced at the right pace and accompanied by the requests that occasion them. At a certain point, Bartleby must "gently disappear behind the screen," which, in a way, is a present rather than a past. In the end, Melville's structure is magical because the lawyer creates Bartleby by *allowing* him to be, a decision of nicely unprofessional impracticality. The competent, but scarcely strenuous, office allows Bartleby, although truly the allowance arises out of the fact that the lawyer is a far better man than he knows himself to be. And he is taken by surprise to learn of his tireless curiosity about the incurious ghost, Bartleby.

The lawyer has a "snug business among rich men's bonds and mortgages and title deeds," rather than the more dramatic actions before juries (a choice that would not be defining today). He has his public sinecures and when they are officially abolished he feels a bit of chagrin, but no vehemence. He recognizes the little vanities he has accumulated along the way, one of which is that he has done business with John Jacob Astor. And he likes to utter the name "for it hath a rounded and orbicular sound to it and rings like unto bullion." These are the thoughts of a man touched by the comic spirit, the one who will be touched for the first time in his life, and by way of his dealings with Bartleby, by "overpowering, stinging melancholy . . . a fraternal melancholy."

A flurry of copying demand had led the lawyer to run an advertisement which brought to his door a young man, Bartleby, a person sedate, "pallidly neat, pitiably respectable." Bartleby is taken on and placed at a desk which "originally had afforded a lateral view of certain grimy backyards and bricks, but which owing to subsequent erections, commanded at present no view at all." This is a suitable

place for Bartleby, who does not require views of the outside world
and who has no "views" of the other kind, that is, no opinions
beyond his adamantine assertion of his own feelings, if feelings they
are; he has, as soon becomes clear, his hard pebbles of response
with their sumptuous, taciturn resonance.

Bartleby begins to copy without pause, as if "long famishing for
something to copy." This is observed by the lawyer who also observes
that he himself feels no pleasure in it since it is done "silently, palely,
mechanically." On the third day of employment, Bartleby appears,
the genuine Bartleby, the one who gives utterance. His first utterance
is like the soul escaping from the body, as in medieval drawings.

The tedious proofreading of the clerk's copy is for accuracy done
in collaboration with another person, and it is the lawyer himself
who calls out to Bartleby for assistance in the task. The laconic,
implacable signature is at hand, the mysterious signature that cannot be interpreted and cannot be misunderstood. Bartleby replies, *I
would prefer not to*.

The pretense of disbelief provides the occasion for *I would prefer
not to* soon to be repeated three times and "with no uneasiness,
anger, impatience or impertinence." By the singularity of refusal,
the absence of "because" or of the opening up of some possibly
alternating circumstance, this negative domination seizes the story
like a sudden ambush in the streets.

Bartleby's "I" is of such a completeness that it does not require
support. He possesses his "I" as if it were a visible part of the body,
the way ordinary men possess a thumb. In his sentence he encloses
his past, present, and future, himself, all there is. His statement is
positive indeed and the *not* is less important than the "I," because
the "not" refers to the presence of others, to the world, inevitably
making suggestions the "I" does not encompass.

Bartleby would prefer not to read proof with his employer, a little
later he would prefer not to examine his own quadruplicate copying
with the help of the other clerks, he would prefer not to answer or
to consider that this communal proofreading is labor-saving and
customary. About his "mulish vagary"—no answer.

As we read the story we are certain that, insofar as Bartleby himself is concerned, there is nothing to be thought of as "interesting"
in his statement. There is no coquetry; it is merely candid, final,
inflexible. Above all it is not "personal"; that is, his objection is not
to the collaborators themselves and not to the activity of proofreading, indeed no more repetitive than daylong copying. The reply is
not personal and it is not invested with "personality." And this the
kind and now violently curious and enduring lawyer cannot believe.
He will struggle throughout the tale to fill up the hole, to wonder
greatly, to prod as he can, in search of "personality." And the hole,

the chasm, or better the "cistern," one of the lawyer's words for the view outside Bartleby's desk, will not be filled.

What began as a comedy, a bit of genre actually, ends as tragedy. But like Bartleby himself it is difficult for the reader to supply adjectives. Is Bartleby mysterious; is his nature dark, angular, subterranean? You are deterred by Bartleby's mastery from competing with him by your command of the adjective. He is overwhelmingly affecting to the emotions of the lawyer and the reader, but there is no hint that he is occupied with lack, disuse, failure, inadequacy. If one tries to imagine Bartleby alone, without the office, what is to be imagined? True, he is always alone, in an utter loneliness that pierces the lawyer's heart when he soon finds that Bartleby has no home at all but is living in the office at night.

(No home, living in the office day and night. Here, having exempted this story from my study of Manhattanism because of its inspired occupation with an ultimate condition and its stepping aside from the garbage and shards of Manhattan history, I was stopped by this turn in the exposition. Yes, the undomesticity of a great city like New York, undomestic in the ways other cities are not—then, and still now. Bartleby, the extreme, the icon of the extreme, is not exactly living in the office. Instead he just does not leave it at the end of the day. But it is very easy to imagine from history where the clerks, Nippers and Turkey, are of an evening. They are living in lodging houses, where half of New York's population lived as late as 1841: newlyweds, families, single persons. Whitman did a lot of "boarding round," as he called it, and observed, without rebuke, or mostly without rebuke, that the boarding house led the unfamilied men to rush out after dinner to the saloon or brothel, away from the unprivate private, to the streets which are the spirit of the city, which are the lively blackmail that makes city citizens abide.

Lodgings then, and later the "divided space" of the apartment house, both expressing Manhattanism as a life lived in transition. And lived in a space that is not biography, but is to be fluent and changeable, an escape from the hometown and the homestead, an escape from the given. The rotting tenements of today are only metaphysical apartments and in deterioration take on the burdensome aspect of "homes" because they remind, in the absence of purchased maintenance, that something "homelike" may be asked of oneself and at the same time denied by the devastations coming from above, below, and next door. Manhattan, the release from the home, which is the leaking roof, the flooded basement, the garbage, and most of all the grounds, that is, surrounding nature. "After I learned about electricity I lost interest in nature. Not up-to-date enough." Mayakovsky, the poet of urbanism.

So Bartleby is found to be living in the office day and night. But Bartleby is not a true creature of Manhattan because he shuns the streets and is unmoved by the moral, religious, acute, obsessive, beautiful ideal of Consumption. Consumption is what one leaves one's "divided space" to honor, as the Muslim stops in his standing and moving to say his prayers five times a day, or is it six? But Bartleby eats only ginger-nuts and is starving himself to death. In that way he passes across one's mind like a feather, calling forth the vague Hinduism of Thoreau and the outer-world meditations of Emerson. (Thoreau, who disliked the city, any city, thought deeply about it, so deeply that in *Walden* he composed the city's most startling consummations, one of which is: "Of a life of luxury, the fruit is luxury.")

To return, what is Bartleby "thinking" about when he is alone? It is part of the perfect completeness of his presentation of himself, although he does not present himself, that one would be foolhardy to give him thoughts. They would dishonor him. So, Bartleby is not "thinking" or experiencing or longing or remembering. All one can say is that he is a master of language, of perfect expressiveness. He is style. This is shown when the lawyer tries to revise him.

On an occasion, the lawyer asks Bartleby to go on an errand to the post office. Bartleby replies that he would prefer not to. The lawyer, seeing a possibility for an entropic, involuntary movement in this mastery of meaning, proposes an italicized emendation. He is answered with an italicized insistence.

"You *will* not?"

"I *prefer* not."

What is the difference between *will not* and *prefer* not? There is no difference insofar as Bartleby's actions will be altered, but he seems to be pointing out by the italics that his preference is not under the rule of the conditional or the future tense. He does not mean to say that he prefers not, but will if he must, or if it is wished. His "I" that prefers not, will not. I do not think he has chosen the verb "prefer" in some emblematic way. That is his language and his language is what he is.

*Prefer* has its power, however. The nipping clerks who have been muttering that they would like to "black his eyes" or "kick him out of the office" begin, without sarcasm or mimicry, involuntarily, as it were, to say to the lawyer, "If you would prefer, Sir," and so on.

Bartleby's language reveals the all of him, but what is revealed? Character? Bartleby is not a character in the manner of the usual, imaginative, fictional construction. And he is not a character as we know them in life, with their bundling bustle of details, their suits and ties and felt hats, their love affairs surreptitious or binding, family albums, psychological justifications dragging like a little wagon along the highway of experience. We might say he is a destiny, without interruptions, revisions, second chances. But what is a destiny that is not endured by a "character"? Bartleby has no plot in his present existence, and we would not wish to imagine subplots for his already lived years. He is indeed only words, wonderful words, and very few of them. One might for a moment sink into the abyss and imagine that instead of *prefer not* he had said, "I don't want to" or "I don't feel like it." No, it is unthinkable, a vulgarization, adding truculence, idleness, foolishness, adding indeed "character" and altering a sublimity of definition.

Bartleby, the scrivener, "standing at the dead-wall window" announces that he will do no more copying. *No more.* The lawyer, marooned in the law of cause and effect, notices the appearance of eyestrain and that there is a possibility Bartleby is going blind. This is never clearly established—Melville's genius would not want at any part of the story to enter the region of sure reasons and causality.

In the midst of these peculiar colloquies, the lawyer asks Bartleby if he cannot indeed be a little reasonable here and there.

"'At present I would prefer not to be a little reasonable,' was his mildly cadaverous reply."

There is no imagining what the sudden intrusion of "at present" may signify and it seems to be just an appendage to the "I," without calling up the nonpresent, the future. From the moment of first refusal it had passed through the lawyer's mind that he might calmly and without resentment dismiss Bartleby, but he cannot, not even after "no more copying." He thinks: "I should have as soon thought of turning my pale, plaster-of-paris bust of Cicero out of doors." Ah. The "wondrous ascendancy" perhaps begins at that point, with the notion that Bartleby is a representation of life, a visage, but not the life itself.

The lawyer, overcome by pity, by troubling thoughts of human diversity, by self-analysis, goes so far as to take down from the shelf certain theological works which give him the idea that he is predestined to "have Bartleby." But as a cheerful, merely social visitor to Trinity Church, this idea does not last and indeed is too abstract because the lawyer has slowly been moving into a therapeutic role, a role in which he persists in the notion of "personality" that may be modified by patience, by suggestion, by reason.

Still, at last, it is clear that Bartleby must go, must be offered a generous bonus, every sort of accommodation and good wish. This done, the lawyer leaves in a pleasant agitation of mind, thinking of the laws of chance represented by his overhearing some betting going on in the street. Will Bartleby be there in the morning or will he at last be gone? Of course, he has remained and the offered money has not been picked up.

"Will you not quit me?"

"I would prefer *not* to quit you."

The "quitting" is to be accomplished by the lawyer's decision to "quit" himself, that is, to quit his offices for larger quarters. A new tenant is found, the boxes are packed and sent off, and Bartleby is bid good-bye. But no, the new tenants, who are not therapists, rush around to complain that he is still there and that he is not a part of their lease. They turn him out of the offices.

The lawyer goes back to the building and finds Bartleby still present, that is, sitting on the banister of the stairway in the entrance hallway.

"What are you doing here, Bartleby?"

"Sitting upon the banister."

The lawyer had meant to ask what will you do with your life, where will you go, and not, where is your body at this moment. But with Bartleby body and statement are one. Indeed the bewitching qualities, the concentrated seriousness, the genius of Bartleby's "dialogue" had long ago affected the style of the lawyer, but in the opposite direction, that is, to metaphor, arrived at by feeling. His head is full of images about the clerk and he thinks of him as "the last column of some ruined temple" and "a bit of wreck in the mid-Atlantic." And from these metaphors there can be no severance.

There with Bartleby sitting on the banister for life, as it were, the lawyer soars into the kindest of deliriums. The therapeutic wish, the beating of the wings of angels above the heads of the harassed and affectionate, unhinges his sense of the possible, the suitable, the imaginable. He begins to think of new occupations for Bartleby and it is so like the frenzied and loving moments in family life: would the pudgy, homely daughter like to comb her hair, neaten up a bit, and apply for a position as a model?—and why not, others have, and so on and so on.

The angel wings tremble and the lawyer says: "Would you like a clerkship in a dry-goods store?"

Bartleby, the unimaginable promoter of goods for sale, replies with his rapid deliberation. Slow deliberation is not necessary for one who knows the interior of his mind, as if that mind were the interior of a small, square box containing a single pair of cuff links.

To the idea of clerking in a store Bartleby at last appends a reason, one indeed of great opacity.

"There is too much confinement about that. No, I would not like a clerkship; but I am not particular."

Agitated rebuttal of "too much confinement" for one who keeps himself "confined all the time"!

Now, in gentle, coaxing hysteria, the lawyer wonders if the bartender's business would suit Bartleby and adds that "there is no trying of the eye-sight in that."

No, Bartleby would not like that at all, even though he repeats that he is not particular.

Would Bartleby like to go about collecting bills for merchants? It would take him outdoors and be good for his health. The answer: "No, I would prefer to be doing something else."

*Doing something else?* That is, sitting on the banister, rather than selling dry goods, bartending, and bill collecting.

Here the lawyer seems to experience a sudden blindness, the blindness of a bright light from an oncoming car on a dark road. The bright light is the terrible clarity of Bartleby.

So, in a blind panic: "How then would be going as a companion to Europe, to entertain some young gentleman with your conversation—how would that suit you?"

"Not at all. It does not strike me that there is anything definite about that. I like to be stationary. But I am not particular."

*Definite?* Conversation is not definite owing to its details of style, opinion, observation, humor, pause, and resumption; and it would not be at all pleasing to Bartleby's mathematical candor. Bartleby is *definite*; conversation is not. He has said it all.

*But I am not particular?* This slight addition has entered Bartleby at the moment the lawyer opens his fantastical employment agency. The phrase wishes to extend the lawyer's knowledge of his client, Bartleby, and to keep him from the tedium of error. Bartleby himself is particular, in that he is indeed a thing distinguished from another. But he is not particular in being fastidious, choosey. He would like the lawyer to understand that he is not concerned with the congenial. It is not suitability he pursues; it is essence, essence beyond detail.

The new tenants have Bartleby arrested as a vagrant and sent to the Tombs. The same idea had previously occurred to the lawyer in a moment of despair, but he could not see that the immobile, unbegging Bartleby could logically be declared a vagrant. "What! He a vagrant, a wanderer that refuses to budge?"

No matter, the lawyer cannot surrender this "case," this recalcitrant object of social service, this demand made upon his heart to provide benefit, this being now in an institution, the Tombs, but not yet locked away from the salvaging sentiments of one who remembers. A prison visit is made and in his ineffable therapeutic endurance the lawyer insists there is no reason to despair, the charge is not a disgrace, and even in prison one may sometimes see the sky and a patch of green.

Bartleby, with the final sigh of one who would instruct the uninstructable, says: *I know where I am.*

In a last urging, on his knees as it were, the lawyer desires to purchase extra food to add to the prison fare.

Bartleby: "I would prefer not to dine today. It would disagree with me; I am unused to dinners." And thus he dies.

Not quite the end for the lawyer with his compassion, his need to unearth some scrap of buried "personality," or private history. We have the beautiful coda Melville has written, a marvelous moment of composition, but perhaps too symbolical, too poetically signifying to be the epitaph of Bartleby. Yet he must be run down, if only to honor the graceful curiosity and the insatiable charity of the lawyer. He reports a rumor:

> The report was this: that Bartleby had been a subordinate clerk in the Dead Letter Office at Washington, from which he had been suddenly removed by a change in administration. . . . Dead letters! Does it not sound like dead men? Conceive a man by nature and misfortune prone to a pallid hopelessness, can any business seem more fitted to heighten it than that of continually handling these dead letters, and assorting them for the flames? . . . On errands of life, these letters sped to death. . . . Ah, Bartleby! Ah, humanity!

Bartleby in a sense is the underside of Billy Budd, but they are not opposites. Billy, the Handsome Sailor, the "Apollo with a portmanteau," the angel, "our beauty," the sunny day, and the unaccountable goodness, which is with him a sort of beautiful "innate disorder," such as the "innate, incurable disorder" represented by Bartleby. Neither of these curious creations knows resentment or grievance; they know nothing of pride, envy, or greed. There is a transcendent harmony in Billy Budd, and a terrifying, pure harmony in the tides of negation that define Bartleby. Billy, the lovely product of nature and, of course, not a perfection of ongoing citizen life, has a "vocal defect," the tendency to stutter at times of stress. By way of this defect, he goes to his death by hanging. Bartleby in no way has a vocal defect; indeed the claim this remarkable creation of American literature makes on our feelings lies entirely in his incomparable self-expression.

So, this bit of old New York, the sepia, horsecar Manhattan, Wall Street. Bartleby and the god-blessed lawyer. They were created by Melville before the Civil War and were coeval with John Jacob Astor's old age and the prime of Cornelius Vanderbilt. And yet here they are, strange apparitions in the metonymic Wall Street district where the exertions, as described by Mark Twain, were, "A year ago I didn't have a penny, and now I owe you a million dollars."

Looking down, or looking up, today at the sulky twin towers of the World Trade Center, "all shaft," the architects say, thinking of those towers as great sightless Brahmins brooding upon the absolute and the all-embracing spirit, it seemed to me that down below there is something of Manhattan in Bartleby and especially in his resistance to amelioration. His being stirs the water of pity, and we can imagine that the little boats that row about him throwing out ropes of personal charity or bureaucratic provision for his "case" may grow weary and move back to the shore in a mood of frustration and, finally, forgetfulness.

There is Manhattanism in the bafflement Bartleby represents to the alive and steady conscience of the lawyer who keeps going on and on in his old democratic, consecrated endurance—going on, even down to the Tombs, and at last to the tomb. If Bartleby is unsaveable, at least the lawyer's soul may be said to have been saved by the freeze of "fraternal melancholy" that swept over him from the fate he had placed at the desk beside him in a little corner of Wall Street. It is not thought that many "downtown" today would wish to profit from, oh, such a chill.

## DAN MCCALL

## *From* The Reliable Narrator[†]

> Somehow, of late, I had got into the way of involuntarily using this word "prefer" upon all sorts of not exactly suitable occasions. And I trembled to think that my contact with the scrivener had already and seriously affected me in a mental way. And what further and deeper aberration might it not yet produce?

The overwhelming majority of modern commentators on "Bartleby" read the narrator of the story in a way that is not only different from mine but quite incompatible with mine. Every virtue I see in the man, they see as a vice; where I see his strength, they see his weakness; what I see as his genuine responsiveness, they see as his cold self-absorption. Some critics read the story as I do, but we are in a distinct minority. There are several reasons this should be so, and I think I understand at least some of them, but first I should like to present as fairly as I can the majority opinion.

Robert Weisbuch * * * refers to the Lawyer as "unnatural," "anti-natural," "lifeless," "self-satisfied," "pompous," and "rationalizing." The Lawyer "investigates Bartleby but refuses authentic emotional commitment in so doing," and "Bartleby rightly refuses to credit the Lawyer's false commitment." The Lawyer is guilty of "toadyism" and his final heartbroken outburst, "Ah Bartleby! Ah humanity!" is no more than "a someways hollow and unfeeling exclamation."[1] Another critic calls the Lawyer a "smug fool" who is "terribly unkind to a very sick man."[2] I had always thought of the

---

† Reprinted from Dan McCall, *The Silence of Bartleby*. Copyright © 1989 Cornell University. Used by permission of the publisher, Cornell University Press.
1. Robert Weisbuch, "Melville's 'Bartleby' and the Dead Letter of Charles Dickens," *Atlantic Double-Cross: American Literature and British Influence in the Age of Emerson* (Chicago: University of Chicago Press, 1986), pp. 44, 45–47.
2. David Shusterman, "The 'Reader Fallacy' and 'Bartleby, The Scrivener,'" *New England Quarterly*, 45 (March, 1972), 118–24, pp. 122–23.

Lawyer as a kind of stand-in for us, a figure we could identify with as we struggled to understand Bartleby. On the contrary, the narrator is "deficient in humanity and quite obtuse towards human beings." I must have had it backwards, for "surely this was Melville's intention: to have his reader *not* sympathize with the Lawyer, *not* to identify with him, *not* to put himself in the Lawyer's place" (*his* italics, not mine).[3] Another critic says, "The narrator attains new heights of vague sentimentality rather than a peak of awareness in his climatic and highly revealing sigh: 'Ah Bartleby! Ah humanity!'" This reader provides dismissive certainty in answering the question

> Who then is Melville's narrator? He is that sort of man one tends to find in high places: the snug man whose worldly success has convinced him that this is the "best of all possible worlds," and whose virtues cluster around a "prudential" concern for maintaining his own situation. The narrator can never fully understand or truly befriend Bartleby because the narrator is simply too complacent, both philosophically and morally, to symphatize with human dissatisfaction and despair.[4]

Still another reader tells us the Lawyer's commentary "rings with blasphemy" and demonstrates "grotesque manifestations of diseased conscience."[5]

Authority is the enemy here. In the extended quotation just above it is taken for granted that the "sort of man one tends to find in high places" is superficial and selfish. Wordly success is bad for the character. The Lawyer has to be bad, or he wouldn't be in an office on Wall Street. Hershel Parker tells us that "our ultimate opinion" of the Lawyer "is not contempt so much as bleak astonishment at his secure blindness. With a bitterer irony than the narrator is capable of, we murmur something like 'Ah narrator! Ah humanity!' In his self-consciously eloquent sequel, after all, the lawyer has merely made his last cheap purchase of a 'delicious self-approval.'" Parker maintains that when "this easy-conscienced" man speaks of kings and counsellors, "he is experiencing a comfortable, self-indulgent variety of melancholy"; when he quotes words from the Book of Job he does so "with prideful aptness," and "characteristically perverts them from profound lament to sonorous urbanity."[6]

This last feature of Parker's argument is interesting to me because

3. Ibid., p. 121.
4. Allan Emery, "The Alternatives of Melville's 'Bartleby,'" *Nineteenth-Century Fiction*, 31 (1976), 170–87, pp. 186–87.
5. William Bysshe Stein, "Bartleby: The Christian Conscience," in *Melville Annual 1965, A Symposium: "Bartleby the Scrivener,"* ed. Howard P. Vincent (Kent, Ohio: Kent State University Press, 1966), p. 107.
6. Hershel Parker, "The Sequel in 'Bartleby,'" in *Bartleby the Inscrutable: A Collection of Commentary on Herman Melville's Tale "Bartleby the Scrivener,"* ed. M. Thomas Inge (Hamden, Conn.: Archon Books, 1979), 159–65, pp. 163–64.

it reminds me of the first time I read the story, at eighteen. I was overwhelmed by the discovery that Bartleby had died, and I didn't know
that "With kings and counsellors" was a quotation from the Book of
Job. The phrase "With kings and counsellors" seemed to me majestic
and solemn and final. That "murmurred I" put a deep hush around it.
But it never occurred to me that the man who said those words was
"easy-conscienced" or "self-indulgent" or the sort of man who "characteristically perverts" a "profound lament to sonorous urbanity." The
figure of Bartleby seemed so weird and funny and painful, his death
at once inevitable and shocking, that I did not see it as an occasion for
the man who was telling me about it to make a "last cheap purchase"
of "delicious self-approval." I trusted that Lawyer.

Thirty years later, I still do. He seems to me extremely intelligent,
whimsical and ironic, generous, self-aware, passionate, and thoroughly competent. But the views of Parker and Weisbuch are not at
all idiosyncratic, and most critics seem to take it virtually for
granted that Melville's lawyer-narrator is not very bright; he is
humorless, selfish, blind, superficial, and bumblingly incompetent.
Liane Norman says the reader "is jolted away from, after having
connected himself with the Lawyer."[7] It must have been a very brief
encounter, for the rupture occurs in the second paragraph when the
Lawyer tells us how he likes to repeat the name of John Jacob Astor,
and "unconsciously betrays himself." This, we are told, is an example of what another critic calls the "unconscious duplicity" of the
Lawyer, for our narrator habitually tells us "far more of the truth
than he intends."[8] Or, as Parker says, what we think of the narrator
is "the product less of what he means to tell than what he unknow-
ingly divulges." Critics poke holes in the Lawyer's words; they quite
literally see through him. It is as if "Bartleby, The Scrivener" is not
a story, it is a lie, and we should examine that lie, to find inconsistencies and contradictions in it. We are the lawyers here, and we
have a hostile witness on the stand. We have to break him, and
expose him for the inadequate and misguided man he really is.

Critics do not so much interpret the story as oppose the narrator's
version to their idea of the "truth." The Lawyer "sees in his imagination the scrivener—but in reality himself—laid out, among uncaring
strangers in a burial sheet."[9] This is a common feature of the critical
readings; Bartleby is not really a person, he is a phantom crawling out
of the unconscious dark pool of the narrator's repressed life. Another
scholar says that "there is something cowardly" in the Lawyer's run-

7. Liane Norman, "Bartleby and the Reader," New England Quarterly, 44 (March, 1971),
22–39, p. 26.
8. William B. Dillingham, "Unconscious Duplicity: 'Bartleby, The Scrivener,'" Melville's
Short Fiction, 1853–56 (Athens, Georgia: University of Georgia Press, 1977), p. 45.
9. Ibid., pp. 31–32.

ning from Bartleby "(assuming he is a real character, not merely a psychological projection)."[1] It is the kind of error Newton Arvin addresses in his commentary on *Moby-Dick* when he says that "taking everything 'spiritually' means not taking it spiritually enough" because the meanings of the work "would not be so wide-reaching and deep-plunging as they are if they were not embodied in a fable of which virtually every detail has a hard, concrete, prosaic, and even naturalistic substantiality."[2] To take Bartleby so "spiritually" makes him a "psychological projection" of the Lawyer instead of the wonderfully drawn character he is. We are told that the Lawyer "is not even 'acquainted'—socially or intimately—with what he himself really is" and that "his prudence and method insure self-deceit." His remark to the grub-man, "No, I was never socially acquainted with any forgers" becomes artificially italicized to "No, I was never socially acquainted with *any* forgers"—as if he were saying don't look at me, I never knew *any* of them—because the narrator himself "is a forger, a self-swindler." The Lawyer literally does not know what he says, and when he quotes the Book of Job, "the words carry an additional significance probably lost on the speaker."[3] Too wrapt up in his own concerns to understand Bartleby's he "likes to avoid trouble" and "finds it more convenient to duck the issue," and "in the end he still does not quite understand what has happened, nor why."[4] The Lawyer is a real scoundrel, for "in bragging that his associates consider him 'an eminently *safe* man,' the lawyer unwittingly suggests that inside knowledge about even financially shady deals would be secure with him."[5] Which is worse?—the "unwittingly" or his tidy silence about "shady deals"? He does not know where his words come from, and he accidentally lets us know he is a crook.

Not only do we know more about the Lawyer than he tells us, we know more about Bartleby than Bartleby himself tells us. He will not go home with the Lawyer because "he has seen something more in the offer than generosity and his refusal indicates his unwillingness to expose himself further to the kind of situation that has repeatedly victimized him."[6] When Bartleby says in the Tombs, "I know you," we are told he means *"I know you for what you are."* The narrator's offer to take Bartleby home is something Bartleby sees through as an offer to provide "at best a *temporary* asylum, not

1. Thomas Pribeck, "An Assumption of Naiveté: The Tone of Melville's Lawyer," *Arizona Quarterly*, 41 (Summer, 1985), 131–42, p. 142.
2. Newton Arvin, *Herman Melville* (New York: Viking, 1950), p. 168.
3. Dillingham, "Unconscious Duplicity," p. 48.
4. Ethel Cornwall, "Bartleby The Absurd," *International Fiction Review*, 9 (Summer, 1982), 93–99, p. 93.
5. R. Bruce Bickley, Jr., *The Method of Melville's Shorter Tales* (Durham, N.C.: Duke University Press, 1979), p. 35.
6. Marvin Fisher, "'Bartleby,' Melville's Circumscribed Scrivener," *Southern Review*, 10 (January, 1974), 59–79, p. 74.

brotherhood."[7] Our Lawyer "exhibits no evidence of contrition," and goes on "fatuously" bragging to the point that he "invites an association with Judas."[8] The Lawyer's sudden realization that Bartleby may be a "victim of innate and incurable disorder" becomes "the lawyer's utter perversion of the basic principles of Christianity."[9] Charity is a sign of weakness, for the Lawyer "is too afraid of creating a scene by throwing Bartleby out at the first sign of insubordination—as a stronger character would have done."[1] The "narrator's stuffy rhetoric depicts a cramped, diminished psyche" and demonstrates "finicky, anal behavior"; his language "quivers at every turn with erotic displacement" and "necrophilic tendencies."[2] In her widely praised book, *The Feminization of American Culture,* Ann Douglas says the Lawyer "is as barren as the scrivener he pities," and he "attempts to force the scrivener to express gratitude for his own benevolence." The Lawyer "is constantly trying to use Bartleby's plight to touch off his own emotions." He ruminates with "a kind of sadistic pity," and operates with "onanistic indulgence."[3]

Even those very few critics who defend the Lawyer do it half-heartedly. One of them says that "the narrator *is good, is* charitable—uncommonly so," but alas he is "all-too-human"; "Bartleby is a kind of personified, continual slap in the face," and the narrator is unable "to go on turning the other cheek forever.[4] The Lawyer is not Jesus Christ, and none of us is, so the story is "about every man's failure—or, more properly, inability to live by Christ's precepts in this imperfect, horological world of ours." Another critic cites some good qualities in the Lawyer, but concludes that the moral of the story is that we can't be our brother's keeper, for self-interest will finally prevail: "Only that reader who knows in his heart that in a similar situation he would have done more for some Bartleby than the lawyer did can claim to be free from 'the inherent selfishness of the human heart.'" As for "the rest of us," each may "find inscribed on his own heart the inexpungeable principle of self-interest—the first law of nature—which Melville intended to reveal here": "Melville sends a ghostly messenger seemingly from the dead not just to show that man would

7. Cornwall, "Bartleby The Absurd," pp. 98–99.
8. Stein: "Bartleby: The Christian Conscience," p. 105.
9. Ibid., p. 108.
1. Cornwall, "Bartleby The Absurd," p. 95.
2. Lewis H. Miller, Jr., "Bartleby and the Dead Letter," *Studies in American Fiction,* 8 (Spring, 1980), 1–12, pp. 8–10. Reading such characterizations, one might hesitate to apply Milton R. Stern's verdict that "the critics who dismiss the narrator . . . are guilty of exactly the same sin of which they indict him": Stern, "Towards 'Bartleby the Scrivener,'" in *The Stoic Strain in American Literature,* ed. Duane J. MacMillan (Toronto: University of Toronto Press, 1979), p. 40.
3. Ann Douglas, *The Feminization of American Culture* (New York: Knopf, 1977), pp. 315–17.
4. Harold Schechter, "Bartleby The Chronometer," *Studies in Short Fiction,* 19 (Fall, 1982), 359–66, pp. 362, 365.

not be persuaded, but, given his common infirmities, he *cannot* be persuaded." Yes, "even a conscientiously good man like the lawyer is finally guided primarily by self-interest."[5]

Today, narrators are unreliable by definition. Fiction told in the first person is inherently deceptive. The great unreliable narrators— that dreadful man who tells us about *The Aspern Papers* or the much nicer but not altogether astute fellow who speaks to us in "The Real Thing"—represent not merely Henry James's wonderful play with perspective but also extreme examples of the condition of first-person narrative itself. This general notion is given a special class-conscious twist by the Bartleby critics, for the Lawyer seems to be wrong because he is a lawyer. The abundant misreadings of the "bad" Lawyer usually reveal an underlying animus toward the profession he represents. For example, one critic tells us the Lawyer is "an unreliable narrator" who "creates the story in order to justify his behavior toward Bartleby." The Lawyer "reduces Bartleby to the status of an object, a commodity." Bartleby's "alienation results from the dehumanizing experience of Wall Street, from the prison of his socioeconomic system." What is eating Bartleby is what is eating his co-workers: they cannot see that they constitute a class. Twentieth-century critics, however, can penetrate that nineteenth-century secret, for they see that "the lawyer reduces morality to a question of money," and he repeatedly offers money to Bartleby. Oppressor and oppressed are blind, both to themselves and to each other; the story is "one of the bitterest indictments of American capitalism ever published."[6]

Ann Douglas says the Lawyer's "sentimental illusion of brotherhood," is an "obfuscation of an essentially class situation, which the narrator demands as the price of his sympathy."[7] The narrator "unwittingly allows us to understand that these copyists are by small and futile oddities of behavior rebelling against the routinized and monotonous quality of their work."[8] In all of Melville's writings that exclude women characters, Melville "is interested primarily in questions of class: the clash between employer and employed, master and slave," and "Melville is dramatizing here the process by which an essentially mass sensibility transforms and assimilates the alien to its own needs."[9]

In all these readings we are asked to see that the Lawyer represents "consumer capitalism"; we are asked to see, too, that the man refuses to recognize—or is simply incapable of recognizing—the

5. Walter Anderson, "Form and Meaning in 'Bartleby, The Scrivener,'" *Studies in Short Fiction*, 18 (Fall, 1981), 383–93, pp. 392–93.
6. James C. Wilson, "'Bartleby': The Walls of Wall Street," *Arizona Quarterly*, 37 (Winter, 1981), 335–46, pp. 339, 346.
7. Douglas, *Feminization of American Culture*, p. 316.
8. Ibid., p. 316.
9. Ibid., pp. 298, 316.

political and economic forces that have made him what he is. Critic after critic tells us that the Lawyer cannot see his own complicity in the ruthless capitalist system and that we should read his every word as deliberate deception or hopeless failure. He is as blind as the poor Governess in "The Turn of the Screw."

But what if he is not? On the opening pages of his narrative the Lawyer spends considerable time and energy bragging about the very thing the critics say he cannot admit. And then the "eminently *safe* man" goes on to tell us that the advent of Bartleby in his life has forced him to question all his old rules. Modern socially conscious readers won't hear of it; they have their man. But they fail to reckon with the wonderfully dramatic quality of the story, the Lawyer's agonizing reappraisal of himself. He does not put it, back in 1853, in any of the language we use so wantonly more than a century later, but we watch him go weak in his knees with his prized "prudence" and "method" as he senses a rich and frightening world that his life-long procedures have shut out. To see him as a representative of a class, an unwitting victim of a social and economic system, is not so much creative interpretation as it is obtuse paraphrase. One of the most interesting dramas in the story is the Lawyer's own helpless intuition that he is not adequate to the challenge of Bartleby, and never has been. His initial boasting about his virtues becomes his tortured exploring of them as weakness and failure. To read him out of his own brave story is to lose what is most lovely and spiritually generous about him.

\*   \*   \*

Two passages are usually quoted by those who denigrate the Lawyer. The first begins with the dire words: "Imprimis: I am a man who, from his youth upwards, has been filled with a profound conviction that the easiest way of life is the best. . . . All who know me, consider me an eminently *safe* man." I am always amazed to see how modern readers use these words to "prove" the narrator's shortcomings. He never addresses a jury, he is unambitious, doing "a snug business" and says that "I do not speak it in vanity" about things nobody in his right mind could speak about in vanity. Why would anyone brag about such cold small potatoes? Even if they were true—especially if they were true.

He invokes John Jacob Astor—with that sly characterization of Astor as "a personage little given to poetic enthusiasm," a man who endows the New York Public Library for "*useful* knowledge." It is Astor's will, and Melville had plenty of fun with it in *Mardi*. John Jacob Astor was a man known to everybody in 1853 as "the landlord of New York," "Old Skinflint," "Moneybags," "Scrooge." How is it possible to read this passage straight? The narrator says John Jacob Astor is "a name which, I admit, I love to repeat, for it hath a rounded and orbicular sound to it, and rings like unto bullion." Melville lays it on with a trowel: "I admit," "I love," "hath," "rounded and orbicular," "rings like unto"—you cannot avoid seeing the narrator sitting there savoring the words "John Jacob Astor" like marbles in his mouth. It is comedy. "Not unemployed," "I will freely add," "not insensible"—this is not the narrator's love of money; neither is it professional vanity or insensitivity to virtue. It is elaborate self-deflation, not puny self-love.

The second passage critics quote is the response to Bartleby's "passive resistance." The narrator tells himself he cannot fire Bartleby, "can get along with him," and "Yes. Here I can cheaply purchase a delicious self-approval. To befriend Bartleby; to humor him in his strange wilfulness, will cost me little or nothing, while I lay up in my soul what will eventually prove a sweet morsel for my conscience." Critic after critic cites this as irrefutable evidence of the Lawyer's dreadfulness. They maintain that only a moral idiot could say such a thing.

But that is true. They are right. Only a moral idiot could. That is just what the narrator tells us. He, not the critics, says "cheaply." He, not the critics, says "delicious." How could a man say "sweet morsel" straight? Look at the verbs—"purchase" and "lay up." The critics insist that to be Christian doesn't really involve personal sacrifice for the Lawyer. But, again, that is just what the Lawyer tells us: it will "cost me little or nothing." The self-irony here is crystal clear. And as soon as he has said it, he goes on, "But"—he could not keep up this bogus benevolence, it was like trying "to strike fire with my knuckles against a bit of Windsor soap," and what he explicitly calls "the evil impulse" mastered him. To take this as evidence of the Lawyer's bad character, words must lose their meaning and context lose its relevance. The Lawyer says to us that he was deceiving himself and letting Bartleby down. The critics shout back, no, you're deceiving yourself and letting Bartleby down.

Allan Silver recognizes the error. Of the "sweet morsel" passage, Silver says, "the lawyer is not merely fatuous; it does not escape him that this test of Christian virtue is mild and easy."[1] Stanley Brodwin has a fresh insight into the Lawyer's last encounter with Bartleby in the Tombs. The Lawyer says, "The Egyptian character of the masonry weighed upon me with its gloom. But a soft imprisoned turf grew under foot. The heart of the eternal pyramids, it seemed, wherein, by some strange magic, through the clefts, grass-seed, dropped by birds, had sprung." Brodwin says "the thematic and con-

1. Allan Silver, "The Law and the Scrivener," *Partisan Review*, 48 (1981), 409–22, p. 414.

notative subtlety of the lines defies" our reading this passage "as yet
another effusion of the lawyer's felicitous Victorian sentimentality":
"Apart from the allusive imagery and poetic tone, the very syntax of
that last line with its choppy, periodic form, phrase by phrase moving to the completing verb 'had sprung' tells us that Melville has
joined his sensibility with his character's."[2] "Melville has joined his
sensibility with his character's" is a stunning, intuitive leap: Brodwin sees that the Lawyer's language is too subtle and beautiful, too
precise, to be a wash of bathos.

This is what Leo Marx saw biographically: the Lawyer—at his
moment of greatest feeling—talks like Melville himself in a moment
of profound self-examination. If the Lawyer were the man the critics tell us he is, we would surely have to finish the story with an
awful thud. The sequel would be just another "sweet morsel." But
that "not-unpleasing sadness" is exactly what the Lawyer opposes to
the "over-powering stinging melancholy" he suddenly feels about
Bartleby.

What the Lawyer actually says, in all his self-denigrations, is so
natural—we all do it, in an attempt to distance difficult experience,
to label it as well-it-can't-be-helped, let's-be-done-with-it. To prove
that the Lawyer is an unreliable narrator the critics merely quote
what he says all along, as a precaution against being unreliable:

> my vanity got the better of my pity

> something from within me upbraided me

> a certain squeamishness, of I know not what, witheld me

> I strangely felt something superstitious knocking at my heart
> . . . forbidding me to carry out my purpose, and denouncing
> me for a villain

Why do we need to be harder on the Lawyer than he is on himself?
I hear him speaking in every line. His training, his practice, his
whole life is backing up on him. The narrator defines himself as a
professional man: he believes in what he does, believes that what he
does is who he is. In the last paragraphs he is reaching for some
explanation, some reason, anything to help. He knows it cannot
really work. He explicitly says to us, "I hardly know whether I should
divulge one little item of rumor." He "could never ascertain" its
basis and "cannot now tell" us "how true it is." He will only "briefly
mention it." With all that stammering qualification, he tells us the
"vague report" of the Dead Letter Office. His heart needs it, his
worn-out and famished brain is hungry for it. Critics are extremely

2. Stanley Brodwin, "To the Frontiers of Eternity: Melville's Crossing in 'Bartleby, the
   Scrivener,'" in *Bartleby the Inscrutable*, ed. Inge, 174–96, p. 188.

suspicious of him here, and they indict him with Victorian cliché. They will not be sidetracked; they want to get on to Chancery and Wall Street, where the real evil of the world lies. No shrewd observer of the human animal believes in its genuine goodness. But Melville really does ask us questions about kindness, about love, about what we can fix and what we cannot. What happens when you run into something you cannot explain and cannot remedy? Where is your humanity then?

Robert Weisbuch sees the Lawyer not only as Dickens but also as Melville's parody of "the typical Dickensian villain." But the typical Dickensian villain looks for weakness to gain power over it, to get an advantage. When the Lawyer sees Bartleby's impoverishment laid bare, he cries out, "His poverty is great; but his solitude, how horrible! Think of it." This is exactly what the typical Dickensian villain cannot do: he cannot "think of it" in sympathetic terms. The Lawyer searches and speculates and probes his own soul; he tries to find his own self-interest and negligence and indifference—all of which vices the critics quote as if the Lawyer were guilty of them, when the truth is that his own negligence is exactly what worries him. The Lawyer, driven crazy by self-doubt, by the most rigorous and extensive self-examination of which he is capable, is seen by the critics as a fool who never questions anything. The critics say that to listen to the authentic voice of the Lawyer is to be tricked into relaxing one's deepest convictions about what is wrong with the world. Bartleby cannot bring us to "a certain hopelessness."

Yes he can. The agony of the story lies in the Lawyer's genuine and terrified account of how the "forlornness of Bartleby grew and grew to my imagination." All through the story the Lawyer is asking what it is that has so damaged Bartleby. At the end, the Lawyer tentatively proposes an answer, hemmed in with qualifications. Many critics find fault with that final explanation. One critic says that "Melville did not let well enough alone" and that "the final long paragraph is the flaw that mars the perfection of the whole."[3] I sympathize with Kingsley Widmer's instinct to preserve a mystery "against which all reason is helpless," but he speaks for the critical consensus when he finds that the final page leaves Bartleby "charitably patronized in memory," in a "thick Victorianism" which marks the Lawyer's "moralizing and rationalizing failure to understand Bartleby."[4]

The last page brings to a focus two of the central problems in the story: the nature of Bartleby's illness and the Lawyer's capacity to

---

3. Charles G. Hoffmann, "The Shorter Fictions of Herman Melville," *South Atlantic Quarterly*, 52 (July, 1953), 420.
4. Kingsley Widmer, *The Ways of Nihilism: A Study of Herman Melville's Short Novels* (California State Colleges, 1970), pp. 118–19, p. 119.

understand it. The "sequel" does help to explain certain details that go before it—for example, as Bruce Bickley says, when the Lawyer asks Bartleby to run an errand to the post office, that is "probably the last place, if the rumor is correct, that Bartleby would ever want to go."[5] But nobody seems to take seriously the Dead Letter Office as an explanation for what went wrong with Bartleby; most critics tell us that the rumor is a boomerang, and it flies right back to the Lawyer, showing us what is wrong with him.

Consider the quiet beauty of the Lawyer's response to the grub-man's question, "Won't he dine to-day, either? Or does he live without dining?"

> "Lives without dining," said I, and closed the eyes.
> "Eh!—He's asleep, ain't he?"
> "With kings and counsellors," murmured I.

Why not end it there? Melville drops down a few lines and says, "There would seem little need for proceeding further in this history"—and maybe he is right. Does the final paragraph really add anything? Indeed, how could one add anything equal to those poignant words?

In his very shrewd preface to "The Turn of the Screw," Henry James proposes the necessity of releasing the reader from "weak specifications." James discusses ghost stories, objecting to their usual superfluity of atmospheric effects—clanking chains and howls in the night. James insists these are not nearly so frightening as what a reader will supply from the depths of his own mind. "Bartleby" is not exactly a ghost story, but Jame's principle applies: what we bring to Bartleby might be more eerie and convincing than the Dead Letter Office and deeper than anything Melville could say. Whatever our author puts in is a "weak specification" compared to what we ourselves provide.

In trying to find a rhetorical model for the Lawyer's speech, I unearthed what seemed to be a source for the final paragraph. At the end of Merton M. Sealts, Jr.'s *Melville's Reading: A Check-List of Books Owned and Borrowed*, I read, down in the W's, item number 546:

> Warren, Samuel. The Moral, Social, and Professional Duties of Attorneys and Solicitors . . . New York, Harper, 1849.[6]

It was listed in the original inventory as "1 Warren's Duties"—which made me think it was a fairly standard text, "Warren's Duties" as, say, "Murray's Grammar" in *Moby-Dick*. At the beginning of War-

5. Bickley, *The Method of Melville's Shorter Tales*, p. 42.
6. Merton M. Sealts, Jr., *Melville's Reading: A Check-List of Books Owned and Borrowed* (Madison: University of Wisconsin Press, 1966), p. 104.

ren's warnings to his prospective lawyers, he speaks of a deceased client in much the same tone, and with many of the same words, that the Lawyer uses in his last paragraph about Bartleby:

> Your unfortunate client shall receive no effectual redress: perhaps none at all. He may be beyond the reach of all earthly redress: he may be moldering in his grave, into which he descended, not knowing, poor soul, that he was leaning on a broken reed, in relying on his professional adviser's competence to arrange his affairs; that his affectionate and just purposes were destined to be all defeated! The "dull cold ear of death" can not hear of a will that is mere *waste paper* . . . of a widow and orphans reduced to destitution, while property, righteously destined for them, is being, through your instrumentality, enjoyed by a comparative stranger, or even by the bitterest enemy of your dead victim! Language, gentlemen, is not strong enough adequately to stigmatize . . .

* * * Warren's italicized "waste paper" might have given Melville the idea for the "Dead Letters"; we hear an exact echo of Warren's "moldering in his grave" in Melville's "moulders in the grave." Warren is saying to prospective lawyers that the property of a man they should have taken care of never reaches those for whom it was intended. Just so: Melville's "bank-note sent in swiftest charity" never gets there, and the ring never reaches "the finger it was meant for." Warren is filling up his young apprentice lawyers with fantasies that are clearly echoed in the images of Melville's elderly lawyer. I was particularly struck by Warren's speaking of "some one suddenly seized with mortal illness, or who has suffered some dreadful accident, hurrying him to a premature death-bed," someone (in Warren's own italics) "suddenly bidden, by the Supreme Disposer of events, to *turn his pale face to the wall.*" Note, too, the 'adequately' in both Warren and Melville; Warren's prospective attorney and Melville's Lawyer cannot find language 'strong enough' to 'express the emotions which seize' them. Melville makes tragically clear what Warren spells out: the 'poor soul,' 'your dead victim,' is now "beyond the reach of all earthly redress."[7]

There are other possible sources for Melville's Dead Letter Office in the newspapers he read, and the imagery is as compelling as any in "Warren's Duties."[8] Hershel Parker discovered "Dead Letters—By a Resurrectionist," which appeared in September 1852 in the

---

7. Samuel Warren, *The Moral, Social, and Professional Duties of Attorneys and Solicitors* (New York: Harper, 1849), p. 114.
8. See John Middleton, "A Source for Bartleby," *Extracts*, 15:9, for a brief item in the Pittsfield *Sun*, February 17, 1853. See, too, George Monteiro, "Melville, 'Timothy Quicksand,' and the Dead-Letter Office," *Studies in Short Fiction*, 9 (Spring, 1972), for an article in the *New England Magazine*, 1831.

*Albany Register*, a story that describes in detail "all the thousand varied emotions, sympathies and expressions that go to make up 'correspondence'" which are "converted into lifeless, meaningless trash."[9] Parker concludes that "accumulating evidence suggests there was a vogue of Dead Letter articles about the time 'Bartleby' was written."

We may discover where Melville found his Dead Letter Office, but not how he used it, and that is what we really want to know. There is something wrong with Bartleby, so badly wrong that he dies of it. He does not expound a doctrine, like "Civil Disobedience," or shake his fist at the sky in protest of cosmic injustice, or hang his head about the difficulties of being a "writer." He starves to death. What the Lawyer says about the Dead Letter Office is the Lawyer's way of answering for himself what we want to know, too. One critic accuses the Lawyer of "inventing" the Dead Letter Office as a "sop to his conscience." That seems to me a desperate confusion about the very status of fiction. It reminds me of a student of mine who read Faulkner's "Delta Autumn" in a similar way. The student attributed Ike McCaslin's "racist" ideas to William Faulkner (who in some measure shared them). But the young woman who delivers a rebuff to Faulkner's racism seemed to the student to walk into the story all by herself, without any help from Faulkner: "Old man, have you lived so long and forgotten so much that you don't remember anything you ever knew or felt or even heard about love?"[1] My student could see that Faulkner wrote Ike's speeches, but saw the young woman as a product of "our" enlightened world, not Faulkner's darkly prejudicial one.

Similarly, against what can we measure the Lawyer's report about the Dead Letter Office? Everything we know about Bartleby comes from the Lawyer. Is this a soul-comforting fabrication, or was he wrong before, and did he tell us a lot of lies back there? Does the Lawyer fade in and out of the truth? Which parts of his testimony should we "privilege"?

The elaborate hedging the Lawyer uses to introduce the rumor tells us that he himself wonders whether it is true. But it is not true or false to some world outside the Lawyer's mind. The question is the adequacy, not the veracity, of the last paragraph. Even if the Dead Letter Office career of Bartleby is "true," something was wrong with Bartleby when he went there. In telling us about it, the Lawyer asks us to "conceive a man by nature and misfortune prone to a pallid hopelessness." Bartleby was that way when he walked in, not when he got kicked out. The Dead Letter Office was the perfect

9. Parker, "The Sequel in 'Bartleby,'" pp. 159–60.
1. The line is said virtually word for word by Beah Richards to Spencer Tracy in the movie *Guess Who's Coming to Dinner?*

place for him. The "business" there was "fitted to heighten" what already was amiss. As Milton R. Stern powerfully argues, the Dead Letter Office "keeps the focus exactly where Melville wants it—on the effect of Bartleby's condition, not on the cause of it."[2]

\* \* \*

Notice the three adverbs in the sentence "'I prefer not to,' he respectfully and slowly said, and mildly disappeared." The first adverb, "respectfully," goes with that phrase repeated by the senior scrivener, "With submission, sir." In Bartleby's mouth it sounds like "haughtiness." There is a funny hum about "respectfully." Then, "slowly"—we watch him go, and we see that the "slowly" is part of the eerie, unhurried stateliness of the man. And "mildly" is a shocker—how do you *mildly* disappear? "Mildly" is genuinely haunting. Various forms, both funny and ghostly, of the word "mild" play through the story. (Melville speaks more than once of the "mildness" of the white whale, and "mild" will become a leitmotif of *The Confidence Man*.) Together, the three adverbs create a leisurely little excursion into the uncanny.

What kind of narrator do we infer from the three adverbs? If you take the view of the critical majority, the Lawyer would be constitutionally incapable of putting the words together. But he speaks this way throughout the story. Most critics say he means more than he says, "unwittingly." Those three adverbs seem to me pretty witting. If this is what we mean by Victorian sentimentality, we are very unlucky to have lost it. A man who says "respectfully," "slowly," and "mildly" like that stakes a claim on our best attention.

The last thing I have to say concerns the story's comedy. Most critics nod at it politely and then go on about their somber business. But the comic quality is one of our chief delights in reading "Bartleby." The anguish in the story is real, of course, and I know of no other word than "anguish" to use. When I read the solemn scholarship, however, I do not find much recognition of the hilarity on the way to the anguish. Perhaps both emotions, the tragedy and comedy, are blinked: failure to deal with one guarantees failure with the other. On the last page of the story you hear a heart breaking, but you would never guess it from those critics who laboriously put on their heavy scholarly armor and say, "Can't fool me—I know that's not genuine emotion, I know that's Victorian gush!" Maybe an inability to mourn goes with an inability to laugh. But one of the greatest comic lines I have ever read—sublimely comic, a line that made me laugh out loud when I first read the story as a freshman,

2. Stern, "Towards 'Bartleby the Scrivener,'" p. 35.

a line that still makes me laugh as a professor—comes when the Lawyer-narrator is trying to get Bartleby to consider other vocational options and asks him, "How then would going as a companion to Europe, to entertain some young gentleman with your conversation,—how would that suit you?" When I first read that question in my freshman dorm, I pictured the "young gentleman" and Bartleby on a slow boat to China or a luxury liner to France. I saw the young gentleman say, "Deck tennis, anyone?" and I saw Bartleby wrapped up in a blanket in a deck chair, staring at the horizon: "I prefer not to." The line goes faster and differently for me now—I don't picture them on the deck of a ship—but one thing has always been true: it is wonderfully funny. The way we encounter Bartleby is analogous to the way the narrator encounters him. Bartleby throws you back on yourself in sputtering exasperation and self-justifying. You cannot "fix" Bartleby, so one thing you do is talk about yourself—it's not *my fault, I'm* a good guy, don't look at *me*.

Richard Chase is right * * * when he says the story "is a starkly simple tale told with great economy of metaphor and symbol." There is no room in it for endlessly proliferating symbology, as in *Moby-Dick*. Melville creates something intentionally bare, dingy, and drab. Chase says "Bartleby" has "a kind of simplicity at once nakedly tragic and wistfully comic." That "at once" is crucial; comedy is not the fringe benefit the critics pass right by. No, the comedy is there "at once" with all the pain, chastening it and transforming it. Chase says, "Melville, we must remember, was a humorous writer, as well as a lyric and epic writer." His humor can be "hearty, jovial, and broad"; it can be "lyrical and heroic"; it can be a "flowing stream of fantasy, alternately gay, grim, festive, erotic, regretful, and sad"; it is often "spare, light-footed, buoyant, and savage."[3]

Robert E. Abrams examines Henri Bergson's theory of "the laughable" in "automatism." Abrams shrewdly points out that Bergson has been popularly misunderstood to suggest that "robotism" is the essential element in the comic. Bergson's real insight was in "the comic dissonance of automatism within the human" so that the funny and the grotesque, "the humorous and the macabre," fade in and out of each other. A good example is the way the word "prefer" creeps into the speech of the other scriveners and into the speech of the Lawyer himself. Bartleby is tragic, in his morbid withdrawal, but "in such grotesque anesthetizations of the self lurks a narcotic charm" and we can see "the hint of something subliminally intimate and wished for in the grotesque."[4]

3. Chase, *Herman Melville*, p. 67.
4. Robert E. Abrams, "'Bartleby' and the Fragile Pageantry of the Ego," *ELH*, 45 (1978), 488–500, p. 493.

As we go through the story, we watch with a certain delight how Bartleby is "catching." We root for the spread of the bug. It is something wonderfully wrong in our boring world. Bartleby stands for our instinctive revulsion from all the commands of that world to "behave." Abrams says, "the deepest loyalty of the subconscious is with such a blind, instinctual figure." The Lawyer's opening remarks about how "eminently *safe*" he is are not an unwitting confession; they are the premise of the comic turn. We feel a delicious, subversive joy in the way the man who won't work works wonderfully well. The straight man in this vaudeville routine is the Lawyer, and he keeps coming back, asking the irrational to be reasonable, trying to get the refractory to cooperate. We love to see him defeated, to watch him as he begins "to stagger" and frantically seeks reinforcement for his own "faltering mind."

To whom can he turn? Who can help in his efforts to understand and deal with Bartleby? An awful vacancy opens up in his life, the vacancy of his "cool tranquillity" and his "snug retreat." He looks around, and there is nobody there. The emptiness of Bartleby's life seems to tally his own. Where is the friend? The wife? The family? The Lawyer has to consult books, Edwards and Priestly. His own life is a bachelor's. This Lawyer prides himself on his balance—"professionally and privately." He instinctively seeks balance and prides himself on the achievement of it. He deals with the world so that "in a manner, privacy and society were conjoined." But now he is getting all unbalanced, yawing dangerously. It frightens him:

> Presentiments of strange discoveries hovered around me.

> sad fancyings—chimeras, doubtless, of a sick and silly brain

> There was something about Bartleby that not only strangely disarmed me, but in a wonderful manner, touched and disconcerted me.

> I trembled to think that my contact with the scrivener had already and seriously affected me in a mental way. And what further and deeper aberration might it not yet produce?

He is quite explicit about his growing fear that he is losing his mind: "The scrivener's pale form appeared to me laid out, among uncaring strangers, in its shivering winding sheet." Note that wonderful "shivering"—the dead man moves! What we sense here is the amazing susceptibility of this "eminently *safe*" man, no longer safe at all, not from Bartleby, and most especially not safe from the haunting voices in his own head. There are, suddenly, deeply frightening voices and images in there. What he thought were brick walls are very slender reeds.

We are inaccurate about the story, and inaccurate about the
Lawyer's mind, if we concentrate exclusively on the pathos and the
tragedy. We must be able to see, simultaneously, how funny it is.
More accurately, we must see a single emotion of great complexity;
only in profound doubleness do we apprehend it truly. Weird little
pairs of words run through the story, sublime little whimpers "wonderful mildness," "great stillness," "sheer vacancy," "wonderous
ascendancy." The mock heroic starts innocently enough in the
genial tone of the opening pages, in that touching image of Turkey
deploying columns, "myself at their head," gallantly charging the
foe, "thus!" with a violent thrust of his ruler. Or Nippers with his
desk at the impossibly sharp angle ("like a man using the steep roof
of a Dutch house for his desk"). All this works in the little self-con-
scious details of the Lawyer's speech, as when he mentions "the proprietor of the face." But, as he gets more and more agitated and
disoriented, he shouts things like "put up your money" to a voice on
the street that says "I'll take odds he doesn't," for it is election day,
and "In my intent frame of mind, I had, as it were, imagined that all
Broadway shared in my excitement." A man whose chief virtues are
"prudence" and "method" literally does not know what he is doing,
does not know what he is saying; "If you do not go away from these
premises before night, I shall feel bound—indeed I *am* bound—to—
to—to quit the premises myself!" That prized balance of mind
becomes absurdly demonic self-contradiction. The Lawyer is walking around "with my hand in my pocket—and—and my heart in my
mouth," and so "I tore myself from him whom I had so longed to be
rid of." The Lawyer is not making sense anymore. The verbal comedy issues into physical comedy: "effectually dodging every one by
the suddenness and rapidity of my flight," the Lawyer rushes from
the building, and runs "up Wall-street towards Broadway, and jumping into the first omnibus. . . . " The Lawyer is running wild.

Or he is brought abruptly to a halt. When he fumbles at his office
door, thinking Bartleby is finally gone, he hears a voice from
within—"Not yet; I am occupied," and

> I was thunderstruck. For an instant I stood like the man who,
> pipe in mouth, was killed one cloudless afternoon long ago in
> Virginia, by summer lightning; at his own warm open window
> he was killed, and remained leaning out there upon the dreamy
> afternoon, till some one touched him, when he fell.

It is a marvelous comic image, elaborately detailed, coming round
to that deadpan climax, "when he fell." It follows the funny little
admission which peeps up when the Lawyer "stood listening for a
moment," and finding that "all was still" assumes Bartleby "must be
gone"—and "I was almost sorry for my brilliant success." If the

Lawyer stands in for "us," he is doing it here. Like him, we would feel very sorry to find Bartleby gone because we need to see this wonderful game keep going. We do not want Bartleby to shape up. We want him, as long as possible, to go on being Bartleby.

As for our Lawyer, he is a man of fine intelligence, keen wit, and generous humor. But he is helpless when fate drops a lonely young man on his doorstep. All the Lawyer's pride in himself blows up in his face, and his whole life begins to malfunction. That is an interesting story. And the text everywhere supports such a reading.

Look, for example, at this not very important sentence:

> Others may have loftier parts to enact; but my mission in this world, Bartleby, is to furnish you with office-room for such period as you may see fit to remain.

If you see that Lawyer as a dolt, you brush right by it. But if you hear the Lawyer's lovely, resonant voice, it is quite moving. In the very next sentence, the Lawyer turns his back on "this wise and blessed frame of mind." That is the way he works; he is not as strong as he wishes to be. He caves in when "a whisper of wonder was running round, having reference to the strange creature I kept at my office." He says, "This worried me very much." And then he goes a little funny in the head. He wonders if Bartleby might be "a long-lived man." Sane man that he is, the Lawyer begins to dream up a totally fantastic situation in which Bartleby will "keep occupying my chambers, and denying my authority; and perplexing my visitors; and scandalizing my professional reputation; and casting a general gloom over the premises"; and, my God, "in the end perhaps outlive me, and claim possession of my office by right of his perpetual occupancy." Anyone who does not see how funny that is will probably miss, too, that "as all these dark anticipations crowded upon me more and more, and my friends continually intruded their relentless remarks upon the apparition in my room; a great change was wrought in me." He is charged up, resolved "to gather all my faculties together," to swing into action "and for ever rid me of this intolerable incubus." An "incubus" might mean merely one dictionary definition of it, "any person or thing that oppresses or burdens." But here it seems to qualify under the terms of another, darker definition, "an evil spirit, supposed to lie upon persons in their sleep." The narrator is having a real nightmare.

And what does he do? Well, "ere revolving any complicated project, however," our Lawyer sits down to discuss, rationally, with Bartleby, "the propriety of his permanent departure." The Lawyer speaks "in a calm and serious tone," commending his remarks to the "careful and mature consideration" of the incubus himself.

After our Lawyer has "denied" Bartleby three times, and moved away from him into new offices, he is called upon by a "perturbed looking stranger," a lawyer who communicates the problem that Bartleby "refuses to do any thing; he says he prefers not to; and he refuses to quit the premises." We smile at our favorite line tucked in there between semicolons; Bartleby-talk is creeping into the speech of strangers now, too: even though we have moved away from him, he's still Bartleby. The Lawyer tells us, "I found several persons waiting at my door in a high state of nervous excitement." Bartleby's "pallid haughtiness" has turned things upside down: "Every body is concerned; clients are leaving the offices; some fears are entertained of a mob; something you must do, and that without delay." The Lawyer is "aghast at this torrent." And then we get the comic payoff:

> Going up stairs to my old haunt, there was Bartleby silently sitting upon the banister at the landing.
> "What are you doing here, Bartleby?" said I.
> "Sitting upon the banister," he mildly replied.

Mildly. Bartleby, the crazy man, is keeping his head while all about him are losing theirs. He is the only one who knows what he is doing. He is "sitting upon the banister"—"upon," not "on." When he answers "Sitting upon the banister" to the question "What are you doing here?" we laugh, for we are paying tribute to the pull of the irrational and to the truth lurking in it. Throughout the story Bartleby's replies subvert and contradict the Lawyer's reality. Of course, we want the Lawyer to save Bartleby. But we really want, just as much, for Bartleby to save the Lawyer. We are about equally divided between our desire to have Bartleby come to his senses and our delight in seeing the Lawyer take leave of his.

In my American Renaissance course it came time for me to teach "Bartleby." Seventy young men and women would be reading it for the first time, and I would have fifty minutes to talk with them about it. I told them I wouldn't give a formal lecture. I told them they would have to write their own "tickets"—one question—and I would try to answer whatever was on the table. I asked them to be simple, to be honest, to say as plainly as they could whatever disturbed or perplexed them when they read it.

On Friday morning I picked up the questions they had placed on the lectern.

> Why does Bartleby stop copying?

> Why did Bartleby "prefer" to be a scrivener in the first place?

> Why does Bartleby stare out the window—is he looking for something?

If the Lawyer is so "safe," why doesn't he throw Bartleby out?

Why does Bartleby copy for three whole days before he stops?

Why does he quit eating?

"Why?"—that's what my students asked—"Why?" I answered them as best I could, but at the end of our discussion I quoted to them the verdict of that excellent literary critic, Albert Einstein: "The most beautiful thing we can experience is the mysterious."

In her "In Brief" column at the front of the New Yorker, Pauline Kael once in a while mentions the movie

> "Bartleby" (1970)—The shock when you first read the story—Melville's "Bartleby, the Scrivener"—may be in the recognition that Melville had this prevision of modern alienation back in 1853. The character is a precursor of Kafka's central figures, of Oblomov, of Dostoevski's underground man, of Camus's Meursault, and you can't grasp how this specifically modern man was formed in that mid-nineteenth-century setting. What is he doing in that world, passively resisting, and withdrawing into courteous, stubborn catatonia?

She is probably right that setting it in modern London "kills the visionary quality right off the bat. . . . The movie was obviously made on a shoestring and with honorable intentions, yet it's tentative and lame; it has little to recommend it but the two actors, Melville's dialogue, and the remnants of his great spooky conception." Kael's phrase "great spooky conception" locates accurately the essential effect of "Bartleby, The Scrivener." It is what I mean by calling the story genuinely haunting. And perhaps we should take that haunting very literally. Bartleby annoys the other characters, and sometimes he provokes them to fury, but he does not haunt them. Bartleby haunts only the narrator. Ghosts do not waste their time on people who cannot see them; ghosts haunt only the people who deserve them. To feel the force of Bartleby's line "I prefer not to," one must hear, in the little silence that follows it, how the line delivers two contradictory meanings, obstinacy and politeness. What makes the line so funny, and so eerie, is the way it stuns the Lawyer every time. He hears its profoundly mixed message, its perfect yes and no. Bartleby's *prefer* creeps insidiously into the speech of his co-workers, and we see it pop up in the messenger from the new tenants in the old office. But only the Lawyer understands, because he can't, quite. He gets used to it, and he does not; he goes on shaking his head in disbelief and nodding it in assent. Bartleby drives the Lawyer out of his mind, for the Lawyer feels as if Bartleby is saying, "I'm what you've got coming to you."

We have to understand the Lawyer's voice because we derive Bartleby through the Laywer and only through him. Misunderstand the Lawyer, and you can't understand Bartleby. The truly remarkable thing about our narrator is just how reliable he really is. To say Bartleby "respectfully," "slowly," and "mildly" disappears is to express the profoundest meaning of the story—to understand not the motive of Bartleby's silence but the dimension of it. Especially that "mildly" affords an oceanic calm. The Lawyer plumbs for us the depth of the surface; he can hear that "Sitting upon the banister" and "I prefer not to" partake respectfully, slowly, and mildly of the awesome silence they lead into. They depend on the Lawyer's being there to hear and complete them. Everybody else hears only what Bartleby says; the Lawyer hears the silence in it. Calling the narrator unreliable is really the same mistake as digging beneath the surface to "explain" Bartleby. We substitute little false meanings for the big true one.

On the last page the narrator is still trying to hear something in the silence that "passively resists" all his efforts to comprehend it. Finally he cries, "Ah Bartleby! Ah humanity!" and falls silent himself. In that concluding act of perfectly responsive audition, the Lawyer is a different man from the one who boasted of his "prudence" and "method" at the beginning. He has had to go through an intense personal loss, a family loss. This is a religious emotion, and it comes from the deepest regions of Melville's heart. Bruce Franklin points to it when he cites the Book of Matthew and connects "this forlornest of mankind" to "the least of these." The traditional religious invitation to "give yourself to Christ" is also a command to "Let the Lord into your life." William James said that all religions must begin with an answer to the single cry for help. Bartleby is the cry *Help* incarnate, or so the Lawyer hears it. In the opening paragraphs of the story the Lawyer brags about what we see as wrong with him. At the end he sees it himself. Bartleby came into his life when his life was not much worth living. When Bartleby dies, "I cannot adequately express the emotions which seize me." Grief awakens the man to his own life, and "humanity" is forever changed.

# Benito Cereno

## YVOR WINTERS AND DARREL ABEL

### On *Benito Cereno:* Opposing Views

\* \* \*

When Cereno is finally rescued by Captain Delano, he is broken in spirit, and says that he can return home but to die. When Captain Delano inquires what has cast such a shadow upon him, he answers: "the negro." His reply in Spanish would have signified not only the negro, or the black man, but by metaphorical extension the basic evil in human nature. The morality of slavery is not an issue in this story; the issue is this, that through a series of acts of performance and of negligence, the fundamental evil of a group of men, evil which normally should have been kept in abeyance, was freed to act. The story is a portrait of that evil in action, as shown in the negroes, and of the effect of the action, as shown in Cereno. It is appalling in its completeness, in its subtle horror, and in its silky quiet.[1]

\* \* \*

Babo is as much the hero of *Benito Cereno* as anyone else; the suppressed forces of life have as much inherent right to assert themselves as the rest, have as much right as the rest to thrust out of sight whatever is antagonistic to them, denies their full reality, and is to *them* the dark—that is the incomprehensible and threatening—half of the world. Aboard the *San Dominick* it was the blacks, not the Spaniards, who exhibited the full range of human vitality. Although Captain Delano had taken Babo for an "indisputable inferior" with "a limited mind," his brain was a "hive of subtlety," and he at last confronted his fate with more dignity than did Don Benito, who fainted when asked to appear in court to identify Babo. The majestic black Atufal was a figure of more personal majesty than any of the whites, and more fit to command than his master. The American

1. Yvor Winters, *In Defense of Reason* (Denver: Allan Swallow, 1947), p. 222.

captain saw in the affection of the Negresses for their babies "pure tenderness and love." "He was gratified with their manners; like most uncivilized women, they seemed at once tender of heart and tough of constitution." It will not do to interpret the mutinous blacks of *Benito Cereno* as the representatives of evil. They represent an oppressed portion of humanity asserting its equal right to life.[2]

\* \* \*

## Epigraph to Ralph Ellison's *Invisible Man*

"'You are saved,' cried Captain Delano, more and more astonished and pained; 'you are saved; what has cast such a shadow upon you?'"

—Herman Melville, *Benito Cereno*

## FREDERICK BUSCH

## [Captain Delano][†]

\* \* \*

It is 1799, and an American merchantman, commanded by Captain Delano, lies near an island off Chile. The sea is "gray," the swells "lead," the sky "gray"; the "gray" fowl fly through "troubled gray vapors," and the scene is summarized by "Shadows present, foreshadowing shadows to come." So the reader is alerted that he will have to read this world and interpret the grays. He is further warned that what he sees are shadows; what casts them is hidden, and the reader must peer: The story is an exercise in, and an essay about, dramatic irony. As much as the subject is slavery and revolution, it is also perception and invention; it is about fiction, the successes and failures and tactics of which are very much on Melville's mind.

Delano is described from the start as having a "singularly undistrustful good-nature," and is virtually incapable of "the imputation of malign evil in man." From the start, Melville wants us to know that Delano misreads the world. So he resorts to the language of gothic romance. The slave ship looks like a "monastery after a thunder storm"; figures aboard her resemble "Black Friars pacing the cloisters"; the vessel is reminiscent of "superannuated Italian

2. Darrel Abel, *American Literature* (Great Neck, NY: Barron's Education Series, 1963) 2:422.
† From "Melville's Mail," in *A Dangerous Profession* (New York: Broadway Books, 1998).

palaces" and her galleries evoke "tenantless balconies hung over the sea as if it were the grand Venetian canal." Delano is placed among the settings in which virgins are pursued by fright figures, and he should be at home—for he is, in terms of the evil and cruelty that Melville wishes to note, quite virginal.

Gothic conventions not only easily signal fright—we may perceive them; Delano cannot—but can serve to remind us at every turn that dying Europe, the worst of it, encounters the most naëïve and imperceptive rawness of the New World. Apocalyptic thoughts bring out the best in Melville, who swims in them as in the sea. So we have such poetry about a ship as "while, like mourning weeds, dark festoons of sea-grass slimily swept to and fro . . . with every hearse-like roll of the hull."

Messages do not get through. And so Delano, maddeningly, scarily, cannot overcome his racism and innocence and see past the virtual *tableaux vivants* arranged for his benefit by the rebel slaves under Babo. The clues that strike us at once are misinterpreted in multiples by Delano. And then the awful symbol, in a story rife with symbols— puzzling rope knots, razors at throat—is uncovered. The ship's figurehead is revealed to be a human skeleton, that of a partner in the slave ship. And we are warned by Melville that what seem to be *only* symbols may be representations of what's actual, that language carries a cargo of the real, and that fiction is a matter of life and death.

The story slips without faltering into another convention, the "true" document that creates verisimilitude (as in the case of Captain Gulliver's deposition or, closer to home, Poe's "MS. Found in a Bottle," or Hawthorne's "discovery" of *The Scarlet Letter* manuscript). The statement by Benito Cereno, a seeming transcript, gives the European account of the slave rebellion, suggests to us how complicated and multifold any actuality is—how difficult to comprehend or relate—and serves to supply small, shuddery details. So we see, for example, that the original figurehead had been a wooden Christopher Columbus; the discoverer (as he was then thought to be, of course) of the New World is replaced by the Old World's grinning corpse: Slavery becomes the emblem of an inescapable fact— that we are haunted by our past, that the New Eden is not free of the old evils, that, as Melville complained to Hawthorne, "the malicious Devil is forever grinning in upon me."

A brief third section follows Cereno's testimony. It contains warnings inferred by Melville (and so many others) concerning the social conditions that will ignite the Civil War. It also offers another, a larger and historical, way of examining the events of the story. And it reminds us how, throughout the first part, we saw menace between the slave Babo and his master (then prisoner) Cereno, while Delano saw affection. Delano saw mastery, and we saw captivity. When Benito Cereno's "symbol of despotic command" is examined, it is seen not to be a sword, "but ghost of one," its scabbard "artificially stiffened." Melville does not, I think, speak here only of command, but of men seen as joined by affection who are later revealed to be acting in reversal of their customary relationships (the more powerful obeys, the slave commands). Melville joins notions of political power and emotional liaison, and not only to warn us that slaves rise up. The metaphor works in reverse as well, I think, and we are instructed that lovers are slaves and masters, that men can be unmanned by love (the limp scabbard), and can, as in the case of wan Don Cereno, even die of it.

The warning note is sounded again as Delano points to a sky he names as "blue," but which Cereno cannot acknowledge; to him, it is the gray, perhaps, of the story's opening. The shadows of that early passage are pointed at again as Delano says, "You are saved: what has cast such a shadow upon you?" Cereno answers, "The negro," and so warns a society of its sin and then its price—only then are we told of the empty scabbard—and points as well to Babo, who took Cereno's soul in partial payment for his freedom. The shadow is national, cultural, and also particular: Cereno dies, as did his partner.

Babo is the genius of the story—compare his invention, his gift for creating a shipwide fiction, to Delano's good dullness—and his head, "that hive of subtlety," is taken from his body. It is his brain the white men fear. He is further reduced by this barbarism, and yet he becomes more of a threat. He stares at the white man from the post on which his head is impaled. He stares at the Old World and the New Eden, at unmanned Cereno, at church and monastery, storyteller and reader. And he stares them down. He began as a man and became a curse. And *his* message, for some, gets through.

\* \* \*

# LAURIE ROBERTSON-LORANT

## [Melville][†]

\* \* \*

During the winter and spring of 1855, Melville composed "Benito Cereno," an indictment of "benign" racism that is one of the

† From *Melville: A Biography* by Laurie Robertson-Lorant. Copyright © 1996 by Laurie Robertson-Lorant. Reprinted by permission of Clarkson Potter/Publishers, a division of Random House, Inc.

masterpieces of his career. His brilliant adaptation of the "ghastly & interesting" *Narrative of Voyages and Travels in the Northern and Southern Hemispheres,* published in 1817 by Captain Amasa Delano, an ancestor of Franklin Delano Roosevelt, opens as the captain of an American sealer discerns a mysterious ship that, from afar, resembles a floating monastery. When the Yankee captain boards the ship, he finds that the strange vessel is a Spanish slaver and that the dark figures who resemble cowled Black Friars, or Dominicans, are actually enslaved Africans. The slaver's captain, a young Spaniard named Don Benito Cereno, tells Delano that most of his crew were wiped out by a plague that also killed the ship's owner, his friend Don Alexandro Aranda, so the Africans have to help with the running of the ship. As Don Benito tells his story to Delano, he faints repeatedly, and his faithful black servant, Babo, supports him with his arm. The "liberal" Delano, a "Massachusetts man" who assumes that Africans are jolly primitives who love bright colors and have a special talent for waiting on white people, constantly compares the "fun-loving" Africans to animals. Boasting that he takes to Negroes "not philanthropically, but genially, just as other men to Newfoundland dogs," he offers to buy Babo from Don Benito by way of complimenting the black for being such an excellent body servant. Despite misgivings prompted by the provocative behavior of several of the remaining Spanish sailors and various other unsettling events, Delano cannot fathom what is really going on aboard the ship.

Melville builds suspense by limiting his third-person narrative to Delano's point of view until the point where Delano himself realizes with a shock that the Africans have taken over the ship and slaughtered most of the whites, and that Babo has woven an elaborate web of deception from the American's own prejudices. By the end of the story, Melville has drawn readers who adopt Delano's view of the *San Dominick* into the same entangling web.

Melville's version of Delano's story differs from the original narrative in a number of ways. He changed the date, and he changed the names of the two ships from the actual *Perseverance* and *Tryal* to the symbolic *Bachelor's Delight* and *San Dominick.* He also invented a number of significant symbols for his fictional adaptation of Delano's narrative: the somnambulistic white noddy, or albatross, in the rigging, a trope for Delano, the white man sleepwalking through history; the ship's shrouded figurehead, covered by a cloth on which someone has scrawled the cryptic words "follow your leader"; the stern-piece showing a "dark satyr in a mask" holding his foot on the neck of a prostrate figure, also masked; the ship's flawed bell, which evokes the cracked Liberty Bell in Philadelphia; the majestic Atufal, who was a king in Africa, and who appears before the Spanish captain in chains and a padlock each time the bell tolls, to beg his freedom; the straight razor with which Babo shaves Don Benito Cereno, and the flag of Spain with which he wipes the Spaniard's blood from the razor; and, finally, the "Gordian knot" that Captain Delano cannot undo.

In this tough-minded story, Melville indicts slavery without sentimentalizing either the blacks or the whites. He makes it clear that Don Alexandro Aranda's having allowed the Africans to move around the decks unfettered does not change the fact that he considered them his property and planned to reshackle and sell them as soon as the ship reached port. Aranda's leniency in keeping his "cargo" on deck, where fresh air and water would ensure a higher survival rate, can be seen as purely self-serving, since better health meant fewer deaths, and fewer deaths meant more profit for the slaveowner. Moreover, freedom within the confines of a slave ship did not protect the women against rape and sexual abuse; in fact, cleaning them up and letting them roam the deck instead of leaving them crammed in a filthy hold made them more accessible to the lustful crew. After Aranda's death, the women, whom Delano imagines to be as docile and sweet as does with their fawns, shave Aranda's bones clean with their hatchets, then hang his skeleton over the carved figurehead of Cristobal Colón as a warning to the surviving Spaniards, covering it with a cloth when another ship draws near.

Melville deconstructs "niceness" as a moral category at the end of the story; when the Americans board the ship, they restrain themselves from maiming or killing the Africans, not because they are kind, but because they plan to claim the "cargo" and want it to be undamaged. The willingness of the American captain to continue the slave trade parallels the willingness of the "enlightened" Founding Fathers to bring the slavery of the Old World into the New.

After Delano and his men overpower the Africans and take control of the ship, the narrative switches to a legal deposition that purports to establish the "facts" of the case—which, of course, means the Spanish point of view. Failing to grasp Melville's reason for including a dry legal document, *Putnam's* editor George William Curtis assumed that the placing of the deposition at the end of the story was laziness on Melville's part, and he complained that Melville did everything "too hurriedly." The deposition, however, actually frames the story to form a mutilated triptych, with the implied third panel being the "voiceless" Babo's version of the story. The legalistic language obscures the moral issues and nullifies the Africans' point of view, as history written by the colonizers always does.

Ironically, Delano's blindness nearly costs him his life and the life of Don Benito, yet, he learns nothing from his experience or the Spanish captain's ordeal, and less about the sufferings of the blacks. In a coda following the conclusion of the trial, Delano blithely suggests that Don Benito can forget his harrowing ordeal, but the Spaniard remains haunted by the shadow of "the Negro." Like Charles V, the Holy Roman Emperor who ordered the first Africans shipped to Santo Domingo to replace the Indians who had been worked to death by Columbus and his men, Don Benito retires to a monastery. In the end, Babo's point of view comes across wordlessly and lingers in the reader's mind. The story closes with the haunting image of Babo's head, "that hive of subtlety," impaled on a pole in the Plaza by the "civilized" Spaniards. The "unabashed gaze" of Babo stares down the long corridors of history in accusation and defiance, a challenge to a nation heading inexorably toward civil war.

Melville knew the scriptural warning, "Those who reap the wind shall sow the whirlwind." He changed the date of the events described in the story from 1805 to 1799 to evoke memories of the revolution in Santo Domingo and altered the description of Babo so that the Senegalese mastermind resembled Haitian patriot Toussaint-Louverture, president of the first black republic in the New World. *Putnam's*, in fact, had just published a lengthy article about Toussaint that was a slap in the face to southerners for whom the words Santo Domingo conjured memories of the slave rebellions and massacres perpetrated by Nat Turner, Denmark Vesey, and Gabriel Prosser in the 1830s.

By suggesting that the rebel Africans were as patriotic as his own grandfathers, Melville echoes a point made by John Quincy Adams in his defense of the *Amistad* mutineers. In words reminiscent of the Declaration of Independence, the narrator implies that the slaves' objective—to commandeer the ship and sail to Senegal, where they could be free—was morally justified. They had to revolt and kill their owner and most of the Spanish sailors, except those whom they needed to navigate the ship, or they had no hope of regaining the freedom that was their natural right. Thus, Melville's version of Amasa Delano's *Narrative* turns colonial history on its head and reflects the legal dramas of the times.

In May 1854, the case of Anthony Burns nearly tore Boston apart, as it had three years earlier. While Lemuel Shaw was hearing arguments in the Burns case, a great throng assembled outside of Faneuil Hall to hear Wendell Phillips and Theodore Parker urge civil disobedience to force the bailiffs to free the fugitive. The abolitionist editor Thomas Wentworth Higginson and his supporters stormed the jail to release Burns, but the attempt failed for lack of numbers, and a volunteer deputy was shot and killed in the skirmish. Parker, Phillips, and Higginson were all charged with "obstruction of justice," but the case was thrown out on a technicality. When Chief Justice Shaw ordered Burns remanded to the custody of his owner, William Lloyd Garrison burned facsimiles of the United States Constitution, the Fugitive Slave Law, and the court decision.

Like Daniel Webster in 1850, Lemuel Shaw considered preservation of the Union more important than the abolition of slavery because he felt that, despite its flaws, the Constitution was mankind's best hope for liberty and justice for all, and that slavery would wither away of its own accord. The scorn heaped on Shaw for upholding the wicked statute put Melville in an awkward position. Not wanting to risk a rift with his father-in-law, he expressed his dissent allegorically instead of openly.

Richard Henry Dana was an editor for *Putnam's* around the time "Benito Cereno" was published, and his Boston Vigilance Committee owned a vessel named the *Moby Dick* that was used to transport fugitives from slavery to freedom, so it's not surprising that Melville's stories reflect the controversy over slavery.

"The Bell-Tower," which was written during the summer of 1855, opens with two epigraphs on slavery. This baroque tale with an Italian setting implies that even the most nobly conceived edifice can be destroyed by a fatal flaw, just as the Union could be destroyed by slavery. John Hoadley, who read the story by a dim lamp, found it "wild, mysterious," and "strangely fascinating," and despite his wife's urging him not to spoil his eyes, he refused to put the story aside until he had finished reading it.

# C. L. R. JAMES

## [The Yankee Captain]†

\* \* \*

A Yankee captain, competent, jolly and good-humored, is at anchor one morning in a harbor off the coast of Chile. He sees a strange vessel come into port and he goes off to pay it a visit. The vessel is a Spanish slaver, with slaves on board and the captain, Benito Cereno, whose name gives the title to the story, tells a sad tale of unfavorable weather, sickness and a hard voyage. The Yankee captain is full of sympathy.

Benito Cereno is followed everywhere by a Negro, Babo, who is

† From C. L. R. James, *Mariners, Renegades and Castaways*, pp. 131–34. Detroit: Bewick Editions, 1978. Reprinted by permission of the publisher.

unfailingly solicitous in his attentions to his master. The Yankee captain, reminding himself how well suited by nature Negroes are to be domestic servants, is very pleased by this.

Benito Cereno is a sick man and at times his behavior is strange. Captain Delano is mystified at many unusual incidents on the ship. But he makes allowances. The Negroes on board and the characteristics of Negroes occupy much of his attention. The slaves are in tumult but some are working. Six blacks in particular, elevated above the general throng, are busy cleaning rusty hatchets. Periodically they clash the hatchets together and the captain recognizes how fond Negroes are of uniting industry with pastime. He sees a mulatto steward on board. Is it true, he asks, that mulattoes are hostile to being placed in a subordinate position to blacks? He sees a Negro slave woman sleeping on deck while her baby sucks at the nipple, and he is pleased at this glimpse of the natural relation between a primitive mother and child. He is so impressed with Babo's unceasing attentions to his master that he offers to buy Babo as his personal servant, a proposal which, as could have been expected, the faithful Babo indignantly opposes. Captain Delano is one of those white men who not only understands but who loves Negroes.

Finally Captain Delano leaves the ship and goes back into his own boat. Suddenly, as the climax of his somewhat strange behavior all day, Benito Cereno leaps into the boat and Babo leaps after him with a knife. Captain Delano fears that his own life is in danger from the ever-faithful Babo, who perhaps believes that his beloved master is being kidnapped. But he soon learns the truth. Babo's knife is intended for Benito Cereno, and after the black is overpowered, the whole story comes out.

The slaves had revolted and seized the ship. They had tried to escape to freedom, but had not succeeded. When they came into the harbor, Babo, the leader, organized a new plot. They would pretend that Benito Cereno was still captain. But he, Babo, would be in attendance on him all day, and if he so much as tried to say a word, he would be immediately killed. All on board, slaves and white sailors, had been instructed by Babo what to do. The slaves kept watch on the sailors. The hatchet-polishers were not Negroes uniting industry with pastime as is the habit of Negroes. They were on guard, ready to intervene in any disturbance. The mulatto steward did not object to Negroes being over him—he was Babo's faithful lieutenant. The Negro women were not kindly primitives—they had taken a leading part in the revolt.

Delano's men finally recaptured the ship and Babo was beheaded. But here, as early as 1855, Melville had, in the opinions of the capable, well-meaning, Negro-loving Captain Delano, itemized every single belief cherished by an advanced civilization (we have selected only a few) about a backward people and then one by one showed that they were not merely false but were the direct cause of his own blindness and stupidity. Under his very nose, Babo had been forcing Benito Cereno to participate in a new plot, aimed at capturing Delano's own ship.

Melville, with his usual scientific precision, does not write of Negro slaves. He writes of the Negro race, civilized and uncivilized alike. Harriet Beecher Stowe, who wrote a few years before, wrote about Negroes, about Uncle Tom and Eva, who mean nothing today. Melville's interest is in a vast section of the modern world, the backward peoples, and today from the continents of Asia and Africa, their doings fill the front pages of our newspapers.

As is usual with him, his protest is uncompromising, absolute. The Negroes fight to a finish, Babo is the most heroic character in Melville's fiction. He is a man of unbending will, a natural leader, an organizer of large schemes but a master of detail, ruthless against his enemies but without personal weakness, as was proved by his behavior after he was captured. Melville purposely makes him physically small, a man of internal power with a brain that is a "hive of subtlety."

*   *   *

# GLENN C. ALTSCHULER

## Whose Foot on Whose Throat? A Re-Examination of Melville's *Benito Cereno*†

Given the rest of the Melville canon one wonders at the difficulty critics have had in seeing *Benito Cereno* as Melville's attack on slavery and racism. Yet difficulty there has been. Several critics, literary descendants of F. O. Mathiessen, view the story as the struggle between pure good and evil.[1] They are embarrassed that Melville chose a slave to epitomize evil, but emphasize Melville's interest in metaphysical and not socio-economic questions. Others see the centrality of slavery to the story but borrow the equation of Babo as pure evil and conclude that the author was an apologist for the system.[2]

† From *CLA Journal* 3 (March 1975): 383–92. Reprinted by permission of the publisher.
1. F. O. Matthiessen, *American Renaissance* (New York: Oxford University Press, 1941), p. 508.
2. Sidney Kaplan, "Herman Melville and the American National Sin: The Meaning of 'Benito Cereno'," *The Journal of Negro History*, XLI (1956), 311–338.

The latter reading is certainly not corroborated by an examination of the rest of Melville's fiction. In the prose supplement to *Battle-Pieces* he proclaimed: "Those of us who always abhorred slavery as an atheistical antiquity, gladly we join the exulting chorus of humanity over its downfall." Those who see *Benito Cereno* as an apologia for slavery must explain the companionship of Ishmael and Queequeg, the cultural relativism of *Typee*, the satiric portrait of slave-holding Vivenza in *Mardi*. Can it be, then, that *Benito Cereno* is not an aberration? The story is a trenchant critique of slavery and the response to it in the North. Those who see Delano as a subtle abolitionist are just as mistaken as those who see Melville as sympathetic to slavery. Perhaps, too, metaphysical and socio-political concerns can be brought together in a unified reading of the story.

Melville was rather faithful to the real narrative of Amasa Delano, but the changes and additions he made are quite significant. He changed the date of the incident from 1805 to 1799, which was the year of the massive slave revolt and take-over of Santo Domingo by Toussaint L'Ouverture. Santo Domingo was the site of the first large-scale importation of slaves in the Americas. Melville changed the name of Cereno's ship to the *San Dominick*, perhaps to make the connection with Santo Domingo more explicit, perhaps, as Bruce Franklin has suggested, to remind the reader of the Spanish Inquisition in which the Dominicans played a leading role.[3] In the sense that senseless violence, oppression and slavery are timeless, Delano is right that "past, present and future seem one."

Let us bracket metaphysical considerations, however, at least for the moment, and examine the specifics of Melville's analysis of slavery. Melville understood the meaning of the "Uncle Tom" and "Black Sambo" roles of the slave long before Stanley Elkins and long before there was a profession called sociology. The novella exists as a warning to the slaveholder that that docile, smiling, loyal servant may be plotting his death. Kenneth Stampp has found that the most trusted slaves, the house slaves, were usually the leaders in plots to escape or revolt—far more than their counterparts in the fields.[4] The revolt on the *San Dominick* would never have taken place if not for Alexandro Aranda's mistaken belief that his slaves were tractable. Southerners carefully passed laws forbidding slave owners to teach their slaves how to read and write, but they were winked at by masters who sought to teach them the lessons of the Bible. Delano and the unsuspecting reader trust Babo who can read and write (and is "less a servant than a trusted companion")—and who, it turns out, can lead a revolt and have his master brutally killed.

---

3. H. Bruce Franklin, *The Wake of the Gods: Melville's Mythology* (Stanford: Stanford University Press, 1963).
4. Kenneth Stampp, *The Peculiar Institution* (New York, 1956), pp. 89–90.

Melville also realized the stupidity of the stereotype of the Negro, a realization that should have been understood by those critics who want to make a case for Babo as pure evil, or pure anything. Delano parrots the traditional wisdom about the Negro—his gentleness fits him to be a good body servant; he is docile and genuinely stupid. Babo is none of these things. In fact, he concocts the ruse against Captain Delano, an extremely complicated plan, in two or three hours—a difficult feat for one whose docility arose "from the unaspiring contentment of a limited mind." When Babo is finally executed and decapitated, his head is described as "that hive of subtlety." * * * As the sailor's knot (significantly not one knot but a combination of several) cannot be untied, neither can one attribute single qualities to one race or one man. The novella provides substantial evidence that good and evil, generosity and viciousness, make all men miscegenated, make everyone and everything gray. Slavery is monopolized by neither race. Babo, we are told, was a slave to his fellow black brethren in Africa. Nor were all slaves black. Cereno, of course, is a slave to his captors, but so is the white on the ship who announces the shaving hour, and who, in status, seems little distinguished from the black slaves. * * *

Melville portrayed the slave in far more realistic terms than the vapid sycophants of much abolitionist literature. He does not hide the brutality of the revolt or the vicious murder of Aranda and many of the passengers. Wanton violence may have been the only way to disprove white notions about the docility of blacks. But Melville also points to the sadistic violence of the whites. Almost matter-of-factly he tells the reader that some negroes were killed "after the capture and re-anchoring at night, when shackled to the ring-bolts on the deck."

Those critics who point to Babo as a symbol of evil admit that slavery might be cause for his violence but assert that because Melville does not specifically deal with it as cause, it should not be regarded as a major theme of the novella. A close reading of the story indicates not only that the slaves at times acted honorably and humanely (although Melville does not excuse or exclude their violence and sadism) but that their actions can only be understood in light of their servitude and desire for freedom. Very early in the work, Melville puts words in the mouth of Delano which are ostensibly directed at Cereno but which have great significance for an understanding of the slave revolt. Delano "noted that there are peculiar natures on whom prolonged physical suffering seems to conceal every social instinct of kindness; as if forced to black bread themselves, they deemed it but equity that each person coming nigh them should, indirectly, by some slight or affront, be made to partake of their fare." What better explanation can be given for the violence of the slaves, they who had to swallow far worse fare than black bread?

But the revolt is not quite an orgy of wanton violence. Aranda is killed only to insure the liberty of the slaves. Every action of the slaves is taken with one aim in mind, to return to a black country. Babo and Atufal "discussed what was necessary for their design of returning to Senegal, whether they were to kill all the Spaniards, and particularly the deponent." Thus, the fate of the captives was explicitly linked to the journey to freedom. The Negroes seemed anxious to draft written agreements with Cereno and their respect for law is indeed ironic. Slaves in revolt and murderers, they yet felt it necessary to have Cereno sign the cargo over to them. The agreements were broken only when there seemed to be a plot against the revolt. For example, the mate Raneds was killed because he made a gesture to Cereno in "the act of handing a quadrant." The slaves could hardly countenance a plot which would steer them away from the promised land. At times Babo and the Negroes showed compassion. Perhaps they did not kill Cereno because he was the sole navigator on the ship. But what reason but compassion did they have for sparing the life of the cook? They had ignored Benito's pleas to spare his friend Aranda because he blocked the path of their liberty, but acceded to his request to spare the cook because they had no reason to kill him.

Those who insist that the violence of the blacks is the epitome of evil point to Babo's plot to take over and rob Delano's ship. Although the possibility exists that the sole motives were greed and the thirst for power, Melville carefully provides alternative hypotheses. First of all, it is Cereno who is the sole witness to the plot (except for the questions he puts to Delano) and we are made to see great gaps in his credibility. Even as he testifies to the court about Babo's design, Cereno admits, "That in some things his memory is confused and he cannot distinctly recall every event." Is it possible that Babo sought to commandeer the *Bachelor's Delight* because it was more seaworthy and better provisioned than the *San Dominick* and could better transport the blacks to Senegal? Is it possible that Babo feared that the captain might eventually discover the truth and pursue him? Given these possibilities, then, it may be that robbery and plunder, if motives at all, were subsidiary motives.

If the story, then, is about the desire of the slaves for freedom and the intermingling of good and evil qualities in men of all races, it is also a powerful warning to the American South that disaster and an orgy of violence might very well await them. At the outset of the story Melville warned the reader that there are "dark shadows present, foreshadowing deeper shadows to come." If, as we later learn from Cereno, those shadows are cast by "the negro," then those societies which bask in the shade of a slave economy, * * * in effect, have as their operating principle the picture on the shield-like stern-piece of the *San Dominick*—"a dark, satyr in a mask, holding his foot on the prostrate neck of a writhing figure, likewise masked." * * *

The picture on the stern-piece is surely the central image of the story, and I shall return to it. Melville realized the mask on every individual prevented full knowledge of his motivation. he recognized that the white man and the black man faced each other masked. Behind the master lay perhaps a timid man, like Cereno, perhaps a more compassionate man. Behind the mask of Uncle Tom lay, per-haps, a Babo. In any event, Melville was acutely conscious of our lack of knowledge of the slave as man. Thus, he ingeniously pre-sented blacks in the only way in which they could be seen in his society—through the eyes of whites. The deposition is included as a remainder of this fact: * * * "On the testimony of the sailors alone rested the legal identity of Babo." * * *

Part of Melville's theme in the novella is a delineation of the problem of separating leaders from followers in the society. At one point, Delano thinks that perhaps Cereno was "some low-born adventurer, masquerading as an oceanic grandee." The United States had, at least in theory, discarded hereditary considerations as a means of determining its leaders but had not found an equally expedient alternative. One method of distinguishing leaders from followers was to make every black man a follower, a solution adopted, in varying degrees by the North and South. The black man would find it exceedingly difficult to masquerade as a leader. "Follow your leader," then, has any number of different meanings. Those blacks who seem to follow their leader may be plotting to become leaders themselves. Those whites who follow their leaders in defense of slavery may follow them in death, as Cereno followed Aranda. Color, then, may for a time be the means of separating leaders and followers, but its death knell would soon be sounded. The system of race subjugation, while it "preserved signs of for-mer state" was certainly "under a decline of masters." Nor does Melville fail to leave other evidence of his gaze into the future. The shaving episode, which does not appear in the Delano narra-tives, relates how Babo draws blood from his master for the first time. Babo drew first blood in the crusade against slavery, as did L'Ouverture and as many thought the slave revolt on the Schooner *Amistad* in 1839 (where Spaniards and Americans fought over cap-tured slaves)[5] was the first blood drawn in the conflict to eradi-

---

5. J. Q. Adams, *Arguments of John Quincy Adams before the Supreme Court of the United States, in the case of the U.S., Appellants vs. Cinque, and other Africans, Captured in the Schooner Amistad* (New York, 1841).

cate the peculiar institution. Finally, Melville alludes menacingly to the tranquil image the South had painted of itself. "Might not the San Dominick, like a slumbering volcano, let loose energies now hid?" Might not Atufal, Benito's "time-piece," exist as a constant reminder of the ultimate intractability of slaves and their unspoken yet all-powerful desire to burst their chains? Melville's warning to the South was unmistakable.

If Melville provided the reader with a telling condemnation of the slave system, he also provided a devastating condemnation of northern complicity in slavery. Anticipating Leon Litwack's *North of Slavery* by more than a century, Melville pointed to the deeprooted, unconscious prejudice of those who claimed they abhorred slavery. Delano comes from Duxbury, Massachusetts, from the seat of abolitionism, yet his first "generous" act is to help the slave-master Cereno secure his ship and cargo so that he might deliver the slaves to their destination. Melville seems to register his recognition of the significance of Hawthorne's rueful observation that the ship which brought the first settlers to Massachusetts made several other trips across the Atlantic with slaves. The conscience of the New Englander is scarcely troubled by his complicity in slavery; * * * he thinks only of his generosity, and perhaps a little of the profits that are to be made. The same man who proclaims, "Ah, this slavery breeds ugly passions in man—Poor fellow!" offers to buy Babo from Benito. Like most Northerners, Delano's anti-slavery stance is merely empty rhetoric. After he sees Babo, bleeding, he thinks at the hands of his capricious master, and makes his proclamation, he "was about to speak in sympathy to the negro, but with a timid reluctance, he re-entered the cuddy." Not only will he fail to chastise Cereno, he cannot even bring himself to say a kind word to the slave.

Delano views the black man in the stereotyped mold constructed by the whites; he follows his leaders in conforming to that mold. He notes the tendency of blacks toward laziness, and urges Benito to "keep all of your blacks employed, especially the younger ones, no matter at what useless task." When he refers to blacks he usually associates them with animals, comparing them, for instance, with Newfoundland dogs. Delano, then, enslaves by perception. If the stereotype is true, then blacks can only be slaves. Not only has he followed his leaders in accepting their stereotypes, but he unhesitatingly accepts the superiority of his race (he is even racist in relation to Cereno) and unalterably opposes alliances with blacks. The harshness of his position should be contrasted with what several critics have seen as Melville's gentle chastisement of his attitude toward blacks as expressed in his observations on their unique musical talent and love of bright colors. At one point Delano hypothesizes that the slaves and Cereno are in league to take over his ship. He quickly

rejects the idea. "Besides, who ever heard of a white so far a renegade
as to apostatize from his very species almost, by leaguing in against it
with negroes?" One can hardly trust Delano's sincerity in his remarks
about the ugly passions engendered by slavery. The "generous" captain takes the lead in recapturing the slaves. Significantly, Cereno
urges his fellow-captain *not* to pursue them. But Delano's sympathies
are not strong enough to overcome his desire not to league with them
even to free them by calling off the pursuit. His sympathies for the
slaves are not strong enough to overcome his desire for revenge, especially when the venture is sweetened by the chance for a little profit.

Melville reverts to the two masked figures on the stern-piece to
underline his assertion that much of the blame for slavery rests with
the North. When the reader first encounters the image, it serves as
an easy analogy to the master Cereno with his foot on the throat of
the slave Babo. When the plot is unmasked he realizes that the roles
were, in fact, reversed. But there is yet another twist. As Babo
jumped into Delano's boat in an attempt to kill Cereno, Captain
Delano "clutched the half-reclined Don Benito . . . *while his right
foot*, on the other side, *ground the prostrate negro*" (italics mine). So
much for the "generous" New Englander.

Had the Captain learned anything from his experience? He had
spent what seemed like an eternity south of freedom but had
emerged neither sadder nor wiser from the experience. Delano, who
is always looking for a "sunny sight" fails to draw any conclusions
from the drama which has unfolded before him, except perhaps that
slaves are violent rather than gentle and docile. Benito Cereno,
who, perhaps has learned Melville's lesson (his scabbard after all,
was now empty) probably says more than he knows when he forgives
Delano for thinking him a monster. "So far may even the best man
err, in judging the conduct of one with the recesses of whose condition he is not acquainted." Applicable to all men, this remark is
applicable to the slave in general, and perhaps Babo in particular.
But the captain, who, let us not forget, eagerly sought to be "a
massa" to Babo, is not to be dissuaded from his sightless optimism.
"But the past is past; why moralise upon it? Forget it. See, yon
bright sun has forgotten it all, and the blue sea, and the blue sky;
these have turned over new leaves." Cereno tries again. "Because
they have no memory . . . because they are not human." Delano's
answer is interesting. "But these mild Trades that now fan your
cheek, do they not come with a human-like healing to you? Warm
friends, steadfast friends are the Trades." If Delano does not mean
the slave trade, Melville wants the reader to remember it. Those
same gentle Trade winds brought slaves to the shores of the Americas. * * * Clearly, Delano will not recognize the harshness in the
Trades as Cereno will. "With their steadfastness, they but waft me

to my tomb, senor." The captain, more and more astonished and pained, tells the doomed man he is saved. "What has cast such a shadow upon you?" "The negro." Silence follows because there was no more that the two could say to one another.

It has been said that Americans recognize no past, that the present exists only as a means of propelling them into the future. Melville recognized the burden of the past * * * and chose a real incident from it to comment on its value and our rejection of it. His portrait of the slave, unlike those of many of the abolitionists, was neither patronizing nor entirely flattering. It was as human as he could make it, given the mask that slavery put on the black man. Melville refused to acquiesce to the neat equation of black and white with evil and good, and refused to make the South the scapegoat for a truly national sin.


# ALLAN MOORE EMERY

## The Topicality of Depravity in "Benito Cereno"[†]

Over the past half-century, Herman Melville's "Benito Cereno" has evoked a kaleidoscopic critical response to which no brief summary could do perfect justice. Nevertheless, one might cast most of the story's commentators into two camps: (1) those who read the tale as a powerful portrait of human depravity, with a sadistic Babo as the prime embodiment of evil, an obtuse Delano as Melville's figure of naive optimism, and a doomed Cereno as his contrasting symbol of moral awareness;[1] and (2) those who view the tale as a stern indictment of American slavery, complete with an amply prejudiced Delano, a guilt-ridden Cereno, and a sympathetic (or even heroic) Babo, driven to violence by an insufferable bondage.[2] The "depravity" critics appear to have a preponderance of textual evidence on

† From *American Literature* 53.3 (August 1983): 316–31. Copyright © 1983, Duke University Press. All rights reserved. Reprinted with permission.

1. See, for example, Stanley T. Williams, "'Follow Your Leader': Melville's 'Benito Cereno'," *Virginia Quarterly Review,* 23 (1947), 61–76; Rosalie Feltenstein, "Melville's 'Benito Cereno'," *American Literature*, 19 (1947), 245–55; and Richard Harter Fogle, "The Monk and the Bachelor: Melville's *Benito Cereno*," *Tulane Studies in English*, 3 (1952), 155–78, rpt. *Melville's Shorter Tales* (Norman: Univ. of Oklahoma Press, 1960), pp. 116–47.
2. Most persuasive are Joseph Schiffman, "Critical Problems in Melville's 'Benito Cereno'," *Modern Language Quarterly,* 11 (1950), 317–24; Allen Guttmann, "The Enduring Innocence of Captain Amasa Delano," *Boston University Studies in English,* 5 (1961). 35–45; David D. Galloway, "Herman Melville's *Benito Cereno*: An Anatomy," *Texas Studies in Literature and Language,* 9 (1967), 239–52: Joyce Adler, "Melville's *Benito Cereno*: Slavery and Violence in the Americas," *Science and Society,* 38 (1974), 19–48, rpt. *War in Melville's Imagination* (New York: New York Univ. Press, 1981), pp. 88–110; and Glenn C. Altschuler, "Whose Foot on Whose Throat? A Reexamination of Melville's *Benito Cereno*," *CLA Journal,* 18 (1975), 383–92.

their side: certainly Babo's "heroism" is difficult to document. Moreover, they appreciate Melville's penchant for "universal" themes. Yet their opponents recall, with equal rightness, his habitual reference to contemporary issues (slavery included) and note as well that "Benito Cereno" appeared in 1855, at a time when slavery was a subject of considerable concern to Melville's audience.

Indeed, these critics imply that slavery was *so* important to mid-century America that a Melville tale published in 1855, featuring slaves and treating depravity rather than slavery, would represent a flouting of historical obligation: a work in which Melville ignored the topicality of his own materials in striving to prove some large "literary" point. To reformulate the suggestion: either "Benito Cereno" treats slavery—or else the author stands convicted of an irresponsible (if temporary) disregard for his own times. Perhaps, however, the "depravity" party should neither quit the field nor admit the charge of authorial fecklessness,[3] for their dilemma is actually false: if "Benito Cereno" treats human depravity, it does so for specific historical reasons. In other words, one need not turn away from history in order to appreciate Melville's universal theme, nor need one adopt an abolitionist reading in order to rescue Melville's tale from "irrelevant" generality. For his depravity emphasis was itself thoroughly topical.

Alert as always to social injustice, Melville did allude to American slavery in his tale—but infrequently, and mainly as a local instance of a far-flung phenomenon. Amasa Delano, Melville's representative American, attempts to buy Babo at one point; eventually he also "[grinds] the prostrate negro."[4] Yet even such impressive details fail to demonstrate an authorial preoccupation with America's peculiar institution. Delano's truthful assertion that "slavery breeds ugly passions in man" seems universally applicable, especially given Babo's original enslavement at the hands of blacks. Moreover, the tableau carved upon the stern-piece of the *San Dominick* shows "a dark satyr in a mask, holding his foot on the prostrate neck of a writhing figure, likewise masked." While this image predicts the embarrassing behavior of the "benevolent" Delano, it also depicts Babo's oppression of Cereno and Babo's own earlier subjugation by blacks *and* whites. Melville's masks serve, then, to make the *San Dominick* symbolic of a worldwide oppression (indicative of a global depravity)—with American slavery as non-"peculiar" illustration.[5]

3. For versions of this admission, see F. O. Matthiessen, *American Renaissance* (New York: Oxford Univ. Press, 1941), p. 508; Margaret Jackson, "Melville's Use of a Real Slave Mutiny in 'Benito Cereno'," *CLA Journal*, 4 (1960), 92; and Kingsley Widmer, "The Perplexity of Melville: *Benito Cereno*," *Studies in Short Fiction*, 5 (1968), 231–32.

4. Melville's tale first appeared in the numbers of *Putnam's Monthly Magazine* for October, November, and December of 1855.

5. See Kermit Vanderbilt, "'Benito Cereno': Melville's Fable of Black Complicity," *Southern Review*, 12 (1976), 317–18.

Nor do the prejudices of Delano prove Melville's overriding concern with the perceptual underpinnings of American slavery. To be sure, Delano's Caucasian confidence that blacks are "stupid" becomes ludicrous in light of a day's events: far from having the "limited mind" of an "indisputable inferior," Babo is the "uncommonly intelligent" owner of a remarkably resourceful brain.[6] Yet if the blacks of the *San Dominick* are smarter than Delano thinks, they are also more fiendish: Delano's chief limitation is not, one remembers, a tendency to intellectual snobbery but a refusal to recognize the presence of "malign evil in man." Though he fails to accurately estimate the black I.Q., he fails, more precisely, to appreciate the "subtlety" of black men in whom intelligence is conjoined to "malignity," in whom "sophistication" merely enhances the ability to oppress. Eminently perceptual, Delano's mistake nevertheless underlines not so much the bigotry of Americans as the calculated cruelty of mankind.

Melville's readers should not suppose, however, that he casually chose blacks to exemplify human viciousness, disregarding the importance of race in 1855. On the contrary, Melville's focus on black ferocity represents an acknowledgement rather than an evasion of American intellectual history. One clue to the topical context of "Benito Cereno" is Delano's emphasis on the "docility," "cheerfulness," and "affection" of blacks; another is Melville's revelatory ending, which, more than heightening our sympathy for Babo[7] or increasing our respect for black intelligence, serves to demolish the notion of black amiability. For by 1855 this notion was hardly unique to Delano. In "Prospects of American Slavery," an article appearing in the influential *Christian Examiner* near the time Melville's tale was composed,[8] one reads: "We . . . point, first, to the affectionate, patient, docile, tractable disposition of the African race,—tolerant of burdens, not apt to harbor deep animosity, . . . and won by the slightest kindness to a grateful and confiding affection. . . . [We point as well] to the example of the British West Indies, which, whatever else they prove, show that violence and hostility are the last things to be dreaded from the blacks when they come to feel their strength. . . . "[9] Similar remarks graced Harriet Beecher Stowe's phenomenally popular *Uncle Tom's Cabin*, first

6. For a reading of "Benito Cereno" as a defense of black intelligence, see Richard E. Ray, "'Benito Cereno': Babo as Leader," *American Transcendental Quarterly*, No. 7 (1970), 31–37.

7. For commiserative treatments of Babo, see Schiffman, Guttmann, Galloway, and Ray; Warren D'Azevedo, "Revolt on the San Dominick," *Phylon*, 32 (1956), 129–40; Ray B. Browne, *Melville's Drive to Humanism* (Lafayette, Ind.: Purdue Univ. Studies, 1971), pp. 168–88; and Marvin Fisher, *Going Under: Melville's Short Fiction and the the American 1850s* (Baton Rouge: Louisiana State Univ. Press, 1977). pp. 104–17.

8. In "The Chronology of Melville's Short Fiction, 1853–1856," *Harvard Library Bulletin* 28 (1980), 391–403; Merton M. Sealts, Jr., offers convincing evidence that "Benito Cereno" was "probably composed during the winter of 1854–1855."

9. *Christian Examiner*, 57 (Sept. 1854), 226.

published in book form in 1852: "[One day] the negro race, no longer despised and trodden down, will, perhaps, show forth some of the . . . most magnificent revelations of human life. Certainly they will, in their gentleness, their lowly docility of heart, their aptitude to repose on a superior mind and rest on a higher power, their childish simplicity of affection, and facility of forgiveness."[1] One could hardly imagine views more akin to those of Delano—or less consistent with the evidence of "Benito Cereno." Apparently Melville was acquainted with contemporary arguments for black docility[2] and sought to attack them by means of his naive protagonist and bloodcurdling plot.

Melville found many proofs of black "violence and hostility"—and few signs of Negro "gentleness"—in Amasa Delano's Narrative of Voyages and Travels (1817).[3] Yet in altering his source for literary purposes, Melville actually heightened the barbarity of Babo and company. According to Delano's Narrative, the blacks of the Tryal refrained from murder after Cereno signed a document promising them safe passage to Senegal;[4] on Melville's San Dominick, the mate Raneds is killed "for a chance gesture" long after the agreement is reached. Likewise, only the San Dominick sports a grisly "figurehead": according to the Narrative, Alexandro Aranda believed his blacks were "tractable";[5] in "Benito Cereno," his bones belie that idea. When embellishing his source, Melville also highlighted particular instances of black depravity with ironic assertions regarding its opposite. Typical is his disquisition on the Negro as "body-servant," which anticipates the disclosure that Jose, Aranda's personal attendant, brutally "stabbed his master" after Aranda had been "dragged half-lifeless to the deck."[6] Melville's account of Negroes as "natural valets and hair-dressers" becomes similarly suspect once one discovers that Babo was not simply barberous in Melville's shaving scene.

Furthermore, Melville changed both the date of Delano's adventure and the name of Cereno's vessel so as to invoke the violent

1. Uncle Tom's Cabin; or, Life Among the Lowly (Boston: John P. Jewett, 1852), I, 259. A similar passage appeared in Stowe's Key to Uncle Tom's Cabin (Boston: Jewett, 1854), p. 41.
2. For a discussion of these arguments, see George Fredrickson, The Black Image in the White Mind (New York: Harper and Row, 1971), pp. 97–129. Fredrickson notes Stowe's emphasis on black docility.
3. Harold Scudder identified Melville's source in "Melville's Benito Cereno and Captain Delano's Voyages," PMLA, 43 (1928), 502-32.
4. See Amasa Delano, A Narrative of Voyages and Travels, in the Northern and Southern Hemispheres: Comprising Three Voyages Round the World; together with a Voyage of Survey and Discovery, in the Pacific Ocean and Oriental Islands (Boston: E. G. House, 1817; rpt. New York: Praeger, 1970), p. 337.
5. Melville incorporated this detail into "Benito Cereno."
6. See Margaret M. Vanderhaar, "A Re-Examination of 'Benito Cereno,'" American Literature, 40 (1968), 186. Delano's Narrative declared simply that Jose "advised the other negroes to kill his master, Don Alexandro" (p. 340); Melville contributed the "stabbing" anecdote.

slave revolt which occurred on the isle of Santo Domingo in 1799.[7]
He invented as well those six "Ashantees" whose hatchet wielding
an ironic author attributes to "the peculiar love in negroes of uniting industry with pastime"—but whose actual function and particular "fury" are described in Cereno's deposition. Not coincidentally,
the Ashantees of West Africa were famous for their ferocity: like the
South African "Caffres" also mentioned by Melville, they had frequently faced white troops in battle.[8] Finally, too, Melville expanded
the character of Atufal, strangely thought by some critics to be
Melville's symbol of the noble black man, ignobly enchained.[9] While
Delano praises Atufal's "royal spirit" and "general docility" and finds
the "chained" Negro a comforting sight, he is obviously laboring
under a misconception. Atufal is nothing less than Babo's "right
hand man," and his chains are a charade. If he has a particular symbolic role, he most likely hints at the power of America's blacks to
break their bonds, to imitate Nat Turner, to stun those innocent
Americans comfortably convinced of the "tractability" of slaves.[1]

Yet Melville's most artful assault on the concept of black con-
tendedness is his continuing emphasis on black muscianship. Perhaps he saw "Negro Minstrelsy," an article praising black music, in
the January 1855 number of *Putnam's Magazine*. The author
remarked upon "the lightness and prevailing good humor of . . .
negro songs," insisting that "a true [negro] melody is seldom sentimental, and never melancholy. And this," he added, "results directly
from the character and habits of the colored race. No hardships or
troubles can destroy, or even check their happiness and levity."[2]
Having read this or some equally dubious declaration, Melville
included in "Benito Cereno" a number of details designed to question both the "lightness" of Negro music and the natural "levity" of
blacks. At one point, for example, he applauds the Negro's "great gift
of good-humor," discovering in the darker race "a certain easy
cheerfulness, harmonious in every glance and gesture; as though
God had set the whole negro to some pleasant tune." Elsewhere,

7. See H. Bruce Franklin, "'Apparent Symbol of Despotic Command': Melville's *Benito Cereno*," *New England Quarterly*, 34 (1961), 471–72, rpt. *The Wake of the Gods: Melville's Mythology* (Stanford: Stanford Univ. Press, 1963), p. 145. Perhaps Melville saw an 1854 *Putnam's* article describing the violent history of Santo Domingo. See "Hayti and the Hay-tians," *Putnam's*, 3 (Jan. 1854), 53–62. According to Merton Sealts, *Melville's Reading: A Check-List of Books Owned and Borrowed* (Madison: Univ. of Wisconsin Press, 1966), p. 87, Melville "probably subscribed" to *Putnam's*, to which he contributed a number of tales, including "Benito Cereno."
8. The Ashantees had defeated a British force in 1824; the bloodiest of the "Kaffir Wars" occurred in the early 1850s. For a contemporary account of the "powerful and fierce Ashantees," see J. C. Brent, "Leaves from an African Journal," *Knickerbocker*, 33 (May 1849), 403–04.
9. See, for example, Galloway, p. 248 and D'Azevedo, p. 130.
1. See Adler, p. 47 and Altschuler, p. 389.
2. "Negro Minstrelsy—Ancient and Modern," *Putnam's*, 5 (Jan. 1855), 74.

however, he nullifies this stereotype by noting that the favorite tunes of Aranda's blacks are anything *but* pleasant. The four grizzled Negroes who, unbeknown to Delano, keep order on the *San Dominick*, emit "a continuous, low, monotonous chant; droning and druling away like so many gray-headed bag-pipers playing a funeral march." And the black females of the *San Dominick* form an even gloomier chorus during and after the revolt on their vessel. Cereno eventually explains: "In the various acts of murder, [the negresses] sang songs and danced—not gaily, but solemnly; and before the engagement with the boats, as well as during the action, they sang melancholy songs to the negroes, and . . . this melancholy tone was more inflaming than a different one would have been, and was so intended . . ."[3] Significant, too, is Melville's passing observation that the murderous Francesco, a person of "good voice," once sang "in the Valparaiso churches." From all these facts, one draws the appropriate conclusion: that, contrary to the claims of *Putnam's*, Negro "minstrelsy" precludes neither melancholy nor maleficence.

Melville did not, then, underline the barbarity of Babo's blacks out of a "literary" disregard for racial implication, or a casual conflation of blackness with evil, but in direct response to the contemporary image of the Negro as more "docile," "cheerful," and "harmonious" than other men: to Melville, black depravity was a matter of "topical" concern. Yet so, too, was white depravity. Aware that the revelations of his tale might instill in the minds of his readers attitudes even more dangerous than Delano's, Melville embedded in "Benito Cereno" considerable evidence that depravity is an essential attribute of all men rather than the private failing of an individual race.[4] Especially noteworthy are his comparison of Cereno's black barber to a "Nubian sculptor finishing off a white statue-head" and his subsequent likening of Atufal to "one of those sculptured porters of black marble guarding the porches of Egyptian tombs." These references accompany Delano's reflection that Babo, a "full-blooded African," seems "not unconscious of inferiority" to Francesco, Cereno's mulatto steward. A pivotal conversation is also nearby:

> Captain Delano observed with interest that while the complexion of the mulatto was hybrid, his physiognomy was European—classically so.

3. Delano's *Narrative* states: "In the act of murder, and before that of the engagement of the ship, [the negresses] began to sing, and were singing a very melancholy song during the action, to excite the courage of the negroes . . . " (p. 341). Melville added emphases of his own.
4. Two critics overlook this evidence when accusing the author of an unconscious racism. See Sidney Kaplan, "Herman Melville and the American National Sin," *Journal of Negro History*, 42 (1957), 12–27; and Joseph Schiffman, *Three Shorter Novels of Herman Melville* (New York: Harper, 1962), p. 235.

"Don Benito," whispered he, "I am glad to see this usher-of-the-golden-rod of yours; the sight refutes an ugly remark once made to me by a Barbadoes planter; that when a mulatto has a regular European face, look out for him; he is a devil. But see, your steward here has features more regular than King George's of England; and yet there he nods, and bows, and smiles; a king, indeed—the king of kind hearts and polite fellows. What a pleasant voice he has, too?"

"He has, Señor."

"But tell me, has he not, so far as you have known him, always proved a good, worthy fellow?" said Captain Delano, pausing, while with a final genuflexion the steward disappeared into the cabin; "come, for the reason just mentioned, I am curious to know."

"Francesco is a good man," [somewhat] sluggishly responded Don Benito, like a phlegmatic appreciator, who would neither find fault nor flatter.

"Ah, I thought so. For it were strange, indeed, and not very creditable to us white-skins, if a little of our blood mixed with the African's, should, far from improving the latter's quality, have the sad effect of pouring vitriolic acid into black broth; improving the hue, perhaps, but not the wholesomeness."

"Doubtless, doubtless, Señor, but"—glancing at Babo—"not to speak of negroes, your planter's remark I have heard applied to the Spanish and Indian intermixtures in our provinces."

Moments later, as Delano and Cereno continue their conversation over a bottle of Canary, the Spaniard alludes "to the different constitution of races, enabling one to offer more resistance to certain maladies than another."

Melville's references (by way of Delano and Cereno) to Francesco's "hybrid" complexion, the moral "wholesomeness" of white "blood," and "the different constitution of races" suggest he was aware of mid-century American interest in "ethnology," or the study of racial characteristics; his references to Egyptian and Nubian sculpture point specifically to Josiah Nott's and George Gliddon's *Types of Mankind*, a massive and much-touted ethnological compendium published in 1854 and extensively reviewed in the pages of *Putnam's*.[5] Nott was a Southern physician, well acquainted (so he thought) with the various deficiencies of the Negro; Gliddon was a retired Egyptologist, eager to buttress Nott's racist arguments

---

5. See *Types of Mankind: or, Ethnological Researches, based upon the Ancient Monuments, Paintings, Sculptures, and Crania of Races, and upon their Natural, Geographical, Philological, and Biblical History* (Philadelphia: Lippincott, 1854); "Is Man One or Many?" *Putnam's*, 4 (July 1854), 1–14; and Carolyn L. Karcher, *Shadow Over the Promised Land: Slavery, Race, and Violence in Melville's America* (Baton Rouge: Louisiana State Univ. Press, 1980), pp. 128–30.

with archaeological evidence. In particular, Gliddon sought to demonstrate that the "types" of men existing in the nineteenth century were no recent development; hence he included reproductions of numerous Egyptian (and Nubian) paintings and sculptures, some of blacks and some of whites, but all proving the antiquity of racial differences.[6] Meanwhile, Nott explored the racial implications of human "hybridity." Sharing Cereno's medical opinion, he noted that mulattoes, like pure-bred Negroes, enjoyed "extraordinary exemption from yellow-fever" when brought to Southern cities. At the same time, he anticipated the views of Delano by insisting that even "a small trace of white blood in the negro improves him in intelligence and morality."[7]

Apparently, however, Melville doubted the validity of Nott's ethnological claims, for the case of Francesco suggests that the intermingling of races does not always produce results favorable to the notion of white preeminence. From Cereno's deposition one learns that, throughout the mutiny, Francesco was "in all things, the creature and tool of the negro Babo"; thus Delano was wrong to accuse the "full-blooded African" of a racial inferiority complex. Moreover, Cereno had good reason for "sluggishly" praising Francesco. As Melville's Barbadoes planter might have predicted, the "worthy" mulatto was "of the first band of revolters" against Cereno's rule, his morals having been un-"improved" by the dash of white blood in his veins. Melville's earlier reference to "a Lima intriguante's one sinister eye peering across the Plaza from the Indian loop-hole of her dusk *saya-y-manta*" and his later mention of Lima's "Plaza" and "Rimac bridge" imply that his own view of human "hybridity" may have derived in part from an 1851 *Harper's* article which contained not only detailed accounts of both the "*saya y manto*" and Lima's architecture but also an assertion regarding what Cereno, careful not to comment on Negroes, calls the "Spanish and Indian intermixtures in our provinces." Wrote the author: "As a general rule the mixed races, which constitute about a third of the population of Lima, inherit the vices without the virtues of the pure races from which they sprung."[8] No Delanovian optimist, he might have said the same for Francesco.

Yet if the mulatto's career discredits the notion of white-blood-as-better, then so does the behavior of Babo's "full-blooded" foes, the

6. *Types*, pp. 141–79, 246–71.
7. *Types*, pp. 68, 373.
8. "Lima and the Limanians," *Harper's Monthly*, 3 (Oct. 1851), 606. According to Sealts, *Melville's Reading*, p. 64, Melville subscribed to *Harper's* throughout his tale-writing years. Significantly, Melville's first mention of the *saya* (by name) occurs in *Pierre*, which he was writing at the time the Lima article appeared. See *Pierre, or The Ambiguities*, ed. Harrison Hayford, Hershel Parker, and G. Thomas Tanselle (Evanston and Chicago: Northwestern Univ. Press and the Newberry Library, 1971), p. 149. Moreover, Melville's own "Town-Ho's Story" appeared in the same number of *Harper's* as the Lima article, making his familiarity with that number more likely.

vindictive Spaniards of "Benito Cereno." The original Delano explained that he was forced to "exercise authority" over Cereno's crewmen in order to "prevent them from cutting to pieces and killing" their black enemies, following the recapture of the *San Dominick*.[9] Melville's Delano is less successful at averting bloodshed. In his deposition Cereno insists that "beside the negroes killed in the action, some were killed after the capture and re-anchoring at night, when shackled to the ring-bolts on deck; that these deaths were committed by the [Spanish] sailors, ere they could be prevented." Nor are Cereno's seamen alone in demonstrating Spanish depravity. In both Delano's *Narrative* and "Benito Cereno," the authorities of Lima flagrantly advertise their own savagery by abusing the bodies of blacks they have lately killed.[1]

More significant for Melville—and more disturbing for his readers—may have been the behavior of Delano's Americans, who likewise indulge in "white-blooded" brutality when seizing the *San Dominick*.[2] The original Delano admitted that the results of American victory were "truly horrid": "Some of [the negroes] had part of their bowels hanging out, and some with half their backs and thighs shaved off." "This," he proudly proclaimed, "was done with our boarding lances, which were always kept exceedingly sharp, and as bright as a gentleman's sword."[3] Melville similarly notes that many of Babo's blacks were "mangled" during the American attack, "their wounds—mostly inflicted by the long-edged sealing-spears, resembling those shaven ones of the English at Preston Pans, made by the poled scythes of the Highlanders." By implication, the actions of Delano's compatriots are in keeping with prior examples of white savagery (unconfined to the Spanish). Consider, too, this mention of a militant exchange: "Upon the second volley, . . . [the negroes] hurtled their hatchets. One took off a sailor's fingers. Another struck the whale-boat's bow, . . . remaining stuck in the gunwale like a woodman's axe. Snatching it, quivering from its lodgment, the mate hurled it back. The returned gauntlet now stuck in the ship's broken quarter-gallery, and so remained." Here white truculence precisely mirrors black truculence—a doubling later reemphasized when "sealing-spears and cutlasses [cross] hatchets and handspikes." Clearly the shout of the invader and the motto of the *San Dominick* speak true: if Babo's blacks are guilty of viciousness, then Delano's whites are all too willing to "follow their lead."

9. *Narrative*, p. 328.
1. See Delano, p. 347; Guy A. Cardwell, "Melville's Gray Story: Symbols and Meaning in 'Benito Cereno'," *Bucknell Review*, 8 (1959), 166; and Max Putzel, "The Source and the Symbols of Melville's 'Benito Cereno'," *American Literature*, 34 (1962), 194.
2. See Vanderhaar, p. 190.
3. Delano, p. 328.

No other detail of "Benito Cereno" so eloquently bespeaks the author's emphasis on universal depravity, unless it be his subsequent notation that the black women of the *San Dominick* were party to the Spanish massacre.[4] Midway through the story, Delano perceives a "slumbering negress" and remarks: "There's naked nature, now; pure tenderness and love." He then proceeds to eulogize all the ladies on board: "He was gratified with their manners: like most uncivilized women, they seemed at once tender of heart and tough of constitution; equally ready to die for their infants or fight for them. Unsophisticated as leopardesses; loving as doves. Ah! thought Captain Delano, these, perhaps, are some of the very women whom Ledyard saw in Africa, and gave such a noble account of." The actual words of the explorer, John Ledyard, were these: "I have observed among all nations, that the women . . . are the same kind, civil, obliging, humane, tender beings. . . . They do not hesitate, like men, to perform a hospitable or generous action; not haughty, nor arrogant, nor supercilious, but full of courtesy, and fond of society; industrious, economical, ingenuous, more liable . . . to err than man, but . . . also more virtuous, and performing more good actions than he."[5] Melville's story casts doubt, however, on both the perspicacity of Ledyard and the sexual suppositions of Delano, for whereas the *Narrative* merely noted that "the negresses of age, were knowing to the revolt, and influenced the death of their master,"[6] a less reticent Melville declares in the deposition that "the negresses . . . testified themselves satisfied at the death of their master, Don Alexandro; that, had the negroes not restrained them, they would have tortured to death, instead of simply killing, the Spaniards slain by command of the negro Babo . . . ". Apparently Melville found the idea of female "generosity" as dubious as the notion of black docility. His tale implies that Delano and Ledyard have erred in thinking that violence and brutality are foreign to *any* segment of humanity since, finally, these traits are as much a part of "naked human nature" as "tenderness and love."

In other words, despite the opinion of Cereno, there is one "malady" to which no "race" offers more "resistance" than another. Humanity is depraved to a man—and woman—or so goes the lesson

---

4. See Feltenstein, p. 254.
5. Quoted in "American Travelers," *Putnam's*, 5 (June 1855), 565. When moving "Benito Cereno" from *Putnam's* to the *Piazza Tales*, Melville substituted Ledyard's name for that of Mungo Park, an English explorer. See Egbert S. Oliver, "Explanatory Notes" to *The Piazza Tales* (New York: Hendricks House, 1948), pp. 235–36. In "Mungo Park and Ledyard in Melville's *Benito Cereno*," *English Language Notes*, 3 (1965), 122–23. Seymour Gross suggests that the substitution resulted from Melville's reading of "About Niggers," *Putnam's*, 6 (Dec. 1855), 608–12, where he could have learned that Ledyard, and not Park, was the original source of those views which interested him. "American Travelers" contained the same information.
6. Delano, p. 341.

of "Benito Cereno." Yet Melville also derived several other "lessons" from this one—all of them significantly topical. Perhaps his ubiquitous animal imagery had its contemporary relevance, for example; mid-century ethnologists were fond, after all, of stressing the animalism of blacks. Nott compared Negroes to "wild horses, cattle, asses, and other brutes," insisting that the intellectual gap between blacks and chimpanzees was no greater than that between Negroes and "Teutonic" types; for him, the "lower races of mankind" formed "connecting links in the animal kingdom."[7] Moreover, Delano appears to side with Nott when he likens Babo to a "shepherd's dog," his favorite black female to a "doe" with "fawn," and one group of blacks to a "social circle of bats," inhabiting a "subterraneous sort of den." Melville, too, sounds vaguely Nottish when comparing Babo's blacks to "cawing crows" and when peering into their "wolf-like" mouths. Yet Melville is also careful to equate Delano's white marauders with "submerged sword-fish" menacing "shoals of black-fish." If "Benito Cereno" supports Nott's contention that blacks are "brutish" (in a moral sense), it also challenges Nott's central thesis by underscoring the brutishness of whites, by exalting no race above another, by treating all men (and women) as equal partners in the "animal kingdom."

Melville's story may contradict as well both the pre-Darwinian evolutionists, who, while noting man's animal origins, also viewed him as clearly superior to beasts, and their orthodox opponents, who commonly emphasized man's spiritual "specialness." Trusting in both evolution and Scripture, the *Putnam's* reviewer of *Types* took issue with Nott over the question of Negro animality, asserting that "a man is a man all the world over, and nowhere a monkey or a hippopotamus, and whatever his rank in the scale of human being, he is entitled to every consideration that properly pertains to man, as separated from ape, baboon, bat, or any other creature that appears to be making a wonderful effort towards his standard." For this writer, man was "inconvertably separated from every other organism, by his anatomy, his physiology, his mind and his heart, which [placed] him, in his lowest forms, at the head of creation."[8] Perhaps Melville read these words, for "Benito Cereno" has something to say about man's pretensions to preeminence of "heart." Observing a general human depravity, Melville simply hinted that God's "noblest" work, the hero of evolution, had clay feet. Man might or might not be better-looking than the baboon, but surely any ape (or bat, or wolf) could meet his moral "standard." And apart from Delano, the human animal might rank high intellectually; but,

7. *Types*, pp. 260, 457.
8. "Is Man One or Many?" pp. 5–6, 14.

morally speaking, all "forms" of man were significantly "low" enough.

Like Melville's focus on black savagery, his broader concern with a universal depravity had, then, its contemporary cause—or, rather, causes. For, indeed, another of Delano's remarks invokes a third intellectual context. Assuming that "stupid" blacks could not have independently conspired against him, Delano goes on to conclude that Cereno and Babo could hardly be in cahoots: "Who ever heard of a white," he thinks, "so far a renegade as to apostatize from his very species almost, by leaguing in against it with negroes?" Evidently Melville realized that, for all its "Egyptian" eccentricities, *Types of Mankind* was no isolated phenomenon, being one of many contributions to a mid-century debate regarding the "unity" of the human race.[9] The English ethnologist, James Prichard, had portrayed the race as a single "species" in two influential works of the 1840s, citing men's common origin (in Adam) and the ability of diverse races to produce fertile "hybrids."[1] The American Presbyterian minister, Thomas Smyth, had sided with Prichard in *The Unity of the Races*, published in 1850; Smyth was opposed by Robert Knox in *The Races of Men* (1850) and, in 1854, by Nott and Gliddon, who meant by "types" the various species to which mankind belonged.[2] The "unity" debate also raged on the magazine front. Readers of "Benito Cereno" (*Putnam's*, 1855) had seen "Is Man One or Many?" in the *Putnam's* number for July 1854, and "Are All Men Descended from Adam?" in the number for January 1855. Meanwhile, *Harper's*, to which Melville likewise subscribed, ran consecutive editorials in September and October of 1854 asking "Is the Human Race One or Many?" and "Are We One or Many?" Thus as he began to compose "Benito Cereno," Melville was everywhere confronted with the question of mankind's "oneness."

That fact helps to explain his emphasis on human viciousness. The earlier *Putnam's* article joined Nott and Gliddon in affirming the multiple origin of races, yet insisted that men were united in having an opportunity for salvation denied to lesser creatures; the second suggested that men were inextricably related by a common

9. William Stanton traces the history of this debate in *The Leopard's Spots: Scientific Attitudes Toward Race in America, 1815–59* (Chicago: Univ. of Chicago Press, 1960).

1. See *The Natural History of Man; Comprising Inquiries into the Modifying Influence of Physical and Moral Agencies on the Different Tribes of the Human Family* (London: H. Bailliere, 1843); and *Researches into the Physical History of Mankind*, 5 vols. (London: Houlston and Stoneman, 1847–51).

2. See *The Unity of the Races Proved to be the Doctrine of Scripture, Reason, and Science* (New York: G. P. Putnam, 1850); *The Races of Men; a fragment* (Philadelphia: Lea and Blanchard, 1850); and *Types*, pp. 81, 465. For reviews of Smyth, see the *Literary World*, 6 (1 June 1850), 533–34; *Harper's*, 1 (July 1850), 284–85; and "Is Man One or Many?" pp. 2–3. A review of Knox appeared in the *Literary World*, 7 (7 Dec. 1850), 453–54. See Sealts, *Melville's Reading*, p. 75, for Melville's acquaintance with the *Literary World*.

parentage. Both *Harper's* articles based arguments for unity on Scriptural grounds. And Melville? In "Benito Cereno" he, too, enlisted on the side of unity—but without the enthusiasm of his allies. Suspicious of contemporary insistences on the moral superiority of whites, the sweet-temperedness of blacks, and the saving virtues of women, he apparently wished to underline the unity-in-depravity of all human beings. Delano assumes that men are of different "species almost"; Nott and Gliddon stressed the "moral and intellectual peculiarities" of races.[3] But Melville's tale proves a single point beyond all else: that when it comes to his remarkable capacity for wrongdoing, man is all too undeniably "one."

Understanding this point—and the interwoven historical roots of "Benito Cereno"—one more fully appreciates the essential dichotomy of the tale: the opposition between Cereno, who knows what depraved men can do, and Delano, who owes his survival to his inability to perceive the truth. Speaking to Cereno after his escape, Delano explains: "[My good-nature, compassion, and charity] enabled me to get the better of momentary distrust, at times when acuteness might have cost me my life . . ." Cereno concurs, noting in his deposition "the generosity and piety of Amasa Delano incapable of sounding such wickedness." In other words, throughout his stay on the *San Dominick*, Delano exhibits the same kindly obtuseness Melville discovered in him at outset. More important, even after Babo has leaped in his direction and a "flash of revelation" has occurred, even after Cereno has testified and the facts of the *San Dominick* are known, Delano *still* refuses to "see" what has been "revealed" to him. Ultimately, he urges Cereno not to "moralize" upon the past—not to seek, that is, the moral implications of his experience. Granted a glimpse of naked human nature, Delano has nevertheless managed to keep his eyes shut. Cereno, on the other hand, has had an eyeful, and it will prove his undoing.  * * * "Benito Cereno" offers a choice of negative alternatives: a life of cheerful obliviousness or an awareness incompatible with life. Having seen his best friend murdered, having felt Babo's fresh-stropped razor pass along the flesh of his own throat, Cereno knows the one thing Captain Delano will never know—"of what humanity is capable." His is a knowledge to die from.

If Delano's primary function is to embody, then, certain naive notions typical of Melville's age, Cereno's is to present Melville's own view of humanity—or, rather, to approximate that view. For, in the end, Cereno makes an understandable mistake: he too closely identifies depravity with blacks. Having observed neither the American attack on the *San Dominick* nor the subsequent Spanish atroc-

3. See *Types*, p. 50.

ities, and unable to control his fear of Babo, he finally insists that "the negro" has cast the "shadow" of death upon him. Cereno might have learned a profounder lesson from his misfortunes. Whatever Babo may represent for the Spanish captain, he was obviously meant to typify the "malign" potential in every man. "Snakishly writhing up" from the bottom of Delano's boat, he is far more than a homicidal black: he is the devilish symbol of *all* the depravity—black, white, male, and female—to be found aboard the *San Dominick*. Cereno's private fixation should not obscure Melville's "larger" point. In "Benito Cereno," "the negro" stands for all mankind.

The author of such a firmly integrationist tale should scarcely be charged with racism. Nor should he be accused of slighting the topical in his haste to proclaim the universal. For if Melville did not produce in "Benito Cereno" an exhaustive treatment of the slavery question, he did consider a host of contemporary issues—and a bevy of prevailing stereotypes. * * * Yet Melville likewise sought to transcend the level of historical particulars. "Benito Cereno" may be more topical than most tales, but it is also more immense, presuming to comment on the nature of man and his continuing tendency to misbehave. It is a work thoroughly in touch with the 1850s—and yet likely to remain relevant in the twenty-first century.

# ROBERT LOWELL

## Benito Cereno[†]

BABU

I was the King. Babu, not Atufal
was the king, who planned, dared and carried out
the seizure of this ship, the *San Domingo*.
Untouched by blood myself, I had all
the most dangerous and useless Spaniards killed.
I freed my people from their Egyptian bondage.
The heartless Spaniards slaved for me like slaves.

[BABU *steps back, and quickly picks up a crown from the litter*]

This is my crown.

[*Puts crown on his head. He snatches* BENITO's *rattan cane*]

---

This is my rod.

[*Picks up silver ball*]

This is the earth.

[*Holds the ball out with one hand and raises the cane*]

This is the arm of the angry God.

[*Smashes the ball*]

PERKINS

Let him surrender. Let him surrender.
We want to save someone.

BENITO

My God how little these people understand!

BABU

[*Holding a white handkerchief and raising both his hands*]

Yankee Master understand me. The future is with us.

DELANO

[*Raising his pistol*]

This is your future.

[BABU *falls and lies still.* DELANO *pauses, then slowly empties the five remaining barrels of his pistol into the body. Lights dim*]

CURTAIN

# MICHAEL ROGIN

## [Mutiny and Slave Revolt]†

\* \* \*

The *San Dominick* slaves carry out the only successful mutiny in all of Melville's fiction. There is near-mutiny on the *Neversink*, comic mutiny on the *Julia*, failed mutiny on the *Town-Ho*, alleged mutiny on the *Bellipotent*, and desertion from the *Dolly*. The metaphoric slaves on all those ships fail to overthrow their masters. Only the

† From *Subversive Genealogy* by Michael Paul Rogin. Copyright © 1979, 1980, 1983 by Michael Paul Rogin. Reprinted by permission of Alfred A. Knopf, a Division of Random House, Inc.

real *San Dominick* slaves succeed. No mutiny occurs during the narrative, however. As with the adultery in *The Scarlet Letter*, the mutiny occurs before the story begins. We learn of it only in Benito Cereno's deposition, after the action is over. *Benito Cereno* recontains a slave revolt inside a masquerade.

The citizens of 1848, as Marx and Tocqueville described them, staged a play about the French Revolution. Putting on the borrowed clothes of their ancestors, they repeated the revolutionary tragedy as a farce. Louis Bonaparte conceived of "historical life . . . as comedy," wrote Marx, "as a masquerade in which grand costumes, words, and postures merely serve as a cover for the most petty trickery." The *San Dominick* slaves also stage a masquerade. "Puppets" held formal political power in the Second French Republic, as they do on the slaver. But there is a difference. Master and slave retain "the contrast in dress, denoting their relative positions," as if those positions had not been reversed. The costumes the slaves wear, and force on the masters, were once insignias of their own servitude. By keeping those costumes, the slaves invert their meaning. 1848 exposed itself as theater, but it left the authority of the French Revolution intact. The slave masquerade is more subversive, as we shall see, both of the American Revolution and of slavery. Imitation may be a comic form, as Marx indicated, but the exchange and restoration of roles is menacing on the *San Dominick*. Unlike the farce of 1848, the slave masquerade takes vengeance on the authority it repeats.

There is no action until the drama on the *San Dominick* is over, only acting. The actors' theatricality calls attention to the artifice of their situation. The story proceeds through a series of tableaux, to use Melville's own word, rather than through dynamic, ongoing, human relations. Don Benito and Babo are continually "withdrawing below," as if they are actors regrouping behind the stage before the curtain opens on the next scene. Once Delano gives too forceful an order. "Instantly the blacks paused, just where they were, each negro and negress suspended in his or her posture, exactly as the word had found them." The motionless frieze is menacing; Delano fears for a moment he will be "massacred." The frozen, artificial stage scenes point to the disjunction between the acting on the surface and the hidden actions underneath. But neither Delano nor the reader has access to the meaning of the drama, since it is absent from the play.

Melville based *Benito Cereno* on an actual slave revolt and masquerade; but he invented staged scenes and stage effects that the real Captain Amasa Delano did not record. Melville placed a chorus of oakum-pickers and hatchet-polishers on the *San Dominick*, for example. The four oakum-pickers "were couched, sphynx-like," in the form of a square. The six hatchet-polishers sat "cross-legged," "along . . . a row, separated by regular spaces." The hatchet-polishers scour hatches; the oakum-pickers unravel old rope. They carry out their tasks with repetitive monotony, conveying the sense that their work is never done. In fact these workers are not really laboring; they are guarding the whites. Unlike the crew of the *Pequod*, the workers on the *San Dominick* are pretending to be a proletariat. Laboring on the surface, the hatchet-polishers and oakum-pickers do not transform nature; they make nothing. They perform static, ritualized motions which, unlike genuine rituals, shut out meaning instead of embodying it.

Melville's slave mutiny as masquerade inserted itself between two opposed perspectives on the master-slave relationship in antebellum America, and unsettled both. Abolitionists invoked the Declaration of Independence to justify slave revolt at sea. Southerners and their Northern sympathizers (like Delano) defended slavery as a familially based alternative to the competitive deceptions of Northern, free society. Both positions appealed to nature and, in the common rhetoric of the time, contrasted the "artificial and spasmodic" motions of a diseased social body to "a natural and healthy vitality." Antebellum fears of social decay are realized on the social body of the *San Dominick*, for there "the muscles and the limbs still move, without their natural nerves and sinews, by the artificial and spasmodic agency of an extrinsic influence." The slaves' extrinsic influence is exposed, to be sure, but not before it has done its lasting work. Neither organic social bonds nor natural rights recover from the artifice of the slaves.

Abolitionists attacked slavery as a violation of natural right. They insisted that slaves, like all individuals, had the right to choose to be free. At the same time, opponents of slavery did not rely solely on abstract theories of contract and consent. They appealed to the authority of the American Revolution. "Liberty is the greatest blessing that men enjoy, and slavery the heaviest curse that human nature is capable of," proclaimed the governor of colonial Rhode Island, Stephen Hopkins. Hopkins was not attacking chattel slavery for, as we know from *The Red Rover*, Rhode Island flourished from the slave trade. He was protesting, in Jefferson's words, the British "deliberate and systematical plan of reducing us to slavery."

The revolutionaries advocated the right of revolution against British enslavement. Abolitionists transferred their arguments to Negroes. "The children of Washington and Franklin," complained Thoreau, "say they know not what to do and do nothing" about slavery. In James G. Birney's words, "Those who approve of the conduct of our fathers in the American Revolution, must agree that the slaves have at least as good a natural right to vindicate their rights by physical force.

John Adams was one of those revolutionary fathers. Neither he nor the son who followed him into the Presidency ever offered the right of revolution to Southern blacks. John Quincy Adams did assert it, however, for slaves who seized their freedom at sea. The horrors of the slave trade, its illegality under American law, and associations of the ocean with nature and natural right all led Adams and others to justify slave mutinies. When slaves seized the *Amistad*, in 1839, Adams represented them. "The law of nature and of Nature's God, on which our fathers placed our national existence," he told the Supreme Court, gave the *Amistad* slaves the right to mutiny for their freedom.

As James Monroe's secretary of state, Adams had opposed freeing the 300 slaves on the *Antelope*, when a pirate which had seized that ship was captured by a United States vessel. But in preparing his *Amistad* defense, in 1841, Adams protested that the *Antelope* slaves had not been permitted to return to Africa (where the *San Dominick* slaves wanted to sail their ship). Negroes also seized an American ship, the *Creole*, in 1841, and sought British protection. Secretary of State Daniel Webster, citing the legality of slavery in American positive law, urged their return to their masters. Joshua Giddings sponsored a congressional resolution opposing Webster and commending the mutiny. Once a ship left its territorial waters, argued Giddings, only the law of nature had validity.

Congress censured Giddings for encouraging slave revolt. Nevertheless, Justice Story ruled for the slaves on the *Amistad*. "We may lament the dreadful acts by which they asserted their liberty and took possession of the *Amistad*," he wrote, "but they cannot be deemed pirates and robbers in the sense of the law of nations." Unlike Adams, however, Story resorted to "the eternal principles of justice and natural law" only because the Negroes were illegally enslaved. He did not use natural rights against valid, positive law. Story had ruled on circuit in 1822 that, since the slave trade was illegal in international law, any slave ship was a pirate. But John Marshall rejected that doctrine for the full court. Like those who attacked *The Red Rover*, Marshall and Webster insisted on keeping slave-trading distinct from piracy. Slave mutiny, not slave-trading was, in Captain Delano's words, "ferocious, piratical revolt." Delano's fears that the *San Dominick* was "of a piratical character" are confirmed, not because the ship was a slave-trader but because the slaves were in command.

*The Red Rover*, by distinguishing illegal piracy from legal slavery, undercut respect for the law. It discredited the positions of Marshall, Webster, and Amasa Delano, and so did *Benito Cereno*. But Melville's tale did not thereby give comfort to the stance of John Quincy Adams. American Negroes who acted upon the fathers' revolutionary principles would destroy the fathers' order.

Melville had introduced the idea of obedience as a form of subversion in *Pierre* and *Bartleby*. But Bartleby only acquired power over the lawyer when he stopped copying. The *San Dominick* slaves destroy their captain by mimicking their obedience to him. Melville did not fictionalize the *Amistad* or *Creole* uprisings, where slaves threw off illegitimate authority and then appealed to the American government for help. He used instead the records of a slave revolt on the Spanish ship, *The Tryal*. On that ship the slaves overthrew their masters only to reenact their own enslavement. Melville fictionalized a mutiny that the slaves had fictionalized before him. As in *Pierre*, he thereby called attention to the fictitious character of allegedly organic human relations. But he did not thereby offer liberation from those false bonds. John Quincy Adams thought that revolutionary fathers like his own gave permission for slaves to be free. On the *San Dominick* the master/father and the child/slave are locked irrevocably together.

When Melville changed *The Tryal's* name to the *San Dominick*, he was calling attention to the slave seizure of power on Santo Domingo, in the wake of the French Revolution. That slave uprising spread terror throughout the American South. "If something is not done, and soon done," wrote Jefferson, "we shall be the murderers of our own children." Jefferson was speaking as a slaveowner, as the author of the Declaration of Independence, and probably as the father of a family of his own slaves. If John Adams gave permission for slave rebellion, Jefferson took paternal responsibility for the destruction such rebellion would visit on his sons. If John Quincy Adams offered an escape from slavery, Jefferson opened and closed doors at the same time.

The carnage finally revealed on the *San Dominick* is closer to Jefferson's nightmares than to John Quincy Adams's hopes. That is one reason why the slave mutiny calls natural rights into question. There is another. Though violence lurks behind the scenes in *Benito Cereno*, the visible and deepest subject of Melville's tale is the inability of its characters to break free. Jefferson acknowledged the trap created by the fathers, but he offered no way out. Neither did Melville. John Quincy Adams helped slaves free themselves from their imprisonment on the *Amistad*. The slaves on the *San Dominick* are trapped. Natural rights theories promised individual freedom; there are no free individuals on the *San Dominick*. Does Melville's fiction thereby lend support to Southerners who insisted that men were "by nature social" not independent, and defended slavery as an organic, familial bond?

George Fitzhugh called his proslavery apology, *Cannibals All!* His epigraph named the fate prophesied for the biblical Ishmael: "His hand will be against every man, and every man's hand against him."

Like Melville in *Moby-Dick*, Fitzhugh connected Ishmael with cannibalism; like Melville he saw all men as cannibals, devouring each other to live. But Fitzhugh believed that the peculiar institution, by making black cannibals into slaves, allowed masters to be Christians. Whereas the capitalist owned only the labor power of his workers, the master owned their physical bodies as well. The capitalist had no reason to care for his workers, for he had no stake in their well-being. Slavery gave the master a personal interest in his slaves. It thereby replaced "the mere cool calculations of the head" with the "pure and regenerate heart." "Man's nature is social, not selfish," wrote Fitzhugh, "and he longs and yearns to return to parental, fraternal, and associative relations." Slavery allowed that longing to be satisfied. It allowed slaveowners to be "philanthropists, and . . . benefit their fellowmen." There was less cruelty under slavery, declared Jefferson Davis, "than in any other relation of labor to capital." Davis explained, "Where ever there is an immediate connection between the master and the slave, whatever there is of harshness in the system is diminished. Then it preserves the domestic character, and strictly patriarchal relation."

The domestic, patriarchal relation between Benito Cereno and his body slave Babo reassures Captain Delano. "His eye falling continually, as from a stage-box into the pit," Delano cannot tell if the common sailors are part of the audience or dangerous actors in the play. The Spanish captain seems like an "imposter. Some low-born adventurer, masquerading as an oceanic grandee." His "stage ceremoniousness . . . seemed not uncharacteristic of one playing a part above his real level." Watching Babo shave Don Benito, Delano wonders if "master and man . . . were acting out . . . some juggling play before him." But "that susceptibility of bland attachment sometimes inhering in indisputable inferiors" reawakens "all his old weakness for negroes." The "affectionate zeal" with which "the negro" performs his services "transmutes into something filial or fraternal acts in themselves but menial." Delano imagines purchasing Babo, and being cared for like the Spanish captain. "Reclining in the servant's arms," Don Benito seems incapable of deviousness. "I have trust in Babo," Benito Cereno tells Delano. The "spectacle of fidelity" in the relation of slave to master assuages Delano's anxiety that things are not as they seem on the *San Dominick*. He will discover that the "spectacle of fidelity" was indeed a spectacle, the confidence a confidence game. Far from standing against deceptive, impersonal appearances, the "parental, fraternal, and associative relations" of slavery are revealed as the heart of the charade.

"Mask torn away," the slave revolt exposes the Ishmaelite cannibal underneath the child-slave. It points to the violence wished away in the stereotype of the happy plantation, a stereotype in which Benito Cereno had himself once believed. "To think that, under the aspect of infantile weakness, the most savage energies might be couched," worries Delano. He is nervous about the Spaniard, however, not the slave; even in the dream on the *San Dominick*, he cannot admit slave revolt into his consciousness. Nonetheless, black violence by itself does not discredit organic theories of slavery. Organicists needed black savagery to justify enslavement. The patriarchal relations of slavery controlled Negro violence, it was argued, and thereby allowed each member of the family hierarchy to find his appropriate place. What organic theories could not countenance was a black intelligence which took revenge on the master in the act of obeying him.

The shadow cast by the Negro over Don Benito is not just the specter of revolt; it is also the stage play of shadows detached from their bodies which has drained the life and color out of his human ties. By forcing Don Benito to play the part of master, Babo has forced him to mistrust the patriarchal, domestic relations which had constituted his identity. By overthrowing slavery and then staging it as a play, Babo has conventionalized the supposedly natural relations of master and slave. He has turned familial intimacy from a stable barrier against marketplace fluctuations into a confidence game. *Benito Cereno* suggests that instead of protecting the master's self, domestic patriarchy opens his boundaries to invasion.

Babo was also the ringleader of *The Tryal* mutiny. But his son, Muri, who "acted as Captain and commander," played the role of Don Benito's confidential servant. Melville collapsed the father-director and the actor-son into a single slave. He was interested not in a slave-father's power over his son, but in a slave-son's power over his father-master. He wanted to accentuate the inverted, personal bond between master and slave. Melville's Benito Cereno is twinned with Babo, "black upholding the white." The slave is a "sort of crutch" for the Spanish captain, performing the function of Ahab's hickory harpoon. Power has shifted from the "cadaverous" figurehead to the slave who supports him. The slave who once obeyed his master now forces the master to "enact the part." Don Benito is a "white statue-head," sculpted by his Negro barber. He is a marionette, manipulated by his slave. The captain is forced to speak the lines that once seemed his by nature. Babo tortures him with an exaggerated fidelity that mocks the paternalism of master and slave.

Like Bartleby's employer, Benito Cereno has the symbols of authority without the substance. "The Spaniard wore a loose Chili jacket of dark velvet; white small-clothes and stockings, with silver buckles at the knee and instep; a high-crowned sombrero, of fine grass; a slender sword, silver mounted, hung from a knot in his sash." The "theatrical aspect" of his costume calls attention to the pitiful state of this "invalid courtier." Don Benito is tortured by his clothing, as Don Pedro in *White-Jacket* was not, for he knows he has lost the authority which his dress claims. "The dress, so precise and costly, worn by" Benito Cereno "had not willingly been put on." The bachelor shirts and buttons in Tartarus with no bodies inside them signify sterility. They point back to the unproductive bachelors in Paradise, but they cause those bachelors no suffering. Don Benito is oppressed by the uniform that he is forced to wear. "And that silver-mounted sword, apparent symbol of despotic command, was not, indeed, a sword, but the ghost of one. The scabbard, artificially stiffened, was empty."

Against an ideology that saw slavery as the most organic of social relations, Melville conventionalized, as stage props, the symbols of authority which slaveowners insisted were theirs by nature. Benito Cereno wore around his neck the key that would unlock slavery—Atufal's chains in the story, "his father's house" in the verse of Isaiah which Melville invoked. Lincoln, after Dred Scott, pictured the "keys" that would free the slave from his "prison house" "scattered to a hundred different and distant places." One the *San Dominick* the master who wore the single key was himself imprisoned. "Manacled" Talus's "clubbed arms were uplifted" on the Bell-Tower, above his "already smitten victim." Chained Atufal, "slowly raising both arms, let them lightly fall." Feigning refusal to beg his master's pardon, the Negro prolongs a living humiliation worse than Bannadonna's sudden death.

"I could not scourge such a form. But I told him he must ask my pardon," Don Benito explains to Delano. The Spaniard had not chained the slaves before the revolt. He appears in this scene to be a philanthropic reformer, replacing the whip by the demand that the reprobate acknowledge his authority. He is imitating those parents who insisted that their children submit emotionally before they were released from confinement. Actually, in an extension of Bartleby's power, the victim is manipulating the paternalist.

In nature a man escapes "the sepulchres of the fathers," wrote Emerson, and "the keys of power are put into his hand." The key close at Don Benito's hand signifies his imprisonment in his patron's sepulcher, the ship with Don Alexandro Aranda's skeleton at its prow. Don Benito's deposition will ultimately provide "the key to fit into the lock of the complications which precede it." "The *San Dominick*'s hull lies open," in that deposition; it casts light on the "shadowy tableau" that Amasa Delano had come upon. But the deposition which exposes the slave masquerade does not reimpower Don Benito. The father's house to which it provides the key is a sepulcher.

Atufal (foreshadowing Talus) is Don Benito's "tall-man and timepiece." Standing watch at his captain's cabin, he is "like one of those sculptured porters of black marble guarding the porches of Egyptian tombs." The tomb is the *San Dominick* itself, we later learn. The masquerade enacted on it is a dance of death. When the mask is torn away, it reveals Don Alexandro's skull.

"So the blind slave obeyed its blinder lord; but in obedience slew him." That moral from "The Bell-Tower" is realized more deeply on the *San Dominick*. Babo tortures his lord by feigning obedience to him. He calls attention to the master's dependence on the support of his slave. Babo's charade fulfills and inverts the dumb show of subservience enacted by the powerless slave. The childlike mask protected the slave from his master, and gave him a kind of influence. Unable to claim power openly, he manipulated through weakness. Babo's imitation of the slave's childlike docility raises the specter of the scheming brain behind the child's innocence.

"You say, 'You know we raised you as our children!' Woman, did you raise your *own children* for the market?" an escaped slave asked her former mistress. Slaves like her left their masters, and explicitly repudiated the familial pretense they had been forced to adopt. Babo takes a different path. Choosing the mask once forced upon him, he still wears his costume and performs his part. Babo stage-manages the play, and gives it a meaning opposite to the one the author-master intended. But he does so with the words he has already been given; the charade gives him no voice of his own. Once the play is over, Babo refuses to "speak words" again.

White men were foolish to be shaved by Negro barbers, according to Thomas Wentworth Higginson. "Behind all those years of cringing and those long years of cheerful submission, there may lie a dagger and power to use it when the time comes." The shaving "play" disorients Delano, to be sure. It is finally so disturbing, however, not because Babo controls the blade but because he cannot use it. Babo's imitation of the master-slave relation keeps him, like Talus, a slave. He is imprisoned, like Bartleby, by the power of weakness. Like the scrivener he takes revenge against his master; he is not liberated from him. The slave who exploited the masquerade is also its victim. "Ahab seemed an independent lord; the Parsee but his slave. Still both seemed yoked together, and an unseen tyrant driving them." Ahab is Fedallah's "abandoned substance" in *Moby-Dick*; the Parsee is Ahab's "forethrown shadow." The shadowy slave has become the master on the *San Dominick*, and turned the master into a shadow as well. But his subversion is an entrapment, and he is still yoked to his former lord.

Organic theorists celebrated the mutual dependence of master and slave. *Benito Cereno* makes slavery a convention, depriving it of its natural ground. But Melville's tale fails to offer the freedom of choice promised by theories which constituted society from human arrangements. The charade is as imprisoning as the organic relationship it undercuts. As the tale strips away the natural bond between master and slave, it locks the two together more closely than before.

Captain Delano is "incapable of sounding such wickedness" as has occurred on the *San Dominick*. His innocence protects him from penetrating the false appearances, and thereby being slaughtered by the slaves. The real Captain Delano (of the *Perseverance*) explained, "As I was deceived in them, I did them every possible kindness. Had it been otherwise there is no doubt that I should have fallen a victim to their power." Like the bachelor lawyers on Wall Street and in the Temple Bar, the captain of the *Bachelor's Delight* remains safely on the surface of appearances. He can no more imagine a slave revolt than the captain of the *Bachelor* can believe in Moby Dick. The ferocity with which Delano destroys the revolt, once its reality is forced upon him, breaks the spell of the masquerade. He protects himself, by violence, from being affected by what he has seen. Captain Delano's foot on the "prostrate negro" at the bottom of his boat, the *Rover*, mirrors the stern-piece of the *San Dominick*, introduced at the beginning of the tale—"a dark satyr in a mask, holding his foot on the prostrate neck of a writhing figure, likewise masked." The stripping away of masks exposes the slave on top during the revolt, and sends him down to his natural place on the bottom. Delano stands for "good order" in "armies, navies, cities . . . families, [and] nature herself." He restores natural order on the *San Dominick*.

Delano turns to nature, after quelling the slave revolt, to reassure Benito Cereno. He points to "yon bright sun . . . and the blue sea, and the blue sky." Nature is serene, and the American wants "Sereno" (as the real Delano spelled the Spanish captain's name) to have "forgotten it all" as well. The Spaniard, however, is forever sundered from nature. He has been forced to play a part which has turned human bonds into deceitful contrivances, and drained them of their natural affection. The captain of *The Tryal*, Amasa Delano reported, was "frightened of his own shadow." The shadow who frightened Melville's Don Benito was Babo. Melville detached Don Benito's shadow from his body, just as Bonaparte's coup detached the shadows of 1848 from their bodies. But Melville's shadow had more power than Marx's. Marx insisted, against appearances, that real power lay in society; he tried to reconnect the political shadow to its social substance. Melville made the Spanish captain's "own shadow" into slavery.

"The negro" has "cast . . . a shadow" over Benito Cereno. Like Hegel's owl of Minerva, Don Benito has acquired philosophic understanding only in defeat and at dusk. The gray-on-gray *San*

*Dominick* has made his shape of life grow old. Benito Cereno is "attended by the monk Infelez," as he was earlier attended by Babo. He retires to a monastery, and soon dies there.

The real Benito Cereno did not retire to a monastery. He fought to regain his slave property, and to stop Delano from acquiring a share of the booty. The real Spanish captain had secreted a dirk, and stabbed a slave after his rescue. Melville has Babo attack Don Benito with a hidden dagger instead. Melville's reversals drained the Spanish captain of his energy. He was modeling him, as Carolyn Karcher has shown, on the enervated Southern cavalier of the plantation novel. Melville's tale commented on the exhaustion of the slaveowning class.

Don Benito's end, in a cloister, mirrors the beginning of his story, for when the *San Dominick* first appears on the horizon, it resembles a "white-washed monastery." The "black friars pacing the cloisters" on the vessel make it seem like "a ship-load of monks." The Spanish captain is a "hypochondriac abbot." Babo resembles a "begging friar of St. Francis." Don Benito has the enervated manner of "Charles V, just previous to the anchoritish retirement of that monarch from the throne." The real Captain Delano complained that the overthrow of the Spanish king, Charles IV, during the Napoleonic wars, deprived him of his reward for rescuing *The Tryal*. Charles IV's dethronement may have suggested to Melville the abdication of the Hapsburg emperor, Charles V. Like Charles V, Benito Cereno will leave his command for a monastery. Charles V's abdication initiated the decline of the Hapsburg empire; it was the beginning of the end of the last feudal effort to rule over all of Christendom. Melville, having identified feudalism with slavery, was allowing the demise of the one to suggest the demise of the other.

Nathaniel Hawthorne was also looking forward to the end of slavery. But the solace he offered contrasted with Melville's gloom. The two friends had become estranged while Melville was writing *Pierre*. Hawthorne was retreating as a writer from the vision of blackness which had empowered Melville. He drew back from their personal closeness as well. *Benito Cereno* can be read as Melville's reproach to his mentor.

Hawthorne wrote Franklin Pierce's campaign biography in 1852, the year his classmate and fellow Yankee ran for President. Pierce had supported the 1850 Compromise. He believed, wrote Hawthorne, that human efforts could not "subvert" slavery "except by . . . severing into distracted fragments that common country which Providence brought into one nation." The Union's destruction, Hawthorne continued, would mean "the ruin of two races which now dwelt together in greater peace and affection, it is not too much to say, than had ever elsewhere existed between the taskmaster and the serf." Pierce's father had fought at Bunker Hill. "Inheriting his father's love of country," the "General" had led "his brethren" of the North and South into Mexico, "to redden the same battlefields with their kindred blood." He would not now, by attacking slavery, favor one section against the other. Franklin Pierce used federal troops to enforce the Fugitive Slave Law. President when Melville wrote *Benito Cereno*, he was Hawthorne's Delano. But while Melville undercut his Yankee, Hawthorne identified with his. If slavery was left alone, promised Hawthorne, "it would by some means impossible to be anticipated . . . vanish like a dream." When the dream on the *San Dominick* vanishes, slavery is still in place.

The dreamlike reveries of the antebellum sentimental novel have been seen as escapes from the ineradicable horror of slavery. Donald Grant Mitchell's *Reveries of a Bachelor* was published the year of the 1850 Compromise; it sold over a million copies. Mitchell's subsequent tale, *Dream Life*, chronicles his retreat from the fugitive slave controversy to a Connecticut farm called Xanadu. Melville turned the dreams of Hawthorne, Mitchell, and Franklin Pierce against the dreamers. No one who has fully inhabited the enchanted world on the *San Dominick* awakes from it. Benito Cereno, who moves on the slave ship "as one in a dream," is haunted to death by that "hive of subtlety," Babo's decapitated head.

"Fixed on a pole on the Plaza," the head of the slave is planted on Aranda's bones. It faces Don Benito's monastery. Towers are Melville's emblems for patriarchal authority, and one of them, Nelson's column at Trafalgar, rises above a group of chained slaves. Babo and his master have changed places, to be sure, but the slave has followed his leader to death; Babo's head is impaled on his tower. The raised head of the slave may portend the end of slavery, but it is a portent of violence, and it does not promise the liberation of the slave.

Melville returned, in *Benito Cereno*, to the feudal nature of naval authority. He located shipboard feudalism in actual masters and slaves, not, as in *Redburn* and *White-Jacket*, in nautical allegorizations. But the exposure of slavery under the aristocratic mask exhausted naval feudalism for Melville; his prose never returned to it again. Medieval Catholicism fails in *Benito Cereno* both as a structure of power and as a source of meaning. The invocation of religion promises a deeper, redemptive significance beneath the mundane tale. It does not deliver on that promise. The *San Dominick* masks provide no access to spiritual truth; only death is underneath them. The *San Dominick* monks are not real monks. Religion is one more phantom, a mask that obscures meaning, not an emblem which reveals it. There was, nonetheless, an actual slave revolt underneath the *San Dominick* masquerade. Beneath the masquerade of *The Confidence-Man*, there is nothing at all. Returning to the theme of shipboard mutiny, in *Billy Budd*, Melville will finally imagine a genuine "monastic obedience" to naval authority. The *Bellipotent* will be modeled, however, not on a feudal Catholic empire but on a modern military state.

# RICHARD E. RAY

## "Benito Cereno": Babo as Leader[†]

When Benito Cereno during the slave rebellion aboard the *San Dominick* responds to the immediate situation and praises Babo's fidelity in the presence of Captain Delano, Babo, in replying that what he "has done was but duty,"[1] makes a statement that contains several interesting features. It serves, first of all, the dual purpose of reminding the Spanish captain of his reversed role while at the same time soothing any suspicions that might have arisen in Amasa Delano's mind. On the other hand, there is a matter-of-factness in the statement reflective of Babo's manner from the beginning of the story until he is finally subdued in the boat, the easy self-confidence with which he does things and the tremendous self-control that he exhibits during Delano's stay aboard the ship. There exists also the possibility that Babo literally means what he says, that his assertion that he is merely doing his duty is, despite its ironical overtones, no more than an acknowledgment of his own view of his role in the rebellion aboard the *San Dominick*.

It is, admittedly, not easy to accept Babo's comment as an expression of purpose, believed by himself, and meant exactly as spoken, and, if accepted, it is equally difficult for many readers to believe that Melville wanted them to share this belief and to sympathize with this leader of the slave revolt. Babo's behavior has often been considered too sinister, his actions too cruel, for him to elicit a sympathetic response. Because of this and because of the sensitive nature of Benito Cereno's character, Babo has been interpreted by one group of critics as a symbol of evil. Considered in this sense, he is a figure who bewilders and endangers the good-hearted but naïve Captain Delano by giving a benign appearance to surface events in order to obscure the malignant evil that, in reality, lurks beneath. The sensitive Cereno, the victim of this evil, is crushed by its

† From *American Transcendental Quarterly* 7 (Spring 1975): 18–23.
1. *Great Short Works of Herman Melville* (N.Y.: Harper and Row, 1966), p. 193. Subsequent quotations are from this edition.

weight. He is morose and inconsolable and generally reacts as Delano observes "like a man flayed alive." "Where," the American captain wonders, "may one touch him without causing a shrink?" The creator of this condition in Cereno, the omnipresent Babo, with cruel and seemingly senseless deeds as his trademark, is easily construed to be a symbol of evil. He becomes, in the words of Rosalie Feltenstein, "a manifestation of pure evil,"[2] or, according to Stanley T. Williams, a man with a "malignant brain," committing atrocities "for the happiness of hatred, evil for the sake of evil,"[3] or he is the epitome, as Sydney Kaplan insists, of the "'malign evil' that Delano at first cannot comprehend."[4]

Many of those who have rejected the above view find in Melville's story a condemnation of slavery and thereby free Babo from the onerous structures placed on his character by an interpretation that makes him a symbolically malign figure. His actions are no longer merely the expected manifestations of an inherently and totally evil creature; rather, they are, as Joseph Schiffman argues "not motiveless" at all but a necessary part of "a rebellion of slaves in their fight for freedom" and, consequently, "dictated by this purpose."[5] Also, once the premise that slavery is an issue in the story is allowed, Babo can become a relatively admirable figure since his cruelty is ameliorated considerably by the merits of his purpose. Allen Guttman, for example, sees him as the hero of the tale since "for all his ruthlessness and savagery" he is "the one person in the story to struggle against a moral wrong."[6]

The chief advantage of this latter school of thought is that it makes of Babo a legitimate human being and offers a scope broad enough to permit an assessment of his character based on merits and demerits, something impossible to achieve if he is to be burdened with the symbolic weight of evil in human existence and thus stripped of a will of his own. In either case, however, limitations are usually imposed on discussions that treat of Babo. On the one hand, the theory of pure evil condemns him completely. Once this thesis has been established, nothing further remains to be said about him and emphasis necessarily shifts to his influence on other characters. On the other hand, in the context of anti-slavery thesis, Babo can too easily become a secondary item of discussion, subordinated to lengthy arguments in support of slavery as a valid issue in the tale.

2. "Melville's 'Benito Cereno,'" *American Literature*, XIX (1947), 247.
3. "'Follow Your Leader': Melville's 'Benito Cereno,'" *Virginia Quarterly Review*, XXIII (1947), 75.
4. "Herman Melville and the American National Sin: The Meaning of 'Benito Cereno,'" *The Journal of Negro History*, XLII (1957), 20.
5. "Critical Problems in Melville's Benito Cereno," *Modern Language Quarterly*, XI (1950), 318.
6. "The Enduring Innocence of Captain Amasa Delano," *Boston University Studies in English*, V (1961), 44.

In both instances what Babo is and what he does in the story rarely receive precedence over other matters.

The intent here is to reject insofar as is possible both of the above approaches to Babo and to accept him, as a starting point, simply as a human being subjected to and motivated by the exigencies of a harsh but real-life situation and to attempt to see him in the light of his own previously cited statement that during the uprising he was doing his duty; that is, as a man who had assumed leadership and, consequently, was immediately confronted with the problems associated with that role. There is sufficient evidence within the limits of the story to suggest that Melville may have had this in mind when he created this controversial figure. Furthermore, a consideration of "Benito Cereno" as a study in leadership with Babo as the central figure is consistent with other details in the story and can account, for example, for such elements as the confusion of mind which leads to Captain Amasa Delano's failure to distinguish between appearance and reality in the events aboard the slave ship.

If one puts aside Babo's cruelty for the moment, the dominant characteristic of this black leader is his extraordinary intelligence. It is he, after all, who creates and sustains the confusing "currents" which, to use Delano's phrase, "spin one's head round." Babo, in fact, because of his intelligence, must have been ripe to the bursting point from having awaited such an opportunity to lead others as the one which presented itself when Don Aranda insisted that the slaves remain unchained because they were "tractable." Up to this point he had always been a slave, even—and this would seem to be the supreme irony for a man of considerable mental capacity— among his own people. This enslavement by his own kind, although ironic, is understandable, however, since a primitive society, lacking the intricate political and economic systems of more highly developed civilizations has much less need of and can thus have less regard for intellect than for physical prowess. In this social environment physical strength would seem to be the important attribute for one who aspired to lead, and a "gigantic" man like Atufal, whose imposing physical appearance and apparent stoicism toward Cereno's pretended punishment cause Delano to see "a royal spirit in him," is appropriately endowed to lead others in a social atmosphere that has few uses for a man of intellect. Thus Babo, the "black of small stature," was forced by his fellow blacks to endure the same menial role given him later by the whites in whose society he also became a slave. There existed no place in the black structure for this physically unimpressive man and no place in the white structure. Once captured by the whites he was destined to remain a slave, despite his keen intelligence, merely because he was black. Babo, the lifelong slave, finally becomes a viable force when given the opportunity to lead, and the blacks gather to him and support him during the rebellion, a situation requiring a capacity for plotting and scheming. He must for many years have dreamed of such a possibility.

Babo leads because of his intelligence and the fact of his intelligence better equips him for the white man's world than for the blacks', but because he is black the only way he can put his intelligence to work within that world is to oppose it. His moment in time comes to him through the forced removal of the blacks from the freedom of their own primitive society to slavery in the new and strange milieu of the white man. Under these new conditions, any desire to escape from the white man's domination tends to cause physical prowess to lose much of its importance. The white man's weapons and chains and the general cunning of his leaders offset the advantages of physical strength. Something more than physical strength is needed if the black man is to resist the white society, and the additional quality is precisely what Babo has to offer, the cunning of intellect.

The willingness with which the blacks obey his orders and respond to his coaching is evidence that they recognize the relationship between his peculiar abilities and their own needs. One of the more interesting features of the story is that Atufal, the magnificent specimen of physical grandeur, should submit himself to the mock-serious punishment routine, devised by Babo, which brings Atufal to parade himself before Cereno and Delano in an effort to impress upon the American what is not true, that the frail Cereno is in power. While Atufal in all his strength stands before the two captains, stoical and proud but in chains, the weak-appearing but all-powerful Babo stands casually and subserviently in the background and looks on. Atufal's ritual is close to, if not, a symbolic acknowledgment on his part and on the part of the blacks in general of the need for a new kind of strength in leadership, the kind that Babo, the small, weak man who is so easily subdued later on by Captain Delano is the boat, is able and eager to provide.

Among the blacks he has supplanted the kind of leadership formerly represented by men of Atufal's timbre, and although, as we learn in Cereno's deposition, Babo "held daily conferences" with Atufal and seems to share his authority with him, the Spaniard's statements make clear that Babo was, in every particular, the man in charge: " . . . the negro Babo was the plotter from first to last; he ordered every murder, and was the helm and keel of the revolt. . . ." Atufal functions as a figurehead of authority only, and quite likely Babo uses him in that role because his awesome physical appearance satisfies the former requisite for fitness to lead and thus commands the respect of the other blacks. At any rate, Cereno describes the former leader as Babo's "lieutenant," and his subordinate position is emphasized when the *Bachelor's Delight* is first sighted. The two confer and, in Cereno's words "the negro Atufal was for sailing away, but the negro Babo would not, and by himself, cast about what to do." Ironically, because he would free himself from slavery, Atufal the strong, purportedly a king in his own land, submits to the leadership of a man he previously would have considered fit only to be a slave.

Once it is admitted that a black intelligence is at work, Delano becomes a man suffering from a special kind of blindness instead of either a weak-witted individual or one who is unable because of his benevolent nature, to believe man capable of malign evil. The latter has sometimes been used to explain Delano's inability to understand what is actually taking place on the *San Dominick*. Richard Harter Fogle, to cite one example, suggests that the good captain "lacks the sense of evil," and therefore cannot "penetrate the meaning"[7] of what is going on around him. Fogle thus finds the story to be one of "delusion, of a mind wandering in a maze, struggling but failing to find the essential clue."[8] This latter assessment is quite obviously true, for Delano is, indeed, "wandering in a maze," and he does fail "to find the essential clue." But his reactions to the events on the slave ship indicate that he fails to find his way through the maze not because he "lacks the sense of evil" but because he discounts the possibility that a ready intelligence might exist among the blacks.

The American captain, despite the narrator's comment that he was a man "not liable . . . to indulge in personal alarms, any way involving the imputation of malign evil in man," is not long in suspecting evil doings aboard the *San Dominick*, but when he does, he directs his suspicions toward the Spaniards. The ominous hatchet-polishers and the disturbance created when the black youth slashes the Spanish boy with a knife, although unsettling, fail to suggest to him the likelihood of a revolt among the slaves. He is too busy concentrating his attention on Cereno's alternately rude and courteous behavior, which he attributes either to an "innocent lunacy, or wicked imposture."

Delano, too, is well aware that evil can present the same face as benignity, and he understands that the reality of the situation on the ship is likely different from what appears to be the reality. He imagines that Cereno might be feigning his illness, for "the craft of some tricksters had been known to attain" this very thing more than once in the past. He knows that "under the aspect of infantile weakness, the most savage energies might be couched—those velvets of the

7. *Melville's Shorter Tales* (Norman: University of Oklahoma Press, 1960), p. 121.
8. Ibid., pp. 121–122.

Spaniard but the silky paw to his fangs," and he finds "a gloomy hesitancy and subterfuge" in the Spaniard's story. He, in short, not only suspects evil but expects it to become manifest through subtlety. Yet, he deludes himself because he doesn't associate a capacity for subtlety with the blacks. He focuses his scrutiny on the Spaniards and makes them the object of his suspicions.

What hides the truth from Delano more than anything else is his attitude toward the blacks, his assumption that if an evil plot is slowly unfolding, then the Spaniards must necessarily be the perpetrators of that plot, for the Negroes are incapable of the necessary cunning. He is easily enough reassured from time to time because the inconsistencies that he observes do not in logical and mathematical fashion add up to an indictment of the Spaniards. If a malign scheme was, in fact, underway, he reasons, "then every soul on board, down to the youngest negress, was his [Cereno's] carefully drilled recruit in the plot: an incredible inference." The implications of this conclusion are clear enough: it is preposterous to believe that the blacks are capable of responding intelligently, even if "carefully drilled." This point is made exceedingly clear in some of Delano's later thoughts: "Was it from foreseeing some possible interference like this, that Don Benito had, beforehand, given such a bad character of his sailors, while praising the negroes; though, indeed, the former seemed as docile as the latter the contrary? *The whites, too, by nature, were the shrewder race.* A man with some evil design, would he not be likely to speak well of that *stupidity* which was blind to his depravity, and malign that intelligence from which it might not be hidden? Not unlikely, perhaps. But if the whites had dark secrets concerning Don Benito, could then Don Benito be any way in complicity with the blacks? *But they were too stupid.* Besides, who ever heard of a white so far a renegade as to apostatize from his very species almost, by leaguing in against it with negroes?" (Italics added).

In the above passage is expressed the underlying cause of Delano's blindness. The blacks are a distinct species whose dominant characteristic is their stupidity. How then with this mental set can he ever fathom the confusion, the ambiguity in circumstances aboard the slave ship? Obviously, he cannot. Happenings that should serve to resolve ambiguities for him tend instead to obscure reality even further. To Delano, Babo just cannot be a cunning thinker and a subtle actor because he is black. Rather, he exemplifies "the docility arising from the unaspiring contentment of a limited mind," as do the other blacks. He has, like so many of his fellows, "the susceptibility of blind attachment," and this explains his careful and continual attendance upon Don Benito. Babo uses the flag of Spain as a towel while shaving Cereno, not as an ironic and insulting gesture, but because it fulfills the black mind's simple requirement that "'the colors be gay.'" The hatchet-polishers are sinister, but only to a point. Then they become ludicrous as Delano's sense of the absurd intervenes. Menacing and foreboding figures one minute, they are transformed in the next to ludicrous "organ" or "scissors-grinders."

What Delano assumes to be a self-evident truth—that the blacks are unsophisticated and lacking in intellect—is the key to his confusion. The blacks as a group are hardly stupid. They were certainly capable of being "carefully drilled," and they knew how to follow a leader in a manner reasonably consistent with the purposes of that drilling. The characteristic that sets their leader off from themselves, and from all others in the story is his intelligence. If he is to be associated with evil, Babo does not represent a symbol of pure evil but functions as a reminder that evil is a by-product of intelligence. Even Delano understands this. He suspects evil and to locate the agents of that evil, looks to the Spaniards under the false assumption that they represent the only source of intelligence. He knows also how misleading reality can be when a scheming intellect is the motivating force in the background. He senses an undercurrent of evil, almost from the start, and until he leaves the ship, his experience is primarily a struggle motivated by suspicions of subterfuge, to make a distinction between the appearance and the reality of events aboard the *San Dominick*. He fluctuates between acceptance of the story he is told and the overwhelming feeling that a mysterious and sinister plot is working its way toward a final conclusion. When he leaves the ship to join his own crew in the boat, he accepts as the reality what appears to be the situation on the *San Dominick*. He does this on the basis of the correct inference that Cereno is too weak to have perpetrated a heinous plot and the incorrect inference that the blacks are not capable of subterfuge. He does not recognize Babo as a prime mover and manipulator of events until the slave leader, knife in hand, lunges at Cereno in the boat.

In presenting the figure of Babo, Melville has given us, among other possibilities, a study in leadership. Joseph Schiffman, who believes that Melville is speaking out against slavery, long ago recognized this, and his description of Babo as "a forceful, clever, courageous leader of his fellow slaves"[9] is a succinct and highly accurate observation. His argument that whatever evil can be found in Babo exists there "because of an evil world" and that he is leading his fellow slaves not into evil but toward freedom is also an especially pertinent contention.[1] In one sense, the name of Delano's

9. "Critical Problems," p. 321.
1. Ibid., p. 318.

ship, the *Bachelor's Delight,* contrary to other interpretations of its significance,[2] supports this very point since, according to certain modes of thought, a bachelor's delight is identical to a slave's delight—his freedom. Babo gives the slaves aboard the *San Dominick* an opportunity for freedom, and they follow their leader toward that goal while he, as any competent leader would, does what he has to do to affirm their faith in him and to insure the success of his undertaking.

Like all leaders, Babo is a man with an end in mind, an illegal end, to be sure, but hardly a morally wrong one. And he leads with acumen. Delano himself, could he have been objective in his evaluation, would have respected this talent in him. In one of the many moments in which he is critical of Cereno's leadership, Delano calls the Spaniard a "hapless man" and wonders if he is "one of those paper captains I've known, who by policy wink at what by power they cannot put down?" "I know no sadder sight," he continues, "than a commander who has little of command but the name." Ironically, at this very moment, Babo, although he has not the name of command, has the command, and he has at the same time the decisiveness to give him the power associated with that position.

What Babo does, after gaining control of the *San Dominick* is, for the most part, consistent with the demands of the situation. He needs the Spaniards to maneuver the ship; indeed, he is completely dependent upon them for navigation, and for this reason he cannot keep them in chains. Yet he must guard against a counter-revolt and because his dependence on their navigational skills is total, it is necessary that he impress upon their minds that no alternative exists for them but complete cooperation with his wishes and absolute obedience to his commands. Unfortunately, to achieve this a man who elects to lead a rebellion cannot afford to rely on gentle persuasion. Thus, Babo is a man who motivates with threats but one who does so only after he has created a background of fear sufficient to give his threats an awful meaning.

On the morning following the uprising, Babo offers the first of several examples of the harsh punishment awaiting anyone who might want to thwart his will when he has three men thrown "alive and tied" into the sea while the Spanish captain looks on. The remembrance of this is then surely in Cereno's thoughts as he responds to Babo's threats after the *San Dominick* first sights land. He made no effort, he explains in his deposition, to "go to Pisco, that was near, nor make any other port of the coast, because the

2. Rosalie Feltenstein (n.2, p. 330, above) suggests that the name is a combination of the names of the two ships, the *Bachelor* and the *Delight,* from *Moby-Dick. Bachelor's Delight* then, as a composite of the two, reflects the happiness associated with the one and the sense of evil associated with the other.

negro Babo had intimated to him several times, that he would kill all the whites the very moment he should perceive any city, town or settlement of any kind . . ." Later when he makes the decision to have Aranda slain, Babo stresses that he does so not only as an additional assurance that the slaves will eventually be set free but also "to keep the seamen in subjection." What he wished to do, according to Cereno's statement, was "to prepare a warning of what road they should be made to take did they or any of them oppose him." Following the killing of Aranda Babo orders eleven more men to be thrown into the sea and with this action his threats take on an even more awesome aspect, for he allows in this instance no faction on the ship room to misunderstand his intentions. His sentences of death fall on Aranda's cousin, on clerks, a servant, and the ship's boatswain as well as upon ordinary crew members.

The deeds of Babo as recounted here are shockingly cruel, but one must, nevertheless, exercise a degree of caution in evaluating them. Babo has for the moment successfully defied a small portion of a formidably strong power structure, but ahead of him lies the difficult task of leading his followers from the relative safety of isolation on the ocean to a secure position ashore, a hazardous task and one fraught with risks. His position is tenuous, and if he is to maintain his position of power, then brute force and the cruelty that accompanies it would seem to be the only course of action open to him. On only one occasion is there evidence in Babo's behavior that his merciless acts are more reflective of an underlying passion that seeks to wreak vengeance than they are a coldly calculated means to achieve an end. This black man who has always been a slave is conscious both of his blackness and the implications of that condition in a white-dominated society, and his extreme distaste for such a state of affairs is glaringly apparent in the grim irony of his words when he takes the Spaniards one by one to inspect Aranda's skeleton and inquires of each "whether, from its whiteness, he should not think it a white's." Yet, this is a secondary response to an act meant to help bring his designed end about, a measure conceived to keep the sailors in subjection and to assure him that should an emergency arise, fear of his awful authority will outweigh any temptations to revolt against him.

Babo's methods are not in any sense unusual. They are, in fact, quite ordinary. He attempts to deceive the good Captain Delano by making the ship appear to be a benign collection of slaves and seamen who have endured the miseries of many days of privation on the ocean. That deceit is an ordinary mode of conduct among civilized whites is supported by the fact that Delano expects deceit from the Spaniards but not from the blacks whom he deigns incapable of such sophisticated maneuvering. And Babo's horribly cruel acts are neither extraordinary nor without precedent. Interestingly, his most vicious deed is the placing of Aranda's skeleton on the bow as a figurehead. Yet, even this is not exceptional, for the use of a gruesome symbol of warning has always been associated with the brutal politics of power when the wills of the conquered and subordinated need to be suppressed. For this Babo had the white man as his pattern. The original source of Melville's story brings this point into focus clearly enough. The process used by Babo when he takes the Spanish sailors to view Aranda's skeleton is, in essence, the same one prescribed by the deputy assessor, Martinez de Rozas, when he passes sentence on the leaders of the slave revolt. All the blacks involved in the rebellion are required to watch the executions, a spectacle gruesomely vivid enough to teach a lesson in obedience through a display of the fearful consequences attendant upon disobedience. The condemned slaves, nine in all, are sentenced "to the common penalty of death, which shall be executed by taking them out and dragging them from the prison, at the tail of a beast of burden as far as the gibbet, where they shall be hung until they are dead . . . that the heads of the five first be cut off . . . and be fixed on a pole . . . and the corpses of all be burnt to ashes."[3] In Melville's story Babo replaces the figurehead of the *San Dominick* with the bones of Don Aranda and uses this grotesque symbol to warn the Spaniards of what fate awaits them if they attempt to revolt against him. In turn, Babo's head is placed upon a pole as a warning to any blacks who might choose to follow another leader like Babo. Both actions have as their base the same motive, and one can only ask the question: which is more macabre—or for that matter more symbolic of evil—a skeleton attached to the bow of a ship or a severed head staring from atop a pole?

Babo's practice of cruelty grows from necessity. The white power structure that he is resisting is eminently formidable and had resisted similar assaults before. It had also provided enough demonstrations in the past of coldly calculated cruelty as a motivational weapon of leadership to provide a model for any new leader to imitate. After Babo's revolt is history, the power structure provides another lesson of the same type for the benefit of Babo's black followers. Babo's flaw was that he received naturally the gift most representative of the white man's success, a ready intelligence. As the white man had used that intelligence deviously to obtain his ends, so did Babo. It would seem that with no suitable place for him in the white power structure it inevitably must follow that he would sooner or later come into conflict with it. Melville in one small but

---

3. Amasa Delano, *A Narrative of Voyages and Travels, in the Northern and Southern Hemispheres,* in *A Benito Cereno Handbook,* ed. Seymour L. Gross (Belmont, California: Wadsworth Publishing Co., 1965), p. 94.

important change from the original source seems to stress this. In Cereno's deposition, he includes the black, Joaquim, who in the original is described as "a smart negro . . . who had been for many years among the Spaniards . . . and a caulker by trade."[4] Melville changes this man's name from Joaquim to Dago and continues to call him "a smart negro" but very significantly changes his occupation and makes him a man "who had been for many years a grave-digger among the Spaniards." For those who insist upon interpreting the story in a strictly symbolic sense, could not the message be that the intelligent blacks will, indeed, strive to be the grave-diggers for their masters? Babo is certainly a case in point.

When seen in the role of a leader "doing his duty," Babo becomes something more than a dusky figure immersed in evil for evil's sake. That his leadership creates evil is not debatable, even if Melville means the story to be a statement against slavery, but the evil that he creates is an indictment, not of Babo, but of the evil created by all men. Evil has always been an ubiquitous companion whenever man has struggled for power and position, and one certainly cannot lead a rebellion and avoid the evil inherent in violence and brutality. If Babo is an evil man, then that evil lies in his decision to revolt, for once this decision has been made and action toward that end initiated, violence and brutality necessarily follow. And to examine individually the brutal acts emanating from Babo's leadership in order to show that he is merciless and inhumane beyond reason is fruitless. One could as well argue that he is not merciless or brutal enough, for despite the barbaric and fear-inspiring killings that he orders, Cereno tells us in his deposition that during Delano's visit to the ship "some attempts were made by the sailors . . . to convey hints to him of the true state of affairs." They are unsuccessful attempts because these men must be cautious. They have before them the spectre of Aranda and the remembrance of the many thrown to die in the sea. Nevertheless, they do attempt to warn Delano, and this in itself is an emphatic reminder that the deaths ordered by Babo were not senseless but sprang from an awareness that complete obedience from a conquered foe is never freely given and can be demanded only under the strongest of motivations.

The revolt on the *San Dominick* was given a chance to start by Don Aranda's mistaken assumption that the slaves were tractable. The history of slavery would seem to make a self-evident truth of the generalization that slaves are rarely tractable when they have a leader, and the slaves in this case had among them a man ripened and ready for leadership. That man was Babo, and his keen intelligence enabled him to seize the opportunity when his moment in

4. Ibid., p. 84.

time arrived. He was almost successful because the interloper in his rebellion, Captain Amasa Delano, was blinded to the possibility of that intelligence. Possibly the most ironic and bitterly understated lines in the story come when Delano and Cereno dine together. Delano is at first disconcerted and then impressed when Babo assumes a position behind his own chair. From this vantage point, the American reasons, the servant can better see what his master seated across the table might require during the meal. Delano, doubtless equating intelligence with the talents necessary for a body servant, whispers to the Spaniard "'This is an uncommonly intelligent fellow of yours, Don Benito.'" Cereno's telling reply comes not from delusion but from an accurate appraisal of the cruel but able Babo. "'You say true, Señor,'" he answers.

Babo's determined efforts eventually come to nothing, and he fails in his purpose, but for a brief moment he is a man with the voice of authority, a leader who speaks through actions. Once his mission has failed, he waits silently for death and ultimately meets a "voiceless end," a manner of dying that is, in his case, particularly appropriate, for he is no longer the leader of a revolt but once again a slave. And a slave is always a man without a voice.

# Billy Budd

## HERSHEL PARKER

### *From* The Plot of *Billy Budd* and the Politics of Interpreting It[†]

The plot of *Billy Budd* is painful and to some even repellent. There will always be admirers of Melville who fervently wish he had abandoned the manuscript in 1889 in order meet the request of the London publisher Edward Garnett that he write the story of his early adventures. Instead, he continued to revise and rearrange many short poems and to rework his story of an innocent young seaman, Billy Budd, who, falsely accused by the master-at-arms, John Claggart, and unable to defend himself through speech, instinctively strikes out and kills his accuser in the presence of his captain, Edward Vere, who at once intuits the essential truth of the situation and (also at once) decides that the boy must be hanged. In rapid sequence the captain leads (or coerces) a hastily convened court martial to conclude what he wants it to conclude, then in a private meeting (to which the reader is denied access) reconciles the boy to his will, so that Billy blesses the captain as he is hanged. At his own death the captain murmurs the boy's name—without remorse.

The issues in this plot are momentous, and seem designed to force the reader to take one of two mutually incompatible positions. One is to agree with the captain that the preservation of law (even military law) overrules all considerations of natural law and justice. The other is to acknowledge that in this world those in power can and often do act as Vere did, but then to insist that Melville's story must be read as an attempt to rouse his readers to protest against any social institution which could sacrifice Billy Budd; such readers despise the captain who all-too-hastily makes his decision and cloaks it in a show of unanimity at a rigged court martial. Readers tend to assume that Melville must have felt about Vere just what they feel, even though other readers with equal conviction are sure that Melville meant just

---

[†] From Hershel Parker, *Reading Billy Budd* (Evanston, IL: Northwestern University Press, 1990) 97–98. Reprinted by permission of Northwestern University Press.

the opposite, and that *they* are the true understanders of the writer. Readers have bent Melville to their political ideologies, whatever they are. The more earnest interpretations of *Billy Budd*, to put it bluntly, are couched in fighting words. Those who disagree with us about the meaning of *Billy Budd* are people we would campaign hard against if they were running for public office; such people (unlike ourselves) are dangerous ideologues, however decorous their appearance and however plausible their language.

\*    \*    \*

# PAUL BERGMAN AND MICHAEL ASINOW

## [On the Movie *Billy Budd*]†

\* \* \* The Articles of War permitted no exception to the rule that a crew member who strikes an officer must be executed. Suppose (though) they acquitted Budd and there was a mutiny, Vere asks. Wouldn't they be blamed for being too lenient? Following Vere on this point proves to be a major boo-boo.

\*    \*    \*

Vere was right in his statement of military law (the death penalty was mandatory for striking an officer), but terribly wrong about the appropriate procedure. Captain Vere had authority only to mete out relatively trivial punishments, such as flogging or banning gum chewing. But what about the mandatory minimum death sentence for striking an officer? Is that a relic of the primitive past? Today American law abounds with extremely harsh mandatory minimum sentences, especially for drug-related offenses. Public fear of crime results in three-strikes-you're-out laws, under which three-time offenders get life in prison, often a grossly excessive penalty. The concern about fairly linking the punishment to the crime is as real now as in Billy Budd's day. In criminal cases judges and juries are permitted to follow their conscience, even if that means not following the letter of the law. It's a lesson that must never be forgotten.

\*    \*    \*

† From Paul Bergman and Michael Asinow, *Reel Justice: The Courtroom Goes to the Movies* (Kansas City: Andrews and McMeel Publishing, 1996), 57–58. Reprinted by permission of the publisher.

# TOM GOLDSTEIN

## Once Again, "Billy Budd" Is Standing Trial[†]

It is a story of innocence and evil, of crime and punishment, of rationality and insanity, of motives tainted and pure. In short, material that lawyers thrive on, and since it was published posthumously in 1924, "Billy Budd, Sailor" has gripped the collective imagination of the bar.

Lately, a cottage industry has grown up in legal circles on the interpretation of Herman Melville's novella. It is taught in courses in jurisprudence, and books and law journal articles delve into whether Billy Budd, the protagonist, was unjustly executed and whether the man who sent him to his death, Captain Starry Vere, was a jurisprudential hero or villain.

Last fall a two-day colloquium on the law and Billy Budd was held at the Washington and Lee School of Law in Lexington, Va. And last week 150 lawyers listened to a prominent judge and professor debate the novel's meaning at the New York City Bar Association.

The novel, said one panelist, Prof. Richard Weisberg of the Benjamin Cardozo School of Law, causes lawyers "to reflect constantly upon our own values."

While some lawyers have long written fiction and some writers have long been fascinated by lawyers, only recently have law and literature become a fashionable and respectable area of legal scholarship. Courses are now offered at the best law schools, legal periodicals are filled with articles exploring Dostoyevsky, Kafka and Melville and at summer retreats, judges are as likely to discuss Shakespeare as Tom Wolfe.

"Literature enriches our understanding of law," said David B. Saxe, an acting Supreme Court justice in New York City.

In the novel, Billy Budd, a popular sailor, has been impressed into service on a British warship. Soon afterward a petty officer, John Claggart, falsely accuses Billy of being a mutineer. When confronting his accuser, Billy cannot speak. The captain comforts him, saying there is no need to hurry. But Billy strikes Claggart dead with a single blow. The captain convenes a court-martial, whose members are inclined to leniency until the captain intercedes. Within 24 hours, Billy is hanged.

Literary and legal critics have often viewed Captain Vere as an honorable man and able administrator who was forced to perform a distasteful task.

† *The New York Times*, June 10, 1988.

This view has been sharply challenged in lectures and articles by Professor Weisberg, who holds a doctorate in comparative literature as well as a law degree. He argued that the captain had acted improperly as witness, prosecutor, judge and executioner. In calling for summary execution, the captain, according to the professor, misread applicable statutes and committed procedural errors.

The professor presented a detailed review of court-martial procedures in effect in the 18th century, when the story took place, and concluded, "From the legal point of view, there was no justification of what Vere did."

His interpretation was disputed by Judge Richard Posner, a Federal appeals judge in Chicago who is a prodigious writer on the side. 13 books and 130 law review articles bear his name. The judge chided the professor for going beyond the text of the book for his evidence. Melville, he said, was "not writing the story for people expected to do legal research."

For Judge Posner, Vere was merely fulfilling his obligation. "We cannot bring a 1980's view of capital punishment to the story," Judge Posner said. "It was utterly routine in the 18th century."

# CAROLYN L. KARCHER

## [Melville and Revolution]†

\* \* \*

*Billy Budd* has probably stirred more controversy than any other work of Melville's with the possible exception of "Benito Cereno."[1] Critics on one side of the fence have interpreted this short novel as Melville's "testament of acceptance," his final reconciliation with all the tyrannies against which he had chafed since his youth: God, Christ, father, captain, naval discipline, and the harsh ways of a flawed world. On the opposite side, critics have cited *Billy Budd* as Melville's "testament of resistance," his deathbed reiteration of the "Everlasting Nay" he had sounded in all the works of his young manhood, from *Typee* to *The Confidence-Man*. It is no accident, of course, that the battle lines between the two camps have often been political, since one can see why conservatives or moderates would

---

† From Carolyn L. Karcher, *Shadow over the Promised Land: Slavery, Race, and Violence in Melville's America* (Baton Rouge, LA: Louisiana State University Press, 1980). Reprinted by permission of the author.
1. Herman Melville, *Billy Budd, Sailor (An Inside Narrative)*, ed. Harrison Hayford and Merton M. Sealts, Jr. (Chicago, 1962). I will be relying throughout on the editors' chronological analysis of the stages the manuscript went through.

agree more readily with the austere, intellectual Captain Vere in setting law and order above the subversive promptings of private conscience, while radicals would tend to find this stand abhorrent and
to sympathize rather with the young sailor victimized by the hatred
of his superior officer and the tyranny of martial law.[2] Yet the controversy could never have arisen had not Melville himself been as
deeply divided at heart as his critics among themselves; for the
moral dilemma central to *Billy Budd*—the dilemma of the Sermon
on the Mount versus the Articles of War, justice versus expediency,
freedom and human dignity versus authority, rebellion versus conformity, social ferment versus despotism, son versus father, Jobian
or Promethean man versus God—is none other than the conflict
Melville had struggled unsuccessfully to resolve throughout his life.

In his early works through *Moby-Dick*, as we have seen, Melville
sided unequivocally with the victims of injustice. Identifying with
common sailors in their rebellion against autocratic commanders,
he consistently drew analogies between the shipboard tyranny he
had experienced at first hand and the tyranny of chattel slavery that
millions of American blacks were then enduring, and a vocal minority of his contemporaries defying. Again and again in these novels,
however, Melville confronted the issue of whether an oppressed
subaltern might justifiably resort to violence against his oppressor,
only to draw back at the brink from endorsing such an act. So strong
a hold, apparently, did some inner authority exert over his imagination that he was never able to let his sailor heroes consummate a
successful rebellion. White-Jacket faced the equally unbearable
alternatives of submitting to the degradation of an unmerited flogging or leaping overboard with his hated captain in his arms, thus
making the supreme reparation for the "privilege" of killing his
oppressor. Steelkilt thwarted the mutiny he had set in motion by
electing imprisonment in lieu of violence and only consenting to

2. This critical controversy is summed up by Hayford and Sealts (eds.), *Billy Budd*, 25–27.
Representative of the "testament of acceptance" school are: Matthiessen, *American
Renaissance*, 508–14; Stern, *Fine Hammered Steel of Melville*, 26–27, 206–39 (with
reservations); and R. W. B. Lewis, *The American Adam: Innocence, Tragedy, and Tradition
in the Nineteenth Century* (Chicago, 1955), 146–52. Representative of the opposite
school are Phil Withim, "*Billy Budd*: Testament of Resistance," and Leonard Casper, "The
Case against Captain Vere," both reprinted in William T. Stafford (ed.), *Melville's "Billy
Budd" and the Critics* (Rev. ed.; Belmont, Calif., 1968), 140–52, 212–15; Merlin Bowen,
*The Long Encounter; Self and Experience in the Writings of Herman Melville* (Chicago,
1960), 216–33; Dryden, *Melville's Thematics of Form*, 209–16; Widmer, *The Ways of
Nihilism*, 16–58; and Franklin, *The Victim as Criminal and Artist*, 67–70. The battle lines
are not always political, of course. Two recent radical critics, for example, reiterate the
pro-Vere interpretation: Gilmore, *The Middle Way*, 182–94; and Ann Douglas, *The Feminization of American Culture* (New York, 1977), 323–26. And the most clear-cut example of an endorsement of Vere growing out of political conservatism comes not from a
Melville critic but from a political philosopher: Hannah Arendt, *On Revolution* (New
York, 1963), 77–83. The best interpretation I have seen of *Billy Budd*, and one that transcends this dichotomy, is Joyce Sparer Adler's "*Billy Budd* and Melville's Philosophy of
War," *PMLA* XCI (1976), 266–78.

violence when it meant certain death. Daggoo's vengeance against his white detractor was forestalled by a storm at sea.

As the slavery crisis had come to a head, making the threat of civil war ever more real, Melville's writings revealed correspondingly less sympathy with rebels and greater foreboding about the consequences of the "agonized violence" needed to overthrow so deep-rooted an iniquity. While he allowed the slave rebels of his short fiction to act out the murderous impulses that White-Jacket and Steelkilt had merely fantasied, Melville denied them, too, the fruits of their rebellion. The insurrection of the Dog-King's subjects in "The Encantadas" eventuated in a "riotocracy" from which many of them sought refuge in the shipboard discipline they had originally fled. Both the slave revolt led by Babo and the revenge that Bannadonna's robot took against his master ended in their deaths. Of these rebels, whose triumph portended the total destruction of the nation, the only one Melville was able to portray at all sympathetically as a human being—and even then solely at the moment of his defeat—was Babo. Yet Melville continued throughout this period to recognize the inevitability, and indeed the necessity, of the revolution his stories heralded, and when the long dreaded Civil War at last broke out, he repressed his misgivings about its outcome, throwing himself heart and soul behind the Union side he perceived as battling for the "Right."

The aftermath of the war, however, seemed to Melville to confirm his darkest fears about the perils of seeking to abolish one wrong by means of another. Overcome by a sense of guilt at the fratricidal passions the war had aroused in him and his countrymen, Melville repudiated radical Reconstruction, with its punitive measures against the South, as a misguided attempt to "pervert the national victory into oppression for the vanquished"[3] and began to identify, as we have noticed, with the southerners he had previously seen as oppressors. At the same time, the blatant corruption of the Grant administration discredited the positive accomplishments of the reconstructionists in his eyes, and like so many of his contemporaries, Melville became disaffected with reformist crusades in his revulsion from their by-products. Hence the characters who became his spokesmen in his postwar poetry were no longer stymied rebels, but disillusioned revolutionaries who upheld the necessity for autocratic governments to control the evil they had come to fear in the human heart.

What this poetry suggests, in short, is that in growing old with the nation, Melville had also grown imperceptibly into the role of the oppressive father against whose authority he had been rebelling in

3. *Battle-Pieces.*

his antebellum fiction. As his letters and other family documents of the 1860s and 1870s tell us, Melville had become a father who, writing home from the middle of the Pacific Ocean, could graphically describe to his eleven-year-old son how a sailor had fallen from the yardarm in a gale off Cape Horn and been buried at sea in a piece of sailcloth weighted with cannon balls, reinforcing the threat implied in such a letter with this cruel admonition: "Now is the time to show . . . whether you are a good, honorable boy, or a good-for-nothing one. Any boy, of your age, who disobeys his mother, or worries her, or is disrespectful to her—such a boy is a poor shabby fellow; and if you know any such boys, you ought to cut their acquaintance."[4] Thus by the time Melville again undertook to formulate in prose the conflict between rebellious youthful idealism and repressive worldly authority that had dominated his literary career, he was writing out of the experience not just of a son thwarted in his efforts to fulfill his ideals, but of a father whose harshness and insensitivity to his children's needs may have driven one son to suicide and the other to a series of flights from home, and from one job to another (uncannily reenacting Melville's own youthful wanderings), that culminated in a lonely death in San Francisco at age thirty-five.

The version of *Billy Budd* that Melville left heavily revised and possibly unfinished on his death poignantly reflects these unreconciled aspects of his personality. The tale had its origin, according to the editors who have made the most thorough study of the manuscript, as a headnote to a ballad recited by a sailor "condemned for fomenting mutiny and apparently guilty as charged," a sailor who, like Babo, had been vanquished after carrying out the rebellion contemplated by White-Jacket and abortively attempted by Steelkilt, and whom one might think of as representing the defeated rebel in Melville. In subsequent stages of the story's composition,[5] this hero gave way to the Billy Budd we now know: the Handsome Sailor, idol of his shipmates, and innocent victim of a false accuser against whom he has retaliated impulsively with a mortal blow, for which he must hang. Meanwhile, two new characters came to the forefront: the evil master-of-arms Claggart, who seeks to destroy Billy because he envies the youth, beauty, and manliness that have won Billy the status of Handsome Sailor; and the ambiguous Captain Vere, who affirms his belief in Billy's moral innocence, but decrees his execution on the grounds that he has committed a capital crime which, regardless of provocation or intent, cannot go unpunished without setting the whole crew a dangerous example, especially during a

---

4. Davis and Gilman (eds.), *Letters of Melville*, 203.
5. Hayford and Sealts (eds.), *Billy Budd*, 1–12.

period of mutinous outbreaks in the navy. As superior officers, the
one about fourteen years older than Billy and the other "old enough
to have been Billy's father," Claggart and Vere both play the role of
the oppressive authority figure Melville had once pitted against his
White-Jackets and Steelkilts. Yet here that authority figure is clearly
split into two halves, onto one of whom Melville could project all his
hatred while seeking reconciliation with the other, a purified and
softened image of the father.

Hence the central problem of interpretation that *Billy Budd* poses
is this: to what extent has Melville actually succeeded in separating
the bad father from the good and in dramatizing what one critic has
called a "reconciliation between an erring son and a stern but loving father-figure"?[6]

To answer that question, one must first look with an open mind
at the evidence on both sides. There is no denying that *Billy Budd*,
as it now stands in its perhaps still tentative state, includes contradictory assessments of Captain Vere. Many narrative statements
about the captain are unmistakably positive and can only be construed otherwise by reading irony into them, as some critics have
attempted to do. A smaller, but crucial number of statements are
extremely negative, and it is hard to explain their inclusion except
as a means of casting doubt on the rightness of the captain's decision. A few passages, finally, can be interpreted either way, depend-
ing on a critic's personal bias.

On the positive side we find: the assertion that Vere had "always
acquit[ted] himself as an officer mindful of the welfare of his men,"
though "never tolerating an infraction of discipline" (BB, 60); Vere's
"unobtrusiveness of demeanor," which "may have proceeded from a
certain unaffected modesty of manhood sometimes accompanying a
resolute nature"; his "honesty" and "directness" (traits Melville also
attributed to himself and for which he had a rueful admiration);[7] his
repute in the navy as a commander especially suited to handling

---

6. Simon O. Lesser, *Fiction and the Unconscious* (Boston, 1957), 92, cited in ibid., 183–84,
n.
7. See Melville's self-portrait as Rolfe in *Clarel* (both the similarities and the differences
between Rolfe and Vere are revealing):

> One read his superscription clear—
> A genial heart, a brain austere—
> And further, deemed that such a man
> Though given to study, as might seem,
> Was no scholastic partisan
> Or euphonist of Academe,
> But supplemented Plato's theme
> With daedal life in boats and tents,
> A messmate of the elements;
> And yet, more bronzed in face than mind,
> Sensitive still and frankly kind—
> Too frank, too unreserved, may be,
> And indiscreet in honesty. (I.xxxi.13–25)

"unforeseen difficulties," where "a prompt initiative might have to be taken in some matter demanding knowledge and ability, in addition to those qualities implied in good seamanship" and to be sure, the affirmation that "something exceptional in the moral quality of Captain Vere made him, in earnest encounter with a fellow man, a veritable touchstone of that man's essential nature"—an affirmation dramatically borne out by Vere's intuitive distrust of Claggart and his acuteness in divining Billy's "liability to vocal impediment." In addition to the virtues the narrator imputes to Vere, various incidents serve to put Vere in a positive light: the admiration Vere expresses for Billy's spirit on hearing how his new recruit, in an apparent "satiric sally," had bade farewell to his former ship with the words "and good-bye to you too, old *Rights-of-Man*" (an admiration one must contrast with the instinctive dislike of the manly sailor that White-Jacket had ascribed to the average sea-officer); the episode in the cabin when Vere, noticing Billy's speech impediment, lays "a soothing hand" on the young sailor's shoulder and says to him in a "fatherly . . . tone," "'There is no hurry, my boy. Take your time, take your time'"; the trial scene in which Vere, betraying his "suppressed emotion" in his voice, makes the unorthodox gesture of publicly assuring Billy that he believes in his innocence of mutinous intent; the picture the narrator conjures up of Vere's possible behavior during his closeted interview with the condemned Billy, when "the austere devotee of military duty, letting himself melt back into what remains primeval in our formalized humanity, may in end have caught Billy to his heart, even as Abraham may have caught young Isaac on the brink of resolutely offering him up in obedience to the exacting behest"; and correspondingly, the peaceful look the narrator describes on Billy's face as a result of "something healing" in the meeting with Vere. Finally, there is a passage in which Melville, under the guise of "a writer whom few know," all but directly exonerates Vere:[8]

> Forty years after a battle it is easy for a noncombatant to reason about how it ought to have been fought. It is another thing personally and under fire to have to direct the fighting while involved in the obscuring smoke of it. Much so with respect to other emergencies involving considerations both practical and moral, and when it is imperative promptly to act. The greater the fog the more it imperils the steamer, and speed is put on though at the hazard of running somebody down. Little ween the snug card players in the cabin of the responsibilities of the sleepless man on the bridge.

8. Hayford and Sealts (eds.), *Billy Budd*, 34–35, and 183, note 282. Recently, however, Stanton Garner, "Fraud as Fact in Herman Melville's *Billy Budd*," *San Jose Studies*, IV (1978), 95–96, has argued convincingly in favor of interpreting this passage ironically.

The weight of all this evidence that Melville endorses Vere is considerable, and it is not surprising that many critics have found it conclusive. Yet the evidence on the negative side is equally convincing, if at times subtler. There is, first of all, the simple fact that Vere is a Man of War, professionally committed to the violence Melville had always abhorred,[9] as he emphasized in changing the name of Vere's ship from *Indomitable* (with its approbative overtones) to *Bellipotent* (with its stark connotation of brute force). There are also the less attractive traits the narrator cites in Vere: a demeanor evincing "little appreciation of mere humor" (BB, 60; surely a failing in Melville's eyes, judging by the prominent place humor enjoys in his writings); a reputation among his colleagues for "lacking in the companionable quality" (another quality Melville ranked high), and for exhibiting "a queer streak of the pedantic" in his intercourse with men to whom the "remote" literary and historical allusions he liked to make were "altogether alien";[1] "settled convictions" that "were as a dike against those invading waters of novel opinion, social, political, and otherwise, which carried away as in a torrent no few minds in those days, minds by nature not inferior to his own"; and not least significant, given its bearing on Vere's alacrity in settling Billy's case in a way that would earn him a name for keeping a close rein on his men in this mutinous era, the possibility that the captain "may yet have indulged in the most secret of all passions, ambition."

As with the positive evidence, however, the most telling counts against Vere emerge indirectly, through little vignettes: the tableau of him covering his face on ascertaining that Claggart is dead, and then slowly uncovering it, to reveal that "the father in him, manifested towards Billy thus far in the scene, was replaced by the military disciplinarian"—a dramatic example of the phenomenon White-Jacket had labeled *"shipping . . . the quarter-deck face,"* when an officer "assumes his wonted severity of demeanor after a casual relaxation of it";[2] the untoward excitement Vere betrays to the ship's surgeon, and the haste with which he pronounces his verdict while in this agitated state of mind—"Struck dead by an angel of God! Yet the angel must hang!"—a verdict he will subsequently present as coldly reasoned, urging the members of his drumhead

---

9. I am indebted for this suggestion to H. Bruce Franklin's comments on my manuscript.
1. See, for example, Melville's description of John Marr: "to a man wonted . . . to the free-and-easy tavern-clubs . . . in certain old and comfortable sea-port towns of that time, and yet more familiar with the companionship afloat of the sailors . . . something was lacking [in the company of his neighbors]. That something was geniality, the flower of life springing from some sense of joy in it, more or less" (Vincent [ed.], *Collected Poems*, 161); also Melville disparagement of Emerson's lack of convivial geniality (Davis and Gilman [eds.], *Letters of Melville*, 80). Contrast this with the description of Rolfe cited in note 7, above.
2. *White-Jacket.*

court not to let "warm hearts betray heads that should be cool"; and most damning of all, the suggestion the narrator advances through the surgeon and invites the reader to "determine for himself by such light as this narrative may afford": "Whether Captain Vere, as the surgeon professionally and privately surmised, was really the sudden victim of any degree of aberration"—whether, in short, his decision to hang Billy, however rationally argued, may not have been the product of temporary insanity.

As several critics have pointed out, this suggestion becomes all the more plausible when juxtaposed with the narrator's analysis of the "mania" he attributes to Claggart, who shares several of Vere's most salient characteristics: an "exceptional nature," austerity, intellectuality, respectability, secretiveness.[3] Of this mania the narrator writes:

> Though the man's even temper and discreet bearing would seem to intimate a mind peculiarly subject to the law of reason, not the less in heart he would seem to riot in complete exemption from that law, having apparently little to do with reason further than to employ it as an ambidexter implement for effecting the irrational. That is to say: Toward the accomplishment of an aim which in wantonness of atrocity would seem to partake of the insane, he will direct a cool judgment sagacious and sound. These men are madmen, and of the most dangerous sort, for their lunacy is not continuous, but occasional, evoked by some special object; it is protectively secretive, which is as much as to say it is self-contained, so that when, moreover, most active it is to the average mind not distinguishable from sanity, and for the reason above suggested: that whatever its aims may be—and the aim is never declared—the method and the outward proceeding are always perfectly rational.

Of course this passage applies specifically to Claggart, rather than to Vere, and occurs amidst the narrator's attempt to define "Natural Depravity," which it would be going too far to ascribe to Vere. But the narrator does ask, with regard to the captain: "Who in the rainbow can draw the line where the violet tint ends and the orange tint begins? . . . So with sanity and insanity." And Melville could not but have been aware that in raising the same question about both men, he was at least drawing a partial analogy between them, if not actually vilifying Captain Vere by association.

Thus the upshot of this exercise in sifting the evidence for and against Captain Vere seems to be an irreconcilably ambiguous view

3. Withim, "*Billy Budd*: Testament of Resistance," 147; Bowen, *The Long Encounter*, 218–21; Franklin, *The Victim as Criminal and Artist*, 68–69.

of him. Unsatisfying though such a conclusion may appear at first glance, this very ambiguity guides us to the heart of the conflict the story embodies; for the key fact, according to the most reliable editors of the *Billy Budd* manuscript, is that the negative view of Vere arises almost entirely from late revisions Melville made in his "final" version of the tale, where Vere assumes a prominent role. That is, Melville apparently introduced Vere in order to dramatize the reconciliation between rebellious sailor and autocratic captain, "erring son" and "stern but loving father-figure," that so many critics have seen in *Billy Budd*. He conceived Vere as a captain who "suffered" more in inflicting the death penalty than the young sailor he condemned to die, a father who pleaded "it hurts me more than it hurts you" delivering his son the mortal blow. And he fantasied this lethal authority-figure, now internalized in himself, receiving forgiveness from a defeated rebel "generous" enough to "feel even for us on whom in this military necessity so heavy a compulsion is laid." Yet at the moment of dramatizing their embrace, Melville recoiled—just as he had always before recoiled on the verge of dramatizing a successful rebellion.

As some critics have observed, the climactic scene of Vere's closeted interview with Billy is fatally marred by "a failure of artistry in its rendering"[4]—a failure to *show* Vere "frankly disclos[ing] to [Billy] the part he himself had played in bringing about the decision, at the same time revealing his actuating motives"; to *show* Billy greeting these tidings "not without a sort of joy . . . [at] the brave opinion of him implied in his captain's making such a confidant of him"; to *show* Vere at last taking Billy into his arms. Patently evading the inherent drama of the scene on the flimsy pretext that "what took place at this interview was never known" and that the sacramental embrace of nature's noblemen ought to remain "inviolable," Melville substituted what one critic has called "a paragraph of thin summarized conjecture" about how Vere and Billy might have acted. He then proceeded, after writing this part of the story, to insert into the recopied manuscript the crucial passage that casts doubts on Vere's sanity and implicitly identifies the self-righteous captain with his malignly jealous master-of-arms, thus fusing the two authority figures into whom Melville had split the ambivalent father image that haunted him. It is as if the rebellious son in Melville resisted to the last the triumph of the father in him who had imagined young Billy going to his death with the cry "God bless Captain Vere!" on his lips.

4. Royal A. Gettmann and Bruce Harkness, "*Billy Budd, Foretopman*," in *Teacher's Manual for "A Book of Stories"* (New York, 1955), 71–74, cited in Hayford and Sealts (eds.), *Billy Budd*, 184, note 287; also Widmer, *The Ways of Nihilism*, 34.

Indeed, true to the younger self who, forty-odd years earlier, in that other man-of-war narrative echoed throughout *Billy Budd*, had pictured himself on the brink of "locking souls" with his tyrannical captain in death,[5] Melville could not end his story without meting out to Captain Vere the death sentence the latter had pronounced against Billy Budd. Shortly after Billy's execution, the *Bellipotent* falls in with the French warship *Athée* ("the aptest name . . . ever given to a warship"), and Captain Vere is mortally wounded in the ensuing battle. His last words, spoken under the influence of an anaesthetizing drug, though "not [in] the accents of remorse," are "Billy Budd, Billy Budd." For Melville, apparently, the deathbed was the only place where a reconciliation between the father and the son in himself, so inextricably intertwined, could be brought to consummation.

If *Billy Budd* ultimately emerges neither as "testament of acceptance" nor as "testament of resistance," at least where the central moral issue it raises is concerned, it does reaffirm the democractic faith of Melville's youth. Unlike Melville's late poetry, with its obsessive focus on human evil, the view of man *Billy Budd* presents is profoundly humanistic, even heroic.

The novel opens with a two-page description of the nautical archetype its title character will personify: the "Handsome Sailor," a sea-faring Hercules and a figure of "natural regality," to be recognized by the "bodyguard" of admiring shipmates surrounding him. The Handsome Sailor, explains Melville, typifies the qualities sailors value most highly:

> Invariably a proficient in his perilous calling, he was also more or less of a mighty boxer or wrestler. It was strength and beauty. Tales of his prowess were recited. Ashore he was the champion; afloat the spokesman; on every suitable occasion always foremost. Close-reefing topsails in a gale, there he was, astride the weather yardarmend, foot in the Flemish horse as stirrup, both hands tugging at the earing as at a bridle, in very much the attitude of young Alexander curbing the fiery Bucephalus. A superb figure, tossed up as by the horns of Taurus against the thunderous sky, cheerily hallooing to the strenuous file along the spar.

He is the apotheosis of the working man, whose "democratic dignity . . . radiat[ing] without end from God" Melville had celebrated in *Moby-Dick*.

No mere paragon of virility, the Handsome Sailor also manifests a "moral nature . . . seldom out of keeping with the physical

5. *White-Jacket*.

make." Without the crowning attribute of virtue, indeed, he could "hardly . . . have drawn the sort of honest homage" his fellow sailors pay him. Billy's comrades, for example, "instinctively" feel that he must have been "as incapable of mutiny as of wilful murder," even if the death penalty "was somehow unavoidably inflicted from the naval point of view," and the image they forever cherish of him is that of a "face never deformed by a sneer or subtler vile freak of the heart within."

Fittingly, this latter-day epic figure who reincarnates Melville's long-dead faith in the essential nobility of man also embodies once again the ardent racial egalitarianism and the commitment to human brotherhood that had always been part and parcel of that faith. The very first instance Melville cites of the Handsome Sailor—three paragraphs before focusing on the Anglo-Saxon Billy Budd—is a majestic African seaman who seems literally to step out of Melville's past. Melville introduces him in his own narrative voice (which he uses in only one other passage of the novel, also reminiscing about a black seaman),[6] and the date and place of the encounter correspond exactly with those of Melville's first voyage to Liverpool, in July, 1839:

> A somewhat remarkable instance recurs to me. In Liverpool, now half a century ago, I saw under the shadow of the great dingy street-wall of Prince's Dock . . . a common sailor so intensely black that he must needs have been a native African of the unadulterate blood of Ham—a symmetric figure much above the average height. The two ends of a gay silk handkerchief thrown loose about the neck danced upon the displayed ebony of his chest, in his ears were big hoops of gold, and a Highland bonnet with a tartan band set off his shapely head. It was a hot noon in July; and his face, lustrous with perspiration, beamed with barbaric good humor. In jovial sallies right and left, his white teeth flashing into view, he rollicked along, the center of a company of his shipmates.

The biographical references recall the experience that long ago liberated Redburn (and perhaps Melville himself) from racism: the encounter with the ship's "black steward, dressed very handsomely and walking arm in arm with a good-looking English woman," which crystallized Redburn's observation that "in Liverpool . . . the negro steps with a prouder pace, and lifts his head like a man; for here, no such exaggerated feeling exists in respect to him, as in America."

The scene Melville depicts in *Billy Budd*, however, where sailors and wayfarers alike pay "spontaneous tribute" to the beauty and

---

6. Hayford and Sealts (eds.), *Billy Budd*, 66. Hayford and Sealts, 135, note 3 (*In Liverpool*), and 156, note 97, also point out these "directly autobiographical reminiscences."

manliness of a fellow being, regardless of race, contrasts vividly with his lament in *Redburn* that "for the mass, there seems no possible escape" from racism. Fulfilling the dream of brotherhood once fleetingly glimpsed by White-Jacket while communing with Tawney in the maintop, and acted out by Ishmael and Queequeg as the alternative to apocalyptic doom, the black Handsome Sailor unites around him "such an assortment of tribes and complexions as would have well fitted them to be marched up by Anacharsis Cloots before the bar of the first French Assembly as Representatives of the Human Race." Moreover, his is the sole Anacharsis Cloots procession in Melville's fiction to accomplish the purpose of its original, unlike both the "Anacharsis Clootz deputation" Ahab leads to death and destruction, and the "Anacharsis Cloots congress" of April Fools the *Fidèle* transports to the wrong New Jerusalem. By creating harmony among his shipmates through their allegiance to him, as the fleshly image of "certain virtues pristine and unadulterate" that once characterized mankind "prior to Cain's city and citified man," this black sailor plays the same role Billy Budd does aboard the *Rights-of-Man*, whose captain describes Billy as "my peacemaker."

The black Handsome Sailor's most obvious fictional antecedents are the "gigantic, coal-black negro savage" Daggoo, who likewise sports "two golden hoops" in his ears and displays the "barbaric virtues" and pride of the native African, and the "grand and glorious" Queequeg, who twice bears witness to human solidarity in this "mutual, joint-stock world" by risking his life to save another's.[7] Although the black Handsome Sailor occupies only the first two pages of *Billy Budd*, he surpasses his more fully delineated predecessors in triumphing over race prejudice—indeed over the very consciousness of race. He testifies that the conjunction of extraordinary prowess, beauty, and virtue that make up the Handsome Sailor can be found—and universally recognized—in men of any race. Even when he fades into his white counterpart Billy Budd, as the lamb-like man fades into Black Guinea, he demonstrates more affirmatively than the Confidence-Man's masquerade that black and white are identical.

Thus in this brief epiphanic opening scene of *Billy Budd*, which fuses the humanistic spirit of *Moby-Dick* with the critical insight of *The Confidence-Man*, Melville has achieved his finest—and final—statement about race. Having transcended both the rage that embittered his devastating attacks on racism in the late 1850s and the paralyzing guilt that marred his vision after the war, he has at last become free to dismiss the phantasm of race with complete serenity, and to embrace once again the dark brothers of his youth.

7. *Moby-Dick.*

# JOYCE SPARER ADLER

## From *Billy Budd* and Melville's Philosophy of War[†]

\* \* \*

In its last stage and final context "Billy in the Darbies" is extraordinarily subtle and complex. Yet Melville is utterly honest with the reader when he calls the gift of the sailor-poet an artless one. For it is Melville's art—as he speaks indirectly through the sailor's artlessness—that is sophisticated in the extreme. To read the ballad as the sailor's creation is prerequisite to appreciating it as Melville's.

The sailor identifies with Billy on the eve of his execution. Like Billy, he feels that the chaplain is good to pray for someone lowly like him. He sees the moonlight; he experiences Billy's fear, his hunger for companionship and food, the pressure of the handcuffs. He intends no symbolism, no irony, no complicated double meanings, only a few childlike puns. Yet, there is the beginning of questioning: "But aren't it all sham?" There is a dawning of consciousness of the grim sacrifice war exacts and men accede to: "But—no! It is dead then I'll be, *come to think*." He sees a correspondence between Billy and another sailor whose cheeks as he sank was also roseate, and feels the tie that unites them all. He has a growing sense of being constricted; the oozy weeds twist about his body and hold him, too, down. He has glimpsed the reality which *White-Jacket* says "forever slides along far under the surface" of the sea on which the man-of-war sails ("The End").[1]

Melville's imagination works through the sailor's; his voice sounds in the overtones with which the narrative has endowed the sailor's simple words. The sailor's descriptive title is Melville's symbolic one: Billy Budd, sailor, lies in the darbies of war, from which he and all other sailors need to be released. He is a pearl of great beauty about to be jettisoned by the man-of-war world and "all adrift to go" like the drifted treasure in "The Haglets." For whom should the chaplain pray if not for "the likes" of him? One of the lowliest on the warship Billy will, in a nonliteral way, go "aloft from alow": as he ascends the yard-end his goodness will convey an inspiration of true glory which at some future time may prove the salvation of all

† Reprinted by permission of the Modern Language Association of America from *PMLA* 91 (1976): 276–77.

1. Herman Melville, *Billy Budd, Sailor (An Inside Narrative)*, reading and genetic texts edited from the manuscript with introduction and notes by Harrison Hayford and Merton M. Sealts, Jr. (Chicago: Univ. of Chicago Press, 1962). All references to *Billy Budd* will be to this edition; chapter numbers do not correspond in every instance to those in other editions.

sailors on what *White-Jacket* in "The End" sees as "this earth that sails through the air."

Suggestive plays upon words, as Melville speaks through the language of the sailor, develop main themes of the prose. The "dawning of Billy's last day" will bring also the dawn of consciousness to the crew. "Heaven knows," indeed, who is responsible for the running of Billy up. The sailor's wondering query, "But aren't it all sham?" is Melville's implied question to the reader: "Isn't it all—the whole religion practiced in the *Bellipotent* 'cathedral'—a grotesque perversion of the religion whose music and rites it exploits but whose God in effect it denies?" A "blur" has been in man's eyes, his vision obscured by war and false songs and stories of war. He has been a child "dreaming."

The sailor-poet's linking of Billy with Bristol Molly, Donald (whoever he is), and Taff the Welshman bespeaks Melville's sense of the common humanity of man for which Billy has stood, the "one heartbeat at heart-core" felt by John Marr,[2] the "common sympathy" with his five hundred "fellow-beings" on the *Neversink* experienced by White-Jacket, his interest "ever after" in their welfare (Ch. xlii), and the real communion and feeling of peace among men that Ishmael knows as he squeezes the whale's sperm with his co-laborers in the *Pequod's* crew and forgets his "horrible oath" to wage Ahab's war (Ch. xciv).

By making the ballad the work of a sailor-poet speaking for the crew whose dormant spirit of harmony Billy has awakened, Melville suggests a coming transfiguration of men and the world. While Billy's body lies bound by the weeds fathoms down, pictorializing the subterranean reality of war as *White-Jacket* pictures it (Ch. lxx), as well as the good submerged in man but still capable of resurrection, his memory prompts in the imagination of the crew a subconscious quest for the meaning of his death, an inquiry that may some day ascend to full consciousness. In contrast to Vere who at the trial had spoken of the "mystery of iniquity" but had turned away from probing it, disclaiming moral responsibility, Melville is engaged in fathoming both the mystery of iniquity in the world and the mysterious potency of good. Since good can inspire mankind, even after the death of one epitomizing it, the ballad about Billy's physical end is not an architectural finial, either of the book or of the world it portrays.

The hanging of Billy has been translated into art (by both the sailor-poet and Melville) which in its interaction with life may give rise to a conscious desire by man to change his mode of existence. The *Bellipotent* form is not an inescapable part of the human condition but the result of the failure so far of man's heart and imagination to attempt to understand its mystery and to seek out the

2. *Complete Poems.*

transforming possibility within it. Melville's imagination, as it makes itself known in all his works, even the most bitter, does not see civilization's forms as static, complete, devoid of all potentiality for "promoted life." It is incapable of "that unfeeling acceptance of destiny which is promulgated in the name of service or tradition."

So Melville in *Billy Budd* has shown the world-of-war, which "fallen" man created and then worshipped, in all its contradictions and potentiality, and his final emphasis has been on the creative in man and on the power of language and art to explore new values and inspire a fresh conception of life. He has written not of original sin but of original good and its continued, though sleeping, existence in man, while evil—outstandingly exemplified in war—has been shown as a depravity in man, a fall from his inborn creative potentiality. As far back as the second chapter Melville had introduced this theme, but its deeper meaning for the work had not then been clear:

> it is observable that where certain virtues pristine and unadulterate peculiarly characterize anybody in the external uniform of civilization, they will upon scrutiny seem not to be derived from custom or convention, but . . . transmitted from a period prior to Cain's city and citified man. The character marked by such qualities has to an unvitiated taste an untampered-with flavor like that of berries, while *the man thoroughly civilized, even in a fair specimen of the breed,* has to the same moral palate a questionable smack as of compounded wine. (Ch. ii)

"Human nature" is not under attack here, but what civilization has done to deprave it is. What we have seen in Vere is that his human nature has been so tampered with that he believes he is "not authorized" to determine matters on the "primitive basis" of "essential right and wrong" (Ch. xxi) and that he must fight against his most natural emotions, his "primitive instincts strong as the wind and the sea" (Ch. xxi). On the other hand, primitive good, as symbolized by Billy, has been seen to be too childlike to be able to survive in the present civilization of the world. To transform the institutions of civilization so that good and beauty can thrive in an environment of peace, the members of the crew of man have to develop the desire to probe civilization's nature and articulate their needs and dreams. They must, in terms of the imagery relating to "Baby" Budd, attain manhood. *Billy Budd* implies that this may yet be.

Thus, in this narrative of man's silence transmuted into poetry Melville uses his art to try to break the spell holding human beings captive in the marble "form" of war, to break the tyranny of the "religion" of war over the minds and acts of potentially creative man. His illumination that a transformation of mankind and of the world is conceivable—may even already be germinating in man's imagination—is the source of the radiance that suffuses the work from Billy's "God bless Captain Vere" on. *Billy Budd* is Melville's most searching exploration of war, reaching back to the beginning of man and his fall into "Cain's city" and forward to a re-creation of the world by humanity reawakened.

## MERVYN COOKE

## [Homosexuality in *Billy Budd*]†

\*     \*     \*

The diametrical opposition of good and evil in *Billy Budd* is inextricably linked with a possible homosexual interpretation of Claggart's and Vere's behaviour towards the Handsome Sailor. As a former seafarer himself, Melville was only too aware of the carnal temptations offered to sailors when cut off from land and confined within the all-male environment of a ship at sea.

\*     \*     \*

The veiled allusions to shipboard homosexuality in the novella (no doubt still derived from Melville's earlier first-hand observations of sexual behaviour at sea) form an undeniably important element of the story. Homosexual lust is a chief foundation for Claggart's hatred of Budd, and even Vere's attitude towards the foretopman is more than altruistically paternal ('he had congratulated Lieutenant Ratcliffe upon his good fortune in lighting on such a fine specimen of the *genus homo*, who in the nude might have posed for a statue of the young Adam before the Fall'). Claggart's sexual attraction for Billy reaches a climax in every sense in the incident described at length in chapters 10 and 13, when Billy spills his bowl of soup at Claggart's feet in a \* \* \* piece of homo-erotic symbolism:

> [Billy] chanced in a sudden lurch to spill the entire contents of his soup pan on the new-scrubbed deck. Claggart . . . happened to be passing along . . . and the greasy liquid streamed just across his path. Stepping over it, he was proceeding on his way without comment . . . when he happened to observe who it was that had done the spilling. His countenance changed.

† From Mervyn Cooke and Philip Reed, *Benjamin Britten, Billy Budd* (New York: Cambridge University Press, 1993). Reprinted with the permission of Cambridge University Press.

> Pausing, he was about to ejaculate something hasty at the
> sailor, but checked himself, and pointing down to the stream-
> ing soup, playfully tapped him from behind with his rattan, say-
> ing in a low musical voice peculiar to him at times,
> 'Handsomely done, my lad! And handsome is as handsome did
> it, too!' . . .
>
> Now when the master-at-arms noticed whence came that
> greasy fluid streaming before his feet, he must have taken it—
> to some extent wilfully, perhaps—not for the mere accident it
> assuredly was, but for the sly escape of a spontaneous feeling
> on Billy's part more or less answering to the antipathy on his
> own.

Another striking sexual symbol is introduced when, at the moment
of his execution, Billy's body hangs motionless and is not convulsed
by the expected spasm. At this moment, Vere stands 'erectly rigid as
a musket'.

With the insight of a practising homosexual aesthete, Auden bril-
liantly pinpointed the significance of the sexual symbolism in *Billy
Budd*:

> . . . the opposition is not strength/weakness, but
> innocence/guilt-consciousness, i.e., Claggart wishes to annihilate
> the difference either by becoming innocent himself or by acquir-
> ing an accomplice in guilt. If this is expressed sexually, the magic
> act must necessarily be homosexual, for the wish is for identity in
> innocence or in guilt, and identity demands the same sex.
>
> Claggart, as the Devil, cannot, of course, admit a sexual desire,
> for that would be an admission of loneliness which pride can-
> not admit. Either he must corrupt innocence through an
> underling or if that is not possible he must annihilate it, which
> he does.

\*     \*     \*

The implications of Melville's final work are remarkably open-
ended, and the story's ambiguities and resonances were to prove a
godsend to an opera composer of Britten's sensibilities.

\*     \*     \*

The three-year gestation period in which *Billy Budd* gradually took
shape was unusually long by Britten's standards and reflects the
complexities of the project and the seriousness with which the
three-man team attempted to hone the Melville story into a work-
able operatic shape. \* \* \* [E. M.] Forster's influence was clearly

considerable throughout and not merely restricted to the libretto: it was partly through Forster's own love of 'grand' opera that Britten elected to return to much larger instrumental forces after the self-imposed restrictions of the two chamber-operas, *The Rape of Lucretia* and *Albert Herring*: Forster wrote to Britten on 20 December 1948 that he wanted 'grand opera mounted clearly and grandly'.

When Forster expressed his view of Claggart in a letter to Britten written in December 1950 ('I want *passion*—love constricted, perverted, poisoned, but nevertheless *flowing* down its agonising channel; a sexual discharge gone evil. Not soggy depression or growling remorse'), his remarks leave little doubt that the homosexual implications of *Billy Budd* were a prime reason for the story's attractiveness to Britten and Forster. \* \* \* The story may be viewed as a homosexual eternal triangle, the violence of Claggart's passion counterpointed with the philosophical—almost paternal—approach of Vere. In the light of Britten's later treatment of the relationship between Aschenbach and Tadzio in *Death in Venice*, Britten must surely have been attracted by Vere's apparent aesthetic, philosophical and sexual predicament. Because of the *mores* prevailing at the time of the opera's composition (homosexuality was until 1967 a criminal offence in the UK punishable by imprisonment), the story's homosexual implications were significantly played down in the opera libretto; but they are never very far below the surface and, without them, the parable of good and evil would be considerably weakened.

# ROBERT K. MARTIN JR.

## [Is Vere a Hero?]†

\*    \*    \*

A majority of readers have found Vere to be the hero and locus of value in *Billy Budd*. Such a misunderstanding is frightening, not so much for what it says about the ability to deal with the text (and Melville did create problems by writing a text without a hero) as for what it says about the society of which Melville had already so despaired. *Billy Budd* is the first Melville text in which the Captain is given real psychological depth, but his place in a hierarchical structure of power in which mutiny—the revolt of the children

---

† From Robert K. Martin Jr., *Hero, Captain, and Stranger: Male Friendship, Social Critique, and Literary Form in the Sea Novels of Herman Melville*. Copyright © 1986 by the University of North Carolina Press. Used by permission of the publisher.

against the father—is the greatest danger renders him incapable of realizing whatever potential for love or wisdom he may possess.

Nothing that we know about the role of the Captain from the earlier works would lead us to believe that Melville would create a captain who represents the moral perspective of the author: every Captain in Melville is corrupt, a tyrant, or a madman. But it is of course possible that Melville came to reject everything he had once believed. Let us look then more carefully at Melville's characterization of Vere. He is a snob. With a "leaning" toward "everything intellectual," he always takes to sea a "newly replenished library, compact but of the best." What texts? Those books that "every *serious* mind of *superior* order occupying any *active* post of authority in the world *naturally* inclines" toward [my emphasis]. His conservatism is not the product of careful reflection on new ideas, but instead "a dike against those invading waters of novel opinion social, political and otherwise." The pomposity of his character is accurately embodied in the language of these passages, language that is employed as a kind of *style indirect libre*, echoing Vere's conceptions of himself and his stilted, self-satisfied phraseology. He is also a tyrant, exercising total political authority, compared by Melville to Peter the Great and his palace intrigues. His speeches to the court are masterpieces of portrayal, illustrating the false protestations and self-proclaimed honor of the prosecuting attorney. His rhetoric here shifts tone and subject with the ease of *Hamlet's* Claudius. But at its heart it is the rhetoric of Ahab: "You see then, whither, prompted by duty and the law, I steadfastly drive." The participial clause is enough to assert his honor but hardly enough to disguise the aggressive energy that it seeks to clothe in virtue.

Vere's behavior in the court is crucial to an evaluation of him, for if he is to be valued, it must be as the man of law, through what Milton Stern has called "his sacrifice of self to the necessities of moral responsibility historically defined." What is important to note about Melville's portrayal of Vere is that he betrays the very code he claims to believe in. It is not even necessary to accept the idea of a moral code higher than military justice (although I am certain that Melville did so) in order to condemn Vere. Revolution may be a legitimate fear, but does it justify the suspension of legal procedure? And if Vere acts only out of a justified fear of mutiny, why not act on that basis instead of cloaking his behavior in legal self-righteousness? Surely the first obligation of a court is to determine evidence; that this court never does. Vere is the accuser, the witness, and the judge; he is even the defense counsel at moments. No witnesses are heard; no attempt is ever made to determine the truth of Claggart's accusation. Of course the fact that the accusation is false does not alter the fact that Billy killed Claggart, but it does determine a great deal about motive and justification. Indeed, it is ironic, as C. N. Manlove has pointed out, that Vere's refusal to consider Billy's intentions argues against any consideration of Vere's intentions when he violates legal procedure. It is hardly the function of courts to make mere determination of facts; as Leonard Casper has pointed out, Vere's rulings make the court function as a coroner's jury, which has no power to sentence anyone. And some investigation might determine whether or not mutiny is really likely on board the *Bellipotent;* the issue is important, since it is Vere's assumption of the danger of mutiny that justifies his suspension of proper procedure, although no effort whatever is made to examine that assumption. Vere has decided Billy's fate before the court meets, and he uses his power to manipulate the court's decision. The trial is a sham, the pretense of justice and not justice itself.

Melville's language makes the situation clear. By what amounts to "jugglery of circumstances," the guilty and the innocent have been reversed. Claggart is only the "apparent victim," while Billy is in fact "victimize[d]." But this is not the appearance of things "in the light of that martial code," or "navally regarded." The question of "essential right and wrong" is too "primitive" to be used as a basis for decision. Melville is not suggesting that essential decisions must await divine justice; he is sardonically portraying what passes for justice under a system of military law. After all, all but the most fundamentalist of Christians accept the necessity of striving for justice, even if they believe that final justice must await eternity; and the word "primitive" can only be applied to the question of right or wrong in an ironic sense.

Vere's own language is a parody of judicial argument, marked by the substitution of the abstraction for the concrete. We know that Vere is capable of adopting other rhetorics, but his use of this discourse of law is Melville's depiction of the corruption of the office: in the courtroom one is faced with the temptation to speak, and hence to think, legally and so betray one's humanity: "Quite apart from any conceivable motive *actuating* the master-at-arms, and *irrespective* of the *provocation* to the blow, a martial court must needs *in the present case* confine its attention to *the blow's consequence, which consequence* justly is *to be deemed* not otherwise than as the striker's deed" (I have italicized the most striking examples of legalese). All of these words amount to saying nothing more than that Billy struck Claggart. It is not possible to imagine that Melville would cast as a hero a man who could so abuse the language. But he could imagine that a man of ambition would use such language to assist himself on his way to a glorious career and that such language would be an effective means of concealing, perhaps even from himself, the immorality of what he does.

At other places Vere argues in terms of "paramount obligations," the very phrase ironic in that it means for him professional responsibility and not moral responsibility. Here he weighs his duties in a series of on-the-one-hand, on-the-other-hand contrasts that again echo Claudius: "though . . . as sailors, yet as the King's officers," "warm hearts" and "heads that should be cool," "private conscience" and "imperial" conscience, "though as their fellow creatures . . . , yet as navy officers." The final contrast can leave no doubt of Vere's abdication of moral responsibility. No one can ever maintain an obligation higher than that to "their fellow creatures," since to do so means to deny one's place as a human being, to make one's political position more important than one's humanity. Vere's justifications for himself echo the reasoning of Melville's father-in-law, Lemuel Shaw, whose decision in the Sims case required the enforcement of the Fugitive Slave Act. Shaw thereby rejected his own prior adherence to natural rights in favor of codified law. A major defense of Vere argues that he represents a "higher ethic" than "justice to the individual," namely "the claims of civilized society." This argument, of course, begs the question of determining who speaks for "civilized society." But it also misrepresents the novel, because Vere cannot be said to speak for society, except insofar as he dictates the microcosmic society of the *Bellipotent*. Vere's decision to hold the court is contrary to law and to the opinion of his officers. It corresponds only to his own desires. Far from establishing a higher social order, Vere imposes the rule of the individual (himself) over social justice. His actions have been compared to the ethical code of Plotinus Plinlimmon in *Pierre*. The analogy is astonishing as an attempt to persuade us of Melville's agreement with Vere. Plinlimmon is one of the many characters in *Pierre* who satirize some element of Hawthorne; he represents the false absolutist, the man who preaches a high truth while secretly accepting the corruption of the world and indulging himself. If Vere is in any way like Plinlimmon, then he is surely one of Melville's nastiest characters. Both of them claim allegiance to a noble code of behavior as a front to deceive others; as Plinlimmon is a false prophet, Vere is a false judge.

The society of *Billy Budd* is corrupt, since power creates greed. The weak serve the strong so that they may profit from them. The Church has been turned into an arm of the state and hence becomes a collaborator in murder (the execution of prisoners) and war. Over and over again Melville has called attention to the role of the military chaplain, who by accepting that post betrays the Church to which he claims allegiance. One cannot serve both God and Mammon. The chaplain on the *Bellipotent* is "the minister of Christ though receiving his stipend from Mars"; by accepting such service he "lends the sanction of the religion of the meek to that which practically is the abrogation of everything but brute Force." The Church, which ought to oppose power, abandons its faith so that it can share in power. The

"war contractors" have an interest in war, since they have "an anticipated portion of the harvest of death." Having invested their money
in preparation for war, and in the production of the instruments of
war, their financial motive leads them to encourage war. Peace might
bring financial ruin. As the Church collaborates and the capitalists
invest, those involved in the hierarchy of the state seek their own
advancement. Vere, that double of Claggart, is driven by "the most
secret of all passions, ambition." But, as Claggart is never able to
profit from his currying of favor with higher authority by denouncing
Billy, since he is killed by Billy, so Vere does not live long enough to
attain to "the fulness of fame," since he is killed in battle by the
French shortly after Billy's execution. The deaths of the two men who
might have gained by the death of Billy add a final turn of the ironic
screw: all that killing, and not even ambition is served.

   Both Vere's defenders and his attackers have pointed to the chapter on Lord Nelson as a model by which to judge Vere. One school
argues that Nelson is an example of "supreme heroism"; another
claims that although Nelson represents "the ideal version of the
governing principle," Vere is "unable to emulate this ideal." But the
issue is not whether or not Vere measures up to Nelson: Nelson is
a false standard from the beginning. One would be surprised if it
were otherwise: a loss of faith in Nelson is one of the most important of Redburn's deceptions in Liverpool. At the base of the statue
of Nelson he sees "four naked figures in chains" which he could
never look at "without being involuntarily reminded of four African
slaves in the market-place." Nelson is thus identified as a hero of
the imperial venture, and that venture is one of the enslavement of
the nonwhite world. Slavery is at the heart of *Billy Budd*.

\*   \*   \*

# ANN DOUGLAS

## [Father and Son in *Billy Budd*]†

\*   \*   \*

It is one of the good fortunes of American letters that Melville's
thirty-year enforced silence in his chosen medium, prose, did not

† Excerpt from "Herman Melville and the Revolt Against the Reader," from "Protest: Case
Studies in American Romanticism," from *The Feminization of American Culture* by Ann
Douglas. Copyright © 1977 by Ann Douglas. Reprinted by permission of Farrar, Straus,
and Giroux, LLC.

stifle him altogether, but rather prepared and disciplined him for a statement for a kind of public balancing of accounts whose powers of condensation have seldom been equaled. In *Billy Budd*, Melville is not a combatant; he is, as never before, at a distance, having calmly assumed the authority he has not officially been granted. We are back at sea in a world of men, we are back in the narrative form, we are back with Calvinism, but with important differences. Probably written in the late 1880s, *Billy Budd* is set, as only *Israel Potter* and "Benito Cereno" were among Melville's earlier works, in the past; and this narrative is uniquely conscious, as its two predecessors were not, of itself as history. Melville's tone is dignified, balanced, formal, legalistic, above all judicious. Despite Melville's frequently stated awareness in the tale that his audience is unfamiliar and uncomfortable with the Bible and with Calvin, theological discussion and definition are here as never before, on their own terms: Melville is explicit on the point that officer Claggart's hatred of the handsome sailor Budd, on which the plot turns, can be explained only by the doctrine of depravity. Captain Vere's rationale for his decision to punish Budd for the unwitting murder of Claggart—"'Struck dead by an Angel of God, but the Angel must hang.'"—draws meaning from a text often used by Calvinist thinkers and repeated by Lincoln in the spare theological cadences of the Second Inaugural Address: "it is impossible but that offenses will come, but woe unto him through whom they come" (Luke 17:1). In the austere literary form which Melville has evolved here, he has apparently discovered an analogue, perhaps a substitute, for the theological discourse which was the substance of America's primarily intellectual tradition. In *Billy Budd*, all experience is ultimately to be marshaled before the faculties of judgment and assessed by them.

This is a narrative not only of the mutual comprehension between two "phenomenal men," a son and a "father,"—the "handsome sailor" Billy Budd and his abstract, intellectual, but fair-minded superior, Captain Vere—but of the understanding between *the* son and *the* father. It is not simply that Budd is compared to Christ, and to Adam, and Vere is cast as his paternal superior, i.e. God. Whether or not he consciously intended it, Melville has given us in *Billy Budd* something close to an allegory of the older Calvinist gubernatorial theory of the Atonement. Just as, in this view, God sacrificed Christ, his innocent son, to dramatize his hatred of man's sin, so Vere suppresses the "fatherly" feeling he has for Billy and becomes the "stern disciplinarian" intent on demonstrating to the rest of the crew the quickness and fierceness with which he will put down any effort at rebellion. Captain Vere refuses to listen to sentiment. Vere's primary concern is not the happiness or even the just deserts of his men as they understand these things. He urges the jury to rule out "the heart," the "feminine in man," and even the "private conscience" in the interest of the "imperial" conscience of their public duties. There are no Bushnellian elements in this Atonement process; Vere sacrifices Budd to instruct his crew and to keep his distance from them, not to win their affection by a display of his love of them.

I am not suggesting that Melville wrote *Billy Budd* as a conscious allegory of the older doctrine of the Atonement; I am suggesting that critics, in denouncing Vere's injustice or in viewing it as evidence of Melville's belief in God's malignity, are in part guilty of just the liberal heresy which Melville opposed—and opposed even in its highest form when it is closely linked, as it is in *Billy Budd*, to "charity." Such critics are like the readers Melville addresses whom he knows are no longer familiar with Calvinist doctrines, the chief of which is that God rules men according to his needs, in the interest of his honor, not in consideration of their desires. Again, it is not that Melville believes literally in these principles, but that he adheres to the rigor of the structures they create. No one could deny that *Billy Budd* is a testament of loss. Billy Budd dies. The re-established father-son relation is damaging as well as sustaining to both participants. Budd is partially speechless, even childish. He feels his fraternal ties less forcibly than his filial ones, and we resist the simplification of justice he finds congenial and perhaps easy. Captain Vere is of course a man, and the human drama is enormously important here. As a man, he suffers from Budd's death: not from "remorse," as Melville is at pains to emphasize, but from grief and loss. As a man, Vere's motives cannot be altogether pure; although Melville stresses his impartiality, his intellectuality, his extraordinary sensitivity, he also points out that Vere is perhaps ambitious, that others even question his sanity. Yet Vere's suffering and his imperfections do not alter the fact that his action in condemning Budd is *analogous* to the Calvinist Deity's in sacrificing Christ. Vere suffers in private for the fact that he has pulled off a totally public gesture: even those readers who condemn Vere can hardly feel that Melville suggests he was motivated by any personal animus against Budd. Since he is human, he pays a price for his determination to operate on the impersonal, even allegorical plane, but it is just this determination which creates the large, although painfully measured, spaces of the narrative. Psychology has given way to judiciousness; everything has its place. Injustice, as we, and even Melville, understand it, is undeniably present. The narrative is not, however, a protest against it. Melville's imaginative energy has unquestionably decreased; but his philosophical vision has gained precision.

Despite *Billy Budd*'s lack of dialogue, its refusal to penetrate the consciousness of the characters, the reader is given almost complete information about the situation in which the story is grounded. We are allowed no interior views, yet this is part of the essential fairness, as well as the remoteness, of the narrative: it is as if Melville can only fathom and bear his own story if presented in an extreme long shot. Yet one should add that Melville respects his characters' privacy as he could not respect Pierre's; Pierre's nightmare was that he had nothing but his privacy. In *Billy Budd*, decorum is the word. Within these limitations, there are no missing pieces of information comparable to the unknown fate of Toby in *Typee*, or the actual paternity of Isabel in *Pierre*, or the real identity of the confidence man; there are no symbols that precipitate and yet absorb events, such as the white jacket or the white whale; there is absolutely none of the sensuous detail which over-runs and destroys the narrative of *Pierre*; the action is not divided between narrative and story as in *Mardi*, *Redburn*, or *Moby Dick*. The process of judgment has become too important, the imperatives of rationalization too strong, for the case to rest on symbols or withheld information. As in no other of Melville's works, the tale simply proceeds, straightforwardly, chronologically; the reader is given whatever it is necessary he know.

The narrative is in some ways dry as a result, and its restraint is a testimony to its impulse toward edification. Because Melville so precisely acknowledges what can and what cannot be known, and because no one thing is less known or unknown than another—we learn as much, or as little, about Claggart's depravity as we do about Budd's innocence or Vere's authority—Melville presents an entire universe to the reader, all parts remote, all parts equally accessible. Melville assumes an audience in *Billy Budd* as he did not in the Dead Sea journals; yet it is not one he pretends to know particularly well. His very audience has become generalized by the unknown possibilities of history: we, the readers of the late twentieth century, are among Melville's rather indifferently hypothesized readers, yet Melville does not attempt to speak personally to us, as Whitman does in "Crossing Brooklyn Ferry." *Billy Budd* represents Melville's established distance from literature as an object to be consumed by a mass audience. The book is extraordinarily helpful to us precisely because Melville was not writing it *for* us, and I think Melville knew this. We may not possess the truth, the conflicting but equally false official and popular accounts of the incident appended at the story's close suggest its inaccessibility. We attain, however, a sense of its dimensions, of the space it occupies. Melville had always been imaginatively preoccupied with bigness, with size; now he is concerned with measurement. We the readers approximate to the "truth" simply because we are not deceived. We are kept to the actual facts and to those rather abstract statements and generalized scenes in which complex emotions and personalities can be presented with the solidity and impersonality of facts.

Despite its lack of dialogue, or perhaps because of it, *Billy Budd* is about communication, and the language and actions which can be trusted to accomplish it. In *Pierre*, where almost no real interaction takes place, incessant talking, singing, and attitudinizing occur among the characters. In *Billy Budd* genuine communication does occur although—and this is significant—only off-stage. Vere presumably explains Budd's fate and his own motivation to the young sailor in an interview whose "inviolable" privacy and "holy oblivion" Melville honors. We are told, however, that "in view of the character" of Vere and Budd, "each radically sharing in the rarer qualities of our nature," we may conjecture with the author that Vere explained himself to Billy, that Billy fully understood, that Vere embraced Billy with the passion Abraham felt for Isaac before offering him up "in obedience to the exacting behest." Two men have met and spoken. There is no doubt that in *Billy Budd* Melville has taken his final leave of abundance; he does not believe, as he once did, that he should try to have everything; he is no longer taking revenge on a public which helped to make such an attempt impossible. Melville has muted his material to master it, but the mastery is itself "phenomenal." Melville's very control becomes emblematic. He achieves what the sentimentalists with their unexamined fascination with process, with biology, failed to do; history, presented in its uncompromised detail, merges, no matter how inscrutably, partially, and ambiguously, with providence.

# THOMAS MANN

## [On *Billy Budd*][†]

"The last thing he [Thomas Mann] wrote was a tribute to 'the most beautiful story in the world,' Melville's *Billy Budd*: 'O could I have written that!'"

† From Anthony Heilbut, *Exiled in Paradise: German Refugee Artists and Intellectuals in America from the 1930s to the Present* (Berkeley: University of California Press, 1997) 496. © 1997 The Regents of the University of California.

# ALBERT CAMUS

## [Melville's Lyricism]†

\* \* \*

The country in which Melville weighs anchor with *Billy Budd* is a desert island. By allowing the young sailor, a figure of beauty and innocence, and whom he himself dearly loves, to be condemned to death, Captain Vere submits his heart to the law. And at the same time, by this flawless story which can be placed on the same level as certain Greek tragedies, Melville tells us, in his old age, of his acceptance that beauty and innocence should be put to death so that an order may be maintained, and the ship of men continue to move forward towards an unknown horizon. Has he then truly secured the peace and final dwelling place which he nevertheless said could not be found in the Mardi archipelago? Or are we, on the contrary, faced with this final shipwreck that Melville in his despair asked of the gods? "One cannot blaspheme and live," he had proclaimed. At the height of consent, is not *Billy Budd* the highest blasphemy? This can never be known, any more than whether Melville did finally consent to a terrible order, or whether, in quest of the spirit, he allowed himself to be led, as he had asked, "beyond the reefs, in sunless seas, into night and death." But no one, in any case, measuring the long anguish which runs through his life and work, will fail to acknowledge the greatness, all the more anguished in being the fruit of self-conquest, of the reply which he has given.

\* \* \*

Melville's lyricism, which reminds us of Shakespeare's, makes use of the four elements. He mingles the Bible with the sea, the music of the waves with that of the spheres, the poetry of the days with the grandeur of the Atlantic. He is inexhaustible, like the winds which blow for thousands of miles across empty oceans and which, when they reach the coast, still have strength enough to destroy whole villages. He rages, like Lear's madness, over the wild seas where Moby Dick and the spirit of evil crouch among the waves. When the storm and total destruction have passed, a strange calm rises from the primitive waters, the silent pity which

---

† From *Lyrical and Critical Essays* by Albert Camus, translated by Ellen Conroy Kennedy. Copyright © 1968 by Alfred A. Knopf, Inc. Copyright © 1967 by Hamish Hamilton Ltd. and Alfred A. Knopf, Inc. Used by permission of Alfred A. Knopf, a division of Random House.

transfigures tragedies. Above the speechless crew, the perfect body of Billy Budd turns gently at the end of its rope in the pink and grey light of the approaching day.

\* \* \*

# THOMAS J. SCORZA

## An Inside Narrative†

In chapter 29 of *Billy Budd*, the next to last chapter of the novel, the narrator presents a journalistic account of the story he has told and is about to complete. Having been written within a "few weeks after the execution" of Billy Budd, the news account "appeared in a naval chronicle of the time, an authorized weekly publication." According to the narrator, the journal's news story "was doubtless for the most part written in good faith, though the medium, partly rumor, through which the facts must have reached the writer served to deflect and in part falsify them." The chronicle's "account of the affair" aboard H.M.S. *Bellipotent* is as follows:

> "On the tenth of the last month a deplorable occurrence took place on board H.M.S. *Bellipotent*. John Claggart, the ship's master-at-arms, discovering that some sort of plot was incipient among an inferior section of the ship's company, and that the ringleader was one William Budd; he, Claggart, in the act of arraigning the man before the captain, was vindictively stabbed to the heart by the suddenly drawn sheath knife of Budd.
>
> "The deed and the implement employed sufficiently suggest that though mustered into the service under an English name the assassin was no Englishman, but one of those aliens adopting English cognomens whom the present extraordinary necessities of the service have caused to be admitted into it in considerable numbers.
>
> "The enormity of the crime and the extreme depravity of the criminal appear the greater in view of the character of the victim, a middle-aged man respectable and discreet, belonging to that minor official grade, the petty officers, upon whom, as none know better than the commissioned gentlemen, the efficiency of His Majesty's navy so largely depends. His function

† From Thomas J. Scorza, *In the Time Before Steamships, Billy Budd, the Limits of Politics and Modernity* (DeKalb: Northern Illinois University Press, 1979). Reprinted by permission of the publisher.

was a responsible one, at once onerous and thankless; and his fidelity in it the greater because of his strong patriotic impulse. In this instance as in so many other instances in these days, the character of this unfortunate man signally refutes, if refutation were needed, that peevish saying attributed to the late Dr. Johnson, that patriotism is the last refuge of a scoundrel.

"The criminal paid the penalty of his crime. The promptitude of the punishment has proved salutary. Nothing amiss is now apprehended aboard H.M.S. *Bellipotent*."

The news account sustains Claggart's charge against Billy Budd, incorrectly reports how Billy killed Claggart, praises the master-at-arms, and applauds Billy's swift execution. Also, the news story denies the English birth with which the narrator had definitely credited Billy and imputes a degree of patriotism to Claggart which implicitly cancels the narrator's earlier expressed doubts about the place of birth of the master-at-arms. In any case, according to the narrator, this news item, "appearing in a publication now long ago superannuated and forgotten, is all that hitherto has stood in human record to attest what manner of men respectively were John Claggart and Billy Budd."

The discrepancies between the "authorized" journal's newspaper account of the events aboard H.M.S. *Bellipotent* and the narrator's own account of those events place his narrative in high relief and ultimately raise questions concerning Melville's intentions in writing the story. In the first place, the obvious contrasts between the newspaper record and the narrator's story have important implications for the narrator's statements concerning the veracity of his own account. He tells the reader that his story "is no romance," that "the symmetry of form attainable in pure fiction cannot so readily be achieved in a narration essentially having less to do with fable than with fact," and that his narration is "truth uncompromisingly told." Thus, from the point of view of the narrator, his narrative and the chronicle's account are related as historical truth to historical falsehood. Both accounts are, however, parts of a work of fiction, *Billy Budd, Sailor (An Inside Narrative)*, and the reader must thus consider in turn the implications which Melville, as author, ultimately seeks to give to the narrator's words, "romance," "fiction," "fact," and "truth." The device of the contrasting journal's account thus both creates historical verisimilitude for the rendering of the main narrative and raises for the reader the question which Melville asked throughout his work, What is truth?

The distinction being made between the narrator and author, and hence the distinction beneath the problem of the levels of truth in *Billy Budd*, is particularly appropriate for Melville's works. Even in his most autobiographical novels, *Typee, Omoo, Redburn*, and *White-Jacket*, Melville carefully created a narrator sufficiently distinct from himself to allow considerable freedom for his artistic expression. In his first two works, Melville's "other self" was dictated partly by prudential considerations concerning his criticism of the South Seas missionaries and his erotic descriptions of life in Paradise, but he continued the practice even in the admittedly romantic *Mardi*, in which the narrator goes nameless until his apotheosis as the demigod Taji. In *Billy Budd*, the distinction between the narrator and the author is the background for the dialogs between the narrator and "an honest scholar, my senior" and "a writer whom few know," dialogs in which Melville is able to cite himself as authority. In all, as used in *Billy Budd*, the device creates a tension between the author's fictional creation and the narrator's "authentic" tale, a tale which purports only to set the historical record straight on Billy Budd.

It is, in part, the failure to distinguish between narrator and author that has led some critics to see *Billy Budd* as Melville's thinly veiled contribution to the recurrent controversy surrounding the *Somers* mutiny affair in 1842. Charles R. Anderson, for instance, read the narrator's claims that his story was "no romance" and "fact" as equivalent to an assertion on Melville's part that *Billy Budd* was the "inside story" of the *Somers* affair, revealed to the author by his cousin, Lt. Gansevoort. Such a reading of the story, however, would see *Billy Budd* as a historical work and, given the controversy over the historical truth about the *Somers* affair, would ultimately reduce Melville's novel to the standing of a mere partisan tract. Further, this reading ignores the implied lesson of the contrast between the naval chronicle and the narrator's tale, namely, that truth is not to be found in recorded history. In fact, the search for historical sources of *Billy Budd* as keys to its meaning actually reverses the lesson Melville would have his readers learn, for such a search assumes that recorded history can plumb the depths of art, while *Billy Budd* asserts in the end that only art can reveal the "inside" truth with which recorded history is unconcerned. Anderson himself, after the damage had been done, went on to say: "In *Billy Budd*, borrowing is reduced to a minimum, and imaginative invention counts for almost everything that makes it, as one critic declares, a masterpiece in miniature."

The opposite reading, the assertion that the narrator and the author of *Billy Budd* are simply and always opposed, was presented by Lawrance Thompson in *Melville's Quarrel with God*. Thompson's reading was an attempt to render an ironist interpretation of *Billy Budd* in the face of all the obstacles to such a reading by creating grounds for a wholesale reversal of the surface tone of the story. Thus, the narrator is seen as "stupid" and "bland," and his view of events and personalities aboard H.M.S. *Bellipotent* may be simply dismissed. In effect, the dismissal of the surface reading of the story can allow the critic to replace the author as the creator of a work's meaning; the burden of proof for such an ironist reading thus must always rest upon the one who would read between the lines. Thompson had good reasons to be dissatisfied with either the historical readings of *Billy Budd* or those readings which complacently set the narrator's story down as Melville's own conservative "testament of acceptance," thereby ignoring the levels of meaning that arise from the distinction between narrator and author. There are no grounds, however, for the assertion that Melville would have the reader simply disregard or reject the narrator's judgments entirely, and, as will be argued here, the effort to work a complete reversal of the story's surface tone in order to arrive at its "inner" truth is far too simplistic an approach to the novel.

In *Redburn*, Melville had one of his earlier narrators note how the historical record of human events, specifically as given by news accounts, drastically reduced the dimensions of human life. Having described the fatal workings of "a malignant fever" among the crowded and impoverished emigrants in the steerage of his ship, young Redburn observes:

> But the only account you obtain of such events is generally contained in a newspaper paragraph, under the shipping-head. *There* is the obituary of the destitute dead, who die on the sea. They die, like the billows that break on the shore, and no more are heard or seen. But in the events, thus merely initialized in the catalogue of passing occurrences, and but glanced at by the readers of news, who are more taken up with paragraphs of fuller flavor; what a world of life and death, what a world of humanity and its woes, lies shrunk into a three-worded sentence!

The naval chronicle's account of the affair aboard H.M.S. *Bellipotent* is witness to the fact that even a news story of more than "a three-worded sentence" can only shrink the "world of humanity." And the whole of which the naval chronicle is a part, the novel which Melville presents as "An Inside Narrative" should not be seen as merely another, albeit still longer "catalogue of passing occurrences," but rather as a different kind of writing altogether. What the narrator presents as a contrast between the historically accurate and the historically inaccurate is actually the author's means of approaching a truth which is beyond the purview of historical writing. The narrator's internal lesson, that a historical record of events does not reveal the truth, must be applied by the critic to Melville's creation, *Billy Budd, Sailor*, as a whole.

\* \* \*

# GORDON TESKEY

## The Bible in *Billy Budd*†

An interesting development in Melville's later fiction is his more favorable attitude to the traditional claims of scripture. Chief among these is the claim that a force for good—a Creator—lies behind the structure of the world and behind most of the events that occur in the world. Of course, what I am calling a more favorable attitude to scripture is so in comparison with that Bible of hell, *Moby Dick* (1851). Melville's greatest work ends in a watery, as opposed to a fiery, apocalypse; and its protagonist, Ahab, holds that behind the apparent world is not a force for good but an elemental malignancy, an evil. Why then in the later work, in *Benito Cereno* and the other *Piazza Tales*, and especially in *Billy Budd*, does Melville withdraw not only from the saturated biblical diction of *Moby Dick* but also from its exuberant impiety, from the cosmic defiance that (as he said in praise of Hawthorne), "says NO! in thunder"? As Hawthorne noted in his journal, it is just this preoccupation with the bible and its spiritual claims that is the problem for Melville the man: "He can neither believe, nor be comfortable in his unbelief; and he is too honest and courageous not to try to do one or the other." The curious thing about *Benito Cereno* and *Billy Budd*, however, is that Melville's very honesty and courage compel him *not* to try to do one or the other, to believe or to be comfortable in unbelief. If either alternative holds out an attraction for Melville the man (and surely, for him, being comfortable in unbelief holds out the greater), the very certainty of such a commitment is perilous for Melville the writer.

We might guess that the change in the later fiction to a less confrontational engagement with the bible may be accounted for by the report of Melville's concern over Evert A. Duyckinck's charge that in *Moby Dick* "the most sacred associations of life [are] violated and defaced." Such an explanation will not take us far. Much of the later fiction, from *Pierre* to *The Confidence Man*, is an exercise in demonstrating realistically, rather than declaring theologically, that an elemental malignancy governs the world. Nor do scriptural references disappear in the later fiction: they are indeed rather more frequent than one might suppose, attesting to Melville's continuing preoccupation with the Bible and with biblical stories.

Shortly after he published the *Piazza Tales*, between the writing of *Benito Cereno* and *Billy Budd*, Melville visited Europe and the

---

† This essay was written for this Norton Critical Edition. It appears here by permission of the author.

Holy Land, or Palestine. (When at the beginning of this trip he met Hawthorne in England, as Hawthorne reported in his diary, Melville spoke with his usual intensity on theological matters and said "he had pretty much made up his mind to be annihilated"—much virtue in that "pretty much." Melville's long poem *Clarel* is, among other things, the record of the spiritual crisis of a young man visiting Palestine, as Melville did himself; and the poem demonstrates Melville's continuing interest not only in scripture but in the actual places where events in the Bible occurred. In his last work, *Billy Budd*, Melville reaches what we may call his final position on the claims of scripture: that although those claims are literally untrue they have moral and psychological validity. They have more than that, for psychology and moral theory claim to have an authority independent of the Bible and of Christian theology. For Melville the stories in the Bible have a mysterious, transcendental resonance which helps him to enter into the mysteriousness of human fate and of the human heart. The possibility of drawing on scripture in ways that will strike a sympathetic chord in his readers is indispensable to him as an artist.

Small wonder then that in *Billy Budd* Melville shows resentment at the growing dislike of scripture among the educated classes of his day:

> If that lexicon which is based on Holy Writ were any longer popular, one might with less difficulty define and denominate certain phenomenal men. As it is, one must turn to some authority not liable to the charge of being tinctured with the biblical element . . . Dark sayings are these, some will say. But why? Is it because they somewhat savor of Holy Writ in its phrase 'mystery of iniquity'? If they do, such a savor was far enough from being intended, for little will it commend these pages to many a reader of today. (Chap. 2)

In these passages—or, rather, in this extended passage from the eleventh chapter of *Billy Budd*, on the question, What was the matter with the master-at-arms [Claggert]?—Melville is making a point that goes against what was becoming then, and is now, the prevailing opinion of intellectuals in the modern world: that the most important things to occur in human life can be accounted for exhaustively by what has been called "immanent critique," without recourse to theological or transcendental language. The world is all that is the case: nothing outside the world is to be invoked to explain anything that occurs in the world. For Melville, however, no synthesis of positive knowledge, no cooperation between, as we might now say, economics, sociology, anthropology, neurophysiology, biochemistry, and physics, can even partly illuminate the mystery of what occurs in life's intensest moments, the moment, for example, when Captain Vere meets alone with Billy Budd, to inform him of the sentence of the drumhead court. It is a deeply human, secret occasion, but with no religious significance whatever. Nevertheless, Melville can speak of it only by employing theological and sacramental language the language of holiness, divinity, and providence: "There is a privacy at the time, inviolable to the survivor; and holy oblivion, the sequel to each diviner magnanimity, providentially covers all at last." (Chap. 22) In Western society, Melville appears to be saying, only the Bible can illuminate the deepest mysteries of life, mysteries "all but incredible to average minds however much cultivated." (Chap. 22) It is therefore the duty of the writer to preserve the force of biblical language, regardless of his own beliefs with respect to its claims.

Melville brings forth this view of the importance of scripture for understanding the human heart in the person of an older man who is described by the narrator in the eleventh chapter of *Billy Budd*. This man is an "honest scholar," probably of the law, who says he is uncertain whether "to know the world and to know human nature be not two distinct branches of knowledge." He adds that he is "the adherent of no organized religion, much less of any philosophy built into a system"; but for all that he doubts one can enter into the labyrinth of a person's heart "without a clue derived from some source other than what is known as 'knowledge of the world'." Worldly knowledge is moreover an actual disadvantage when it comes to understanding persons in extreme spiritual states: frequent intercourse with society, with institutions, with the marketplace, with the multifarious business of life "blunts that finer spiritual insight indispensable to the understanding of the essential in certain exceptional characters, whether evil ones or good." (Chap. 11) The old scholar goes on to observe, with delightful urbanity, that "Coke and Blackstone"— famous commentators on English law—"hardly shed so much light into obscure spiritual places as the Hebrew prophets. And who were they? Mostly recluses." Having recounted the older man's assertions, the narrator says he was perhaps too young at the time to see his drift; but he may see it now. He then proceeds to make the observation I have already quoted concerning the inadmissability among fashionable intellectuals of "that lexicon which is based on Holy Writ." (Chap. 11) Without the lexicon of scripture containing such words as sin, redemption, faith, despair, sacrament, holiness, divinity, providence, heaven, and hell, it is all but impossible for the writer to illuminate regions of experience we think of as most intensely human and assign to the "heart."

I have spoken so far of what Melville perceives to be the writer's duty with respect to biblical language. What about the critic? To give critical considerations to the use of biblical allusions in any work of literature it is necessary to distinguish between allusions made by the narrator and those made by the characters; and, among those made by the characters, it is necessary to distinguish between allusions that make the characters typical of a social class and allusions that set characters apart. And of course even when these distinctions have been made we must be sensitive to moments when allusions that are apparently being used for one of these purposes are secretly being used for another as well—or for a purpose exceeding the bounds of representational or mimetic consistency. But in most instances it is almost impossible without ambiguity to assign an allusion to one of these purposes while sharply excluding the others. One could describe all the problems of interpretation as flowing from the uncertainty that underlies every use of allusion, even the most apparently straightforward.

In *Billy Budd* it is the narrator's employment of scriptural allusions to complicate our unfolding response to the tale that demands closest study. How much does he mean by these allusions? To choose a relatively straightforward example, when Claggert makes his accusation to Captain Vere and Vere looks away, he gazes on the captain with a look that betrays assiduous calculation: "a look such as might have been that of the spokesman of the envious children of Jacob deceptively imposing upon the troubled patriarch the blood-dyed coat of young Joseph." (Chap. 18) By supplying a spokesman for Joseph's brothers, who have sold Joseph into slavery, Melville is sorting out an ambiguity in the biblical text, where it says that the brothers of Joseph both *sent* the coat to Jacob and *brought* it themselves: "And they took Joseph's coat, and killed a kid of the goats, and dipped the coat in the blood; And they sent the coat of many colours, and they brought it to their father; and said, This have we found: know now whether it be thy son's coat or no. And he knew it, and said, It is my son's coat; an evil beast hath devoured him; Joseph is without doubt rent in pieces." (Genesis 37.31–32) By comparing Claggert not to the wicked brothers of Joseph but to an anonymous, poorly attested messenger sent by them to accomplish their wickedness, Melville suggests the multifarious ways in which evil operates through relatively inconspicuous agents following orders—a lesson we have learned well in the twentieth century. But whose orders is Claggert following? The biblical allusion, as Melville gives it, suggests a conspiracy rather than an autonomous act. And yet we know another man, one of the afterguard, a man on whom this allusion would more properly fall, has been suborned by Claggert. (Chaps. 14–15) The allusion has the purpose not so much of intensifying our understanding of Claggert's evil as of dispersing our attention from him onto other, rather different, manifestations of evil.

It would be possible to discriminate in this way among all the allusions to scripture that Melville's narrator employs; and to make such discriminations is one of the most important things criticism can do. But the very uncertainty into which the different classes of allusion descend suggests that the heart of the matter lies elsewhere: not in distinctions between more and less significant allusions but in the total relationship in the tale between literary and scriptural language.

The same applies to characters who are represented making biblical allusions. In *Billy Budd* it is Captain Vere alone who habitually does so. When Vere speaks of Claggert's accusation of Billy as a "mystery of iniquity," "to use a scriptural phrase," he alludes to 2 Thessalonians 2.7. (Chap. 21) While we should not suppose Vere can recall the exact biblical passage, it is doubtless a phrase he has heard often. Likewise, when Vere speaks of the ocean as "the element where we move and have our being as sailors," (Chap. 21) he appropriates the language of Acts 17.28: "for in him [Jesus] we live, and move, and have our being." Again, Vere employs the phrase without much awareness of its original context; and it is mildly surprising that a reference to Christ should be appropriated by him to refer to the ocean. In using such phrases without any particularly religious intention Vere speaks as a man of his day, and especially a man in authority. He is not being pious; he is being grave, speaking as he is at Billy's trial before the drumhead court.

More unusual is Vere's exclamation upon Claggert's being pronounced dead after Billy's single blow: "It is the divine judgment on Ananias! Look!" (Chap. 19) This alludes to Acts 15.1–11, in which a member of the early Christian community, Ananias, having attempted "to lie to the Holy Ghost" by keeping back from the community some of the price of a house he has sold, falls dead at Saint Peter's feet. In this instance Vere speaks not as one in his social position would speak but to reveal what makes him different from the run of practical men in command of warships. Vere's biblical cast of mind flares up spontaneously at a moment of astonishment and horror. Not only does Vere's remark show that he believes, as the other officers do, that Claggert's accusation is a lie; it shows an inclination to believe Claggert's unlikely death to be a divine judgment. But is this merely the expression of passion, or does Vere actually believe it? If he does, are we supposed to accept it as such or put it down to naivety in Vere? Are we to think that the force for good which lies behind the world (in which Vere believes) shows itself in this act of retribution, using Billy as its instrument? Supposing it has, or supposing only that Vere thinks it has, what then are we to make of the sequel: the hanging of the instrument of divine justice, after vigorous prosecution by the very man who recognized the act as divine? The question, the uncertainty, is expressed by Vere himself in bizarrely contradictory language. Alluding to the angel of the Lord which killed the Assyrians by night, he says Claggert is "struck dead by an Angel of God. Yet the angel must hang." (Chap. 19).

At moments such as this Melville forces upon our attention biblical allusions that leave us not only uncertain of his meaning but uncertain whether they have any meaning. One thing that will help us to interpret biblical allusions with more, if not with complete, assurance is an understanding of the larger context of biblical thinking from which they are drawn. To that end I give in the following section a brief, necessarily schematic account of the Bible's structural divisions and of the total narrative that the Bible tells.

It is well to recall that nineteenth-century America was still a biblical culture. Most people heard readings from the Bible at least once a week (often more frequently); and conversation was as littered with biblical allusions as it is now with references to television shows. Moreover, most people had, from their elementary Christian education, an understanding of the parts of the Bible and a familiarity with the narrative running through it. They would have learned that the Christian Bible is divided into two major parts, the Old Testament and the New. The Old Testament, as Christians polemically termed it, is the Hebrew scriptures, which were originally written in ancient Hebrew and Aramaic, and which contain books of law, history, wisdom, and prophecy. The New Testament, originally written in Greek, is the Christian part of the Bible; it contains the four gospel accounts of the life of Jesus, an historical book (Acts of the Apostles), books of teaching in the form of epistles, and the final, prophetic, book Revelation. Through all these books, divided as they are at the "middle" between Old and New Testaments, runs a single narrative. The narrative covers the full course of human existence in the world, from the creation of that world to its final, apocalyptic destruction. As I have mentioned, a broad familiarity with this narrative structure could be taken for granted by Melville as part of his readers' early education, as it was of his own.

By "the claims of scripture," which I mentioned at the outset, I mean those doctrinal assertions, anchored in the biblical writings, which Christianity makes about seven fundamental things: God, humanity, Satan, the Fall, history, Christ, and redemption. Of these only two—humanity and history—belong to what Melville's legal scholar terms "knowledge of the world." In the Bible humanity and history are entangled with four things which do not belong to the world and cannot be deduced from any positive evidence derived from the world; they are instead brought from outside the world to impose on it a radically coherent explanation: God, Satan, the Fall, and redemption. The narrative of the Bible, from the first book, Genesis, to the last book, Revelation, is the story of humanity's fall into and redemption from history. The Fall is not a single event at the beginning but a continuous one, extending up to the moment when Christ reverses the direction of history and humanity begins its long climb upward toward its redemption. The narrative of Christian history thus has a parabolic, or "V" shape, with Genesis and Revelation at the two upper points and Christ at the point at the bottom. Schematically, the left arm of the "V" designates the Old Testament, the Hebrew scriptures, which begins with Genesis and ends with the prophets. The Old Testament tells the story of the nation of Israel and looks forward to the coming of the Messiah, who will make Israel supreme among the kingdoms of the earth. The right arm of the "V" designates the New Testament, the Christian gospel, which begins with the four accounts of the life of Jesus and ends with the prophetic book, Revelation. Jesus is seen as the Messiah who was foretold by the Old Testament prophets. However, his kingdom is not to be established on earth, inside history, but rather in heaven and outside history, in eternity. In the mean time the vessel of salvation in the New Testament is no longer (as in the Old Testament) the Hebrew nation, but the Christian church.

So much for the schematic structure of the Bible, which reflects the structure of history as conceived by Christians. Let me now summarize the biblical narrative by means of the seven things I have mentioned. First, God creates a perfect world and a perfect humanity. Satan tempts humanity away from obedience to God, with the result that humanity becomes mortal and sinful and the natural world becomes the brutal, destructive force we know it to be. This is the Fall, the beginning of history, but the Fall continues in history as events go from bad to worse. After a long period of time, most of which is taken up with the history of the nation of Israel, God sends his son, Jesus Christ, to become human himself and to accomplish the redemption of fallen humanity. As a man, Christ can redeem the rest of humanity by dying on the Cross and rising again out of death. But the life of Christ on earth is only the first step in the redemption of humanity. The Redemption is not completed until the last book of the Bible, Revelation, which is the English meaning of the Greek-based word *apocalypse*, or "unveiling." In Revelation history is brought to a violent end—it is torn back, like a veil, to reveal the spiritual reality behind it—and the world as we know it is destroyed by fire. After a cosmic battle in which Satan and his adherents are defeated and cast into the bottomless pit, humanity—or rather that portion of humanity which is saved—is joined with the Son in the heavenly city of Jerusalem, which has replaced the world and become a cosmos unto itself. In the heavenly Jerusalem is the tree of life, more properly the tree of immortality, which assures immortality to the inhabitants of heaven. In Revelation the tree of life grows, rather strangely, on either side of the river of life, which flows from the throne of God: "In the midst of the street of it, and on either side of the river, was there the tree of life, which bare twelve manner of fruits, and yielded her fruit every month: and the leaves of the tree were for the healing of the nations." (Revelation 22.2). How does a tree grow on both banks of a river? The author of Revelation is drawing from Ezekiel's vision of the heavenly Jerusalem, in which trees whose fruit is never consumed grow on either side of the sacred river (Ezekiel 47.12). The author of Revelation wishes at once to evoke this vision from Ezekiel and to retain the traditional singular of the tree of life in Genesis. This is a good example of how the collage-like nature of the Book of Revelation makes small inconsistencies inevitable while reinterpreting those inconsistencies as mysteries. This is the tree which grew in the garden of Eden, near the tree of the knowledge of good and evil; it is jealously guarded after the Fall: "And the Lord God said, Behold, the man is become as one of us, to know good and evil: and now, lest he put forth his hand, and take also of the tree of life, and eat, and live for ever: Therefore the Lord God sent him forth from the garden of Eden, to till the ground from whence he was taken. So he drove out the man; and he placed at the east of the garden of Eden Cherubims, and a flaming sword which turned every way, to keep the way of the tree of life." (Genesis 3.24) With the restoration to humanity of this formerly defended tree of life the Bible comes full circle, uniting the ideal garden, Eden, with the ideal city, Jerusalem. However, it is not just a circle but an ascending spiral: the celestial city of Jerusalem, with the essence of the garden of Eden inside it, represents a plane of human existence that is even higher than the "perfect" one which we are shown in the garden of Eden.

In scripture the goodness which stands behind the fabric of the created world is opposed by a transcendental force of evil—Satan. Although Satan is never equal to God and is fated to be destroyed in the end, he has a part to play in every significant human event after the Fall. Melville reminds us of Satan's ubiquity in human affairs when describing Billy's "organic hesitancy," his, in the event fatal, defect of speech. The defect is an instance of how even the most perfect-seeming man will bear in some part of him the debilitating effects of original sin: ""In this particular Billy was a striking instance that the arch interferer, the envious marplot of Eden, still has more or less to do with every human consignment to this planet of Earth. In every case, one way or another he is sure to slip in his

little card, as much as to remind us—I too have a hand here."
(Chap. 2)

Satan is particularly associated by Melville (as evil in general is in
the Old Testament) with cities, the first city having been founded by
the first murderer, Cain. Billy's relative innocence comes from his
having had little acquaintance with cities or with civilized life. He is
described as "a sort of upright barbarian, much such perhaps as
Adam presumably might have been ere the urbane Serpent wriggled
himself into his company." (Chap. 2) (The nonbiblical epithet of the
serpent as "urbane" associates him with cities, *urbs* being Latin for
"city.") Melville goes on to say that "the doctrine of man's Fall, a
doctrine now popularly ignored"—there's that resentment again—
accounts for the fact that the purest expressions of virtue "will upon
scrutiny seem not to be derived from custom or convention, but
rather to be out of keeping with these, as if indeed exceptionally
transmitted from a period prior to Cain's city and citified man."
(Chap. 2) After the Fall, humanity becomes the field of conflict
between evil and good, between the Cain and the Abel in us all, and
the conflict is what we call history. (Whereas Abel is a shepherd, like
the pastoralist nation of Israel, Cain is an agriculturalist, intensive
agriculture being necessary to the large urban societies in
Mesopotamia, Egypt, and Philistia, all of them Israel's enemies.)
But the conflict for Melville is much more than historical; it is the
defining condition for everything important that occurs in human
life and in the human heart, including the life and fate of Billy
Budd.

For Christianity the struggle between God and Satan over
humanity is decisively changed when God becomes human himself
in the person of his son, Jesus Christ. By dying on the Cross Christ
reverses the direction of history, ensuring that humanity will eventually be freed—redeemed—from Satan's grasp. Christ is even
called the "second Adam" because he undoes the consequences of
the first Adam's sin. I have mentioned one occasion on which Billy
is compared to Adam before the Fall. The other is when Lieutenant
Ratcliffe is congratulated by Captain Vere for impressing, that is,
forcibly obtaining for service on the warship *Bellipotent*, "such a
fine specimen of the *genus homo*, who in the nude might have posed
for a statue of the young Adam before the Fall." (Chap. 18) Billy
*looks* like Adam in the time of innocence, before the Fall. But he is
not quite as innocent as the prelapsarian Adam. The effects of the
Fall in him are invisible and, so to speak, acoustic, being connected
with his speech impediment. That it is necessary to change the field
of perception from the visual to the acoustic to understand the fal-
lenness of Melville's character suggests that Billy's bivalence is a
deliberate effect. He is at once an innocent and a fallen Adam, thus

expressing the truth that each of us bears within or without some of
Adam's innocence and some of Adam's sin.

Adam is not, however, the only biblical figure to which Billy is
compared. In suffering death unjustly Billy becomes like Christ, a
perhaps inevitable association in the intensely biblical atmosphere
of Melville's story. Billy's violent effort to speak when accused by
Claggert brings to his face "an expression which was as a crucifixion to behold." (Chap. 19) When the rope that draws Billy upward
by the neck brings him to the yardarm he is pinioned there in a
manner that is intended to remind us of Christ's Cross. (Chap. 25)
The effect is increased by the decision "for special reasons," to hang
Billy from the mainyard rather than, as is customary, from the foreyard. (Chap. 25) That main yardarm, or spar, is kept track of by the
common sailors over the years as it falls to different uses. Even
when reduced "to a mere dockyard boom," it is revered as if "a chip
of it was a piece of the Cross." (Chap. 30)

What are we to make of this association of Billy with Christ,
which is so much more problematic than the association with
Adam? To compare Billy with Adam before the Fall is to underline
Billy's innocence, his naivety, his vulnerability, and of course his
physical beauty and strength. These qualities are necessary to the
impact of the story; and they are restricted to the demands of the
story. But to compare Billy with Christ is to bring into view a range
of possibilities that extends far beyond the demand of the story,
tempting the credulous to suppose Melville has a dark, allegorical
intention; it is to suppose that Melville is chiefly interested in Christ
and only secondarily in Billy. This is most unlikely. In the Christian
faith Christ is the Son of God; he became incarnate as a man in
order to preach, to prophesy, to heal, and to die as a sacrifice to pay
for the sins of mankind. He rose on the third day and ascended into
heaven. He will return at the end of history to judge all mankind.
And he will at last unite mankind—the part of it that is saved—to
himself for eternity, in the heavenly city of Jerusalem.

Unlike the qualities I mentioned in Adam, these basic tenets
about the person of Christ have very little to do with Melville's tale
about Billy Budd. What does? Billy is a peacemaker like Christ; he
has a personal magnetism not unlike that of Christ; he is an innocent victim, though not for the sins of mankind but for the sake of
naval discipline in the year of the great mutiny; and at the last
moment Billy says, "God bless Captain Vere," which vaguely recalls
Christ on the Cross asking God to forgive those who have crucified
him, "for they know not what they do." (Chap. 25; Luke 23.34) As
always occurs with an over-determined symbol, the association of
Billy with Christ is one in which the effective similarities are less
consequential than the differences, leaving us, so to speak, hanging.

Are we to see Billy as being like Christ in a few ways but different from Christ in most of the ways that matter? Or are we to try to reconcile the imbalance by interpreting the text allegorically, so that the ways that matter *will* matter on the plane of a wholly unapparent but primary meaning? Such questions are more general than that of how to interpret *Billy Budd*: they go to the heart of the problem of the relation between literary and scriptural language.

Chapter 25 of *Billy Budd*, which recounts Billy's hanging, covers the period of time from just before dawn to the moment when the rosy light has lit the sky from over the horizon—the light into which Billy ascends as the halter draws him up. In anticipation of the strange, rising movement at its climax, the chapter opens with a beautiful allusion to the prophet Elijah's ascension into Heaven and the falling of his robe to his successor, Elisha (2 Kings 2.11–13): "the luminous night passed away. But like the prophet in the chariot disappearing in heaven and dropping his mantle to Elisha, the withdrawing night transferred its pale robe to the breaking day. A meek, shy light appeared in the East." (Chap. 25) In the story alluded to, the prophet Elijah, accompanied by his acolyte, Elisha, crosses the Jordan River into the wilderness, striking the waters with his prophetic mantle which then part for the two of them to cross. Arrived in the wilderness, a fiery chariot, drawn by fiery horses, descends from heaven and takes Elijah up. Elisha assumes the prophet's fallen mantle and crosses the Jordan River back into Israel, striking the waters so that they again part.

In comparing the change from night to dawn to the transferring of the mantle from Elijah to Elisha, Melville establishes the feeling of a blessed ascension which will be transferred to Billy when he too "ascends." To this feeling, moreover, is added the idea a benefit conferred on those who remain on the earth. Elijah never dies but is taken up into heaven, from whence he is expected (as we see in the New Testament, John 1.21) to return one day; and in the meantime. Elisha and the prophets after him will carry on Elijah's holy work. Billy's execution bears traces of this blessedness, of this rising and this transmitting; and much is made, though in an intriguingly ironic way, in an exchange between the purser and the surgeon, of the unaccountable absence of "mechanical spasm" in the body as it is hanged: "'You admit, then, that the absence of spasmodic movement was phenomenal.' 'It was phenomenal, Mr Purser, in the sense that it was an appearance the cause of which is not immediately to be assigned.'" (Chap. 26) Billy's stillness may be attributed either to a preternatural and spiritualized act of the will, or it may be that there is a scientific explanation, one similar in character to the hypothesis that his heart "abruptly stopped—much like a watch when in carelessly winding it you strain at the finish, thus snapping the chain." (Chap. 26) With this hypothesis of the surgeon's Melville is making fun of a worldview in which a human heart is like a watch, with nothing mysterious to it; and he is raising the question he raised earlier by means of the old, honest scholar, who doubts whether to know the world and to know human nature are not two distinct things. Do we require a transcendental hypothesis to explain Billy's stillness, one to which biblical language can point? Or is there (as the surgeon is confident there is) an immanent explanation, a natural cause that is, however, "not immediately to be assigned"? (Chap. 26)

Either alternative has power to tempt. On the one hand, because physical suffering is distressing to contemplate, we can be comforted to think Billy instantly died and that even mechanical spasm in his body was suppressed by a natural cause. On the other hand, because the execution is unjust, we are attracted to the possibility that its victim rose above it (so to speak), transforming the brute physicality of that event into a spiritual act—let us say, a sacrifice generating harmony in the navy and reverence in the sailors. I am well aware that Melville's readers will be divided on the relative attractions of these alternatives: to some, the first is defeatist and reductive; to others, the second is obscene. But to be repelled by one of these alternatives is not to find perfect happiness in the other. Melville gives just enough scope to each, and withholds just enough value from each, to make impossible any final decision between them.

It is vital to keep this point in mind when we turn to the most remarkable, the most mysterious, biblical allusion in *Billy Budd* which occurs at the climax of the tale: the allusion to the apocalyptic Lamb of God in the Book of Revelation. That allusion is prepared for as Chapter 25 begins, in a passage continuing the one I quoted concerning the prophets' mantle. Here, Melville just mentions that thin bank of clouds which later will be shot through with the radiance of the dawn, as Billy is hanged: "a meek, shy light appeared in the East, where stretched a diaphanous fleece of white furrowed vapor. That light slowly waxed. Suddenly *eight bells* was struck aft, responded to by one louder, metallic stroke from forward. It was four o'clock in the morning. Instantly the silver whistles were heard summoning all hands to witness punishment." (Chap. 25) With the whistles summoning the ship's crew we forget that "diaphanous fleece of white furrowed vapor" through which the dawn palely shines, as through a veil. But it is brought back at the moment Billy is hanged. Here in its entirety is the penultimate paragraph of Chapter 25 in which the fleecy cloud is compared to the fleece of the Lamb of God:

> The hull, deliberately recovering from the periodic roll to lee-
> ward, was just regaining an even keel when the last signal, a
> preconcerted dumb one, was given. At the same moment it
> chanced that the vapory fleece hanging low in the East was
> shot through with a soft glory as of the fleece of the Lamb of
> God seen in mystical vision, and simultaneously therewith,
> watched by the wedged mass of upturned faces, Billy ascended;
> and, ascending, took the full rose of the dawn.

I shall return shortly to the biblical allusion in this passage. But
to understand its effect in the tale it is necessary to understand
its context, which is one of physical motion. Two motions are communicated to us: the lateral rolling of the ship on her beam and
Billy's vertical ascent to the spar. The first motion is connected to
the execution as the means of its timing, the signal being given
when the ship regains an even keel. It is the motion of the physical world, of which the brute factuality of the hanging is a part.
The second motion, Billy's "ascension," seems to have something
in it that is nobler than the first: let us say, the possibility of transcendence and of spiritual hope. Yet for all its transcendental
promise the rising motion is at last absorbed in the ship's "periodic roll to leeward" as the dead body sways at the yardarm. By
the careful management of these different, contradictory motions,
the possibility of transcendence is briefly shown us before falling
back into the pathos of a dead body whose only motion is imparted
to it by the moderate swell. It is with that pathos that Chapter 25
ends, decisively canceling the possibility of apotheosis which had
been briefly raised:

> In the pinioned figure arrived at the yard-end, to the wonder of
> all no motion was apparent, none save that created by the slow
> roll of the hull in moderate weather, so majestic in a great ship
> ponderously cannoned. (Chap. 25)

The possibility of transcendence to which I referred is strongly
conditioned by the reference to the Lamb of God and the apocalyptic scene of rosy light and mystical vision. Even the play of colors in the scene suggests the martyred saints of the apocalypse
who have "washed their robes, and made them white in the blood
of the Lamb." (Revelation 7.14) Because of the curvature of the
earth, the light of the dawn has not yet illuminated the deck of
the ship but shines above it, in the rigging, thus making possible
the dramatic effect of Billy's rising vertically into that light:
"watched by the wedged mass of upturned faces, Billy ascended;
and, ascending, took the full rose of the dawn." (Chap. 25) The
biblical resonance of the passage is augmented by the use of those
strangely active verbs to describe what Billy must passively suffer:

"Billy *ascended*; and, ascending, *took* the full rose of the dawn."
(Chap. 25)

Again, Melville sets before us a contradiction between what is
happening in fact and what is happening, so to speak, in the spirit.
On the one hand, Billy is being executed by being drawn up by the
neck in a halter, so that the dawn light shines on his helpless body
at the end of a rope: that is what the scene represents. On the other
hand, Billy is described as if he were ascending by his own power
and gathering the light of the dawn to himself: that is what we are
told by the grammar of those active verbs. It is as if Billy were making a sign, rather than being made an example.

In addition to the grammar of the description there is its lexis, in
particular the choice of the word *ascended*, which is used in scripture to describe Christ's ascension into heaven: "When he ascended
up on high, he led captivity captive." (Ephesians 4.8; cf. John 20.17)
More important still for the readership Melville would have
expected is the fact that the Ascension is an article of the creed
which is recited at every service in church, stating that Christ
"ascended into heaven," where he sits on the right hand of God.[1]

We may turn now to Melville's unexpected, disturbing, sublime
evocation of the apocalypse in his reference to "a soft glory as of the
fleece of the Lamb of God seen in mystical vision." To understand
what he would have expected many of his readers to associate with
this image it is necessary to summarize the complex identity and symbolism of the Lamb in the Bible's final book, Revelation. The "mystical vision" to which Melville refers is not any mystical vision but this
one, the vision of Saint John the Divine, recorded in the Book of Revelation. The Lamb to which Melville refers is the central figure of
that mystical vision and the symbol to which (so it seems when we are
reading Revelation) every other symbol in the Bible is directed and in
which every symbol is fulfilled. Who or what is this Lamb?

The Lamb of God in the Book of Revelation is Jesus in his final,
apocalyptic form at the end of time: he is the Son of God who
defeats Satan, judges mankind, and establishes his eternal kingdom
in a mystical marriage to the heavenly city of Jerusalem. Jesus is
symbolized by the lamb because he is a sacrificial victim and
because his sacrifice—the Crucifixion—occurred during the feast
of the Passover, when a lamb is to be sacrificed by every family. The
sacrifice commemorates the lamb which every Hebrew family in

---

1. See Mark 16.19 for Christ's sitting on the right hand of God. For the Ascension, see Acts
1.1–9, the episode in which the risen Christ, having appeared to the apostles and given
them his final commands, is at last "taken up" into heaven, where he will remain until the
Second Coming. Although the verb, *to ascend* (*anabainein*), is not used in this episode—
Christ is instead "taken up" (Acts 1.9)—the episode is referred to as the Ascension. It is
distinguished from Christ's Resurrection. That event is his rising out of the tomb in which
he was laid and appearing to various persons before the Ascension.

Egypt slaughtered and ate on the night when God slew the Egyptian firstborn. God "passed over" those households in which the blood of the slain lamb was used to mark the doorposts and lintel: "Then Moses called for all the elders of Israel, and said unto them. Draw out and take you a lamb according to your families, and kill the passover. . . . For the Lord will pass through to smite the Egyptians; and when he seeth the blood upon the lintel, and on the two side posts, the Lord will pass over the door, and will not suffer the destroyer to come in unto your houses to smite you. And ye shall observe this thing for an ordinance to thee and to thy sons for ever." (Exodus 12.21–23). This is the annual Passover feast, during which Christ chose to enter Jerusalem to be sacrificed himself.

Melville was fascinated by the image of the Lamb and by the texture of its fleece, which he appears to have found as seductive to the touch as spermaceti. For him the fleece of the Lamb gave a premonition of what Heaven would be like if it existed and one were to get there: a burying of one's face and hands, of one's entire body, in the deep, snowy fleece about the body of God. There are notable allusions to the Lamb in *Moby Dick*, in *The Confidence Man*, in *Clarel*, and in the most famous of Melville's letters, the one in which he tells Hawthorne of having completed *Moby Dick*: "I have written a wicked book, and feel spotless as the lamb." (To Hawthorne, 17 Nov. 1851) In *Clarel* Melville refers to the "Ecce Homo" arch on the *Via Crucis* ("Way of the Cross") in Jerusalem: "The same, if childlike faith be true, / From which the Lamb of God was shown / By Pilate to the wolfish crew." (1.13.25–27)

The symbolic identification of Jesus with the Passover lamb originates in the last and most mystical of the four gospels, the Gospel According to John, which was long believed, as Melville knew, to have been written by the same John who wrote Revelation. In this gospel John the Baptist repeatedly identifies Jesus with the Passover lamb: "The next day John seeth Jesus coming unto him, and saith, Behold the Lamb of God, which taketh away the sin of the world." (John 1.29) Just as the Passover lamb in Exodus dies in place of the firstborn child of the family, so Jesus dies in place of all mankind. Mankind is thus redeemed, as we read in one of the epistles, "with the precious blood of Christ, as of a lamb without blemish and without spot." (1 Peter 1.19) A lamb that is without blemish or spot is a perfect sacrificial victim and more highly valued by God. Christ's perfection is not physical but moral: as the only human who was ever free of sin, Christ is the only victim worthy to die for all the sins of mankind.

In Revelation the Christ-Lamb becomes a much more tremendous, cosmic, and surreal figure, being provided, for example, with seven horns and seven eyes, and somehow standing "as it had been slain." (5.5–6) Even his sacrifice takes on cosmic proportions, since he is slain now not at a moment in time but before time, "from the foundation of the world." (13.8) Nor is he just a sacrificial victim. The Lamb is a figure of power and wrath, "the Lion of the tribe of Juda," "The Lord of lords, and King of kings." (5.5;14) The Lamb alone has the power to open the seven seals of the book which is in the right hand of God the Father, thus pouring out his, the Lamb's, wrath on the world. (6–8) The Lamb brings about the end of the world, defeats the warring kings of the beast of the apocalypse, and causes the downfall of the great, evil city, Babylon. (17–18) The Lamb feeds the hosts of the righteous in Heaven who have washed their robes white in his blood, and he quenches their thirst for justice in "living fountains of waters." (7.14–17) The Lamb conducts the final judgment, admitting into Heaven those whose names "are written in the Lamb's book of life." (21.27) The Lamb becomes the husband of "that great city, the holy Jerusalem, descending out of heaven from God" (21.10), in which the saints will live. The Lamb is the temple of the city and also the light that shines through it and in it, being the "glory" or brilliance of the Father: "And the city had no need of the sun, neither of the moon, to shine in it: for the glory of God did lighten it, and the Lamb is the light thereof." (21.23) When Melville speaks of the dawn light shining through the cloud "with a soft glory as of the fleece of the Lamb of God," he is using *glory* in this biblical sense, as if we were briefly being given a glimpse of the heaven of the righteous and of the innocently slain, into which Billy will ascend.

How much of this do we need to know to read the sentence in *Billy Budd* in which the Lamb of God appears "in mystical vision"? All of it, of course. But how much of it may legitimately be brought to bear on interpretation of the passage? Probably very little, so far as its details are concerned. What we do need to know, and we can know it only by reviewing the details of the Book of Revelation, is that Melville intends to evoke, briefly but intensely, so that it is over almost before we have noticed, a Christian apotheosis, an ascension into Heaven. For an instant, we have a vision of a sublime movement upwards which seems not to end, as if Billy were being received, in the manner of a baroque religious painting, directly into Heaven. It is an apotheosis not unlike that with which Milton's "Lycidas" concludes, with its vision of the drowned Lycidas in Heaven, received among the saints, who "wipe the tears forever from his eyes." (line 181)

The difference is that Melville does not allow us to rest in the comfort that Milton achieves. He raises the possibility of transcendence only to bring back the other, darker possibility symbolized by the lateral rolling of the ship, a possibility that, as I said earlier, decisively cancels the first. Billy's ascent is abruptly terminated at the yardarm, where he is left pinioned, the dead body swaying with the roll of the ship. The "fleece of the Lamb of God" sentence should not be read apart from the ponderous physicality, the majesty, of the sentence that follows it, canceling visionary rapture with the force of the real. The danger to an unvigilant criticism is in failing to notice how brutally the possibility of transcendence is canceled. Nevertheless, it would also be a misreading of this episode to suppose that the rapture awakened in us by that possibility is annihilated. Rather it is drawn back into, and preserved within, the very physicality that was its undoing. From where else comes the *majesty* of "the slow roll of the hull in moderate weather, so majestic in a ship ponderously cannoned"? Majesty—from the Latin *maiestas* "greatness"—is no physical thing, like the weight of cannons. In the alchemy of Melville's writing majesty is communicated to the rolling ship by the "soft glory" of the mystical vision, a glory which descends into the ship and conceals itself in the slow roll of the hull.

Together, the two sentences—the one following Billy's ascension into the dawn, the other noting the roll of the ship in moderate weather—compose one of the great moments of literary irony. I mean a moment when a spiritual hope, the possibility of transcendence, is raised, only to be negated by the physical truth. But because the physical truth alone can never gives us a world in which the trouble of living is worth it, the spiritual hope is preserved, as it were, under erasure. Absurdly, ironically, transcendence is at once affirmed and negated. For Melville, it is the duty of the writer to acknowledge fully the unyielding authority of the physical world without dismissing the claim on the human heart that spiritual hope has. To do both these things, to avoid the reductiveness of scientific positivism on the one hand and, on the other hand, the credulousness of a religious belief which must live in denial of the physical world, is not a question of steering a middle way between those possibilities. It is a question of awakening the power of literary language continually to suppress the possibilities it raises, while allowing those possibilities to live on within, and to transform from within, whatever it is that survives them. Such is the parasitic afterlife of scriptural language in Melville's fiction.

One final biblical allusion in *Billy Budd* may be mentioned in illustration of this point. When Melville's narrator conjectures what may have transpired in private between Captain Vere and Billy when Vere delivers the verdict of the court, he mentions that Vere was of an age to be Billy's father; he then alludes to God's commanding Abraham to sacrifice his son, Isaac, giving us a picture of Abraham at the last moment clasping his beloved son to his breast. The Bible, which is the most unsentimental of books, gives us no such picture. Abraham receives the command and proceeds efficiently to carry it out: "And they came to the place which God had told him of; and Abraham built an altar there, and laid the wood in order, and bound Isaac his son, and laid him on the altar upon the wood. And Abraham stretched forth his hand, and took the knife to slay his son." (Genesis 22.9–10) At this moment an angel calls to Abraham to stop him, and Abraham looks up to see a ram with its horns caught in a thicket, which he sacrifices instead of his son. (The ram becomes for Christians a type of Christ dying for the sins of mankind and as a symbol is fulfilled in the Lamb of Revelation.) In Erich Auerbach's famous discussion of this episode he speaks of the remarkable spareness and taciturnity of the biblical narrative, causing the reader to supply human feeling, to imagine what unrecorded expressions, and what affecting gestures, might have transpired between the actors of the scene.

When Captain Vere communicates to Billy the sentence of the court, he speaks with him alone: "Beyond the communication of the sentence, what took place at this interview was never known. But in view of the character of the twain . . . each radically sharing in the rarer qualities of our nature . . . some conjectures may be ventured."(Chap. 22) The last of the conjectures is this:

> The austere devotee of military duty, letting himself melt back into what remains primeval in our formalized humanity, may in end have caught Billy to his heart, even as Abraham may have caught young Isaac on the brink of resolutely offering him up in obedience to the exacting behest. But there is no telling the sacrament, seldom if in any case revealed to the gadding world, wherever under circumstances at all akin to those here attempted to be set forth two of great Nature's nobler order embrace. There is a privacy at the time, inviolable to the survivor, and holy oblivion, the sequel to each diviner magnanimity, providentially covers all at last.(Chap. 22)

In the spare, biblical tale there is, as we have seen, nothing of this which is why Melville says Abraham *may* have caught Isaac to his heart, as Vere *may* have caught Billy. What transpires when "two of great Nature's nobler order embrace" is a "sacrament" that is private and inviolable; it is lost to recorded history in "holy oblivion," which "providentially covers all." It does not belong to the world, although it is in it; and we sense that for Melville it will belong even less to the world with the coming modernity. There is an almost emblematic fittingness in Captain Vere's receiving his death wound in a fight with a ship named the *Athée* (the *Atheist*), and from a shot fired from the porthole of the enemy's main cabin. Although he is a nonbeliever, Melville needs the theological language of sacrament, of holiness, of providence, and of faith, when he reflects on what is most important to him.

## Appendix *on* Benito Cereno

In *Benito Cereno* we encounter several explicit biblical allusions: the decrepit slave ship seems launched from Ezekiel's Valley of Dry Bones; Benito Cereno's refusal to dine on Captain Delano's ship calls to Delano's mind, by contrast, "the Jew [Judas], who refrained not from supping at the board of him whom the same night he meant to betray"; Delano's suspicions are partly allayed by the benign sight of the evening sun shining through the clouds, "like the mild light from Abraham's tent"; the remark that Babo's hand passing the bottle of Canary wine is as "mute as that on the wall" alludes to Belshazzar's feast in Daniel 5; Babo's name suggests "Babylon," the evil city where Belshazzar's feast takes place; and finally, in a more doubtful allusion, the common sailor's undergarment, "edged, about the neck, with a narrow blue ribbon," recalls Numbers 15:38, in which the Israelites are commanded to edge their garments with blue. There is nothing particularly recondite about most of the biblical allusions in *Benito Cereno*; nor, at first, do they seem to be marshaled to any consistent literary purpose.

But a disturbingly sanctimonious aura hangs over the tale, enforcing a sharp division between the human characters in it: Captain Delano and Benito Cereno are associated with traditional Christianity, the slaves with paganism, ferocity, and demonic guile. The effect is disturbing because it is not always clear how Melville would wish us to take it: "'You are saved,' cried Captain Delano, more and more astonished and pained; 'you are saved: what has cast such a shadow upon you?' 'The negro.'"

Benito Cereno is very far from being "saved" in either the physical or the theological sense. He will die in three months time, evidently from the effects of his ordeal, and in some deeper, indistinct sense, his infirmity manifests a sickness in his soul for which the only explanation he can give is, 'The negro."

The Negro is of course Babo, who after trial in Lima is beheaded, his body burned, and "his head, that hive of subtlety, fixed on a pole in the Plaza" where it "met, unabashed, the gaze of the whites," Meanwhile Babo's victims, Aranda and, after three months in a monastery, Benito Cereno himself, are buried in the vaults of St. Bartholomew's church. (The church is appropriate. St. Bartholomew was martyred by being flayed, as was frequently represented in art, and Benito Cereno is through much of his story like a man being flayed, as is suggested in the famous shaving scene, and as Captain Delano remarks to himself: "He is like one flayed

alive." In the direct association of blackness with evil and whiteness
with the community of the good, Melville might seem to be attempting to undo the spell cast by Chapter 42 of *Moby Dick.* "The Whiteness of the Whale," in which whiteness itself becomes the most
powerful symbol of terrifying evil. In a note to that chapter, for
instance, Melville remarks on the whiteness of the polar bear, in
which the "ferociousness of the creature stands invested in the
fleece of celestial innocence and love." "And hence," he goes on to
say, "by bringing together two such opposite emotions in our minds,
the Polar bear frightens us with so unnatural a contrast. But even
assuming all this to be true; yet were is not for the whiteness, you
would not have that intensified terror."

In *Benito Cereno* all appears to be set right again as these opposites are driven apart: white people are associated with the Christian church, black slaves with demonic intelligence and Hell. Yet at
the close of the tale the whites appear helpless, or at least ineffectual, before the severed head of Babo. The head retains the power
of action, not only in meeting the gaze of the whites but also in looking toward St. Bartholomew's Church, where Aranda's bones are
interred, and towards the monastery on Mount Agonia, from
whence the grisly stare summons Benito Cereno to his grave: "the
head . . . looked towards St. Bartholomew's church, in whose
vaults slept then, as now, the recovered bones of Aranda: and across
the Rimac bridge looked towards the monastery, on Mount Agonia
without; where, three months after being dismissed by the court,
Benito Cereno, borne on the bier, did, indeed, follow his leader."

Aranda's skeleton had been suspended by Babo from the bow of
the ship, as a figurehead, with the inscription chalked beneath it,
"follow your leader" (*"Seguid vuestro jefe"*), not only as a warning to
the Spanish sailors, especially Benito Cereno, but also as a statement of intent. In the closing words of the tale the action Babo had
begun is completed and his menacing promise is kept, a sinister
accomplishment which Melville communicates with masterly economy in that single word, *indeed*: "did, indeed, follow his leader."

The tale ends with a disguised but intriguing Biblical allusion.
"Mount Agonia," on which the monastery in Lima stands, is named
after the Mount of Olives outside Jerusalem, on which Christ's
agony in the garden took place, on the night before he was crucified
(Luke 22.39–44). The page heading in the King James Version of
both Matthew and Luke's gospels names "Christ's agony in the garden"; in Luke's gospel Christ is described "being in an agony" (verse
44) as he prayed, meaning, in the Greek sense of the word *agōn*, a
contest or struggle with himself. As we see in *Clarel*, Melville knew
that there was a monastery on the Mount of Olives too.

What are we to make of Benito Cereno's vaguely Christlike agony, his death caused by the melancholy effect on his soul of the resolute ferocity, unswerving even in death, of "the negro"? To term Benito Cereno a "Christ-figure," in the manner of an older, naively interpretative criticism, raises more problems than it solves. To say, on the other hand, that in alluding, at the close of his tale, to Christ's agony in the garden Melville is deliberately travestying a Christianity for which commerce in human beings evidently is not a sin seems hardly less naive. Yet as readers we would not wish to be deprived of the strange resonance or glow that is afforded by the momentary evocation of Christ's agony in the garden, however incomparable it is, by any conscious effort of interpretation, with Benito Cereno's last three months in the monastery. If Melville is saying anything at all in the reference to Mount Agonia, or in any of the other biblical references in the tale, it is that there is a difference between scripture and the claims of scripture. Scripture itself, he would say, is indispensable to literary expression if it is to have any serious, permanent impact. But the claims of scripture—that is, the abstract, dogmatic principles derived from the biblical writings—are either irrelevant to literary expression or are put in question by it.

Both *Benito Cereno* and *Billy Budd* are set against the background of the French revolution, which was shocking to many because of the resolute atheism of its ideology. Melville shares the atheism but not, as a writer, the resoluteness. In the first of the three concluding chapters of *Billy Budd* we learn that Captain Vere, the tale's most developed, human character, dies at Gibraltar from wounds received in an engagement with a French line-of-battle ship; formerly called the *St. Louis*, the ship has been renamed the *Athée* (the *Atheist*). Melville's comment on this appellation is that it is, though unintentionally, a singularly appropriate one for a warship: "Such a name . . . while proclaiming the infidel audacity of the ruling power, was yet, though not so intended to be, the aptest name, if one consider it, ever given to a warship." (Chap. 23) Melville the man is a nonbeliever, an atheist, but as a writer, and perhaps also as a man, he is not on the side of "infidel audacity," of that vulgar aggression towards spiritual things (or, it may be, spiritual delusions) which motivates the change of the ship's name. But in this instance, where it is a warship that is being renamed, he notes the ironic appropriateness of the change, for there is something hypocritical in giving the name of a Christian saint to a machine for dealing death. What is telling is Melville's compulsion to invent, and then to mediate on, the change of a warship's name from *St. Louis* to the *Athee*. He is nervous about the quality of the human world whose emergence is indicated by such small but significant events.

Melville thus finds himself in the uncomfortable but honest position of many thinking people of the time (honesty is more often

uncomfortable than not): that of being without faith but also
unwilling to abandon everything for which that faith stands, including the human wisdom that resides in the scriptures. With the death
of Captain Vere in the fight with the *Athée* Melville shows us the
older, worldly wisdom represented by Vere undone by an aggressively innovative and dismissive modernity. For Melville, it is not the
end of Christian faith in itself that is cause for concern but rather
the end of the "measured forms" of human life, of human understanding of itself; and for such understanding scripture is the most
enduring source. Vere is reported as saying, in a classical rather
than a biblical example, that "'With mankind . . . forms, measured forms, are everything; and this is the import couched in the
story of Orpheus with his lyre spellbinding the wild denizens of the
wood.'" "And this, the narrator adds, "he once applied to the disruption of forms going on across the Channel and the consequences
thereof." (Chap. 27) Yet it is just this dedication to the forms in all
circumstances which leads to the tragic death of Billy Budd. In *Billy
Budd*, his last work of fiction, Melville engages in a deeper reflection on the emotional power of scriptural language, even (perhaps
especially) in the absence of belief; for belief is, in the end, only a
matter of the head, that is, only of a portion of what we are. As he
said in another letter to Hawthorne: "I had rather be a fool with a
heart, than Jupiter Olympus with his head. The reason the mass of
men fear God, and *at bottom dislike* Him, is because they rather distrust His heart, and fancy Him all brain like a watch." In *Benito
Cereno* and *Billy Budd* biblical references are more sparing so that
the mind may freely play about and meditate on the fewer examples
that occur. Hence what would appear, on a superficial examination,
to be evidence of a decline of interest in the Bible in Melville's later
fiction is necessary to his more serious engagement with it as a
writer. He is no longer just using scripture but meditating on it.

# HANNAH ARENDT

## [Compassion and Goodness]†

\* \* \*

Compassion and goodness may be related phenomena, but they are
not the same. Compassion plays a role, even an important one, in

---

† From *On Revolution* by Hannah Arendt. Copyright © 1963 by Hannah Arendt. Used by
permission of Viking Penguin, a division of Penguin Putnam, Inc.

*Billy Budd*, but its topic is goodness beyond virtue and evil beyond vice, and the plot of the story consists in confronting these two. Goodness beyond virtue is natural goodness and wickedness beyond vice is "a depravity according to nature" which "partakes nothing of the sordid or sensual." Both are outside society, and the two men who embody them come, socially speaking, from nowhere. Not only is Billy Budd a foundling; Claggart, his antagonist, is likewise a man whose origin is unknown. In the confrontation itself there is nothing tragic; natural goodness, though it "stammers" and cannot make itself heard and understood, is stronger than wickedness because wickedness is nature's depravity, and "natural" nature is stronger than depraved and perverted nature. The greatness of this part of the story lies in that goodness, because it is part of "nature," does not act meekly but asserts itself forcefully and, indeed, violently so that we are convinced: only the violent act with which Billy Budd strikes dead the man who bore false witness against him is adequate, it eliminates nature's "depravity." This, however, is not the end but the beginning of the story. The story unfolds after "nature" has run its course, with the result that the wicked man is dead and the good man has prevailed. The trouble now is that the good man, because he encountered evil, has become a wrongdoer too, and this even if we assume that Billy Budd did not lose his innocence, that he remained "an angel of God." It is at this point that "virtue" in the person of Captain Vere is introduced into the conflict between absolute good and absolute evil, and here the tragedy begins. Virtue—which perhaps is less than goodness but still alone is capable "of embodiment in lasting institutions"—must prevail at the expense of the good man as well; absolute, natural innocence, because it can only act violently, is "at war with the peace of the world and the true welfare of mankind," so that virtue finally interferes not to prevent the crime of evil but to punish the violence of absolute innocence. Claggart was "struck by an angel of God! Yet the angel must hang!" The tragedy is that the law is made for men, and neither for angels nor for devils. Laws and all "lasting institutions" break down not only under the onslaught of elemental evil but under the impact of absolute innocence as well. The law, moving between crime and virtue, cannot recognize what is beyond it, and while it has no punishment to mete out to elemental evil, it cannot but punish elemental goodness even if the virtuous man, Captain Vere, recognizes that only the violence of this goodness is adequate to the depraved power of evil. The absolute—and to Melville an absolute was incorporated in the Rights of Man—spells doom to everyone when it is introduced into the political realm.

\* \* \*

# PAULINE KAEL

## Billy Budd[†]

*Billy Budd* is not a great motion picture, but it is a very good one—
a clean, honest work of intelligence and craftsmanship. It ranks as
one of the best films of 1962. * * * *Billy Budd* not only has a
strong story line; it has a core of meaning that charges the story,
gives it tension and intellectual excitement.

In the film version of *Billy Budd*, Melville's story has been
stripped for action; and I think this was probably the right method—
the ambiguities of the story probably come through more clearly
than if the film were not so straightforward in its narrative line.
* * * The film could easily have been clogged by metaphysical
speculation and homo-erotic overtones. Instead, it is a good, tense
movie that doesn't try to tell us too much—and so gives us a very
great deal.

Terence Stamp is a remarkably intelligent casting selection for
Billy. If he were a more feminine type—as the role is often filled on
the stage—all the overtones would be cheapened and limited.
Stamp, fortunately, can wear white pants and suggest angelic splen-
dor without falling into the narcissistic poses that juveniles so often
mistake for grace. Robert Ryan gives a fine performance in the difficult role of Claggart.

\* \* \*

Melville, with all his circumlocutions, makes it overwhelmingly
clear that Claggart's "depravity according to nature" is, among other
things, homosexual, or as he coyly puts it, "a nut not to be cracked
by the tap of a lady's fan." Billy's innocence and goodness are intolerable to Claggart because Billy is so beautiful.

Neither Stamp nor Ryan can be faulted. Unfortunately, the role
of Captain Vere as played by Ustinov is a serious misconception that
weakens the film, particularly in the last section. Ustinov gives a
fine performance but it doesn't belong in the story of *Billy Budd*: it
reduces the meanings to something clearcut and banal. Ustinov's
physical presence is all wrong; his warm, humane, sensual face
turns Melville's Starry Vere into something like a cliché of the man
who wants to do the right thing, the liberal. We *believe* him when
he presents his arguments about justice and law.

† From *I Lost It at the Movies* (Boston: Little, Brown and Company, 1965). Reprinted by
permission of the author.

Perhaps it is Ustinov's principles that have prevented him from see-ing farther into Melville's equivocations. Ustinov has explained that he was concerned "with a most horrible situation where people are compelled by the letter of the law, which is archaic, to carry out sen-tences which they don't wish to do. That obviously produces a para-dox which is tragic." This is, no doubt, an important subject for Usti-nov, but it is not the kind of paradox that interested Melville. Melville, so plagued by *Billy Budd* that he couldn't get it in final form (he was still revising it when he died), had far more unsettling notions of its content. As Ustinov presents the film, the conflict is between the almost abstract forces of good (Billy) and evil (Claggart) with the Captain a human figure tragically torn by the rules and demands of authority. Obviously. But what gives the story its fascination, its greatness, is the ambivalent Captain; and there is nothing in Usti-nov's performance, or in his conception of the story, to suggest the unseemly haste with which Vere tries to hang Billy. In Melville's account the other officers can't understand why Vere doesn't simply put Billy in confinement "in a way dictated by usage and postpone further action in so extraordinary a case to such time as they should again join the squadron, and then transfer it to the admiral." The sur-geon thinks the Captain must be "suddenly affected in his mind." Melville's Vere, who looks at the dead Claggart and exclaims, "Struck dead by an angel of God. Yet the angel must hang!" is not so much a tragic victim of the law as he is Claggart's master and a distant rela-tive perhaps of the Grand Inquisitor. Sweet Starry Vere is the evil we *can't* detect: the man whose motives and conflicts we can't fathom. Claggart we can spot, but he is merely the underling doing the Cap-tain's work: it is the Captain, Billy's friend, who continues the logic by which saints must be destroyed.

Though it is short, *Billy Budd* is one of the most convoluted, one of the strangest works Melville wrote (in some ways even stranger than *Pierre*). Among its peculiarities is a chapter entitled "A Digres-sion," which is given over to a discussion between the ship's purser and the ship's surgeon after Billy's death. Their subject is why Billy's body during the hanging did not go through the movements which are supposed to be invariable in such cases. The absence of spasm—which is a euphemism for ejaculation—is rather like a vari-ation or a reversal of the famous death stink of Father Zossima in *The Brothers Karamazov*. I don't want to stretch the comparison too far, but it's interesting that Melville and Dostoyevsky, so closely con-temporary—Melville born in 1819, Dostoyevsky in 1821—should both have been concerned in works written just before their own deaths with the physical phenomena of death. Billy Budd, by the absence of normal human reactions at the moment of death, turns into a saint, a holy innocent, both more and less than a man. Father

Zossima, by the presence of all-too-mortal stench after death, is robbed of his saintliness. Melville's lingering on this singularity about Billy Budd's death didn't strike me so forcibly the first time I read the story, but reading it again recently, and, as it happened, reading it just after William Burrough's *The Naked Lunch*, with all its elaborate fantasies of violent deaths and gaudy ejaculations, Melville's treatment seems odder than ever. Billy Budd's goodness is linked with presexuality or nonsexuality; his failure to comprehend evil in the universe is linked with his not being really quite a man. He is, in Melville's view, too pure and beautiful to be subject to the spasms of common musculature.

Before this rereading I had associated the story only with that other work of Dostoyevsky's to which it bears more obvious relationships—*The Idiot*. It is, of course, as a *concept* rather than as a character that Billy resembles Prince Myshkin. It may be worth pointing out that in creating a figure of abnormal goodness and simplicity, both authors found it important for their hero to have an infirmity—Myshkin is epileptic, Billy stammers. In both stories the figure is also both naturally noble and also of aristocratic birth: Myshkin a prince, Billy a bastard found in a silk-lined basket. And in the structure of both, the heroes have their opposite numbers— Myshkin and Rogozhin, Billy and Claggart. For both authors, a good man is not a whole man; there is the other side of the human coin, the dark side. Even with his last words, "God bless Captain Vere," Billy demonstrates that he is not a man: he is unable to comprehend the meaning of Vere's experience, unable to comprehend that he will die just because he is innocent.

What's surprising about the film is how much of all this *is* suggested and comes through. What is missing in the film—the reason it is a very good film but not a great one—is that passion which gives Melville's work its extraordinary beauty and power. I wonder if perhaps the key to this failure is in that warm, humane face of Peter Ustinov, who perhaps, not just as an actor, but also as adaptor and director, is too much the relaxed worldly European to share Melville's American rage—the emotionality that is blocked and held back and still pours through in his work. Melville is not a civilized, European writer; he is our greatest writer because he is the American primitive struggling to say more than he knows how to say, struggling to say more than he knows. He is perhaps the most confused of all great writers; he wrestles with words and feelings. It is probably no accident that Billy's speech is blocked. Dostoyevsky is believed to have shared Myshkin's epilepsy, and when Melville can't articulate, he flails in all directions. Even when we can't understand clearly what he is trying to say, we respond to his Promethean torment, to the unresolved complexities.

The movie does not struggle; it moves carefully and rhythmically through the action to the conclusion. Its precision—which is its greatest virtue—is, when compared with the oblique, disturbing novella, evidence of its limitations. Much of what makes the story great is in Melville's effort to achieve new meanings (and some of the meanings we can only guess at from his retreats and disguises) and it is asking rather too much of the moviemakers to say what he wasn't sure about himself. But as Ustinov interprets Vere, Billy is just a victim of unfortunate circumstances, and the film is no more than a tragedy of *justice*. There's a good deal in the film, but the grandeur of Melville is not there.

# NEWTON ARVIN

## [Departure]†

\* \* \*

There are not many final works that have so much the air as *Billy Budd, Foretopman* has of being a Nunc Dimittis. Everyone has felt this benedictory quality in it. Everyone has felt it to be the work of a man on the last verge of mortal existence who wishes to take his departure with a word of acceptance and reconciliation on his lips.

It was begun, according to Melville's own notes, a little less than three years before his death—begun as a shortish tale, "Baby Budd, Sailor"—and it must have been present to his mind during almost all the time that followed. Discontented with what may have seemed to him the meagerness of the shorter tale, he revised and amplified it to more than twice its original proportions, slowing down its movement but enriching its inner interest, and a few months before he died dismissed it as finished at last. Doubtless he would have had it privately published, as he did the poems, if his health had made this possible.

If there is a great deal of the Nunc Dimittis in the essential feeling of *Billy Budd*, there is a great deal of the Backward Glance in its subject. After so long an interval during which he had lingered over other themes, Melville's mind was turning back more and more in these late years to the sea and to sailors, to thoughts of his own days on a man-of-war and of the men he had known there: happy thoughts of Jack Chase, for example, and grimmer thoughts of the man, whoever he was, whom he represents in *White-Jacket* as the

† From *Herman Melville* (New York: William Sloane Associates, 1950).

knavish master-at-arms, Bland. *Billy Budd* is dedicated to the memory of Jack Chase, "that great heart," and the character of Claggart is a kind of redoing of the figure of the master-at-arms on the *Neversink*. For the action of his tale, moreover, Melville had turned back to an event that had occurred more than forty years earlier, while he himself was in the South Seas, and that had a curiously personal and poignant association in his own memory. This was the famous case of the brig *Somers*, the American naval vessel on which, in 1842, a young midshipman, Philip Spencer, with a boatswain's mate and a common seaman, had been charged with mutiny and, after being haled before a drumhead court, had been hanged at the yard-arm. A cousin of Melville's, Guert Gansevoort, a few years older than he, the executive officer of the *Somers*, had presided over the court that found young Spencer guilty, and many of the sympathizers with the unfortunate (or reprehensible) midshipman—Fenimore Cooper, among others—regarded Lieutenant Gansevoort as little less to blame for a shocking piece of injustice, as they felt it was, than the commander of the vessel himself. Whether they were right or not, Guert Gansevoort appears to have brooded remorsefully over the incident during the rest of his life; to have been embittered and even broken by it. The case of the brig *Somers* had come home to Melville in an intimate and probably a painful way.

Now, almost half a century after the hanging of Philip Spencer, and more than two decades after Guert Gansevoort's death, Melville's imagination, doubtless reawakened by a magazine article on the old affair, was suddenly stirred to an awareness of what a tale like that of the *Somers* could be made to signify. For reasons that are easy enough to understand, he placed the action of his story, not on an American brig in the 'forties, but on a British seventy-four at the end of the eighteenth century, a short time after the famous Mutiny at the Nore. All these, however, are matters of the surface; they have a genuine interest, but they say little about the real feeling of *Billy Budd*. This feeling is very deep and very affecting; it triumphs even over the stiff-jointed prose, the torpidity of the movement, the excess of commentary, and Melville's failure to quicken any of the scenes with a full dramatic life. In spite of these blemishes of form and manner, the persons in *Billy Budd* and the moral drama they enact have too much largeness, as well as too much subtlety, in their poetic representativeness, not to leave a permanent stamp on the imagination.

For the tale of the Handsome Sailor and his unhappy end has an archetypal depth and scope that no reader can quite mistake; it is Melville's version of a primordial fable, the fable of the Fall of Man, the loss of Paradise. There are vibrations in it of the Book of Genesis, of the *Works and Days*, of Milton; there are other vibrations that are pure Melville. Billy himself, at any rate, is on one level Primal Man; he is Adam; indeed, it is said of him that, in the nude, he "might have posed for a statue of young Adam before the fall." His physical beauty, certainly, is such as the First Man's would necessarily be; but so, too, and of course more vitally, is the purity of his innocence, his incapacity so much as to imagine evil, his utter freedom from all malice and envy, and his helplessness in the presence of the wrong. His goodness, moveover, is not mere blank innocence; it is an active and disarming *good nature* also, and it draws upon him the spontaneous affection of his mates. But there is a complete absence from it of any intellectual element whatever; the illiterate and mindless Billy is "radically" a barbarian. And perfect as Billy is in the innocence of his heart, he is touched nevertheless by the primordial imperfection of humanity. His stutter is a symbol of this, and there is a mysterious justice in the fact that this stutter is his undoing.

If Billy is the Adam of this naval Eden, Claggart is of course its Satan. Malign as he is, Claggart, like the great Enemy in *Paradise Lost*, has a certain nobility of form and type. In physical presence, with his tall figure, his shapely forehead, and his curling black hair, he is quite without meanness, and it is only his strangely protuberant chin and his unwholesome pallor of complexion that hint at the depravity of his being. That depravity is inherent and terrible, but it does not express itself in what are called vices or small sins. As a naval officer, Claggart is a model of dutifulness and patriotism, and intellectually he is a man of marked superiority. He is dominated, indeed, by his intellectuality; dominated by it, at any rate, in his *means*, for his aims are mad; with all his "rationality," he is completely exempt, at heart, from the law of reason. Instinctively he hates the good; hates Billy precisely because he is innocent and guileless. In the deepest sense Claggart is a rebel and a traitor, like his great exemplar; a rebel against the law of reason and a traitor to the image of man. There is a Guy Fawkes, as Melville says, prowling in the hid chambers of his nature, and it is wholly suitable that the charge he brings against an innocent man should be the charge of mutiny. It is true that Billy has been guiltless of what he is accused of; guiltless of rebellion and disobedience; but was not that the sin to which Satan tempted the first of men? and is it not fitting that Claggart should now impute it to Billy? There is a strong suggestion of the old serpent in the master-at-arms, and when, after his death, Billy and Captain Vere attempt to raise his body to a sitting posture, "it was like handling a dead snake."

Now that he has struck dead an officer of the Navy, Billy is indeed objectively guilty, under the Mutiny Act, of a crime of exactly the same heinousness as that with which he was falsely charged. It may be that, as the officer of marines protests, Budd *intended* neither mutiny nor homicide; Adam did not *intend* disobedience either, and, as Captain Vere observes, "Budd's intent or non-intent is nothing to the purpose." The Mutiny Act, like war, of which it is the offspring, "looks but to the frontage," and Captain Vere, as the embodiment of naval authority, the Jehovah of the drama, has no choice but to administer, dutifully and grimly, the harsh terms of that Act. In order to do so, he must suppress not only the heart within him but his private conscience: it is the "imperial" conscience, formulated in the Naval Code, under which he officially proceeds. This means adjudging to death a youth toward whom he is drawn emotionally as a father to a son. Imaginably, Billy might *be* his son, for Billy is a foundling and one in whom noble descent is as evident as in a blood horse; and the aristocratic Captain Vere, a bachelor, "was old enough to have been Billy's father." The sacrifice of Billy by Captain Vere is a re-enactment of the sacrifice of Isaac by Abraham, though it is a completed one; and Vere does not turn aside from his duty, anguishing though it is. Billy is hanged at the yard-arm, and Vere, a few months later, mortally wounded by a shot from the *Athéiste*, dies with Billy's name on his lips.

Such is this rewriting of the first three chapters of Genesis, this late-nineteenth-century *Paradise Lost*. *Billy Budd* owes much of its subliminal effect on the imagination to the fact that it repeats, with variations, that primordial pattern. Yet quite as real as the repetition, and at least as vital, are the variations. There is no Eve in this Eden, for one thing, but far more importantly, the tale does not have, after all, the unequivocal spiritual and moral simplicity of the Christian legend or of any of its theological formulations. It abounds in what Melville himself calls ambiguities; it suggests no unambiguous dogma. There is a strain of irony in it that has no parallel in Genesis or in Milton; it is made explicit in a manuscript sentence that Melville later struck out: "Here ends a story not unwarranted by what sometimes happens in this incomprehensible world of ours—Innocence and infamy, spiritual depravity and fair repute." Unlike the world of theology, Melville's world is insuperably incomprehensible, and he makes no claim to comprehending it.

The drama of the Fall of Man is a drama in which divine and absolute justice is countered by infernal evil in a contest for the immortal soul of God's creature, Man, and in which Man, yielding to the temptation of the evil spirit, turns rebel against God's will, disobeys it, and involves himself and all his posterity in the guilt of Original Sin. Billy, on the contrary, is no rebel against divine justice, and he is not guilty, even symbolically, of disobeying some transcendent will. He is an unwitting, impulsive offender against the Mutiny Act, the child of war, itself an evil and infecting with evil everything that relates to it. Captain Vere makes no mistake about that. To the protest of the officer of marines that Billy intended no mutiny, he replies: "Surely not, my good man. And before a court less arbitrary and more merciful than a martial one that plea would largely extenuate. At the Last Assizes it shall acquit." If there is a divine justice, Billy is innocent in its eyes; he goes to his death as a penalty for breaking a law that has no absolute sanction whatever. His impediment in speech is a symbol of his irreducible imperfection as a man; it is not a symbol of total depravity, and Vere's real feeling about Billy breaks out when, gazing at Claggart's dead body, he cries: "Struck dead by an angel of God."

There is a far more enigmatic intertangling of good and evil in this universe of Melville's final vision than in the universe of theology or of dogmatic ethics: evil and good, as Rolfe had said, do indeed play, braided, into one cord. Billy may be as blameless as Oedipus of any conscious evil intention, yet a malign fate, working upon his inevitable limitations as a human being, brings it about that he commits in fact a capital crime. Meanwhile, Claggart's iniquity, terrible though it is, is not the absolute and transcendent wickedness of the principle of Evil itself, the Evil of the Father of Lies. It is, as Melville insists, "a depravity according to nature," born with him and innate, not the product of training; but it embodies some mysterious principle in human experience that "by no means involves Calvin's dogma as to total mankind." It takes chiefly the form of an instinctive hatred of the innocent and the good, but a hatred so spontaneous and so insane that it suggests a dreadful perversion of love. Claggart's glance, indeed, sometimes follows "belted Billy," moving about the deck, "with a settled meditative and melancholy expression," his eyes strangely suffused with tears. At such moments the diabolic master-at-arms looks like the man of sorrows. "Yes, and sometimes the melancholy expression would have in it a touch of soft yearning, as if Claggart could even have loved Billy but for fate and ban."

It is his miserable destiny, however, to be incapable of loving the good, indeed to be incapable of love itself, and there is no greater misery. For there is a solid reality in this incomprehensible universe, this universe of equivocations and contrarieties; it is the reality of "the heart within you." To mind "the issues there" is to know that, even in the dark midst of evil and hate, goodness exists, and that its essential reality is that of love. Neither goodness nor love can flourish in a nature "dominated by intellectuality," as Claggart's is, and certainly not in a nature like that of the ship's surgeon, with his materialistic, scientific rationalism. They attain their fairest form, perhaps, in a nature as pristine and even primitive as Billy's is, but they are not irrevocably at war with the life of the mind, and indeed they attain their highest form in association with it. Captain Vere is a man with "a marked leaning towards everything intellectual," a passion for books and learning, and a habit of abstracted meditation. Yet he is an image of the high virtue in which the sternest sense of severe and painful duty is united to a capacity for the purest and tenderest love, the love of father for son. And it was in the full imaginative realization of that love, given and received, that Melville brought his work as a writer to its serene conclusion.

After the drumhead court has pronounced its just and inexorable sentence, Captain Vere and Billy have a final interview alone together in the stateroom where Billy is confined. What occurred there was never known, says Melville, but he adds that "the austere devotee of military duty, letting himself melt back into what remains primeval in our formalized humanity, may in the end have caught Billy to his heart even as Abraham may have caught young Isaac. . . . But there is no telling the sacrament . . . wherever . . . two of great Nature's nobler order embrace." Whatever took place in the stateroom between the ideal father and the ideal son, its effect was indeed sacramental, an effect of the purest unction and the most complete reconcilement. When, during the night that follows, the chaplain of the vessel comes upon Billy lying asleep on the upper gundeck, he gazes down on the sleeping countenance and feels that even he, "the minister of Christ," has "no consolation to proffer which could result in a peace transcending that which he beheld." Ishmael, in the end, after so long a banishment, had been taken back to his father's heart. Billy's final words, as he stands the next morning with the noose about his neck, are an expression of rapturous surrender: "God bless Captain Vere!"

# Selected Bibliography

• indicates works included or excerpted in this Norton Critical Edition.

## GENERAL

• Arvin, Newton. *Herman Melville.* New York: William Sloane Associates, 1950.
Bloom, Harold, ed. *Herman Melville's "Billy Budd," "Benito Cereno," "Bartleby the Scrivener," and Other Tales.* New York: Chelsea House, 1987.
Franklin, Bruce. *The Wake of the Gods, Melville's Mythology.* Stanford, Calif.: Stanford University Press, 1963.
Gale, Robert L. *A Herman Melville Encyclopedia.* Westport, Conn.: Greenwood Press, 1995.
Newman, Lea Bertani Vozar. *A Reader's Guide to the Short Stories of Herman Melville.* Boston: G. K. Hall & Co., 1986.
• Rogin, Michael. *Subversive Genealogy: The Politics and Art of Herman Melville.* Berkeley: University of California Press, 1985.

## BARTLEBY, THE SCRIVENER

Abrams, Robert E. "Bartleby and the Fragile Pageantry of the Ego." *ELH* 45 (1978): 488–500.
Barber, Patricia, "What If Bartleby Were a Woman?" In *The Authority of Experience, Essays in Feminist Criticism.* Ed. Arlyn Diamond and Lee R. Edwards. Amherst: University of Massachusetts Press, 1977.
Beja, Morris. "Bartleby and Schizophrenia." *Massachusetts Review* 19 (1978): 555–68.
• Bergmann, Johannes Dietrich. "Bartleby and *The Lawyer's Story." American Literature* 47 (1975): 432–36.
Brodwin, Stanley. "To the Frontiers of Eternity: Melville's Crossing in 'Bartleby, The Scrivener.'" In Inge, ed., *Bartleby the Inscrutable.*
Foley, Brian. "Dickens Revised: 'Bartleby' and *Bleak House." Essays in Literature* 12 (Fall 1985).
• Hardwick, Elizabeth. *Bartleby in Manhattan.* New York: Random House, 1983.
Inge, M. Thomas, ed. *Bartleby the Inscrutable.* Hamden, Conn.: Archon Books, 1979.
  Contains 12 critical essays on "Bartleby."
  Especially valuable is Bruce Bebb's "Checklist of Criticism," which covers 240 essays and notes from 1863 to 1976; Elizabeth Williamson's "Supplement" cites 30 more such essays.
Jaffe, Leo. "'Bartleby the Scrivener' and *Bleak House."* In Inge, ed., *Bartleby the Inscrutable.*
• Marx, Leo. "Melville's Parable of the Walls." *Sewanee Review* 61 (1953): 602–27.
• McCall, Dan. *The Silence of Bartleby.* Ithaca, N.Y.: Cornell University Press, 1989.
Oliver, Egbert S. "A Second Look at Bartleby." *College English* 6 (May 1945): 431–39.
Sten, Christopher W. "Bartleby the Transcendentalist: Melville's Dead Letter to Emerson." *Modern Language Quarterly* (March 1974): 30–40.
Stern, Milton R. "Towards 'Bartleby the Scrivener.'" In *The Stoic Strain in American Literature.* Ed. Duane J. MacMillan. Toronto: University of Toronto Press, 1979.
Sullivan, William P. "Bartleby and Infantile Autism: A Naturalistic Explanation." *Bulletin of the West Virginia Association of College English Teachers* 3.2 (Fall 1976): 43–60.
Vincent, Howard P., ed. *Melville Annual 1965: A Symposium: 'Bartleby, the Scrivener.'* Kent, Ohio: Kent State University Press, 1966.
Weisbuch, Robert. "Melville's 'Bartleby' and the Dead Letter of Charles Dickens." In *Atlantic Double-Cross: American Literature and British Influence in the Age of Emerson.* Chicago: University of Chicago Press, 1986.
Zelnick, Stephen. "Melville's 'Bartleby': History, Ideology, and Literature." *Marxist Perspectives,* 2 (Winter 1979–80): 74–92.

## BENITO CERENO

- Abel, Darrel. *American Literature*. Great Neck, N.Y.: Barron's Education Series, 1963.
- Altschuler, Glenn C. "Whose Foot on Whose Throat? A Re-Examination of Melville's *Benito Cereno*." *CLA Journal* 3 (March 1975): 383–92.
- Busch, Frederick. "Melville's Mail." In *A Dangerous Profession*. New York: Broadway Books, 1998.
- Emery, Allan Moore. "The Topicality of Depravity in 'Benito Cereno.'" *American Literature* 55 (1983): 316–31.
- James, C. L. R. *Mariners, Renegades and Castaways*. Detroit: Bewick Editions, 1978.
  Matlack, James. "Attica and Melville's 'Benito Cereno.'" *American Transcendental Quarterly* 26 (Spring 1975): 18–23.
- Ray, Richard E. "'Benito Cereno': Babo as Leader." *American Transcendental Quarterly* 7 (Summer 1970): 31–37.
- Richardson, William D. *Melville's 'Benito Cereno.'* Durham, N.C.: Carolina Academic Press, 1987. Includes a selective bibliography of well over a hundred interpretive essays on *Benito Cereno*.
- Robertson-Lorant, Laurie. *Melville: A Biography*. New York: Random House, 1996.
- Sundquist, Eric J. "'Benito Cereno' and New World Slavery." In *Reconstructing American Literary History*. Ed. Sacvan Bercovitch. Cambridge, Mass.: Harvard University Press, 1986.
- Winters, Yvor. *In Defense of Reason*. Denver: Allan Swallow, 1947.

## BILLY BUDD, SAILOR

- Adler, Joyce Sparer. "*Billy Budd* and Melville's Philosophy of War." *PMLA* 91 (1976): 276–77.
- Arendt, Hannah. *On Revolution*. New York: Viking, 1962.
- Bergman, Paul, and Michael Asinow. *Reel Justice: The Courtroom Goes to the Movies*. Kansas City: Andrew and McMeal, 1996.
- Cooke, Mervyn, and Phillip Reed. *Benjamin Britten, Billy Budd*. New York: Cambridge University Press, 1993.
- Cover, Robert M. *Justice Accused*. New Haven, Conn.: Yale University Press, 1975.
- Douglas, Ann. *The Feminization of American Culture*. New York: Farrar, Straus & Giroux, 1977.
- Goldstein, Tom. "Once Again, 'Billy Budd' Is Standing Trial." *The New York Times*, June 10, 1988.
- Hayford, Harrison, and Merton M. Sealts Jr. *Billy Budd, Sailor (An Inside Narrative), Reading Text and Genetic Text, edited from the Manuscript with Introduction and Notes*. Chicago: University of Chicago Press, 1982. The best text so far.
- Kael, Pauline. *I Lost It at the Movies*. Boston: Little, Brown & Co., 1965.
- Karcher, Carolyn L. *Shadow over the Promised Land: Slavery, Race, and Violence in Melville's America*. Baton Rouge: Louisiana State University Press, 1980.
- Martin, Robert K. *Hero, Captain, and Stranger*. Chapel Hill: University of North Carolina Press, 1986.
  Milder, Robert. *Critical Essays on Melville's Billy Budd, Sailor*. Boston: G. K. Hall & Co., 1989.
  ———. *Billy Budd, Sailor, and Selected Tales*. New York: Oxford University Press, 1997.
- Parker, Hershel. *Reading Billy Budd*. Evanston, Ill.: Northwestern University Press, 1990.
- Scorza, Thomas, Jr. *In the Time before Steamships: Billy Budd, The Limits of Politics and Modernity*. DeKalb: Northern Illinois University Press, 1979.
  Vincent, Howard P., ed. *Twentieth Century Interpretations of "Billy Budd."* Englewood Cliffs, N.J.: Prentice Hall, 1971. Contains twenty-four critical essays and a selected bibliography of another twelve essays.